"Women a[illegible]
will try [illegible]
Washington Post

KATHLEEN E. WOODIWISS'
FOURTH STRAIGHT
MULTI-MILLION-COPY ROMANCE

ASHES IN THE WIND

Over One Year on
The New York Times Bestseller List

Enjoyed by more than 2½ million readers
in the $4.95 edition . . . Bringing
Kathleen E. Woodiwiss' bestselling success
past the 12-million-copy mark!

SELECTED BY THE DOUBLEDAY
BOOK CLUB

Other Avon Books by
Kathleen Woodiwiss

THE FLAME AND THE FLOWER
A ROSE IN WINTER
SHANNA
THE WOLF AND THE DOVE

KATHLEEN E. WOODIWISS

ASHES IN THE WIND

AVON
PUBLISHERS OF BARD, CAMELOT, DISCUS AND FLARE BOOKS

ASHES IN THE WIND is an original publication of Avon Books. This work has never before appeared in book form.

AVON BOOKS
A division of
The Hearst Corporation
1790 Broadway
New York, New York 10019

Published by arrangement with the author
Library of Congress Catalog Card Number: 79-51351
ISBN: 0-380-76984-0

First Avon Trade Printing, September, 1979
First Avon Mass Market Printing, April, 1981

Printed in the U.S.A.

WFH 15 14 13 12 11 10

Dedicated to the memory of my parents—

Gladys and Charles

In love—

KEW

PART ONE

Lament

Oh, my home!
My land of sunshine,
Of loving folk and
Gently passing days.
You are gone!
Gone beneath the booted
Heel of WAR;
The million-legged worm
That crawls mindlessly across
My land and leaves behind
A tangled waste of broken lives
And lifeless bodies.

You have left me! Alone! Forlorn!
Atoss like a leaf upon the flood.
Wherever I would set my feet and rest,
I find—Despair.
You have rent the very fabric
Of my soul with your going.
You have fled my grasp,
And everywhere I turn, I find—
The hated smell of WAR,
That acrid scent of
Ashes! Ashes!
Ashes in the wind!

Chapter 1

September 23, 1863
New Orleans

THE wide, muddy river lapped with deceptive laziness at the foot of the levee, while a heavily laden riverboat ponderously picked a path through a bevy of Union warships. Two hundred yards away, the main body of the fleet lay anchored midstream, apart from the city and its sometimes hostile inhabitants. Squat, ugly gunboats with decks nearly awash wallowed like swine amid their more graceful sisters of the open sea, the tall-masted, slim-hipped frigates. Several of each type stood with steam up and cleared for action should the occasion warrant it.

A brownish haze hung over the city and the humid air pressed the sweltering heat down upon the detachment of blue-clad soldiers waiting on the dock for the arrival of the sidewheeler. Its once-bright trim of red and green now faded and chipped, the steamboat resembled some lumbering beast grown gray with age as it threshed toward them with towering black horns spouting smoke and flame. It wallowed ever closer until it cautiously nudged against the low quay where the Mississippi touched the port city. Great hawsers snaked out like giant feelers, and pulleys and blocks creaked above the shouts of laborers as the vessel shouldered closer against the jetty.

In the last moments of their journey, the passengers had gathered belongings and pressed forward in anticipation of their landing. Each one seemed to have a specific end in mind and was working toward it with diligence, though it was impossible to perceive any definite goal in the churning crush of people. These were the eager-to-be-rich, the scavengers, the harlots, the rogues of society descending upon New Orleans to squeeze what wealth they could from her impoverished citizenry, and as much as they might from the Yankee invaders. When the gangway formed a bridge to land, they moved as one body to leave the vessel, rudely jostling and elbowing each other aside in their haste until they found their progress halted by a rank of Union soldiers who held them at bay. A second rank formed immediately behind the first, then the two lines of soldiers stepped apart, opening a corridor from the cargo deck to the gangplank. The first angry murmur changed to caustic jeers and catcalls as a single file of thin, ragged, unwashed Confederate soldiers began to pass through the aisle, shuffling along in unison, the only pace their fetters and chains would permit.

Halfway down the once elegant staircase from the promenade deck, a slender lad stood where he had been stopped with the rest of the passengers. Beneath a battered slouch hat pulled low over his ears, wary gray eyes stared out of a begrimed face. Overlarge garments emphasized the smallness of his frame, and the baggy trousers were gathered about his thin waist with a rough rope. He wore a loose cotton jacket over a voluminous shirt, and though its long sleeves were rolled back several times they still flopped over the narrow wrists. A large wicker case stood on end near his outsized boots, which turned up at the toes. The lean face was smudged with the soot of the deck passage, and through the smut the first signs of a sunburn showed across the bridge of his thin nose. His claim to years appeared no more than a dozen, yet the deliberateness and quiet reserve in his manner belied his apparent youth. Unlike the other travelers, a pensive frown marked his youthful brow as he watched his defeated countrymen led from the boat.

The prisoners were met on shore by the waiting detachment, while aboard the riverboat the Federal soldiers fell in behind their officers and followed them ashore, at last allowing the other passengers to disembark. Dragging his eyes from the shuffling prisoners, the boy lifted his valise and began to make his way down the steps. The case was clumsy and repeatedly bumped against his leg or snagged the clothes of others who came in its path. Avoiding the glares tossed his way, he fought to control his burden and advanced as best as he could. Behind him a man with a gaudily dressed and overpainted woman on his arm grew perturbed at the slow progress of the youth and sought to press past. His haste caused the boy to stumble. The heavy wicker case caught the balustrade, then rebounded heartily against the impatient one's shin. A vicious curse exploded from the man and he whirled, half crouched, with a knife suddenly glittering in his fist. The startled lad drew himself up against the balustrade and stared with widened eyes at the long, slim blade that threatened him.

"Gauche cou rouge!" The man's French was slightly misaligned in the Cajun way and guttural with rage. Black, restless eyes glared in arrogance from a swarthy face while he scathingly perused the youngster. The rude man's wrath slowly dissolved, for he found nothing even remotely menacing in the frightened youth. Sneering, the man straightened himself to a height barely half a head taller than the boy and replaced the blade in its hiding place beneath his coat. "Be careful with your trash, eh, *buisson poulain*. You 'ave almost send me to the surgeon."

Clear gray eyes flared hotly at the insult while the youth's lips grew thin and white. He understood all too well the slur to his parentage and longed to throw it back into the other's face. Grasping his valise more tightly, he gave the two a disdainful scrutiny. The woman was obvious, and though the man wore a coat of rich brocade, the bright print shirt and red bandanna knotted about his neck marked him as one of the backwater riffraff whose presence in the city was usually occasioned by a mysterious rise in fortune.

Pricked by the boy's sneer of contempt, the harlot huffily reclaimed her companion's arm and crushed it to her ample bosom. "Ah, give him a couple of cuffs, Jack," she urged. "Teach the lil' piker to mind his betters."

The man flung up his hand in exasperation and fixed the trollop with an impatient stare. "The name is Jacques! Jacques DuBonné! Remember it!" he bade her heartily. "Someday I will own this town. But no cuffs, *ma douceur*. There are those who watch—" He gestured upward where the Yankee captain of the sidewheeler leaned on the quarter rail of the top deck. "And who remember too well. We do not wish to offend our Yankee hosts, *chère*. Were the whelp older, I might enjoy taking him on, but he ees barely weaned. He is not worth our bother. Think no more of him. We go, eh?"

The ragamuffin watched the two go ashore, his loathing apparent in his smut-blackened face. To him the two were worse than the Yankees. They were traitors to the South and to everything he loved.

Conscious of the captain's stare, the lad lifted a quick glance toward the quarter rail. The gray-haired captain gazed down upon him with more compassion than the boy was willing to accept from a Yankee, and he could not find it in him to give even a small gesture of gratitude. The officer was a distasteful reminder of the defeat the Confederates had suffered in the Delta. Unable to bear the weight of the captain's regard, he gripped his valise with determination and hurried down the stairs to the main deck.

A landing ran along the waterfront to accommodate the low decks of the river steamers. A few yards of level space gave room for loading and landing, then the levee rose abruptly to the main warehouse level. Its steep stone face afforded steps for people and ramps for wheeled vehicles. As the lad laboriously hauled his case toward the nearest steps, a short caravan of Federal wagons rattled down an adjacent ramp. At a brusque command from a sweating sergeant, a handful of soldiers dismounted and started toward the sidewheeler.

The youth eyed the closing Yankees nervously, then forcing his gaze downward, he carefully kept his pace slow and deliberate. But as their footsteps neared, his trepidation mounted. They seemed to be coming straight for him. Did they know?

The lump in the lad's throat grew until the first soldier went on past and clamored across the gangplank, leading his fellows with him. Glancing around furtively, the boy saw that the men were pairing up on heavy cases stacked on deck, then carrying them to the wagons.

Just the same, the lad reasoned to himself, *it's best to get clear of these Yankees as soon as possible.*

On reaching the top of the levee, he saw a huge stack of barrels which he hurriedly put between himself and the packet and then hastened toward the shelter of the warehouses. Black scars marred the cobbled wharf. Fire-stained warehouses, a few displaying the new lumber of recent repair, were a harsh reminder of the thousands of cotton bales and hogsheads of molasses that had been set ablaze by the citizens of New Orleans in an effort to keep the blue invaders from seizing them. More than a year had passed since the river city had bowed to Farragut's fleet, and it was not a pleasant thought for the youth that he must now live in the midst of the enemy.

Shrill laughter drew his attention to the hired carriage into which Jacques DuBonné was helping his buxom companion. As the barouche swept briskly away from the dock area, the youngster experienced a genuine surge of envy. He had not the coin to purchase a ride for himself, and it was a goodly distance to his uncle's house with, no doubt, more Yankees along the way.

The oppressive presence of Yankee blue was everywhere. He had not ventured into New Orleans since its fall, and he felt much the alien. The unceasing bustle of the waterfront exceeded what it had ever been before. Soldiers moved supplies onto boats or into warehouses. Gangs of black laborers abounded, and sweat flowed freely as the men strained in the steaming heat. A vulgar curse made the youth jump swiftly aside, and he waited as a six-in-hand of huge, plodding horses, their foam-flecked sides heaving, drew a large wagon piled high with casks of gunpowder along the cobbled wharf. The skinner swore again and swung his whip against the broad back of the drays. Heavy hooves struck sparks from the stone as the animals struggled harder.

Intent upon staying out of the team's path, the boy heedlessly stepped backward into a loitering group of Union soldiers. Their presence was first marked when a slurred voice called loudly:

"Hey, looky here! An up-country brat come to town."

The young Southerner turned and stared, half in curiosity, half in hatred, at the foursome, the eldest of which could have barely been called a man, while the youngest's cheeks were still covered with the light down of youth. The one who had spoken passed a nearly empty bottle to a companion and stood forth, his feet spread, his thumbs hooked in his belt. He towered over the slim lad who eyed him apprehensively.

"Whatcha doing here, yokel?" he called boldly. "Come ta see the big, bad Yankees?"

"N-no, sir," the boy nervously stammered, his voice breaking and dropping in key on the last word. Uncertain and dismayed at this unexpected confrontation, he glanced uneasily toward the others. They were more than tipsy. Their uniforms were in sad disarray, and for the most part, they seemed only to be seeking some diversion from boredom. The lad could not be too careful and sought to make them more cautious.

"I'm supposed to meet my uncle. He should be here—" He let his voice trail off in the lie and gazed about expectantly as if seeking some trace of his kin.

"Hey!" The Yankee private grinned over his shoulder. "This kid's gotta uncle around here. There, boy!" He jabbed a finger painfully into the other's shoulder and pointed to a team of mules nearby. "Do you suppose one o' them could be your uncle?"

The lad yanked the brim of his floppy hat lower, bristling under the uproarious laughter of the four. "Excuse me, sir," he mumbled, not intending to remain the target of the Yankee's drunken humor, and started to turn away.

In the next instant the hat was snatched from his head, baring a mop of shaggily cropped dark reddish brown hair. The lad threw his hands over his head to hide the uneven thatch, at the same time opening his mouth to vent his outrage. For some reason he seemed to think better of it and clamped his jaw tightly shut. Angrily he grabbed for the taken item, only to see it sail high in the air.

"Man oh man!" the soldier hooted loudly. "That's some hat!"

Another caught it and began to inspect it closely. "Hey, I think I saw an ol' mule downriver with a hat better'n this. Maybe that was his cousin."

As the boy reached him, the hat was sailed off again. The lad was incensed and stood with small fists clenched, a snarl of rage baring gnashing white teeth. "You bluebellied woods colt!" he shrieked, his voice piercing a high tenor. "Gimme back my hat!"

The first soldier caught it and, with loud guffaws,

upended the wicker case and sat on it, bowing the flimsy sides until it threatened to burst. His laughter exploded into shouts of pained fury as a well-directed boot found his bony shin and, another, his knee. With a roar he came to his feet and seized the slight youth roughly by the shoulders.

"Now you listen, you sow-belly brat!" he snarled, shaking the lad and bending near until his whiskeyed breath choked the other. "I'm gonna turn you over—"

"Atten*hut!*"

Immediately the boy found himself sprawling free, almost stumbling over the case. He saw the hat fall to the ground and scurried to retrieve it, jamming it securely on his head before he whirled with doubled fists, ready to do battle. His jaw slackened as he stared amazed by the sight of the four soldiers standing ramrod stiff. The whiskey bottle smashed on the cobblestones, and in the wake of its shattering, the silence was ominous. A tall figure strode into view, resplendent in dress-blue uniform with shiny brass buttons, bright braid on cuffs, and gold epaulettes bearing the rank of captain riding on wide shoulders. A red and white sash was bound about a lean waist beneath a wide black gun belt, and a Hardee hat was pulled down over his scowling brow. As the man came forward, the yellow stripes that ran down the sides of his trousers flashed against the blue of the cloth.

"You men!" he barked sharply. "I am sure the sergeant of the guard can find more worthy chores for your attention than abusing the children of this city. Report to your quarters at once!" His gaze sternly raked them as they struggled to maintain a rigid stance, then he curtly ordered, "Dismissed!"

The officer watched the scrambling departure of the four before turning to the boy who found himself meeting eyes of bright azure blue set in a face bronzed golden by the sun. Long, light brown sideburns were neatly trimmed, accentuating the leanly fleshed cheekbones and firm angular jaw. His nose was thin and well formed, slightly aquiline, and beneath it were generous, but at the moment unsmiling, lips. There was an air of the professional soldier about him, a quality that displayed itself in his crisp manner, almost painfully neat apparel, and rather austere mien. The handsome features bore the look of good breeding appropriate to some princely head of state and those eyes, fringed with dark lashes, seemed capable of piercing to the lad's innermost secrets, causing a chill of fear to go through him.

Gradually the captain's stern visage softened as he stared at the raggedy urchin. When a smile tugged at the corners of his mouth, he quelled it as quickly as it came. "I'm sorry, boy. These men are a long way from home. I fear their manners need as much improvement as their judgment."

The youngster was overwhelmed by the presence of a Federal officer and could muster no reply. He glanced away as the man's gaze ranged upward from his oversize boots.

"And you, boy. Are you waiting for someone?" the captain inquired. "Or running away from home?"

The youth fidgeted beneath the other's close inspection but remained mute, pointedly ignoring the questions as he stared off into the distance. His ragged, ill-fitting garb and turned-up boots suggested a serious lack of coin, prompting the man to draw his own conclusions.

"If you're looking for work, we can use an extra hand at the hospital."

The youth wiped his nose on the back of a dirty sleeve and let his eyes roam derisively over the dark blue uniform. "I don't fancy workin' fer no Yankee."

The officer smiled leisurely. "We won't demand that you shoot anyone."

The translucent gray eyes narrowed with hatred. "I ain't no lackey to wipe some Yankee's boots. Go find you someone else, mister."

"If you insist." The man casually produced a long cheroot and took his time lighting it before continuing. "But I wonder if all that pride of yours keeps your belly full."

The youngster lowered his gaze, too aware of the painful gnawing in his stomach to make any denials.

"When was the last time you ate?" the captain queried.

The urchin's retort came sharply on the heels of a piercing glare. "Cain't see it's any of your business, blueleg."

"Do your parents know where you are?" The man watched the youngster thoughtfully.

"They'd turn over in their graves if'n they did."

"I see," the officer said with more understanding. He glanced about until his gaze fell upon a small eating establishment located near the wharf, then he looked back to the boy. "I was about to have a bite to eat. Would you care to join me?"

The boy raised cold, bright eyes to the tall captain. "Don't need no handout."

The Yankee shrugged. "Consider it a loan if you must. You may reimburse me when your fortunes improve."

"My ma learnt me never to jaw with no strangers ner Yankees."

The officer responded with a low chuckle of amusement. "Unable to deny the latter title, I can at least present myself. Captain Cole Latimer, assigned as surgeon to the hospital."

Now the clear gray eyes betrayed a wide measure of distrust as they swept the officer. "I ain' never seen no sawbones younger'n fifty, mister. Betcha you're filling me full o' rot."

"I assure you, I am a doctor, and as to my age, I'm probably old enough to be your father."

"Well, you sure ain't *my* pa!" croaked the youth irately. "Not any damned Yankee butcher!"

A long, lean finger was thrust into the boy's face, almost meeting the tip of the slim, arrogant nose. "Now look, boy. There are some folks here who would not take kindly to your choice of titles. You can bet they'd use stern measures to take some of the starch out of you. I've fished you out of one scrape, but I have no intention of playing nursemaid to any quick-tempered little whelp. So have a care for your manners."

The grimy cheeks flexed with irritation. "I can take care o' m'self."

Captain Latimer scoffed in disbelief. "By the looks of you, somebody needs to take you in hand. When did you last wash, anyway?"

"You're the nosiest bluebelly I've ever seent!"

"Ornery little runagate," Cole Latimer muttered and gestured officiously. "Grab your bag and come with me." He left the waif staring after him in dumb surprise and strode purposefully toward the eating establishment he had espied earlier. He had gone only a few paces when he sharpened his voice and, without glancing around, barked, "Hop to, boy! Don't stand there gawking."

The urchin scrambled in the officer's wake, crushing the hat tighter on his head and struggling with his heavy case. Before the entryway of the wood frame structure, Cole Latimer paused. The youngster was a quick step behind, almost treading on the heels of the shiny black boots, but halted abruptly when inquiring blue eyes turned upon him.

"Do you have a name?"

The lad squirmed uneasily and glanced around him.

"You do have a name, don't you?" Cole Latimer inquired with a hint of sarcasm.

A brief, reluctant nod gave him an affirmative answer. "Uh—Al! Al, sir." The nod became more vigorous.

Throwing away his cigar, the captain arched a brow as he peered at the lad. "Is something wrong with your tongue?"

"N-no, sir," Al stammered.

Skeptically eyeing the battered hat, Cole reached to push open the door. "Remember your manners, Al, and find a place for that thing besides the top of your head."

The boy made a sorry attempt at a smile, glared at the Yankee's back, and glumly followed him in. The stout matron of the place paused in her work to watch the two cross the room where they settled themselves at a small table that stood before a window. Her face betrayed no emotion as she contemplated the Yankee's crisp, neat uniform and the lad's ill-fitting garments, but when she returned to the task of chopping vegetables, a slight frown flitted across her brow.

Reluctantly copying Captain Latimer's manner, Al pulled his hat off and slid into the chair indicated. In wry disbelief Cole surveyed the unevenly cropped thatch of mahogany brown hair, and his expression grew obviously pained.

"Who cut your hair like that, boy?" he asked. He missed the bottom lip which trembled at his question and caught only the croaked answer.

"Me."

Cole laughed. "Your talents must lie in other directions."

Silence answered him as the thin face turned to the

window, and gray eyes brimmed with threatening tears. Not noting the lad's distress, Cole beckoned the woman to their table where she stood with arms akimbo.

"Y'all get shrimp today," she drawled roughly. "Bisque or creole. We got beer or coffee, tea or cow's milk. What's your choice, suh?" she asked, stressing the last word.

Cole ignored the satirical inflection in her voice, having grown accustomed to the disdain Southerners bore him or any soldier in blue. He had arrived in New Orleans when General Butler governed the city, and the public animosity had been worse then. The General had tried to run the town like a military garrison, issuing orders and mandates that were supposed to solve any situation. Unable to understand or cope with the stubborn pride of the citizenry, he had failed miserably. Indeed, the city had been near a state of revolt when the general was recalled. Yet the man had been equally severe with his own troops, had even hung a few who had been caught stealing from civilians. New Orleans was not an easy city to manage and certainly not by the weak-willed. Because Butler had been harsh in his measures, he had been doubly unpopular, but the Southerners would have hated any Yankee placed in the general's position.

"I'll have the bisque and cool beer," Cole decided. "And for the lad, anything he wishes with the exception of the beer."

When the woman left them, the captain again studied his young companion. "New Orleans seems an unlikely destination for a boy who hates Yankees as much as you do. Have you kin here, or someone else to stay with?"

"Gotta uncle."

"That's a relief. I was afraid I would have to let you share my quarters."

Al choked and had to cough to clear his throat. "Ain't gonna bed down with no Yankee, that's fer sure."

Sighing impatiently, the captain came back to the subject of work. "I would assume you have need of some sort of income, but most of the civilians are in a hard way themselves. The Union Army is about the only source capable of hiring you, and the hospital seems a good choice for one such as you. Unless, of course, you desire to join the sanitation crews and sweep the streets."

Al controlled his glare only slightly.

"Can you write and cypher?"

"A little."

"What does that mean? Can you pen your name, or can you do more?"

The boy stared at the officer with bristling anger, and his voice was flat as he retorted, "More, if'n I gotta."

"We did have some blacks to clean at the hospital, but they enlisted in the army," Cole commented. "We don't have much of an Invalid Corps since the wounded that are capable of getting about are either returned to their units or sent back east to recover."

"I ain't gonna help heal no Yankee!" the boy hotly protested. A hint of tears brightened the translucent eyes as he spoke. "Y'all killed my pa and brother and drove my ma to her grave with yer infernal thievin'."

Cole felt a pang of pity for the ragged lad. "I'm sorry, Al. My task is the saving of lives and the mending of men, whatever uniform they may wear."

"Huh. I ain't seen a Yankee yet who wouldn't rather ride across our lands, burning and lootin'—"

"Just where are you from to have gained such a high opinion of us?" the captain interrupted brusquely.

"Upriver."

"Upriver?" Sarcasm was bold in the captain's tone. "Not Chancellorsville or Gettysburg? You've heard of those places, haven't you?" Despite the tightening lean jaw and the lowered gaze of the other, he didn't ease his mockery. "Why, from your answer, I could assume you were a damn bluebelly just like me and had seen some of those Johnny Rebs swarming over our lands. Just how far upriver do you mean, boy? Baton Rouge? Vicksburg? Perhaps Minnesota?"

Stormy gray eyes flew to meet his and snapped with irate sparks. "Only a braying ass would come from Minnesotee!"

A warning finger made a reappearance beneath the lad's slim nose. "Didn't I tell you to mind your manners?"

"My manners is jes' fine, Yankee." Boldly he slapped the hand away. "It's your'ns what got me riled. Ain't yer ma ever tole you it weren't nice to point?"

"Be careful," the officer cautioned almost gently. "Or I'll take down your britches and blister your backside good."

With a gasp Al came half out of his chair, then

crouched like a wild animal at bay. Indeed, a feral light gleamed in the lucid depths of his eyes. He jerked up his hat again and jammed it over his shabby hair. "You lay a finger on me, Yankee"—he ground the words out in a low, husky voice—"and you'll draw back a nubbin. I ain't taking no guff off'n no damned blueleg—"

In the face of this dire threat Cole Latimer rose and leaned forward deliberately until blue eyes stared into gray from a little more than a hand's breadth apart. The captain's eyes grew hard and flintlike. Yet when it came, his voice was soft and slow. "You dare me, boy?" Before the urchin could move, the hat was snatched from the ragged head and slapped onto the table. The gray eyes grew wide in sudden distress. Cole continued, his tone unchanged. "Sit down. Shut up. Or I'll do it here and now."

The lad swallowed and could find no trace of anger to bolster his flagging courage. Quickly he sat down and, with considerably more respect, cautiously watched the Yankee.

Cole lowered himself into his chair and, studying the humbled one, spoke carefully and distinctly. "I have never been an abuser of children, nor of women—" The lad's gaze never left the captain's face, and he sat rigidly erect. "But if you tempt me enough, I might change my ways."

The suddenly uncertain boy searched for his best manners. Lowering his eyes before the man's regard, he folded his hands in his lap and sat meekly silent.

"That's better." Cole nodded his approval. "Now, how far upriver?"

The reply was barely heard. "A few miles north o' Baton Rouge."

Captain Latimer's mouth softened into a lazy smile as the boy carefully avoided meeting his eyes. "I shall hope in the future that you will revise your opinion of me, Al." The lad raised his gaze and appeared somewhat bemused until the officer explained. "My home is farther upriver—Minnesota."

Embarrassment joined confusion in a rapid play over the sprig's face. He was rescued from his predicament when the portly matron returned to their table, skillfully balancing a huge tray on one hand. With a total lack of fanfare, she placed large steaming bowls of the spicy bisque before them. Shortly, these were joined by a plate of warm biscuits and another of cornmeal-battered catfish, deep fried to a golden brown. The woman had hardly retreated from their table before the boy began munching on a piece of fish and as rapidly spooning the rich broth into his mouth. For a long moment Cole watched in amusement until the ravenous youngling became aware of the officer's attention. Suddenly abashed, Al laid down the fish and slowed his spooning. Captain Latimer chuckled lightly, then turned his interest to the tantalizingly delicious food.

Though the boy had eaten heartily at first, he seemed to satisfy his hunger quickly and dallied with the remainder of his food while Cole consumed his portions more leisurely, savoring each taste fully. When he finished the meal, the captain sat back and wiped his mouth on a napkin.

"Do you know where your uncle lives?"

A quick nod answered him, and Cole rose, tossed down several bills, and picked up his hat. He gestured for the lad to follow. "Come on. If I still have a horse outside, we'll see about getting you to your uncle's."

The youngster readily hoisted his case and hurried out the door after the tall man. He could hardly refuse the captain, and besides, riding was infinitely better than walking. Struggling with the valise and the weight of the heavy boots, he staggered behind his guardian. The unlikely procession of unwashed ragamuffin and impeccably groomed officer made its way to where a tall, long-legged roan stood tethered in the shade. Gathering the reins, Cole turned to consider the slim lad and his burden.

"Do you think you can stay on behind me and hold your gear?"

"Yeah." The boy swaggered a bit. "I been riding since I was little."

"Get up there then. I'll hand you the valise."

Cole held the horse while the lad attempted to step into the high stirrup, but once in it he had not the span to throw his other leg over the saddle.

"Since you were little, huh?"

With a start of surprise, Al felt a broad hand beneath his buttocks, hoisting him up. The gray eyes widened considerably, and some distress showed in his face as he was settled on the back of the steed. Angrily he jerked around to snap at the Yankee, but the captain was already lifting the case. He set it before the youth with an offhand remark. "I would guess that you've had an easy life until now, Al. You're as soft as a woman."

The captain placed the reins without further comment and swung onto the horse, throwing his leg over the horn of the saddle. For a moment, they adjusted things, then the captain asked over his shoulder, "All set?"

At the answering, "Yup," Cole reined the beast around and rode away from the dock. The roan was magnificent and well trained but unaccustomed to the extra load, slight though it was. The youth was proud but had to fight the large case in his arms, the slippery back of the animal, and a reluctance to touch the captain. His efforts made the steed more skittish. Finally Cole lost his patience and snapped curtly over his shoulder, "Al, get your butt settled and be still back there, or we'll both end up in the street." Reaching around, he caught the smaller hand in his and pressed it firmly against his side. "Here, grab a handful of my jacket. Now hang on with both hands and sit still."

Gingerly the youth took hold of the proffered garment and adjusted himself. The horse quieted some, and the ride was easier. The wicker case sat on end between them and was held in place by the boy's arms. The lad was satisfied. At least he didn't have to rub against that hated blue coat.

Chapter 2

THE city had been relatively untouched by battle. Along the river the scars of strife were visible, but as they moved away from the dock, life appeared to go on much as it had before, unhindered by the presence of Union soldiers. Shops and narrow houses, adorned with iron lace-trimmed balconies, huddled close against each other. Well-tended gardens were visible in courtyards behind exquisitely wrought iron gates, and trees grew in odd places. As the boy's directions led them away from the Vieux Carré, the avenues grew wider, then small lawns became evident. Magnolia trees laden with large, waxy blooms mixed their heady fragrance with that of jasmine, sweet shrub, and crepe myrtle. Further on, the lawns grew wide and spacious, and great houses spread their galleries beneath towering, moss-festooned oak trees.

Cole peered over his shoulder and spoke with some doubt. "Are you sure you know where you're leading us, Al? This is where the wealthy live."

"Huh. What little wealth you Yankees leave." The boy shrugged and pointed. "I've been here before. It's just a little ways further. Down there."

A few moments later he gestured to a lane that led through a tall hedge behind which loomed a brick house of considerable proportions. Brick arches shaded the first floor gallery, and near one end of the porch, a curving wrought iron staircase led to an upper filigree-adorned balcony that stretched across the face of the manor. Massive live oaks shielded the whole from the hot sun, and beneath their spreading limbs, the carriage house could be seen beyond the intricate iron gate that led into the grounds.

Cole sensed the boy's rising eagerness as he turned his steed onto the curving brick path. Halting the animal before the wide gallery, Cole swung down and looped the reins through the iron ring of the hitching post, then reached up to take the case. As he set it down, Al bounced to the ground and fairly flew to the front door to pull vigorously upon the bell. Like any good servant, the captain was left to heft the bag and follow behind.

Al cast an apprehensive glance over his shoulder as Cole joined him and impatiently rang the bell again. A sound of footsteps came from within and the door was opened by a striking young woman, slightly taller than the boy. As she looked at them in confusion, Cole swept his hat from his head and tucked it beneath his arm. A Yankee officer's presence on the gallery was bewildering, but not half as much as the pleading grimace she saw on the lad's face.

"Ma'm." Cole had seen nothing that resembled recognition in the beautiful visage and began to suspect the urchin's credibility. "This boy says he knows you. Is that true?"

The woman returned her astonished gaze to the youth and appeared repulsed by what she saw. She wrinkled her nose in disgust. "Gracious me, I surely should hope n—" Suddenly she gasped. "Al—Al—"

At the boy's startled expression, she choked off the name but was obviously flustered. She glanced nervously toward the captain then back to the lad.

"Al?" She tried out the name gingerly and was encouraged by the boy's responsive smile. "Why, Al, it is you! We hadn't—ah—expected you. My goodness! Won't Mama be surprised. I declare, she'll simply be aflutter when she sees you!"

The raven-haired beauty faced Cole again and gave him a charming smile. "I hope Al hasn't done anything too terrible, Colonel. Mama always said Al had a mind of his own. Why, there's just no telling what he'll do next."

"Captain, ma'm," Cole corrected politely. "Captain Cole Latimer."

The boy threw a thumb over his shoulder and explained gruffly, "The doc, here, give me a ride from the boat."

The young woman's eyes widened in amazement as she shifted her gaze from the Union officer to the roan tethered to the hitching post. "My goodness, you don't mean to say you rode together—"

Al coughed loudly and half turned to the Yankee. "This here's my cousin, Roberta. Roberta Craighugh."

Cole had already taken in the black hair and dark eyes, the summer gown of flowered peach muslin cut daringly low across a full bosom, and responded in the gallant fashion of a gentleman, clicking his heels as he bowed. "I'm honored to make your acquaintance, Miss Craighugh."

Roberta's mother was French, and that amorous blood now rose under the manly perusal of this handsome Yankee officer. The war had curtailed many of the pleasures in her life, and she was approaching the spinsterish age of twenty-two. She had become convinced that without male companionship a girl could waste away to nothing. It seemed like ages had passed since she last received a gentleman caller, and she was hopelessly bored with her existence. But her spirits steadily revived as her prospects of making another conquest loomed brighter. What made it more intriguing was that he was in the ranks of the forbidden harvest, the hated Yankees.

"I can't say I've entertained too many Northern soldiers, Captain," she stated brightly. "I've heard so many disturbin' stories about y'all. Still"—she nibbled pensively at her fingertip—"y'all don't look like the sort of man who would go about the countryside frightening poor, defenseless women."

White teeth gleamed in a reckless smile as Cole responded. "I try hard not to, ma'm."

Roberta blushed with excitement, and her thoughts ran rampant. He seemed far more manly and self-assured than those silly boys who had feverishly plied her with proposals before marching off to war for the Confederacy. She had found no challenge in winning their hearts, but this Yankee might prove better sport.

As if suddenly reminded of her cousin, Roberta faced him. "Al, why don't you run along in. Dulcie will be glad to see you, I'm sure."

Dismissed but reluctant to go, Al glanced worriedly from his cousin to the Yankee. Al had seen that certain look come into Roberta's eyes before on prior visits and he knew it boded ill for himself, if not for the captain. To have the enemy pay court to Roberta was like looking down the wrong end of a rifle. He'd just as soon not be on the dangerous end when it went off.

Wiping a grubby hand on his dingy trousers, Al extended it toward the man. "Thank ya kindly for the ride, Cap'n. I 'spect you can find your own way back jes' fine." Al nodded toward the sun shining through the trees. "Looks a bit like rain, though. Guess you'd best be gettin' back befo'—"

"Nonsense, Al," interrupted Roberta. "The least we can do is repay this nice gentleman for his kindness. I'm sure he would enjoy some refreshments after that long, hot ride." She smiled warmly at Cole. "Won't y'all come inside where it's cooler, Captain?" Ignoring her cousin's distress, she opened the door wider and beckoned sweetly, "This way, Captain."

Al stared after the two as they entered the house, his teeth clenched in rage, his gray eyes flaring. He hefted the heavy case and wrestled it through the door, but in the process banged his elbow and mumbled several words the captain would not have approved of had he heard. Fortunately, that one's attention was well occupied as Roberta led him into the sparsely furnished parlor.

"You must forgive the appearance of this room, Captain. Before the war it was much more grand." Demurely she spread her wide, hooped skirts before Cole's chair and perched with ladylike poise on the edge of the faded silk settee. "Why, my father has been left with only a little bitty store to make ends meet after we had so much. And who can afford to pay such exorbitant prices as he must charge. Imagine paying a whole dollar for a bar of soap, and I grew so fond of Parisian scents. I can't bear to even look at those rough ol' cakes Dulcie makes."

"War seems to get the best of everybody, ma'm," Cole commented with irony.

"The war wasn't so hard to bear until that dreadful General Butler descended upon us. Excuse me for being blunt, Captain, but I hated that man."

"Most Southerners did, Miss Craighugh."

"Yes, but few had to endure what we were put through. My father's warehouses were seized by that beastly man. Why, he even had our furniture and valuables confiscated just because Daddy wouldn't sign that miserable ol' loyalty oath. They were even going to take away this very house, if you can imagine but Daddy gave in—just to keep me and Mama safe. Then, there was that awful affront to all of us when Butler issued orders that the womenfolk of the city should be treated less politely by his men. I just can't imagine a gentleman like yourself, sir, following such a command."

Cole knew General Order Twenty-Eight by heart, for it had caused a great furor among the civilians. Butler had issued it to protect his men from the insults of the women of New Orleans, but his actions had backfired and eventually won more sympathy for the South. "And I, Miss Craighugh, cannot envision you deserving such treatment."

"I must confess that I was afraid to set foot outside this house for fear of being accosted. I was most relieved when the Union Army decided to replace General Butler, and now they have that other nice general in command. I've heard that Banks gives the most lavish balls and is far more cordial. Have you ever been to any of those affairs, Captain?"

"I'm afraid I've been too busy at the hospital, Miss Craighugh. It's a rare day I have to myself, but I've been most fortunate today. After the general's inspection of the hospital this morning, I was able to take the afternoon off. I shall hereafter consider it as my good fortune."

Al stood through Roberta's chatter and the captain's replies, attempting to catch her eye while at the same time trying to stay out of the man's range of vision. But the lad realized his cousin was totally engrossed with entertaining the Union officer and refused to be interrupted. Forcing the woman to remember her manners, Al dropped the valise on the marble floor with a disrupting clatter.

Roberta started. "Oh, Al! You must be starving, child, and supper won't be for ages yet. Go tell Dulcie to find you something to tide you over." She smiled brightly at Cole. "Gracious, it's been so long since we've entertained, I've nearly forgotten my upbringin'. Captain Latimer, won't you stay and join us for dinner? Dulcie is just about the best cook in New Orleans."

Al rolled his eyes in total incredulity. How could Roberta do such a thing?

Surprised by the invitation, Cole was slow to reply. Usually it was only the women of the back streets who would lower themselves to consort with the enemy, and even they were not always the most congenial. Though it had meant long months of celibacy, he had not been inclined to indulge himself with some pretty, knife-wielding Confederate sympathizer. Nor, for that matter, had he been tempted to crawl into bed with those proven safe by countless numbers in the Union ranks. He was not uneager to be in the company of such a beauteous lady, but there were things to be considered. Her father, for instance. He would just as soon refrain from getting himself into a forced marriage.

"I just won't hear of you rejecting my invitation, Captain," Roberta pouted winsomely, confident that he would accept. After all, she had never been refused before. "I suspect that you've been shown very little hospitality here in New Orleans."

"One can hardly expect it under the circumstances," Cole smiled.

"Well, it's settled then," Roberta replied happily. "You must stay. After all, you did bring Al home, and we are indebted to you."

Unable to regain Roberta's attention, Al gave a subdued snort and made his way toward the back of the house. The oversize boots clumped noisily against the floor, marking his passage through the mansion. The sound of his stride was like a death toll echoing through the stripped rooms, and he softened his steps. The house was hardly more than a shadow of its former splendor, and it was painful to look about at the bare walls and empty nooks and crannies where once treasured pieces had been displayed. Absent, too, was the usual bustle of servants. Al could surmise that except for Dulcie's family, all the slaves had gone.

He swung open the kitchen door and found the black woman busy preparing a stew for the evening meal. Dulcie was a large-boned woman, broad but not fat, and stood a good head taller than the slight youth. She paused in scraping a carrot and wiped her brow with the back of her hand. From the corner of her eye, she caught sight of the unkempt lad and frowned heavily in displeasure as she looked him over.

"Whad yo' doing here, boy?" she questioned suspiciously. She threw down the carrot and rose to her feet, wiping her hands angrily on the large white apron. "If'n yo' wants some vittles, yo' comes to de back do'. Doan come traipsin' through Mastah Angus's house like some lord almighty Yankee."

Fearful that her voice might carry to the parlor, Al tried to shush the Negress and gestured toward the front of the house. But seeing the open bemusement on the servant's face, he stepped closer and laid a hand on the woman's arm.

"Dulcie, it's me—Al—"

"Law-w-w-sy!" The screech of recognition seemed to ring through the whole manse before it ended abruptly as the wide-eyed youth clapped an anxious hand over the old woman's mouth.

In the parlor Roberta glanced worriedly toward the direction of the kitchen before meeting Cole's wondering gaze. Coyly she murmured behind her fan, "Al always did have a way with Dulcie."

Avoiding any further inquiries, she engaged him in bubbling conversation. The color of his uniform she had already discarded as irrelevant. He was a man, completely and totally. It showed in his walk, his speech, his gestures. The easy rich timbre of his voice sent delightful shivers down her spine. His manners were smooth and polished, yet she sensed in him that which brooked no impertinence. He was at ease with her. Still, she surmised that he would be equally relaxed in a group of men. She had barely met him, yet her blood was warmed by his presence, and she thrilled with the idea of being actively courted again.

Cole had resigned himself to a wasted day when the misplaced waif became his responsibility. It was rare enough that his duties at the hospital permitted his absence for even an afternoon. And he found it difficult to resolve this splendid turn of events. To be here in a cool parlor enjoying a pleasant repartee with a desirable woman was a greater reward than he might have expected from giving aid to an orphan whelp. He relaxed as he listened to Roberta's light and animated chatter until a few moments later a carriage rattled to a halt before the house, immediately silencing the effervescent woman. Concern creased her brow, and she came to her feet, at once nervous and more than a trifle distraught.

"Excuse me, Captain. I do believe my parents have arrived home." She was about to hurry into the hall when the front door burst open and Angus Craighugh came charging through the portal, followed closely by his wife. Angus was a short, stocky man of Scottish descent, with whitening tawny hair and a broad, ruddy face. Leala Craighugh was a distraught woman whose small stature had grown plump with the passing years. Her dark hair was lightly streaked with gray, and her sudden distress clearly showed in her large, dark eyes. Indeed, the anxious expressions the elders wore gave mute evidence that both had seen the roan with its Federal trappings. They could only think the worst.

Roberta had no chance to halt her parents out of earshot of the captain and explain his presence. He had decorously risen with her and now faced the two who could hardly do more than gape at him.

"Is there trouble?" Angus Craighugh demanded. He shot a quick glance toward his daughter but gave her no pause to answer before his anger was again turned on the Union officer. Craighugh's stubborn, square jaw tightened as he hotly declared, "Sir, my daughter is not in the habit of entertaining your men in the absence of a proper chaperon, and most especially, Yankees. If you have business with me, we'll go into my study where we won't disturb the ladies."

Cole was about to allay the man's fears when Roberta interceded. "Daddy, dear—this is Captain Latimer. He met *Al* at the dock and was kind enough to escort *him* here."

Rumbling in confusion, Angus scowled darkly at his only child. Some of the indignation apparent in his ruddy face yielded to obvious bewilderment. "Al? Him? What is this, Roberta? Some tomfoolery of yours?"

"Please, Daddy." She took his hand and her black, shining eyes stared intensely into his. *"He's* in the kitchen getting a bite to eat. Why don't you and Mama go and greet him."

In some consternation the elder Craighughs acceded to their daughter's urgings. Roberta relaxed a bit as she found herself once more alone with Cole. She graced him with a fetching smile and was about to comment on the heat of the day when, from the rear of the house, there came a shrill scream followed, after a breath's pause, by a rush of confused French. Roberta jumped as if stung, but recovered herself quickly as she realized the captain was already moving past her.

"No! Please!" she gasped, grasping his arm. She was saved from the need of further physical effort by the reappearance of her father supporting his distraught wife against him and patting her cheek while she continued to babble a stream of incoherent words. Angus hastened to lower his burden to the settee and managed to calm her flood of garbled verbiage.

"Perhaps I could be of assistance, sir," Cole offered, stepping near. "I am a doctor."

"No!" The answer was sharp and sudden. Angus waved away the other's help and, struggling to control himself, continued more calmly. "No, please. Forgive her. It was just the surprise—there was a mouse." He shrugged lamely.

Cole appeared to accept the excuse until he looked pointedly toward the door where Al had come to lean against the molding, then he nodded. "I think I understand."

Roberta twisted her hands anxiously, nervously eyeing the youth. "Al has changed so much, it would give anybody a shock—"

Leala had regained a small bit of composure and struggled to sit upright. Carefully keeping her gaze away from the lad, she tried to maintain some semblance of poise.

"You must forgive us all, Captain," Angus said rather tersely. The older man appeared rather strained as he faced the doctor. "We don't often have Union officers visiting here. We were sure there was some difficulty, then to see the—ah—boy, Al—"

The youth sauntered casually into the room, his large boots dragging on the threadbare rug, and gave them his own dirty-faced grin, showing small, sparkling white teeth for a moment. He shrugged and gave the excuse, "Sorry, Uncle Angus. I ain't never been too good at writin', and 'sides, I couldn've sent a letter nohow."

Angus flinched slightly as the lad spoke, while Leala's

bewildered gaze fastened on the boy and followed his every movement.

"It's all right, Al," Angus managed to reply. "These are hard times."

Roberta smiled somewhat tremulously at Cole. "I do hope you don't think we're a bunch of ninnies with this display, Captain."

"Of course not," Cole assured her politely, though his eyes, raising to the slim lad, gleamed with amusement.

Angus moved between and stood where the Yankee could no longer survey the youth. "I hope you will accept our gratitude for bringing Al to us. No telling where the boy would have ended up had it not been for you."

Al strolled jauntily across the room, seeming to challenge some comment from the Yankee. Cole responded by giving the youth a twisted grin. "In truth, sir, he was having himself quite a tussle with some soldiers when I interrupted."

"Oooh!" Leala gasped and, seizing her fan, plied it with great verve.

Angus momentarily directed his attention to his wife. "Are you all right, Mama?"

"Oui," she choked and nodded stoutly. "I am fine."

Angus turned his concern to the boy. "Was there some difficulty? Are you—all right?"

"Sure!" Al swaggered and showed a small doubled fist. "Given a chance, I'da whupped them bluebellies."

His uncle gave him a strange look. "Well," he sighed, "I'm glad you're here safely and it's all over."

Al smiled slyly. " 'Tain't over." All eyes swung round to him and, except for the captain, no one breathed. The gamin grinned broadly. "Roberta asked the doc to stay fer supper."

Leala's fan rattled to the floor, and she slumped back in her chair with a forlorn groan. She could only stare in numb disbelief at her offspring. Angus's face darkened ominously as he, too, looked at his daughter. It was a long moment of awkward silence.

Cole thought it best to relieve their distress. "I am on duty later tonight at the hospital, sir. I'm afraid I cannot accept the invitation."

"Oh, Captain," Roberta mewled, ignoring her parent's displeasure. "Surely you will let us show our appreciation for you bringing Al to us. When will you be free again?"

Cole was amused at her persistence and determination. "If no difficulty occurs, I will have an evening liberty Friday of next week."

"Then you must come and share a meal with us Friday evening," Roberta urged sweetly despite her father's warning scowl.

Cole could hardly mistake the reluctance of her parents and turned his consideration to the other man. "Only with your permission, sir."

The elder silently conveyed his disapproval to the daughter but could only resign himself. Short of blunt discourtesy, he could find no way out. "Of course, Captain. We do appreciate your service to the boy."

"The least I could do, sir," Cole replied politely. "It seemed the lad needed someone to take him firmly in hand. I am much relieved to see him with his kin."

"Huh!" Al scoffed. "One less brat on your mind. You bluebellies make enough orphans and then have the gall to prance yer rears into parlors laid bare by your thieving men—"

Leala's wavering voice whined fearfully, and she wrung her hands disconcertedly, looking plaintively toward her husband. Angus hastened to pour a strong sherry for his wife in hopes of offsetting her shock. He pressed the goblet into her trembling hand and waited until she took a deep drink, then looked at Al reprovingly. "I'm sure that Captain Latimer had nothing to do with that, Al."

"Of course not," Roberta agreed, surreptitiously glaring at Al. The captain was the most exciting person she had met since the occupation of New Orleans, and she was not about to let her cousin make a mess of her best chance since this boring war had forced her into a spinsterish existence. Indeed, she intended to use all her wiles to bring about a relationship that would be completely advantageous to herself. Dipping her dark lashes coquettishly, she turned a smile upon Cole and warmed with pleasure as he perused her in that ageless way in which a man looks at a handsome woman. He was ripe for the plucking.

A witness to this exchange, Angus stiffened and could not disguise his angry flush of color when the other man looked at him squarely. Cole smiled pleasantly. "Your daughter is very beautiful, sir. It's been a long time since I've enjoyed such gracious and fair company."

Through Angus's blustering discomfiture, Al snorted like an angry calf, drawing the captain's quizzical attention. Cole could well understand the father's displeasure, but the boy's manner puzzled him. Their eyes held for a long moment, the gray ones cool and derisive beneath the probing orbs of blue. Almost arrogantly the slim lad turned and strode to the settee where Leala sat. The glass of sherry stood on the table beside her, and in a contemptuous salute to the captain Al raised it and, still glaring his hatred, deliberately drained the contents.

"Al—" Cole's voice was subdued, and only the lad realized the threat in it. "You are distressing your aunt. And I'm sure it would be nice if you remembered your manners. In the presence of ladies, a gentleman should remove his hat."

Leala wrung her hands in renewed anxiety and glanced fearfully at her husband. She appeared on the verge of hysterical tears.

"Captain, it's quite all right," Angus was quick to insist, but Al's hand was already reaching toward the battered hat. Visual gray daggers pierced the Yankee before the thing was snatched off and sailed furiously across the room. Roberta gasped. Angus froze in horror before he found his voice. His bellow shook the rafters. *"What in the hell have you done?"*

A low moan started from his wife, rising in pitch and volume. She threw wide her hands and then clasped them tightly together as if seeking divine help. "Oh, Angus, Angus, Angus, what has she done? Ooooh!"

Angus quickly poured another glass of sherry and thrust it at his wife. "Here, Leala, drink," he bade and, with rare presence of mind, added, "Roberta hasn't done anything. It's that fool boy chopping away at his hair again."

His frown was fierce and deep as he directed it toward the youth, but he spoke aside to the captain. "Al has always been afraid someone might mistake him for a girl."

His nephew choked and turned away, but Angus addressed him curtly, "Al, I think it's time you had a bath. You can have your usual room. And"—he pointed to the wicker case—"take that baggage with you."

When the boy was gone, Angus shook his head in bruised wonder. "The youth these days! I just don't know what it's all coming to. They have no discipline." He raised his arms and seemed eager to vent his tirade. "They do just as they please!"

Cole meant to allay the man's fears. "He appears to be a good lad, sir. Hardheaded, perhaps. Stubborn! Dirty! All true. Yet he should grow up to be quite a man."

Several months would pass before Cole would come to understand the pained frown that Angus Craighugh bent on him that moment.

Chapter 3

AL placed the large wicker case on the bed and slumped wearily beside it. On the riverboat a cotton bale had doubled for a bed, and it was an everlasting mystery how a thing that began so soft could be made so hard and uncomfortable. What little sleep had come had been brief and fitful. The coolness of early morning had been the only respite, and as the day grew hotter and more sultry, it was necessary to remain alert lest an uncautious moment destroy the best of plans. The game had been well played, and even the test of Roberta was past.

Al rose and moved to gaze out the window as the door opened and Dulcie's two daughters struggled to haul a small brass tub into the room. There was no way to determine if they had been warned, but it was best to avoid further commotion while the Yankee was still in the house. The girls could not suppress curious glances at the slim, forbidding back of the guest as they carried in water and prepared a tepid bath. But nothing was said, and after laying out towels and soap they left the room, closing the door gently behind them.

Grimy hands scooped into the bath and cupped the water, bringing it to the smudged face. A long sigh of pleasure escaped the weary lips as a flagging spirit was refreshed. With renewed attention, the gray eyes surveyed the room. A few pieces of furniture were gone, but what was left was familiar. The room seemed to welcome the wanderer like an old friend, evoking fond memories of old. They were needed to dull the stark ones of more recent origin. It was not home, but it was the best this one had sampled in a fortnight.

The slim figure slowly turned to confront the cracked mirror that stood beside the tub. A rueful smile spread over the pensive face. As if with a will of their own, hands raised and thin fingers ran through the shaggy mop of deep russet hair. The boots were kicked off with vigor, the loose trousers quickly followed, and the jacket was tossed on top of them. The shirt reached almost to the knees, and nimble fingers feverishly loosened the buttons until that, too, was discarded with the rest.

Alaina MacGaren stood before the mirror in plain, straight pantaloons and a child's chemise, her youthful breasts bound almost flat by the snug fit of the latter. Sweat-stained and dirty, the undergarments joined the growing heap and finally, free of restraint, she enjoyed a long, deep breath. Her reflection reaffirmed the fact that the past year and its toils had made her thin to a fault. She didn't care to be reminded how starved she looked, but she could hardly bemoan the fact. It had lent well to her disguise. Though seventeen, she had masqueraded as a stripling lad beneath the very noses of the Yankees. Captain Latimer had not even been suspicious.

Alaina, with some irritation, remembered Roberta's warm and congenial acceptance of the captain. Her cousin's flirtation would almost guarantee his return to the Craighugh home. Yet for Alaina, his visitations would pose definite problems. Without warning she might be called on to resume her charade.

Then, too, the subject of work had to be considered. After seeing the near poverty of the Craighughs, she could not freely accept their charity. She was determined to provide for herself, but what the captain said was true. There were few civilians who could afford to pay her a wage. Besides, what better place for a wanted woman to hide than as a lad in the Union hospital? The idea stayed with her and began to tickle her imagination.

Under closer inspection, Alaina studied her image. How long could she pose as a boy at the Yankee hospital? Was there something in her face that would betray her? The thin, pert nose that seemed almost an adjunct to her face with its sunburned brightness, and the lean, slightly squarish face with its high cheekbones could possibly pass for a boy's features, dainty though they were. Perhaps the large and sparkling gray eyes that slanted upward beneath long, silky black lashes were not even a liability. But the mouth! It was too soft! Far too pink and delicate! Certainly not boyish!

Musingly Alaina puckered, grimaced, and tightly smiled at her reflection. *There!* she thought. *If I just hold my lips firm—it just might work.*

Alaina considered her features only for what hazard they might pose. In spite of her mother's best efforts, she had been much of a tomboy most of her young life. Then, these last years of overwhelming responsibility, a meager diet, and hard work had all but smothered the customary changes to womanhood. In the face of this hindrance, nature, with infinite patience, bided its day. This was a time for survival, not girlish longings. With a hardness of mind born of necessity, Alaina gave her thoughts over to how best she might carry out her mummery. She entertained no concept of a day when these selfsame, though now inconvenient, features might cause a man to forget what other goals he had in mind.

The sound of the front door opening and closing caught Alaina's attention, and she went to peek through the louvered slats of the French doors that led onto the balcony overlooking the front lawn. Captain Latimer came into view and strode toward his horse, settling his hat on his head. Reluctantly Alaina admitted to herself that he was a splendid and somewhat exceptional figure of a man. Tall, ramrod straight, lean and muscular, he lent to the uniform a dignity and bearing that few men could. She would even concede that he was rather handsome with his crisp, clean features and vivid blue eyes. But he was a Yankee and that, in Alaina's opinion, was an unpardonable sin. She dismissed him easily as she returned to her bath. If Roberta was infatuated with him, *this* cousin was most certainly not. She could accept him no better than she could that arrogant lieutenant who months ago at Brian Hill, had threatened to see her hanged for a spy. In fact, were the truth made known, Captain Latimer would probably seek the same end for her.

Lowering herself into the bath, Alaina scrubbed hard and worked the homemade soap into the snarled thatch that covered her head. Cutting her hair had been the hardest part, but the long, softly curling tresses had become a liability she could ill afford. Hiding in an old barn by the edge of the river, she had lopped it short lest a stray breeze or a brush in a crowd sweep the hat away and betray her.

How innocently it had all started. In the beginning the Confederate soldiers had only asked for food and shelter, sometimes a night or two of rest before they moved on. Her mother had dutifully taken them in, and Alaina had continued on after Glynis MacGaren's death, hoping somewhere some woman might be as kind to her brother, Jason, now the only other survivor of the Louisiana MacGarens. Banks and his scavengers had left precious little after their occupation of Alexandria, but Alaina had persisted, sharing what she could after the Yankees ravaged Briar Hill. But then, more than a fortnight ago, a young soldier had died in her barn, leaving in her care a message for General Richard Taylor. It had seemed simple enough for her to deliver it to the Confederate camp. That deed, however, proved pure misfortune. The eldest son of her white-trash neighbors, repeatedly rebuffed by her somewhat caustic tongue, discreetly followed her to the camp and home again. Once more he had proposed that he move into the MacGaren house and set himself up as lord and master of it, offering to wed her now that she had no kin left to care for her. He had retreated quickly enough when Alaina took up her father's pistol and drove him out of the house at gunpoint. The rejected swain had wasted no time in carrying the tale of her deed to the Yankees, receiving no doubt a goodly sum for his . . . loyalty.

Hate beat a more bitter note in Alaina's heart as she remembered the Yankee lieutenant who had ridden up the lane to Briar Hill with his handful of black soldiers. He had sat back in his saddle to watch in glee as his men circled close about her on their mounts, frightening off the milk cow she had been leading. But when he had grown bored with her defiant stare, the lieutenant had brusquely commanded his men to search the out buildings for Confederate soldiers, then loosening the flap of his holster as a warning, he had directed her ahead of him into the house and there, after barring the door behind him, had made a proposition in such crude terms as to be grossly insulting.

Alaina had replied in curt, cool disdain that her agreement would be conditional upon it being so cold a day that a certain unlikely locale would freeze over. The gallant lieutenant had cast aside his innate gentility and tried to force himself upon her in the parlor. Her screams had brought Saul crashing through the back door, and in the face of the huge black servant's rage, the chickenhearted coward had fled like a cur with its tail tucked between its legs, calling his men after him and vowing to see her hanged and that damned black right along with her. They would be back, the lieutenant had promised quite vocally, and with reinforcements. Then, just before he departed down the lane, he drew his pistol and shot the cow between the eyes. If his threat had not stirred enough fear, that unwarranted cruelty had brought cold terror to Alaina's insides. Ruthlessly he had taken pettish revenge, not caring who might suffer.

The pain of leaving her home still haunted Alaina. It seemed like ages since she had thrown what she could into the aged valise, assumed her boyish identity, and scrambled up behind Saul on Briar Hill's only remaining horse. For more than a week they had roamed the countryside, going to ground whenever Union troops were in the vicinity, only daring to return home once for food in the wee hours of morning. They were in Baton Rouge when Saul, about to cross the street to join her with their precious knapsack of food, was stopped by a shout. Glancing about, Alaina had spied the lieutenant rushing toward him and gesturing wildly for other soldiers to halt the black's escape. There were few men who could delay the powerful man, much less hold him secure. As he fled down the street away from her, Alaina drew back into the alley and slowly measured her retreat until well assured no one gave her notice, then she clambered onto the back of the nag and lit out. That night she kept a vigil for Saul, roaming the streets and finally camping on the outskirts. No more was seen of him, and after two days of scouring the countryside for him and eating nothing but a few handfuls of raw corn found in an untended field, she had traded the horse for the fare on the riverboat and headed for New Orleans.

The memories sharpened the pang of homesickness, and Alaina actively set her mind to something less disturbing. Finishing her bath in a rush and donning a threadbare garment, she laid out her meager possessions. The black dress she had worn to her mother's burial was her best, while the two muslin gowns she owned had been repeatedly patched. Alaina shook her head in rueful recollection. That fool soldier on the dock had nearly squashed the case open, and she had worried that it might fall from Captain Latimer's horse when she rode behind him. A young boy would have found a valise full of women's garments hard to explain. The captain had been so sure he had rescued an orphan lad. Instead, he had delivered to safety a young woman branded a spy by his own army and hunted like a dangerous animal.

A light rap sounded on the door and, at her call of admittance, Leala bustled into the room followed closely by Angus and Roberta.

"Alaina, child! You gave me such a start!" the older woman tenderly scolded before placing a kiss upon the girl's brow where the short hair was beginning to dry and curl in soft, feathery wisps. "And your hair! Your beautiful hair! All gone!"

"What made you leave Briar Hill?" Angus questioned brusquely. "When we came to see your mother buried, you were determined to remain. It's been almost a year since Glynis passed away. What happened to change your mind? Surely Jason hasn't been—"

"No!" Alaina didn't want to consider that her oldest brother might have perished like her other brother Gavin, and her father. "No," she said more calmly. "It's just that when the Yankees occupied Alexandria, they rode through our crops and tore down the sheds, enlisted our slaves in their army, slaughtered the cattle to feed their gluttony and took the horses for mounts, leaving nothing to make ends meet. Saul managed to hide one old nag from them, but I traded that to get here. Why, they even dragged away the mules, but whether to eat or to ride I'm not sure." Pacing the floor, she continued relating the story, gesturing and at times wringing her slender hands when the memory disturbed her greatly. "There's no way of knowing what happened to Saul. If the lieutenant caught him, he might be either dead or in jail."

"But what do you intend now, Lainie darling?" Roberta asked with wide, innocent eyes.

Angus cleared his throat and, seeing no other choice,

magnanimously yielded a declaration. "She'll stay here with us, of course. There's little else she can do."

"But, Daddy," Roberta implored. "Captain Latimer will surely come back. What is he going to think if he finds out that Al is really a girl?"

"You shouldn't have invited him, Roberta," her father mumbled discontentedly.

"Oh, Daddy," Roberta smiled and affectionately pinched his cheek. "Think of all he can do for us. Isn't it time we started taking from the Yankees instead of giving up everything that we own? Haven't they stolen enough from us? With butter four dollars a pound, and eggs five dollars a dozen, how can we afford to exist? Dulcie has been going to the French Market less and less, and your customers have become quite stingy with trading their foodstuffs and paying their bills. Why, I haven't had a new gown in months, and now we have another mouth to feed."

"Roberta!" her mother gasped.

If any lagging uncertainty remained in Alaina's determination to find work, Roberta's crudity strengthened her resolve. "I don't intend to be a burden," she announced. "Captain Latimer is looking for a boy to work at the hospital, and I'm going to accept the position—as Al."

"You'll do no such thing!" Leala was aghast. "I've never heard of anything so ridiculous! Imagine! A young, innocent girl working for those dirty Yankees! Why, your dear mother would come back to haunt me if I consented to anything so foolish. Poor Glynis, she was so in hopes you'd learn to be a lady. And now look at you! *Ma petite*, what's to become of you?" The woman dissolved into tears, unable to bear what this dreadful war had done to her niece.

"Now, Mama," Roberta soothed, patting Leala's shoulder. Although always rather thin and bony, Alaina had drawn, with her brightness of wit and easy charm, a covey of young men continually about her and Roberta could not bear to share the tiniest bit of masculine attention with her cousin. She could only think that Alaina, dressed as a boy, would be no competition at all. Indeed, the situation might lead to a bit of fun. Alaina always was too uppity for a country cousin, anyway. "The Yankees won't know it's Lainie. They'll think it's just a boy—Al—

that's all. And she plays the part so well, no one will ever know. What a trick to play on those nasty ol' Yankees."

Angus silently agreed with his wife. His sister, Glynis, had often despaired because Alaina refused to conform to a more genteel way. The girl had found far greater pleasure romping with her brothers, and Angus did not doubt in the least that she could shoot and ride about as well as most men. If anyone could pull such a farce off, Alaina was the one to do it.

Chapter 4

ALAINA stared wistfully out as the rain made long, wavering runnels down the windowpanes. Finding the right hospital had been difficult enough, but waiting for Captain Latimer had proven even more time consuming. She was beginning to wonder if anyone had bothered to inform the doctor that Al had come to inquire about a job. But what could one expect when a dirty-faced urchin asked to see a busy surgeon? Had she come wearing wide hoops and a fetching bonnet, Alaina wagered herselt, she would have had better results.

The room into which she had been ushered was obviously one in which the doctors spent their leisure moments. The narrow cot, the sparse and stark furnishings, however, indicated little time spent in relaxation.

In the hallway outside the dayroom, brisk footsteps stopped abruptly at the door. Quickly Alaina stepped down from the high stool where she had perched and, hat in hand, faced Captain Latimer as he entered. Seeing the scowl that drew his brows sharply together, she became suddenly wary of her foolishness at being here. Whatever else she might think of the man, she knew that Captain Latimer was not really a fool. How long could she hope to hide her identity behind the guise of unwashed scamp?

Recognizing the young lad, the captain curbed his irritation at being summoned from his duties and crossed the room to the washstand. Pulling off the long, white coat that was liberally smeared with blood, he tossed the garment into a basket before he met the youth's uncertain gaze.

"At least you appear to have learned a few manners since last we met," he commented a bit more tersely than he had intended. Seeing the apparent confusion of the other, he indicated the tattered hat.

"I done thought about that there work you offered," Alaina began politely, though she chafed at having to ask anything of a Yankee. "And seein's how my uncle can't afford another mouth to feed, I 'spect it's the only right thing fer me to do. That is, if'n you still need me, suh."

"Of course we need you, Al. Right now, if you can begin." At the quick, answering nod the captain briefly smiled. "Good, I'll show you what needs to be done, then I must get back to work. A riverboat was ambushed a few miles upriver, and they're bringing in the wounded. It would seem that your countrymen have difficulty recognizing the color of our uniforms. Several civilian passengers were brought in with the soldiers."

Alaina bristled as if rubbed the wrong way with a burr. "Them civilian-whatevers ain't no more'n packrats! They go upriver jes' to steal cotton from the plantations, and you bluebellies sit back and let 'em."

Cole splashed water into a porcelain basin and peered askance at the untidy youth. "Whatever they are, they're still human."

"Huh! Jes' barely!" Alaina snorted derisively. "I ain' gonna shed no tear over none of 'em."

"Perhaps I shouldn't trust you in the wards," Cole said, stripping off his shirt and splashing cool water over his face and shoulders. Sunlight glanced off a small, gold medallion which hung on a long chain about his neck, sending tiny flecks of light dancing across the wall. "I'm wondering if you might do more harm to our soldiers than they can bear."

The gray eyes narrowed. "Jes' as long as I don't have to play wet nurse to none of 'em, I'll do my work and do it good," she assured him sharply. "You needn't worry on that account. Of course—" She drew the last word out while she gave the man a scathing regard. Had she been of such a mind, she might have admired the wide, furred chest or the fascinating play of muscles that rippled along his ribs and arms. She relished more her hatred of Yankees. "If you think yer fellas got something to fear from an orphan boy, well, mister, you jes' better not hire me on."

Cole laughed aloud at the youth's audacity. He had already come to the conclusion that Al was as blunt and honest as any boy he had ever known. And twice as dirty! "I thought your uncle told you to wash."

Al's lean jaw flexed with irritation. "You show me what you want cleaned, bluebelly, and I'll see it done. But leave me outta your plans. A little dirt never hurt nobody."

Cole grunted in derision. "I can't even tell what you look like beneath all that grime."

"You don't need to, Yankee. Jes' cause you favor water and bathing, there ain't no need fer me to take up yer vices." Alaina didn't care for the way he contemplated her filthy garb and the washbasin and asked harshly. "Whatcha want me ter do 'round here? Ya did say you had to get back ta work, didn't ya?"

Cole slipped into his shirt again and, over it, donned a fresh white coat. He led Al through eight wards of the hospital, pausing in each to give brief, pertinent instructions as to what would be expected. The wards were large rooms, crowded with cots and, upon these, bandage-bedecked men. A thick layer of dust had accumulated beneath the beds, and old, discolored dressings were strewn upon the floor.

"We ain't discussed wages yet," Alaina pointed out. "How much you gonna pay me?"

"Same as any good Union soldier," Cole replied. "A dollar a day and found."

"I'll take the meals," Al stated flatly. "But since I ain't gonna sleep here, make it a dollar ten and you got yerself a deal."

"That sounds fair enough," Cole conceded, half amused. "But you better be worth it."

Alaina shrugged noncommittally. She wasn't about to go out of her way to reassure any blasted Yankee. When the captain left her, she did not tarry. She filled a bucket from the cistern pump and into it pared thin shavings from a bar of lye soap. With a heavy broom she reached into every corner, beneath every bed, stand, and chair, raking out the piles of trash and dirt. Her activities were ignored for the most part by soldiers more engrossed in the boredom of their pain than in the presence of this tight-lipped lad. A rare attempt was made by an occasional soldier to exchange some brief word with the boy, but since Al was no more inclined to pleasantries than the others, these attempts were met with grim silence, and the lad hastily took himself elsewhere.

The day's labor saw two wards clean. The filth and

grime had collected for several weeks and had become almost a natural fact of life in the wards. It was near dusk when Alaina wearily surveyed the well-scrubbed floor she had just finished. Her knees were raw; her hands burned from the strong soap. It was a dismal thought that she had only six more wards to clean. But that, she told herself firmly, would have to wait for another day. Even for a young lad, it was quitting time, and she had no wish to travel the streets after dark.

Feeling a bit frazzled and worn, she plodded down the hall in her oversize boots. At least the results of her hard work were readily discernible. The two wards almost gleamed with their new tidiness. The floors were scrubbed, the windows washed, the tables dusted. Even Captain Latimer would find it hard to fault her labors. But then, she hadn't seen him since early morning, and perhaps that was just as well. If the two wards were clean, she could hardly say the same for herself—and he did seem to resent her lack of neatness.

The ride home on the scrawny back of Ol' Tar (short for Tarnation), her uncle's ancient nag, did nothing for her fatigue. When she arrived home, Roberta was at the back door to meet her with her hair done in style and wearing a fetching gown of mint green muslin. Alaina felt the sharp contrast between them. Before leaving the house that morning she had rubbed a muddy mixture of dirt, grease, and water lightly through her own hair to disguise her dark, burnished curls. It was a disgusting mess that she longed to wash out, and as she passed her cousin, she hid her reddened hands with their short, broken nails and hurried to closet herself in the small pantry just off the kitchen. With the abrupt reduction of the Craighugh larder, the sizable cubicle had been made into a bathing chamber for the family, being conveniently near the kitchen hearth where a hot bath could be prepared without the laborious hauling of water. It was here that Alaina whiled away a good part of the evening instead of taking supper with the family. She lazed away the time, washing her hair, cleaning and trimming her nails, and rubbing a soothing salve on her red hands. It was a small luxury she permitted herself, but after playing the part of a boy these weeks in her bid for freedom, it was a great relaxation just to be a girl again. Where the pleas of her mother had failed, the enforced confinement in the boyish garb was beginning to show some results, to make her long to be a lady.

On the fifth day of work at the hospital, Alaina started over again and cleaned the first two wards. This time her labors went quickly, as the depth of debris was less. She placed empty tins for the trash and the soldiers began to use them. She even had help from a few who were mightily bored with their humdrum existence.

Much to her discomfiture, she found her midday meal intruded upon when Captain Latimer brought his plate of food and joined her at the table. With a baleful eye, Al peered up at him and considered the other tables in the mess hall. They were the only two people in the room.

"What's the matter, bluebelly? You cain't find no place else to sit?"

"Excuse me, Al, I didn't know you had a penchant for eating alone," the captain apologized dryly but made no attempt to leave.

"Whatcha think I come in here so late fer?" Al queried impertinently. "I'm particular as to what kind o' critter I eats with. Never had a stomach for takin' down vittles with polecats."

"Stop your caterwauling and eat," Cole ordered tersely. "You won't grow much bigger than you are now if you don't learn to pay more attention to food." Cole pointed to the leather pouch on the table beside Al's plate. "What do you carry around in that?"

"What's it to ya?"

The captain shrugged casually. "Well, I guess I'm curious. It's not a change of clothes, I'd wager, since I haven't seen you in anything but what you're wearing."

"If ya gotta know, it's vittles," Al grumbled. "What I can't eat here, I take home." She looked at the doctor narrowly and rubbed the tip of her nose with a thin finger. "You got some objection?"

Replying in the negative, Cole took a sip of coffee before he reached beneath his white coat and produced a narrow tan envelope with an official-looking stamp over the sealed flap. He tossed it on the table in front of her, and she noted that it bore the name Al Craighugh.

"What's that fer?" Alaina questioned suspiciously.

"Your wage for the week."

She tore open the missive. "But there's seven dollars here," she remarked, counting it out.

"The paymaster decided to make it an even amount. You've earned it." He watched the lad tie the money carefully in the corner of a worn handkerchief. The captain continued eating for a thoughtful moment before he inquired, "What are you going to do with all that wealth? Buy new clothes?"

"Half goes to Uncle Angus to pay fer lodging, then I plan to save what I can from the rest," Alaina stated matter-of-factly.

"If you'd like to earn some extra money, I have quarters in the Pontalba Apartments, and I could use someone to clean it during the week while I'm on duty."

"You're sure you can trust me, Yankee?" Al prodded.

"Do you want the work or not?" Cole asked impatiently.

"How fur a piece is it ta your what-cha-ma-call-its?"

"Apartment." Cole supplied the word and the information. "It's right on Jackson Square. You know where that is, don't you?"

"Yup." Al nodded. "How do I get in?"

"With a key," the captain responded with sarcasm and fished into an inside pocket for the mentioned object, giving it over. "I can get another from the landlord, so you can keep that. I will expect the same degree of cleanliness as I have seen here at the hospital, and for that, I will give you three dollars a week."

"Three dollars a week?" Alaina repeated in amazement. "You rich or somep'n?"

"I can afford *you*."

Alaina shrugged. "Makes no difference if you are or ain't. I'll clean yer 'partment and won't do no thievin' neither."

"Didn't expect that you would. Would you like wages in advance?"

"I can wait. 'Sides, you'd best hang onto what you can, jes' in case Gen'ral Taylor takes New Orl'ans. Likely you could buy yo'self someplace to lay yer head when the Johnnies capture ya."

"I'll worry about that when the times comes, if it ever does," the captain replied.

Alaina rose to her feet and hitched her britches. "Gots

ter get back to work now, Yankee. Cain't say as it's been nice talkin' to ya."

Despite himself, Cole smiled as he watched the lad amble off. Sometimes the urchin could be completely exasperating, yet there was something about him that was likable, too. He just had the usual difficulty defining the latter.

The days sped past, and with each Roberta grew more restive and impatient for the arrival of the appointed evening when she and her parents would entertain Cole Latimer. She repeatedly inspected her best gown lest some flaw mar her grand display. Indeed, no bird of paradise ever lent more attention to her preening than did Roberta. Insistent upon perfection, she scolded Dulcie on the eve of the captain's intended visit because the dining room and parlor had not been tidied for two days, as if, the black woman grumbled, there were not more important matters to be seen to than sprucing up the house for a Yankee.

Time progressed, as one might expect, and the day of Roberta's challenge arrived, much to Alaina's chagrin. While the older cousin dozed peacefully behind carefully drawn drapes, the younger girl dragged an indignant Ol' Tar from the stall, mounted astride his knife-edged spine and laboriously prodded him into a reluctant saunter, directing him toward the hospital. Once under way, the ornery nag settled into a bone-rattling trot, punctuated by grunts and wheezes, until he was convinced that no amount of fakery would regain him the comfort of the carriage house.

Though it was still early in the morning when Alaina arrived at the hospital there was already a train of ambulances before its doors and attendants were unloading wounded by the score. Alaina could guess the reason. Although the Mississippi River had been open to Federal shipping since mid-July and Baton Rouge was considered secure, General Taylor was recruiting for the Confederacy in up-country Louisiana and was making himself felt by waging a continuous guerrilla battle against the outlying fringes of the Yankee Army.

The blood and gore soon forced Alaina to retire from the crowded hallways, and the last she saw of Captain Latimer that morning, he was sorting out the wounded and determining which could afford to wait a few hours, or even a few days. The latter cases were rare, for only the more seriously injured were sent back to the hospital for treatment. The rest were treated in field hospitals nearer the action.

Though the morning progressed, Alaina refused to venture near the surgeon's wing and the persistent odor of chloroform grew stronger by the hour. How the captain could manage to be the sparkling guest Roberta expected that evening, Alaina could not begin to guess, and since she had determined not to be present at dinner, she would have to wait and hear the results at some later date.

In the late afternoon, it became difficult to carry out her chores, for she could no longer avoid the wards where the newly arrived wounded were being treated unless she totally disregarded her duties. As she worked, she often had to glance away as a running or gaping wound was uncovered, and her stomach heaved at the stench of putrid, rotting flesh. But when an oozing stub of a limb was brought into view, the sight proved too much, and she fled outside through the nearest door with a hand clutched over her mouth, helplessly retching. Her exit was badly timed, for Cole had taken a moment of rest outside and was there to witness her humiliation as she discarded her lunch behind a convenient bush. Too mortified to meet his amused gaze, she accepted the handkerchief he dunked in the watering trough. With trembling hand she dabbed the cool, wet cloth to her brow and face, then after a moment found the courage to peer up at the captain.

"Feel better now?" he asked solicitously.

Alaina's pride had been pricked, and she was hardly in the mood to forgive the captain for being at hand to watch her abasement. "You owe me three dollars, Yankee."

"Of course." Unable to stop grinning, Cole counted out the bills and handed them over with a teasing gambit. "I would say you take to cleaning better than you would doctoring. I don't think I've seen anybody quite as squeamish as you."

"You got somep'n to say 'bout the way I cleaned yer 'partment?" Alaina questioned angrily.

Cole shook his head. "No."

"Then I'll thank ya to keep yer comments to yerself, mister." With that, Al stomped back into the hospital, almost threatening to let him find someone else to clean his blamed apartment. But then, it was probably the easiest money she would ever make, for Captain Cole Latimer was as neat as his appearance suggested. And three dollars seemed like a lot to waste for pride's sake. As it was, she took pleasure in avoiding the captain for the remainder of that afternoon. Small revenge to be sure, but revenge she could afford.

The ride home on the narrow back of Ol' Tar that evening was a further test of endurance. The old horse's skill at finding his stable was unerring, and he grumbled only slightly as Alaina led him back to his stall. In the light of the dim lantern that hung from an overhead beam, she saw that Jedediah, Dulcie's husband and the Craighugh's coachman, had remembered her and left new hay in the manger and a fresh pail of water beside it. It was a relief that her labors were shortened this much, and she made a mental note to thank the man. She scooped a handful of oats into the grain box for the already dozing Tar, knowing that if Uncle Angus learned of it, he would sorely protest this squandering of the precious grain.

To date, her uncle's sole use of Tarnation was when he had hitched the animal up to a decrepit cart and went to plead his poverty with the Yankees. Perhaps Angus had been wise, for he had managed to retain possession of at least two horses, one a fine gelding of moderate spirit, which the man used on his own high-wheeled gig, and the other, Ol' Tar. The beast seemed a random collection of bones connected by rawhide sinew, the whole of which masqueraded in a worn and well-scarred horse's hide. He had two gaits. A loose-jointed shuffle appeared to be his normal one. It was perhaps faster than a walk. But when an unusually winsome mare happened by, the blood stirred in his veins, he arched his scrawny neck, flagged his tattered tail, and with great effort actually lifted his hooves from the ground, all of which resulted, if a rider was present, in a spine-snapping trot.

In her dirty, ragged garb, Alaina felt much akin to the unhandsome steed. A handful of Angus's grain now and then was her tithe to the aging mount. She tried not to strain the Craighugh's larder either and made it her habit to eat her meals at the hospital, stowing portions of the more delectable fare in her leather pouch for use in the kitchen or, occasionally, a late snack. It was her rule to pay Uncle Angus at each week's end. His Scottish frugality displayed itself as he murmured a few embarrassed words on the hardships of war before tucking the coins away in his purse. Alaina was fully aware that available goods for the store were sharply curtailed since the occupation and that his account books were heavy with entries of unsatisfied credit. It gave her a sense of freedom knowing that she did not further burden his resources.

The lantern was doused, and through the darkness Alaina groped her way along the flagstone walk from the stable to the house. A thoughtful extravagance on Dulcie's part met the weary late arrival in the form of a candle stump left aglow in the kitchen and water simmering on the hearth for a bath. Hopefully she would not be expected to work the later hours very often, but with the overload of wounded this day there had been no chance to escape the rapidly mounting chores and no sympathetic ear to listen to her complaint. Doctors apparently had little compassion for the healthy and able.

In the converted pantry, the boyish garb fell into an indiscreet pile on the floor, given no more notice by the one who gradually lowered her aching body into the water. Alaina moaned a soft mewl of delight. After the long, tiring day, when she had to drag herself through the last hours of work by keeping the thought of a bath uppermost in her mind, she intended to enjoy it now at her leisure. Slowly she lay back and closed her eyes, letting the heat seep into her tired limbs.

Only a moment of this revelry had passed when the rattle of the doorknob made Alaina sit up and snatch for a towel. Without so much as a knock, Roberta came boldly in, beautifully clothed in a red crepe de chine dressing gown. As she paused and shaded her eyes against the lamp, the wide sleeve fell back, displaying exquisite white, ruffled lace at her wrist.

"I thought I heard you come in."

Modestly Alaina tucked the linen towel over her bosom, not wishing to contrast herself with Roberta's roundly proportioned form. Her cousin began to pace fretfully, a difficult task considering the narrow space left by the tub.

"Do you have any idea what kind of day I've had?" Roberta demanded. "Why, it's been terrible! Terrible! I declare, Lainie darling, I just don't know what this world is coming to!"

It had all the appearance of being a long session, and though Alaina objected to this intrusion, her voice was casual and chatty. "Your situation sounds dire, Robbie. I thought you were having a guest this evening?"

"I am not!" Roberta whirled in high agitation. "Oh, posh! I wish these damned Yankees would get their war over with!"

"I think they're trying their best," Alaina retorted, growing a little annoyed herself. Sometimes she wondered where her cousin's loyalty really lay, but then, Roberta had given nothing to the war but hours of complaint about her highly vocalized inconvenience.

"The sooner the better, I say!" Resentfully Roberta folded her arms beneath her bosom. "Then the rest of us can get back to doing things the way they were before!"

"I believe Mister Lincoln has other ideas," Alaina reminded her dryly.

"That backwoods oaf!" Roberta railed and faced the tub. "I'm sick to death of that man's name! I'm sick of all this—this killing!"

Alaina's eyebrows raised as she stared at her cousin. Roberta rarely, if ever, concerned herself with the casualties of war. "Whatever has upset you, it must be serious."

"I'll tell you what has upset me! Just look at this!" Roberta pulled a crumpled note from the pocket of her wrapper and waved it beneath Alaina's slim nose without giving the girl a chance to comply. "For some damn reason, Captain Latimer couldn't come tonight! He sent this instead." She shook the missive angrily above her head, making the flame flicker in the lamp which sat high on a shelf. "A righteous excuse! An emergency! Bah! All the Yankees ever do is march about Jackson Square or ride their horses up and down the streets to look threatening. How can anybody get hurt that way? All Gen'ral Banks does is steal cotton or some such thing! Why, there hasn't hardly been anybody killed since Cock-eyed Butler hanged William Mumford and no one has come down sick with yellow fever since that terrible ol' Yankee got so scared he would catch it. Imagine, gettin' all those men out to sweep the streets! Why, New Orleans never had such a cleaning! And here we all were hoping the Yankees would come down sick and die."

Alaina's bath was becoming increasingly tepid, not to mention the fact that she was beginning to feel slightly waterlogged. It went against her grain to defend a Yankee and his reasons for not coming, yet Alaina realized her own comfort was at stake. Despite her great reluctance, she relented. "There was a skirmish upriver, Roberta. The wounded were brought back, and the doctors were kept busy trying to tend them all. I had to haul away bloody bandages and muddy clothes all afternoon just to keep an open passageway through the wards."

"Muddy clothes!" Roberta's mind grasped at Alaina's statement like a vulture at raw meat. "Lainie! You don't mean you're there when they undress men!"

Offended by the way of her cousin's mind, Alaina gritted, "I haven't seen a naked man yet! And I wish you would stop calling me Lainie. You know I hate that name."

"I guess you always did prefer 'Al' to anything more genteel," Roberta simpered and, ignoring her cousin's frown, flounced down upon the low stool that sat beside the tub. "What's so hellishly important about Cole tending those men anyway? Surely other doctors are there to bandage up those men."

"There are other doctors," Alaina conceded. "But it seems they were all in demand today."

Roberta sensed her cousin's growing irascibility and changed the subject, though not adroitly. "You must have learned a lot about Captain Latimer."

"I hear the other doctors talking."

"You spy on them?" Roberta queried, leaning close.

Alaina glared. "I do not! I'm just not deaf, that's all! They don't care who's around to hear."

"Tell me more about Cole," Roberta urged.

"Cole?" Alaina looked at the other woman wonderingly.

"Is he rich?" the older cousin questioned excitedly. "Real rich?"

"How should I know?" Alaina snapped. "I only know that he can afford to pay me three dollars a week for cleaning his apartment, and he never seems to have a shortage of money."

"You didn't tell me you cleaned his apartment!" Thoughtfully Roberta tucked her tongue in her cheek. "I bet Daddy doesn't know about it either."

"I can ill afford to turn down three dollars for a few

hours work," Alaina said crisply. "And I see nothing wrong with it since Captain Latimer is not there when I am."

"You mean he trusts you in his apartment alone?"

"And why not? I've never stolen a thing in my life!"

"But he can't be sure of that."

"He was confident enough to give me a key."

"A key? To Captain Latimer's apartment?" Roberta's interest rose with every passing second. "How do you manage to work all week at the hospital and then clean his apartment, too?"

"I do it after work the nights he has duty. He doesn't live far from the hospital, so I don't have to go far out of my way."

"And where does the captain live?" Roberta sweetly inquired.

Alaina looked at her suspiciously.

Smiling pleasantly, Roberta warned, "If you don't tell me, Lainie, I'll inform Daddy you're cleaning that Yankee's apartment. I don't think he'll approve. He might not let you work there after he finds out."

"I don't know what you have in mind, Roberta," the younger girl snapped, "but I really don't care. If you want Captain Latimer so much, take him."

"Where does he live?" Roberta questioned eagerly.

Alaina shrugged. "Pontalba Apartments. Anything else you'll have to find out from the good captain himself."

"You're mean, Lainie," Roberta pouted. "You always did like to tease me and be hateful about things. You're getting just what you deserve for being so spiteful."

"Da' ye say now?" Alaina retorted, affecting the Scottish burr of her father. "The truth ne'er hurt me nane, but ye'll na be hearing more aboot his lordship from these here lips!"

Roberta sulked for a long moment, but realizing even a fine pout would not impress her cousin, changed her tactics. "I'll ask Captain Latimer when he comes."

"Comes?" Alaina straightened in the tub and grasped the linen cloth more firmly when it threatened to fall from her bosom. "You mean Captain Latimer—is coming—here—despite this evening?"

Roberta was the epitome of angelic goodness now that her tirade was spent. "Didn't I tell you, Lainie? He wrote that he'd try to make it next week if the invitation is still open." Her voice took on an edge of command. "Now you be sure and tell him next Friday is just fine. Daddy said it would be."

Alaina wrinkled her nose as if she smelled something sour. "What do you see in that Yankee, anyway?"

"Everything." Roberta laughed gaily. "But most of all, a way out of this miserable hole!" She leaned forward, her dark eyes asparkle, and spoke as if she confided a deep, dark secret. "Did I tell you that he addressed the letter to me and signed it simply, 'Cole'?" She hugged her knees and rocked in sheer joy.

"Not until now," Alaina murmured wryly. She propped her elbow on the rim of the tub and leaned her chin in her palm. She could almost spell out what was coming next.

"The way he looked at me," Roberta sighed, her eyes half closed with the blissful memory. "And right in front of Daddy, too! You saw that, didn't you, Alaina?" She ignored the girl's perplexed frown and rushed on. "Oh, he's a bold one, that Cole! And I tell you, Lainie, I'm going to wrap that long-legged Yankee right around my little finger."

She rose with a delicious giggle and kicked the ruffled lace at the hem of her nightgown before she danced out of the cubicle.

"Would you mind closing the door?" Alaina called in exasperation.

Roberta leaned in with a smile on her face. "Right around my little finger!" she crooned, crooking the mentioned member to make the point. Waving her fingers coyly, she pulled the door shut, leaving Alaina at last to her bath.

Alaina climbed from the now-cool water and ruefully regarded her own water-wrinkled fingers. "Right around my little finger," she mimicked with sarcasm. "Right around—" She suddenly scowled and stamped her bare foot, hissing to herself, "Jaybird Yankee!"

Chapter 5

IT was not difficult for Alaina to avoid the busy doctor, yet far too often for total peace of mind, she found herself forced into his companionship. A certain animosity flourished between the boy, Al, and the man, Cole, and more than once Alaina felt the bite of the captain's reproof. Though it gavc her some assurance that he had not yet guessed her secret, she wondered if all he saw was the soot on her face, for it was there his criticism thrived. He could not know, of course, of the effort she took to smudge her face every morning or of the treatment her short mane received. The dirt and grease had proven an excellent replacement for the old battered hat that he had forbidden her to wear in the hospital, but it only aggravated his ambition to see the urchin clean.

"One of these days," he threatened, "I'm going to teach you how to properly wash yourself. Look at your hair! It's so stiff you could pound a strand through a fence post."

"Betcha you was born with a chunk of soap in your mouth," Alaina retorted with a fervor to match the doctor's. "I ain't never seen a body so attached to washing as you."

"That raises the question of what you were born with," Cole returned with sarcasm before striding away beneath her glare.

The night the captain came to call on Roberta, Alaina took herself far from the house. She had no intention of joining the group for dinner. Dressed as a filthy boy, she would simply be subjected to the Yankee's disapproval if it didn't arouse his curiosity as to why Angus would allow the child to appear in such an untidy state at their table.

If Alaina managed to escape that evening's festivities, she was not able to avoid hearing all about them from Roberta. The older cousin sought her out as soon as possible, not caring that Alaina was just dozing off to sleep when she burst into her room.

"Oh, Lainie, it was the most exciting evening ever! And do you know, Cole's father is also a doctor and has been a widower since shortly after Cole was born. I'm sure they're rich, too."

"Did you ask him?" Alaina yawned sleepily as she snuggled deeper into the soft bed.

"Of course not, you silly child. That would be rude. But I know they are," Roberta smiled slyly. "Cole has traveled abroad and was educated in the East where he and his father have properties, besides their home in Minnesota. I imagine when the old man dies, Cole will inherit all of his fortune. Why, he already owns properties of his very own. Now tell me, what man without money can boast of that?"

Alaina peered up at the ceiling thoughtfully. "He boasts?"

"Oh, Lainie, you're exasperating!" Roberta snapped. "Of course not. But I know how to ask subtle questions to find out things."

"I think I'll ask him if he's rich," Alaina mused aloud. "That's what you really want to know, isn't it?"

"And why not?" Roberta questioned defensively. "A girl must look out for her own best interests these days. And I'm tired of wearing these rags the war has left me. I'm going to find me a rich man who can afford to buy me all the things I want."

Alaina stifled another yawn. "It's late, Roberta, and I'm tired. I nearly fell asleep by the bayou waiting for that critter to leave. Can we talk about this some other time? I have to get up with the sun."

Roberta sighed as if in sympathy with her cousin. "Poor Al, you do have your hardships. But then—"

"I know! It's nothing more than what I deserve!" Irritably the girl fluffed her pillow and punched a small fist into it. "And Captain Latimer seems to have been sent here for the special purpose of destroying my sleep!"

By now Al made the rounds of her wards in two days, cleaning and scouring and scrubbing as if only to show one Captain Latimer that she was worth every cent of her wage despite her own untidy appearance. The wounded soldiers began to welcome the break in the otherwise endless monotony. Al began to exchange quips with them, sometimes biting remarks returned in anger, but as the soldiers became known as individuals instead of faceless enemies, the tones softened.

Questions of home and family were asked, of origins and leanings, political and otherwise. Some soldiers struggled to retain some humor in this dismal place. With these Al exchanged light banter. Others were dismayed at their wounds and disappointed with the pain and effort of life. To these Alaina gave a challenge, a dare to live. To those who were deeply injured, she grudgingly gave pity and sympathy and an odd sort of bittersweet tenderness. She ran errands for those who couldn't go for themselves, sometimes purchasing a comb, a shaving brush, or a bottle of lilac water for a girl back home. The packet of letters she carried to the post became a daily thing, and the appearance of the youthful lad with his bucket, brooms, and mops was awaited with eagerness by those who were trapped in the wards. It gave the day a brightness, a spark so small yet brightly seen and cherished. The dull gray silence of the wards had yielded to a youthful and oftentimes rebellious grin. The musty, cloying odor of molding debris became the pungent scent of lye soap and pine oil. The moans of pain were now more often hidden beneath a muffled chuckle of laughter or the low-voiced murmur of shared experiences.

For Alaina, it had begun as a simple chore—a job, a task, a way to earn money. It soon became for her a time of conflict. Her sympathies were firmly with the struggling Confederacy, yet against her will she found herself liking some of these men, many within a year or two of her own age, and several much younger. Bold and brazenly righteous, they had marched off to do battle, much like her own father and brothers, thence to lie on narrow beds of pain and helplessly wait either healing and its rewards—or death.

There had been times at Briar Hill when death seemed what every Yankee deserved. Now she found it an agonizing experience to watch one of those same struggle through their last moments of life. She knew them! They were human! They ached! They suffered! They died! More than once she was forced to seek privacy where she stood with trembling hands clasped desperately across her mouth in an effort to hold back the sobs, while tears flowed unchecked down her cheeks. Her attempts to harden her emotions failed. Instead, she seemed to become more vulnerable to the hurt and agony of watching death have its way.

On this morning in early November, Alaina vowed to keep her distance from any who were close to that dark door. She carefully reasoned it through and came to the decision that the only way to avoid such disturbing grief was not to get close to it.

It was a mild, pleasant day as she hopped onto the mule-drawn streetcar to continue her journey to the hospital. Roberta had begged her father for the use of the gelding and carriage, leaving Angus no alternative but to hitch Ol' Tar to the rickety buckboard and take himself to work and Alaina as far as the store. From there she walked to St. Augustine's Church where she caught the streetcar and finally swaggered past the orderly at the hospital door.

"You're late," Cole commented offhandedly as he brushed past her in the hall.

"Yeah, well, it ain't easy to pay for a ride on the money you Yankees pinch out," she called to his back as he strode briskly down the hall. She opened her mouth to throw another retort but quickly snapped it closed when Doctor Mitchell, the surgeon general, stepped abruptly from one of the wards. He looked at the suddenly red-faced youth, then frowned down the hall toward the tall, ignoring back of the captain.

"Do you have a complaint, son?" the gray-haired officer asked kindly.

Alaina tried to swallow her discomfort. "No, suh."

"Then I suggest you get about your duties. Several ambulances arrived during the night, and there's some tidying up to be done. Captain Latimer is far too busy now to discuss your wages."

"Yes, suh," Alaina mumbled. General Clay Mitchell was the only Yankee yet she had not dared to stand her ground with. He was a tall, barrel-chested Irishman, and though he demanded the respect of every man in the hospital, there was something kindly about the man. It just wasn't in her to be rude to such a gentleman, even if he was a Yankee.

Closer to the surgery rooms, cots had been set up to accommodate the new arrivals, some of which writhed and moaned with pain while others wept softly. One lay apart from the rest; he was so still Alaina could have taken him for the dead. A bandage covered his eyes, and a thin trickle of dried blood trailed from the corner of his mouth. His belly was covered with a sheet to keep the flies away from the wound that slowly turned the whiteness of the cloth to a dark, forboding red. Here was one who was so far gone the doctors had chosen to delay treating him until those soldiers with a better hope for life could be tended and perhaps saved.

The sight made Alaina back slowly away. *No more,* she thought. *I've seen enough!* She fled to where she kept the cleaning equipment, determined to keep her resolve, and busied herself with scrubbing the wood floor at the end of a ward where she was sure no soldier teetered near the brink of death.

Her promise to herself, however, was not to be kept. Even in the safe haven she had found, she began to hear the faint call of a desperate plea. She tried for some time to ignore it. Surely someone else would fulfill the man's need. A simple task to fetch the soldier water. But not her task! Never again!

Yet it seemed she could hear nothing else, and no one gave him water. Rallying her determination, she dipped her coarse brush into the murky liquid and began to scrub harder. But nothing could drown out the thin, weak call.

"Blast it all!" she swore beneath her breath and jumped to her feet. She hurried down the hall to where the soldier lay, still so motionless that it frightened her. Then she saw his tongue flick weakly across parched, cracked lips.

"Wait." She bent beside his ear, afraid he was too deep in pain to hear her. "I'll get you water."

She touched his thin hand reassuringly, then rushed off to the mess hall to find a glass. When she returned, she carefully slipped an arm beneath his head and raised him enough that he might sip the water. But suddenly she found her wrist seized.

"Don't!" Cole commanded sharply and, taking the glass from her, set it aside. "You'll do him more harm than good." He saw the bewilderment in the dirty face and gentled his tone. "You never give a gut-shot man a drink. Here, I'll show you."

From a nearby cabinet he took a clean cloth, dipped it into the water and carefully wiped the dry lips. He dipped the cloth again, but this time dribbled a few drops into the soldier's mouth. Alaina watched Cole quietly as he began to speak to the man in a tone that was strong yet cajoling.

"This is Al. He's going to stay with you for a while." As she shook her head with her own desperate need to be gone far away, Cole frowned sharply, warning her to silence. "Rest easy. We'll be able to tend your wounds in just a few moments. They're clearing out the surgery room now."

Cole straightened and took Al's thin hand into his larger one and pressed the damp cloth into her palm. "Be here when I get back. If anyone asks, it is on my order."

She nodded lamely.

"Make him as comfortable as possible. It won't be long."

Again she nodded and even as the captain turned away, she was reaching to the washstand for the basin and pitcher. Ever so gently she washed away the dried blood running along his cheek and, with long, cooling strokes, wiped his brow and cleaned around the bandage covering his eyes, shooing the flies that were forever gathering.

"Al?" The faint rasp made her lean down to him.

"Yeah, right here," she half-whispered.

It took an effort on the soldier's part to utter the next word. "Thanks."

Alaina was suddenly glad she had taken a moment for mercy, and she bit her lips to still their trembling before she managed in her boyish vernacular, "Anytime, Yankee."

Cole paused in the doorway of the officer's dayroom as the medical sergeant called his name. Sergeant Grissom hurried to catch him.

"There be a young lady to see you, Cap'n. She's waiting in the vestibule for ye."

"I haven't time—" Cole began tersely.

"She says it's urgent, sir. Claims it can't wait."

Cole frowned harshly. He was mystified by such a summons, but he had work to do. "Is she injured?"

Sergeant Grissom grinned. "I would say most definitely not, Cap'n."

"Then is someone else injured?"

"She did not say that, sir."

"Well, see if one of the other doctors is free to attend her."

The sergeant raised bushy eyebrows. "She said it must be you, Cap'n. And she's been waiting near come an hour."

Cole sighed and pulled out his pocket watch. "I have only a moment to spare. Tell the lady I will be down directly."

Cole hurriedly doffed his blood-stained smock. His uniform was also marred with darkish blotches, not the proper dress to meet a lady, but there was no help for it. He hadn't time to change. Buttoning the top of his blouse, he strode quickly down the hall.

Roberta rose from a bench in the foyer and bestowed a brilliant smile upon Captain Latimer as he came across the vestibule toward her. "You seem surprised to see me, Captain." She lowered her lashes demurely. "I suppose it does seem forward of me coming here like this."

"Indeed not, Miss Craighugh." Cole took her hand solicitously. "I was just now told a lady was waiting. Had Sergeant Grissom mentioned how beautiful the lady was, I might have taken a moment more to prepare myself. But you must understand, I have been quite heavily detained."

"You need not impress me with the cause, sir." Roberta did not try too hard to suppress a rather pretty wrinkling of her nose as she glanced daintily away from his blood-stained blouse. She was well aware of her expressions, having spent many hours practicing them in front of a mirror. "I came here hoping I could be dreadfully presumptuous, Captain."

"Continue, Miss Craighugh." He smiled his consent. "Your voice is the sweetest I've heard all day, and I try not to question my rare moments of good fortune."

"You are most gallant, Captain." Roberta tilted her wide-brimmed hat slightly so the captain could admire her fine, aristocratic profile. She knew the beauty of her long, down-turned nose and high cheekbones, the red sultry curves of her lips. "I was just passing by in my carriage when it came to me just how hard you work. No time for relaxation it would seem, or even a leisurely meal. A man does have to eat, doesn't he, Captain? And you can hardly be blamed for taking a few moments to do so. I know of a divine little place in the Vieux Carré where they serve the most delicious shrimp. Would you care to join me, Captain?" Though she was all smiles and coy looks, she held her breath awaiting his answer. She had secretly planned for this all week, and she would be crushed if he disappointed her now.

"I must humbly apologize, Miss Craighugh. I have wounded left to attend to. Otherwise, I would be most anxious to enjoy your company."

Roberta hid her annoyance. This was no mewling schoolboy she could lead about on a string and expect him to obey her whim. She tried another ploy. "It wouldn't be a terribly great distance for you to ride out and join us for supper this evening."

Cole smiled at her persistence. "What would your father say about my coming, Miss Craighugh? I have the distinct feeling he'd just as soon not have his daughter consorting with a Yankee."

The corners of Roberta's mouth turned upward coquettishly. "Why, Captain Latimer, you don't impress me as a man who bothers himself with what fathers think."

Cole laughed, his eyes glowing as they lightly caressed her. "On the contrary, Miss Craighugh. I do worry about what fathers may think. As to your invitation, I would rather avoid the surprise and not come unannounced."

"Now don't you worry about that. I know how to handle Daddy. Dulcie is cooking up a nice bouillabaisse, and you won't want to miss it."

A lazy grin twisted his handsome lips, lightening her heart. "If nothing further develops, I should be free later this evening."

Roberta was coolly poised despite her elation. "I shall look forward to this evening then, Captain. Now, I really must let you get back to your duties." She waited briefly in hopes of hearing protestations, but she had to conceal her disappointment again when he glanced almost imperceptibly toward the large, standing clock in the vestibule. She laid a hand tenderly across his lean knuckles as he strolled with her toward the entry. "I've held you away from your work long enough, Captain. You will forgive me, won't you? I must not know much about doctoring to imagine you can come and go as you like."

"I am destroyed," Cole responded as he guided her from the door and handed her into her carriage. "But I assure you that you have made my day considerably brighter."

"This evening then, Captain?" she murmured demurely.

"This evening." Cole smiled and saluted her, then spinning on a heel ran back into the hospital without a backward glance.

Roberta watched him go, and the thought of that lean form guiding her across a ballroom floor was almost overwhelming. *And all that money!* She could not suppress a delicious shudder at the thought. She rapped the back of the driver's seat with her parasol.

"Jedediah, take me around by Jackson Square before we go home. I haven't been for a carriage ride in a month of Sundays."

As the carriage lurched into motion, Roberta raised the parasol to shield her carefully protected skin from the sun but not enough to hide her beauty from the soldiers who paused to stare.

Chapter 6

MAJOR Magruder was waiting for Cole at the head of the stairs, his hands clenched behind his back and his legs braced wide apart. It was obvious he had been watching. "Quite a bit of fluff you've picked up there, Captain Latimer."

"Miss Craighugh," Cole informed him and raised an eyebrow at the man's apparent curiosity.

"A Southern wench, I presume."

"Wench, hardly! Southern, yes. Al's cousin, and I would be more selective in what is chosen for adjectives when the lad is within hearing. He has a way of setting one back on his heels." Cole smiled at the idea of the short, rather heavyset major nose to nose with the small, wiry Al.

"Humph!" Magruder said. "Uppity little beggar for tidewater trash."

"Not tidewater trash, Major," Cole corrected. "He comes from a farm upriver somewhere. Lost his parents in the war."

"You're quick to defend the rebels," the major sneered. "Next thing, you'll be feeling sorry for Lee."

Cole faced the major squarely. "I sympathize with all men when they are hurting. It is for that reason I became a doctor. And I consider my oath most sacred."

"Humph!" Magruder said again and followed Cole into the day room where the younger man poured water into a basin and began to scrub his hands. "You should get some combat experience, son." He dampened his own hands from the ewer and ran wet fingers through his graying hair while considering himself in the mirror. "Fourteen years I've spent in the military. Went with the army down to Mexico. Eight years a lieutenant." He glanced aside at Cole's rank. "And here you are a captain after two." He leaned against the commode and folded his arms as if he were about to impart some vital wisdom to his junior. "Your fancy oaths won't do you much good in the heat of battle with men falling all around you. You pick the ones you can do some good for, and ethics be damned. You give a swig of laudanum to the rest and put 'em in the shade. If they're still alive when you get back to them, then you try to patch them up."

Cole shook his head in rejection of the advice. He was aware of his own lack of experience in the field but held strong doubts that he would accept such a callous attitude should the event present itself.

Magruder straightened. "I was looking for you to invite you to join us." When the captain glanced up in mild surprise, the major shrugged. "It was Mitchell's suggestion, not mine. The rest of the doctors are going to Sazerac's for a bit of celebration. You've heard of the Confederate defeat at Broad Run, haven't you?"

"Defeat? Humph! I've also heard of Old Rosey's at Chickamauga—what would you call it—tactical retreat?"

"We only celebrate the victories." The major sniffed. "Before this war is over we'll pay those damned rebs back tenfold."

"Only one thing is certain now." Cole spoke through his hands as he splashed water on his face. "Whichever side wins, there's a lot more bloodshed to come."

"Squeamish, Captain?" Magruder smirked, raising a brow.

Cole reached for a towel. "No, Major. I just see it as a damned waste, that's all."

"Then you refuse to celebrate with us?" Magruder waited much like a hawk for the captain's answer.

"Right now, I'm going to take the blinded boy into surgery and see what I can do for him. Then, if there's anything left of the evening, I plan to join Miss Craighugh and her parents for dinner."

"You're wasting your time on that boy," Magruder chided. "He'll be gone before another day is out. You might as well leave early and enjoy the lady's company."

Cole hung the towel and took out a fresh smock. "Be that as it may, Major, I am still committed to my oath. The least I can do is try."

"Suit yourself, Captain, but you'll only cause him more

misery before he dies. Besides, it's a task requiring at least two doctors—"

An orderly pushed open the door. "We got the last one in the surgery room, Cap'n, and the chloro' is started."

Cole nodded and turned to Magruder as the door swung shut. "Doctor Brooks has already agreed to assist.

"Brooks! That old rebel? You'll have to watch him close. He's more likely to slit the boy's throat."

"He took the same oath I did." Cole's voice was firm. "And he takes it every bit as seriously as I do." He rested a hand on the door knob and continued thoughtfully, "He's not a rebel, you know. In fact, he lost quite a few friends when he spoke out against seccession." He opened the door. "Now if you'll excuse me, Major, I have to get on with it."

Magruder followed him out in a less than pleasant mood. It always aggravated him when the young fools wouldn't listen to his advice. He caught sight of the cleaning boy through the doorway to the surgery ward, a wet rag in his hand and a worried frown on his skinny face. It sharpened Magruder's irritation to know that good Union dollars were supporting the irresponsibility of the filthy little brat. "Get on with your work," Magruder ordered gruffly. "You've had enough lagging for one day."

Cole glanced over his shoulder at the frowning man and resisted snapping back a retort. To Al's questioning gaze, he jerked his head, and the slim lad went hurrying off.

"You seem to have a penchant for picking up lost strays," Magruder smirked. "From now on, resist the temptation to bring them among us. That little beggar's not to be trusted."

Cole smiled benevolently. "I don't know about that, Major. I've never had any qualms about turning my back on him." He shrugged. "Couldn't do much damage if he tried. He's hardly bigger than a mite."

"Hah!" Magruder scoffed. "The little ones do the most damage. Hit you where it hurts."

Cole laughed at the other's unintended humor. "I shall keep that in mind, Major."

Nearly three hours passed before the stretcher bearing the blinded soldier was carried from the operating ward. "Be careful," Cole warned the orderlies. "He has more stitches than a quilt and is far more delicate."

Doctor Brooks dried his hands on a towel. "Do you think you got everything?"

Cole sighed and dragged off his bloody smock. "We'll know soon enough. At this point, we can only hope and pray that peritonitis doesn't set in."

" 'Twas the boy's good fortune you were here to tend him. I've seen less gifted and less patient doctors in my time."

Cole shrugged away the compliment. "If you're going to make the effort, you might as well do the best you can."

Doctor Brooks pulled out his watch and noted the time. "Nearly six. I'll give a last check about the ward upstairs and then go fetch some vittles. I don't suppose a young man like yourself would care to join an old fool for supper."

"I've already promised this evening to a young lady," Cole smiled.

Brooks chuckled. "She'll be much better company for you than I." The old man approached the stairs, then paused, half turning. "That cleaning boy I've seen flitting around here—you're not of a mind to share him, are you?"

"You mean Al?"

"I don't know his name. Don't even know what he looks like. Every time I pass through the hospital, he's on all fours scrubbing floors. If there's any part of him I could recognize, it's his hind end."

"I'm not sure, but I'll think about it," Cole assured the man.

The older doctor nodded understandingly. "Well, if you should decide in favor if it, bring him up."

When Cole left the hospital and came around to untether his roan, he found Al perched on the hitching rail. The captain raised a wondering brow at the lad. "I thought you'd be gone by now. What are you doing here this late?" Cole glanced over the back of the horses tied to the rail. "Where's that nag you call a horse? Don't tell me he threw you off his scrawny back."

"Ain't got him today." The answer was short as Alaina broke pieces from a twig and tossed them into the dust. "Roberta took the carriage, and Uncle Angus had to hitch up Ol' Tar for hisself."

"So you're left to find your own way back."

"Ain't as bad as that. I was gonna catch the next streetcar over to the store. Uncle Angus should still be there."

"And if he's not?" Cole peered at the lad questioningly.

"I didn't come here to beg no ride from you!" Alaina hotly declared, just in case the captain was suggesting it. She cringed at the very idea. Riding behind the captain without the wicker case between them might well get her into more trouble than she was ready for. Indeed, she was well aware that she was beginning to look more and more like a grown woman without her clothes to disguise her.

"Then what are you waiting around here for?" Cole questioned.

"I was wondering—" She found it hard to admit that she worried about a Yankee. "I was wonderin' if—if 'at last fella made it through all right."

Cole led his horse around and stood staring at the young, unkempt lad. Finally Al shrugged away her shame.

"I gots my weak moments jes' like everybody else."

Cole chuckled. "You do surprise me, Al."

"He did make it, didn't he?" Shading her eyes against the lowering sun, Alaina tried to see his face.

"Bobby Johnson made it," Cole conceded. "If he survives the next few days, he just might make it home."

" 'At's all I was wantin' to know." Al straightened herself to slide off the hitching post but in the process felt herself losing the heavy boots. In an attempt to keep them on, she raised her legs. It was surely not the most graceful descent she had ever made in her life, but it might have been the quickest. The hard ground was there to meet her soft backside when she landed unceremoniously in the dust. Her yelp of pain made Cole's horse shy. Suddenly seeing that she might be trampled on by the huge beast, Alaina quickly forgot her agony and scrambled up, leaving her boots behind. It was all too much for Cole's control, and he burst into amused laughter, winning Al's outraged glare.

"You sorry Yankee! You'd just as soon let that mule stomp me into the ground!"

"Now, Al." Cole chuckled, trying to stem his urge to levity. "I was just watching you dismount that hitching rail. You were the one who frightened Sarg. Don't blame me."

Alaina ruefully rubbed her bruised posterior and

wished she could groan her misery in her own natural tones.

"You're going to be sore." Cole offered his wisdom freely. "If you would accept a Yankee doctor's treatment, I've got some liniment in the dayroom I could massage—"

"No, suh!" Alaina shook her head and was most serious in rebuke. "I ain't taking down my britches fer no Yankee!"

Cole was sure Al's voice carried the whole length of the street and back. He sighed and painfully closed his eyes. "Now that you have everyone staring and no doubt think the worst, are you satisfied?"

Al cackled gleefully and hooked her slim thumbs in her rope belt. "Gotcha, didn't I, Yankee? Fer once, I gotcha. And you know somep'n?" She sauntered arrogantly close. "I'll laugh when they hangs ya."

"Major Magruder warned me about you," Cole remarked dryly. "I should have listened."

"Yeah, well, I don't like him none neither."

"If you care for a ride home," Cole said tersely and wondered why he should trouble himself, "I'm going that way shortly. You can wait at my apartment while I change my uniform—"

Alaina looked at him narrowly. "Ya goin' out ta see Roberta?"

"She invited me to dinner." Cole leisurely raised an eyebrow. "I need not ask if you mind. Your feelings are apparent."

Irritably Al folded her arms across her bosom. "Ain't no skin off'n my nose what critters Roberta fetches in fer supper. She always was one fer taking up with skunks and whatnot. Anyway, it ain't my table. Just don't figger on me joinin' ya, 'at's all. I don't eat with Yankees less'n I can't help it."

"Do you want the ride?" Cole questioned impatiently.

"I ain't of a mind to ride the rump of 'at high steppin' nag clear to home," she replied, rubbing her backside.

"I had planned to take a buggy from my apartment." Cole shrugged. "Suit yourself, though. I guess when a boy is as soft as you are, he might just as well take to wearing dresses. As to that," he gestured casually to the slim, bare feet, "I've seen a lot of lady's slippers bigger than your feet."

Self-consciously Alaina curled her thin toes into the

dust. "You were gonna fetch up a buggy to ride out?"

Cole nodded. "Do you want to come along?"

"I'll meetcha over your 'partment maybe," Al said sheepishly. She didn't like taking favors from Yankees, but it would save her a penny or two, and nowadays a penny seemed like a fortune.

"If you're not there when I come out," Cole said as he swung onto his mount, "I won't wait for you."

Alaina retrieved her boots. "I'll be there, Yankee."

And so she was, and early enough that she waited some moments across the street for him to appear. Keeping an eye on his apartment window, she strolled around the square until she was pushed roughly aside by several soldiers who brushed boisterously past. Through the gathering darkness, she glared at their backs, then turned to stare angrily at the words General Butler had added to the dedication on the base of the statue of Andrew Jackson —"THE UNION MUST AND SHALL BE PRESERVED."

"Just like a Yankee to rub it in," she sneered.

Hearing the rhythmic clip-clop of horse's hooves and the rattle of carriage wheels, she turned and, recognizing the captain in the buggy seat, waved and hastened toward him. He drew rein beside her. "I was wondering if you would make it."

She saw his face in the deep dusk and the soft yellow glow of the buttons on his uniform as they reflected the lights from the gaily illuminated apartments. It sometimes surprised her just how handsome he was. "You sure this is free?"

Cole pulled a long, slim cigar from his blouse and leisurely rebuttoned the brass. "Seems to me, Al," he spoke as he struck a sulfur match and puffed the long cheroot alight, "that you'd know when to keep that sharp tongue sheathed, especially when you could lose that which you want."

Al indignantly protested. "You was the one what offered! Did I beg ya? Did I, huh?"

Cole raised the reins to slap them against the horse's back. "If you don't want the ride—"

"Wait!" Alaina bit her lip as Cole leaned back in the seat and grinned. She yielded. "I wouldn't mind a ride."

He tossed his head. "Hop in."

She took a step toward the back of the buggy where she intended to hike herself up on the luggage boot, but

Cole's terse inquiry halted her. "Where are you going?"

When she shrugged lamely and gestured to the back, he slapped the seat beside him. "Right here where I can keep an eye on you. From now on I think I'll heed Magruder's advice."

Hesitantly, Alaina eased into the seat beside him. She didn't like sitting so close, not when he smelled so fresh and clean, and she had the awful odor of rancid grease in her hair. Self-consciously she tugged down the floppy brim of her hat and sat mutely silent for most of the way home. The contrast between them was excruciatingly painful when she allowed herself to forget that he was a Yankee and remembered he was a man and she, a young woman.

Chapter 7

THE evening was laden with the sound of tree frogs and chirping crickets, of blended voices drifting up from the parlor below, and of masculine laughter, deep and rich. A cool, languid breeze gently swayed the branches of the huge oaks, rustling their leaves and sweeping the fragrance of sweet shrub through the open balcony doors of Alaina's bedroom. The soft, silvery radiance of the moonlit night touched the delicate but pensive features as the girl stood in the open balcony doors. She was a prisoner in her own room, trapped by the presence of the Yankee below. And she was lonely, so miserably alone and forlorn she felt the sharp ache of it deep within her chest. Never before had she known such confinement, and the tinkling brightness of Roberta's laughter made the very walls close in about her. It threaded its way with merciless mockery through her head, turning the room into a torture chamber.

Alaina rolled her head against the door molding and with misty eyes stared back into the tall mirror that stood in her room. She found no comfort in what she saw. Despite Captain Latimer being in the house she had managed a bath in the pantry, then had slipped through the bushes skirting the house and stealthily climbed the gallery stairs to her bedroom. The solitary figure in the silvered glass looked more like a young woman than her usual attire allowed her, but the dark, softly curling hair was unsuitably short, and the loose, threadbare nightgown far from flattering.

Alaina's gaze roamed to the armoire that held her meager belongings, and she knew a strange yearning to dress in something pretty and feminine, to be treated as a woman, to be able to smile and laugh with her own girlish gaiety, instead of having to curb the softer looks and lower her voice to a deepness that made her throat ache.

This guise of stripling lad was the charade she must play. Yet it was becoming increasingly difficult to don those wretched clothes and assume the personality that was more repugnant each morning. Bit by bit the masquerade was robbing her of her womanhood.

An illusion increasingly haunted her. In her mind she saw the tall, lean form of Captain Latimer sweep past and on his arm, a woman clothed in deep red silk. His face was animated and alive as he paid court to the lady, and on his knee he vowed his love. The woman's hand reached out as if bestowing knighthood upon the handsome head, and his lips touched the slim fingers and traced a path along the bare, white arm. The vision widened and the full red lips he kissed became the visage of her cousin, Roberta.

Alaina wandered out onto the balcony, seeking the cool evening breezes and fleeing the apparition in which "Al" could have no part. Doubts drummed with heavy blows upon the already crumbling walls of her confidence. She could never hope to be the woman Roberta was, a woman who attracted men wherever she went. She was destined to be just plain Al, scrawny, boyish, unattractive. Painful as it was to accept, scrubbing floors seemed her future, while Roberta need do nothing more than smile helplessly and have the whole world offered to her.

Slowly Alaina meandered down the balcony stairs until she could survey the lower gallery. A shaft of light streamed from the parlor, illuminating the lower steps, and she dared go no farther for fear she might be seen. At the far end of the portico sat the bench and chairs around which, on those rare visits to the city, she and her brothers had played as children, while Roberta tirelessly dressed china dolls in clever gowns and frilly bonnets.

Roberta's laughter intruded upon the stillness of the night, and joining it was the captain's deep, rich chuckle and the reluctant chortle of Uncle Angus.

"Captain, it seems you've been nearly everywhere," Roberta crooned. "Besides your home, what is your favorite place? Paris perhaps?"

Leaning down, Alaina peered through the parlor window and watched Cole as he responded with a gallant declaration.

"There were none in Paris more beautiful than the one before me now, Miss Craighugh."

Alaina raised her eyes heavenward and made serious consideration about praying for his soul. It was Angus's rather heavy clearing of his throat that prompted the captain to rise to his feet.

"However, as much as I've enjoyed your charming company," he took Roberta's hand decorously, "the hour is late, and I must be going." He bestowed a light kiss on the soft, pale hand, and self-consciously Alaina gripped her work-reddened hands between her knees. She was too caught up in watching Captain Latimer's departure to think of escaping.

"I hope you will come again," Roberta murmured demurely, slipping an arm through Cole's and walking him to the front door. Alaina drew herself into a small knot as she realized the captain was opening the door and stepping out. Roberta followed, and it was not so dark that Alaina could not see her cousin stroke his chest and lean into him provocatively, pressing her bosom closely to that blue uniform. "You will come again, won't you, Cole?"

Alaina's cheeks burned as she found herself in the next moment an unwilling witness to the doctor's passionate response. Roberta was crushed against that hard chest. His mouth came down upon those red lips with a fervor that made Alaina breathless just watching. She had never before in her life watched a man kiss a woman in such a fashion and felt much the intruder, yet at the same time a strange excitement began to pulse through her veins. Suddenly the thought of being kissed in the same manner by Cole Latimer made her warm and dizzy. When he touched Roberta's breast, it was her own that tingled until the nipple rose taut beneath her nightgown.

"You'll come tomorrow, won't you, Cole?" Roberta whispered the plea. "You won't let me sit here all by my lonesome, will you?"

"I have duty," he breathed as his lips traveled along her cheek.

"Duty?" Roberta's appeal was soft and muted. "Can't you forget duty for a while, Cole? I'll be here all alone tomorrow. Mama's going to the store, and Dulcie has to go to market. Won't you come, please?" Her lily white hand covered his, pressing her bosom almost to overflowing her décolletage. "We'll have the whole afternoon to ourselves."

It amazed Alaina that Roberta could remain so purposeful beneath his caresses when she herself, only observing, was as much atremble as a willow in a windstorm. The warm, yearning tide of feeling that throbbed within her loins was strange and alien to her, and reluctantly she conceded that if she were the one within his arms, she'd be nearly swooning by now.

Footsteps in the hall intruded, and Roberta snatched free and began smoothing her hair.

"I must be going," Cole whispered. "Your father is growing fretful."

"I'll be expecting you tomorrow," Roberta smiled tenderly.

About to turn away, Cole paused. "I'm sorry, Roberta. I really have duty."

Then he was gone, leaving Roberta pouting petulantly as she watched him ride away. Being caught alone in a house with the captain would have been a surefire way of bringing this spasmodic courtship to a quick marriage, and her mother would probably have been the one to find them, having expressed her intentions of staying away only an hour or two.

"Daddy?" she called into the house. "I need a new gown, something real pretty."

"Roberta! I must protest!" Angus came to stand in the door. "You know how hard it is to come by even the few coins we manage to make at the store. I don't have enough to spare."

"Oh, Daddy, don't be such a worried goose. Alaina pays you tomorrow, and I'm sure Madame Henrí will wait for the rest of the money if you promise to pay her each week."

"Roberta, I can't! It wouldn't be right!"

"Daddy, I'm going to catch me a rich man," the young woman stated matter-of-factly. "And I'll need all the help I can get. If I wear rags, he'll think I'm just after his money."

"If you're thinking about that Yankee—" Angus's anger was genuine. "Rich or not, I don't want him in this house again! This evening has upset your mother. And besides, what will the neighbors think?"

"Oh, what do I care about them? They're a bunch of old fuddies anyway."

"You should show more respect, Roberta," Angus chided.

"I know, Daddy," Roberta sighed laboriously. "But I'm so sick of having to scrimp for pennies."

"Come in, and go to bed, child. No use fretting your pretty head."

"I'll come in a moment, Daddy. It's so nice out here, I'd like to enjoy the evening a bit longer."

"Very well, but not too late."

Roberta hummed softly to herself as she waltzed gaily about the gallery. She could almost imagine herself at a grand military ball such as Banks was purported to give, wearing the most beautiful gown there and, of course, having as her escort the most handsome man.

Suddenly she gasped and came to a frightened halt as a pale apparition on the stairs took on human form. "Al!" she hissed, recognizing the small shape. "What are you doing here? I thought you were in your room."

"The name is Alaina," the younger cousin corrected and turned on bare feet to climb the stairs. "Would you mind using it?"

Roberta sneered bitingly, enraged that the girl had been eavesdropping. "You always did look more like an Al than any Alaina, anyway."

The younger cousin half whirled at the caustic comment, stared at the shadowed, smirking face, then continued on up the stairs, tossing back over her shoulder, "At least you don't see me throwing myself at a Yankee."

"You're just jealous!" Roberta followed her to accuse. "You're jealous because you'll never be able to catch a man like Cole Latimer. You and your scrawny—why, he'd laugh you right out of bed!"

Alaina flinched at the cruelty of her cousin's words, half convinced that what Roberta said was true.

"And I'm going to tell you something else, Alaina MacGaren," Roberta continued emphatically. "I'm going to get Cole Latimer to marry me."

Alaina half turned, and Roberta smiled triumphantly until the smaller woman asked almost calmly, "And what will be your excuse when he finds out you're not a virgin?"

Roberta gasped in shock. "How did you know?" Her voice shrank to a hushed whisper as she demanded again, "How did you know?"

Alaina shrugged casually. "I overheard Chad Williamson boasting about it to the Shatler brothers. Of course, they're all dead now, so I guess I'm the only one who knows."

In open threat Roberta clenched her fist and held it before the other's face. "If you tell Cole, I swear he'll hear all about your little secret!" Roberta calmed slightly, reclaiming her power over the other. "Besides, that was a long time ago. I was only fifteen—and it was only that once." She made a face of disgust. "I didn't like it anyway. All that panting and pawing. I was completely exhausted afterward, and I couldn't sit down properly for a week."

"Captain Latimer is a doctor. Perhaps he'll realize—"

Roberta cut her short. "I'll figure out something to convince him. I'll make him believe!"

Alaina entered her room, throwing back over her shoulder. "I don't think he's inexperienced with women."

Roberta was a quick step behind her. "I'll make him believe, I tell you!"

Alaina looked at her and calmly pointed out, "But first, you have to make him want to marry you."

Roberta scoffed. "That's as easy as snapping my fingers. In fact, he's probably well on his way—"

Alaina nodded reflectively. "You may be able to pull off your schemes. You may even fool him in bed, as you say. But I wonder, Roberta, if you'll ever be happy—I mean, really happy."

"Don't be absurd! Of course, I will. He has money—"

Alaina laughed disdainfully. "Do you think that makes for real happiness. A wife must share her husband's bed with joy, bear his children—"

"Children! I'm not going to ruin myself for anybody's brat!"

Alaina gazed somewhat pityingly at her cousin. "If you really loved a man, you'd want his children."

"That's the way *you* feel! And you, poor little goose, will be lucky if a man even looks at you!"

"If you're through with your insults," Alaina murmured, unable to find any firmness in her voice. "I'd like to go to bed now. I have to be at the hospital early."

"Of course! You must rest a lot to be able to scrub all those floors. Cole mentioned that you scrub them real good."

Perceiving that her thrust had hit its mark, Roberta swept gracefully into the hall, closing the door behind her.

Alaina stood with angry tears gathering and spilling over her thick lashes. Bruised by Roberta's assault, she slowly put out the lamp, and in the darkness, stared at the shaft of moonlight spilling into her room. The insults had cut to the quick, and they were even more frightening because the same disparaging thoughts had found no denial in her own mind.

Chapter 8

FRIDAY morning came in a disorganized rush for Alaina. She overslept, and from there the day degenerated into a mad frenzy. Her mops were unusually clumsy, and once she even tripped backward over a full pail of dirty water, spilling herself and the murky liquid onto the floor. She rubbed her bruised elbow and, muttering sourly, got back to her feet. Out of the corner of her eye she caught sight of Captain Latimer as he stepped into the hall to see the cause of the commotion. His sharp, clear disapproval was, no doubt, meant to shame her for her clumsiness. It almost bought him a bucket over his head. When he was gone, Alaina sneered to herself and tried to wring some of the grimy water from her baggy garments. She could do without his fatherly discipline.

It was midmorning when she found time to check on the progress of Bobby Johnson. He was still under the effects of a heavy dosage of morphine to ease his pain and to keep him still while his wounds mended. It was enough for Alaina to find him alive.

In the early afternoon she became the object of the captain's perusal once again. She was polishing the last pane of a window when she noticed that he was watching her thoughtfully. It certainly didn't settle her any. Of course, another Yankee might have seen past her disguise and laid bare her secret, but with Captain Latimer, she could only surmise that he was contemplating her filthy garb again. He seemed blinded to anything else.

Deliberately she continued wiping the glass as he strode toward her, never turning until he was a short step away, then she whirled and looked at him suspiciously, as if expecting some dire mistreatment from his hands.

"I'm not going to beat you," Cole assured tersely. "At least, not yet."

Alaina wiped her slim nose along her sleeve with an appropriate sniffle to accompany the action. "My pa warned me never to turn my back on a bluebelly." Her derisive gaze swept him from toe of polished boot to handsome head. "Yank-kee!"

"You must surely find that difficult with all these good Union soldiers about," Cole quipped with sarcasm.

"You said it, Yankee, I didn't." Alaina searched in her back pocket, dragged forth a ragged cloth, and proceeded to loudly blow her nose into it. "Can't rightly find a spot where my backside ain't turned to a fureign'r."

"If you're finished," Cole said impatiently, "I've some more work for you to do, though it goes against my better judgment."

"I shoulda known," Alaina lamented with a feigned groan. "You're either a-fussing 'bout my looks or wantin' me to do somep'n. What's it now, bluebelly? Wiping up more Yankee puke?" How she hated that word!

Cole smiled sardonically. Al's ever-primed contrariness had a tendency to wear on one, but in view of the lad's squeamish nature, Cole translated it more as bravado. The boy deliberately challenged out some rebuke or punishment, and since that seemed to be his wont, Cole concluded it must be the last thing he received. He held his temper and answered the impertinent question. "Something worse, I think."

Inwardly Alaina cringed. She didn't take it as an idle threat and vowed that if he set her to cleaning the room where the doctors did amputations, she would quit. She had no stomach for such gore.

"Follow me." Cole stepped toward the door, then turned as Alaina paused in indecision. His voice cracked sharply in command. "Well! Get a move on!"

Alaina chafed bitterly. This man knew how to get under a person's skin. "I thought you might be gone ter visit Roberta this afternoon. What made ya stick around here?"

Cole raised a wondering brow at the youth. "I think you were misinformed."

Alaina shrugged. "Seein's as you were so hot and eager to get out to the Craighughs' las' night, I jes' figured you'd try to see her as much as ya can."

"I was sent here for the prime purpose of taking care of the wounded, not to pay court to the ladies, however much I would enjoy it. And you"—the blue eyes bore into gray—"were hired to clean. Now come along."

Much to Alaina's relief, they climbed the stairs to the third floor, a place where she had never been allowed before. It was a hot day, and here the heat was more intense. Perspiration seemed to pop from every pore, making the coarse cotton shirt cloyingly clammy against her shoulders and back. Small beads of moisture began to trickle down between her breasts, and it was an agony not to scratch. Even Cole, as he strode down the hall with his highly polished boots and immaculate garb, was not unaffected, and his blouse began to show a dark, damp streak down his spine.

Alaina had to hustle in her oversize boots to keep up with the captain's long strides. She followed him down a main hall, then they came to another where a sergeant sat at a small desk. The short corridor ended in a doorway that stood half open and betrayed a whole squad of Union soldiers lounging and playing cards within the room. Behind the sergeant, a soldier stood guard in front of another door. The air was stifling here, and sweat darkened the soldiers' blouses. When he saw the pair, the sergeant wiped his brow with a red kerchief, nodded to Cole, and rose to unlock the guarded door, ending Al's bemusement. A ward fully twice as large as those below was revealed. But here the beds were filled with soldiers of the Confederacy, recognizable by various articles of the gray uniform many of them wore. Some lay still and quiet, staring upward in a daze, while a few moaned on their beds of pain. A hoarse rasping came from a young soldier whose cot was near the door. As they entered, he struggled to turn his head on the pillow, and even as a lame smile quivered across his thin lips, he was seized with a fit of painful coughing. Alaina knew too well that these men were prisoners, mending here before they were sent on to Ship Island or Fort Jackson.

"This is Al," Cole announced to the men. "He's going to tidy your quarters." He reached back to draw the slim figure forward, but Alaina snatched angrily away.

"Git your hands off me, Yankee!" she barked. "Jes' keep to yerself, and we'll get along fine."

A tall, lanky reb hooted with laughter. "Ooooee, Cap'n, you sure got yourself a mean kid there. Where'd you manage to catch him?"

"In a scuffle with some of our soldiers," Cole responded dryly. "My mistake was thinking he was outnumbered. I didn't know then that I saved the others from certain disaster."

From the back of the room a burly man growled. "Hey, pup, why you working for them Yankees? Didn't your ma teach you better?"

Al shrugged. "She tried, but I gotta eat somehow."

The man leaned back in his bed and tucked in his chin thoughtfully. " 'Pears to me that they ain't feedin' ya enough. The last time I saw a little bitty runt like you, he was on his mammy's knee. Maybe you're too young to know that respectable people would rather starve than clean up bluebelly rot."

Leisurely, Al sauntered to the foot of the man's cot and stared pointedly at the filth that surrounded it. "Ain't bluebelly rot in here, mistah. It's all Johnny Reb."

The soldier scowled at her, but the bright gray eyes never wavered. A low chuckle of laughter came from his fellows and, red-faced, the man gruffly commanded, "Get to work 'fore I take a broom handle to your scrawny backside."

Alaina's gaze casually marked the man's good leg which was drawn up beside the one that wore a long wooden splint. "Try it, Johnny, and you'll be needing planks fer your other leg."

Any concern Cole might have had for the lad's safety faded quickly as he witnessed the exchange. Al handled himself like a small, banty rooster, full of fight and about as easily subdued.

Alaina glanced around as an older man, white of hair and thick of frame, entered from a small room at the back of the ward. It was with more than a little alarm that she recognized him to be Doctor Brooks, the Craighughs' physician and friend.

"Captain Latimer," he called. "If you have a moment I would like your opinion on a matter." The doctor moved to the bedside of a soldier, spoke to him in a low voice, then began to draw back the sheet that covered him. Alaina didn't wait to see if the soldier wore anything more than the bandage across his stomach. But in her haste to make her glimpse as brief as possible, she whirled and stumbled into the captain.

"Al!" he snapped, steadying her. "What's wrong with you?"

Alaina fumbled for an excuse. "Guess it's the heat."

"Then take off that blasted coat. You look hot enough to roast." He reached out as if to flick the shirtfront, and there was a loud slap as Al struck the hand away.

"Told you not to touch me!" Her tone approached a strident screech.

A chair clattered in the hallway, and the guard rushed in, followed by the sergeant. Both appeared ready to quell whatever disturbance might be brewing. Cole's angry frown bore into the youth as he rubbed the smarting member.

"One of these days, Al," he gritted. "One of these days."

"I warned ya, didn't I? Don't touch me! I said it! You jes' don't listen! It's yer own blame fault."

"Al!" Cole's lean cheeks flexed tensely and the blue eyes narrowed. "Do you have any notion how exasperating you are?"

The slim shoulders shrugged indifferently, and finally Cole spoke over his shoulder to assure the sergeant. "It's all right. Just be prepared to watch this hotheaded imp while he's here. He'll have another war starting before you can stop him."

With a last glance of warning to the youth, Cole brushed past and went to converse with Doctor Brooks. Alaina kept her gaze carefully away from the thin, bare form lying on the bed and the wound Cole was examining. She began to tidy the room and stooped to pick up several volumes of poetry that lay scattered beneath the cot near the door.

"Hey," the soldier rasped, too weak to raise his head from the pillow. "Are you from around these parts?"

"Upriver," Al replied, scrubbing around on her knees as she picked up the books. "Close to Red."

"Rednecks, I betcha," the burly one tossed sourly.

Alaina bristled but didn't glance his way. Straightening the volumes, she rose with them in her arms.

"You wouldn't happen to know a young lady who lives about ten or so miles from Alexandria, do you?" the soldier beside her wheezed, interest lighting his eyes. "Pretty little thing. No bigger than you. She gave the bunch of us some food one time." He swallowed heavily. "And let us bed down for the night in her barn. I never—knew her name, but she had—a big black man who always made sure—we showed her respect. She called him Saul—"

Alaina turned aside and mumbled over her shoulder, "All the people have gone from there now. She's probably moved on like the rest of us."

"That's too bad." The soldier coughed before he continued. "I was thinking that—maybe, when this war is over—and I'm released from prison—that I'd pass that way again. She was a real lady—sharing with us—what little she had. I'd like to repay her—somehow."

Alaina's hand trembled as she put the books aside. A young man, full of dreams that all too soon would be crushed behind the walls of a prison. How could she tell him that this scrawny, scraggly haired youth was all that remained of that girl?

She started in surprise as a hand came upon her shoulder, and with reluctance she faced Doctor Brooks.

"So, you're the young lad Captain Latimer has been warning me about," he chuckled. "It took an effort on my part, but he finally brought you up here to help me out."

The kindly blue eyes twinkled as Alaina lifted her gaze, then amazement dawned in his face, and his mouth sagged slowly open. "My lord!"

Alaina grimaced sharply as he recognized her. Doctor Brooks had often been at the Craighugh house when she and her family were visiting there. On several occasions he had teased her about gathering in with the young boys as if she were one of them.

Abruptly, Doctor Brooks cleared his throat and turned back to Cole, catching the younger man's arm and leading him to the door. "There was another matter I wished to discuss with you, Captain. The morphine is almost gone—"

The two men walked out into the hall, and Alaina slowly released her breath. Doctor Brooks would guard her secret as jealously as he guarded the lives of these men who filled the Confederate ward.

A light breeze caressed her, bringing her to the awareness of her surroundings. It suddenly dawned on her how much cooler it was here in the ward than in any other room in the hospital. Lifting her eyes, she saw the open skylight high above her head. There, the hot air was allowed to escape while the cooler breezes from outside were drawn through the room.

"Them dumb Yankees ain't figured it out yet," the lanky reb chuckled, catching the lad's contemplation of the air vent. "They stuck us way up here to keep us from climbing out the windows, but they ain't yet realized we got the coolest room in the place."

Alaina grinned at the humor of it, remembering the sergeant sweating in his airless corner. Lately, it was a rare day that they could snatch even a small victory from the Yankees.

When Doctor Brooks returned to the room, his pale blue eyes met hers. "I would have a private word with you, 'Al,' when you've finished with your chores."

On Saturday, Alaina worked in her uncle's store under Roberta's supervision. Since most of Al's chores were finished by that Friday night, the captain granted the boy the day off. When this was found out, Roberta contrived to trap Alaina into volunteering her services at the store since she had been asked to work as well. Through much of the day, Roberta made it her personal duty to see that no undue frivolity resulted, while she bent the quickness of her mind to the accounting books, bringing the figures up to date. Sitting at her father's large store desk, more often than not she became the interest of Yankee soldiers who wandered in. She derived great pleasure when these same brushed roughly past the tattered boy who swept and cleaned and neatened the stock.

Sunday was a day for church and socializing. Since Alaina could hardly groom herself and accompany the Craighughs, she found a few hours when she could be free of Roberta's scrutiny and ceaseless baiting. Dulcie and her family went to their own church, and that was usually an all-day affair. Thus, Alaina had the house to herself. In her leisure she bathed, perfumed herself, put on her old but best muslin gown, and, for a small space of time, enjoyed being a woman.

It was early afternoon when she glanced out a front window and to her dismay saw Captain Latimer riding up the lane. In sudden panic Alaina flew to her room. There was not a moment to lose! The gown and slippers were thrown aside, and the detested britches and shirt dragged on. The boots came well above her ankles and hid her stockinged feet. She rubbed a handful of ever-ready dirt over her face; the floppy hat would serve to cover her clean hair. There was no time to muddy it again, nor could she bring herself to do it.

The doorbell clanged and after a few moments was heard again. Alaina held her breath, hoping he would go away. Finally she heard his footsteps crossing the gallery. She waited, anxiously counting the moments. From the French doors she could see no sign of the Yankee or his horse. Carefully she crept down the gallery stairs so the oversize boots would not clump against them. To avoid any possible meeting, she dashed through the tall bushes toward the back of the house. Sighting the carriage house, Alaina headed for it, jumping over the low shrubs and sprinting for the open door. She glanced back over her shoulder and darted inside, intending to saddle Ol' Tar and head out to the bayou where she wouldn't be disturbed. But in the next moment she charged full bore into the back of Captain Cole Latimer. She hit him with such force that she knocked him away from the water pump and sent him sprawling in the dust and dirt of the stable floor.

Alaina stared in mute surprise as Cole rolled and with a growl came to his feet. Spitting chafe, the captain recognized his assailant and flung out a hand to catch the thin arm as Alaina attempted an escape.

"You bumbling little roughneck!" he barked. "What are you trying to do?"

His fingers bit painfully into her arm, and Alaina's fear came back full force as she realized that in her haste she had left on her corset and feminine undergarments. The soft chemise held her bosom to a full roundness while the corset tightly cinched her small waist. If he touched her, there was no way she could explain it away. Her arm ached under his tight grip, and this manhandling was more than Alaina had ever taken from anyone. Her own orneriness came to her defense.

"Get your hands off me, Yankee!" she shrieked. "You got no right to lay a finger on me!"

Hotly irate, Alaina snatched her arm away and was immediately afraid she had left some skin behind. Some meager sense returning, she hunched her shoulders in the outsized shirt and crossed her arms to rub the offended member. She moved away from him slightly, into a deeper shadow of the barn.

Cole was somewhat chagrined at his own quick temper. "I'm sorry." He began to dust himself off. "I'm sure it was an accident and—" A sudden thought struck and he looked up sharply. "It was an accident, wasn't it?"

"Yeah," Alaina relented a bit. "I didn't see ya in the dark."

"What were you running away from, anyway?" Then Cole chuckled. "I'll bet you saw me and were afraid I'd come to fetch you for extra work."

"I ain't afraid o' work," Alaina snapped testily.

"I guess you're not, at that," Cole conceded. He unbuttoned his blouse halfway down, folded the collar under, and rinsed his face and hands under the pump. "I brought my horse around for a drink before I headed back. Actually, I just have a few hours off and thought I'd pay my respects to your cousin." He missed Alaina's expression of disgust as he splashed water onto the back of his neck, then wiped it dry with a handkerchief. He retrieved his gauntlets and glanced about for his hat. He found it in the dust just outside the stable door. Brushing it off, he came back to Alaina.

"Since no one else seems to be home, I'll be going back. You can inform Roberta of my visit." He watched as the lad moved away, the slim shoulders oddly hunched. "What's the matter?"

"You hurt my arm," Alaina snapped, her clear gray eyes narrowed and accusing.

"I'll apologize for that—if you will apologize for knocking me down." He waited, his bright blue eyes gleaming with amusement.

"I guess," was the most Alaina would relent. She was considering how well she might enjoy swinging a heavy boot against the bluebelly's rear.

Suddenly a perplexed frown came upon Cole's face. His brow raised wonderingly as he bent toward Alaina and sniffed. "What in the world? Have you taken to a lady's way?"

Alaina's heart gave a frantic leap and lodged in her throat until he continued. "You smell as if you bathed in a tubful of perfume."

"Oh! Well!" Alaina stumbled in search of an explanation, then gave a small, reluctant shrug. "It's Roberta's.

She said I stunk too much and dumped some of her rosewater on me."

Cole began to chuckle. "I begin to understand why you ran away from me." He gathered his horses reins, set his Hardee hat jauntily upon his head, and rebuttoned his blouse. "Rest assured, Al, your secret is safe with me. But all the same, I wouldn't come to the hospital smelling like that—if I were you."

Alaina bestowed upon him an unappreciative glare. She followed him to the front of the house but only because she wanted to make sure that he left. They were rounding the corner of the house when the Craighughs' carriage halted before the stoop.

"Why, Captain Latimer," Roberta called gaily and waved. "What brings you way out here today?" Her smile froze into a fixed grin as she saw Alaina bringing up the rear. "Don't tell me you came out here to see little bitty Al."

Cole gallantly offered a hand to assist her to the ground. "I had a few hours free and thought I might find you at home."

"Ahem!" Angus cleared his throat loudly and descended to help his wife down. "I'm afraid our daughter is committed to joining us this afternoon, Captain."

"But, Daddy!" Roberta moaned and was bent to argue, but her father's angry look silenced her. She dared not continue for fear of creating a scene that would discourage the captain from coming again.

"We plan to visit friends, and they asked especially that Roberta join us." It was an outright lie, but he was not of a mind to bend to his daughter's whims again and allow this man to eventually become his son-in-law. He granted his daughter almost everything she asked of him, but her hand in marriage to a Yankee was something else entirely.

"I hope you have not been waiting overlong, Captain." Roberta managed to smile dazzlingly. She had gotten around her father before; this presented no mean challenge. Only time was needed.

"Al entertained me quite fairly," Cole chuckled, "until I vow I could bear no more of his attention."

"Al?" Roberta hurled a glare in the lad's direction, immediately suspicious. "What has he been—ah—telling you?"

"I'm sure he will relate the tale with relish, thus I leave the telling to him." Cole paused and glanced at Angus's stiff back. The elder Craighugh's hospitality appeared very limited, and not caring to start a family quarrel over his presence, he spoke rather ruefully. "I'm afraid, however, that I must be going. I have overstayed as it is."

Regretfully Roberta watched him to the saddle and smiled demurely as he touched the brim of his hat. "I bid you good-day, Miss Craighugh." He glanced at Al. "I'll see you tomorrow."

With a clatter of hooves he was gone. Roberta waited until her parents had entered the house, then turned on Alaina in a fury. She managed to keep her voice low but it was sharp and demanding.

"Just how well did you entertain Captain Latimer? You little bitch, if you've told him about me—"

"My goodness! I don't know what got into me." Alaina feigned the innocence of a simpleton. She was well aware of what her cousin feared and if, for a brief moment, she delayed her answer for the sake of revenge, it was understandable.

"Alaina MacGaren! I'll tear that ragged mop out of your head by the roots!"

The younger girl shrugged. "It's not what I said but what I did."

Roberta's eyebrows raised sharply, her thoughts running rampant.

"We had a tussle in the carriage house." Alaina licked her lips as if savoring the torment she was putting her cousin through. "He even liked my perfume."

"Lainie!" Roberta nearly screeched. "You're teasing me again! I just know it! And if you don't tell me just exactly what happened, you'll be sorry."

"Oh, calm yourself," Alaina chided. "You look as if you're about to explode. I only knocked him flat on his face."

"That better be all!" threatened the woman. "That just better be all!"

Chapter 9

IT was cooler now; the awful heat of late autumn had fled. Alaina's hair had grown to a length that brought stares of disapproval from Cole Latimer, and reluctantly she lent herself to Aunt Leala's talents at trimming hair. The short, neat style proved very becoming to her small face, accentuating the beauty of the large gray eyes, the slim fragile features, and high delicate cheekbones. With the improved diet, her slight, willowy frame began to ripen beneath her baggy garments but she continued as before, uncomfortable in her disguise as boy, yet unable to discard it.

The day was Monday, and as was their custom, the surgeons gathered early in the morning to tour the wards. This was, in part, a time meant for the men to air their complaints and indispositions. However, as was his custom, Major Magruder stationed himself close at the general's elbow with a readied pen and a warning glance for those who would criticize the staff overmuch. It was also the time when the doctors made their decisions on which soldiers were well enough to yield their beds and return to the limited-duty units.

Alaina had barely begun her labors when a brief column of gray-clad soldiers, once more in irons, came shuffling down the stairs. Doctor Brooks fought a running battle to keep these men until they were fully recovered, realizing that if they were sent to the prisons in a weakened state, it was tantamount to a sentence of death. As she watched, Alaina felt an ache within her chest. For most of them, the war was over. Unless they managed an escape from the well-guarded Yankee prisons, they would see no more of battle, but would spend their days fighting the privation of brutal confinement. As the prisoners passed, a few of them grinned or spoke to her. The burly sergeant, whose leg she had threatened, raised his clenched fist.

"Buck up, lad." He smiled at the dirty-faced chore boy. "The war ain't over yet." His words rang hollow and flat, and it was more as if he tried to cheer himself.

Alaina struggled to find some worthy retort, but then they were gone, and the hall was empty, though the rhythmic jangle of linked iron continued to echo down its length. Such high hopes had gone to war with these men only a swift year or two past. Her throat felt tight, and tears threatened to course down her cheeks. Quickly she brushed at her eyes, then glanced up to find Cole watching her. The glare she tossed him hardly did justice to the bitterness that raged within her. At the moment her hatred of Yankees was supreme. Watching the prisoners file past had been like seeing her own brother being taken away in chains. She hated this war! She hated the enemy! She hated Cole Latimer most of all!

Cole wisely turned his back and continued with his duties. He would let time be the balm for this ragamuffin boy. Whatever he said now would only serve to deepen the rancor of the lad.

Much to Alaina's consternation, the morning also brought an influx of prisoners to fill the emptied beds. Several were brought in on litters and taken into surgery. Among them was a young Confederate cavalryman who had taken a minié ball in his leg and was left with a jagged, gaping wound that formed a gruesome marker leading from mid thigh to knee. General Mitchell had departed the hospital after the morning inspection, leaving Major Magruder in charge. It was the latter's decision, along with Major Forbes, to amputate the leg near the hip since they were unable to extract the lead shot that had lodged in the vital joint. Cole learned of it from a casual comment made by an orderly and made haste to join his superiors.

"It's got to come off!" Magruder declared angrily after the younger man had offered his opinion.

"Dammit, Major!" Cole struggled a moment with his own rising ire and managed to continue more calmly. "It's a man's leg, not the hindquarters of a mule! There's no infection."

"The shot's in there deep, and it's only a matter of time

before lead poisoning sets in. There is no way we can get it. Major Forbes and I have already tried."

"Then try again," Cole urged. "At least that much you can do."

"We've got other wounded to attend to," Magruder responded sharply. "Some of our own men are waiting. We can't waste the time."

Cole became incensed. "There are none who can't wait. A minor wound here and there, that is all. Gentlemen, this man may very well need his leg after the war. Are you butchers to be so callous about it?"

"Butchers!" Magruder's reddened face betrayed his outrage. He had never cared for this upstart who seemed to consider his own opinion higher than those of more rank and experience. The man was obviously unaware of the many matters even now pressing; the sheer weight of administration alone was awesome. This only roused his hatred of the captain until it coiled like a savage viper within his belly. He would not stand for this interference and questioning his judgment.

"Captain, if you do not desist, I'll put you on report for insubordination," he threatened. "Your sympathies for the enemy will be the end of your career. Now, I order you to get out of here. We have work to do."

Abruptly Cole left the room, nearly overturning Alaina who had been scrubbing the hall floor nearby. The argument had been impossible to ignore, and she gave no excuse as she glared at the captain for a second time that day.

"You're jes' gonna stand there and let 'em do it, ain't-cha?"

"Go fetch Doctor Brooks," Cole snapped sharply. "And quickly!"

Alaina needed no other urging. Despite the heavy boots, she sprinted across the hall and flew up the stairs to return in a brief moment with the puffing, wheezing doctor. Snatching the old man's arm, Cole drew him into the room where Magruder stood ready to start the amputation.

"Gentlemen, if you proceed further," Cole interrupted curtly, "I believe you will have to answer to Doctor Brooks and be held accountable for the inhumane treatment of a prisoner."

Major Magruder threw down the scalpel and incredulously demanded, "Do you threaten me, Captain Latimer?"

"No, Major," Cole replied almost gently. "But neither do I believe that the surgeon general will tolerate such treatment of a prisoner-of-war."

"You take too much upon yourself, Captain," Major Forbes warned.

Cole calmly folded his hands behind his back. "Perhaps I do, sir, but I can only hope that if a similar decision ever has to be made on my behalf, someone will take into consideration that I greatly value my legs."

Magruder snarled, "If you have so much love for this Johnny Reb, Captain, then you and your good *Southern* friend can try to save his damn leg, though it can well mean the man will lose his life for it."

Cole Latimer did not refuse the challenge. With Doctor Brooks's assistance, he set to work. Alaina kept reappearing at the door where the captain worked, anxious to know if the young soldier would survive. When Cole finally emerged from the room, he found the ragged lad close by. The clear gray eyes anxiously questioned, and it was a long, thoughtful moment before Cole replied, "He'll live."

"And the leg?" Alaina asked, fearing the worst.

Slowly Cole smiled. "He has that, too."

Cole saw a quick flash of white teeth in a happy grin and was sure the lad moved toward him a step, then the usual scowl returned to mask it all. Al gave a short, embarrassed nod and hastened back to her duties, leaving Cole much bemused. The boy was obviously reluctant to show any softer emotion such as gratitude and seemed to find ease in an almost perverse belligerence.

Bobby Johnson's condition had improved somewhat. The dosages of morphine were being continually eased. But whenever Alaina paused beside his bed and tried a comment or two, the young soldier only rolled his head away and refused to answer her.

It was early on a storm-drenched morning when Alaina found him struggling with pen and paper, trying to write a letter. As she dusted, she worked herself around to where she could see what his efforts had produced. Dark splotches of ink marked the sheet of paper and the lines of writing ran together uphill and downhill.

"They ain't gonna be able to read that," she offered.

The writing stopped abruptly, then slowly his hand crumpled the paper. With a sudden sob, Bobby threw the wad, bouncing it off the wall.

"Hey, Yankee! You're making a mess fer me to clean up."

The retort came sharp and bitter. "You Johnny Rebs made a mess of me that nobody can clean up."

Alaina snorted. "The graveyards are full of worse messes 'an you, and it ain't jes' bluecoats neither."

The soldier rocked his head listlessly on the pillow. "I'd rather be dead. I'll go home now for my wife to bring me meals all my life. I can't ask that of Jeannie! What woman wants a blindman for a husband?"

"Seems to me, Yankee, she'd be mighty happy jes' to have ya home."

"My name isn't Yankee!" he barked.

"Yeah, I know. It's Bobby Johnson. We met outside the surgery ward."

A long, quiet pause intervened. "Are you Al?"

"Yup."

Bobby Johnson heaved a sigh. "I guess I've had too much time to feel sorry for myself."

Alaina stared down at the young man, yearning to console him but afraid to get involved. Still, she was led to do the kinder thing. "I ain't much fer reading, but sometimes I gots nothing better to do. Would ya like me to read to ya—sometimes?"

"That would be nice.

In the next several days Alaina rushed about to finish her work so she could sit beside the young soldier to read to him. He began to respond to her quick humor and even conceded dictating a letter to his mother and another to his wife. It was not until she had read the last page of a short novel and folded the book that Alaina glanced up and saw a troubled look on Bobby Johnson's face.

"What's the matter? You didn't like it?" she asked, somewhat disheartened.

"I liked it," Bobby replied slowly. "But I noticed as you read that your voice—softened. I would guess that you've been well schooled despite your attempts to hide it."

Alaina knew a sudden cold chill and held her breath, realizing she had blundered badly.

"I also know that you are no Al." He reached out a groping hand to take her wrist. "You are small—a small woman. Yes! Yes! You are a girl! Where did you come by the name of Al?"

"Alaina," she whispered.

"Young?" His fingers passed along her finely boned hand. Though rough from work, it was not a hand of an old person.

"Seventeen." Alaina bit her lip and asked shyly. "Are you going to tell anyone?"

"Explain to me why you want the others to think you're a boy, and I will judge for myself."

Reluctantly trusting to the blindman's wisdom, Alaina related her reasons, leaving nothing out. "I am not guilty of spying," she murmured. "But as you say, you are my judge now. My freedom depends on what you decide."

A long, dreadful, and anxious moment passed, then—"I always enjoyed the tale of *Oliver Twist*. Will you read it to me?"

Tears of relief rushed to Alaina's eyes, and in distraction she began to smooth his sheets. "My uncle has the book in his study. I'll bring it tomorrow."

She started to move away, then paused. "You won't tell Captain Latimer, will you?"

"Not unless I see a need," he assured her.

The rain continued to fall upon the city, and by Saturday, when there seemed to be some hope of it clearing, the heavy mists of early morning coalesced to a soaking rain. Leaden skies pressed close above the rooftops, and even the cobbled streets grew rivulets of mud. Al was to have the afternoon off. Her labors during the week had brought everything to a gleaming tidiness, and even after a careful inspection, she could find nothing more to occupy her in the wards. But as she stepped from the last, the grimy, filthy marble floor of the wide foyer just inside the front door caught her eye. Here was a challenge indeed. It would take the best of her cleaning talents to bring out the original beauty of the pale-veined pattern.

Some time later, Alaina stood back and surveyed with satisfaction the meticulously scrubbed floor. *A final mopping with rinse water ought to do it,* she thought, *and then I can go home.*

The task was nearly done and the mop was being wrung out for the last time when voices sounded outside and the door swung inward to herald the entry of several officers and a pair of officious-looking civilians. They crossed the entryway and took no note of the angry glare that followed them as they left their passage marked with muddy footprints.

Ominously, Al hefted the mop and heaved it back into the bucket. She started over again to erase the muck, dipping the mop often to rinse the dirt free. Little progress had been made when the door was flung open again and another pair of mire-caked boots advanced across the floor.

The mop froze in mid stroke, and Alaina loudly complained, "Hey, c'mon, Yankee. Can't you wipe your—"

"Out of my way, you little fool!"

Alaina was roughly pushed aside and went sprawling as her feet became entangled with the mop. Jacques DuBonné strode arrogantly past, unconcerned that his boots threw dark, wet slime across the clean marble floor. Several steps past the urchin, he paused and half turned, demanding, "Where is a doc—?"

His last word ended abruptly with a wet *shlop* as the sopping rags of the mop took him full in the face and twined about his head. Dubonné flung up an arm to rake away the mess, then gasped as he was drenched from head to foot with the filth-thickened contents of the pail. He spluttered in outrage and reached beneath his coat for his slim blade, snatching it forth. In the dim light, the sharp edge winked evilly.

Alaina stepped back, still holding the bucket, and began to chuckle at the dripping Cajun, then suddenly she was engulfed by two huge black arms that came from behind her, pinning her own to her side. She struggled to free herself and let loose a series of definitive expletives that would have made a mule skinner pause in awe. She kicked wildly in the black's grasp as she saw the twisted snarl frozen on Jacques's face. The small man crept forward, turning the knife threateningly in his hand.

"Here now! What's going on?" Cole's sharp bark came from the stairs, and he hurried toward them. He had been about to leave and wore his regulation uniform and the Hardee hat which came down across his scowling brow.

Furtively, Jacques slipped the knife out of sight, but the black made no attempt to release his captive. Alaina's arms had grown numb beneath his merciless grip, and the bucket slipped from stiffening fingers and clanged to the floor, rattling noisily as it rolled away.

Cole halted a short pace away. "Put the boy down," he demanded and gestured to the black. "If there is a need, I will discipline him." The giant man only stared at him, and the captain sharpened his voice. "Put him down, I say!"

As the Negro made no move to obey, Cole lifted the flap of his holster and laid his hand on the butt of his pistol before Jacques spoke to the black in a tongue unknown to Alaina. The giant smiled and spread his arms wide, spilling her to the floor. A grunt of pain was jolted from her, and she sat where she landed, gasping for breath.

Jacques's eyes suddenly narrowed as he looked at her more closely. "I know you from the riverboat!" he snarled. "You build a great debt to me. Next time I collect all that is due, eh?"

As Alaina struggled to rise, Jacques peeled back the sodden jacket from his shoulder and whirled angrily to the captain. "You see?" He gestured to a blood-soaked sleeve. "I am wounded. I came here for a doctor, and this little —many-fathered snipe—!"

Her jaw squared ominously, Alaina drew back a fist and lunged forward, but Cole grabbed a handful of her britches, drawing a yelp from her as he caught some bruised buttock as well. Despite her struggles to get free, he dragged her back, still holding her firm.

Warily eyeing the irate youth, Jacques continued, "He attack me with the mop and bucket!" He scraped disgustedly at his befouled brocade vest. "Look! My clothes! They are ruined!"

Alaina snorted, snatching her backside free of Cole's restraint and tossed both men a glare. "He needed a washing."

"That whelp will pay!" railed Jacques, stepping menacingly toward Alaina.

Cole moved between the two and caught the man's arm as he tried to reach for the youth. "I doubt the boy can afford your kerchief, let alone the rest. He will be disciplined, rest assured."

Alaina glared as Cole snapped, "You're here to clean up messes, not make them."

"That's just what I was a-doing when this jackass

stomped in from the barnyard. That lame-brained mule ain't never been taught to wipe his feet."

Cole's quick glance about the hall allowed him some understanding of the youth's irritation, yet it was a doctor's duty to tend the wounded. He gave the small Frenchman no chance to argue further. "Let me look at that." He plucked at the bloody sleeve and briefly examined the injury before he peered down at the man curiously. "This looks like a saber cut. How did you get it?"

"Bah!" Jacques threw up his good hand. "I took a house in the country for payment of a debt. The sheriff, he is a city man. He would not serve the papers, so I do it myself. Huh, Madame Hawthorne! She is crazy ol' woman! She would not take them. She hid a sword behind her skirt, and when I try to give the papers so"—he stuck out his wounded hand indignantly—"she take a swing at me. Zing!" He laughed derisively. "Now the sheriff will have to arrest her. I show that old lady, eh?"

"You blackhearted—!" Alaina cried hotly, but a sharp glare from Cole silenced her. She sulked, glowering at his back.

"I was just leaving," Cole announced brusquely. "But I suppose I can delay a moment." He half turned to the urchin and promised direly, "I'll talk to you later. Now get this mess cleaned up."

Alaina bristled like an enraged porcupine. She snatched up her mop and with eyes narrowed watched the captain escort Jacques down the hall. The black followed them, tossing a wide grin back at her.

"We'll clean that and put some carbolic on it." Cole's comment drifted back. "It's not deep. A simple compress should do."

Alaina's work was done in a rush, and the tools put hurriedly away. She had no mind to wait for further castigation but grabbed her hat and hurried on her way. Captain Latimer had threatened her much too often. This time he might just carry out his promise.

A bit of indignation still showed in Alaina's tight lips when she arrived at the Craighughs'. With more energy than was warranted, even for one so petite, she slammed the kitchen door and ignored the windowpanes that rattled threateningly in their wood casings. She was hardly in the mood to exchange banalities with Roberta, but since their argument her cousin had made it a habit to wait near the back entrance for her. With Angus at the store and Leala frequently helping him, Roberta had nothing more than trivia to occupy her. She rose late, whiled away the hours attending to her person and long before the dinner hour, began to dress with exacting care. By the time Alaina arrived home every strand of hair had been artfully curled, the long white fingers carefully manicured, and a fresh and pretty gown donned. It was no different this early afternoon.

"I declare, Al." Roberta had begun to enjoy using the masculine sobriquet. "I never know if it's you or some errand boy coming to the back door. You do play your part so well!"

"Yeah! And I'm gonna take to toting me a gun, too!" the younger woman retorted with virulence. The boyish slang only added emphasis to her wrath. "Jes' might kill me a few polecats afo' I'm done."

Roberta was momentarily stunned into speechlessness. It was Dulcie who quickly turned from the hearth where she had been stirring a squirrel stew and demanded, "Whad yo' gone and done now, chile? Ain' yo' in 'nuff trouble widout killing yo'self some Yankee critter?"

Alaina kicked off the heavy boots and sent them sliding across the brick floor toward the pantry. "I've been mauled, bruised, and threatened. I've spent the morning on my knees scrubbing floors, only to have some dirty, sneaking river rat go traipsing across it. Got my backside abused and manhandled by that long-legged Yankee—"

Roberta gasped, truly scandalized.

"He's li'ble to be the first one I punctuate!" Alaina warned, wagging her finger toward Roberta. "Just you watch. And then I'm going to take my gun to that reprobate Jacques DuBonné, and make him crawl on his belly all the way back to Mrs. Hawthorne's so that lady can finish what she started!"

Roberta was aghast. She had never seen her cousin in such a temper. "Alaina! What has gotten into you?"

"Righteous anger, that's what's gotten into me! Righteous! Do you know what that means, Roberta?" She advanced on her cousin, her jaw squared dangerously. Mumbling incoherently and shaking her head, Roberta stumbled back into a ladder-back chair where, with jaw aslack, she stared agog into those blazing gray eyes.

"It means I have just cause!" Alaina railed at her

quivering cousin, then she straightened, almost calmly, and strode arrogantly about the kitchen. She threw up a hand dramatically. "Just cause! Yes! I can plead that at my trial!"

"Whad trial is dat?" Dulcie squawked, planting her hands firmly on her broad hips and thrusting out her jaw. "Whad yo' gone and done, Miz Alaina? Yo' tell me right now!"

"Nothing, yet," Alaina replied smugly. She took a peeled turnip and bit into it, then gestured with the vegetable, chewed, and waited until she had cleared her throat before she continued. "But I'm going to do something. Before I'm through, Jacques DuBonné"—she spit the name out with loathing—"is going to wish he'd never laid eyes on Mrs. Hawthorne."

"You mean that old woman who comes to Daddy's store?" Roberta questioned uneasily.

Alaina's attention perked. "You know her?"

"Well, she doesn't come in that often when I'm there," Roberta hedged, not quite sure just how much she should tell Alaina. After all, her cousin might well jeopardize what seemed to be a most promising relationship with Cole.

"But you know where she lives," Alaina pressed.

"Not exactly." Roberta shrugged lamely. "Out north on the old river road somewhere, I think—"

The girl strode to her boots and snatched them on. "I'll find out where if it takes me all night!"

"Now, Lainie, don't! Don't do anything foolish!" pleaded her cousin fearfully.

The girl slapped the floppy hat on her head and grinned, showing small, sparkling white teeth. "That all depends on what you call foolish, Robbie. I guess I jes' don't consider shooting a few blackhearted varmints foolishness." She shrugged nonchalantly. "It all depends on them."

Before she left the house, Alaina went to the armoire in her room and lifted out her father's army pistol. None of the Craighughs knew she had it. She had carried it into the house in her valise the first day she arrived. It was a long-barreled Colt .44 that was almost too heavy for her, but she knew how to use it, and with accuracy. She tucked it carefully within her leather pouch and pulled the strap over her head and arm. Despite her threats, it was not in her plan to use the weapon but—just in case—she added the powder flask, caps, and ball box to the pouch. It gave her a sense of assurance to feel the weight of the piece solidly against her hip.

It was more than an hour after Alaina dragged Ol' Tar out of the stables and rode off on his back that Roberta faced Cole Latimer across the threshold of the Craighugh home.

"Why, Captain Latimer," Roberta beamed, having fully recovered from Alaina's tirade. "I thought for sure you had forgotten about little ol' me."

"I'm afraid this is not a social call, Roberta," he stated as gently as possible. "I would like to see Al, if he is here."

"Al?" Roberta was crushed. She had thought that Alaina, disguised as a boy, could give her no competition in her efforts to win Cole, but she had not reckoned that this warring animosity between the two would draw Cole's attention away from her. She covered her irritation with a winsome pout and coyly fluttered her lashes. "Why, Captain, you mean to tell me that all you came for was to see that runty little boy. And here I was thinking you had come calling on me. I'm dreadfully put out."

"I'm sorry," Cole said apologetically, "but the boy threw a bucket of dirty water over a wounded man today at the hospital." Roberta's gasp of horror was genuine. "What I have to say to Al won't take long. May I speak to him?"

"Why, Al's not here, Captain." Roberta smiled hesitantly. "He was, but he left some time ago."

"Did he say where he was going? I must get this straightened out before he comes to work Monday. I can't allow anything like this to happen again."

Roberta pondered a brief moment whether it was better to claim her own innocence and tell all, just in case Alaina really carried out her threats, or appear ignorant of the girl's whereabouts. The trouble with lying was that it might get back to Cole.

"I tell you, Captain, that boy was in such a temper." Roberta wavered in her telling when she thought of what Alaina's reaction might be, but bravely proceeded. "He plumb scared the life out of me and Dulcie. Why, he was a-threatenin' to shoot some varmint named Jacques, and I'll swear to it, he went off looking for trouble."

Despite himself, Cole felt responsible for the boy. "Which way did he go?"

"Why, off down the river road." Roberta stepped out onto the gallery and lifted her arm in the same direction Alaina had taken. "You go down there about a mile, then turn north a mile or two. You can't miss it. A big old board house with a steep roof and only a single porch across the front. It has an iron hitching post like a black boy with a ring in his hand."

Cole was about to turn away when she laid a restraining hand on his arm. "You will be careful, won't you, Captain? Al is a pretty good shot, and he did mention he was thinking of putting a hole through you."

"Hot-headed little scamp!" Cole muttered beneath his breath. Jacques had said that he intended to return to Mrs. Hawthorne's with the sheriff. It would be just like Al to get into more trouble than he could handle.

Chapter 10

THE rain had stopped much earlier, but had left the streets and dirt roads a muddy hazard. The shuffling gait of Ol' Tar kicked up clods of mud and only nibbled at the miles, much to Alaina's festering impatience. She was not in the mood to contend with the nag's single-minded determination to return to the stable, though her angry prodding gained her little more than sporadic jolts of a knock-kneed canter, and she applied the smart taste of a heavy willow switch to his scarred hindquarters in hopes of speeding him on his way. The worst of her fears was realized as she came toward the end of the muddy lane. Tall shrubs allowed only a glimpse of the steeply pitched roof of the Hawthorne house, but afforded a clear view beneath the overhanging limbs of the massive oaks that bordered the road. Two empty carriages waited there, one a fancy landau, the other a plain buckboard. Alaina could only surmise that Jacques had arrived ahead of her and possibly, as he had threatened, with the sheriff.

Alaina turned Tar off the lane and slid from his bony back. She left her boots beside the bush where she tethered him and, feeling the coolness of the wet grass beneath her bare feet, made a furtive approach along the tall hedge until she could view the front yard through the tangled growth of a wisteria vine. Her eyes readily found Jacques DuBonné, and she noted with a certain satisfaction that he had delayed long enough to effect a complete change of clothes. The enormous black was present, lolling indolently against the far side of the fancy carriage, and another man, almost as big, stood near Jacques at the foot of the front steps.

Facing them off near the edge of the long, raised porch was a tall, white-haired woman of sixty years or more.

She bore herself proudly, with a firm, almost haughty demeanor, while she rested her crossed hand in imperious grace upon the hilt of a downward-thrust, brightly gleaming saber. The unspoken challenge was clear; she'd use the sword if there came a need.

Alaina ran along the bushes until she could slip through a break to the back of the house. Rounding the structure, she stopped to choose the best vantage point. A few low shrubs grew alongside the house, and she crouched behind their cover where she would miss no word of the exchange.

Jacques was waving his arm wildly and demanding some show of action from the sheriff. "I tell you I have the paper that say I purchase thees property from the bank!" he declared, withdrawing a packet from inside his coat, and, snapping the back of his fingers sharply against them, ranted on. "I have it all here, Sheriff. Now, I insist you arrest thees woman!"

The slow, pondering deliberation of the law officer seemed to infuriate the smaller man, for when the sheriff only stared at him, leisurely mouthing a cud of tobacco, the Frenchman railed, "Will you do something?"

"Well now," the sheriff drawled. "I've been trying to hear what this old lady has to say for herself, but you just ain't giving her much chance, Mr. Bonny."

"DuBonné!" Jacques corrected irately. "And what you think she to say, Sheriff, that will discount this?" He shook the packet beneath the other man's nose. "I demand you do the thing, or I am forced to highest authority."

The sheriff grumbled and, peevishly tugging his hat off, stepped closer to the long porch where the woman stood. "Ma'm, I'm sorry, but I have my duty, just like the man said."

"Of course, Sheriff," the woman replied in a firm, but oddly pleasant rasping voice. "But I wonder if Mister DuBonné has made you aware of my skill with my husband's sword. As yet, I haven't had a chance to use it on a gentleman of the law."

"Ma'm," he shook his head sadly, "I sure would prefer it if you'd just come along peacefullike."

The aged chin raised proudly. "I must respectfully decline, of course. I knew your mother well, Sheriff Bascombe. She was a fine woman." Mrs. Hawthorne paused for effect, then twisted the well-set prod with vicious intent. "Were she alive today, I'm sure she would be highly distraught if she learned that you dispossessed me without due cause or course."

"Well—uh, ma'm—I—I—" The sheriff stuttered into silence, and his face went red.

"You must enforce the law!" Jacques cried, striding forward a short space. "I have pay the good money to the bank for thees place! I will not be denied! Arrest the old hag!"

"The debt you rave about, young man, was paid a good six months ago," Mrs. Hawthorne doughtily informed him. "I have a receipt—"

"Receipt, bah!" Jacques said. "You have declare the existence of such a paper, but I 'ave seen no such proof."

The woman continued calmly, as if she had not been interrupted. "A letter of receipt, duly witnessed, from the bank."

"It doesn't exist!" Jacques exclaimed as he dared to step nearer.

Mrs. Hawthorne smiled ruefully. "In either case, sir, you will be a bit more frayed if you set a foot on that step."

Shaking his head irascibly, Jacques muttered a few unintelligible words. They meant nothing to the sheriff and Mrs. Hawthorne, but they struck a cord in Alaina's memory of the moment just before the black released her, when Jacques had uttered a similar-sounding verbiage. And as before, the black was moving on command—sidling to one side behind the carriages to where he could take the woman by surprise. Digging into her pouch, Alaina quickly withdrew her father's pistol and, with trembling fingers, checked the loading and slipped fresh caps into place.

The negro was almost even with the end of the porch now and was stealthily working his way around the sheriff's buggy while Jacques continued to argue with the woman. Alaina stepped out from behind the bushes, bracing her small feet wide apart and squared her sights on the black's wide chest with both hands clutching the handle of the pistol, then carefully drew back the hammer. The black froze as he heard the double click and slowly searched with his eyes until he saw the threat. True worry furrowed the broad, glistening brow and tiny beads of sweat stood out as he gaped at the thin lad and the huge pistol.

Alaina gestured with the gun, and the black carefully complied, stepping sideways toward the others as she moved forward. Jacques, at first seeing nothing more than his servant's return, irately spouted several more commands in the tongue of unknown origin. Then the ragged lad came into sight, and he sputtered into gawking silence.

"*You!*" He regained his voice with force.

The sheriff whirled, and Al calmly nodded a greeting.

"Aftahnoon, y'all."

"What's the meaning of this?" barked the sheriff. "Put down that gun, boy, before you hurt somebody."

"Might at that"—Al puckered her lips thoughtfully—"if'n y'all don't back up a ways from the porch and give Miz Hawthorne a breathing space."

Jacques hastily followed the youth's directions, having already tasted of that one's contrariness. But the sheriff ignored the scruffy sprite and lifted a foot to place it on the lowest step.

"Now, Mrs. Hawthorne—"

The report of the pistol numbed the ears, and a large splinter flew from the plank beneath his foot, leaving a wide gash of fresh wood. The sheriff stumbled back a few steps as the pistol was immediately recocked, and the black halted in a forward stride when it again took his chest as a point of aim. The negro obligingly lowered his foot and relaxed, while the sheriff gaped at the lad, well assured that the youth had lost his mind. Then his face darkened, and furiously shaking a fist, he railed, "You little half-witted bindlestiff! I'll break that pistol over your backside before I throw you in jail! I'm an officer of the law and—!"

His words were cut short by a shout and the thundering approach of horse's hooves. Horse and rider came toward them, and much in the manner of a flamboyant calvary officer, Captain Latimer swung off his still-prancing roan.

"What goes on here?" he demanded as he looped the reins through the ring of the iron hitching post. Dragging off his gauntlets, he strode forward, taking in the scene that greeted him.

"Well now, I just don't see where that it's any of your business, mister." The sheriff spat a stream of black juice onto the grass and peered at the Yankee with a less than grateful frown.

Cole tucked the gauntlets beneath his belt and casually rested a hand on his holster. "May I remind you, sir, that the entire occupied area is under martial law. By definition, that suspends all civil authority and affairs. You can be held responsible for what transpires under your offices without the approval of the military governor."

The sheriff swore softly beneath the prodding of his memory and gestured toward the lad. "I came out here to do my duty as an officer of the law and that young whelp took a shot at me."

Alaina shrugged innocently as the captain turned and raised a brow at her. "I coulda shot him clean through if'n I'da wanted to." She gestured toward the black with the gun. "Coulda shot him, too, while he was a'trying to sneak up behind that po' woman."

"Al, put that gun down," Cole commanded.

Undismayed, Alaina laid the still-cocked pistol on the porch and rested an elbow on the planks without removing her hand more than a few inches from the well-worn grip. For the moment at least, she'd let him handle the situation.

"I repeat!" Cole remonstrated, facing the others. "Just what is going on here?"

Jacques burst out in a rush of outraged explanations. "That old woman, she don't pay her debt. The bank put the house up for sale. I bought it! Here are the papers! All legal!"

"Do you mind if I look at those?" Cole asked.

"You will see," Jacques handed them over with open satisfaction.

After a moment of studying the documents, Cole glanced up at the old woman. "What do you have to say about this?"

"I pay my debts," Mrs. Hawthorne informed him loftily. "All of them. I have a receipt!"

"Bah!" Jacques snorted. "She say she has such a paper, but nothing has been seen of it!"

"Sir, I do not lie," she informed him bluntly, raising an audacious brow. "And I do not cheat people either."

"May I see the receipt you speak of?" Cole requested.

Mrs. Hawthorne gazed down at him coolly. "And why should I trust a Yankee, sir?"

A gleeful cackle from Al won the captain's glare. "Now

there be a woman what's got a good head on her shoulders."

Mrs. Hawthorne accepted the compliment with a gracious nod. "Thank you, child. I've often thought the same thing myself."

Al gestured casually. "I guess as Yankees go, though, he's fit to be trusted." She caressed the handle of the pistol tenderly. "At least, as much as them other fellers."

"I am beholden to your kindness, child, but I'm a bit confused. Perhaps I have cause to trust you, seeing that you stopped that black oaf, but why should I take your word?"

"Well, I ain't a friend o' that there fella," Al nodded toward Jacques, "so I must be a friend of yours."

"For some reason, that sounds reasonable to me," Mrs. Hawthorne responded in wry amusement. She lifted the sword briefly toward Cole. "You know him that well?"

"Yeah, I know him." The information came reluctantly. "He's a sawbones at the Union Hospital."

Faced with a choice, Mrs. Hawthorne paused a moment, then as if coming to a decision, she reached into the bodice of her dress and handed over a sheet of paper to Cole with a rueful comment. "Considering my age, I thought it was the safest place to hide it."

"Yes, ma'm." Cole won a private battle not to smile and unfolded the letter to study it for a few moments. "This seems to be well in order, sheriff," he commented, scanning it once more briefly. He half turned to the man. "Perhaps the bank is in error."

"No!" Jacques shouted and shook his own papers. "I have purchased thees property!"

"If that be true, the bank owes you a reimbursement, sir, for Mrs. Hawthorne's receipt seems well in order. It's a statement that this property is free of debt and promises a clear deed. It is dated well before any of your papers."

"Sheriff!" Cole turned, leaving Jacques to sputter into silence. "There seems to be adequate cause to believe an error has been made."

"You damned right, Yankee!" Jacques spat venomously. "You and this filthy little bastard have made it! You have interfere with Jacques DuBonné." The Frenchman clenched his fists in rage. "An' Jacques, he promise your blue coat will be your death!"

The captain bent a chilly stare on the Cajun. "My usual task is protecting life, sir." His voice was low and silky smooth, and even Alaina held her breath. "I could make an exception for special cases, however."

Jacques struggled between his desire for revenge and a knowledge of the pure foolishness of any such attempt at this moment. Finally he controlled himself and retreated to his carriage.

"I will be at the bank when it opens Monday to clear thees thing," he promised, bowing deeply, then jabbered to his man who mounted to the driver's seat. "We will have some talk then, Monsieur le Capitaine." He seated himself and, with a wave of his hand, signaled the black to take him from this scene of defeat.

Cole faced Sheriff Bascombe. "If Mrs. Hawthorne will permit, I shall present this paper to the bank some time next week and evoke an explanation and redress."

"Make him sign fer the paper!" Al's sharp nasal tones cut through the abating tension. "Make the cap'n sign a what-cha-ma-call-it thing, like you got from the bank."

Cole turned sharply and met the impertinent stare. Almost gently he warned, "Don't press me."

Petulantly, Al leaned back against the porch. "You'd best give him the paper, Mrs. Hawthorne. That Jacques fella could jes' come back after the cap'n is gone and take it for hisself." Al shrugged. "It'll be the safer thing to do."

"Thank you for that bit of confidence," Cole said with chiding mockery.

" 'Tain't confidence in you," Al objected tartly, "it's jes' a matter of choices."

"I stand corrected."

Cole glanced at the museful sheriff. Al never made anything easier, especially when it pertained to getting him out of trouble. "I'm sure as a gentleman of the law, Sheriff, you can understand that the boy was only trying to protect the lady's rights. He meant no real harm."

"Well, I dunno—" The sheriff scratched his head.

"Good!" Cole took the decision from him. "The boy works at the hospital under my direction, should you need to question him further."

Reluctantly the man heaved his heavy shoulders. "I guess he didn't hurt me none." He gestured to the splintered board and directed a frown at Al. "You better be careful with that iron, boy. We ain't hung anyone your age for—oh—eight or ten years, at least." He turned aside with a grin and winked at Cole, then nodded to Mrs. Hawthorne. "I'll be checking back to find out how this all comes out, and if I visit again, it won't be with the likes of Mister DuBonné a-taggin' at my heels. Good-day, ma'm. Doctor!"

The sheriff stepped up into his buckboard and clicked his horse into motion.

"I'll have your signed receipt now, Captain," Mrs. Hawthorne stated. "And I will be anxiously awaiting word from you as to what you have found out."

"Yes, ma'm. I'll see to it as soon as I can." After the necessary papers were signed he glanced around at Al. "Can I see you home before you get into more trouble?"

"What do you think you are, my guardian angel or somep'n? I can take care of myself. And I don't need your help gettin' home. I got Tar."

"Perhaps I should return to your uncle's and assure your cousin that you've come to no harm. It will be a while even if you manage to get that beast headed in the right direction."

Al's eyes narrowed. "You do that, Yankee."

Cole drew on his gauntlets. "I'm glad I have your approval," he laughed as he swung into the saddle.

"Jes' don't do nothing what'll getcha hitched in the family," Al called.

Cole pulled the steed around and grinned mockingly. "You needn't worry, Al. I can take care of myself."

"Huh!" Alaina snorted derisively, then frowned as she watched him ride out of sight.

"Come in, child," the woman's rasping voice intruded upon her thoughts, "and have some tea before you go. It's rare enough these days that I have visitors, much less those of a friendly nature."

For the first time since she arrived, Alaina could take a moment to consider the woman. The face was wrinkled and ancient, yet a bloom of rosy color still touched the cheeks, and there was a sparkle in the soft, brown eyes that age could not dim.

"What name may I attach to you?" the woman asked.

"Al."

"Al? Nothing else?" An elegant brow raised.

"The res' don't matter none."

"That's a matter of opinion, child."

"Well, you can jes' call me Al fer right now."

"All right, Al." She stressed the name oddly as she gave the younger one a casual scrutiny. "Now tell me, for what purpose did you traverse this narrow dirt lane? As the road ends at the levee, I can only assume you came to see me."

"Yes'm. That polecat Jacques came slinging his mud onto my clean hospital floor and was spoutin' off 'bout bringing the sheriff out here to arrest you. I jes' figured I owed him one. That was a fine piece of cuttin' you did on his shoulder, ma'm."

"Thank you, my dear," Mrs. Hawthorne graciously replied and considered the sword. "I hated to soil it on such vermin, but I'm sure Charles would have understood."

"Charles?"

"My husband. I'm a widow now." She waved a hand toward the carefully tended, exquisitely flowered garden across the lane. "He's buried yonder with my daughter, Sarah. They died of the yellow jack before the war."

"I'm sorry," Alaina murmured.

"Oh, don't be. Both had a good life, and it is my belief that they're enjoying a better place now." She held the door wide. "I hope you like tea. I can't abide that chicory they pass off as coffee nowadays."

Alaina followed her into the house, and the woman led her through a cool hallway. Without pausing, Mrs. Hawthorne asked over her shoulder, "Has anyone ever explained the decorum of hats to you?"

Alaina swallowed and, dragging the offending article from her head, mumbled, "Yes'm."

"How old are you?"

"Old enough to know a little and guess some more, ma'm."

"I believe that." She gestured for Alaina to take a chair at a tea table in the parlor. "Sit there, child. I'll be only a moment. The water is hot. I was preparing tea when those awful men arrived."

Alaina looked down at the tapestry seat of the chair that she had been bidden to take, then glanced around until she found one that her soiled clothes would not damage and exchanged them. Gingerly sitting on the edge, Alaina surveyed the room with more appreciation. Everything seemed in order, nothing missing, no telltale rectangles on the walls where paintings once had been. The furniture was intact and in good condition. A rarity these days to be in a parlor that no Yankee had savaged.

Mrs. Hawthorne returned bearing a tray upon which reposed a most handsome porcelain tea service and, with a clatter of china, set it before Alaina and began to fill a cup. The woman seated herself in a tall-backed chair across from Alaina and stirred a teaspoon of sugar into her cup, while she carefully perused her tattered guest. Uneasy beneath the woman's regard, Alaina sipped her tea. When she again raised her gaze, Mrs. Hawthorne's stare was just as intense.

"Why do I have the feeling you're playing games with me, child?"

Alaina swallowed with difficulty and managed to ask innocently, "Ma'm?"

"Your clothes! Why are you running around masquerading as a boy?"

Alaina opened her mouth to answer, then as she realized the full import of the words, her composure crumbled. She sat as one stunned, her mind stumbling and forming no logical thought.

Mrs. Hawthorne smiled and tasted her tea. "I suppose I have an unfair advantage. Before I married, I taught at a school for young girls. None of them managed to fool me for very long either." She sipped her tea again and nodded her head. "You're good. You're very good. I think your liberal use of dirt"—she wrinkled her nose in mild distaste—"disarms most people. But there's a softness in the way you step and the way you handle yourself." She laughed briefly. "And I've never known a man who cared about a chair or wasn't clumsy with a teacup.

"Now," she leaned forward, her soft brown eyes glowing with expectant curiosity. "Will you tell me why?"

The sun had dipped low in the sky when Alaina crossed the Craighughs' back yard. Once she had been able to gather her wits about her, she had felt no hesitation about Mrs. Hawthorne and tirelessly recounted the tangled chain of events that had led to her present circumstance, while the woman listened with rapt attention. It was an afternoon preferable to one spent under Roberta's heckling. That one was waiting for her in the kitchen with a smug, complacent smile.

"Where have you been all this time, Lainie? You missed Captain Latimer's visit."

"Good." She nodded stoutly. "I've had enough of ol' striped-pants for one day."

Roberta laughed and examined her fingernails closely. "I declare, Lainie, there just doesn't seem to be anything at all feminine about you."

"If you mean I make my own bed, wash and iron my own clothes, and work for a living, you're right. When have you ever brought a dollar into the house?"

Roberta sniffed delicately. "Hmph, a lady has other responsibilities."

Dulcie rolled her eyes and, with a rattle of pots and pans, loudly busied herself.

"Yeah," Alaina grunted laconically. "Like being lazy and getting fat."

"Lazy! Fat! How dare you!" Roberta's ample bosom contested the restraint of her bodice as she drew her shoulders back in stunned amazement. Before she could air her outrage, the pantry door slammed loudly, shutting off any further rejoinder. As Dulcie giggled over her labors, Roberta glared at the woman's broad back and petulantly stalked out of the kitchen. She was passing the parlor door when her father looked up from his newssheet and gazed at her over his glasses.

"Who was that?"

Roberta paused in the doorway. "Oh, Lainie just came home."

Leala glanced up from her embroidery. "Sometimes I think Alaina works far too hard, Angus. Here she's been out all day again. That poor girl."

"Humph!" Angus returned to his paper. "The work will do her good. Teach her some responsibility."

Roberta was a trifle piqued. "Maybe I should find some work, too, Daddy."

"Not you, my dear." Angus favored his daughter with a doting smile. "You're a different kind of lady."

Satisfied with her parent's indulgence, Roberta leisurely retired to her bedroom to dream about life as a Yankee officer's wife, and for several pleasurable moments, Alaina was able to savor the cleansing heat of her bath before the door swung open. She glared back over her shoulder, an angry word ready on her tongue, but when she saw it was only Dulcie with a clean towel draped over her arm, her irritation eased. The woman set a large block of homemade soap on the table beside the tub, then bustled about, humming to herself as she picked up Alaina's cast-off clothing and smoothed the frayed nightgown the young girl would wear. Alaina puzzled at the woman's manner but found no explanation for it until she took up the bar of soap and began to wash. From the soap wafted a scent strangely familiar, not unlike the perfume Roberta owned and jealously guarded.

Alaina raised her gaze in amazement. "Dulcie! You didn't!"

"I sho' 'nuff did. Miz Roberta has been raisin' such a ruckus 'bout de soap I been makin', ah jes' figgered she'd squall only a mite mo' if'n ah showed her dere ain' no difference, 'ceptin' a little sweet-smelling rosewater, betwixt my soap and all dem fancy bars her pa used to bring home fo' her."

Regretfully Alaina laid the soap back, picking up another smaller piece. "You'd best save it for Roberta. 'Al' would have some tall explaining to do if the Yankees noticed he smelled like a flower garden." It had been bad enough when Captain Latimer had caught her smelling like one.

Dulcie grunted obstinately. "I sees it a cryin' shame dat Miz Roberta gets all dem fancy clothes and parfums, and yo' ain't got nothing but de dirt and dese heah boy's clothes. Mister Angus been skimpin' pennies and mos' times takin' de money yo' make scrubbing dem Yankee floors jes' so he can get dat chile some cloth for a new gown."

"What money I give him," Alaina murmured, "is barely enough to pay my keep."

"Yo' ain't 'round here 'nuff to cost Mastah Angus the time o' day," Dulcie protested. "An' mos' times yo' look like some tidewater orphan. When is yo' gonna stop traipsin' 'round in dem boy's clothes and start actin' lak a lady?"

Alaina heaved a sigh. "I don't know, Dulcie. Sometimes I think never."

Alaina had left the cleaning of Cole's apartment for Sunday, knowing the captain was scheduled for duty until the late afternoon. She sought the time away from the Craighugh house, wishing to avoid any further confrontation with Roberta. She found it necessary, however, to seek Cole out at the hospital and admit that she had misplaced his key.

"You needn't say what's on yer mind," she warned. "I can see it in yer eye."

"After yesterday, I'm trying to refrain from saying anything to you," he retorted, handing over the key. "Because once I start, I might not be able to stop."

"You gotta chance to visit with Roberta," she reminded him rancorously. "That should've made you happy."

"Not nearly as much as turning you across my knee would."

She glared at him. "You got them papers of Mrs. Hawthorne's seen aftah yet, Yankee?"

"If you don't know better, the banks are closed on Sundays."

"Don't get 'nuff money to put in banks," Al goaded. "How should I know what their hours be?"

Cole peered down into the gray eyes, his own narrowed suspiciously. "Are you complaining again?"

Alaina shrugged petulantly. "Jes' stating fact."

"What do you do with your money, anyway? Haven't you earned enough by now to buy yourself a change of clothes?"

"Cain't see doing that 'til these wear out." Cole opened his mouth to retort, but Al cut him off abruptly. "Gotta go now if'n I'm gonna finish yer 'partment afore nightfall. Yo' ain't paying me to stand here jawing with ya."

"Be there to let me in," Cole called to her back. "Or else bring the key back here."

"Yeah, yeah."

Sometime shortly after noon, Cole paused over his meal to receive a packet of letters Sergeant Grissom brought to him. After briefly testing the perfumes of the two from Xanthia Morgan and Carolyn Darvey, he tucked them into his blouse, saving them to read at home at his leisure. He felt a mild disappointment at the absence of a correspondence from his father, then noticed the painstaking script of Oswald James, a lawyer and close acquaintance of the family. The date was nearly two weeks ago. He chose to relieve his curiosity as to the lawyer's purpose in writing and slit open the envelope. A crushing weight descended upon him as he read the first line.

"I regret to inform you that your father passed away during the night—"

Roberta directed Jedediah to a halt beside Jackson Square and, after bidding the black driver to wait, continued by foot, loftily ignoring the Union soldiers who paused to stare. She had other purposes on her mind and was not bent toward petty flirtations this afternoon. She was after richer game than that. A Yankee doctor, to be exact.

She had taken the key from Alaina's coat, and the cool weight of it inside her glove reassured her that all would go smoothly. Even cajoling her father into allowing her to take the carriage for a Sunday afternoon outing had been relatively simple. By the time Cole Latimer reached his apartment, she would be garbed in such a manner as to eliminate any reluctance he might have. Though he had thus far betrayed none, one could never be too sure about a single man's objection to being caught.

The rapid tap of her sharp heels gave evidence of her haste. Now that she had laid out her strategy, she was eager to be about it. Even the repugnance of submitting herself to that undignified end by which men proved their virility did not dissuade her. Once Cole bedded her, she could claim herself with child, and even if he proved unwilling to do the honorable thing, she knew her father would convince him.

A prior afternoon spent discreetly questioning proprietors of nearby shops had supplied the information she needed to find her way to Cole's door, for the man himself had been casually evasive. Indeed, the captain appeared to have a strong sense of self-preservation.

Footsteps behind her made her hastily tuck away the key and chance a surreptitious glance askance. Her hopes were momentarily darkened as she recognized the tall, broad-shouldered form of Cole Latimer coming toward her. His brief, stiff smile as he swept off his hat was discouraging, but she plucked up her resolve and turned to face him with a coy laugh.

"Why, Captain Latimer, would you believe that you're just the person I was hoping to see?"

"You're not here to see Al?" He remembered distinctly telling her that he would be on duty all day. That he was here at all was due to the fact that the surgeon general, upon learning of his father's demise, had ordered him to take the afternoon off since there were no duties pressing.

"Al?" Roberta questioned apprehensively. Her plans were going astray faster than she could remedy. "Why, I thought that runty little boy had gone fishing or something."

"He's here," Cole stated and, reaching past her, turned the knob and pushed open his door. The overlarge boots stood just inside the entrance, and the bristly swish of a scrub brush could be heard from an adjoining room.

Roberta was through the door before Cole could invite her in, and he followed, closing it behind her.

"Al?" he called.

A noise much like the outraged squeal of a little piglet preceded the sound of running bare feet. "I thought you had to work, Yankee!"

Alaina came to an abrupt halt in the parlor door as she saw Roberta. Each woman stared at the other with something less than pleasure, then Al leaned cockily against the doorjamb and scratched her nose with a forefinger.

" 'Pears to me you got company, Cap'n. I suppose now you'll be wantin' me to finish up and be on my way, is that right?"

"No, that isn't right." Cole scowled at Al before stepping out onto the balcony. His eyes searched the street below until they found the carriage with Jedediah waiting in the driver's seat. Cole returned to meet Roberta's questioning gaze. "Not wishing to jeopardize your reputation, I'll let Al escort you back to your carriage." He put up a hand to plead his case as she opened her mouth to protest. "Forgive my manners, but I just received word that my father passed away and this afternoon I fear I'd be poor company at best."

"Your father?" Roberta asked. "Dead?" At his answering nod, her mind caught on to the fact that there was now no one who stood between Cole and all that money.

Alaina nudged her cousin's arm gently. "Come on, Robbie, I think the cap'n wants to be alone." She turned back to the man hesitantly. "I'll come back and finish up what I started, then go home. Maybe I can do the res' tomorrow, or maybe the next day."

Roberta was highly miffed at being led from the building like a naughty schoolgirl. Alaina refrained from comment and was greeted enthusiastically by the black driver.

"Miz Al!" He chuckled. "Lawsy, I sho' glad it was you Miz Roberta was a-comin' to see. I been sittin' here ponderin' what I was gonna tell Mastah Angus should his chile come ta harm by all dese here scalawag Yankees."

"Take her home, Jedediah, and don't stop for anything. I'll be along directly."

"Yas'm." The black grinned broadly. "Doan stop fo' nothin'. Yo' hear dat, Miz Roberta?"

"You'll do as I say, Jedediah," Roberta informed him sullenly. "Now take me home, and be quick about it."

"Yas'm. I intend to do jes' dat, Miz Roberta."

Chapter 11

WORD had filtered down to New Orleans that Grant was guffawing because Law's command, mistaking it for a cavalry charge, had been stampeded by a bunch of frightened Federal mules in a night battle around Wauhatchie, Tennessee. But a more dignified Confederate explanation had it that the gray troops had already been driven back by Orland Smith and Tyndale when the "mule charge" took place. To the groaning chagrin of the South, however, it was the Yankees' hearty recommendation that the mules be commissioned as horses.

The city was quiet, almost hushed, and what faces Alaina saw as she pushed Ol' Tar through the early morning streets were drawn and downcast with the bitter taste of another defeat. It would be a bleak Christmas season for the South this year. It was a bleak enough Monday.

In the hospital stable, Alaina found an empty stall where she could tether Ol' Tar and clandestinely appropriated a few handfuls of sweet clover hay from an overfilled manger nearby. Noting that Captain Latimer's roan was present, she affected a boyish whistle and made her way into the hospital by the back door, pausing to hang her pouch and hat on a peg near the entrance before dragging out the mops, brooms, and buckets. As she backed out of the closet, her arms full of cleaning utensils, she was forced to step lively to avoid being knocked down by a rushing medical orderly whose arms were as full as her own, but with fresh bandages. He gave neither pause nor apology but hastened off down the hall to disappear into one of the surgery rooms.

Alaina glared after him until he was out of sight, then with a few mumbled words about rude Yankees, she leaned the mops and brooms beside the closet door. With her best nonchalant air, she sauntered toward ward 5.

She was early enough that she could pay Bobby Johnson a visit before setting about her day's labors.

The greetings of the Union soldiers were strangely reserved this morning and contained nothing of the usual coarse humor. The ward grew hushed and still as she entered. Her eyes found the empty bed, then the sheet that had been spread over a large stain in the aisle. The dull, vividly familiar color of drying blood marked the cloth where it touched the floor. Refusing to meet anyone's gaze, Alaina spun on her heel and fled the room, struggling to defeat the haunting nightmares that threatened to invade her mind. She let the door slam behind her and ran down the hall to the surgery room in use. She knew "Al" could not enter and leaned against the wall beside the door, panting to ease the ache in her chest, then Cole's angry voice came from inside, startling her.

"Who was on the late duty last night?"

"Major Magruder." Alaina could put no face to the voice that answered.

"I'm not going to let you blame this one on me!" The named one quickly set forth a heated defense. "I made my rounds, and everything was as it should be. Especially him!"

Alaina raised on tiptoe to peer through a clear spot in the etched glass of the door. Cole and Doctor Brooks were working over the midsection of the man on the table while the orderly reached between them with white pads that came away bright red. She could see the patient's chest rise and fall in shallow breathing. Near his head, the medical sergeant sat on a tall stool and let an occasional drop fall from a small, brown bottle onto a cloth mask that covered the mouth and nose of an otherwise heavily bandaged face.

"Slower!" Doctor Brooks admonished the sergeant.

"Why, 'especially him'?" Cole questioned as he plied the curved needle and catgut.

Magruder replied from his corner where he rested casually against a cabinet, making no effort to assist. "When I made my ten o'clock round he was caterwauling something about his wife and baby."

Cole glanced up from his work briefly, his lips twisted in an acid grin. "And what did you say to him, Major?"

"I simply told him to shut up and try to act like a man." Magruder paused, then continued as if he felt a need for more excuse. "He was disturbing the rest of the ward."

The two working doctors straightened, Doctor Brooks to watch Cole closely, and the younger man to fix Magruder with an accusative glare. Alaina could see between them for the first time and caught sight of the long, oozing wound where torn, ragged edges gaped wide across the patient's lower belly. Her stomach heaved, and she stumbled back to lean against the wall, steadying knees that had suddenly turned to jelly. Cole's voice came to her as if through a long tunnel, tightly controlled, but with an undertone of savage satire.

"Major, how can you expect a mere boy to act like a man?"

"He is man enough to have a wife!" Magruder's own anger, or perhaps fear, began to show. "Anyway, I told you he was a waste of time from the very beginning."

At that moment Alaina wanted to hear the sounds of a Yankee major being brutally beaten, but much to her disappointment, when Cole's voice continued, it was low and almost gentle, though muffled as he bent again to his task of repair.

"Who found him?"

The major volunteered the information. "The sergeant, at his four o'clock check."

"What happened to the two o'clock check?"

Again, it was Magruder who answered. "I checked each bay briefly and saw nothing out of order."

Cole's voice came in crisp, curt tones. "One of the other men said he was awakened by someone calling out shortly after midnight. Johnson's bed was empty then, but the man heard nothing more and went back to sleep. You missed a man lying on the floor in the middle of a ward?"

"I tell you, I saw nothing!" Magruder protested.

There was silence thereafter, except for an occasional command or an exchanged word as the operation continued. Strength refused to come back into Alaina's limbs. Had she been able to find even a small measure of it, she would have fled. Then, the door beside her swung open, and Captain Latimer's shoulder held it so.

"Let him rest there for a while before you move him," he instructed the orderly.

Doctor Brooks came to stand beside him. "You've done

all you can, Cole. Whether he lives or dies is a decision God must make."

"I can't understand why—" A frown from Doctor Brooks warned him to say no more as the other's gaze strayed behind the door. Cole turned abruptly and met the agonized gray eyes. His manner immediately gentled as he took note of the tear-streaked grime on the thin cheeks and the trembling lips.

"It's Bobby Johnson." His voice was soft and understanding. "He fell. Tore most of the stitches out. Half bled to death." His clipped, disjointed sentences made him angry at himself, and he rubbed a hand across his brow in chafing frustration. "We patched him up—but I just don't know." He reached out to console the lad, but the small, work-roughened hand made a vicious swipe of negation as Al's lips curled back in an unemancipated sob. Utter pain showed naked on the young face.

"Take the rest of the day—"

"No!" The half-choked word interrupted with finality. Al plucked courage from somewhere and strength came anew. She turned her back on the doctors and trudged down the hall, narrow shoulders sagging as if with the weight of the world. Buckets rattled echoingly in the hall, and a moment later the old cistern pump began to clank.

Everybody in the wards knew of the attachment that had formed between the cleaning boy and the blind soldier, although Al had yet to admit it as fact. Sympathetic eyes followed her through her duties, and when she was absent for brief spells, no one sought the urchin out. The attempts at banter were halfhearted and stilted.

Private Bobby Johnson was returned to his bed with the tenderest of care. When no other duty pressed, Doctor Latimer was to be found at the boy's bedside. The young soldier lay motionless and pale. He showed no signs of regaining consciousness as the day wore on. Alaina was torn between a strong desire to be far away, should the worst happen, and a need to be near if he should come around. She was never far from ward 5. Though she found many reasons to check on something near the last bed on the window side, she could not watch the still form for very long and her visits were short.

Cole heard the whisper again and realized Bobby's lips had moved slightly to shape a weak, "Who?"

"Doctor Latimer." Cole rose from his chair and leaned closer. "How is it, Bobby?"

"Hurts!" The answer was simple. "Like fire!"

"Why—did you get up?" Cole searched for more words to clarify the question.

"Thirsty!" The boy understood. His tongue licked at cracked lips. "Like now! Couldn't ask the major." The hoarse whisper shook, and Cole wet the parched mouth with a moist cloth. "I had to do something for myself, just for once. Had to—act—like a man."

Cole touched the boy's hand. "Rest now. Don't worry. I'll be here."

A wan smile was his answer, and that too faded as Bobby Johnson retreated into the blissful darkness of sleep once more.

Angry at his own helplessness, Cole turned away to find Al standing at the foot of the bed. Alaina stared at the ashen soldier with a far-off look in her eyes.

"I hope Magruder trips and falls headfirst into a privy some dark night," she hissed.

"You can't blame the man." Cole sat back in his chair and tried to explain. "He couldn't have known what would happen."

Al seemed not to hear. A slow smile curved her lips as she added with wishful relish, "An' I hope I'm the one who trips him!"

"Aren't you about done for the day?" Cole asked as he swung around to face the unrepentant lad.

"I guess." The gray eyes moved slowly to meet his.

"I'd better warn Magruder to be careful on dark nights."

The gray eyes never wavered. "Y'all jes' do that, Yankee." The words were what Cole expected, but something of the old bite was missing.

"You're slipping, Al," Cole taunted. "I thought you hated all us Union bluebellies."

"Go to hell, Yankee!" This time the old spirit and sting were boldly in attendance.

"I'll be here at the hospital all night," Cole called after the departing youth.

The comment came back loud and clear over Al's shoulder. "Then maybe I ken get some peace fer once't."

For the first time that day, honest chuckles were heard in ward 5.

The next day passed much as the one before. Expectant hope that the young soldier might recover thrived in everyone's heart. When Alaina looked in on him, his stomach was distended, making an obscene hump beneath the blanket. The stain that wet the bandages over his wound was no longer red, but black and malevolently odorous. For the most part, he lay in a stupor, partly induced by heavy draughts of laudanum, though he was given to spells of such groaning and twisting that it seemed that a great rodent gnawed at his vitals. Alaina could abide neither the sight of these spasms nor the thought that she might be elsewhere should he rouse. The hours passed with a tortured, springhalt gait. No change was noticeable in Bobby Johnson's condition, and when a misty rain began to fall late in the afternoon, it seemed to Alaina that the whole world mourned in gray dismal grief.

The ride home was wet and cold, and Alaina sat for a long time by herself in the dark stables. In part, she had no desire to face Roberta, and in part she needed the time to come to grips with her own tangled emotions. She failed on both accounts, and it was a late hour when the distraught young woman finally sank into a troubled sleep.

It took an effort of sheer will for Alaina to draw herself from the warm bed in the cold, dark, predawn hour. Even then, it was not until she splashed her face with ice cold water from the ewer that her brain began to function. The usual application of grime, soot, and grease was accomplished amid shudders of revulsion, and it was small solace that Roberta still snored loudly when Alaina crept down the stairs. It was a further test of her will to get Ol' Tar to move from his snug stall and venture out into the chilling, light rain that had continued throughout the night.

A full hour of her workday had passed before Alaina was free of the shivers that had started with the ride to the hospital. Bobby Johnson lay as still as death except for an occasional shudder that passed through his limp body. Cole hovered near but would answer no question and grew angry when Al pressed for a reply. The day stumbled along on leaden limbs toward the noon hour when, though her appetite decried the effort, Alaina choked down a few bites of food. It was midafternoon when she descended the stairs from the Confederate ward and caught sight of the orderlies carrying a blanket-draped litter out of ward 5 toward the gruesome, brick-lined vault that was loosely referred to as the "morgue." She did not have to be told the news, for a quick glance into the ward confirmed her fear. Doctor Latimer sat slumped in the chair beside Bobby Johnson's empty bed. Though the sense of loss made a gnawing pain in the pit of her stomach, Alaina's eyes were strangely dry as she paused beside a uniformed officer who also watched the departing detail in silence. A moment later Cole Latimer came from the ward, a grim, angry frown set on his face. He brushed past the slight figure that stepped forward with upraised hand to question him, then strode down the hall and into the dayroom. Alaina slumped in misery as he disappeared from sight, then stiffened as a broad, blunt-fingered hand came to rest on her shoulder.

"I warned him, of course," the officer stated. "He made a mistake."

" 'Tain't so!" Alaina glared up into the offending one's face and angrily shrugged off his grasp. "Cap'n Latimer is the best surgeon here!"

"Such loyalty," Magruder mocked. "I'm sure the captain would appreciate your comments. But I meant that the doctor has allowed himself to become too deeply involved with a case that could have had no other end." He shrugged his shoulders to free them of concern. "I warned him."

Alaina set her jaw and gazed down at her oversized boots. The agony would have been less for herself had she been able to harden her own heart, but then she might have found herself more akin to Magruder, incapable of any of the softer emotions that made living worthwhile.

"Why don't you take the rest of the day off, boy?" the major suggested magnanimously.

"I'd jes' as soon keep busy, thank ye." Her rejection was curt.

"Suit yourself." Major Magruder smiled thoughtfully and gazed in the direction of the dayroom. "The captain tried the same thing after receiving word that his father died, but he drove himself too far. Who knows but what it might have cost a life?"

He strode off before Alaina could give hot retort, and

perhaps it was just as well there were no privies close about.

Al was unusually quiet the rest of the day. The bed in ward 5 was soon filled with another Union soldier. Somehow she could not bring herself to look in. Instead, she chose to tidy the officer's dayroom, a much-neglected place since most of the doctors were far too busy to utilize it. She had not seen Captain Latimer since he left the ward in such a rush, and the other doctors, living as close to death as they did, did not press the lad.

Without knowledge of her secret, however, their reasoning was slightly astray. Alaina's confusion ran far deeper than any of them guessed. She had a natural dislike of Northerners which had been focused by the war to a deep hatred. Now she knew her enemies by name and by face. They were no longer anonymous bluejackets, bright with braid and shiny buttons; they were men and boys, smiling and sad, happy or angry, laughing, joking, hurting, crying, dying, just the same as the friends she had waved good-bye to, just the same as her own beloved father and brothers. Human and with bodies that proved so terribly frail when pelted by fragments of metal. She had to rummage deep to find the memory of her hatred and deeper still to feel its stirring as of old.

Distractedly Alaina rubbed an oiled rag along the arm of a chair, trying to sort out her own feelings. She could offer no solace to the mother or wife of Bobby Johnson, but fervently hoped that someone, somewhere, had laid a kind hand on the breasts of her father and brother in their last moments. She felt the start of tears in her eyes, but sniffed them away as she heard footsteps in the hall. A young private passed the doorway, then halted and came back to peer in.

"There you are, Al. Doctor Brooks wants to see you in his office when you finish work."

Before she could question him, the orderly was gone. Alaina gave a last quick dusting to the chair and packed her rags, mops, and buckets away. It was nearly quitting time anyway, and she might as well see what the doctor wanted. It was the first time he had ever summoned her.

The climb to the third floor was less tiresome now that the weather had cooled. Trying to gain some respite from her feeling of disloyalty, she paused a moment to banter with the soldiers in the Confederate ward, then sauntered on down the hall toward Doctor Brooks's small office. The door was open, and she managed an urchin's grin as she entered. The elderly man hastily rose from his chair and came across the room to meet her.

"Didja want somep'n, doc?" she asked in her rough, boyish vernacular.

He did not speak but passed behind her. Alaina heard the door close and raised an eyebrow at the click of the latch. Turning, he came back and, taking her arm, led her to a chair.

"Forget that kind of speech for now, Alaina. We're alone, and no one can hear. Here, child, have a seat."

Alaina complied, then watched in great confusion as the man puttered about his office. Several times he opened his mouth to speak but failed and grew angrier with each attempt. Finally he came forward, snatched a thick volume of papers from his desk, and thrust them at her. His manner was now apologetic.

"We receive these each week, Alaina. The armies exchange them by special messenger."

Somewhat at a loss, Alaina lowered her eyes and began to read.

Confederate States of America
Compiled by:
Headquarter's Staff
General Lee's Army of Virginia
Subject: Casualty Report
A. Complete listing of:
1. Wounded
2. Killed
3. Missing in action
4. Deserters.
Note: This section for the Union occupied areas of Louisiana, Mississippi, and Alabama.

A cold, tight feeling began to form in the pit of Alaina's stomach. She had only one brother left! Jason! And she had seen these same reports twice before. With fearful slowness, Alaina raised her gaze until she met Doctor Brooks's worried frown. She clenched her jaw tightly to keep it from trembling, then hastily flipped through the alphabetical listing until she came to the M's. Her finger traced down the left hand column until she saw what she dreaded.

MACGAREN, JASON R., CAPTAIN. MISSING IN ACTION, PRESUMED DEAD. OCTOBER 4, 1863.

The rest blurred before her eyes. October the fourth! More than a month ago! Jason! Jason! Eldest child Jason! Tall, strong Jason! Beloved older brother Jason! She remembered the time when Gavin, the younger brother by three years, had put burrs under her saddle; it was Jason who had snatched her from the bucking horse. Jason! Her hero! Poor, dead Jason!

"Alaina! Alaina!" The words broke into her trauma. She realized the doctor was rubbing her hands between his own. "Are you all right, child? You are so pale!"

Wearily Alaina nodded, wondering vaguely why no tears came. She braced back in the chair, withdrawing her hand and, as if it had become something vile and tainted, pushed the volume from her lap. It fell to the floor unheeded. Her lips curled back, her nose wrinkled as if some odorous stench invaded her nostrils.

"Alaina, have hope!" Doctor Brooks commanded. "It just indicates that he's missing, not dead. Have hope, child."

"It's the same!" Alaina half snarled, half sobbed. "It's just the same as before. First, it's missing, then later a letter saying his body is buried somewhere and he's officially dead."

Doctor Brooks could not deny it. He had seen too many of these reports. They were usually made before the heat of battle cooled and rarely were all the dead accounted for. He could only shake his head sorrowfully and try to comfort her, but the sobs were coming, dry and racking.

"He didn't—really want—to leave us. It was just—the thing to do—All the men went." Alaina tipped her head back, and the tears streamed down her face in a sudden rush. She cried out in agony as the pain of it hit her full force.

"Aaarrrgh! Damn the war! Damn the fighting! Damn the killing! When will it end? Oh, Jason! Jason!" Her head fell forward, and Alaina covered her face with her hands, sobbing freely. Doctor Brooks pressed a soft cloth into her grasp and gently patted her shoulder, wiping his own cheek with the back of his hand.

"In God's good time, Alaina," he murmured softly, "when men have played out their foolish charades and grown sick with the slaughter, then it will end. He gives us free choice and full rein on our lives, and we do with it what we will. I beg of you, my child, don't blame God for man's folly."

Alaina leaned her head against the comforting shoulder and let her anguish flow. Doctor Brooks raised her gently from the chair and half led, half carried her to a small couch. He pressed her down upon it and sat beside her, resting a hand on her shoulder, while she wept out her grief. When her trembling finally subsided, she fell into an exhausted slumber.

The windows were dark and the hour late when Alaina opened her eyes again. Doctor Brooks rose from his desk and came to her side.

"Are you ready to go home now, child?"

Alaina rubbed her puffy, reddened eyes and nodded wearily.

"I'll have my carriage hitched and brought around for you."

"No!" Her reply was sudden. "No thank you, Doctor Brooks. I have Ol' Tar. Besides"—she smiled tremulously at the old friend—"a ragamuffin lad has no place in a fine buggy."

The doctor heaved a sigh. "As you wish, Alaina." He studied her for a long moment before reaching out to take her hand. "You're a rare one, Alaina MacGaren. Many young women could not have borne what you have, and surely not with such spirit." He straightened. "However, even a lad can get into trouble this late at night."

"I'll be careful," she reassured him quietly. She caught a glimpse of her reflection in a window and paused, seeing her eyes swollen and red. She glanced up at the doctor and ventured a timid question. "Is Captain Latimer still here?"

"No, Cole left early this afternoon," he replied. "Magruder accused him of letting his grief for his father interfere with his good judgment. I think the major still smarts from the leg incident. This time he openly accused Cole of being careless with Bobby Johnson's life."

"But that's not true!" Alaina declared. "It was Magruder!"

"I know that, of course. Magruder had to blame someone else, though, to be sure that he was not accused himself." The doctor waved his hand with an angry flourish. "When I last spoke with Cole, he made mention that his plans were to go out and let propriety go to hell."

A short time later, Alaina mounted Ol' Tar and turned him toward the river. She had no wish to return to the Craighugh residence just yet. Uncle Angus and Aunt Leala had made plans to attend a political meeting this evening, and she had no desire to contend with Roberta's sniping comments. Instead, alone and lonely, she meandered along the water's edge. The slow lapping of the water and the oily ripples of the Mississippi made it seem deceptively gentle. Yet it had the strength of the fall rains behind its current, and the river had been known to change its course overnight, ripping a new flow way where none had been before.

The rain had stopped some time ago, and a bright, three-quarter moon now hung high above the flitting clouds, shyly showing its face and sending a thousand tiny fragments of light shimmering across the molten surface of the river. Alaina forced her mind away from the morass that seethed with her own problems. She dismounted and sat on the bank, wrapping her arms around her knees and resting her chin upon her forearm as she stared at the silent black hulks of the distant Union ships. Rage and fury roiled within her anew. Bitter tears stung her eyes.

"Traitor!" She spat into the river. "You brought the Yankees to our door. Shameless hussy! Have you no honor? No loyalty?"

From the stygian depth no answer came, but through Alaina's mind there flowed apace a long, marching column of blue and gray figures, each with some horrible disparity, as if the artist had not completed them, some missing arms, others legs, or sometimes an eye or half a face. Unfinished caricatures! Leftovers of the war! Halfmen! Or less! It was a nightmare, the essence of which she could find in any hospital, Union or Confederate.

Strangely, from the darkness of the river, a shadow took form. Alaina blinked until she recognized it as a large tree drifting toward her down the river. As it came close to the bar, it struck the shallows, then rolled heavily in the current. Suddenly an arm flashed in the moonlight, and

Alaina came to her feet, realizing this had nothing to do with imagination. There was sputtering and thrashing as a hapless man struggled for a fresh grip on his tumbling raft.

Quickly Alaina glanced about her. Very shortly the man would be moving well beyond her reach, and there would, then, be little she could do to save him. The log swirled in an eddy and started to roll, threatening to dump its passenger in the water again. The man flung an arm wide and gave out a weak call before his head went under. The words were lost to her, but the sound of the voice set her to action.

Snatching off her heavy cotton jacket, she ran along the spit of land to its farthest point and splashed into the water. She swam out, fighting the strong current that sought to drag her under as it swept the log and the man toward her. Taking a deep breath, she dove under the swirling liquid and felt the water thread through her fingers as she plunged deeper. The trunk passed over her, and she shot up, desperately clutching for the man. She broke the surface of the water beside him.

There was no time for amenities, or breath for them left in her lungs. She caught a handful of his hair and channeled all the strength she could muster into her strokes, pulling him with her, not fighting the current but riding with it. Her feet sank into the oozing mud of the bottom, yet still she supported the man's head above water while she gasped precious air, then floated him into waist-deep water. Her strength was nearly spent, and it was all she could do to tug him onto the bank. Another log lay on the edge of the river, and with dogged perseverance, she managed to drag him over it until his head hung down the other side.

A cough followed by a violent retching brought up the brackish water he had swallowed and assured her that life still resided in the limp body. She reached out a hand to lift the lolling head and stared agape. It was Cole Latimer! Her mind stumbled. She had saved a Yankee, blue as a jaybird and wearing nothing more than his long johns. Now a vision assailed her. One of Jason lying twisted and gazing forever sightless under this same dimly lit night sky. Her eyes misted, then sobbing and shivering with anguished frustration and the chill of her wet garments, Alaina collapsed to her knees beside him. She wept and cried and gnashed her teeth, but no easing came, only a dull persistent thought of what must be done. With an effort she regained her composure and wiped at her wet cheeks, brushing away the tears that mixed with the water dribbling from her short hair.

"You m-muleheaded, gator-bait Y-Yankee," she croaked tearfully. "You s-sure picked a rotten c-cold night to go swimming." She rolled him over until he sat braced against the log. He groaned and groggily dropped his head back against the waterlogged wood. A trickle of something dark and sticky to the touch began to course down his brow from his hair, and a quick search with her fingers found a large lump beneath his scalp. "Someone laid a g-good one on you, Yankee. 'Pears to me you got yerself stinkin' drunk to boot, and in this neck o' woods, that's pure foolishness. I thought ya said you could take care of yerself."

The problem now was what to do with him. She had lost the key to his apartment, and it was obvious he was without his. Besides, she could hardly parade a Union officer in his underwear through Jackson Square. No telling what the ramifications would be for them both if she did.

There appeared to be no alternative other than taking him to the Craighughs'. It was her uncle's usual custom to remain at the political rally until a late hour, sometimes returning when dawn was almost upon them. If that were the case tonight, she might be successful in smuggling the doctor past Roberta. There would be some tall explaining to do in the morning, and Uncle Angus would be furious, but she would leave the matter of soothing him to Roberta, who was far more effective at it anyway.

Alaina ran back toward the spit of land where Tar waited, tied the laces of her boots and threw them across his bony back, then led the animal back to the captain. By now, he was shaking uncontrollably from the chill of his wet underwear. The only dry article she had was the large cotton jacket, and she labored for some moments putting it on him, though her own teeth chattered apace with his.

Taking his arm across her shoulders, she got him to his feet, then staggered precariously beneath his weight. It took a tremendous struggle on her part to steady his tall, broad-shouldered frame. It was a further labor of patience to get him mounted on the back of Ol' Tar, who snorted in high disgust at this abuse. Any grace Cole might have achieved once astraddle, quickly disappeared as he slumped forward over the beast's neck. Alaina groaned in angry exasperation as Tar bolted away, nearly losing his rider. Catching the nag's bridle, she led him once more to the log, which provided a step for her to mount.

"Come on, Yankee. Sit up!"

Her command finally penetrated his deep torpor, and sluggishly Cole raised himself to a sitting position on the horse's back. Alaina settled herself with deliberation before the Yankee captain, then glared over her shoulder as he leaned heavily against her back. His hand slipped with angering familiarity around her hips, but she refrained from prodding him upright with her elbow. In his condition, if she knocked him off the horse, she might never get him mounted again.

They traveled the back alleys and unused roads until they reached the Craighugh house. No lights shone from the mansion itself, and only a dim lantern glowed from the stable. Alaina could well surmise that Roberta had gone to bed, having no one except the servants to keep her company. Urging Tar onto the lawn to deaden the sound of his hooves, Alaina rode him directly into the stable. She slid off his back and, with unswerving tenacity, dragged the captain from the horse's rump. Fearfully she clamped her hand over Cole's mouth as he mumbled a recognition, peering at her with reddened eyes, and testily shoved him against the wall near the door.

"You ought to be ashamed of yerself. Gettin' yerself drunk, then letting someone hit you over the head and take yer clothes. That beats all, Yankee."

She left him braced against the wall and led Ol' Tar into his stall, giving the steed an extra measure of precious grain for his unusual efforts this night. Angus's carriage was still out, and for that bit of good fortune, Alaina was extremely grateful.

She rounded the end stall, then stopped in bewilderment for the captain was not where she had left him or anywhere to be seen. Her mind flew in a thousand different directions. Where the devil had he gone? She called softly, passing the water trough, and suddenly she felt him stagger against her back. Her slight weight was not enough to stop them both from sprawling headlong into the trough. She went under first and thought she would be drowned before Cole rolled off her. Finally free, she choked and wheezed in air, almost strangling on the water she had swallowed.

"Bluebelly!" she railed and swung her arm around, knocking him off balance. Her anger was not so easily vented, and she pushed his head under the water for a thorough dousing and sobering. When she pulled him up again, coughing for breath, she leaned down into his face, her small jaw thrust out obstinately, and warned, "Next time you try to give me a bath, Yankee, you'd jes' better head out running. The only reason I don't drown ya now is 'cause you're too drunk to be scared."

"C-cold," he strangled, and his violent shivering attested to his claim. Alaina relented and, with her own teeth chattering, climbed out of the trough. She dragged at him until she got him seated on the edge, then lifted one of his legs out and turned him about as she lifted the other. Worriedly, she glanced up toward Roberta's windows, hoping her cousin had not been awakened by the commotion. The windows were closed against the crisp night air, and Dulcie's quarters above the carriage house were still dark.

When she got him to the house, Alaina carefully opened the back door, cringing as it squeaked slightly. Drawing Cole's arm about her shoulders again, she staggered into the house with him. Halfway across the kitchen, she realized they were leaving wet trails behind them. That would never do!

"Wait here," she whispered to Cole and settled him in a chair. "I'll get a couple of quilts." She ran into the pantry where that morning she had noticed a freshly aired stack and came back with two. As she passed the hearth, she swung the huge kettle over the coals and laid several sticks of wood beneath it. If she ever got the captain to bed, she had every intention of returning to the pantry for a hot bath.

Wrapping a warm quilt about Cole and the other about herself, she took his arm again and hauled him up from the chair. They progressed clumsily through the house and began to climb the stairs. After ascending several steps, Alaina stumbled over the tail of the blanket she had flung about herself, banged her shin, and lost her grip on Cole. Fearfully she clutched at the balustrade, missed, and descended belly-down several steps, bumping painfully along the edges. It was a moment of complete havoc as Cole followed after her. Tears of pain stung her eyes, and she clenched her teeth against moaning aloud as she found herself beneath him near the bottom of the stairs. She twisted out from under him and desperately clutched her hand over his mouth again as he muttered unintelligible words.

"Be quiet!" she hissed. "If I leave ya in the stables, Uncle Angus might jes' shoot you for an intruder. The safest place for ya is upstairs in the guest room. But we can't wake up Roberta. Do you understand?" She had great doubts that her words penetrated, and as she dragged the quilt about his shoulders again, she fussed in an angry whisper. "I never woulda thought you'd get yerself so stinkin' drunk."

Alaina tried the stairs again, this time managing them very well, considering she half carried a man who outweighed her twice over. She led him to the guest room near her own. It was just down the hall from Roberta's bedroom but far from the one belonging to the elder Craighughs. Moonlight brightened the room, and Alaina had no need of the bedside lamp to show her the placement of furniture. Jerking down the covers of the tester bed, she let Cole fall back upon it. With a wry word of thanks for the shadows deepened by the moonlight, she pulled the sodden underwear from his body, lifted his legs onto the bed, and drew the covers over him.

"For once, Yankee," she said, smiling ruefully, "ya ain't a-fussing at me."

She left him and closed the door quietly behind her. In a matter of moments she was in the tub. The steaming bath took her weariness and transformed it into a languid half stupor. Deliberately she took the scented soap she had avoided and began to lather her hair and body. Her disguise was the last thing she wanted to contend with this night, and at the moment she was numb to all the dangers of discovery. With a ragged sigh, she leaned her head back against the rim of the tub and watched the candle's flame make fluid shadows on the ceiling. She was like an empty shell, drained of strength, senseless to grief. What the morrow held for her she could neither fathom nor rouse a care for. It seemed an eternity away.

Her thoughts meandered through fantasy. A beautiful gown! Her hair long and shining! A man holding her as they danced! Suddenly she remembered Cole's strong, muscular arms about her as they rode together, and it became his face above her own, his eyes gleaming with warmth into hers, his embrace that she welcomed.

Alaina shook her head furiously. This was madness! Cole Latimer was a Yankee!

Angrily she rose, dried herself roughly, and snatched on her nightgown. She spread the boy's clothes before the kitchen hearth to dry and sat before the warmth of the fire to comb and fluff her hair. It was some time before she calmed her thoughts and made her way through the quiet house to her bedroom. The mansion was like a tomb of silence as she eased her aching body between the sheets. She guessed the time might be close to eleven or twelve; she couldn't say for sure, but the moon steadily arched its way across the night sky as her bruised mind settled into the haven of sleep.

The clock had marched away at least two hours when a muffled thump and a rolling noise startled her into full awareness. Muted sounds of movement came from the room next to her own, then a man's voice sounded in a low curse.

That fool will wake Roberta yet! Alaina thought frantically as she leapt from her bed. She snatched up a robe to throw over her thin, threadbare gown, then carefully eased open her bedroom door. Seeing no one, she ran on bare feet down the hall and slipped quickly into the guest room.

Even as Alaina closed the door behind her, she gave a mental curse at her own stupidity for blundering in wearing feminine garb. Cole Latimer was not in a heavy stupor as she had supposed, but was standing near the bed, fumbling with the lamp. The glass chimney lay on the rug near her feet where it had rolled, and it was obvious he was trying to light it.

Bright moonlight streamed in through the parted curtains, lightening the room until all was visible. Though the lingering essence of intoxicants still clouded his brain, Cole became aware of the woman who leaned against the door. His mind felt slow and listless, and he could find no reason for what he saw, nor could he explain his presence in a strange bedroom, nor that of the woman. His situation struck him as extremely precarious. For all he knew he might momentarily find himself confronted by an outraged husband or an irate father bent on restoring his daughter's honor. As to that, she did appear to be a young thing.

"Ma'm," he began, sorely chafed at the thickness of his tongue. "I fear I have intruded."

Alaina realized escape was impossible and knew she would have to brazen it out. Yet it was fortunate that she had come. The Craighughs could return anytime now, and if they encountered a naked Yankee roaming through their house, the ensuing furor would be disastrous for all concerned.

Cole's confusion was apparent, and Alaina played upon it, her quick wit shaping a plan. Through the rough talk of the soldiers at the hospital, she had learned things that had set her ears to burning.

Her soft laughter broke the silence of the room. "Surely you haven't decided to leave us after you vowed to stay the night, Captain. Can it be that you have forgotten so soon?" She mimicked the relaxed familiarity of the most successful courtesan and her voice was as honey, smooth and cultured. The deception seemed simple enough; she could play this part as successfully as that of ragged urchin. Yet she was thankful for the shadow that shrouded Cole's nakedness, for the game might have dissolved in her own embarrassment and flight.

Though he could not fathom how he came to be in such a place, Cole's benumbed mind accepted the obvious situation. If he had chosen to avoid the brothels for his own continued health, this was such a comely companion he could easily be induced to stay the night. After all, it had been some time since he had felt the pleasures of intimate companionship. Surely no great mental prowess on his part was required to satisfy his sudden hunger. His wit, though numb, was quite pragmatic and, having found an explanation, settled on it with relish.

Alaina remembered her uncle had kept a crystal decanter of brandy hidden away in the guest room, and she went to search the bureau for it. This was no time for the captain to sober up. If he would just drink enough and go back to bed, she was sure he would sleep the night through.

As she passed before the window, a shaft of silvery

moonlight penetrated her garments. The slim but well-curved figure whet Cole's appetite and imagination no small amount. The lust flared through his starved senses, and he felt a familiar tightening in his loins.

"Here, Captain," the silky voice urged as the woman came back. "Have another drink." Alaina pressed a water glass, liberally filled with brandy, into his hand, then slipped quickly away as he reached for her. Her soft laughter teased him. "Drink first, Captain."

Cole lifted the glass and tasted deeply of its contents. He was rather pleased at its quality but accepted that too as logical. In the captive city, brothels were the only establishments that continued to operate affluently, and it was evident that this one was a step above the others he had seen.

"Now really, Captain." She rested a hand on his furred chest and pushed him back lightly. "You should return to bed. There's a chill in the air, and you'll surely catch your death." Cole tried to focus on her face, but it was only a vague blur. "I've an errand to do downstairs, but it won't take long, then I'll be back."

Alaina mentally grinned at her own cleverness. There was no errand, of course, but in his drunken state, he'd be happily dozing soon after she left him.

The idea was not to Cole's liking. It had been a long time since he had been closeted with one so fair, and though he could not see her face distinctly, her fragrance and those silken syllables stirred his ardor until he burned with eagerness. He finished the brandy in an impatient gulp, hardly feeling its warmth with the heat that already throbbed through his veins, and set the glass aside.

"You rest yourself a moment, Captain," Alaina coaxed softly, moving away. "I really must be about my errand."

Cole cursed his stumbling gait but caught her arm as she reached the door. Alaina looked up at him in surprise, not daring to speak. Her heart pounded turbulently within her bosom. He seemed so tall and immense as he loomed over her like a threatening dark avenger.

"A kiss I would have," he murmured thickly, "lest I grow weary of the wait. Come." He pulled her hard against his chest. "Give me a sampling of your wares that I might better anticipate your return."

Had it not been for the insistent pressure of his body washing away any feelings of confidence, Alaina would have sighed in relief. But this man was far too bold to allow even a small measure of comfort. Moments before she had thought herself knowledgeable about men, but now, as Cole laid his hand upon her buttock and pressed her to him, she became acutely conscious of her innocence. The instinct to snatch away from the alien hardness was almost overwhelming. Yet a well-versed lady of the night would hardly react in shock or refuse to kiss a customer. Though this path certainly did not lead where she wished to go, she could find no way out.

Resolutely Alaina raised on her toes to meet his lips and saw his blue eyes translucent in the ghostly moonlight, his lean and handsome features starkly etched. A strange feeling, until this moment unknown to her, fluttered within her breast, and she was halted for a brief passing of time by the flood of excitement that surged through her. With renewed determination, she forced it down; she would answer him quickly, then go.

She found her lips entrapped with his, and though they were soft and gentle, they flamed with a fiery heat that warmed her whole body. Her eyes closed and the strength of his embrace, the brandy taste of his mouth, the hard pressure of his loins made her all too aware that this was a strong, living, healthy man, that he was treating her like a woman, indeed desiring her. Her head swam as he drew back slightly, and she wondered vaguely if she might swoon. In the quiet moment that passed between them, she tried to still the violent tremor that had seized her.

"You do overwhelm a girl, Captain," she breathed unsteadily. "But, really, I must go now."

Suddenly he was frowning down at her. "Not—another?"

Alaina stared at him, confused, until the sudden realization dawned. She blushed furiously but managed to give him a tantalizing taste of the velvet laugh. "Of course not, Captain. But I do have other duties, you know."

Cole's scowl relaxed, and he gathered her to him again impatiently. Her arms found no place to rest, and hesitantly Alaina laid them around his bare neck.

"Another sip," he murmured against her ear and brushed warm kisses along her throat, "then perhaps I will let you go."

The fool! the back of her mind smirked. He had chastened and dragged her about these past few weeks, finding no trace of womanhood. Well, she would give his besotted mind a taste of that unseen twit.

Almost eagerly Alaina came full against him, little realizing the devastating effect her softly clad body had on him. Cole's arms crushed her to him, and his mouth turned across hers, invading, demanding, taking hers with a sensual, leisure thoroughness. His hand slipped up to cup her head while he greedily devoured her moist, yielding lips. He felt the shortness of her silken hair, the stirring pressure of soft, round breasts against his chest, and even in his befuddled state, he ached to sample this woman more thoroughly.

Alaina's mind reeled from the intoxicating potion of his passionate kiss. The trembling weakness in her limbs attested to its potency. His head raised slightly, and his tongue passed slowly along her parted lips, then penetrated to softly search, slowly, languidly possess. The odor of brandy filled her brain, and reality retreated from her grasp. She felt no need to struggle. He would be sated soon, she rationalized naively, and he could wait the night out in his bed. For this moment, she nestled in those all-encompassing, wished-for arms, and the long-suppressed woman in her was free to enjoy the embrace of a man. Not just any man, but Cole Latimer.

Cole loosened his crushing vise, and Alaina found she had to lean against him for support. His lips brushed her temple and pressed ardently upon her throat. He moved, and Alaina suddenly realized his arms were inside her robe and that the garment gaped open, offering her no further protection. The tie belt had been neatly slipped, and the only thing between them was the thin batiste nightgown. His thigh rubbed familiarly against her own, while his hands dipped low to caress the soft hollow of her back.

Reason flooded back to Alaina. Turning slightly, she slipped her arm downward, inside of his, then with her elbow she held away his arm. She twisted the other way until her shoulder pressed against his hard chest, freeing her own hands to counter his. Before she could react, his hand moved upward and cupped her breast, his fingers teasing the soft crest beneath the cloth as his head dipped downward toward it.

Smothering a shocked gasp, Alaina stepped away from him, at the same time catching both his hands, pushing them against his chest, and patting them gently as if to make them stay there.

"Captain Latimer, your eagerness astounds me. To the bed, Captain, and have another drink. Rest assured I will fly to you in but a moment's passing. But for now, I must go."

A half frown, half smile crossed his face. "I have no knowledge where your duties call you, girl, but I daresay they will wait. But right now"—Alaina saw the hard, flint-like gleam in his eyes—"I must have you."

His arms swooped her up, and in a single lunge, they were on the bed. Alaina started violently as her gown came up, and her bare thigh brushed the scorching heat of his manhood. They had not stopped bouncing on the mattress before she rolled and came to her feet on the far side. She had every intention to keep right on going, but her breath was jerked from her abruptly as he halted her flight. The skirt of her robe was firmly twisted in Cole's grasp, while the top cut into her shoulders. Desperately Alaina shrugged and yanked one arm free, meaning to leave the whole of it behind. But the wicked garment whipped tightly about her other arm and held her prisoner where she stood. Now, with definite panic rising, she crouched and braced her feet against his effort to bring her back. Cole was on his back and could not gain leverage to draw her nearer. Frantically Alaina yanked at the twisted fabric with her free hand, while Cole fought to disengage his arm from the tangled sheet.

"Captain, please," Alaina begged, managing to keep her voice from betraying her alarm. "There will be plenty of time later. Let me go for just this moment." Her arm was almost free, and she took heart. "Rest assured, Milord Yankee," she cajoled in the warmest tones, "I shall return to you as soon as my tasks permit."

The robe slipped. She was free! But so was he!! His arm flashed out, catching her above the elbow with a strength she had not thought was possible in those lean, well-scrubbed hands. Though she pried at his fingers, she could not escape, and purposefully he drew her toward him. The betraying robe, having spent its effort to the utmost, fell to the floor. Slowly Alaina was pulled downward until she lay upon him, her tensed thighs twisting to escape the pressure of that bold blade of passion which seared her through the weblike thinness of her gown. His head dipped, and through the straining cloth, his lips toyed hungrily with the soft peak of her breast. The single tie at the neck snapped, and the top split open, spilling the full glory of her bosom before him. His mouth, hot and moist, traced a molten path across the soft, heaving mounds, and Alaina's breath caught as he lazily caressed the nipples with his tongue. A shuddering excitement passed through her, and the strength ebbed from her limbs. Weakly she sank upon him, and Cole rolled to bring her beneath him. Raising his head, he stared down into her eyes and smiled slowly.

"Madam, I will have you now."

Alaina shook her head in frantic denial. Some fear mixed with the awesome pleasure of the hard body pressing down upon hers. "I must go," she protested breathlessly and, in a half sob, again whispered, "I must go."

"Nay, girl. I will have you now. I have paid the night away, and 'tis my right."

Though she made no gain in her struggle to preserve her modesty, Alaina seized upon his words with new hope. She tried to push her gown down below her hips again, but his hand was in the way, caressing her flat belly and wandering over her hips and thighs with the boldness that made her quake.

"But therein lies my cause, Captain," she whispered urgently, knowing he had no purse or anything else to barter with. "You have not paid."

Cole frowned at her, then glanced back over his shoulder. No sign of his clothes. If he freed her now, she would fly. And he wanted her in a most desperate way. As a thought came to him, he tugged the gold chain and its medallion from over his head and held it before her eyes. "This is worth more than thrice your cost. It will be my security."

"No! I cannot!" Alaina gasped, but he slipped the chain over her head. The warmth of the medal seared her breast. "Please. Captain, I beg you—"

"Cole," he murmured, his lips hovering closely above hers.

"Please, Captain—I can't!"

"Cole!" His whisper was insistent.

"Cole." Her own whisper was filled with dread.

He smiled and closed the distance between them in a wink. A blinding madness seized Alaina as he grew more purposeful. He lowered his hips between her thighs, and her eyes widened at the burning heat of his maleness. That blunt hardness touched her intimately, intruding upon the privacy of her soft, woman's flesh.

"Oh!" she moaned in a strangled voice, afraid of that which probed with gentle but unrelenting pressure at the tight, resisting flesh. She heaved beneath him and strained against the broad, expanse of chest. "Cole, listen to me—"

A burning pain exploded in her loins, and there was a sense of fullness as he plunged deep within. Alaina pressed her face against the base of his neck, biting her lip until she tasted blood, while tears of pain trickled down her cheeks unheeded. Then his hungering mouth searched out her lips, and he kissed her with a long, leisured thoroughness until the ache of the intrusion began to subside. He did not rush, but savored each passing moment of pleasure, and in the waiting, a strange new, budding ecstasy began to bloom and grow within Alaina, a feeling which she could neither quench nor deny. His tarrying attacked her senses; the throbbing heat of him warmed her, and she began to respond to his wild, ardent kisses. Her arms crept about him, and her tongue played timidly with his. She was not even aware of the precise moment he began to move; it seemed all so effortless on his part. But suddenly she was incapable of reason! She arched against him and met his consuming passion instinctively and with a raging fire of her own. Each thrust, now forceful and hard, brought her to a new plateau of pleasure, and each level was so completely filled with bliss she was sure she could go no higher. Yet higher did she go—and higher—and higher. Her world tore itself free of restraint and soared on to almost unbearable joy. His hoarse, ragged breathing echoed the pounding thunder of his heartbeat, and the fierce, wild fervor swept them on and on. They were two beings blended together in a whirling eddy of passion, yet set apart from the world and soaring on effortless wings. He groaned aloud and her lips returned to possess his. Somewhere she had lost the fumbling uncertainty of innocence, and was driven by licking flames of desire. Lips and bodies were merged in a fiery fusion that touched to the depths of their souls and left them spent cinders that drifted on the wind and settled ever so slowly back to earth.

Much later, everything drifted back into place. Cole

knew a much-needed release for his mind and body, and though there was no strength left in his limbs, he sought to hold fast to this moment in time lest he lose some portion of it to the oncoming forces of sleep. But its relentless pursuit wore at him, and he felt himself drifting away, losing contact with reality.

Alaina's mind came together from the nether ends of the universe where it had fled until she was again aware and knew that she lay nestled against a warm, hard body. His arm was flung across her, and his breath stirred the wispy curls upon her brow.

"Cole?" she murmured, half awake, then in the next millionth of a second, Alaina MacGaren realized full well what she had done. She! Herself! That bright-born daughter of the Confederacy had brazenly bedded a Yankee officer!

A shriek of anguish tore itself from her lips before she could strangle it. She threw off the sheltering arm with a snarl and, coming to her knees, struck Cole's shoulder with the heel of her hand, rolling him onto his back, but the best she got from him was an incoherent mutter. He had tumbled deeply into that same heavy slumber she had earlier sought for him.

Choking on angry sobs, she clasped the torn gown over her bosom and snatched up her robe. At the door, she glared back through brimming tears to where he lay sprawled naked on the bed, then weeping bitterly, dashed from the chamber, not caring that she left the door half open behind her. Her own room offered shelter and familiarity. Within her bed, she burrowed deep beneath the covers, curled into a tight ball, jamming a pillow tightly over her ears. There, in absolute exhaustion, she sobbed out her dismay; and much sooner than she would have guessed, the sweet peace of slumber overtook her.

Roberta had roused when a shriek penetrated her sleep, and she had groggily opened her door just as the portal down the hall was flung open. The pale glow of Alaina's gown had been sheathed momentarily in moonlight as the girl paused in the doorway of the guest room, then the younger cousin had fled weeping to her own room. The muffled sobs drifted back, arousing Roberta's curiosity no small amount.

Roberta lit a lamp and made her way to the door her

cousin had left open. Her hand flew to her throat as she saw the long, male form lying on the bed. His face was turned away, but his furred chest rose and fell in heavy slumber. The room reeked of brandy, and she found the evidence of its use on the bedside table where the decanter and glass had been left. Cautiously Roberta moved closer until the light cast its glow upon the bed, until the dark specks of blood marring the bleached whiteness of the linen sheets became blatantly obvious to her.

Why, the little tart's been bedded! Roberta's bosom trembled as she laughed to herself. Then a gasp of horror was wrenched from her as she suddenly recognized the slumbering one. Captain Cole Latimer!

The tramp! Vicious rage welled up within her. *She's gone behind my back and taken him! The bitch! She's had him! And he was mine! Mine!*

Oh, how she yearned for vengeance! She wanted to rake her nails across the girl's visage, to slap the thin cheeks until they were red and raw. She almost ran to Alaina's room then, to snatch the younger woman from her bed, but the small spots of blood made her pause. Thoughtfully she stared at them, and her mind began to race. This might be her chance to set a snare for the captain. If he was drunk, as he must have been to bed the twit, he might not remember everything that had happened when he woke in the morning. And if he did and made a protest?

No matter, she smiled smugly. *Daddy will take care of that.*

She put out the light and cast her gown carelessly to the floor. She snuggled against Cole's firm chest. He did not rouse, and Roberta's eyes gleamed over her own shrewdness. Alaina had solved all her problems, even to the point of leaving evidence of departed purity.

Chapter 12

AN enraged bellow shattered Cole's slumber. He blinked red-rimmed eyes at the dimly lit room, then suddenly meaty fists were pummeling about his head. More than a little stunned at this attack and completely disoriented, he threw up his arms to protect himself lest the blinding pain within his brain split it asunder. All manner of vile names and curses were hurled down upon him, and through the epithets, he could hear a shrill, discordant screeching of a woman. The whole of it was most effective in jangling the raw ends of his nerves. But that was not the end of his torture, for the man's fingers clawed feverishly at his throat and began to squeeze.

"Daddy! Don't!" the woman's voice wailed and grew more piercing. "Listen to me, Daddy! Please!"

Of a sudden, Cole was fed up with this nonsense. With the back of his arm, he flung off his assailant. Angus, being not well known as a teetotaler and having imbibed considerably at the rally, tottered halfway across the room before he regained his balance. He stared in wide-eyed rage, yet some ray of reason penetrated his brain. He gave up the idea of killing the Yankee with his bare hands. By damned, he would get his gun!

Cole watched the man dash from the room, then slumped wearily against the pillows, pressing the heels of his hands against his temples as he sought to ease the throbbing ache that bloomed there. Gingerly he felt at the long lump on his head, wincing as he touched a particularly tender spot. From beneath sandpaper lids, his eyes came upon Roberta who clutched nothing more than a quilt over her nakedness. It was a full moment before everything began to dawn.

Muttering a curse, he sat up and glanced about him. The stained sheet caught his eyes, and his mind rebeled. What the hell had he done?

He had no time to find a logical explanation, for Angus Craighugh came charging through the door, clutching an oversize Colt revolver. The man stopped a pace away from the bed and, seizing the piece in both hands, struggled to pull back the heavy hammer.

"Say your prayers!" Angus bellowed, his dewlap aflap. "You—you child molester!"

"Just a damn moment!" Cole barked, his own rage mounting. He came to his feet, the sheet snarled around his hips. He didn't have any idea how all this had happened, but he sure as hell wasn't going to get shot lying down. He couldn't very well deny what he had done during the night; the blood on the sheets gave evidence of that, and from his muddled memory came the remembrance of a woman warm and vibrant beneath him. But there his confusion mushroomed. He found difficulty fitting the shape to Roberta. Her dark eyes lowered shyly before the onslaught of his stare, and the evidence was overwhelming even to him.

"Angus, no! You can't!" Leala pleaded. "Think of our daughter's reputation! The Yankees will have it spread abroad before light. And they'll hang you besides."

Roberta struggled with the blanket in an effort to maintain her modesty, but finally made herself heard. "He promised to marry me, Daddy. And I love him."

Cole looked at her sharply, wondering what stupidity he had babbled in the night, but Angus's frenzy was renewed.

"A Yankee!"

"Angus, calm down," the usually flustered Leala cautioned. "Remember your dyspepsia! You'll be in bed for a week."

"A Yankee!" Angus moaned and waved the pistol precariously.

"I love him, Daddy, and I want to marry him."

Both men stared at Roberta, much agog. But the father, never having denied his child before, could only consider that this was the least he could do for her, to see the marriage performed posthaste.

"Get your pants on." Angus commanded sharply, pointing the pistol at Cole threateningly. "Make yourself decent for the parson."

Cole glanced about him, and the pandemonium in his

head burgeoned. No sign of his uniform! "It seems I am without proper attire."

Angus's reddened face darkened to a raging purple. "Where have you hidden them?"

"Ask your daughter," Cole suggested calmly.

The older man's eyes seemed to protrude as he strangled on several combined curses. He had to mightily restrain himself from falling on the Yankee and beating him to a pulp. The strong uncertainty of whether he could accomplish this was all that held him at bay. Irately he looked to his daughter who stammered and shrugged in confusion.

"Al's britches are in the pantry," Leala stated as her husband turned to her for wisdom. "Otherwise, there are no other clothes but yours."

"Never!" It was more a reluctance to have the girth of his belly and the shortness of his stout legs contrasted to the Yankee's tall, lean torso that made Angus voice a strenuous objection.

"Al won't mind," Leala said sweetly, then glanced hesitantly toward the captain. "After Jedediah fetches the parson, perhaps he might stop by the captain's quarters for more suitable clothing. Al will be needing his clothes in the morning."

"I fear if I am without my clothes, madam, I am without a key to my apartment." Cole was not in the mood to be charitable or accommodating.

"Uh—I'll take care of that, Mama," Roberta offered. "Why don't you go get Al's britches, and I'll talk to Jedediah."

His brow furrowed, Cole watched the daughter follow her mother out. Something nagged at him about the way her long, dark hair flowed around her shoulders. He remembered a time of struggling, as if from the bottom of a dark pit, or up from a pool of water; Al—and the stable! Cole rubbed his aching head. It just wouldn't come together. There had been a woman in the dark, then an eager body beneath his, answering his passion with a vivacity that had brought him searing, unforgettable pleasure. Why couldn't he equate that woman with Roberta?

When Leala returned, she handed in Al's damp britches, and disdainfully, Cole took the proffered garment.

"Now get dressed," Angus demanded.

Despite the threatening gun, his throbbing head, and the fuzziness in his brain, Cole managed to don the pants. Besides being uncomfortably wet, they were short, snug across his hips, and blatantly flaunted his manhood.

"They'll do," Angus said, waving away Cole's doubtful expression with the bore of the Colt. "Let me assure you, sir, we're not having too many witnesses to this affair, not if I can help it."

Jedediah was sent to rouse the parson, and even managed to beat the latter back, despite having to travel to the Pontalba Apartments and back again. But Parson Lyman had never been known as a speedy man. Indeed, he was much of a procrastinator, and had it been Angus Craighugh out to fetch him, he might have pleaded a timely wait to get himself organized. But since the message was carried by Jedediah and that one seemed somewhat in a dither, Parson Lyman thought it best not to delay too long. Still, dawn was lightening the eastern sky before he arrived to perform the service. By that time, Angus was chomping anxiously at the bit and Cole was modestly garbed in the uniform Jedediah had been sent for. It was a full-dress uniform, one Cole reserved for formal occasions or inspections. But whatever its use, it served him better than Al's britches, which he left hanging reflectively on the urchin's doorknob.

The ritual proceeded with rigid formality for all but Roberta who waxed gleeful and ecstatic. When the final words were spoken, sealing them in wedlock, it was she who threw herself in Cole's arms and presented a generous kiss upon his lips. Having gained her end, Roberta forgot the means and, in high spirits, clutched Cole's arm and stayed close to his side.

Into the midst of her gaiety intruded the sharp, heavy rap of a fist upon the door. Dulcie, sniffling in her apron, answered the door and ushered a cavalry sergeant into the parlor. The man nodded a brief, curt greeting, then, catching sight of Cole, gave a sharp salute.

"Your hat, Sergeant," Cole reminded him tersely. His head still hurt, and he felt in dire need of a good night's sleep. "There are ladies present."

The sergeant's neck reddened above his yellow kerchief, but he swept the offending item from his head before he spoke again. "Beggin' your pardon, Captain," the trooper pressed on. "We have orders to search every house we can. Confederate sympathizers, dressed in our uniforms, broke into the hospital early this morning and helped some rebels escape. No telling where they might be hiding out, sir."

Cole's brows raised sharply. "Was anybody hurt?"

"The C.Q. sergeant and the guard. The band was led by a man dressed as a doctor, and they took only those prisoners who could walk. It looks as if they got away clean, sir."

"I have spent the night here, Sergeant, and I have not been accosted by any rebels. However, it would be advisable to search the carriage house and stables. Somebody might be hiding out there."

"Yessir!" The sergeant paused a moment and grew uneasy.

"Well?" Cole demanded.

"All officers and men have been recalled and are to report at once to their duty stations, sir."

"See to your duty, Sergeant," Cole instructed. "And when you are ready, I'll leave with you. I believe I am without a mount."

The man saluted stiffly, spun on his heel, and hurried out, his saber sling slapping against his thigh.

"I think it's just too disgusting for words!" Roberta angrily stamped her foot. "Just married! And here you are running off to that stinking old hospital!"

Cole half turned and raised a brow at her, but said none of the things that came to mind. He excused her ire as disappointment. But there was a war going on, and she would do well to acknowledge that and remember he was not his own free man.

"Mama?" The daughter pleaded, turning for support to that one.

"Captain Latimer must go, Roberta," Leala spoke firmly.

"Daddy?" Roberta's voice was plaintive now.

Angus would stand much relieved to see the Yankee gone and could yield his offspring no solace. "Work before pleasure, my dear," he prattled, then bit his tongue as the parson shamed him with a look of mild reproof. Red-faced, Angus cleared his throat sharply. "Let the captain be on his way."

"Ooooohhh!" Roberta wailed. "You're all against me!" She whirled and fled, sobbing with such volume that even from her room, her cries could still be heard.

Alaina came sharply awake, her exhausted sleep shattered by the harsh weeping. The sounds of masculine voices and movement in the front yard disturbed her further, and she ran to the window to look out. Several Yankee troopers had dismounted before the house, and a sergeant was gesturing about the grounds as he barked instructions. Her first frightened thought was that Cole had found out who she was and had summoned them.

Someone had thrust Al's ragged garments in her room, and she found the britches hooked on the doorknob. She donned them quickly, smearing dirt over her face and through her hair. She hastened to the head of the stairs, but paused as Dulcie, coming into the foyer, threw a meaningful frown upward, jerking her head toward the parlor. Accepting the warning, Alaina jammed the floppy hat on her head and made a cautious descent.

On the threshold of the parlor, she leaned casually against the doorframe and tried to keep her eyes away from Cole. He was resplendent in his uniform and most handsome despite the scowl that drew his brows together. She was very curious as to how he had gotten his clothes.

"What's all the fuss 'bout?" she asked innocently.

"Al! Don't you ever bathe?" Cole snapped in exasperation.

Alaina snorted. "Might ketch yer kinda vermin if'n I did."

"Mind your manners!" Angus barked, betraying his own lack of patience. "There has been enough disaster heaped upon us this morning without tempting more."

"Disaster?" Alaina scanned the faces present, paused on Cole's tensed features. "What disaster? All I did was bring him here after—"

"You what?" Angus railed, coming out of his chair. "You! You brought that Yankee here? To my house? Do you know what you've done?"

Alaina shrugged helplessly, glancing briefly toward Cole whose attitude of stiff restraint made her all the more confused. Worry puckered her brow as she tried to explain. "He musta got hisself drunk and robbed, then dumped in the river. I jes' fished him out. I didn't know where else to bring him, him bein' in his johns and all." She looked at Cole and fussed. "Don'tcha know they's some streets what ain't safe? Even for a highfalutin Yankee captain?"

Angus growled in rage and stepped menacingly forward, but Leala caught her husband's arm.

"Go easy, Angus. The child did nothing more than we might have done."

"Bah! A Yankee?" Angus groaned. "You could have let him drown." In his mind, Angus fixed the source of all his woes. His eyes burned with his wrath as he glared at Alaina who scuffed a foot uncertainly against the rug while he continued to berate her. "You brought that Yankee to this house the first time, too." He fed on his own righteous rage. "If it weren't for you, you little *tramp,* this marriage would not have—"

"Angus!" Leala gasped in horror at her husband's conclusion. Angus mumbled in frustrated disgust and stomped out of the room, making his way with ponderous tread to his bedroom.

"Marriage?" Alaina was even more bewildered now. "What marriage? Who?—You!" She stared at Cole, a sick feeling of horror welling up within her. Carefully she asked, "You been leadin' some gal 'round on a string?"

"Not until this morning," Cole muttered.

Leala's cheeks flamed with hot color as she tried to explain. "Captain Latimer and Roberta were—ah—found —together this morning. Angus thought it his duty to send for Parson Lyman."

"My gawd!"

The minister's coffee cup clanked loudly as he set it down firmly on the saucer. This lad was far too young to be allowed such freedom with language. He would speak with Mrs. Craighugh on the subject of the boy's tutelage immediately.

A sound of running feet left Leala gaping at the empty doorway where Alaina had stood only a second before. "Was there something amiss with the boy? He left so quickly."

Parson Lyman rose. "The lad fled in much of a dither, I fear. He seemed most embarrassed by what happened here last night."

Cole's brows came together in confusion. He could have sworn he saw tears start in the gray eyes before the boy whirled. "Perhaps it's time somebody told Al the facts of life," he muttered. "He seems unusually naive."

The pastor scowled in disagreement. "You'd never guess it from his language."

Leala could not bely them, but she sought to temper their judgment of Alaina. "We must make allowances," she bade them. "Only last night Doctor Brooks dropped by to tell us that—uh—Al's oldest brother is on the missing list and presumed dead. Both of Al's parents are gone, the middle boy, and now the older brother, too. There has been much of grief and pain for that poor child."

Cole rubbed at his brow as if he sought to soothe away the persistent ache that throbbed there. He could better understand the lad's tears now, and Al had a right to them. The boy had lost so many of the ones he loved.

Alaina sat in her room and further strained the sorry condition of her hat, twisting it in anguished hands against the need to cry out. Sobs racked her body, but she had to choke them back. She could hear Roberta's wails of disappointment piercing the heavy walls of the house, and she longed to give vent to her own bitter hurt. But many questions would be raised by a chorus of bawling females.

There was no question in her mind what had happened. Roberta had vehemently vowed that she would marry Cole, and Alaina groaned within herself, knowing she had witlessly trussed him up like roasting fowl for the woman.

Cole's voice came from the front yard, and Alaina rose and went to stand beside the French doors. The sun was climbing over the treetops in the east, and the sky was a vibrant hue of fuchsia. Her eyes followed Cole as he moved about in the yard below. After a moment's discussion with the sergeant, he took a trooper's horse, swung into the saddle and departed the Craighugh estate. As he rode away, Roberta ceased her caterwauling, and then, in a moment, the squeak of her bed betrayed where she would spend the greater part of her day. Leala's weary footsteps marked her passage to her bedroom, and the house grew quiet. There would be no opening of the store today.

Chapter 13

MIDMORNING found Alaina finished with a leisurely bath that had been free from even Dulcie's attention. The housekeeper was understandably petulant and uncommunicative. She didn't like the idea, any more than her master, of a Yankee in the family. The house was strangely silent, and Alaina could guess the events of the early hours had unduly wearied the Craighughs.

With a ragged sigh, Alaina laid out the black gown she had worn too often for her age, tossing beside it the black-veiled bonnet, high-heeled slippers and corset. She could not bring herself to return to the hospital this morning. Instead, she would go and see Bobby Johnson put to rest, since his own loved ones could not be there. At his graveside, she would pass a silent tribute and a moment of mourning for her brother. Then, as before, she would put the sadness behind her and carry on.

She made so bold as to have Jedediah bring about the Craighughs' carriage and fine-spirited horse, for there was small chance the family would be using them before noon. Several blocks away from her destination, she left Jedediah with the buggy and, lowering the dark veil over her bonnet, walked the rest of the way alone. At the cemetery a long row of whitewashed brick "ovens" stood ready to receive the caskets. It was in these three-tiered kilnlike tombs that the dead were laid to rest.

Alaina halted near the end of a row of tombs, her heart suddenly lurching within her bosom. Cole Latimer stood with the burial detail, and the sight of his tall, lean form made her feel suddenly faint. Though other men were close about him and similarly dressed, she saw only him, for he had become as familiar to her as anything she could name. But there was no reason for dismay, she chided herself. If he noticed her at all, he would never associate her with Al beneath the covering of her veil, nor with the woman he had made love to in the night, for he believed that to be Roberta. Yet the quaking in her limbs could not be stilled.

Biting a trembling lip. Alaina gathered courage from an unknown source and mingled with other black-garbed women, many with young children at their skirts. She wanted to remain as inconspicuous as possible while the burial proceedings were conducted. There was a long line of simple pine caskets, all neatly draped with Union flags. For some fallen soldiers, this was only a temporary resting place until their kin could claim the bodies or the war was over.

The chaplain finished his prayers over the first coffin, and the detail, at a command from Captain Latimer, pushed the box into the chamber, then moved to the next. Under the present stricture, the only way Cole had been able to attend Bobby Johnson's funeral was to volunteer to be in charge of the burial detail, definitely not one of the more popular chores.

He was still several ovens away from the private's coffin when he glanced around and saw a small, slim woman pause before it. She wore the black of mourning, and after bowing her head in a brief prayer, she tenderly placed a small nosegay of flowers on the head of the bannered box. In some puzzlement, Cole watched the trim figure quickly withdraw into the shadows of a huge oak where she remained as the procession drew nearer. Though he roweled his memory with cruel spurs of will, he could put no face or name to the woman, yet there was an elusive familiarity about her, something about the way she moved with a bold, almost boyish grace.

As the burial detail made ready to put away Private Johnson, Cole turned, intending to exchange a word with the strange woman. But the chaplain, seeing the direction of the captain's eye and the comeliness of the figure it rested upon, tugged at his sleeve to hurry the proceedings along.

"Come now, Captain," the man chided. "Duty first, you know. These men deserve our attention for this moment. Time enough for condolences later."

As the chaplain drew Cole back, Alaina let out her breath slowly in relief. Her present costume was enough to disguise her from a distance, but she was not willing to yield Cole the benefit of close scrutiny.

The flag was removed and neatly folded. Cole replaced the flowers, and the pine coffin, with its meager remembrance of beauty, was slid into its niche. Cole excused himself, but by the time he pushed through the men, the slim, black-garbed woman was well down the path and was hurrying farther away. He hastened his long strides, compelled to follow by reasons unknown even to himself.

Alaina glanced anxiously over her shoulder, and her heart thudded anew as she realized he was coming after her. She waited until she passed the gate of the cemetery, then she lifted her veil and let her feet fly. Indeed, she was so intent upon reaching the carriage before Cole caught up with her, that she failed to see the small, dark-haired man in her path until too late.

"Mon Dieu!" Jacques DuBonné cried angrily, stumbling back from the collision. "Watch where you go!"

Somewhat dazed, Alaina put a trembling hand to her brow to steady her reeling head. It was then that Jacques noticed the petite and curvacious figure in black and was struck by the enchanting beauty of her face. He repeated the expletive, this time in a tone of admiration, and his gaze warmed with interest as it moved boldly over her soft curves. It was rare to meet a beautiful woman who, by her diminutiveness, made him feel so large and manly.

"Mademoiselle!" He bowed, sweeping his low-crowned hat from his black head. "Permit me to introduce myself—"

It was as far as he got. Glancing frantically over her shoulder, Alaina saw Cole rapidly approaching. She had no time for Jacques DuBonné in any case. She brushed past him and fled around the corner. Reaching the carriage, she climbed in and breathlessly bade the black man, "Hurry, Jedediah! On your way! Captain Latimer is behind me!"

Jedediah slapped the reins against the horse's back and shouted, "Giddap, mule! Yankee's a-coming!"

They were careening onto another street when Cole came around the corner. His only glimpse of the woman was the black bonnet, its veil fluttering out behind her like a taunting gonfalon.

Frowning, Cole turned back and found Jacques Du-

Bonné gaping at him. It was a full moment before the Cajun regained his tongue.

"We meet again, eh, doctor?" He thrust out his chin toward the departing carriage. "You know *la petite* mademoiselle?"

Cole arched a brow. "Do you?"

The Frenchman laughed. "It seem we agree on one thing, eh, monsieur? She is quite a piece of sweetmeat, eh?"

"I presume you have been informed of Mrs. Hawthorne's clear title to her property." Cole deliberately ignored the man's comments and withdrew a cigar from his blouse as he watched the reddening face of the man. "No one at the bank could explain how it happened. An oversight, they said." He flicked his thumbnail against the head of a sulfur match, touched the small flame to the cheroot, and leisurely puffed the rolled tobacco leaf alight. "But upon further investigation, I learned a most interesting coincidence. Similar occurrences have happened through the bank, with the decision favoring one Jacques DuBonné, because no other proof has been available. Strange, isn't it?" His eyes lifted to the small man. "If Mrs. Hawthorne had not taken the precaution of watching after that piece of paper, she would have found herself evicted from her home and you would have owned it for a pittance of what it was worth." He shrugged casually. "Of course, I don't have proof, but I would say offhand that you have been most fortunate in finding a friend at the bank."

A sneer came to Jacques's lips. "Like you say, monsieur, you 'ave no proof."

As Cole slowly smiled, the man curtly touched the brim of his hat, glared, then abruptly turned and stalked away.

Cole cast a glance over his shoulder to the corner where the widow's carriage had disappeared, then thoughtfully returned to the cemetery. For some reason, that slim form interested him greatly.

When all chance of pursuit was lost, Jedediah slowed the headlong pace, and Alaina collapsed back into the seat, closing her eyes as she tried to slow her pounding heart. The lesson had been bluntly slammed home, that whatever it was about her that had caught Cole's eye, she had undoubtedly whetted his curiosity. In the future she would have to be far more careful where she went as a woman.

"Where to now, Miz Alaina?"

"To the hospital, Jedediah. If the captain is gone, perhaps I'll be able to see Doctor Brooks a moment."

But when they arrived, the burial wagons were just entering the stables, and from a distance Alaina could see Cole in the buggy with the chaplain. She knew he would soon be about in the hospital, and she could not risk being seen by him again.

As it was the old doctor's custom to return to his home at noon for a midday meal, Alaina directed Jedediah to take her to the Brooks's residence. There, a dour-faced black woman answered the door and showed Alaina into the doctor's study to wait.

The noon hour had chimed before the doctor's buggy entered the courtyard and its white-haired driver alighted. He came into the house frowning thoughtfully. Doctor Brooks was greatly loyal to those soldiers who were in his ward, and he could not be too unhappy that those few who had excaped would avoid spending the remainder of the war in a Federal prison. But there were other matters to deal with.

Doctor Brooks paused as he saw the young woman who waited for him. Almost hesitantly he asked, "Alaina?"

In response, the girl untied the bow beneath her chin and slipped the bonnet from her head, shaking the dark, silky hair out with a toss of her head.

"Good heavens, child," the doctor chortled. "You play the part of Al so well, it's difficult to keep in mind that you are, after all, a very beautiful woman."

Alaina tossed the hat into a chair and snatched off her gloves. She had had far too much time to think. "Your words are kind, Doctor Brooks," she finally managed with grace. "But of late, I find I have the same trouble myself. This role of lad wears on me."

"My child! My child!" He would have consoled her, but Alaina faced him wide eyed, anguish etched in every delicate feature.

"I am not a child!" Her lips trembled with her declaration. "I am a woman full grown!" She twisted her slender hands. "And I long for a man to treat me like one."

Suddenly Doctor Brooks understood and watched her

closely as she strode away in anger. "Captain Latimer, perhaps? I heard that he married Roberta this morning."

Alaina's gray eyes came quickly back to him.

The old doctor shrugged. "The captain mentioned it this morning."

Alaina's frown faded to be replaced by a sad introspection. She wandered listlessly to the window and stood gazing out. A long sigh that was oddly broken in the middle lifted her narrow shoulders. Futilely she folded her arms, and her voice was barely heard in the quiet room.

"What am I to do?" She did not pause for an answer. "I see Roberta and other women dressed in their finery and with long, glorious hair." She considered her own work-reddened hands before she raked the slim fingers through the short-cropped hair. "And I must hack mine to a boy's length and wear these widow's weeds or lad's rags and never let myself enjoy the very thing that I am."

The doctor was still considering what his reply should be when the housekeeper entered the room, bearing a large tray weighted down by a pot of tea, a bowl of grits, another of greens, a platter of batter-fried chicken, and a smaller one of hot cornbread. The delicious aroma wafted up to tempt the young girl who had taken nothing to eat since the previous midday. Gratefully accepting a plate from the black woman, Alaina forgot her consternation for the moment. Her youthful spirit rebounded. She slipped into the chair graciously held by the doctor, and, as they ate, gave a brief recounting of events that had occurred after she left his office the previous evening, leaving off any mention of her intimate involvement with Cole.

"Uncle Angus blames me because I brought Captain Latimer into the house. I fear my welcome at the Craighughs' has worn severely thin. I must seek other employment and residence. I have managed to save some money, but I can hardly support myself on a scrub boy's pay. I'll need to pay for room and board wherever I go, and I came here to ask if you know of some employment I might take."

The doctor rose from his chair and paced the study, greatly troubled. He rubbed his fingers through his thick, white thatch of hair, mussing it terribly in the process. Finally he spoke of what worried him. "Alaina, I have already had to defend Al this morning lest he be considered to have taken part in the escape. Should he disappear now, an investigation would ensue that may well uncover your true identity. That would be most difficult to explain." He leaned his knuckles lightly on the table before her and caught her eyes with his own. "Nor can I recommend that you be anything other than extremely secretive about who you are. There is now a two-hundred-dollar reward being offered for one Alaina MacGaren."

Alaina's eyes widened, and she watched the older man closely.

"It seems," he continued, "that the Confederate prisoners commandeered a steam packet. It had over a hundred thousand dollars in payroll money aboard. The half dozen Yankees set to guard it were killed, and those who fled from the hospital forced the captain to put them ashore upriver. The steamer arrived back late this morning, and plans are already afoot for a pursuit."

"But why—"

Doctor Brooks raised a hand to halt her questions. "There was a dark-haired woman of small stature who waited with horses on the far shore. One of the rebels was heard calling out to her, and the name he used was none other than—Alaina MacGaren."

Alaina sat as one stunned, staring unseeing across the room. The doctor held his silence, letting the full import of the tale settle in her mind. When at last her gaze rose, he met it.

"Your masquerade cannot be dropped. If Alaina MacGaren is caught, she will be hanged, or at the least spend many years in a Yankee prison. There is no safer place to hide than at the Craighughs', for that is where the boy, Al, is known to reside. Al must return to work, or he will be sought for questioning. If he is not found, things will go very hard for Angus and Leala."

Alaina shook her head vehemently and clenched her hands into fists. She wanted so badly to find some flaw in his reasoning and escape her increasingly odious role, but she knew his logic was deadly true.

The week drew out, and still all Federal troops were held on duty. Even the new bride had to spend the evenings without her groom. Roberta chafed at this harsh cruelty and ridiculed Cole's notes of apology. This was too much for her to bear, she whined, and retired to her room to sulk in solitude, much to the relief of everyone else in the house.

If Roberta fretted with the absence of her husband, then Angus chafed with the presence of Alaina. The latter's cause grew more perilous with each passing hour. A tale was brought back by the soldiers who had set out in pursuit of the band of rebels and what they reported fairly curled the hackles of everyone's ire. All the wounded escapees from the hospital had been found not far from where they had left the riverboat. They had been shot in the back and left where they had fallen, all sixteen of them. Items of blue uniforms were scattered over the carnage, and the uniform of a medical captain was with the rest. The woman, the horses, the money, and the men who had lured the wounded soldiers out of the hospital were nowhere to be found. The trail could not be followed beyond where it plunged into a dense swamp. It was almost an afterthought that Captain Latimer's roan was found wandering near the dock where the riverboat had been seized.

A hue and cry was raised among the Southern citizenry. Where a week ago, Alaina MacGaren had been touted as a genteel heroine of sorts, now she was branded as a vicious traitoress and even debauched as the common harlot of a mysterious band of brigands and pirates who, with unbiased cruelty, laid waste the stores of honest men, both blue and gray.

From the outlanders, the reward was raised to a staggering thousand Yankee dollars in gold, and from the residents the quiet promise of enshrinement as a hero of the city, all for the one who would point a finger and bring Alaina MacGaren to justice. The Briar Hill plantation was confiscated by the Federals, and notice was given that it would be sold. Until then, it would be boarded up to preserve it from those who, in hatred of Alaina MacGaren, might be bent on destroying it.

On street corners angry citizens gathered and carefully watched passersby with open suspicion. It was fortunate they sought a striking young woman and not a drowsy lad on an ancient nag, when Alaina made her way to the hospital through the early morning mists. The general air was one of tension, and irate murmurings could be heard wherever a group collected.

The feeling did not abate in the hospital, and even the wounded Yankees were aroused at the callous butchery that had occurred. Alaina had just laid out her mops and buckets when a fully uniformed and armed corporal sought her out and insisted she accompany him. She was led at a brisk pace to the third floor again and was fairly panting when he stopped before a guarded door.

"Wait here!" he bade the scrub boy tersely, then knocked on the panel. The door was opened a crack, and the corporal leaned in to converse briefly with someone on the other side of the door.

"Come along." He gestured to Al and, pushing the door wide, ushered her in.

A gasp came from Alaina, and the sudden panic in her eyes was not in the least feigned. She had never seen as much brass, blue, and braid as was contained in the long room. Cole sat at the near end of a lengthy table, and his face was taut with concern even though he gave her a reassuring smile and nod. Beside him sat Doctor Brooks, and the old gentleman's face was pale with his own anxiety over Alaina being summoned. He and she bore the weight of a secret that could destroy them both, Captain Latimer, and untold others.

Alaina was agonizingly aware that much rested on her performance in the next few moments. She remembered what Mrs. Hawthorne had said and wiped her nose on a sleeve with a loud sniffle. As she was offered a chair, she seemed to stumble toward it in awed bewilderment.

Surgeon General Mitchell leaned forward in his chair at the head of the table, and Alaina fixed her eyes with a glazed stare at his stars.

"Rest easy, boy," the general uttered in a kindly tone. "This is not a court or trial. It is merely a panel investigating this affair."

Alaina nodded jerkily and wiped her nose again, scratching an ear with her other hand.

"We need to ask you a few questions. Doctor Brooks has informed us of your recent loss. I can only give my own humble condolences."

The nose met the sleeve again, and the wide, frightened eyes never left the oversized gold stars on the general's shoulder.

"I am led to believe that you rescued Captain Latimer from the river the night of the escape."

"Yessuh!" The words burst out in a torrent as she plunged into her statement with an overanxious rush. "He was a-floatin' on a tree down by the railroad levee. Kept goin' under when the branches caught on the bottom. When ah got him ashore, he was in the altogether 'ceptin fer his long skivvies, o' course, an'—"

"Slow down, boy," the general admonished with the barest hint of a smile. "We'd like to get this all straight. What time did you see the captain in the river."

"Musta been afore eleven," Alaina mused, chewing a fingertip as she rolled her eyes upward. "Yeah, that old clock was strikin' eleven when I got him in the house." She stared at the star again and let her voice slowly pick up speed again. "Ya see, him bein' in his skivvies an' all, and what with the cap'n gettin' me the job an' all, I didn't have much a mind ter haul him 'cross the square, in his skivvies and all I mean. So's I took him home with me. It were afore eleven. Maybe ten or so." She nodded her own acceptance of her logic and pursed her lips in sudden surety.

"And Captain Latimer spent the entire night at the Craighugh house?" The general pressed for his point.

"Oh, yessuh! Ya see, suh, that there is the problem! I mean, he spent the night with—uh—I mean—Uncle Angus, he fetched his old pistol an'—uh—well—I was asleep some o' that, ya know! An'—well, the cap'n got hisself hit on the head an' maybe it sorta scambled his—uh—" Alaina waved a hand in a circle around her ear and glanced askance at Cole who had leaned his elbows on the table to rest his head in both hands, while Doctor Brooks was seized with a fit of coughing. Most of the rest of the officers present were steadfastly studying the ceiling.

"And—uh—well, anyway—he got hitched ter my cousin, Roberta, an' well, yessuh, I rightly guess y'all could say he was there all night, I guess." She let her voice taper off in growing uncertainty.

"That's all, Al." The general toyed with a stack of papers in front of him. "You can go now, and thank you."

She rose to her feet with a mumbled, "Welcum, suh."

The corporal opened the door for her exit, and it was not until she was alone in the dayroom that her knees gave way. She sat trembling in a chair for some time, trying to compose herself. She had succeeded to a small measure and was just lifting the mops and buckets again when a shadow fell across her, and she looked up to see Cole. Slowly she put down the utensils and straightened.

"I guess I got ya in a lotta trouble."

"No." Cole stared at the urchin and let out a long breath as he ran a hand through his hair. "I had already told them as much as I remembered. They only needed your verification."

"Huh?"

"You did fine! Look! Put that stuff away. I want you to run an errand for me. I don't know when I'll get out to Mrs. Hawthorne's again, and"—he pulled an envelope from his blouse—"she may need this, though our friend Jacques will not be troubling her again. They have found the man who was responsible, and he is henceforth without employment. At least, by any bank around here, and her deed has been verified by the bank. It's with her letter here." He looked at Al closely and tapped his knuckles with the packet. "Do you think you can make it out there without getting lost or something?"

Alaina worried the button on her cotton coat. "I guess I really got ya in a lot o' trouble."

"No, dammit!" Cole snapped. "I got myself in a lot of trouble! And stay away from the river! I may try it myself this time!" He turned his back, then halted a pace away. "And you can take the rest of the day off."

He went down the hall quickly, and Alaina did not hesitate, for at least with Mrs. Hawthorne, she could wash her face and act halfway human.

Chapter 14

NOW, more than ever, Alaina felt the stricture of her masquerade. Her name was on everyone's lips, and how cruel the brunt of the lie that shamed the family name. Alaina MacGaren, wanted by both the Union and Confederacy. Each side desired to see her hanged. The least of her punishment, if she were caught, would be banishment to Ship Island or Fort Jackson. But there, all-too-loyal Southerners were sent, and she would fare worse by their hands if they thought she had helped murder the escaped Confederate prisoners.

Both she and the Craighughs were caught together in this irony of events. Alaina could not leave, for their good as well as her own, and they were obliged to accept her company. After all, she was blood kin, and they did know her innocent of the deeds. Still, Angus found it impossible to stay for very long in the same room with his niece. Leala could only shake her head sadly, being the only one in the family who even pretended any sympathy for Alaina. Leala could not bear to see the young girl hurt. But even she worried what Alaina's presence in the house would mean to the rest of the family. They had suffered enough since the occupation; she dreaded giving up anything more. To their neighbors, who knew they were akin to one Alaina MacGaren, the family openly deplored the girl's actions. They could not take the chance of denying Alaina's guilt. If everyone else thought she was a renegade, then so must they.

It was the eighth night that Cole had been at the hospital, and for the eighth night in a row, Roberta had retired to her room to wail herself to sleep, making it virtually impossible for anyone else to find the peace of slumber until she had.

Sipping from a glass of buttermilk, Alaina strolled

musefully across the foyer and paused at the door of the parlor to glance about the empty room. It was no more than eight in the evening, but the Craighughs had retired to their bedroom for the night, perhaps hopeful they could forget their troubles for a brief time or, behind their closed doors, reduce the noise of Roberta's bawling.

Alaina stopped, her bare foot poised upon the first step of the stairs, as the clip-clop of a horse's hooves leisurely rang on the cobbled drive. Peeking out the narrow window beside the front door, she saw the gold-trimmed blue of a Yankee officer's uniform.

"Cole!" Her mind raced. "He's finally coming!"

Alaina quickly checked her appearance in the ornate mirror hanging in the foyer. The boy, Al, wrinkled his nose back at her, much in repugnance, and for an added touch, Alaina held the glass to her lips, raising it high until she had a wide, buttermilk mustache to sport. Grimacing at herself, she mussed her hair, then sauntered to the front door. Casually she opened it and leaned against its frame to watch the captain dismount and hitch his horse to the post.

"Thought ya'd deserted us," Al commented brashly. "And by all that yowling Roberta's a-doing, I guess she figgered the same."

Cole glanced at Al sharply, pulled the saddlebags off his horse, and threw them over his shoulder without comment.

Alaina was in such a mood to extend his discomfort to the limit. "That caterwauling's been going on for eight days now—night and day." She shrugged lamely. "Ain't seen ya that much at the hospit'l to be sure ya was even around. Why, ya mighta gone someplace. Maybe upriver! Even clear to Minnesotee!"

"Wipe your mouth," Cole said tersely, striding past her to enter the foyer.

Alaina backed around to lean against the wall, eyeing him speculatively as he laid the saddlebags in a chair. "Cain't rightly see why ya'd come back to that bawling." She nodded in the direction of Roberta's bedroom where the wailing loudly continued. "But then, I ain't sure jes' how ya managed it all after I put ya to bed that night. You was drunk as an old coot. Why, ya nearly drowned me in the watering trough befo' I gotcha in the house."

Cole peered obliquely at the tousled-haired youth, recalling for himself a small memory of that event. "Seems to me you were intent upon drowning me."

"Ah-ha! So ya do remember!" Alaina chortled boyishly and swaggered forth toward the well-groomed captain, hooking her slim thumbs in her rope belt and looking him up and down. "Weren't so high and dandy that night, ya weren't. In fact, as I recollect, ya looked pretty damned stupid—for a Yankee sawbones."

Cole chafed beneath the lad's gloating pleasure. "You haven't wiped your mouth," he reminded curtly.

Alaina drummed her fingers against her hips. "What I'm wondering is, would ya've rather stayed in the river now that ya find yerself hitched and all."

"Don't be absurd!" Cole snapped.

Alaina caught the uneasy, almost imperceptible glance he cast toward his bride's chamber from which flowed Roberta's droning whine. "Ya can relax," she assured him impertinently. "Robbie's almost finished. Cain't go on much longer."

Cole patted his pockets as if he had forgotten something and glanced about him.

"Ya ain't looking for an excuse to leave, are ya? I told ya, you can relax."

Cole shot the urchin a glare. "Don't you ever stop talking?"

His rebuff brought a cackle of glee from Al. "Kinda touchy, ain'tcha?"

Cole opened his mouth to retort, but before he could utter a word, Roberta's bedroom door was snatched open, and the woman appeared. Catching sight of only Alaina above the balustrade, she frowned. "I thought I heard voices—"

Then she saw Cole. With a glad cry, she flew down the stairs, unheedful of her skimpy silk nightgown that strained into transparency across her bosom. She threw herself into his arms and smothered him with ecstatic kisses.

"Oh, Cole! Darling! I've been so worried about you."

Painfully Alaina averted her eyes from the exuberant bride greeting her groom. She wanted to be a thousand miles from where she was now, anyplace but here witnessing this.

Cole glanced at the urchin's forbidding back. There was almost a cringing attitude about the small shoulders, and he could see only one cause. "Roberta, we seem to be embarrassing the boy."

"What boy?" Roberta seemed genuinely perplexed until Alaina's brooding gray eyes turned, then she laughed gaily. "Oh, him! Why, I guess I was so thrilled when I saw you, Cole, that I just didn't stop to think." She feigned a blush as she passed a hand across her bosom, leading his eyes to the ripe, swelling fullness. In the past days she had been plagued by one fear, and that was the flaw in their marriage vows; they were unconsummated. She had worried that Alaina would fly to Cole and tell everything. After all, the twit had fallen into bed with him when he was too drunk to know what he was doing. She wouldn't put it past her cousin to go a step further and try to separate them.

Now that the consummation was only moments away, Roberta's dark eyes gleamed tauntingly at Alaina, boasting of the victory she had won. The younger cousin faced away again and disconcertedly jammed her hands in her pants pockets while Roberta crooned to Cole.

"Come, darling." She slipped her arm within his. "You must be exhausted."

"I should stable my horse."

"Nonsense! Al can do that." She threw a coy wave over her shoulder as Alaina glanced at her sharply. "He's good at it."

After a restless night, Alaina rose at her usual time and glumly donned her dirty garb. She avoided the mirror as she rubbed the soot from the fireplace onto her face and arms, not wanting to see her red-rimmed eyes and be reminded of the tears she had shed during the night. Like a coward, she had buried her head beneath a pillow for most of the night, fearful that some sound might venture from Roberta's bedroom and remove any doubt as to the activity of the newly wedded couple.

Solemnly Alaina made her way down to the kitchen, her heavy boots dragging. The aroma of hot biscuits, mingled with the surprising but deeply appreciated smell of strong, savory coffee, hit her as she pushed through the door. Her amazement mounted still further when she saw Cole sitting at the table. She had thought that he would sleep late this morning and not return to the hospital immediately. But he was already dressed and ready to meet the day. At least, that was her first impression, until she drew nearer. He had not even glanced up when she came into the kitchen, and as she pulled out a chair across the table from him, she saw that he was so preoccupied with his thoughts that he was stirring an empty cup, while he stared unblinkingly into the crackling fire that blazed in the hearth. Her questioning eyes turned to Dulcie who shrugged in bewilderment.

Cole had obviously brought the coffee, and he seemed in the greatest need of it. Thinking to be helpful, Alaina fetched the pot and poured the black liquid into his cup. She had never seen him so engrossed in his musings before, and she couldn't help watching him. But in the next instant, Cole was torn painfully from his trance as his stirring overturned the cup, spilling scalding liquid into his lap. He yelped and shot to his feet, wiping furiously at his lap with a napkin, while Alaina gaped at him.

"What are you trying to do, you young fool! Make a damn eunuch of me?" Cole shouted. The wool of his uniform was still steaming, and in considerable discomfort, he was nearly dancing.

Unable to think of anything better, Alaina grabbed a bucket of cold water and threw it on him where the coffee had spilled. It was a full moment before Cole released his breath. He glared at Al menacingly, while Dulcie beat a tactful retreat, her hand clutched over her grinning mouth. It was a rare day one could douse a Yankee and get away with it.

"I'm sorry," Alaina shrugged lamely, drawing herself up into an even smaller form. "I didn't know ya was gonna do that! You just looked like ya needed some coffee."

"I don't think I can bear any more of your favors," Cole growled, jerking open the buttons of his blouse.

"All right!" Alaina's own ire rose at his apparent ungratefulness. "Next time I'll leave ya in the river."

"I might fare better," Cole muttered and winced as he picked at the wet fabric covering his groin. "Hell! I've been burned to the core."

Alaina's cheeks took on a vivid hue of red. "Guess it's time for me to be leaving."

Cole flung up a hand to halt her. "You're not escaping so easily. Go upstairs and ask Roberta for my saddlebags. There's some salve in them."

"But she's probably sleeping!" Alaina whined in protest, not wanting to venture near their bedroom. "An' she hates to be woke up!"

Cole bit his tongue as a caustic comment threatened. After the first initial submission, Roberta had proven herself dully unresponsive in bed. Indeed, he had gotten the impression that she rather loathed exerting herself. She was certainly different from that warm and intoxicating creature his muddled mind remembered from that night.

A heavy frown came onto his face, and seeing it, Alaina fled, not daring to protest further. She had angered him enough for one day. There might be serious consequences if she persisted.

At her timid knock on Roberta's door, a sleepy voice mumbled from the other side, "Who is it?"

"It's me, Al. The cap'n sent me after his saddlebags."

In the next moment the portal was snatched open, and Roberta stood in the doorway, wearing a thin, silk gown. Her eyes narrowed as she questioned suspiciously, "Why didn't Cole come for them himself?"

"Got hisself burnt," Alaina stated bluntly. She gestured impatently. "He wants them saddlebags, if you're of a mind to fetch 'em."

"Really, Al, must you use that vulgar language when there's no need?" Roberta chastened, portraying no concern for the depth of Cole's injury.

"When there's a Yankee in the house, I ain't takin' no chances."

The older woman smiled superciliously. "I believe I forgot to thank you, Lainie, for bringing him home. Who knows but what you didn't save me a considerable amount of time and effort."

Alaina glared. "You got them saddlebags handy?"

Roberta stepped back into the room, and Alaina kept her eyes carefully averted from the bed while the woman searched about for the saddlebags. When she found them, Roberta came back to the door and handed them over. "You made it so easy for me, Lainie, I just couldn't resist. And Cole will never know the difference. Just to make sure of that, I'd better warn you. If you think you'll be able to tell him without having the Yankees know who you are, then you greatly underestimate me—Al."

"You can relax, Robbie," Alaina admonished mockingly. "Since I don't want it spread about any more than you, it will be our deep, dark secret."

"Then we understand each other." Roberta raised a brow as she queried, "And you'll stay away from him?"

"Not likely." Alaina answered flatly and, turning, hurried toward the stairs, flinging back over her shoulder, "We not only work at the same place, but *now* we live in the same house."

The noise of her boots on the stairs drowned out the comment Roberta hurled, and in a quick moment Alaina returned to the kitchen. Cole was in the pantry with the door closed behind him, and she called through the wood, managing to sound more brash than she felt.

"Got yer saddlebags, Yankee. I'ma leaving 'em here at the door. Now I gotta run befor' them bluebellies dock my pay fer being late."

Snatching up her floppy hat, she did a lickety-split scamper out the back door, not waiting to hear if Cole had anything to say.

When some time later Cole strode through the foyer at the hospital, Alaina jauntily braced her arm on the handle of the mop and gave him the best of a boyish smirk. "You're late, Yankee. Major Magruder's been askin' where you was at."

Cole glared at her. "I've no doubt you explained everything with your usual relish."

"You can bet on it, Yankee." Al grinned and cackled gleefully. "Guess you'll be known around here from now on as Mister Hotpants hisself."

Cole briefly cast his eyes upward as if seeking some divine help for keeping his control. "If I let myself think about it too long," he growled, "I might consider that you intended it as some sort of prank."

"'Tweren't me what done it," Alaina denied. "You done it yerself when you was a-moonin' over Roberta."

"I wasn't mooning over Roberta," Cole corrected sharply.

"Well, you sure was acting like ya was!" Al accused. "Sittin' there stirring an empty cup! What was I suppose to think?"

"I had other things on my mind besides Roberta," Cole stated heatedly. "And it's none of your damned business what."

"Did I ask ya? Huh?"

"You didn't need to. I saw the curiosity burning in your eyes."

"You was a-seeing nuthin' more'n seething hatred, Yankee!"

"If you hated me so much," Cole mocked, "why did you pull me from the river?"

"Didn't see who 'twas 'til I pulled ya out. Then I came close to throwing you back. Now I'ma thinking I shoulda done it while I had the chance."

Cole snorted impatiently and brushed past, convinced that Al would never admit to having a kind thought about a Yankee, even if the twit was capable of any.

Her day at the hospital done and seeking some excuse to delay her return to the Craighugh home, Alaina turned Tar onto the old river road. But it seemed that she was not meant to escape Cole's company, however much she tried to avoid him. She was nearly to her destination when a thunder of hooves behind her made her turn in the saddle, and as she recognized the roan and its rider, she groaned aloud.

"Yankee!" she barked as Cole drew near. "Ain'tcha got a home to go to? Whatcha comin' out here fer?"

"This is the first opportunity I've found to talk with Mrs. Hawthorne. Do you mind?" he asked sardonically.

"The whole reason I was a-comin' out here was 'cause I thought ya'd be home with Roberta," Al complained. "Ain't she expectin' ya?"

"I wasn't specific about what time I'd be home." Cole shrugged. "And I had to see to this."

Petulantly Alaina turned Ol' Tar toward the iron hitching post. She had hoped for a little free time in which she could relax and just be herself. Those moments she could spend as a woman were becoming more and more important to her, and she was not pleased when she had to give them up. Cole's presence only heightened her discomfiture.

"If ya was a lil' more anxious to get yerself home, it wouldn't bother me none," she grumbled, sliding from the saddle. "I seen more enthusiasm in an ol' steer my pa had."

Cole grunted obstinately. "Thanks to you, I'll have to abstain from being the loving husband for a few days. And if you can't grasp my meaning—" He frowned intently into the wide gray eyes that turned upon him. "You damn near ruined me."

Alaina ducked her head and hunched her shoulders as she hurried toward the porch. She had a feeling that life was going to be rather bumpy around the Craighugh manor for a while, and perhaps it would not be unwise if tonight she stayed close to the shelter of Cole's shadow, just in case Roberta was waiting to talk to her. At certain times, it was best to avoid trouble rather than charge full-bore into it.

But on the way home, Cole broached a subject Alaina would have preferred avoiding. He was silent and thoughtful as he kept the roan's prancing pace attuned to Tar's stable-bound gait. Then thoughtfully he turned to the sprig. "Al, are you sure you didn't take me someplace else before you got me to the Craighughs'?"

Alaina found it difficult to answer him casually and, in a croaking voice, inquired, "Jes' what kinda place were ya thinkin' ya was at?"

Cole peered at her, trying to see her features in the dark, but Alaina kept her face averted and fidgeted with her hat, thwarting his efforts.

"How old are you, Al?"

"How old do ya think I am, Yankee?"

"Thirteen at the outside—maybe."

"That'll do." Alaina yanked the brim of her hat down low, uneasy beneath his casual glance. Sometimes darkness had a way of revealing more than it ought.

"Do you know about houses of—ill repute?" Cole asked.

Alaina choked and coughed to get her breath, strangling out a reply. "Maybe."

"I seem to remember finding myself in one," he stated bluntly.

"Let me ease yer mind, Yankee. You weren't in any."

"Are you sure?"

"Yup. As sure as I'm sittin' here on Ol' Tar." Alaina shrugged concedingly. "Unless, of course, ya was there afore I found ya. Maybe ya went there first, got robbed by some o' them fancy fillies."

Cole found no balm for his troubled thoughts. There was still the matter of his missing medallion to be dealt with, but he just couldn't put anything in sequence. It was only a scattered set of impressions that he struggled with.

Much later that evening Alaina was in her bedroom waiting for the household to settle for the night when the door burst open without warning and Roberta stalked in, forcing her presence upon the unwilling cousin.

"You little sneak," the woman sneered. "You did it on purpose, didn't you?"

Alaina met the threatening daggers that came at her from Roberta's glower, smiling leisurely. "If you're talking about this morning, Robbie, had I thought of it, I might have done much better. There's just something about having that Yankee under the same roof that makes me more than a bit jumpy." She spread her hands helplessly. "I can't even take a bath until he's gone or in bed. And that reminds me." She hurried about the room, gathering her nightwear. "I'd better get my bath now that he's tucked away for the night."

"Alaina!" Roberta exploded. She reached out to halt her cousin, then froze when she saw the steel in the suddenly dark gray eyes.

"Say what you will, Roberta." Alaina unconsciously mimicked Cole's soft, threatening tone and glanced pointedly at Roberta's outstretched hand. "But don't ever touch."

"Stay away from Cole," Roberta spat in frustrated rage. "Do you hear me, you little brat!"

"Like I said," Alaina stressed the last word coldly. "I don't see how that's possible now."

She slammed the door and hurried down the stairs before her cousin could catch her. Once within the haven of the pantry, Alaina released a long sigh of relief. Whatever Roberta's new status happened to be, the woman seemed bent upon making it even more pronounced.

Though only moments before Alaina had seemed assured of herself, her countenance now hinted of uncertainty and dismay. It was strong in her mind that a real lady would never have entered such a shameful charade as she had done with Cole, and most certainly would never have let it progress so far. But Cole's inability to distinguish between the two women he had most recently made love to savaged her pride and fed her anger, possibly more than Roberta's trickery.

Alaina snatched off her boyish garb and crushed it disdainfully beneath her feet. A tall mirror had been moved into the pantry, and in it she saw the incongruous vision of Al's dirty hair and besmudged face and, beneath it all, the ever-maturing form of a young woman clad in childish undergarments. The long gold chain gleamed around her neck and, weighted by the small, shiny medallion, dipped between her round breasts. With trembling fingers, Alaina lifted it and went closer to the lamp to inspect it. A coat of arms was in bold relief on one side, its main element being two winged ravens. She turned the piece and stared. Engraved in fine, ornate script under the smooth, polished gold were the words, PROPERTY OF C. R. LATIMER.

The words tore into her brain with a rending impact that fairly staggered her. Yet she could not afford to put the thing aside. If Roberta was the one who had taken the key to Cole's apartment, which Alaina highly suspected now, no hiding place in the house would be safe from the woman's snooping. If worse came to worse, and she found herself with child, the babe would have need of a father while the mother rotted away in prison. Cole would deserve to know what he had begotten and with whom. The medallion would remove any doubt that the babe belonged to him. This much Alaina would claim for herself, the confidence that her child would be somehow cared for. She wouldn't ask for more.

Sunday morning saw the Craighugh family in church, and though Cole had worked until the wee morning hours, Roberta vehemently insisted that he join her. She did not dare leave him alone in the house while the younger cousin was there.

His absence allowed Alaina some time to relax, but even that was harshly reduced when the family returned early with Roberta squalling angrily. Cole had tried to warn his new bride that she might be heartily snubbed by old friends and acquaintances because she had married a Yankee, and yet Roberta had been so intent upon showing off her new possessions, as well as her handsome husband, that their stiff-necked disdain came as a shattering blow to her pride.

"I'll never go there again!" she vowed, slapping down her hat on the kitchen table.

"Now, now, Roberta," Leala soothed, glancing hesitantly toward Cole who calmly went about lighting a cigar from the hearth.

"Just watch me! I'll pay them all back! I'll give the

grandest, most lavish ball this city has ever seen! And I won't invite any of them! I won't!"

Cole casually raised his gaze and squinted through the smoke as it curled from the glowing tip of the cheroot. "And just whom will you invite, my dear?"

"Why—" Roberta paused a long moment in thought. There didn't seem to be any acquaintances left to ask. "Why, I'll invite General Banks and his wife." And more emphatically, "I'll invite the Yankees!"

Leala gasped and, feeling suddenly faint, sought a chair and fanned herself fervently. Dulcie turned from the hearth with her brow gathered ominously and stared at the young woman. It was rather a blessing that Angus was still out in the carriage house.

Cole leisurely examined the long cigar. "That should impress everyone."

Roberta missed the mild sarcasm and beamed. "Of course."

"Whut's all the ruckus 'bout?" Al questioned from the doorway.

"Never mind!" Roberta glared.

Alaina shrugged and sauntered in. "Guess it weren't any o' my business, nohow."

"Huh," Dulcie grunted obstinately. "Miz Roberta done got some foolish notion in her head 'bout invitin' a whole passel o' Yankees fo' a party."

"What!" Alaina forgot her hoarse, boyish tone in her amazement.

Cole half turned to look at her curiously, and she quickly fetched a cup of coffee to sip. The first taste burned her tongue, and she winced and abruptly set the cup on the saucer. Meeting the gray eyes, Cole smiled lazily and silently saluted the urchin with his cigar.

"Cole! Throw that thing in the fire!" Roberta demanded caustically, having witnessed the brief exchange. "It makes me nauseous!"

"Nauseous?" Angus stepped through the kitchen door in time to hear his daughter's statement and looked at her aghast. "Can it be that you're already—with child?"

Roberta's jaw dropped in surprise, while Alaina fought to keep a firm grip on the cup and saucer. It was not Roberta's condition she was concerned about, but her own. Dismayed, she glanced at Cole who was smiling his amusement. He would not find it so funny, Alaina thought miserably, if he were faced with the sight of Al growing potbellied with child!

"Daddy, you'rc so indelicate," Roberta chided. She saw Alaina move to the door and couldn't help needling in exaggerated concern, "Why, Al, you look plumb peaked. Don't tell me you're feeling sick, too."

"Yeah," Alaina managed dryly. "But it's the idea of ya askin' all them Yankees here what makes me ill."

"What Yankees?" Angus demanded, providing an escape for Alaina as he turned square-jawed to his daughter. That one suddenly appeared less confident of her lavish party.

Chapter 15

COLE Latimer's presence in the Craighugh household brought with it a rich abundance long forgotten by all, except perhaps Roberta. The meals improved considerably, and Dulcie no longer had to scrounge for such items as salt or sugar. Even Angus mellowed a small degree as a good supply of bourbon and brandy once more filled his cabinet. From one of the old families in the city, Cole purchased a buggy and several fine horses, and the next day a large ration of grain was delivered to the stable. Cole proved far less stingy with its dispersal than Angus had been, even in good times. The gelding gleamed with a new luster, and even Ol' Tar lost some of his mulish mien.

Roberta's biggest and loudest complaint now was that when she had the money to purchase them, there were few really extravagant gowns to be had. Still, the day was rare when she did not venture out and return with at least a new hat or a pair of fancy slippers, which immediately upon Alaina's arrival, were tried on and shown off.

It was through her own restlessness in the long hours of the night that Alaina realized Cole also suffered from insomnia. While Roberta slumbered peacefully, he was given to prowling the house, as if he sought something more than the sweet succor of his marital couch. Indeed, his mind was greatly troubled. Roberta accepted his caresses with the absolute minimum of response and, once committed, seemed in a hurry to get the whole thing over with. She had nothing of the fire and spirit with which his memory betrayed him. Even the show of passion she had displayed before their marriage cooled now that she bore his name.

"My goodness, Cole," Roberta had gasped in shock after his tongue passed possessively across her lips. "You don't think a lady would kiss like that, do you? It's revolting!"

Cole frowned. "But there was a time when you enjoyed it."

Roberta was aghast. "I never!"

Cole ran a hand behind his neck, kneading the tense muscles there. He found little ease with Roberta, even in the most casual conversations. "Whatever happened to that medallion I gave you, anyway? I miss wearing it."

"Medallion?" Roberta repeated blankly.

Cole opened a window. "You know, the one I gave you that night." He scowled darkly, irritated with his own inability to remember that time clearly. Pieces and parts of that half-dream were beginning to come back to him, yet there was no orderly sequence, and as now, he could find no reasonable explanation for what he recalled. It seemed he had slipped the medallion about her neck because he had been without money. But that was not logical. He could hardly claim that Roberta sold herself for a golden trinket, however much she enjoyed spending his money. "At least, I think I gave it to you."

"You must have lost it." Roberta shrugged. "If it's in the house, I'll find it for you."

The next day, when Alaina came home from the hospital, she found her room torn topsy-turvy. Every nook and corner had been thoroughly searched; her mattress and bedcovers ripped from the bed and left in a heap on the floor. She could only stare in mute amazement at the chaos.

"She could have been more tidy, at least," Alaina hissed testily, having no doubts as to the identity of the culprit and what the woman had sought. Angrily Alaina returned her clothes to the armoire and began straightening out the disorder, but the sharp click of Cole's booted heels sounded in the hall outside her room. Before she could reach the door to slam it closed, he passed the open portal. A long silence followed his abrupt halt. When he stepped back to the doorway, there was an expression of amazed incredibility on his face.

"Al! This is a disgrace! You ought to be ashamed."

Alaina slowly closed her eyes in frustration, fighting an urge to scream at him and call him the blind, stupid ninny she was sure at the moment he was. "Jes' 'cause ya buy them army rations for us to fill our bellies with," she railed, "there ain't no call for ya to start running the household! I keeps my room jes' the way I wants it; and when the notion hits, I clean it up. I ain't gonna have some bluebelly brassbuttons watchin' over me every stinkin' minute he's around! Now git outta here!"

She slammed the door in his face and stood trembling as she listened to his footfalls moving on down the hall. With shaking fingers she clutched the medallion that drooped between her breasts. It was the only thing that Roberta could have been after. That meant Cole was beginning to recall more of that night. Given enough time, he might remember all of it, and where would they be then? And where would her child be, if indeed she had conceived?

The tension between Alaina and her uncle eased a trifle, no doubt aided by the fact that she spent much of her time at the hospital or at Mrs. Hawthorne's. At least, at those places she was able to find some escape from Roberta's sharpening glares and the supposedly innocent remarks that cut to the quick. But life at the Craighughs' was far from tranquil. After a few brief weeks of questionable marital bliss, arguments began to arise more frequently between the young wedded couple. Having managed to collect a sizable wardrobe of rich gowns and other accoutrements, Roberta wanted now to show them off at the fancy affairs and elegant balls the Federals were wont to give. Angus, with staunch Southern stubbornness, had refused to open his house for the entertainment of Yankees, only frustrating Roberta more.

General Banks's wife and many of the officers' wives were rumored to wear fashionable gowns, and Roberta longed desperately to bedazzle them with her own collection. She was tired of the disapproving stares of the Southern ladies. Besides, it was hardly a challenge to show her gowns off to black-garbed widows and those whose men fought in far-off places. If she could only attend one of those important affairs, she knew she would be touted as the best-dressed woman in New Orleans. And to attend those social festivities on the arm of a handsome Federal officer would be the crowning achievement. The greatest problem was that Cole's profession lent him little time for leisure hours, and she had to content herself with a sparcity of engagements, a bitter vetch for her to swallow.

Instead of staying home as she had done in the past, she had expected her life to be once again exciting and gay. But she soon realized that though Cole was generous enough with his money, his time was carefully rationed. It became her goal now to demand more of that since he seemed to value time more than money. If he did not come home when she expected him, Roberta sulked and threw tantrums. Indeed, if he had acted anything but totally convinced that Al was a dirty-faced boy in need of some discipline, she might have accused Alaina of trying to steal Cole away by keeping him at the hospital.

A date had been settled on for the Federals to sell Briar Hill, and Alaina grew restive. She swore to herself that somehow she would buy it back, but with her meager salary, that seemed an impossibility. She saw the necessity of once again dressing herself in widow's weeds and going out. But first, she had to convince Cole to let her have a day off from the hospital, and this was her intent this morning.

Alaina tugged on her garb and fussed silently as she struggled with the tight chemise. Luck had been with her, and she no longer had to worry about being in a child-bearing state. Still, it was becoming increasingly difficult to hide the unboylike bounce of her bosom. It was a laborious and time-consuming chore to drag the old chemise on, and this morning it seemed even more difficult because she hurried to catch Cole before he left.

Except for Dulcie, Cole Latimer rose first in the house. Alaina was next, and the two of them were usually gone when the rest of the family stirred. Roberta trailed them all, waking at a late hour. She then complained that the others had taken the best of the food her husband had bought. Indeed, it had been the source of several arguments when Dulcie drew on the enriched larder as if it belonged to a common cause. It had taken a firm statement by Cole that such was definitely the case before Roberta grudgingly yielded the point.

Casually Alaina entered the kitchen, her bosom sufficiently subdued and heavy boots scuffing on the wood floor. Cole sat at the kitchen table eating the hearty breakfast Dulcie had prepared for him. After Cole's assertion that what he had provided was to be shared by all, Dulcie reluctantly began to reconsider her opinion of Yankees and now allowed that there were some possibilities for this one. Though she was still somewhat reserved in her friendliness toward him, the silence that greeted Alaina was one based almost on mutual respect, which from Dulcie had been grudgingly won.

Alaina plunked herself down on the woodbox beside the warm hearth, giving Dulcie a morning greeting. After a long moment, Cole's eyes slowly raised, and he lowered his fork to the plate as he found the lad watching him curiously. Dulcie glanced wonderingly back and forth between them, trying to determine what was amiss now.

"Something on your mind?" Cole asked and waited expectantly until Alaina shrugged. She spun a chair about across the table from him and straddled it, laying her arms across the top and resting her chin low in such a way that only the pert nose and sparkling gray eyes showed between the sleeve and the bedraggled mop of filthy hair. Her answer came in a muffled rush of hasty words.

"I gots all my work caught up and bein' as that's the case, I was wonderin' if'n I could have the day off."

Cole frowned at the dirty-faced sprig. "What have you to do that's so all-fired important?" Quickly he held up a hand to halt the answer. "Don't tell me. I know! You're going to take a bath and need the whole day to get all that dirt off."

Dulcie's shoulders shook with an ill-suppressed chuckle, but she quickly busied herself slicing more ham as Alaina's brows dropped dangerously low. The gray eyes narrowed and grew a shade darker. The boyishly garbed girl sniffed and rubbed the smudged nose against her sleeve.

"I got things ter do." Her gaze roamed the ceiling rafters rather than meet his amused regard. "I could get me a new pair o' boots." She scuffed the floor absently. "I saved some o' my money, an' I gots a couple o' other things to buy. I gots a fren or two to look up. Anyway, I ain't hardly had a day to m'self since I comed here."

"New boots!" Cole drew back as if in amazement. "New clothes! A washcloth and soap perhaps? Here, let me see if you're ill." He reached out a hand to feel Alaina's brow.

"Keep to yerself, bluebelly," she warned crisply, avoiding his touch as she would a fiery brand. "I ain't sick. I just ain't going ter work terday, that's all."

"I guess you've earned it." Cole pushed back from the table and rose. "I've got to be going." He drew his buckskin gauntlets from his belt and slipped them on as he crossed to the rear door. There, he paused to look back. "If you do take a bath, drop by the hospital before you get dirty again. I'd like to see how you look when you're clean."

He ducked out the door and missed the import of what was hurled after him. The tone of the snarl was enough to guess it was not a compliment.

A young bank clerk was deeply engrossed in copying entries into a ledger when he realized the sound of high heels clicking on the marble floor had ceased in front of his desk. He withdrew his pen from the page and raised a bespectacled gaze to confront the intruder. His breath slowed in his chest, for the figure that stood before him was shapely and trim to that degree which men talk about but rarely have the fortune to view. The garb was all too familiar throughout the South, that of the mourning widow, the dark gray or black and the severe cut. What he could see of the smallish face and wide, dark-lashed eyes through the black veil made him wish she would raise the gauze and allow him some assurance that the beauty of the face would compliment or exceed the fairness of form.

Immediately his manner changed from one of piqued annoyance to that of ingratiating servitude. "May I help you, madam."

"Sir, I was informed I might seek assistance from you." The voice was silky smooth and so soft and fluid it fairly sent shivers down his spine.

"Of course, madam." He rose and hurriedly sought a chair for his comely guest, then resumed his own seat. "And what may I do for you this morning?"

Alaina carefully lifted the veil and managed an expression of helplessness. There was a need to exercise great care lest she give away her identity. The clerk forgot all matters of importance as he gazed directly into those gray translucent depths.

"My father passed away, sir, and left me a small inheritance." She affected a most genteel drawl. "I have been considering moving away from New Orleans, perhaps to some outlying district, perhaps even upriver, and I wonder if there might be some properties soon to be sold that would be appropriate for a widow of limited means. I do have to be careful with my money, for it is the very last that I have. You must understand, I can't afford anything too expensive." She smiled engagingly. "Now I'm wondering if you know of a place, say north of here, that is to be sold? I heard some talk about a deserted plantation almost clear to Alexandria. It seemed like it was on a river. I do love the river, don't you? Any river."

"Oh, yes—yes, surely, madam." He nodded eagerly. Clearing his throat, he took on a manner of importance. "Now, let me see." He sorted through a sheaf of papers. "There was a place that came available not too long ago, but you wouldn't want that one."

"My goodness, sir, why not?" She fluttered her lashes, appearing innocently confused. "Is something wrong with it?"

"Why, no! But it belonged to the family of that woman renegade, Alaina MacGaren."

A surge of excitement raced through her, and she had to wait a moment before she could speak calmly. "I wonder how much a place like that would sell for. Is it terribly expensive?"

"Oh, not really, madam," the man chuckled. This sweet young thing could use all the assistance he could offer. Why, she was barely twenty, at the outside, and in these cruel times, a woman would do well to depend on a strong man. "This one is being put up by the Yankees for auction, and the minimum they're asking is only five thousand dollars. Uh, Yankee dollars."

Alaina gulped and her hopes shriveled into despair. *Only* five thousand Union dollars! At that rate and considering her salary from the hospital, she just might be able to afford the hitching post.

"This place is going on sealed bids, and the closing date is, let me see—April—April twelfth, ma'm. The results will be posted at all banks in Union-held territory around this area."

"My goodness." Alaina let the dismay sound in her voice. "I don't think I can afford that. Is there anything cheaper perhaps?"

The teller's face fell somewhat. "No, ma'm, nothing

at all. The rest are to be auctioned, and you'd have to take your chances there."

"I will have to talk this over with my uncle," Alaina murmured as she rose on trembling limbs. She gave a weak smile. "Thank you for your assistance, sir."

Feeling sick at heart, Alaina moved away from the man's desk. The sum of money was so far above her means it seemed like a dream. In fact, the only person she knew who might possibly have that much money was Cole Latimer, and she could think of no way to even broach the subject to him.

Eager to be away and think, Alaina stepped from the bank and was too engrossed in her dilemma to notice the man who moved to block her path until she was abruptly halted by his presence close in front of her. Glancing up in surprise, she found herself staring into Jacques DuBonné's black, shining eyes.

"Mademoiselle!" He swept a low bow as he spoke, then when he straightened a smile flashed rakishly across his swarthy face. He had at last found the young widow he had been searching for. "We meet again!"

With pointed brevity, Alaina lowered her veil and stepped aside to pass on her way, but the man moved quickly into her path again.

"Your pardon, mademoiselle." He spread his hands in a helpless gesture. "I dare not let you escape again. The last time, I find no trace of you. It was as if you drop from thees earth."

Alaina fixed the man with a dispassionate stare. "I cannot imagine your cause in looking for me, sir, but it seems you have wasted your time. I do not know you, nor do I wish to correct that condition. Now, if you will let me pass—"

"Ma chérie!" Jacques was quick to argue. "Can you not guess that I am enamour with you? Now that I find you again, I be most stubborn to free you until I get the promise of your company. Perhaps this evening—"

"Don't be absurd! Can you not see that I wear the dress of a widow? Your invitation is quite improper, sir, and if you do not let me pass, I will most definitely scream." The boldness of this wiry, little man was beginning to wear on her temper. She tried to brush past him, but found her arm firmly seized.

"Thees is too public a place to discuss such things of

delicacy, *ma chérie.* I have my carriage and my man across the street. I will take you wherever you wish to go, and we may have a bit of privacy on the way."

Jacques lifted his hand and gestured to the black who sat atop the elaborate landau. At the Frenchman's signal, the servant slapped the reins and began to ease nearer.

"You presume far too much, sir! I do not offer my company to strange men." Alaina had had quite enough of the man's obstinate impositions and was most anxious to be on her way. Several passersby had paused to stare, and if it was not unsettling to Jacques, it most definitely was to her. She jerked her arm from his grasp and fixed him with a cold, silver glare that pierced the veil. "Stand aside."

"Come, *ma petite.* Do not be difficult," he laughed, offhandedly dismissing her protests. Among his entourage of doxies, most had capered prettily for a few coins, and never having been associated with a lady, he had no concept of a gentleman's way of courtship. He savagely used women for his own egotistical whims and, when he tired of them, thrust them aside in disgust. This widow whet his interest, and he was not to be denied. He slipped an arm familiarly about the slim waist and began to draw her with him toward the carriage. "I will take you for a ride in my grand carriage, then we can—Aaaagh!"

This last was torn from his throat as the sharp, dainty heel came down full force on his instep. He jerked his pained foot away from her and caught her arm again, but only briefly. He staggered back, his ears ringing from the sharp slap carried to him by the flat of Alaina's slender hand. He had not guessed such strength could come from one so small. But this was enough! His own rage clouded his judgment. No wench abused Jacques DuBonné! He found his balance and stepped forward to grasp her roughly, intending to repay her well for his smarting face.

In the next moment, a gasp was wrenched from the man as he was seized roughly by the scruff of the neck and lifted back with enough force to spill the hat from his head. The small man clawed for his stiletto. But the hand at the nape of his neck blocked his access to it, and Jacques suddenly felt the slim blade pressing between his own shoulder blades as the coat was twisted backward. He knew the well-honed edge and feared that the thin blade might snap or taste his blood. His toes barely brushed the sidewalk, and held rigid, he could not twist to see who it was who held him.

The huge black halted the landau and, bracing his arms to jump down, made to join the fray. But he froze as the gaping bore of a Remington .44 came around to stare with singular intensity at his broad chest. Slowly, carefully, the black resettled himself in the driver's seat.

Cole Latimer set the gaudily garbed man to his feet with a shove. "It seems, Monsieur DuBonné," he drawled leisurely as his blue eyes took on a flinty hue, "that I ever find you assaulting women or children."

Jacques straightened his coat with a jerk and retrieved his hat. Dusting it off with his cuff, he fixed Cole with a baneful glare. "You have interfered with me thrice, Capitaine Docteur." He placed his hat jauntily on his dark head. "I am not one to overlook such a debt for long."

Cole let the hammer down easily and slid the pistol into the holster, deliberately leaving the flap open. He tipped his hat to the black-clad woman. "Are you all right, madam?"

The face was barely visible behind its heavy veil. An almost imperceptible nod answered him.

"Do you wish to press for redress from this man?"

The bonneted head slowly indicated a negative.

"Then I shall assume this affair over and done with."

Alaina chanced a reply. "You have my undying gratitude, Captain."

The low, velvet soft voice stirred something in Cole's memory, but he had no time to dwell on it, for Jacques sneered, "Have a care, Capitaine Docteur, I am not used to interference. The next time, it will be different."

Cole pressed the flap of his holster shut. "And you, Monsieur DuBonné, you take care of yourself. It has been my experience that bullet wounds are much more difficult to repair than saber cuts."

Jacques gave a derisive snort, then glanced around. "I think, monsieur, we have both lost the cause." He pointed down the street toward the fleeing figure of the trim widow. Cole watched her disappear around a corner and missed the quick gesture Jacques made to a tall, thin man who had emerged from a building across the street. The fellow returned a quick nod, then hurried after the departing widow.

Casually, Jacques strolled to his waiting carriage and gazed back to the Federal officer. "Good-day, Capitaine Docteur Latimer. Another time perhaps."

Cole touched the brim of his hat. "Perhaps."

The carriage swung about, and Cole frowned. His moment of conversation with the widow had been far too brief. Like Jacques, he wanted to know more about her. And that voice! Something about it was like sharply pungent smoke drifting through his head, elusive as the very wind. But somewhere he had heard it before, and he would not be satisfied until it came to him just where.

Alaina slipped into the Craighugh house, unaware that she had been followed by a man who would later report to DuBonné that the widow lived in the same house where the Federal doctor was known to reside. This information was thoroughly confusing to the Cajun and thwarted any plans he might have had to seize her. But even more baffling was the fact that she was not seen leaving the house again, though the tall man spied upon it for several weeks thereafter.

Lifting her skirts, Alaina hurried up the stairs, only to be confronted at the landing by Roberta. Despite the late afternoon hour, the woman still wore a nightgown and wrapper.

"Where have you been in that garb?" the older cousin demanded sharply.

Alaina brushed past her, slipping off the bonnet. "I went to the bank to ask them about Briar Hill."

"You what!" Roberta screeched and stormed into the bedroom after Alaina. "You endanger us all for that pitiful farm? How dare you!"

The younger woman whirled, and her eyes darkened into pools of stormy gray. " 'That pitiful farm,' darling," she said in a low, flat tone, "was my home. It is the place my family labored to build. In its soil rest the weary bones of my mother. When you speak of it to me, it will be best to use a more reverent tone lest some terrible fate befall you."

"You dare threaten me! Were it not for you, we'd have no cause to worry now. You ought to be careful that we don't turn you out."

"If not for me, darling, you'd never have wed precious

Cole," Alaina bitingly reminded her. "Isn't that worth some danger?"

The glaring heat from the dark eyes was enough to convey that Roberta resented the harsh jarring of her memory. "Someday Cole and I will be gone from here."

Alaina turned away and spoke over her shoulder as she pushed off a dainty slipper. "That Mrs. Mortimer who was here yesterday when I came from work—I overheard you talking to her about Washington. Is that where you're planning to take Cole?"

Roberta smiled smugly. "You do have big ears, darling."

"When you entertain Yankees in the house, I have to keep my ears open." The corners of Alaina's mouth lifted briefly in a substitute smile as she faced the woman. "Call it self-preservation."

"Mrs. Mortimer is the wife of a Union officer," Roberta corrected.

"As I said, a Yankee."

"She's going to talk to her husband about sending Cole to Washington. Perhaps he'll even be on the President's personal staff. He has the intelligence—"

"My! My! You sure are ambitious for him. Have you talked it over with him?"

"There's no need right now. He'll be informed soon enough."

"How good of you. No doubt he'll be forever indebted to you for helping his career along."

"Don't be sarcastic," Roberta snapped. "I'm doing it for his own good. At least, it's more than what you would have done for him had you been able to carry out your schemes to take him for yourself. The best you could have given him was a passel of brats to hang on to his coattails."

"You're right," Alaina agreed, flinging up her hands dramatically. "As always!"

Chapter 16

THE captive city on the Mississippi reflected the fortunes of the Confederacy and, to the chagrin of the cupying troops, the misfortunes of the Union. Last Sepnber had found the city cheering when the news of the ion collapse at Chickamauga came, and October found citizenry almost arrogant in the hope of rescue when Lee crossed the Rapidan on his way north again. November opened, and Lee went into winter quarters at the same spot he had departed a month earlier. The city grew silent and its people sullen, then Grant sent Bragg's army fleeing south from Chattanooga, and Longstreet failed to crack the Union front at Knoxville. New Orleans gave up its dream of early reunion with the Southern cause.

Christmas and the beginning of the new year had been dreary and celebrated only in the privacy of homes, if at all. The year grew darker still in the second month as Sherman raided deep into Mississippi while the eastern armies still lay dormant. The Yankee frigate *Housatonic* was sunk by the small submersible Hunley, and though the deed was meager in import, it was great in heroism, and thus was seized upon for its brightness. The news of the Confederate success at Olustee, Florida, was overshadowed when the Yankees appointed, as Governor of Louisiana, one G. Michael Hahn who, though a native, was an ardent anti-secessionist.

Now the winds of March came as if to dry the land and make it firm for the boots of marching soldiers. The fifth of the month dawned brash and breezy, and this Saturday had been chosen to embrace the inauguration of the new governor. When the ceremonies were completed in front of massed Union troops in Lafayette Square, the ensuing celebration awed the citizens of the city with its unbridled extravagance.

A chorus of a thousand men had been assembled, and their voices were raised in a full rendition of the "Anvil Chorus" with all the bands of the army in accompaniment and hundreds of cannon fired in unison by electrical devices. All the churches had been ordered to ring their bells, and the din was magnificent, if somewhat tuneless.

It was earlier in the morning when Alaina settled herself near the kitchen hearth while Dulcie prepared her a plate of grits and sausages. The bright flames danced around the bottom of a black kettle that hung over the fire, sending bubbles rolling over the surface of the water that filled it.

"Ain't he later'n usual?" Alaina asked, nodding toward the pantry door.

Dulcie came to the table to set the plate down and confided in a low whisper. "Mistah Cole's gotta work late tonight, and Miz Roberta ain't hardly gib dat man a bit o' peace since he got up. The Yankees is gettin' demselves all duded up to celebrate dat traitor being 'lected gov'nor, and she wants Mistah Cole to take her to dat highfalutin ball Gen'ral Banks is givin' tonight. Now dat she and Mistah Cole's movin' ta Washin'ton, Miz Roberta got it in her head she's one o' dem Yankees. She had Jedediah fetch her over ta Miz Bank's house jes' yestahday, while you and Mistah Cole was at de hospital. An' she come back a-ravin' over dat woman's genteel manners."

Alaina snorted in derision and stirred melting butter into the steaming grits. Dulcie set her massive arms akimbo and frowned sharply as she watched the girl sprinkle a heaping spoon of sugar over the cooked hominy. "Dat's de way dem Yankees eat grits, chile! Doan yo' go turnin' yo'self inta one o' dem critters, too!"

"Dulcie?" Cole called from the pantry where he had gone to bathe.

"Yassuh, Mistah Cole?" The black woman sauntered nearer the door.

"Ask Jedediah to bring that water in here now, if it's hot."

"Jedediah ain't here, Mistah Cole. Miz Carter, down the road, was ailin', and she ask Mistah Angus if Jedediah could fetch her ta da doctor."

"I thought I heard Al. Is he out there?"

Dulcie exchanged an apprehensive look with Alaina who had straightened in her chair with sudden alert attention.

"Yassuh," the black servant answered slowly. "Mistah Al's sitting right heah."

"Then have him bring the water in. This bath is freezing."

Alaina's distress showed in her smudged face and widened eyes. After a brief moment, she collected enough of her wits to call back, "Ya wants it, bluebelly, come get it yerself. I got a day o' totin' water ahead o' me widout starting now."

"Al!" Cole's bark came with the sharp edge of anger. "Get that water in here now!"

Alaina threw down her fork and railed at the door. "I ain't fetchin' it, bluebelly!"

"Get it in here now!" Cole commanded in a barely subdued bellow. "Or I'll tan that skinny rump of yours!"

"Gotta ketch me furst, Yankee!"

"I'll catch you," Cole warned. "And I'll not only tan your bottom, I'll show you what a bath is for!"

At that threat, Alaina stuttered into silence. She wouldn't put it past the Yankee to do just that.

"Al!" The captain's patience was wearing thin.

"All right! All right!" Alaina moaned in the petulant tones of a yielding teenager. She went to the fireplace and tested the steaming kettle with her finger. Then suddenly a glow of mischief brightened her eyes. Pouring cold water into the hot, she slipped her hand into the water. Just about right! After she was through with him, that Yankee would never ask this of her again. She dipped a bucket into the kettle, filling it full, then caught the tip of her tongue between her teeth as she struggled with the weight of the pail across the room.

"Al!"

"I'm coming!" she wailed in answer. "Keep yer suds up, Yankee. I'm hurryin'."

She avoided Dulcie's horrified stare and shuffled into the pantry, pushing the door wide. "Gotcha yer water, bluebelly."

Before Cole had a chance to reply, Alaina emptied the whole bucketful down his back. A hoarse gasp was torn from him at the sudden shock. It was just hot enough to be very noticeably uncomfortable. His roar of rage made Alaina drop the bucket, and as he grasped the sides of the tub to heave himself out, she quickly decided the moment was at hand for a hasty retreat. A gay torrent of laughter followed her as she fled. The enraged doctor snatched a large towel around his hips and charged after her, nearly slipping as his wet feet made puddles on the floor. The menacing look in those startling blue eyes squelched the rippling sound of gaiety the very moment Alaina shot a hurried glance over her shoulder. She did a spritely scamper across the kitchen to place Dulcie's bulk between herself and the nearly naked and furious Yankee.

"You little whelp! I'll blister your britches good!" Cole cried.

"Whatsa matter, Cap'n?" Alaina asked, her chuckling voice a pure shade of innocence. "Weren't it hot enough?"

"You witless little vagabond!" Cole's longing for vengeance was more than apparent as he began to stalk her. "It's about time you learned what a hot bath is for!"

Alaina solved Dulcie's dilemma by leaving that shelter and strolling across the room, carefully keeping the large cooking table between herself and the enemy.

"Jes' 'cause ya think ye're some kinda relative now," Al informed him haughtily and rubbed a slim finger through some flour on the table, "don't think ya got a right ter handle me anymo' than befo'."

"I'll handle you, all right!" he warned direly and lunged around the table for her.

A moment later Cole had to duck as Al kicked a boot off, sending it flying toward him. The second boot followed on its heels, catching Cole on the bare shin. His grunt of pain brought a quick grimace from Alaina who hadn't really meant to hit him so hard, but she had no time to pause in consideration of his injury before he charged after her. Her giggles floated back over her shoulder as she circled the table.

"What is going on here!" a shrill voice demanded, and all turned in abrupt silence to see Roberta in the doorway.

"That brat nearly scalded me again!" Cole gritted through clenched teeth. "And when I'm through with him, he'll need a cold pack for his rear!"

"Cole! Stop it!" his wife railed as he lunged toward the dodging waif who sprinted quickly away from the kitchen table to retrieve her boots.

"Not until I teach him some manners!" Cole flung. "It's high time somebody did!"

The man followed the laughing imp and raced toward the back door just behind the ragged form. The portal slammed closed, and in the next instant, Cole found himself facing Roberta who, fearing that her husband would follow Alaina into the yard, spread her arms across the portal, barring his escape.

"I want to talk to you!" she said sharply. "Upstairs, if you don't mind."

"I was taking a bath," Cole retorted and turned toward the pantry. "And I plan to finish it, now that I've gotten rid of that little menace."

"And paraded yourself naked around the women of this household," Roberta sneered.

Holding the towel firmly around his hips, Cole caught himself in mid stride, turned slightly and gave a brief, apologetic bow to Dulcie. "Your pardon. I did forget myself in my quest for revenge."

Dulcie's chuckling merriment could not be restrained as she busied herself stirring the grits. "Dat Al, he sho' can scamper."

"Cole!" Roberta warned him tautly. "Stay away from that boy!"

Cole arched a brow toward his wife. "Now, I can't very well do that, my dear. It seems I brought him to the hospital as a hireling, and I have yet to find cause to dismiss him. And as you should know, my dear"—his voice was pleasant but held more than a trace of sarcasm—"that *is* where I work."

"Too much!" Roberta gritted. "You could just as easily take me tonight, but you're more devoted to that damned hospital than to me."

Cole refused to comment on that statement. Of late, it was the only place he could escape from Roberta's ceaseless harping. He noticed that Dulcie had quietly slipped from the kitchen, giving it over to them.

"You don't deny it, then," Roberta sneered. "You can't!"

He shook his head slowly. "Don't start that again, Roberta. Just the other night I had Major Warrington take my duty hours so I could go with you."

"And you were miserable, weren't you?"

"If you'll remember, my love," he stressed the endearment, "we went to the theatre the night before and Antoine's afterward. My total hours of sleep were three. I was tired!"

"Anytime you go with me you're tired!" Roberta flung petulantly. "But you can chase that—that *boy* around the kitchen!"

"Now what does that have to do with it?" Cole threw up his hand in resignation. "Don't tell me you're jealous of that pint-sized ragamuffin?"

"Don't be ridiculous! It's just that you never seem to find time for me, but you're always with *him.*" She jerked her head toward the back yard.

"Don't worry." Cole's sarcasm had thickened. "He won't be going with us to Washington."

"Huh!" Roberta tossed her dark mane over her shoulder. "You'd just as soon stay here than be attached to Mister Lincoln's personal staff."

Cole sighed wearily and shook his head. "Roberta—I doubt that I will be on the President's staff. He has colonels aplenty to serve him. For your information, Washington has a large hospital which General Grant keeps well stocked with wounded. The only thing you can be sure of is that I'll probably have more paperwork to keep up."

"It's still an important advancement. And if not for me, you'd have thrown away the chance. Now, as it is, you'll probably make general, and we can live in Washington and meet all the people who surround the President. That is, of course, when the Union wins."

"I wish Grant were as sure as you are." Cole gave a wry, lopsided grin and considered Roberta more closely. It seemed that she had progressed quite far in her plans for them. "You should also know that after the war, I'll be returning to my home to take up my practice again."

"What? To be slaughtered by the Indians just like all those other poor people? Oh, I heard about all those wild savages roaming the countryside. I'll never go there to live! Never!"

Angrily, Cole turned his back upon her and strode into the pantry, slamming the door behind him. With a curse, he threw aside the towel and got back into the tub, but Roberta was in a bit of a temper herself and followed him.

"You'll not escape me so easily, Cole Latimer!" She marched straight to the tub. "And we still have to settle the issue about tonight. I want to go to that ball!"

Cole flung up a hand irritably. "Then go! But I've got work to do!"

"You wouldn't care if some other man *did* take me!" she wailed with a sob of rage. "You're cold! Unfeeling!"

He gave her a sidelong look of disbelief. "Madam?"

"Ice runs in your veins!" she accused tearfully.

"Well, my dear," he drawled leisurely. "I've seen ice thaw quicker in a Minnesota January than you in bed."

"What do you mean?" Roberta demanded in outrage.

"Let's face it, Roberta. Since our marriage you seem to have become bored with it all. If you want to know the truth of it, I liked you better the first time, after Al fished me from the river."

For a stunned moment Roberta gaped at him, then the next instant the air cracked with the sound of her open palm meeting Cole's cheek. "How dare you! How dare you!" she railed in high agitation. "Just because I don't act like some eager little trollop who falls into bed with you for a trinket, you insult me like this. I am a lady, Cole Latimer, and don't you ever forget it! I assure you, a lady does not enjoy being pawed and petted!"

He frowned at her curiously as he passed a hand down his reddened cheek. "Strange, I seem to remember giving you a trinket for your favor. A medallion, as a matter of fact." His gaze lightly skimmed the heaving bosom above the low décolletage of her lace dressing gown. "And sometimes, Roberta, I get the feeling there are two sides of you, each completely different. Where is that woman I held in my arms that night, Roberta? Has she retreated now that the vows have been spoken and sealed?"

Roberta straightened indignantly, gave him a scathing regard, whirled on her high heels, and stalked out of the room, taking her turn at slamming the door. Cole leaned back in the tub and listened to her heels clicking in rapid staccato across the brick floor in the kitchen. That woman, he mused, was turning his life into a living hell.

Idly he picked up a bar of homemade soap from a dish that held a vast assortment of scented bars Roberta had recently purchased. A fragrance wafted from it, filling his head and stirring in the very depths of his soul some twinkling memory he could not quite grasp hold of. A phantom form swam through his mind, and from its soft, beckoning lips came the ripple of sweet laughter mingled with honeyed words—

"But therein lies my cause, Captain. You have not paid."

Cole's eyes flew open. That voice again! He must be going mad! He had not even seen the young widow's face, and here he was already having illusions of holding her in his arms!

Presenting herself at the general's residence shortly after Cole left for the hospital, Roberta played upon Mrs. Banks's sympathies and gained an escort for that evening's affair. She spent the afternoon preening herself, trying on countless gowns and casting them off in distaste until she found one that met her mood. Before dressing herself for the grand affair, she napped in order to be fresh and rested for the long evening ahead. She would teach that Cole Latimer a lesson he would not long forget.

Though Dulcie had been hard at work all day, cutting and preparing to smoke the meat of a hog that Cole had purchased and sent out, Roberta gave the black woman stern orders to make sure the bedroom upstairs was neat and tidy before she returned. Dulcie was still grumbling about the command when Alaina came home that night after helping Mrs. Hawthorne with some heavy chores.

"Miz Roberta gone off a highfalutin it wid some Yankee colonel widout tellin' Mistah Cole, Mastah Angus, or Miz Leala, and there her pa and ma went off visitin' wid kinfolk for the night. Dere sho' is gonna be some fur flyin' in dis house if'n Miz Roberta ain't fetched herself home befo' Mistah Cole." The woman slapped down a long length of sausage she had just finished stuffing and shook her head sorrowfully. "An' ah is gonna see some feathers flyin' myself if'n I ain' cleaned up dat room befo' Miz Roberta gits back. Cora Mae and Lucy went off to sit with Miz Carter cause de doctor tole dat ol' lady to rest in bed. I jes' ain't got around to cleanin' upstairs yet wid all dis heah po'k a-needin' to be smoked befo' hot weather sets in. Miz Roberta don't care if de rest o' us eats or not."

Despite her own weariness, Alaina offered assistance, well understanding the woman's plight. Since Cole had portioned out a comfortable salary for the black family and had taken over the expenses of running the household, Roberta had assumed for herself the role as mistress of the manor. Now that she was a woman of affluence, Roberta had become a rather domineering figure and expected Dulcie and her family to cater to her every whim above that of the elder Craighughs. More and more it was ceasing to be a home that could be enjoyed by all who occupied it.

Late into the night Alaina helped hang the hams and meats and clean the kitchen, then seeing that Dulcie was near exhaustion, she propelled the older woman off to bed with the assurance that, after her bath, she would straighten up Roberta's bedroom herself.

Alaina had no inkling just what she had volunteered herself for until she stood in the doorway of her cousin's room and stared in amazement at the jumble of clothes, shoes, petticoats, hoops, and a vast assortment of accessories left helter-skelter about the floor and over the furnishings. Beneath heaps of petticoats and silk stockings, the bed was unmade and rumpled. But in the disarray, Alaina noticed there was nothing of Cole's. His clothing was neatly arranged in the tall armoire that had been moved into the room to accommodate his possessions.

Alaina placed cool fingers against her temples. She was bone tired and dearly longed for sleep, but she had promised Dulcie that she would see the room neat and presentable before she went to bed. Despite the monumental task laid out for her, she had to keep her word.

The soft patter of raindrops that began to hit the windows was a prelude to the storm that soon swept down upon the house. Lightning flashed and thunder rumbled swiftly on its heels, making Alaina jump as it loudly cracked the silence. She worked by the light of one lone kerosene lamp that sat atop the bureau beside the door. Angus had exacted a bit of revenge upon the Yankee, though it was little noticed by the one to whom it was directed, and had taken all but one lamp from the room. The late hours Cole usually kept saw him making his way through a dark house and finding the path to bed without aid of a light.

Alaina carefully folded the silk stockings and put away the rich gowns, allowing herself the luxury of holding a few before her as she passed the tall, standing mirror. In sharp contrast, her threadbare robe was a disillusioning mark of her own poverty. It brought to mind that she had failed thus far to raise enough capital to buy Briar Hill. Unable to think of a logical explanation as to why Al would need so much money, she had not dared to approach Cole on the matter of a loan.

Almost self-consciously Alaina doffed the tattered robe. Her gown still bore a bit of pretty lace across the bodice, even though the carefully mended rent Cole had put into it caused the garment to pucker untidily.

Silently Alaina worked, admiring the expensive clothes while she put them away. Though they belonged to another woman, it was a luxury just to touch the fine silks, the rich velvets, the seed pearl-encrusted bodice or the jet-trimmed crimson ball gown.

A bolt of lightning streaked across the night sky, and the rain washed down the window in sheets. The small clock on the bedside table delicately chimed in the late midnight hour, and Alaina stared at it in amazement, wondering where the time had flown. A few last articles to put away, the bed to straighten, and then she could go to bed.

Moments later, as she was tucking away the vast folds of a petticoat, Alaina paused to listen. Had she heard a noise in the hallway, or was it the rumble of distant thunder? Whatever it might have been, she decided it was best to hurry. She had no wish to be caught by either Cole or Roberta.

Quickly Alaina closed the armoire door, then halted abruptly. This time she could not mistake the creaking of the wood floor in the hallway as someone came toward Roberta's bedroom. No scuff of boots were heard, nor the sharp click of high heels. But it was raining hard. Cole would have stopped at the back door to remove his boots, whereas Roberta would have tracked mud through the house rather than trouble herself.

Her heart thumping wildly in her chest, Alaina flew to the lamp and blew out the flame. But he'd only light it again, she thought frantically. Carefully, trying not to make a noise or worse yet, drop the lamp, she put the glass hurricane lantern on the floor behind the dressing screen. The room was now totally black, but she knew Cole had the advantage. His eyes were accustomed to the dark!

Alaina stood in the middle of the room, turning about indecisively. She couldn't pass him in the hall! He'd probably mistake her for Roberta and stop her. A place to hide then! Under the bed! Heaven forbid! She'd be trapped there as an unwilling witness should he and Roberta become amorous. The dressing screen! Of course!

The doorknob turned, and Alaina flew to join the hidden lamp. But not fast enough. As the door swung open, Cole's eyes caught the pallid glow of her white gown as she dashed behind the screen.

"Are you still up?" His voice still bore an edge of sharpness that bespoke of a lingering vexation.

A jagged ripple of lightning touched the sky as Cole dropped his wet blouse over a straight chair that sat before the fireplace. Alaina, fearfully peering around the edge of the screen, saw him doff his shirt and move to where the lamp should have been. He searched the top of the bureau, patting it carefully in the dark so he wouldn't knock anything over. Failing to find the lamp, he swore and opened a drawer in the chest, took out a cigar and match. He turned, lighting the cheroot, then raised the small, flickering light high. Alaina ducked back and held her breath as he looked about the room for the lamp.

"Where has the lamp gone to?" he growled. He walked to the windows and threw the draperies wide before opening a window a crack. The scent of rain mingled with the aromatic smoke as he stood gazing out onto the ebony, storm-tossed night, leisurely enjoying the cigar. Finally he turned, unfastening his trousers, and sat down on the edge of the straight chair to pull them off. He was about to doff his underwear when he turned thoughtfully to face the corner of the room where the screen was.

"Roberta? Are you ill?"

Alaina waited in trembling disquiet as she listened for his approach. Cole was puzzled by his wife's uncharacteristic taciturnity. If she was still sulking because he had been unable to attend the ball, then he was in for another night of argument and strife.

Cole tossed the cheroot into the fireplace and neared the screen. He was just reaching to fold it back when the whole thing fell forward, pushed by a decisive force from behind. The top caught him squarely across the chest as a pale shape leapt past him. Angrily Cole tossed off the screen, reached out an arm and snatched a handful of thin cloth. A rending tear preceded a startled gasp, then a small, slippered foot kicked at his shins.

"Dammit, Roberta! What's gotten into you?" He ignored the hands that slapped at him and jerked her around roughly. Alaina stumbled against the bed and, in great trepidation, quickly scampered across it. Cole was just irritated enough to lunge after her, his fingers reaching to ensnare her. In the next moment, her gown was all he had. The batiste was fragile with age and needed no more than a gentle tug to separate it completely. The strain Cole placed upon it was not light by any measure, and the whole thing shredded apart like the most fragile gossamer.

Cole tossed the gown aside and swung around the massive bedpost to fling himself toward the now naked woman. The vague blur of pale bodies in the dark room gave away their movements, and seeing him near her, Alaina abruptly changed directions and scurried to the opposite side of the bed. Cole was faster and leaped around the corner post in time to catch her full against him. The sudden contact of their bodies came as something of a shock to both of them. There was only the briefest meeting of soft, bare bosom against hard, furred chest before Alaina tore away with a gasp. But in that abbreviated encounter, Cole became certain of one thing. This was *not* Roberta! The form was too small, too slim, too light. He reached out a hand, brushing her hair, and immediately it all came back to him. The short hair! The slim body! His mind rebelled in disbelief.

"Who the hell!" His eyes probed the darkness for her features as he demanded in a hoarse whisper, "Who are you? Who—are—you?"

Lightning seared the sky in a brilliant, almost blinding flash, and in that moment, her hair tousled and unkempt, Al was plainly visible.

"Good lord!" Cole cried. There was a glimpse of her pale, heaving breasts with the gold medallion gleaming tauntingly between. "Al!"

"Alaina!" The whisper was like a pained scream in the room.

"It was you! It was you that night!"

Alaina tried to snatch away, but he caught her wrists. She fought him, wildly twisting and writhing in an attempt to gain her freedom.

"Will you be still!" he cried and, when she would not, increased the pressure of his grip upon the delicately boned wrists. Stubbornly Alaina resisted the pain until finally Cole gave up the tactic, not wishing to hurt her unduly. Instead, grasping both her wrists into one hand, he gathered her close with his free arm and stifled her struggles against him. Alaina's eyes opened wide with alarm.

"No!" she railed, suddenly afraid of his intentions.

They were in the house alone, and there was no one to stop him if he chose to take her again. "Let me go!"

"Be still then," he commanded.

Slowly she quieted, and Cole loosened his hold, but as soon as he did, Alaina came alive with a flurry. She escaped his grasp and, without pause, sought to extend that condition with further flight. She was just reaching for the doorknob when he caught her again. Cole's memory was like a book being opened wide for the first time, and he wanted some answers.

Blindly, insanely, Alaina fought him, trying to claw his hand away from her arm. The night he had taken her virginity was far too vivid in her memory. She would not misjudge his strength or his ardor again! In her state of undress, she was far too vulnerable, and she wanted to be safe in her room with the door barred between them.

"Stop it!" He caught her hand in his. "I just want to talk."

He pressed her back against the wall and tried to still her frantic threshing with the weight of his own body, but he was too conscious of her warm body and of the soft nipples that seemed to burn into his chest. He was becoming increasingly aroused, and her struggles only sharpened his desires. Moisture popped from his pores, and it was a labor to remember that he was even partly a gentleman.

"Ooooh n-o-o-o!" Alaina moaned in dismay. His thighs crushed her own quaking limbs, and his excitement was blatantly obvious to her.

Cole snatched away and pulled her to where he had seen a white garment on the bed. It was her robe that he thrust at her.

"Dress yourself!"

Alaina hastily complied, though she found it impossible to stop her violent shaking and the robe offered her meager protection.

"Where is the lamp?" Cole questioned sharply, as provoked with himself as he was with her.

Alaina's voice quavered as she answered. "Behind the screen."

"Don't run away again," he warned darkly. "You owe me that much, and I'm just in the mood to tear this damn house apart to find you."

"I owe you nothing, Yankee," Alaina sniffed with open mutiny in her tone.

"Stay where you are!" Cole commanded sharply. After setting the screen upright, he felt around until he located the lamp and returned it to its place on the bureau. "I intend to find out just what the hell is going on here."

He touched a sulfur match to the wick and, replacing the chimney, turned it up until its glow drove the shadows back into the corners. Reaching out, he pulled Alaina close to the lamp and cupped her chin in his hand, raising her face full to the light. Tears streamed down her cheeks at this rude examination, but Cole could only stare in wonder.

"By damn! I should have known!"

The dark brown hair, with highlights of red, framed a creamy-skinned visage. The lips were soft and sensuous; the eyes a clear sparkling shade of gray fringed by thick, black lashes. Even with the undisguised fullness of womanhood, the features were unmistakably Al's.

A chuckle started deep in Cole's chest. "I should have given you a bath the first day we met."

"Fool! Idiot!" Then as if these words were not bad enough, she spat, "Yankee!"

He seemed oblivious to the epithets as he turned her face first to the left, then to the right. "How old are you?"

She glared up at him, grinding her teeth as she answered bitterly, "*Seventeen* . . . going on eighteen."

Cole heaved a sigh of relief. "I feared you were much younger." Another light dawned in his skull. "Alaina!" He raised a brow. "Perhaps Alaina MacGaren?"

"Of course!" She flung his hand away from her and rubbed her arm where his fingers had bruised it. "Alaina MacGaren! Spy! Murderess! Enemy of both North and South! What is it now? Two thousand for my head? What will you do with it all?"

"Dammit, girl, if you were with me, then you couldn't have—"

"You are so swift in your deductions," Alaina sneered derisively. "But tell me, Captain Latimer, who will be my defender? I carried a dead man's effects to his commander and became a spy for refusing a Yankee's fondling. I was forced to flee my home and become a lad! Will you destroy Roberta's name to clear mine?

Or will you make up some lie to tell, then stumble over your hidebound honor in its telling and trap me all the more firmly? Will you condemn the Craighughs to prison for having aided a fugitive? Will you plead you mistook the virgin, decry your vows, and make the whole thing seem right in your muddled mind?"

Alaina sidled away from him and silently vowed to shred his arm if he tried to touch her again. Glaring at him, she hissed through clenched teeth, "Do you think I will plead for my salvation from a Yankee? Do what you will! Seek out your pride and honor, but do not hope to find your conscience clean and laundered upon my couch! Go find your loving bride, the one you chose. But leave me be!"

She choked on the sobs that welled up, and blinded by tears, she whirled and flew to the door, flinging it wide. Her gasp of horror made Cole look around. Roberta, in all of her finery, stood before the door with jaw hanging aslack. For a stunned moment, the woman could do nothing more than stare wild eyed at the girl, then her gaze traveled downward to the transparency of the skimpy robe before her eyes flew to Cole and took in his indecent attire.

"The minute my back is turned"—she advanced like a raging hurricane, while Alaina stumbled back before the onslaught of her fury—"you two are at your dirty little games! There's no telling just how long you both have been—" Her next words were such obscene accusations, Cole's temper flared.

"Roberta! Shut your damned mouth!"

She turned to him, and her voice became a wheedling whine. "How could you? How could you go behind my back with this—this tramp? Do you take to bed every little hussy who offers herself?"

Alaina gasped in outrage. "I never!"

"Whore!" Roberta screamed stridently, and in the next instant Alaina's ears were ringing from the vicious slap hurled against her cheek. Before Cole could step between, Alaina came around full circle with her small fist clenched tight. She was not as genteel as Cole had been that morning. Indeed, she had mimed the lad far too long. Her knuckles met Roberta's jaw with a solid *thunk* and with enough force to spin the larger woman about. Roberta stumbled away and collapsed into an overstuffed chair, instantly losing all desire to engage in further combat with her irascible cousin. Closing her eyes, she stayed carefully still.

Cole quickly stepped to the washstand, wet a cloth, and reached to dab at the small, red trickle of blood that ran from the corner of Alaina's mouth, but she ducked away.

"Don't touch me, Yankee!" she snarled the warning. "Just keep your hands to yourself." She yanked the cloth from him and glowered. "You've done enough damage!"

With a last smug smirk at the recumbent Roberta, Alaina pulled the robe snugly about her and, spinning on her heel, made a haughty exit from the room, closing the door quite forcefully behind her.

Cole dampened another cloth and approached Roberta's chair. She proved rather spritely herself as she snatched the rag from his hand and fairly flew to the mirror. Worriedly, she leaned close to inspect the damage and dabbed gingerly at the visible red mark on her jaw.

"Ohhh!" she wailed. "I'm marred for life! I'll never be the same! She's ruined my face!" Her eyes narrowed menacingly. "If it's the last thing I do, I'll get even with that little bitch."

"At the rate of exchange just witnessed, my dear," Cole returned dryly, "I would suggest a careful approach to this matter of revenge, lest you find yourself hopelessly in debt."

Roberta tossed her head arrogantly. "Lainie's always been jealous of me. She's always envied my beauty and, every chance she's gotten, has tried to hurt me. If that little whore thinks she can get away with this—"

Cole firmly shut the window against the chill breeze. The main storm had moved away, leaving in its wake a light drizzle that splattered against the glass.

"Since she was the virgin in my bed and you were not, Roberta," he smiled at her stiffly. "I would further suggest a more accurate choice of appellations. Those you toss about so casually have a way of coming home to roost."

Roberta grew worried and fretful. "Whatever do you mean, Cole darling? What did Lainie tell you? You, of all people should know she can't be trusted. Why, she even betrayed those poor, helpless prisoners—"

Cole looked at her sharply, and she stumbled to a mute halt. Scowling, he selected a pair of dry trousers from his wardrobe and jerked them on. "She told me nothing, Roberta. And you, my dear, of all people"—the words stung more on the return—"stand witness to the fact that Alaina had no part in that slaughter upriver."

He removed a heavy woolen campaign shirt from the armoire and as he slipped into it, Roberta searched his face for a hint of meaning.

"How would I know that?" she asked cautiously.

Cole paused in buttoning the shirt. "Is it so difficult to understand, madam? The simple truth is that Alaina was the woman I made love to that night—the only one. Therefore, my dear, it was you who played your dirty little trick on us."

"That's a lie!" Roberta panted and struggled to conjure some evidence to bear out her untruth. "A vicious lie! I tell you, Cole, Alaina has filled your head with lies! You were too drunk to remember, but—"

Roberta jumped in trepidation as Cole threw down his boots in front of the straight chair. "You do err, madam. I may have been drunk, but that I do remember." He sat down to tug on the boots. "It always confused me because you were so different from the girl I held in my arms that night. But until this very evening, I could not imagine anyone else in this house being the one. At least, now I know the truth."

Roberta accepted his words with dismay. What she had done was out in the open. Her greatest fear was that Cole would set her aside. Without his money, she would go back to a dowdy and boring existence. She would never go to Washington. She was distressed at the idea of being made the laughingstock of all those drearily garbed widows she had haughtily snubbed.

Plaintively she held out her hands to Cole. "Oh, darling! I only did it because I loved you so much." She decided a mild wringing of her hands and a confused countenance would enhance her plight. "Why, Cole, you just don't know how I yearned for you." She smiled helplessly as she moved to him and slipped onto his lap. "I was beside myself when I found you had been with Lainie. I just couldn't give you up without a fight." She tugged at his hand and brought it to her breast. "Am I not more beautiful? Am I not more of a woman?"

Cole met her gaze without any warmth. "Madam, that little twit of a girl, for all her boyish mien, could give lessons on the art of being a woman at the local bawdy house." He smiled dispassionately. "At least, she's not afraid of a man mussing her hair."

With an indignant gasp, Roberta shot to her feet and drew back her hand to strike him across the face. Cole's eyes never wavered as they rested coldly upon her. But with the most recent experience still fresh in her mind, she thought better of it. She had other ways of cutting through a man.

"She must have proven herself an eager little beggar for you to remember her so well. But then, you seem to have a preference for lewd women, and I can imagine she performed her chores well."

"Chores!" Cole laughed shortly. "Egads, it's true! You approach making love as a labor!"

Roberta lifted her nose primly. "You don't think a lady enjoys being pawed, do you?"

"If sharing some pleasure in the act of marriage is beyond the confines of a lady, then to hell with ladies!" Cole growled. He threw his leather case onto the bed before continuing ominously. "Whatever Alaina is, be assured it was her performance that night that snared you a husband."

"What do you mean?" Roberta hotly insisted, grabbing his sleeve and trying to turn him. "What do you mean?"

Cole faced her and leaned forward until Roberta was forced to sit quite abruptly in the overstuffed chair behind her. Disregarding the tapestry covering, he propped a booted foot on the seat beside her hips and, bracing an arm across his knee, bent down to meet her eyes squarely.

"The one thing that stood out from that night was the pleasure I had with that woman. So, whatever the reason you claim for plotting your trap, you have Alaina to thank for its success."

"I don't believe that," Roberta scoffed. "As I remember it, Daddy took the matter entirely out of your hands."

"Madam, I am a doctor, but then, I am also a soldier.

Do you honestly think a doddering old man is going to frighten me witless? Whatever you might think, my dear, your father was not the most proficient of wardens. I might have escaped had I not gotten my mind entangled with those blissful moments I spent with Alaina."

Roberta twisted her hands in honest dismay as Cole returned stoically to his packing. The silence dragged out an eternity, and she could not stand the suspense any longer. Almost tremulously, she asked, "Are you leaving me?"

"Never fear, my dear," he smiled sardonically. "I will take you to Washington and parade you on my arm as is your wish. I've made my bed and I must lie in it."

"Then where are you going?"

"General Banks is going on a campaign up the Red River. Until a few moments ago, I was undecided as to whether I should volunteer. I have made my decision to go."

"But you could be gone for months! What am I going to do in the meantime?"

Cole leisurely surveyed her ball gown as he hefted his case. "I'm sure you will find some form of entertainment in my absence. I can't believe you'll be greatly deterred from having a good time while I'm gone."

"But, Cole," she whined and followed him to the door where he paused to look at her. "What if something should happen to you? Are there not certain matters you should attend to before you go?"

"If you mean the arrangement of financial matters, my dear," his tone was harsh, "I see no cause to leave my estate to you. You'll be suitably cared for, and if there should be an heir, everything will be held in trust for the child by my lawyer. Otherwise, you'll receive a monthly pension from my holdings." He smiled briefly. "The rest will be donated to charity since there is no further kin."

"What about Alaina?"

"That, madam, is none of your damned business," he returned crisply.

Anxiously she stepped into the hall behind him. "But I'm your wife."

"I'll leave the buggy at the hospital, and when you get word we've moved out, you can send Jedediah for it," he said, ignoring her statement. His eyes moved impassively toward Alaina's closed door as he strode to the stairs. He could hear the click of Roberta's sharp heels behind him and faced her at the head of the stairs. "You might brace yourself, madam, for the move to Minnesota when the war is over."

Roberta's jaw sagged. "Minnesota! That godforsaken place? You can't ask that of a gentle born lady!"

"Madam, I'm not asking. If you wish to go with me, that is your decision, but whatever, I've made up my mind."

Chapter 17

FAR to the northeast, the last squall line crouched like a low range of mountains and dissipated its angry energy with flashes of jagged light. The storm tumbled and roiled, grinding its way across the coastal swamps, moving away from the crystal clear sky of the western quadrant where the moon hung high and bright. In the hushed aftermath of the storm, mists rose from the rivers, lakes, and swamps until a dense blanket of fog lay over the entire Delta. From any lofty pinnacle in the main portion of the city, the tops of taller buildings and houses could be seen as great black boulders in a fretful channel of cottony white, and beyond them, the spidery rigging of topmasts marked where the Yankee fleet lay at anchor on the river.

Across the sleeping city, only a few blocks from the Craighughs' house, Cole Latimer guided his horse and buggy through the eerie, luminescent mists, and the steady clip-clop of hooves and the rattle of wheels were the only sounds that rent the muffled shroud of silence. Tense-faced, he peered into the grayness and silently cursed his own addled brain. Over and over in his mind he berated himself for a fool. How could he have failed to recognize the difference between the two women? They were as dissimiliar as east and west, or, he grimaced, maybe north and south.

He had traveled only a short distance when, in the haze ahead, he espied a dark shape flitting quickly across the road. It disappeared behind a large live oak that grew close upon the curb. As he drew near no other movement could be discerned, and cautious of being waylaid, Cole halted the buggy and drew his pistol.

"You there! Behind the tree!" he barked. "Step out where I can see you."

Though a long moment passed, he received no response. Cole raised the gun, and the double click of the hammer being drawn back echoed sharply along the fog-endued avenue. He was about to call out again when grudgingly a small, slim black figure stepped into view. Cole quickly lowered the pistol, recognizing the trim form of the widow he and Jacques had shared an interest in. Holstering the gun, he tied the reins to the dashboard and stepped down. Politely he touched the brim of his hat as he neared the curb where she had stopped.

"Madam, it seems a foul night and a late hour for a lady to be about unprotected. May I give you assistance in any way?"

The black-bonneted head gave a negative reply, prompting Cole to wonder if everyone was bent on giving him mute answers.

"Do you wish to be taken somewhere, perhaps?"

Again the same movement of the head came as an answer. What else could Alaina do when the moment she uttered a word recognition would dawn with it. She cursed her luck and was beginning to doubt that she would ever be rid of this Yankee. Everywhere she turned, he seemed to be there, ready to ensnare her.

Cole drew off his gauntlets and tucked them beneath his belt. "Madam, as a gentleman I can hardly leave you here without escort. I do not wish to pry, but if you will name a destination, I will deliver you there without further ado. I assure you most humbly that you need have no fear of me."

Alaina scoffed in silent derision. If she could only change the character of her voice as easily as her garb, she would give him an answer. One he would not soon forget.

Cole reached into his shirt for a cigar, then searched in his pocket for a match. This had all the appearances of evolving into a long, decidedly one-sided conversation, and at the current rate of reciprocation, he would do just as well talking to himself.

"Shall we wait together then, madam?" he inquired dryly. "At least until you decide where I may take you. I give you my word, I won't be going until I am assured of your safety."

Inwardly, Alaina groaned her frustration as he

reached back to strike the match on the metal frame of the buggy. The small light flared, and Cole turned to stand patiently in the street before her. He was about to touch the flame to his cheroot when the irritated tap of her toe against the curb drew his attention. His brow raised sharply as he realized the widow's slight stature was just about the right size for—Al—or Alaina. And that little chit—

His jaw clamped firmly on the cigar, he moved the match closer to her veiled bonnet and, with his free hand, lifted the thin gossamer barrier. He stared into Alaina's snapping gray eyes, forgetting the match until the heat of the flame seared into his fingers. Mouthing a startled oath, he flipped it away and shook his hand.

"Did you burn yourself, Captain?" Alaina patronizingly plied him.

"Yes!" he snapped irately, throwing the cigar into the gutter.

"He who plays with fire, Captain—" she chided. "Well—you know the saying."

"I have grown most cautious of wayward lads and warming pots," he observed gruffly. "I shall have to lengthen the list to include widows and matches, or perhaps shorten it to one, Alaina MacGaren."

"As you will, sir. But it was not my doing," she reminded him. "You were the careless one."

"I don't suppose it has occurred to you that you might have told me what really happened that night?" he prodded ill-humoredly. "As I remember it, there was plenty of time for you to warn me before the consummation of the marriage."

"But, Captain," Alaina purred with a tight smile of malice. "You seemed so eager and content. How could I disturb such a blissful state?"

"Dammit, woman!" he barked, then cautiously lowered his voice. "Are you so simple that you cannot imagine why I married her?"

"Uncle Angus did have something to do with it, I believe," she returned flippantly.

"Forgive me," he snorted contemptuously, "for ever thinking that you and Roberta were so different. It seems, after all, that you both think alike."

"And what do you mean by that?" Alaina questioned indignantly.

"Never mind," he grumbled. "It shall be my everlasting secret. I doubt if you'd believe me anyway." Irritated, he indicated her black gown. "Did you take time to pack anything? Or is this it?"

Alaina stepped behind the tree and brought forth her wicker case, but when she glanced up, she found the large, darkly clad form of Cole standing close in front of her. His arms were akimbo, and though the shadow of the wide-brimmed hat hid his face, she detected a note of disapproval in his stance.

"Miss MacGaren, I do not claim to be a gentleman of blood," he stated firmly. "And you most certainly have never professed to be a lady. Nevertheless, let us, in common agreement, strive to portray ourselves as being both gracious and mannerly." He stooped and took the valise from her hand. "If you please, mademoiselle." He bowed, clicking his heels, and swept a hand about in an invitation for her to proceed.

Pricked by his rebuff, Alaina tossed her head and adjusted her woolen shawl more securely around her shoulders. She could well do without this Yankee's advice or assistance. If he wanted the case so badly, she'd leave it with him and make her own way unencumbered through the night. Indeed, she had every intention of walking away from him, but the gutter directly in front of her was filled with water, and she could not easily step across it unless she turned toward him. Lifting her skirts almost to her knees, she drew back a foot, preparing to leap the obstacle. But of a sudden, the night lurched askew, and she was swept from her feet by iron-thewed arms and clasped against a broad, hard chest she remembered far too well.

"How dare you!" she gasped. "Let me go! Put me down!"

"Try harder at being a lady then," Cole admonished, showing not the slightest inclination to obey her. His long stride easily cleared the moat as he mockingly lectured her on the proprieties of being a lady. "A gentlewoman would hardly display her ankles so readily nor carry her own valise when a gentleman is present."

"And do you suggest that a gentleman would handle a lady so rudely?" she scoffed with rancor, yet she deigned to put an arm about his neck and, with a small movement, settled herself more securely in that not unwelcomed cradle. "I declare that in spite of the many threats against his person, Al was treated more gently than this. Perhaps I chose the wrong disguise. You would no doubt have been more at ease with the lad."

"That may be," he murmured distantly and paused beside the buggy. "But I mightily favor your present form above that of scarecrow boy."

His face was so close, Alaina had no difficulty discerning its every detail, and the soft, lazy smile it bore awoke burning memories that, while thrilling, were also most disturbing. The shivery warmth that ran through her completely disrupted her composure. She turned her own face away and thus betrayed the sudden blush that would have gone unseen in the misty darkness.

"Captain, if you please—" She struggled to set a foot to ground. "Your everlasting fondling wears on me. And you, if I dare remind you, are a married man."

Cole placed her quite ungently upon the buggy seat, his anger once more kindled. "A fact which weighs more certainly upon your discretion than mine, Miss MacGaren."

He passed to the rear of the carriage, tossed the wicker case into the boot beside his own baggage, and jerked the canvas cover over them. He returned to her sight and lit another cheroot with quick, taut movements, the flare of the sulfur match displaying a frowning, pensive visage. Alaina glanced away, reading his ire, and slid across the seat to make room for him. As he lifted a foot to the step, however, she placed a hand upon the tufted leather, and when he glanced up in wonder at her delaying gesture, she smiled condescendingly.

"I do miss the case between us, Captain."

"Is it magical, then, that it will protect your virtue?" His tone grew curt. "Shall I fetch it?"

Demurely Alaina folded her hands in her lap and stared down at them. Her voice was soft and low but almost a scream in the misty darkness. "What virtue, Captain?"

His answer was an explosive, "Damn!"

Finding no better comment, Cole mounted into the seat and lifted the reins. After a long moment, he dropped them again and leaned back, resting a booted foot on the dashboard. "You have not yet named your destination, Miss MacGaren. This does make it rather difficult to proceed."

"I have no place in mind, Captain," she confessed.

"I've precious little coin to squander for lodging, as you may well know. I had hoped that perhaps Doctor Brooks might afford me a night's shelter."

"I still have my apartment at the Pontalba place," Cole informed her tersely. "Since I shall be absent for some weeks, you are welcome to make use of it. At least, it would offer you privacy and some time to settle your circumstances."

Alaina jerked her head up with curt laughter. "Of course, Captain, and in those weeks I shall become well established as your paramour. When you return, it will take but a moment or two to bring that fact into being. Oh, wherefore art thou, gentle man?"

"Dammit, girl!" Cole seized the reins again and slapped the horse into motion. "The dregs of your virtue are the greatest stumbling block my temper has ever known." He glared down at her. "I feel most deeply the burden of your present distress and accept that it is in the greater part my fault. I offered the apartment only with the kindest intent." He clamped his teeth down hard on the cigar but, after a pause, continued. "I've had enough of your pettish mewling. You'll stay there, and I will hear no further argument."

Alaina met his dark scowl with a heated glower, but she held her silence, neither yielding nor denying. For a time they wove the streets in stilted truce, while Cole smoked his cigar and let his irritation ebb, finding in its place much provender for thought. Alaina was startled from her own musings by his brief, dry chuckle that did not lend itself to humor but rather some unspoken vexation.

"The night besets you, Captain?" she ventured.

"It has come to mind, Miss MacGaren, that in the past few months three people have entered and affected my life. They had no face I could define, yet each bore the mark of this war. First, there was the ragged boy driven from his home and, I thought, well in need of my attention. Then, I came across a convincingly wayward wench who seared her brand upon my mind and left me searching for a face and a form. And lastly, there was the widow who, though well veiled, had a shape so refined that it stirred my imagination and made me seek her out." He glanced aside at Alaina. "Now I find they are all one and the same. Tell me, Miss MacGaren, am I the richer or the poorer for my new-found knowledge?"

Alaina's frown gradually softened into a bittersweet smile as she stared straight into the mists. "Has it yet been put to pen, Captain, that war is hell?"

The buggy passed on in the darkness, the wheels whirling over the cobbled avenue, the steady clatter of hooves rattling, the seat squeaking, but no further word was spoken between the two as they jounced along. The streets were deserted; the ferocity of the storm had driven even the drunkards to shelter, and for a brief time, in this small hour of the morning, it seemed a city devoid of life.

Cole drew rein and halted the buggy in front of the red brick structure where he had once resided. He stepped down, retrieved her valise, and came around to help her down. She sat stiff and rigid on the seat, and he saw her fine-boned profile tilted obstinately to betray her mutinous thoughts. He could not help but wonder at the grit of this young woman. He had known no other quite like her, and the disturbing fact was that she seemed capable of disrupting his whole life no matter what character she portrayed.

"Are you going to be difficult, Miss MacGaren?" he questioned and recognized the cool disdain of those clear, gray eyes as they turned upon him.

"Is it your desire to see me packed off to Ship Island, Captain?" she asked in a low, hushed voice.

Cole braced a hand on the dashboard and stared at her with a puzzled frown. "I think not. I know you to be innocent of at least part of the charges."

"Then I implore you, sir. Give me some other title. I fear my own is being bandied about in a most frightful manner."

"Of course." He touched the brim of his hat obligingly. "My apologies, madam. I shall be more careful." She could see the shadow of a smile playing across his lips. "Do you have a preference in the matter?"

"None at all, Captain."

With a wry smile, he offered his hand to help her down. "Al doesn't seem to fit anymore. Then, of course, there's Lainie." At her glare, he shook his head and laughed. "I think not."

Cole refrained from resting a hand on the small of

her back as he escorted her to his apartment door, no matter how natural the urge was to lay it there. As for Alaina, she was apprehensive about entering his apartment, for she no longer had the guise of Al to protect her from those eyes that touched her like she had never been touched before. She waited in troubled silence as he unlocked the door, then glanced around as hurrying footsteps came toward them.

"Captain! Captain Latimer!"

A young lieutenant rapidly approached Cole with a hand held out in greeting, prompting Alaina to turn quickly aside. She sensed Cole moving to block the man's view of her and was grateful for that small bit of consideration.

"I heard that you had gotten married and moved out, Captain," the man chortled, eagerly pumping Cole's hand. "What are you doing back here at this unsaintly hour?"

Cole frowned, realizing the lieutenant had not given up his inquisitive ways or altered his reputation as the worst gossip in the Union Army.

"It's been a long night, lieutenant, and my wife has had a considerable shock." And that certainly was no falsehood. "Will you excuse us?"

"Of course, sir. I didn't mean to impose—"

Cole held the door open for Alaina to precede him, set the wicker case just inside the entrance, and lit a lamp before turning to close the portal. The soldier still lingered in the hall and was craning his neck to get a better glimpse of the black-garbed figure. Cole's gaze cooled, and he left the man no other choice but to make a hasty departure as he bade in a flat tone, "Goodnight, Baxter."

He pushed the door shut and listened to the fading footsteps, then turned to find Alaina staring at him accusingly.

"I gave you freedom with my name, but I think you've carried it a bit far, sir. You let the man think I was Mrs. Latimer."

Cole shrugged indolently. "If I let him think you're my wife, you won't be bothered by other men while I'm gone, and Baxter will have little to gossip about when I'm here."

"How cozy for you," she observed with arid sarcasm.

Cole's brows came together in a harsh scowl as her

words pricked his anger. "Perhaps I should consider that you owe me some recompense for letting me marry another woman." His ire grew as he thought about it. "Should I be grateful? Did you enrich my life by your silence? Girl, I would have been far better off had you not played your game with me."

Eyeing him uncertainly, Alaina removed her bonnet and ran trembling fingers through her short-cropped hair. He stood before her, tall and powerful, his face austere, his eyes challenging. Knowing he was right, she found no worthy retort or other trace of the reckless bravado that had brought her through thus far.

"I'll go," Cole announced more gently, recognizing her fear. He carried her valise into the bedroom where he lit another lamp on the bedside table. He looked at her as she came to stand at the end of the bed and found it hard to drag his eyes away from that fascinating visage. How could she have fooled him so completely? "You know where everything is," he stated slowly. "I'll leave a key for you. Be sure to lock the door after I've gone."

"I will," she murmured timidly, lowering her gaze from his.

"Alaina—" The name came from his lips like a wind sighing through the trees. He reached out to caress a short, silky strand of hair between his fingers, but she snatched away and self-consciously covered her head with an arm.

"I told you!" Her voice caught in a ragged cry. "I don't like to be pawed!"

Cole dropped his hand and let out a long, steadying breath. "I'll be back later on this morning and bring some food."

"I don't need your handouts," Alaina murmured. "I can take care of myself."

Cole's gaze skimmed over her casually. "I made my assessments regarding your success at doing that the first day we met, when you were half starved. I haven't changed my opinion since." Returning to the parlor, he removed a slicker from an armoire and moved to the door where he promised, "I'll be back."

He strode out, closing the portal behind him, and Alaina quickly locked it and leaned weakly against it. She could not bear to stay the night in his apartment, to sleep in his bed, to know his possessions surrounded her. He belonged to Roberta, and she could have no part of him.

Anxiously she set to work. She knew what she must do. Though she was weary, she could not stay longer than the moments it would take to change her disguise. She flung open her valise and, stripping the garments from her body, carefully folded them into the case, then donned in their stead the boy's clothes. A long shudder of revulsion passed through her as she once more sooted her face and arms from the blackened fireplace and jammed the filthy hat down over her hair.

As soon as she felt it safe, she left the apartment. This time it was Al who stealthily crept on bare feet down the stairs, but as she rounded the last corner, she found herself face to face with Lieutenant Baxter, bleary eyed and wrapped in a flannel robe and carrying a porcelain pitcher in his hand. Giving not so much as a pause, she spoke his name clearly and accompanied it with a brisk, "Good-morning, suh," and brushed quickly past him. Before the young man's muddled brain could sort this out, the lad had ducked down the stairs and was gone from sight.

Lieutenant Baxter stared dumbly after the boy, considering the dozen or so courses of action open to him, the more rabid of which entailed rousing the whole complex for a search and chase. In his mind he imagined the dour faces of the colonels, majors, and captains as they were rudely roused from their slumber at this ungodly hour. After a moment Baxter shrugged, mumbled a soothing word to himself, and returned quietly to his bed.

Alaina paused in the shadow of the portico to slip on her woolen socks and outsized boots, then moved away from the Pontalba Apartments as casually as a ragamuffin urchin could without bringing unwanted attention down upon his head. She had left Jackson Square well behind when she espied a heavy dray wagon lumbering northward on some early morning delivery. The driver dozed in his seat and took no notice of the lad who swung himself up on the tailgate nor his descent when they crossed the river road.

It was Mrs. Hawthorne's custom to rise early to enjoy the hazy mists of the Deep South's dawns. She usually greeted the sun with a stroll in her flower garden, but this morning she was surprised when she opened her back door and found the small form of "Al" seated on a wicker suitcase and huddled sound asleep against the railing of her porch. With tender compassion, the old woman knelt and, placing her arm about the other's shoulders, gently shook Alaina until the gray eyes fluttered open.

"Come, child," she urged. Raising her guest to her feet, Mrs. Hawthorne guided Alaina to a settee in the parlor where she gently pressed her down and spread a huge knitted shawl over her. The young face gave a brief smile of thanks, but the exhausted Alaina could muster little else.

"Sleep, child," Mrs. Hawthorne commanded softly. "You are safe, and I will wake you when breakfast is ready."

Much refreshed after a hearty breakfast, Alaina leaned back to sip the hot, strong but effective coffee the woman had made especially for her and glanced briefly at the clock. "You shouldn't have let me sleep so late, Mrs. Hawthorne. It's almost ten."

"The rest did you good, Alaina." The woman did not seem in the least bit sorry. "But what's this you tell me about your captain? You wish to avoid him, too?"

"Him, most of all!" Alaina snapped vehemently. "I've just had enough of that simpering bluebelly lording it over me wherever I go."

"I see." Mrs. Hawthorne considered the suddenly irate and nervous young girl for a long moment. "Well! Have you made any plans?"

"I'm going home. Before Briar Hill is sold, I'd like to take a last look at it." It was as much as she would admit, and the thought of some Yankee slouching in her mother's parlor made her throat tighten to a degree that further words would have been difficult.

"But, child, how will you travel?" Mrs. Hawthorne insisted.

Alaina chewed her lip in consternation. "If I told you, the Yankees could make you tell or put you in jail. I just can't place you in that kind of trouble."

Her hostess burst out into carefree laughter, and

when the woman leaned forward, the brown eyes were bright with anticipation. "Listen to me, young lady. I haven't had so much fun and excitement in years. Why, since you came, my blood has started flowing again. I was afraid I was doomed to a dreary, fading end, but now I can hardly wait to see what happens next. In my day I handled better men than any I've seen lately, with the possible exception of your Yankee captain. Do you honestly think I'd let you wander off without helping you? Anyway"—the old woman made an imperious gesture to Alaina's garb—"Doctor Latimer knows about your disguise now."

Alaina chafed at the reminder. "And he knows about the widow, too. That mangy critter will probably track me down just for the meanness of it."

"You've been a boy too long, Alaina," Mrs. Hawthorne observed. "A young lady watches her language more carefully."

Alaina lowered her gaze, remembering Cole's objection to her less than ladylike ways. She had gotten too far into the habit of Al to shake it quickly.

The older woman consulted the clock. "I daresay, your captain will be here before dark. We'll have to move with some speed to see you gone from here before he arrives."

"We?" Alaina's eyebrows rose sharply, but Mrs. Hawthorne had already bustled off into the kitchen. She came back after a moment bearing a small crock filled with a dark brown, ichorous fluid which she placed ceremoniously in the middle of the table.

"This is butternut stain," she explained. "It's used to color wool and other fabrics but few realize it can stain the skin, too. It's quite durable and lasts perhaps as much as a week or two." She paused and her eyes gleamed again with excitement. "If you mixed it with cottonseed oil and applied it right, you could pass as a mulatto."

"But that would be even more dangerous. I could get waylaid or caught as a runaway slave." Alaina had a right to be apprehensive.

Mrs. Hawthorne could hardly contain her bubbling spirit. She leaned closer. "I have a friend across the river in Gretna. He's wealthy and quite independent. He thinks all Yankees are fools and all rebels misguided. I know he will help."

Cole had caught a few hours of sleep in the dayroom at the hospital, then had been tied up setting his various affairs in order for the coming campaign. As soon as he was free, however, he returned to his apartment with a bundle of food and a large clothier's box beneath his arm. To purchase a gown and suitable accessories on Sunday had been difficult, but he had managed to bribe a couturiere to open her shop.

His first light rap on the door brought no response, and though he knocked louder, no sound of movement could be detected in the apartment. It suddenly dawned on him that Alaina might be gone. Dragging forth a key, he opened the door and entered, setting his purchases aside on the table as he called out.

"Alaina? Alaina!" His voice sharpened as he strode rapidly through the rooms. In another moment he found that his first assumption had been correct. She had gone with her meager possessions, not even staying long enough to rest, for the bed was only rumpled slightly where he had left her case.

"Damn!" He was angry with himself for having trusted her, for allowing her to slip through his fingers so easily. He could only surmise that she was well on her way to her destination, wherever that happened to be.

Seeking out Lieutenant Baxter, Cole was told that no one had been seen leaving around the hour he indicated except a tattered little beggar boy. Cole didn't wait to answer the man's inquiries about the youth, but left in a rush. He ran back to his buggy, this time wheeling it about and heading toward Doctor Brooks's. But at the older man's door, the black housekeeper only shrugged at the question put to her.

"No, suh. De doctah ain't here, and no one's been calling terday."

Cole's scowl deepened as he retreated from the house. There was one other place he knew of where Alaina might be, and that was Mrs. Hawthorne's. Anxious to catch the girl before she extended the distance between them to parts unknown to him, he grew increasingly frustrated at the delays and the slow pace of the buggy. He chided himself for having been so misguided as to believe Alaina would actually stay where he had bade her. The little vixen was bound to drive him ragged before the day was out.

When he arrived at Mrs. Hawthorne's, his long strides carried him quickly across the porch where he pounded a fist upon the door until he heard sounds of movement from within. He waited, slapping his gauntlets irritably against a lean thigh, and was soon met with a bright, welcoming smile.

"Why, Captain! What brings you out here?"

"Has Alaina MacGaren been here?" he asked as the woman led him into the parlor.

Mrs. Hawthorne turned wonderingly. "My goodness, Captain, what could you be wanting with her?"

His frown grew ominous, and she saw his eyes flit toward the ragged case which stood where Alaina had left it. He faced her, and the question blazed in his countenance.

"The girl is gone, Captain. There's no need for you to search here for her. She left the baggage behind."

"Where?" he roared. "Where did she go?"

Mrs. Hawthorne shrugged, smiling sweetly, "Texas maybe. She had some friends over there. Or maybe it was Mississippi. Seems like I heard her say her father's people came from there. Or maybe—"

Cole growled, raising the woman's eyebrows, and strode angrily to the wicker case. Squatting down, he flung it open and searched through the widow's weeds, petticoats, pantaloons, threadbare robe, and lastly, the ragged garments of the boy. He came to his feet with a curse. Who the hell was she now? He whirled and found the woman watching him calmly.

"How did she go?" he demanded. "What did she look like? Is she garbed as a boy or girl?"

"So many angry questions, Captain. Tsk! Tsk! No wonder the girl ran away from you," she chided.

"Did you give her a horse?" he inquired sharply.

"Will you have some tea, Captain?" she inquired, pouring a cup.

Cole waved it away impatiently. "Has she horse or buggy?"

"A horse, I think." Mrs. Hawthorne nodded. "But then, it might have been a buggy. She rides very well, did you know that?"

"I don't doubt that in the least," he retorted. "But what disguise is she wearing?"

"Now, Captain." The elder smiled benevolently. "The

girl made me promise not to tell you. And I am a woman of my word."

"And you won't tell me where she's gone?"

"Alaina didn't want me confiding in you at all, Captain." Mrs. Hawthorne spread her wrinkled hands in apology. "I'm sorry. I can see that you are distressed. Do you fear for her safety?"

"Of course," he snapped. "She has no money, no food—"

"I did pack a basket for her, so she won't starve for three or four days at least, but she refused to take coin. She assured me that she could take care of herself."

Cole snorted derisively.

"Captain?" Mrs. Hawthorne looked at him closely. "You seem overly concerned about the girl. Is she kin to you?"

"Only distantly by marriage," he replied absently as he began to pace restlessly about the room.

"A special person then? Perhaps your mistress?"

Cole whirled to face the woman at her bold suggestion. "Hardly!" He hurled the blunt denial. "I thought she was a boy until yesterday."

"Well, that leaves only one thing." Mrs. Hawthorne seemed to settle the fact in her mind and folded her hands together as she made the firm accusation. "You're in love with her."

Cole folded his own hands behind him and struggled to contain his laughter at the ridiculous idea. He leaned forward and began as if to lecture a wayward orderly. "Madame Hawthorne—"

"You needn't be so formal, Captain. I give you permission to use my given name, if you so desire. Tally is what most everybody calls me." She seated herself primly to await his continuance.

"Tally." Cole paused to re-form his thoughts and tried again. "I am a married man of only a few months, and I knew Alaina only as 'Al' before that. I simply feel responsible for the girl. She—uh—has a way of getting herself into the thickest fray and has too much temper to avoid trouble. I only wish to offer her my continued protection."

"Of course, Captain." Her voice and smile were sublimely innocent. "And you've done such a wonderful job, at that."

As he stared down into those warm, shining brown

eyes, Cole had the distinct impression that Tally Hawthorne was both for him and yet against him. From that confusion, he could draw no further argument. He retrieved his hat and gauntlets, then paused beside the door. "Good-night, Tally."

"I really do wish you good fortune in your endeavor to find your girl, Captain. Now good-night."

Cole opened his mouth to reply, but Mrs. Hawthorne was already picking up the tea service as if she had already dismissed him. He left.

Chapter 18

CAPTAIN Cole Latimer rose early in the morning on Monday, the seventh day of the windy month. With a last glance about his apartment, he hefted his saddlebags and departed, relieved that the night of dissatisfied, restless pacing was at an end and that he had some purposeful activity to set his mind to. At the hospital he picked up the orders assigning him as physician to the First Division of the 19th Corps under General William H. Emory and accepted the issue of a surgeon's field kit, a heavy, bulky, leather case curved on the bottom to fit behind the cantle of a saddle. He paused briefly in the doorway of the officer's dayroom to look in, just in case "Al" might have decided to return. His doubts were magnified into disappointment, no less bitter for the fact that he had expected as much.

Passing the posting board, he plucked a handbill he had only casually noted before, but it was not until he had secured passage on the Gretna ferry and found a private moment to himself that he withdrew the parchment from his blouse and read it with more care.

BRIAR HILL

LEGALLY CONFISCATED
estate of the renegade

ALAINA MACGAREN

1500 acres, approximately
600 tillable (appraised)

House, stable, carriage house
intact. Other outbuildings in
need of repair.

Minimum acceptable bid:
$5,000 U.S. Currency
Sealed bids only.
Auction: 12 April, 1864

Cole leaned against the railing of the small steam packet and stared into the roiling river that flowed beneath his feet. He was as sure now as this grunting little boat made noise that Alaina was headed back to her home, if only for a last look. The route of the march would take the army through Cheneyville, from whence, he had been assured, it was only a few miles to Briar Hill. Just maybe, in the passing, he would be lucky enough to catch a glimpse of a familiar slim form.

At Gretna, Cole led the roan into a stockcar of the train bound for Brashear City and the waiting army, then settled himself in a seat in the passenger car in hopes of reclaiming some of the sleep he had lost during the night. But failing to find succor for his tired mind, he was a victim of the sluggard, time. It dragged on interminably.

Major Magruder was anxiously awaiting his arrival at the Brashear City station. The man had stridently protested the orders assigning him to the campaign, but now with Cole as a willing volunteer, he was impatient for his comfortable quarters in New Orleans. As soon as the younger man stepped down from the car, he was at the captain's elbow and bypassed all usual forms of greeting.

"You'll find the medical camp about three miles west on the lakeshore. It's a choice spot, but I must warn you about the mosquitoes. They've grown quite barbarous with so much Yankee blood to feed on." His voice droned on in a rapid-fire summation of orders, directives, and the general state of readiness of the medical cadre, which, he assured Cole, were ready to move on a moment's notice. It was several moments before he paused and cleared his throat. "Any questions, Captain?" At Cole's negative reply, Magruder cheered up a bit. "Good! Then you won't need me, and I'll see to my horse." He took a few steps, then turned back with a languid smile. "I'd wish you good luck, Captain Latimer, but I think your first real campaign will prove to be devoid of any such frivolities."

Most of the units Cole passed on his way to the medical encampment appeared to be in a state of permanent repose rather than readiness for an impending march. Those who had avoided the labor parties lazed about and indulged in pastime inactivities. The medical camp was no exception. In fact, there was even more of a flavor of a Sunday outing that existed in the hospital corps.

The sun was just touching the treetops when the charge of quarters directed Cole to Major Magruder's recently evacuated tent, and the brief southern twilight had flown by the time he returned from the officer's mess. A single oil lantern provided him light as he entered his name in the unit's log and settled himself in.

The eighth of March dawned bright and clear, bearing the promise of continued fair weather. Captain Latimer had risen before the sun and, after a hearty breakfast, returned to the cantonment area to inspect the small detachment that would form his command. He could find no rosters of assignment, and a corporal in the administration tent informed him that no such thing existed and that Major Magruder had been responsible for the organizational matters of the medical unit. With a sense of hovering doom, Cole sought out the sergeant major and together they went out to the vehicle park. There were twenty-five supply wagons and as many ambulances of the sturdy "rucker" type, along with five medicine vans. Cole satisfied himself that these last were well provisioned. The ambulances were new and in good condition. But when he lowered the tailgate of a supply wagon and peered inside, Cole immediately hoped that Magruder had finally fallen into that privy Alaina had mentioned. He turned curtly to the sergeant major, and his first question was as cool as a leftover breath of winter wind.

"Where are the lading bills for these wagons?"

"Ain't no bills, sir," the burly man stated without fanfare. "We just loaded 'em with whatever was handy. The major said it didn't matter. If we came onto a fight, all the wagons would be grouped up anyway."

"And how will we find anything without unloading them all? Perhaps you would like that duty, Sergeant." The sharp tone of Cole's retort left little doubt in the sergeant's mind that an error had been committed. "I suggest you break out the men and get these wagons unloaded so we can sort out this mess."

"But, sir!" The sergeant major subsided into silence under the captain's chilled glare.

"Sergeant," Cole began slowly, almost gently. "If a shell hits this wagon, we'll bandage about four acres of swamp, but not another soldier. The next one contains all the alcohol and laudanum. If that one tips into the bayou, you'll have the happiest bunch of gators for miles around."

"Yes, sir." The sergeant major was properly chastened. "I'll round up the men, sir. Right away, sir."

It was a day to try any man's soul. Rosters had to be made up detailing five supply wagons and five ambulances to each divisional wagon train, as ordered. Drivers had to be assigned to all vehicles, two stretcherbearers and a medical orderly for every ambulance. A surgeon's assistant went with the pharmacy vans, and the vans were to accompany the division commander's staff. Then, all the supplies had to be sorted, apportioned, and reloaded so that the loss of any one wagon would not jeopardize the entire campaign.

By nightfall, a semblance of order had been restored, and the wagons were all reloaded, this time properly. Cole arranged his mosquito bar and was busily assigning random titles to one Major Magruder when a messenger arrived at his tent. The young private saluted smartly and informed the captain that the Headquarters group and the two divisions of the 13th Corps would lead out on the march at sunrise on the ninth. Cole's division, the first of the 19th Corps, would follow the corps staff as soon as the road was clear past the intersection.

It might have been termed an ominous portent that the sun rose in a blood red sky. The day cleared as the mists disappeared with the first warmth, and dark thoughts were forgotten. The division broke camp and moved out on the road in midafternoon, yet was still in sight of the camp that they had just departed when the corps ahead called a halt for the night bivouac. Cole groaned within himself, wondering ruefully if Magruder was heading this campaign.

The tenth dawned gray and foggy, and before the breakfast fires were doused a light rain began to fall.

Cole donned his oilskin slicker and pulled the Hardee hat low as he mounted the roan. Until it was needed elsewhere, he had claimed one of the ambulances as his quarters and left the bulky kit and his saddlebags in that venerable conveyance.

General Franklin's army, though mostly seasoned men, had not been together long enough to meld as a unit. The columns accordioned as they marched, and halts had to be called more and more often as the once-firm, red clay roadway turned into an insidiously treacherous sea of mud. The Bayou Teche bordered on the right, and the dark, black muck of a swamp lay on the left. To leave the road was to pass from doubtful into hopeless.

The rain quickened from a light misting to a genuine downpour and, having attained that state, held it throughout the remainder of the day. The red mud took on a special quality of its own and tenaciously clung to whatever touched it. Indeed, it seemed to be everywhere. When a halt was called for the night, the wagons stopped where they were, and the men sought out the nearest solid, or at least semisolid ground whereon to rest their weary bodies. Campfires flickered into existence as a few found dry tinder, then, with the darkness, a dense fog crept out of the swamp to muffle the twenty-mile-long column. One of Cole's last thoughts before he sank into a much-needed slumber was that the forces of nature appeared destined to keep him from reaching Briar Hill while Alaina was still there. And in the next days he had more cause to despair, for the rain continued without ceasing.

That same drizzling moisture fell on the subject of his musings as she stared with brimming eyes down the long avenue of oaks. The windows of the white house were shuttered and boarded, the front door criss-crossed with planks of wood. It was a large, raised cottage of West Indian influence, possessing a long, sloping roof with dormers and pillared porches on three sides. For Alaina, it was home! Briar Hill! It had taken her almost five days, but she was finally, at last, home.

She slapped the reins against the horses' backs, and the decrepit team splashed on through the puddles that marked the lane, pulling the rickety hearse behind them. One look at the black-draped coffin inside the glass-enclosed burial wagon was enough to dampen the curiosity of onlookers, but barely a handful of people had given any notice to the reed-slim mulatto boy who sat high in the driver's seat, for the yellow banners that waved from the staffs at each corner warned that the hearse bore a yellow fever victim, and most of those she passed had been anxious to keep a respectful distance.

A tall, stovepipe hat came down close over Alaina's shaggy hair, and a long-tailed coat obscured the feminine shape of her. The dye of the butternuts had been used to darken her fair skin, allowing her to successfully pass as a young servant boy taking his dead master home. The hearse had belonged to Mrs. Hawthorne's acquaintance who had proven to be an undertaker. Like the old woman, he had taken to the idea with humor, brushing off Alaina's concern about returning the hearse. "If you're a friend of Tally's, my dear," he had assured her, "I shall count it an honor to be of service. Besides, the wagon is nearly as old as I am, and not worth the bother to bring it back. Don't trouble yourself."

Thus, Alaina had made her way home and in a slow, plaintive voice, had warned away any who had witlessly drawn near. "Stay away! De massah done passed on from de fever, an' de Yankees say he gotta be burned if'n he stays. But de missus jes' want him buried in de ground near de home where he was born."

A canopy of moss-bedecked branches arched high above her head, sifting raindrops of moisture down upon her as she passed beneath them. Memories came flitting back of her last days at Briar Hill and of her hardships when the Yankees had occupied Alexandria in the spring of '63. The enemy had swept away the harvest of the land, confiscating livestock, cotton, and lumber where they could find it and burning homes as it met their moods. Though Briar Hill had escaped the torch, it had not escaped the devastation of its fields and the theft of its livestock and cotton. A few of the planters had managed to hide barges of cotton in the swamps, but Banks had come away well supplied just the same. Still, her own losses had been only superficial when she took into account what she had given up to

Captain Latimer. That night had scored its memory on her soul.

The leaves of the trees were new green, their growth no doubt spurred on by the endless spring rains. The azaleas were in bloom and, even in the heavy mists, were still the same rich, vibrant fuchsia of happier days. But then, it was only circumstances and people who changed in times of trouble. Spring still came with its burst of color and fragrance; the trees remained standing staunchly through grief to bring new life beneath a warming sun or pelting rains.

As she neared the house, Alaina's eyes fastened on the bold red cross that had been painted on the front door of her home, and her spirits struggled beneath the weight of judgment against her. She had been condemned as a traitoress by her own people without benefit of a hearing. The cross bore out their verdict; they would kill her if they could.

On trembling limbs Alaina climbed down from the hearse and mounted the steps. The elusive laughter of her mother drifted through her mind, while the faces of her brothers and father passed wraithlike through her memory. She had been happy living in this house with her family, but nothing was left of the gaiety she had known here. Its charm, like the rest of her loved ones, was gone forever.

Slowly Alaina walked along the gallery to the side of the house, her eyes inspecting every boarded window. Sweet olive shrubs grew thick against the house, and their fragrance wafted up, mingling with the fresh scent of rain. It even smelled like home.

The cookhouse was to the rear of the house, detached from the main structure, and she found only one plank of wood blocking the back entrance to the house. Alaina ducked beneath it, thrusting her shoulder against the portal that had always been hard to open in damp weather. Once inside, she closed the door quickly behind her and blinked at the unfamiliar darkness that enveloped the dining room. Only a ray or two of dreary afternoon light filtered in through the shuttered windows, but an empty, hollow sound echoed with her footsteps as she crossed the room. When her eyes became accustomed to the meager light, she realized that a good many of the furnishings had been removed from the house. She ran to her parents' bedroom and then the parlor, but both rooms were almost barren, only vacant shadows of her memory. Her eyes could not seek and touch and linger on those familiar bits and pieces of memorabilia that had been as much a part of her life as anything that remained. It was like the death of a loved one, and her throat tightened with contained grief.

She wandered listlessly to her own bedroom where most of the furniture remained much as it had been before her departure. In despair she sagged to the edge of the bed, weary, bone tired, and aching inside. A low sob escaped her, and tears trailed down her darkened cheeks. Her thin hands closed in tight fists, grasping the ticking of the bare mattress, as if by dint of will she could hang on to the remembrances associated with her home. Then, she straightened apprehensively as the floor behind her creaked beneath a heavy foot. In sudden fear she sprang up to face the intruder. But as recognition dawned, she stared agog, her tears forgotten, her eyes wide in disbelief.

"Miz Alaina?" the familiar voice questioned uncertainly as the giant black man stepped hesitantly closer. "Is dat you, chile?"

"Saul!" Her shriek of joy pierced the stillness of the house, and in the next instant, she had thrown herself into his bearlike embrace. She wept now with happiness and relief as he clumsily patted her back. "Oh, Saul, I thought you were dead!"

"No,'m," he grinned as she stood back. "Dem Yankees hung onto my tail for the better part of a week, but ah finally threw 'em. Ah didn't dare lead 'em back to you, Miz Alaina."

"I thought you had been taken, so I went to Uncle Angus's," she sniffed.

"Ah been keeping an eye out for you 'round here all along. Ah figgered yo'd come back sooner or later. All dem rumors ah's been hearing, ah knowed yo' was in a heap o' trouble. It jes' seems, Miz Alaina, de lies keep gettin' worse and worse." He tilted his head and chuckled as he surveyed her. "Nobody'd know ya though. Yo' look almost like me."

Laughing and brushing away her tears, Alaina gestured to a bare corner in the room where once an armoire had stood. "But where has everything gone, Saul? It doesn't look much like home anymore."

Saul snorted in disgust. "Dat pack o' jackals down the road loaded up dere wagons and when ah comed back, dey had already taken dere pick o' everything. Ah sneaked over to the Gilletts to have me a look-see, and sho' 'nuff, they got a good parcel of what's missing. When Mistah Jason comes home from de war, we'll go have a gun-to-gun talk wid dem white trash folks. That young whelp, Emmett, he been laudin' it 'round dese parts dat he's de one what run yo' off. He won't be talkin' so fine and mighty when Mistah Jason comes back."

Alaina heaved a tremulous sigh. "I'm afraid Jason won't be coming back, Saul."

"Ah, nooo," he moaned sorrowfully. Tears gathering in his eyes, the black man hung his head and slowly shook it.

"How have you been managing?" Alaina questioned in a quavery voice.

Saul wiped his face on his sleeve and swallowed his tears. "Oh, ah ain' had no trouble gettin' along, Miz Alaina. Ah been living downstairs mostly, and when somebody comes pokin' 'bout, ah hides up in de attic. Dem Gilletts got to nosin' 'round here one night, and ah took some chains and rattled dem all through the house and made spirit noises. Dey hightailed it off ta home right quick. And dey ain' been back since."

"Serves 'em right," Alaina muttered. "They're nothing but a passel o' chicken hearts."

"Yas'm, dat dey is," Saul agreed. "Den a while back a fancy fella come riding up on horseback wid some other men, one of 'em was dat Yankee who said we was spies. Well, dat fancy man said he was gonna buy Briar Hill when it comes up for auction. Him an' the other two men an' a woman wearing britches went off in de woods. Ah followed 'em an' got as close as ah could. Dey buried something out dere, an' ah guess it was one of the men 'cause only three of 'em come back, de fancy man, de lieutenant, and de girl. Ah ain' found nerve enuff to go diggin' up any grave to make sho' what dey buried."

The idea that a murderer would own Briar Hill was bitter gall for Alaina to swallow. Somehow she would have to prevent it. With grim determination, she gritted, "We'll just have to find out what it was they buried."

The black man looked at her dubiously. "Yo' gonna dig up a dead man, Miz Alaina? He's been in de ground fo' some time now."

"If I ever clear my name, I might have to prove those people are murderers in order to get Briar Hill back. It's my home, and I'm not giving it up without a fight!"

"Yas'm," Saul mumbled uncertainly.

"We'll hide the hearse and horses in a shed, then come night, we'll take a lantern out to the woods and see if we can find what that fancy man has hidden."

That evening the pair of vagabonds dined on palatable fare. A few dozen ears of corn were discovered in the barn, and the old gristmill soon reduced the hard kernels to a coarse meal. Several nests remained in the old hen house, and some of the chickens had found their way back after being scattered by the Yankees. From these Alaina purloined a half dozen eggs, and in the cookhouse pantry, she found salt and leavening which, blended with eggs and cornmeal, produced a rich golden cake of delectable flavor. Dried beans were cooked with a thin strip of bacon cut from a slab Saul produced from his knapsack, and to top the meal several large bass that Saul had caught were dipped into the cornmeal and fried. For a few moments at least, the two were able to forget the hardships the war had inflicted upon them as they enjoyed the repast.

The moon climbed on its laborious path into the night sky and gave silvery halos to the low-hanging clouds that flitted across its face. Alaina gathered the wooden bowls and washed them in a bucket of water, then taking up a lantern, she faced the black man expectantly.

Saul heaved a sigh and rose to his feet, displaying no spirit for the task at hand. But obligingly he nodded, "Ah'll get a shovel."

The strange pair began to beat the woods in hopes of finding some trace of what they sought, yet they were almost surprised when Saul came upon a soft spot of ground between two blaze-marked oak saplings. Someone clearly had planned to return to the place.

Most reluctantly Saul set about his labors while

Alaina held the lantern high. The rain had lightened to a fine, sporadic mist, but the soil was soggy and weighty to lift. Almost three quarters of an hour had passed before Saul's shovel struck something—something very hard. For all of his misgivings about the deed, new interest took hold of the black. This was no body the miscreants had buried.

"Miz Alaina, hold the lantern closer," he urged. "Dere is somep'n else here."

He scooped away a spadeful of mud and immediately lost some of his enthusiasm as he uncovered the remains of a hand. It was still loosely attached to an arm that was flung over a large metal-bound strongbox. Alaina recoiled and stumbled back, holding a hand clutched over her mouth. To this point, her bravado had been based on an unwillingness to believe that murder had been committed on the lands of Briar Hill and that Saul had somehow been mistaken. Now, it all came upon her with a crushing truth that made her weak and sick.

"Oh, lawsy, Miz Alaina. Ah was right. Dey kilt him."

Shuddering, Alaina remained mute as the black worked at loosening the heavy chest from the grave. When finally he set it before her, she brushed away the damp soil that clung to the top and held the lantern close. The letters "U.S.A." were stenciled across the face of the box and identified the piece as the Union's property. Curiosity whet her impatience and she twisted at the piece of heavy wire that held the cask shut. The way the hasp was bent suggested that a padlock had once secured it but had been forcibly torn away.

"Stand back, Miz Alaina," Saul directed and, when she complied, swung the heavy shovel against the knot of wire. It broke away after a second blow, and the black threw back the lid. Alaina gasped in surprise and knelt beside Saul. Within the chest were paper-bound packets of Yankee bank notes, several layers deep, which covered a bottom tier of neatly bagged twenty-dollar gold pieces.

"Lawsy me!" Saul whispered in awe.

"It's Yankee money!" Alaina stated the obvious in as much amazement. From between the pouches she drew a sheaf of papers and scanned them briefly. "It's a payroll. Ordered to be shipped out of Washington to New Orleans and from there to the troops under Brigadier General T. Kilby Smith. There's more than a hundred thousand dollars here!" She paused as it suddenly came to her. "Why, this must be it!" She waved the papers at Saul excitedly and hastened to explain as he stared at her in bewilderment. "This is the payroll that was stolen in New Orleans and blamed on me!"

"Ain't dat somep'n? Why, it's jes' like dat fancy man knows fer sure he's gonna be buyin' dis place, and is already movin' in."

Alaina sat back and thoughtfully chewed on the corner of her lip. Her eyes slowly narrowed, and the determined gleam that came in them began to worry Saul. What she was thinking could well mean trouble ahead for them both.

"Miz Alaina—?" he began in an anxious tone, but she stared him down, the gray eyes glowing brightly.

"I'll tell you, Saul, that if Alaina MacGaren is going to be hanged for stealing, no one else is going to enjoy this money either."

"Whad we gonna do with it all, Miz Alaina?"

"For the time being, we'll hide it someplace where we can grab it in a hurry and light out just in case the fancy man comes back."

Saul snorted. "We gonna be in a fine kettle of fish if'n we're caught wid dat money. Wid dat box beneath our nose, it's like havin' a noose 'round our necks just waitin' for somebody to come along and give it a tug. And if dat fancy man ketches us, we ain' gonna be no better off'n dis fella in dis here grave."

"We'll just have to take care that we're not caught —by anyone."

The dirt was pushed into the grave again, and the spot was carefully disguised as before. For the time being, an old trunk in the stable handily received the payroll chest. The tray of the trunk had collected its own trove of broken harness straps and buckles, and this was carefully replaced over the box. Since neither of the fugitives was of a criminal bent of mind, they did not consider that only a frightfully honest man could pass an unopened lid or door and not yearn to know what it conceals.

The turgid river swirled muddy red beneath the lowering sun on March fourteenth. Above the deep green of the trees, the sky was a blaze of color; vibrant pinks and brilliant golds with a patch of bright blue shining forth here and there. The dusty blue-gray haze on the eastern horizon deepened with each passing moment, and from the same direction came a low rumbling noise, like distant thunder, though no flashes of lightning could be seen. Alaina met Saul's apprehensive frown.

"Do yo' hear it?"

She nodded and again scanned the treetops to the east.

"Guns!" Saul stated bluntly. "Big ones! Comin' from 'way over the other side of Marksville. Maybe twenty miles or so off yonder."

"Fort De Russy," Alaina murmured. "It's been manned again, and you can bet the Yankees are trying to take it."

"Dey jes' might be comin' dis way, Miz Alaina." The outsized black twisted his hands in anguished fretting. "Lawsy me, we ain't got nothin' mo' to spare. Dey'll burn us out fo' sure, dis time."

"Nail that Yankee 'No Trespassing' sign on the door again." Alaina launched into the process of decision making with bitter perseverance. "They'll think twice about burning their own property. We'll move into one of the dogtrot cabins for a while." She grinned up at Saul with gleeful malice. "If the bluebellies come riding 'round, I'll just have to pass off as your kinfolk, or some such."

The following day the sound of gunfire stopped. The small fort had been reduced, the garrison taken prisoner, and on the sixteenth the flotilla of Yankee warships moved on up the Red River, guarding thirty-odd transport steamers that carried two divisions of seasoned veterans under the command of General A. J. Smith. Another division, under another Smith, this one General T. Kilby, stayed behind to raze the remains of Fort De Russy and, in exuberant largesse, extended their activities to the surrounding countryside.

Fresh from Sherman's guiding hand, the bluecoats proved expert in their trade of war. Simsport had felt the heat of the Yankee torches, and the lush Avoyelles prairie was not to be spared. Inhabitated by the gentle Acadians who held a rich tradition of freedom and who were generally sympathetic with the Union cause, the area was soon well dedicated with "Sherman's monuments," the stark, charred chimneys that stood unsupported where once spacious plantation homes had been.

The rain continued to muddy the fields of the plantations, while the Yankees laid waste to the prairie. In Shreveport, the headquarters of the Confederate Army of the West, Lieutenant General Kirby Smith, the third of that auspicious surname to be involved, worried and fretted, but could not release General Taylor and his thin Louisiana division to the attack until the scattered grayback Army of the West could be collected from its far-flung posts and concentrated against the advancing Union Army. Major General Richard Taylor, son of Zachary and brother-in-law of Jeff Davis, could only fall back, recruiting volunteers as he went, hoping that somewhere he would have a chance to defend the soil of his native state.

Alaina worried about much the same thing—how to protect her home from the rampaging hordes of blue that came ever nearer. The smell of ash was heavy in the air, and even the rain could not wash the stench away. In her half of the dogtrot cabin, she tried to relax on a hard, lumpy, cotton-filled pallet, but she could only wonder at what new test might beset her now with the Yankees all about them.

When the rain abated, the night grew still. The smell of ashes and smoke became oppressive as an eastern breeze freshened. She pulled the blanket over her head in a vain effort to shut out the hated essence of war. It was a dismal thought that in her attempt to escape Cole she had thrust herself directly in the path of a greater threat. But this time she had her back to the wall, and there was no place else to run.

She waited. The dread was oppressing. Neither she nor Saul dared venture far from the cabin. They lived with the agonizing fear that any moment the enemy would descend on them with flaming torches.

Then, just as it seemed Briar Hill would be next, Kirby Smith's division tired of their sport. The men reloaded onto their steamers and journeyed northward to join the rest of the river-borne army already in Alexandria. But there was hardly a moment of respite before another swarm of Union blue traversed upon familiar soil.

Urging every bit of speed he could from the wearied nag he rode, Saul came on a frantic race toward the cabin, waving his hat and yelling, "Dey's coming! Dey's coming! Far as de eye can see, dey's coming!"

Alaina pressed a trembling hand over her pounding heart and stared at the gasping man as he threw himself onto the porch.

"Dey's got wagons and men as far back as yo' can see, Miz Alaina!" He paused a moment to catch his breath. "Ah seen 'em! A little ways past the creek where ah was huntin'."

"Are they coming this way?" she questioned in a restricted voice.

"We're bound to see some of 'em, Miz Alaina. Dey's sending out patrols right and left."

"Then we'll stay close to the cabin until they pass." Her hands were clenched into fierce, desperate fists. "Pray God they're not bent on burning."

It was the twentieth of March before Franklin's infantry slogged their way as far as Cheneyville and nearly noon before the van of the 19th Corps entered the small hamlet on the northwestern corner of the Avoyelles prairie. Cole arranged to be absent for the afternoon and joined a cavalry patrol that was leaving to scout in the general direction of the Briar Hill plantation. The patrol had gone a little more than two miles when the road bent sharply to the west where it came into conjunction with a creek. A narrow dirt lane led off to the right, and some distance down a crowded group of rather large, sprawling shanties could be seen. All of them bore the appearance of having been assembled of whatever material was at hand and at whatever whim struck the builder. The inhabitants, at least those who were visible, seemed to be white, although the color of the local soil, which was liberally affixed to random portions of unclad anatomy, made that a doubtful observation. As the patrol passed, several naked tots were snatched from the mud of the lane where they had been playing and were quickly taken out of sight. The older children and adults made no effort to approach the road. In fact, they seemed to prefer a goodly distance between themselves and the mounted strangers.

A little farther along the bayou road, several well-built cabins stood in a neat row. Most of them appeared deserted and had apparently been ransacked, for shattered pieces of splintered furnishings were strewn about the yards. Weeds sprouted where once small gardens had been tended, and doors hung askew from broken hinges. Cole noted that a cabin at the far end of the row displayed the only sign of habitation. A thin wisp of smoke curled from the brick chimney, and on the front porch a large black man leaned lazily against a post while he watched the approaching Yankee patrol. Beyond the cabins, another lane penetrated a dense, wisteria-tangled hedge of briars, and the steep roof of a sizable house was visible amid the tops of towering live oaks. A broken sign, dangling from a post near the entrance, still bore the faded letters ______ HILL.

Alaina watched through the dirty window as the Yankee patrol splashed along the muddy road. The two officers who led the short column were almost identical with their Hardee hats and the gray-blue slickers that protected them from the misting rain. But the one on the near side rode taller and straighter astride a roan that was just like—

Her eyes lifted to the man's face, and she used the heel of her hand to clear a spot on the grimy pane. Then she gasped and flattened herself against the wall beside the window.

Cole Latimer! The name flared blindingly bright in her mind. How could he have known where she was? How?

Cole lifted a hand to his companions to signal his departure from the patrol and reined the roan into the front yard of the dogtrot cabin, stopping near the porch where the black stood.

"You belong to this farm?"

"Ah did, but ah is free now," Saul stated. "An' dere ain' nobody 'round here to say any different."

"Have you seen anything of the girl who used to live here? The one they call Alaina?"

The black scratched his head. "Lawsy, Mistah Yankee, it was a while back when she left. All dem white folk what lived in the big house is either dead or skedaddled. Ain' been a white soul 'round here in a long time. Jes' dem Gilletts down de road apiece. But dey's mean folk, an' gen'rally it's trouble when dey comes a-callin'. Massah MacGaren didn't cott'n to dose people 'tall."

"Are you sure you haven't seen anything of the girl?" Cole pressed.

Saul chuckled and shrugged his massive shoulders. "Mos' everybody what stops here asks de same question, Mistah Yankee, and ah tell 'em de same thing."

Cole glanced about in frustration. The black would have no reason to trust one garbed in Yankee blue, and Alaina was too stubborn to come out of her own accord. Yet Cole had hoped for the improbable.

"If you do happen to see the girl, will you tell her that Cole Latimer was here asking about her? Tell her —I'm not going to give up so easily."

The black peered at him closely. "You lookin' to fetch up dat reward for yerself, mistah?"

"Just tell her. She'll know what I mean."

Wheeling his horse about, Cole guided the roan into the overgrown drive and rode toward the house. Beyond the tall hedge, it was like entering a different world. He sat the back of his mount, thoughtfully surveying the house and grounds. He could understand Alaina's hatred of the people who had snatched away her world and reduced her to the level of poverty. Indeed, he was considerably amazed that she had controlled herself well enough to masquerade in the midst of her enemies for better than six months.

The huge, moss-draped oaks rose high above a wide, thickly grassed lawn that almost echoed with the laughter of children at play. For a moment he could imagine a slim, tomboyish girl playing tag with her brothers. The vision faded to be replaced with one of tear-filled gray eyes and the remembrance of a lithe, young form in his arms, then of another time when an all-too-feminine shape flitted past a moonlit window. It seemed he would never be free of those ghosts; they haunted him wherever he went.

Drawing closer to the house, Cole saw that the lower windows and doors were boarded up. A handbill fluttered on the front door over a boldly painted red cross. It was this that roused a feeling of anger in him. Good lord, the girl could hardly bear the sight of blood! How could they condemn her as a murderess?

He urged the roan on into the back yard, bringing a muttered curse from Alaina. She flew to the back door of the dogtrot cabin and carefully slipped out, clutching the wool coat close about her neck. She ran along the line of cabins until she came to the row of magnolias that bordered the yard. At the back of the house, she crouched behind some shrubs where she could watch him as he looked about. She was not about to trust a Yankee, no matter how intimately she had known him.

Cole's eyes flitted over the stable and carriage house. As warranted, they were still intact, though both stood open with sagging doors. Behind these buildings, at the edge of a wide field, more sheds and barns stood, some of them in a sad state of repair. He halted his mount at the gate that opened on to the field and gazed about him, suddenly plagued by a feeling of sadness that he had missed meeting the MacGarens as a family. To have nurtured such an interesting individual as Alaina, he could only consider that they had been well worth knowing.

As he turned his mount away from the gate, his eye caught an odd shape in one of the sheds. Curious, he drew rein and dismounted to inspect the tarpaulin-draped conveyance. It proved to be a glass-sided hearse complete with coffin inside and well splattered with dry, red mud, the same with which he had lately become overly familiar. Yellow flags hung from the staffs at each corner, and Cole knew the portent that they carried. Reaching a gloved hand in, he lifted the lid of the coffin. Much to his relief, the thing was empty. He grimaced and dropped the dusty canvas back into place. At least he wasn't ready to ride in one of these contraptions yet, or, he hoped, anytime soon.

He passed his hand reflectively over the mud-crusted wheel, then slowly returned to his mount. An image taunted his thoughts and began to jell into a firm belief. He could almost see the yellow-bannered hearse emerging from the mists of his mind with its small, slim driver. Disguised as a boy, came the answer that settled his long-unsatisfied question; she was wearing britches again.

He swung onto the roan's back. The patrol was far ahead by now, and he would have to hurry to catch them. Lone Union officers were not particularly popular in these parts, and Briar Hill roused memories that were best put aside for the time being.

Alaina held her breath as he rode leisurely past her hiding place. He seemed in no rush to call back the patrol, and it was only after he had gained the main road that he kicked his horse into a gallop.

She could not resist going back to check on the hearse, and on the way passed the shed where she had stabled the horses before Saul had moved them to a hidden copse in the swamp beyond the fields. A small flutter of white high on one of the doors caught her eye, and when she drew near, she saw it to be a folded piece of paper wedged into a sheltered crack. Unfolding it, she stared at a handbill that announced the pending sale of Briar Hill and which gave her name in bold print as a renegade. Turning it over, she found a penned message.

> "Al: You should cover the fresh manure in here. It's a dead giveaway. Wish to see you in N.O. when I return. We have matters of importance to discuss.
>
> C.L."

"What was dat Yankee pokin' 'round here for, Miz Alaina?" Saul questioned as he hurried toward her.

She refolded the note and tucked it within her bodice. "I guess he was just curious about Alaina MacGaren like everyone else is."

"He sounds a mite more determined 'an mos'," the black grunted.

Alaina nodded in silent agreement. This was one Yankee she had the feeling she wasn't going to shake so easily.

Chapter 19

THE war ground inexorably on. The armies in the east still faced each other across the Rapidan and prepared for the spring offensives. The same Butler of New Orleans fame, led an army up the James to threaten Richmond. In the central theater, Sherman refined his tactics on a march through northern Mississippi to Meridian and back, while Steel set out from Little Rock toward Shreveport to divert some of Kirby Smith's forces away from Banks's thrust up the Red River.

For the South, there was little to cheer about. General Forrest led his small band of cavalry on a raid northward through western Tennessee and Kentucky. Bragg, having been driven back across the Chickamauga, was relieved of his command and replaced by General Joe Johnson, who proceeded to fight a flawless retreat to Atlanta. In Louisiana General Dick Taylor reluctantly fell back ahead of Banks and bided his time waiting for reinforcements.

General Banks, on the other hand, proceeded quite leisurely in the execution of his campaign. After he dallied in New Orleans to attend the inauguration festivities, he joined his troops in Alexandria, arriving by steamer, and ordered them to march on the twenty-ninth, while he himself, an ex-politician, stayed to witness the April first election. He chose the easier form of travel once again and joined his men the evening of the second. Finally, on the sixth, General Banks and his troops marched out of Natchitoches on what was designed to be the last leg of their journey. Their aim was to take Shreveport and it was obvious to Banks, and he said as much, that the Confederacy could field no army capable of defeating his thirty thousand–plus, tried and true, brave and blue.

But Dick Taylor had reached the end of his tether

and refused to leave his state without a battle. The place was Sabine Crossroads, and many a Union soldier would remember the name henceforth with a shudder. It was here that Banks allowed his lengthy column, the units separated by two- and three-mile-long wagon trains, to be attacked by a determined force of some nine thousand Confederates. The gray army executed well, rolling the long blue lines back upon themselves until the battle became a rout. Darkness gave Banks a breather, and he collected his dispirited force at the small village of Pleasant Hill where he braced himself in readiness. The next afternoon before dusk Taylor launched another attack on the Union's left flank in a left-wheeling movement. On the verge of another rout, the Confederates were caught on their own right flank by A. J. Smith's veterans and were themselves set to flight. It was a repeat of the day before, but in reverse, and as on the prior day, darkness put an end to the conflict.

Banks was elated with his success, but his generals advised retreat, all but Smith who had to be ordered to cease his pursuit of the rebels. Across the field of conflict, Taylor retreated to the nearest water and made camp, only to be roused in the early morning by his superior Kirby Smith who, having learned of the defeat, ordered Taylor to withdraw his force to Mansfield. Thus it was that both armies retreated from the battlefield, Taylor in disgust, Banks in disgrace.

The Union Army withdrew to Grand Ecore and the protection of the heavy guns of Porter's fleet, that same which had suffered a severe chastisement from the Texan, Green, and his western horsemen as the flotilla tried to force its way up Loggy Bayou. The blue-clad soldiers proved much swifter on the countermarch and reached Natchitoches in a single day, but it was a wry footnote to the battle that most of the non-walking wounded had to be left to the tender mercies of the Confederates as some unthinking soul had ordered the wagons back before the onset of the battle and sent the medical supplies with them. It was this predicament that caught Captain Latimer between the cruel jaws of fate from which he was not to escape unscathed.

A diet of catfish, chicken, eggs, and an occasional snared rabbit had sufficed for the occupants of Briar Hill for three weeks or more. The thought of the sugar-cured hams hanging in the Gilletts' smokehouse whetted the palates but gave no sustenance to the body. A planned foray to the Gilletts' curing shed seemed the only way to satisfy their cravings.

Alaina reapplied the butternut stain with as much repugnance as when she had dressed the part of Al. Saul fetched one of the horses from the hiding place in the swamp, and the two miscreants set out as dusk descended on the land. Some distance away from the Gilletts' dwellings they left the mount securely tied at the edge of a stand of trees from which, if necessary, a rapid flight could be made. The approach to the smokehouse was made stealthily, for the members of the loose-knit family were given to wanderings at odd hours. The sun continued to sink, touching the horizon, as Alaina and Saul snaked their way beneath thick brush and found shelter behind a fallen log at the edge of the Gilletts' poorly defined back yard.

A dozen feet away stood the sturdy log structure that served the clan as a smokehouse, and beside the waist-high door, lazed the redoubtable figure of Emmett Gillett, that selfsame one whose proposal to Alaina a year earlier had roused such mirth as to cause her to laugh in his face before she got down to the matter of driving him away at gunpoint. He also had the honor of being the one who had reported her as a spy to the Yankees.

A door slammed, and a cheery whistle wheedled its way through the deepening darkness as a smaller, slimmer lad drew near, bearing a lighted lantern which he hung on a pole near the smokehouse.

Emmett straightened and hitched up his pants. "Wha'cha doin' out hyar, Tater?" he demanded authoritatively.

"Brought ya a light." The lad adjusted the lantern's wick until the flickering stopped. "Yer pa didn't want ya to hurt yerself in the dark, an' all."

Emmett eyed the youngster suspiciously, but failed to pin down the insult. He decided his neophyte needed to be impressed by a recount of his derring-do. He sucked in his sagging belly, drew back his narrow shoulders, and rocked up on the balls of his bare feet.

"Yassuh, Tater. Ah jes' 'bout captured this hyar Yankee all by m'self." The young man strutted and patted the black Union holster belt that fitted tightly about his broad waist.

"Ah, Emmett! Ah knows ya seen dat Yankee a-floatin' in a boat down on the bayou this morn'n, and you comed arrunnin' up hyar screechin' fer yer pa."

"Ah didn't screech!"

"Did so! I heerd ya."

"You listen, Tater Williams. Pa gived me this gun 'cause ah captured this here Yankee."

"Aw, Emmett, yer pa jes' let ya wear it for a lil' bit whilst ya watched the door, so's ya wouldn't squall so loud 'bout being in late fer supper. Why, if dat Yankee comed out hyar, yer skin'd fall empty right here in the dirt 'cause you'da outrun it."

" 'Tain't so! I ain't skeerd o' no Yankee. Y'all jes' watch!" Emmett picked up a heavy cane pole and, thrusting it through the narrow slot in the door, whipped it around viciously, then bending low, he called in, "Hey, Yankee. You awake in there?"

The stick jumped and jerked inward a little bit as if someone weakly tugged on the other end. Tater whooped and Emmett seized the thick butt of the pole with both meaty paws lest it be snatched away from him. A split second later, his eyes flew wide as he was hauled smartly forward. His forehead slammed against the rough logs of the smokehouse, and he let out a bellow of pain as his knuckles were scraped hard against the narrow slot and the cane pole disappeared within. Before he could gather himself and rise from his knees, the pole reappeared with a vengeance, catching him in mid abdomen and throwing him backward into a slickery puddle of mud.

"You open this door, toad," a hoarse voice rasped from inside, "and I'll show you just how wide awake I am."

Behind the log where she crouched, Alaina's hand tightened on Saul's arm. Glancing at her in wonder, the black saw her face taut and rigid in the meager light. Her lips barely moved as she whispered savagely, "We've got to get that fool Yankee out of there."

"Miz Alaina?" Saul whispered back. "We don' need no ham dat bad. Let's go find us some nice chickens."

Angrily Alaina turned to stare at Saul, then she realized he had not read her mind and did not comprehend her reasoning. She rolled over and leaned her head against the log. "No. Forget the ham. I mean we got to get that Yankee out of there."

Emmett got to his feet with a curse and sucked his skinned knuckles, glaring toward the slot in the door. "You jes' better watch it, Yankee," he mumbled above Tater's uproarious guffawing. "I might jes' shoot you clean through with this here gun."

"Yer pa said if you so much as pulled that pistol outa that holster," Tater reminded his cousin breathlessly, "he'd strap yer backside good."

"You get yerself up to the house wid the rest o' the chilluns," Emmett barked. "Ah is got mah work to attend to, an' ah cain't be jawin' wid no youngun's."

Tater seemed willing to comply, and the evening grew still as Emmett strove to ignore the drying mud on his backside. In the darkening shadows another form soon approached, and a young girl of rather startling proportions moved into the circle of light cast by the lantern.

"Hi, Jenny." Emmett waxed more cheerful. "Ya want me ter bring the Yankee out fer a look?"

"Yer pa said ain't nobody to touch that door," the girl informed the young man tersely.

"Uh—Jenny—uh, ya want to go over behind the smokehouse an'—uh, talk fer a while?"

"Ya knows ah is spoke fer, Emmett. Willy'ud break yer head fer jes' sayin' that—if'n he knew."

"Aw, Jenny, he don't have ter find out." The young man scuffed his feet in the dirt.

"Anyway, yer ma sent out some soppin's an' a glass of milk ter tide ya over." Jenny held out a mug and a tin plate heaped with biscuits and gravy.

"Cain't ah come in and eat supper now?" Emmett moaned.

"No! Eddie will be out to spell you in an hour or two," the girl replied.

"An hour or two! Why, I've been here all aftahnoon!"

"You ain't been out here no more'n hour as yet, an' yer pa says ter keep walking so's yo' don't fall asleep standin' up."

"Well, guarding this Yankee is hard work!" Emmett protested.

"Hard fer you, maybe. Course keeping awake is hard enough for you."

"Hain't nobody else working this hard," Emmett called after her departing form.

The last of the brief twilight faded, and Emmett was alone with his charge. The chore was wearisome. and he yawned until his jaws fairly cracked. He paced back and forth well out of reach of the cane pole. The clouds were thick overhead, and the lantern's weak light made long, eerie shadows shift and move as it swung in the light breeze. Small sounds came with the darkness, and the young man struggled with an imagination that filled the night with stealthy Yankees. He wished heartily that his pa hadn't been so specific about taking out the Remington pistol. He could have used the succor of the well-oiled butt in his hand.

He jumped as a small, scuffling sound came from the shrubs, and he thought he caught a glimpse of a fleeting skinny shadow. "Tater? That you?" A long silence answered him. "Tater Williams, y'all come out here, right now! Don't you hassle me none, you li'l pinkie. Ah got a dangerous chore ta see to."

There was only more silence, and the man shrugged, trying to whistle through dry lips. He turned to resume his strolling, and a trembling gasp choked in his throat. An immense black giant who towered head and shoulders above him, stood less than an arm's length away. The ogre's eyes flashed with yellow fire in the reflected lantern light, and massive arms raised up to seize him. With a quaking squeal, the terrified Emmett wheeled and fled a full four paces before he measured his length solidly and with a meaty *thunk* against the unyielding wall of the smokehouse. Slowly, languidly, he sagged into the dust, having escaped his demons the hard way.

Saul bent and rolled the limp form over, nodding his head in relief as he took in the slow, shallow breathing and the rapidly swelling knot on the young man's forehead.

Alaina came to Saul's side like a flitting shadow and gestured for him to take the holster and pistol from the still form. She bent at the door, struggling to shift the heavy log propped against it, then stepped aside quickly to avoid the sudden threshing of a bamboo pole.

"Here! Stop that!" she hissed into the slot. "We've come to help you."

She tapped Saul on the shoulder and pointed to the log. He moved it away with an easy swing of his powerful arm, then the black returned to the task of binding the slumbering Emmett while she pulled the low door wide, knelt, and gestured for the occupant to come out.

Cole Latimer dragged himself through the half-sized portal and leaned weakly against the outer wall, sucking deep breaths of clean, fresh air into his lungs, while his benefactors gagged the erstwhile guard and thrust the trussed one into the dark hole he had just evacuated. The smaller of the pair entered the smokehouse, and a moment later reappeared with a ham. The door was closed, and the log propped carefully back into place.

Saul took Cole's arm over his shoulder, while Alaina followed with a leafy branch, carefully erasing all signs of their presence. They passed across spongy ground, through a thick grove of trees, and came at last to where the horse was tethered. Cole was hoisted unceremoniously onto the steed's bare back and given a handful of mane. Saul led the horse out across open fields and Alaina came behind, rearranging sod, replacing twisted grass, brush, and otherwise disguising their passage.

They pushed through a thick hedge where the smell of magnolia blossoms was heavy in the air and to the back side of a large, unlit house. There was something familiar here, but through his feverish haze Cole could not quite place it. He was lifted down, and the small one led the horse away to a hiding place, while the big one again took his arm and half carried him into the deserted structure. After a while the little one returned, and there was much scrabbling in the darkness. There was a rasping scratch of a match. A candle was lit, then another. The dim forms of his companions moved about the meagerly furnished room. The two came to squat beside him, then the small one began to laugh, while the large one, whom he saw now as a black man, joined the mirth with a broad white-toothed grin. Cole could not find the joke, and stared at them in confusion until the smaller one reached up and snatched off the hat, shook out the dark hair of a short yet unmasculine length and turned so the light could strike her face.

"Alaina!" Relief flooded through Cole. "My God, Alaina!" His words seemed a prayer of thanksgiving.

Alaina grew serious as she reached out a trembling hand to touch his thigh. The front of his right trouser leg, from outer hip to knee was split and showed the darkly stained cloth of a makeshift bandage. In the dim light the entire leg looked greasy wet with fresh blood. His boot was sticky with it, while the rest of his uniform bore the dried mire of the swamps through which he had wandered. Weakly he slumped back against the floor, and with a sigh, closed his eyes, yielding up his tenuous grasp on consciousness as he gave in to the peace of security, however temporary, and the utter fatigue that raked him.

Alaina stared down at the sleeping man, and when she spoke her voice was sharp in the darkness of the room. "Saul," she opened with sudden resolution, "I think we had better get the captain into a bed."

"But, Miz Alaina." Saul was agog at her suggestion. "De only bed in de house is—!" It would have been unheard of in a day long past that a young lady would have suggested that a man occupy her bed, whatever the cause. Yet it was a clear statement of the times that such gentility was no longer practical, and Saul finally accepted as much.

Alaina sensed his surrender. "Hurry, Saul! He may be bleeding to death."

With no further reservation or objection Saul gathered the wounded Yankee in his stout arms and followed up the stairs as Alaina led the way with a lamp. She opened the door to her own bedroom and ran to throw back the bedcovers, then stood aside as Saul lowered the mud-crusted captain to the mattress. She winced as Saul straightened the blood-soaked leg, bringing a disturbed moan from Cole.

"You'd better see how bad it is first, then we'll try to clean him up." Alaina began to tug off a dirt-caked boot. She knew the bounds of her limitations and relied upon the black to pry away the bandage that was stuck fast to the wound. Her stomach tightened precariously as the filthy rag was lifted away, revealing a gaping hole in Cole's thigh. Dread shivered through her with a coldness that was oppressing, and a vision of a sheet-draped litter being taken to the brick morgue flashed through her mind. Angrily she pushed the thought away, rejecting the possibility, yet her lips moved in a silent, fervent prayer.

"Ah ain't no doctah, Miz Alaina," Saul commented as he examined the wound. "But ah guess it's bad enough so's we gotta get him to someone who can take care o' dis here wound proper."

Alaina chewed her lip worriedly. "We can't trust any doctors around here. We'll have to get him back to a Union hospital—"

"But where is dat, Miz Alaina? 'Ceptin' dis un, ah ain' seen a Yankee for days—jes' Confed'rates beatin' the bushes. Ah heerd dey is holed up in Alexandria, but dere's a lot o' gray 'twixt here an' yonder. How we gonna get him through?"

"I don't know. I don't know," she moaned. "Doctor Brooks is the only one I would trust, but he's in New Orleans—and it's a long trip."

"No tellin' when dem Yankees are gonna pull out o' Alexandria, Miz Alaina. We might get him dere, and dere wouldn't be no Yankee doctah to tend him. 'Pears to me it might save us a lot o' runnin' 'round if we head straight fer New Orl'ans."

"Maybe you're right, Saul," she sighed.

" 'Til den, maybe I jes' better wash up dis here leg o' his, and see what ah can do to patch it up."

"I'll start a fire and boil some water. As long as we're at it, we might as well give him a bath."

"Yo' think yo' might be able to fetch up a needle and thread to sew dese britches back together again if'n ah rip open de seam?" Saul asked as she crossed to the bedroom door. "It might hurt him a mite if ah tries to pull dem down over dis hole in his leg."

"I'll lace it with twine if I have to," she returned with determination. "Go ahead."

Alaina fairly flew out to the cookhouse. Swinging a caldron of water over the heap of dead, gray ashes in the large hearth, she set about making a fire. With the Confederate patrols ranging the countryside, there was even more reason to be cautious, but with darkness deeply upon them, it was fairly safe to light a small fire.

She utilized the lift located in the fireplace wall in the main house to haul up a tray of salves and implements her mother had used for tending the minor cuts and scrapes of her family, then threw in a stack of linen towels and sheets, items which the Gilletts cared little about since they were too lazy to use anything more than a few filthy quilts in the wintertime and completely shunned bathing with soap and water. Her bedroom was directly above the dining room, and the chute, hidden behind small doors beside the fireplaces, ran from first floor to second. A rope on a pulley worked the moving shelves that could be raised or lowered to either elevation. She rapped her knuckles on the inside wall of the shaft to signal Saul that it was coming up, then she pulled on the rope until the shelf reached her bedroom.

Hurrying upstairs with a large pan of hot water, she found that Saul had stripped away Cole's filthy clothes and left them in a heap beside the bed. As she entered, he hastened to cover the captain's bare midsection with a towel, not wanting to shock her sheltered values as well as protecting his own naiveté. Alaina did not pause.

"I'll bathe him," she stated bluntly. "You tend his leg."

"Miz Alaina, if yo' don't mind me askin'," the black approached the subject hesitantly. "Why is dis here Yankee so all-fired impo'tant to y'all? Ain't he the one what come lookin' fer ya?"

Alaina began ripping up one of the sheets for bandages. "Why, he's Miss Roberta's husband."

Surprise etched the black's visage. "Miz Roberta done married a Yankee? An' wid Mistah Angus hatin' 'em?"

"He still does, and he found out why with this one," she answered, then wrinkled her nose as she glanced briefly at the raw flesh of the injury. "We'd better get to work before the captain bleeds all over the mattress."

"Yas'm," Saul agreed, yet with concerned curiosity, he contemplated his young mistress as she bent over the Yankee. He had seen her this distressed only once before, when she had tended her dying mother. Yet it was equally true, as it was with all the MacGaren clan, that whatever venture Alaina set herself to, she approached it with a simple but complete commitment.

"He's feverish," she said, pressing her hand alongside Cole's neck.

"Maybe ah better put a poultice on dis here wound jes' ta draw out any infection."

"Anything to help him," she murmured in distraction as she gazed down at Cole. An occasional groan parted his lips, and at times his eyes would flicker open briefly as if he wandered through a mild delirium. There were dark circles beneath the thick lashes, and his face looked gaunt and ashen beneath the bristly growth of a beard. *Don't let him die,* the prayer went through her mind over and over. *Don't let him die.*

For a time they worked over him with only the murmur of an occasional word spoken between them, while in his stupor Cole groaned and twisted away from the large, black hands that diligently cleaned and worked at his savaged flesh. The muscles jerked in the leg as the pain seared through the unconscious man, rousing him momentarily to awareness. He stared with fever-glazed eyes at the small, shaggy head bent over him as she gently washed the hard-thewed arms and furred chest with warm, soapy water. Weakly he raised his hand from the mattress, reaching to touch her and murmuring her name, but the effort cost him much in strength, and almost as quickly his arm fell back upon the bed and he retreated once again into the soft, dark world of oblivion.

Saul glanced wonderingly from Yankee to mistress, then frowned and gestured to the wound. "Yo' can bet dere's somep'n still in dat hole. Doan know jes' what, but if it's lead shot, it'll poison his blood if it ain't got out."

Worry drew Alaina's brows together. "But can't you take it out?"

"It's in dere too deep, Miz Alaina—near to the bone, ah'd say. 'Sides, ah ain't got nothin' ter get it out with."

"Can we get him to New Orleans?"

"Doan know, Miz Alaina. Maybe wid a poultice and wrappings on his leg, we can get him back dere in no worse fix dan he's in right now—maybe even a li'l better."

"Come daybreak, you'd best scout around and see just where we can get him through. We're likely to see less Confederates going south."

The black laid a poultice on the wound, and bound it all tightly in order to press the ragged edges of the gaping hole together, then held him up while Alaina smoothed a clean sheet beneath the captain. Once the balm had been applied to the injury, Cole rested easier, having entered into a deeper sleep that even their ministerings could not disrupt. Alaina shaved the dark stubble from his face, and with his cheeks devoid of the prickly growth, he looked more like himself, making her suddenly and acutely conscious of his near nudity. In the dim lamplight, his bronze-hued skin showed dark against the sheet. The long, muscular form was superbly proportioned, with broad shoulders tapering to narrow hips and lean thighs, and a furring of hair dwindling to a thin line that traced downward over his flat belly. Alaina felt her cheeks grow hot as she realized that her gaze was lingering overlong, and she hastily unfolded a sheet over him.

"You sit with him for a while, Saul. I'll make us some supper." She excused herself quickly and left without waiting for the black's nod. She sought the night air to cool her flaming cheeks, and it was a long time before the trembling in her fingers ceased.

Chapter 20

COLE Latimer lay still for a moment. A small sound from somewhere nearby convinced him that he was awake. It was daylight, and from the comfort of the mattress beneath him, he guessed that he was in a bed and naked between clean sheets. It was beyond his ken how this could be. The leg still ached with a dull, throbbing pain, but when his finger touched it, he found it snugly wrapped in a neat bandage. Slowly he opened his eyes, and his amazement was complete as he saw the lace-edged canopy of the tester bed wherein he lay.

A slender form dressed in boy's clothing moved past the bed, and though the skin was stained brown, he'd have known that pert profile anywhere. He tried to wet his dry, parched lips with the tip of his tongue and called out to her.

"Al?" His best effort was a hoarse croak.

Alaina turned quickly and hurried to the bedside, her eyes questioning as they searched his face in anxious concern. "How do you feel?"

"Can you get me a drink?" His voice was little more than a rasping whisper.

"If it's permitted, doctor," she teased gently.

He nodded slightly and smiled, closing his eyes again. Her footsteps moved away from the bed, then returned. He opened his eyes to find her watching him closely. Accepting her assistance, he raised slightly and drank deeply to satisfy his burning thirst. The fever was gone, but every muscle in his body ached, and there seemed no ease from the pain that ebbed and flowed through his leg.

"Would you care for something to eat?" she asked. "There's some soup and cornbread down in the cook-house."

"Enough to spare?" He searched her face as he leaned back into the pillow.

Alaina chuckled ruefully. "Whether they know it or not, the Gilletts have been contributing to our welfare. They helped themselves to our livestock right along with the Yankees, so I figure they owe us."

"I could stand some food," he admitted. "My backbone has been rubbing a hole in my stomach for the past few days."

The thick bean soup, seasoned with ham and vegetables, was accepted with ravenous appreciation. After Alaina folded a quilt behind his back and fluffed the pillows over the padding, Cole ate heartily, brushing away her attempt to assist him. When she took the tray away several moments later, he felt much strengthened by the nourishment. Still, he was reminded of his limitations by the piercing pain that stabbed through his leg when he tried to move it.

Alaina's face mirrored his grimace. "Still hurts?"

Cole lightly kneaded the bandage over the wound. "I fear I've taken a piece of a cannon shell."

"What happened? I thought doctors usually worked well back from the battlefields."

It was a story as frustrating as the inspection of Magruder's carelessly packed supply wagons. After the first day's defeat and the second day's victory, to be ordered to leave the wounded and pull back, he had found the whims of command too much to bear. He remembered the beginning of it all rather vividly. He had been called to assist the wounded of a forgotten battery that had been badly mauled, and as he was so involved, an argument with an arrogant colonel, Franklin's provost marshal, had developed over the proprieties of deserting helpless casualties. With stubborn tenacity he had remained with the injured, and with the assistance of the private who had found him and a lightly wounded sergeant, he had labored to drag a pair of wagons from the swamp where the rebels had pushed them. They had chased the unit's hobbled mules through the woods until four had been caught to form a pair of teams. The loading of the wounded into the wagons had just been accomplished when a Confederate patrol appeared on the brow of the hill above the glade. He had ordered the sergeant and private to flee with the wagons while he himself seized one of their new Henry repeating rifles and tried to hold off the adversary, giving the wagons as much of a head start as he could afford. Unfamiliar with the rapid-fire rifle, the rebels had taken cover, apparently confused as to how many they faced. But they had lost no time in bringing up a breech-loading rifled cannon that they had captured from the Union cavalry on the first day's battle and were soon lobbing explosive shells down into the clearing.

From that point on, Cole's memory was somewhat vague and confused. After giving the wagons the lead they needed, he had scattered the gun crew with a final volley from the Henry, then had smashed the rifle on a shattered cannon barrel and had sprinted for the roan. He had just vaulted into the saddle when another shell struck a pile of powder kegs, and it had seemed, then, as if the whole clearing had exploded. He had a vivid recollection of a tall pine beginning to topple toward him and a heavy blow on his thigh. There had been a time of clinging to the back of the crazed horse as it thrashed through the swamp while shots and shouts rang out from the rear. He remembered discovering his injury and effecting a crude bandage, then nothing but long hours of blinding sun and sweltering heat, gnawing flies, stinging mosquitoes, and a variety of animals who had not seen enough of man to do more than stare at the strange apparition that passed. A grinning alligator had raised its head and, with slitted, cold-blooded eyes, had watched his cautious progress as the horse gave it wide berth. Darkness had come, then the sun again, and a night of shivering beneath a moss-bedecked live oak during a downpour, after which everything seemed to run together in a kaleidoscope of fleeting visions, steaming days and bone-chilling nights filled with gnawing, stinging insects of every sort, and the horse stumbling along the road. He had tried to guide the steed generally southward and eastward, reasoning that sooner or later he had to hit the Red River. There had been a vague familiarity about the area, but his dazed mind had not been able to pin it down. When he had come across a pirogue on the bank of a bayou, he had traded the wornout roan for a chance to lie down and let the sluggish current carry him along.

The sun had baked him, and his parched lips had cracked painfully as stark branches and long, swaying fronds of moss passed with stately dignity overhead. Then, there had been rough hands clawing at him, and a blinding white pain had shot through his leg. When next he woke, it was in the dark sweltering heat of the Gilletts' smokehouse.

Alaina's patient silence went unrewarded as Cole finally shook his head and shrugged. "It's still rather confused, and anyway there just isn't that much to tell." He glanced about him. "Are we at Briar Hill?"

She nodded. "In my room." Half embarrassed by her blunt revelation, she rushed on to explain. "It's the only room left with a whole bed in it."

His eyes flicked over her. "It's not proper for a gentleman to take a lady's bed, but I thank you just the same. It's the best I've slept in for quite some time." Soberly contemplating her garb and darkened skin, he suddenly frowned in bemusement as a thought struck him. "Did you bandage my leg?"

"Saul did. I only washed and mended a few clothes and bathed you—" She halted abruptly, biting her lip as his brow raised questioningly. In the beginning she had felt no qualms about bathing his long male form. She had been far more concerned with his health than the impropriety of an unmarried young woman washing a naked man. War had a way of taking the innocence from the land and the people. Only, she wished he'd stop looking at her like that.

"You must admit that's a turnabout," he smiled leisurely. "I was sure it would end up the other way around."

"You threatened often enough," she retorted, uneasy beneath his continued perusal.

"What I'm wondering is why you bothered to save me from the Gilletts—" He peered at her thoughtfully, wondering just what to believe of her, if she hated him as much as she professed.

The gray eyes snapped with fire. "Maybe I shouldn't have! Because you're the most ungrateful, bull-headed, bluebelly Yankee I've ever seen!"

She spun on her heel, having every intention of leaving the room, but he seized her hand and relentlessly tugged her back.

"Believe me, I'm grateful. I can only consider that with what the Gilletts had planned for me, you just might have saved my life. It was a relief to wake up this morning—"

"It's afternoon," she corrected aloofly, not yet ready to forgive him. She disengaged her fingers and stood back, self-consciously jamming her hands in the pockets of her oversize coat. "You've slept through most of the day. Now if you'll excuse me, I have some chores to do."

She stepped away quickly, not giving him any opportunity to draw her back, and took herself out to the cookhouse where she stalked about, forming many aspersions on her tongue about the man upstairs in her bed. She worked at her feelings of injury, trying to mold them into a good, healthy hatred for the bluebelly; she would have felt more comfortable with those emotions than any she had been experiencing lately.

Dusk had deepened over the land, and the west blazed with the brilliance of gilt-framed magenta and melon pink clouds when she went out for a last hopeful search of the nests in the hen house. She had prepared a sack of food for their journey and boiled what eggs she had earlier found, but a few scrambled for Cole's supper would help him to regain more of his strength. He would need it for the trip south.

She was near the end of the shed when through a wide gap in the rough, planked wall, her eyes caught the movement of shadows furtively flitting along the edge of the woods.

"Emmett, I bet," she said to herself. "Up to no good again." She pressed close to the wall and watched through the crack until she was sure it was two men on horseback. Deserters? The question rose up in her mind. Either blue or gray, their kind boded ill. Depending on where their loyalties lay, a disabled Yankee might seem fair game for the killing.

Cautiously she returned to the house. Saul had taken her pistol with him, and that left only Cole's Remington for their protection. The door was open wide to her room, and when she entered, she found Cole seated on the edge of the bed. He had managed to don his underwear and was attempting to pull on his trousers over them. His pallor and the tensed muscles in his jaw were visible proof that the effort cost him much in pain.

"We've got company," she announced in a low voice.

"It might be the Gilletts, or perhaps deserters." She lifted the holstered pistol from the bureau. "Stay in bed and be quiet. I'll keep an eye on them."

"What are you going to do with that?" He nodded toward the gun.

"Use it, if I have to," she stated simply.

"Give it here." He motioned for her to bring the weapon to him. "If there's going to be any shooting, I'll be doing it."

"You're in no condition to even be out of bed," she protested.

"Good lord, woman," he rasped. "I've dragged myself through the swamp getting here. I can certainly move from the bed. Now give it here."

She paused in indecision beside the door, reluctant to yield to him. With laborious effort, Cole raised himself to stand on one foot, dragging up his trousers and wavering unsteadily as he tried to fasten them.

"Will you lie down!" she groaned in fretful worry and quickly stepped to his side to push him gently back upon the bed.

As she did so, Cole reached out a hand and took the pistol from her. "Thank you, Miss MacGaren."

"I know how to use it," she complained. "And besides, I wouldn't shoot anybody."

"That's the difference between us." Cole pulled the weapon to half-cock and spun the chamber, checking the caps and loading. "Where are our visitors?"

Alaina gestured lamely toward the bedroom window that overlooked the wooded area, and Cole rose once more to an unsteady but upright stance. "Can you help me over to the window?"

Sensing his determination, she reluctantly stepped close to that broad, muscular chest and tentatively slipped an arm behind his waist, bracing her other hand against his leanly fleshed ribs. As he laid an arm over her shoulders, a memory came winging back to haunt her, and she became dizzyingly aware of a time when his hard-thewed arms had clasped her to his chest, and taunting, warm lips had played with hers—

Alaina dropped her head and forced her attention on the task at hand. He belonged to Roberta, she kept telling herself, and all her wants and needs could come to naught.

Despite his agonized, shuffling gait, they reached the window, and Cole leaned against the wall beside it while she ran back for a chair and stool. Sliding them both to the window, she firmly bade him to sit, and steadied him as he complied. A darkish stain began to seep through the bandage, warning that undue stress on the leg would not be tolerated.

"Are you all right?" she questioned anxiously and was not greatly reassured by his brief nod. Careful not to disturb his leg, she perched beside it on the stool where she could observe the meanderings of the visitors with him.

Night crept in with its stealthy cloak of darkness, and though they strained to see, no movement was detected in the outer edges of the copse, or the yard below. Then, a wavering, shifting light moved through the trees and came ever closer until it was recognizable as a lantern being carried by one of the men. The two paused on the outskirts of the woods, facing each other, and gestured wildly as if in a heated debate. Both wore duster coats and hats, but the lantern was held too low to allow any light to touch their faces. One was shorter and seemed almost petite from a distance. A woman? It was he—or she—who bore the hooded lamp and waved his free arm accusingly. A brief moment of violence ensued when the small one slapped the other, then almost immediately staggered away from a return blow.

"They're coming toward the house," Alaina said.

Cole watched the pair's progress closely. "They seem to be searching for something. They're going into the carriage house."

"You don't suppose they're the ones who—" She bit a thin knuckle as she realized what she had been about to say. Saul had stated that he had seen two men and a woman leave the woods where the grave had been found. These were two men—or possibly a man and a woman—without the treasure—but perhaps looking for it.

Cole tried to see her face in the ebony shadows that surrounded them. "What were you going to say?"

Alaina hunched her shoulders diffidently. "Nothing."

Several moments passed before the two again emerged from the carriage house, this time shaking clenched fists threateningly at each other.

"Whatever it is they're after, I doubt that they've found

it," Cole observed, wincing slightly at the burning pain of his wound.

"It's not any of the Gillett clan," Alaina mused aloud, wishing that the pair would hold the lantern higher so she could see their faces clearly.

"They're going into the stable now."

"The stable!" Alaina sprang to the window, and her fears were realized as she saw the light of the lantern disappearing into the same outbuilding where she and Saul had hidden the chest.

"They'll find it for sure," she gasped.

"Find what? What is in there, Alaina?"

"Some old harnesses and things," she mumbled, rumpling her hair in abject frustration. Why hadn't she and Saul thought of hiding the chest in a more secretive location? Why did the thieves have to return so quickly for it? Why? Why? Why?

"You're not worried about a bunch of old harnesses," Cole pressed. "What are you afraid they'll find?"

She groaned and wrung her hands. "Saul and I found something buried out there in the woods and put it in that old trunk in the stables."

"What was it?"

"A chest of some type." She avoided the more significant answer by rushing on. "Saul was here when they buried it, and he said they left one of their own men out there. We found him in a grave with the box."

"They murdered him?"

"I would say."

Cole grimaced and kneaded his leg as the pain continued to sear through it. "They're coming out of the stables now. Carrying something heavy."

Alaina knew exactly what the two had found. She pressed closer to the window and watched them, then her blood took on a sudden chill as the miscreants turned toward the house. She gasped. "They're coming this way."

Cole struggled to rise, but she pressed him back down into the chair.

"Be still," she hissed. "You're as weak as a starved kitten and certainly not strong enough to hold them off by yourself. All you'll do is get yourself killed." He made an attempt to argue, but firmly she settled the matter. "We'll wait here together, or by heavens, you'll have to walk over me to get to the door. Now stay where you're put."

She flew across the room and closed the portal, quickly locking it against any casual intrusion. As she came back to him, she opened the small cabinet door in the side wall that framed the fireplace.

"Sometimes voices carry up through the chute," she offered the information in a detached frame of mind, more worried and frightened than she cared to let on.

They waited in breathless silence as a sound of splintering wood was heard, and Alaina knew that the board that barred the back door was being ripped away. The portal creaked as it was pushed open, and a moment later something heavy was dragged into the room below them.

The voices of the men echoed through the house, raised in a savage argument, though the words themselves were unintelligible. Cole reached up and reassuringly gripped the slender hand that clutched his shoulder. The thin fingers relaxed in his grip as if surrendering the weighty responsibility of their defense.

After a while a hush fell over the house and they realized that one of the men had left by the back door. From the window, a tall, dark form could be seen running back toward the woods. The man disappeared into the trees and a moment later emerged with two horses. As if anxious to rejoin his companion, he came back toward the house at a run, leading the animals. As soon as he stomped through the back door, the dining room became once more a center of verbal strife, yet only the words of the man nearest the fireplace could be distinguished clearly. His angry rebuttals evidenced the accusations of the other.

"If I had hidden it there, do you think I would have led you to it again?" The one who spoke laughed shortly. "Why, I would have taken it far away from here." His tone became soft and wheedling, almost cajoling. "Good lord, I was the one who sent the little bitch scurrying away from here in the first place, and without me, you would never have thought of getting the whole countryside in an uproar looking for a female traitor while we made our escape."

Alaina frowned deeply. That voice was strangely familiar to her, and what he said was most peculiar.

They were obviously talking about her, but who besides Emmett—

"Didn't I inform you of the shipment? And let me remind you, that it was I who stuck my neck out the night we dumped that fellow in the river. Had I been caught wearing his uniform—hell! This whole thing is too absurd for you to accuse me. If Banks's troops hadn't been driven back, this property would still be up for auction, and it could have been yours, just as we arranged. But you're running scared now that the rebels have pushed us back."

Us? A Yankee? Alaina canted her head, listening more intently.

"Oh, sure, it was a good thing we came after the chest, because somebody undoubtedly planned to come back for it. But don't go stampeding me because a few of our plans have gone awry. The property may yet be taken and put up for auction. In the meantime, the chest is safe with us, and we can split up our shares right now."

As if his words finally appeased the other, the two quieted, and only the sound of some mild labor being performed issued upward through the shaft. After a while, the muted noise ceased, and the voices sounded again in laughing relief. Then abruptly, the gaiety was broken by a shout, the noise of a struggle, then silence.

Alaina held her breath as she and Cole strained to hear some sound from the room below. A single set of footsteps, heavy and uneven as if under a considerable burden, left the house and, in a moment, returned quick and light, only to leave again with another load. Then quietness reigned for an eternity of time. No sound of horses' hooves came to indicate any departure from the house, yet all was stillness until a slight noise came from the front porch. After a while, the steps returned to pause again near the back door. A new sound intruded, a splashing and gurgling, and the heavy, cloying essence of coal oil seeped into the bedroom, prompting a mutual fear.

Alaina's nails dug into Cole's bare skin, but he hardly noticed as he struggled up from the chair. In too brief a time, choking smoke roiled up through the chute, and the crackle of flames confirmed their fears. The rattle of hooves was heard outside, moving away, and Alaina ran to close the small cabinet door.

"Blast them! Blast them all!" she railed. "I should have killed them the first moment I laid eyes on them!" She choked on the sobs of bitterness and at the airless, breath-restricting smoke. All of her being seethed with hatred for those who had set fire to her home. Her pained, keening moan trembled from her shaking lips, the cry mingling with the growing roar below. Cole grasped her roughly by the shoulders, his hard fingers biting into her flesh, and shook her until some sense returned.

"Alaina—listen! We've got to get out of here before we're trapped. Do you understand?" He gave her a quick shake, demanding her answer. "Do you understand?"

She nodded a confused answer barely discernible in the deep shadows. She coughed on the choking smoke and took his arm over her shoulder, ready to help him, but at the door, she let him lean against the wall while she flew back to the bed.

"Alaina! Come on!"

"You can't go gallivanting about the countryside half naked!" She came back to him with his garments and boots and a patchwork quilt from the bed. Quickly snatching on his blouse, Cole slipped a small miniature which his hand had brushed on the wall into the folds of his shirt, while Alaina fumbled with the key in the lock with no results. Cole reached out and brushed her trembling hands aside then, unlocking the door, flung it wide. Heavy dense smoke rolled upward from the stairs, filling their nostrils and stinging their eyes, nearly driving them back.

"Let's get out of here!" He caught her arm, and hobbled painfully into the hall.

"Look!" Alaina gasped and pointed. "They must have touched off a fire at the front of the house, too! It's all in flames!"

"Let's try the back!"

She led him down the stairs, bearing as much of his weight as her slight frame would allow. Hobbling around the balustrade as he left the bottom step, Cole paused a moment in the hall. The far side of the dining room was in flames and the back doorway was engulfed in a fiery inferno that prevented any passage to the safety beyond.

Alaina smothered a scream and quickly drew Cole's attention to a pair of legs that jutted out across the doorway near the hall. Cole dragged his own injured leg behind him as he struggled to reach the portal. The man was oddly hunched over an open, empty chest that bore the letters "U.S.A." boldly stenciled on the side of the coffer. Cole bent, briefly examining the two stab wounds in the man's back, and reached to find a pulse in the neck. There was none.

"Is he dead?" Alaina questioned, trembling as she came to stand beside Cole.

"Yes." He rolled the man over from the awkward, half-crouched position. The legs straightened slowly, and a bright yellow stripe flashed on the britches of dark blue as the long coat he was wearing spread open.

"A Yankee!" Alaina gasped. Then she saw the face and recognition dawned. "Why, it's Lieutenant Cox! He was the one who branded me a spy!"

The officer's half-drawn pistol was tangled in the bulky coat, while his other hand clutched a corner of bright, brocade silk. Cole pried the dead man's fingers open, taking its prize, then reached within the chest to draw out the only thing that was left in it, the sheaf of papers.

"Saul and I found it," Alaina rushed to explain. "It was the gold shipment taken from New Orleans. They buried it out in the woods with the body, and Saul and I, we hid the chest in the stables."

Cole tossed the papers back into the box. "Well, there's one less to share it now."

"Saul said there was a fancy man and a woman who came out here with Lieutenant Cox the night they buried it."

The fire roared up suddenly, scorching their faces and driving them back a step. Cole grabbed Alaina's arm, stumbled across the hall, and pushed open a door leading to the opposite side of the house. The room was relatively free of smoke, and he swung her inside, closing the door behind him as he hobbled in after her. They had stepped through the only door in the room, and there was no escape from here except through the boarded windows. Cole wrenched a wooden leg from a broken table and smashed the windowpanes, then began to pry at the closed shutters that were boarded shut from the outside. Then suddenly from without strong hands began to pluck the planks away as if they were thin shakes and soon the shutters were flung wide. Saul's black face briefly appeared in the opening before Cole reached back and, lifting Alaina bodily, unceremoniously stuffed her through the window. As soon as she was clear, he thrust his own head and shoulders out and found himself taken in the black's powerful grasp. He gritted his teeth in pain as his bandaged leg was dragged over the windowsill, then gratefully leaned on Saul as the man whisked them away from the house to the shelter of the stable. Cole collapsed beside Alaina on a pile of musty straw where they coughed the smoke from their lungs. Absently Cole wondered if he would ever again savor the taste of a good cigar.

He found Saul's anxious gaze on them and waved away his concern. "Did you see," he gasped, "another man ride away from the house?"

"No, suh! Ah comed lickety-splittin' it across the field when ah seen de fire comin' from de back do'. Ah ain't seen hide nor hair o' nobody."

Alaina sat huddled in a small heap staring at the burning house. The fire was licking upward from the back door, curling toward the second level, while the front of the house was nearly encased in flames. Tears trickled down her cheeks and muffled sobs began to shake her slim form as she relented to the turmoil of sorrow roiling within her. Seeking to hold her close and give her comfort, Cole slid an arm about her, but with a ragged snarl, Alaina ducked away.

"Don't touch me, Yankee!" she snarled and glared at him with tears flowing unchecked down her cheeks. "You and your damnable blue army have cost me almost more than I can bear!"

He let her sob out her grief, his face grim with the knowledge that he could not stop this fiery ravishment of her home. "Don't you think we'd better get out of here," he suggested after a while, "before someone gets curious about the fire?"

Alaina stopped crying with a choked gasp and shot to her feet. "The Gilletts! They'll be coming down here as soon as they see the fire. We've got to get away from here!"

"Yas'm," Saul agreed fervently. "But which way? Dem white trash gonna be comin' up de road, and dere's Confed'rate cavalry patrols in de other d'rection. An' anyways we ain't gonna get fur in de dark."

Alaina felt much like a fox being hounded from its den, but found welcome distraction from her sorrow as she rose to the challenge. "Hitch the team to the hearse. We'll head back across the fields and hide out by the bayou tonight."

She turned abruptly and presented Cole his boots, then brushed quickly past to gather their supply of food from the cookhouse, not caring to lend her assistance as he struggled to pull them on.

Putting the beacon of the burning house behind them, the oddly matched trio set out to cross the wide field in the hearse. Saul had pushed the heavy casket aside, and Cole lay beside it where he could stretch out his leg. An eruption of sparks and flame shot high above the treetops and made the tears sparkle in Alaina's eyes when she turned back to look. As they crept across the open space, the wavering light of the fire brightened the field, stretching fluid, black shadows ahead of them. They could hear the excited shouts of the Gilletts as they swarmed down the road toward the burning house, and it seemed that any moment the hearse would be seen, and a hue and cry raised, but the Gilletts were too intent on watching the fire, allowing the escaping party to make it safely to the woods.

In the pitch black darkness beneath the trees, Saul's unerring skill brought them to a well-masked grove beside the bayou. The black dismounted and, after seeing to the horses, went back to the edge of the copse to post a watch lest one of the Gilletts stumble on their path and a pursuit develop. Hunching in her oversize coat, Alaina curled up on the seat and stared sadly at the crimson glow of the low scudding clouds.

Sometime around midnight the fire died down and not long after a light misting rain began to fall. Saul gathered a slicker around his broad shoulders and settled himself against the bole of an ancient oak. Alaina climbed down from her perch and sat in the open rear door of the hearse, resting her head on her drawn-up knees and keeping the best distance from Cole she could manage. At least with the advent of rain, the voracious mosquito attacks abated, and some sleep could be found.

Morning came, but the day remained dark and gray as the low clouds and drizzle persisted. Cole dragged himself out of the hearse and stretched to ease the aches and cramps born of a night on its hard floor. Saul had started a small fire and was warming some ham over it, but Alaina was nowhere to be seen. Saul lifted his gaze as Cole hitched himself around to lean against the front wheel of the hearse. The black laid a slice of ham and a hearty chunk of cornbread on a tin plate.

" 'Tain't awful fancy, suh," he said, grinning as he offered the breakfast. "But it'll stick ta yer ribs till nightfall."

Cole indulged his curiosity as he accepted the plate. "Where's Alaina?"

"Oh, Miz Alaina she took h'self off fo' a walk." Saul fixed a plate which he covered and carefully tucked beneath the seat of the hearse, then began preparing another for himself. "Ah 'spect she done gone back to de house. Ah'll hitch up de team in a bit, and we'll meander 'round dat way afo' we leaves."

The remains of the house could not be seen until they were nearly to the gate, then the charred ruins came into sight. The nearest of the large oaks that had once sheltered the house from the sun were denuded and seared into twisted, grotesque caricatures of their former shapes. The charred beams that thrust up from the cinders resembled the bones of some gigantic beast that had died in agony. Wisps of smoke curled upward, while the droplets of rain hissed on still-smoldering embers. The stench of wet ash was heavy in the early morning air.

They found Alaina just beyond the stables, on her knees in the red mud, her hands clasped tightly in her lap. The top hat lay unheeded beside her. Saul swung down and went to her, placing a huge, gentle hand on her shoulder.

"Miz Alaina?" He spoke softly, as if reluctant to disturb her. "We gots to leave now—afo' dem Gilletts git up and about."

She lifted red-rimmed eyes, and her lips trembled as she took a deep breath. "It's all gone, Saul. There's nothing left."

"Ah know, Miz Alaina." He nodded, then stared at the smoking rubble, his own eyes filling with moisture. "But ah ain't gonna say good-bye. Someday ah is gonna come back an—"

His throat thickened, and he swallowed as the lump of sadness made further words impossible. He heaved a laborious sigh and turned away from the sight of the ruin. "But we's got to be goin' now, Miz Alaina." He lifted her to her feet and bent to retrieve the hat, wiping it on his sleeve before handing it back to her. She jammed the thing on her head and turned up the collar of her bulky coat, becoming in that instant a tawny-skinned, spindly boy. From where he sat at the open end of the hearse, Cole could only stare at her, amazed at the transformation. Where, now, was the soft, yielding woman he had once upon a night bedded and thereafter yearned to recapture?

Alaina came around to the back of the hearse and cocked her head thoughtfully as she considered him. After a moment, she turned to Saul who joined her.

"Whatever, on this green earth, are we going to do with him?" She asked the question quite innocently, but Cole had the distinct and uneasy feeling that she had already arrived at an answer.

"Wal," the black drawled as he rubbed his chin reflectively. "Ah been doin' some powerful thinkin' 'bout dat." His eyes went to the coffin, then he raised a questioning brow to Alaina who nodded slowly in agreement as an evil smile spread across her countenance.

"Oooh nooo!" Cole moaned as he caught the drift of their unspoken pact.

"Just how far do you think we're going to get, Yankee, with all that bluebelly blue and brass shining across the whole countryside?" Alaina questioned impatiently.

Cole rolled his head back and heaved an exaggerated sigh of submission. "Lord save me from this woman!"

"Get him in there." She gestured to Saul and smiled smugly as the captain, with narrowed blue eyes, silently warned of some recompense. Cole lifted his leg over the side as Saul came to help him. As soon as the captain was laid in the coffin, the black lowered the lid, placing small pieces of board along the edge to provide a crack for air. The black crepe was carefully arranged to hide the space, and the back of the hearse closed. Cole sighed to himself as the hearse jounced into motion. At least he was warm and dry, but it was small solace when Alaina's giggle still rang in his ears.

As they headed back across the field to the lane that wandered along the bayou, Alaina rose on one knee and turned to stare back over the body of the hearse. She could see the still-smoking rubble that bore no hint of the home it once had been. The beautiful wisteria vines had gone with the rest and would never grow there again. The heavy ash would leach out its lye in the rains to sour the spot for months to come. Briar Hill was now a cluster of barns, stables, and dogtrot cabins. The great white house that had been the MacGaren pride was gone. All that remained of it were the years of memories that drifted through Alaina's mind.

She sat down on the seat again beside Saul and huddled deep into the oversize coat against the morning's dampness. No heed was given to the tears that streamed down her cheeks, for the weight of this young day was already heavily oppressive. A freshet breeze stirred the trees and brought a stench of smoke and ashes. It embellished what would be her last memory of home for a long time.

Chapter 21

THE hearse had just turned onto the Marksville road when a rapidly approaching clatter of hooves warned them to pull off and hide behind a stretch of brush. Saul climbed down to muffle the horses, while Alaina ran back to warn Cole. Presently the rotund shape of Emmett Gillett came into sight riding a mule that was more inclined to saunter lazily along despite the obvious dither of haste his master was in. Though the beast was whipped into a disjointed trot with a stout willow cane, he quickly tired of the pace and gave a series of arched-back crow hops that completely disrupted Emmett's decorum. Then, for a space, the animal strolled leisurely along as was his wont until the man recovered enough poise and breath to use the cane again. It was in such a manner that Emmett gradually wound his spurtive course past the trees and brush where the hearse was hidden, and finally jolted out of sight.

"I don't know where he's going," Cole remarked dryly as Saul came around to the back of the van. "But I doubt if he'll arrive with his mount."

"That way is Marksville," the black grunted.

"He's probably gone to warn the sheriff that there's a Yankee roaming loose hereabouts," Alaina enlarged upon the blunt statement. "We'd better head toward Cheneyville in case there's any Confederate troops around."

Cole peered at her wonderingly from beneath gathered brows. For one so staunchly Southern, she had thrust herself wholeheartedly into the task of getting him through. Yet her reasons were most confusing.

Alaina turned and found him watching her. Disconcertedly she snatched the brim down low over her brow and mumbled sourly, "What are you staring at, Yankee? A body would think I had two heads the way you're gawking."

"Sorry," he apologized gruffly. "I was just trying to decide which side of you is the real Alaina MacGaren."

In the late afternoon they came to the outskirts of a small town and quietly eased the hearse into an empty shed near some deserted railroad tracks. Saul closed the wide doors behind them, and they had just settled themselves on upended boxes and pallet to share a cold supper of ham and boiled eggs when the thunderous approach of a large group of horses brought them to a startled rigidity.

"It's a Confed'rate patrol," Saul whispered as he peered through a crack in the boards and, after a long moment, added, "Looks like dey is plannin' to make camp right smack dab on top of us."

Alaina swallowed, hardly tasting the bite of ham she had only half chewed.

The crunch of gravel nearby warned them to silence, and they waited, scarcely breathing, as an officer and a sergeant passed the shed.

"You checked this place, Sergeant?"

"Got it earlier, sir. Didn't even come across a cockroach. We searched all the barns and sheds in town, too. It's not likely anyone will be getting through with all four roads covered by our men."

The captain walked on, while the sergeant strolled around the corner of the shed and began to relieve himself against the boards. Alaina had been listening intently, but as the sound intruded upon the tension-filled silence, she turned away from her companions with a blush that made her ears burn, absolutely refusing even to glance toward Cole.

With the Confederate soldiers wandering about so close to the shed, the fugitives crept about with the utmost caution lest some careless noise give them away. Feed bags were hung on the horses' noses to muffle a chance snort and keep them docile. Cole kept his pistol within easy reach, while Saul wove strips of cloth in the trace chains to keep them from jingling.

Their nerves stretched taut with the tension. It seemed only a matter of time before some curious explorer would throw open the door to discover them. Indeed, it was like being naked in the town square and waiting for some passerby to point out the fact. A young soldier sauntered near and rested his hand on the door latch for several moments while he chatted with a companion. The three in the shed waited breathlessly, hearing his voice but oblivious to his words as they stared at the metal latch bar that rattled and strained when the young private leaned against it.

The door banged and rebounded with a crash as the Confederate straightened from his rest and answered the call to chow. Weak with relief, Alaina sank onto a small wooden box as the soldiers strolled away together. Cole stowed his pistol back in its holster, while Saul danced a loose-footed shuffle in the dirt.

Suddenly a muffled thump came from the far end of the shed, and in the meager light, the outline of a small door, low in the wall, appeared as the portal was pushed open against a pile of dirt that blocked it. Alaina's and Cole's pistols came around to cover the intruder, and Saul seized a hefty length of wood as thick as his forearm for his weapon. When the door was pushed wide, a slight form wiggled through and stood up to dust the dirt from his pants. It was Tater Williams.

Cole relaxed against the wheel of the hearse as the youth moved toward them apprehensively eyeing the two guns that followed his movement. The boy jerked a thumb over his shoulder and hastened to explain. "Thar's a wood box outside." He let his gaze rest on the captain's pistol. "Anyhows, ah didn't come ter do yez no harm."

"How did you find us?" Cole questioned.

"Followed yez." The ragged boy seemed unconcerned by the inquiry. "Ol' man Gillett sent Emmett to Marksville and me here. Emmett took the mule and left me afoot." He grinned wisely. " 'Course, dat ol' mule and Emmett ain't never had no common ground atwixt 'em. Ah figger ah beat him, even afoot. Ah were s'posed to tell the deputy 'bout the cap'n gettin' 'way, an' all." At their suddenly suspicious stares, he quickly added, "Ah did, too! 'Course, ah ain't said where ye was."

Alaina peered at him narrowly, curious as to what end the boy served. Tater scuffed a bare foot in the dust and looked at her sheepishly.

"Ah don't like Emmett none too much, and when y'all left him trussed up in the smokehouse, I figgered I owed ya somep'n. Haw!" The boy clamped a hand over his own mouth to smother the sudden outburst, then gave a low giggle. "When ol' man Gillett found Emmett hog-tied and they take dat rag outa his mouth, Emmett set in ter squallin' 'bout how's a boogerman and a dozen Yankees got him and how he fought 'em all 'til the boogerman squashed him. Ya could jes' see ol' Gillett astewin' and afumin'. He say, 'Put dat rag back in his mouf.' " The giggles threatened again. "His pa left Emmett in dat dirty ol' smokehouse 'til mornin', and Emmett were as mad as a scorched woods hog when he got hisself out. His pa made him scrub down in the horse trough afore he could come in an' eat. Emmett swore if'n it was the las' thing he'd ever do, he was gonna shut the cap'n in dat smokehouse 'til he is cured up like a ham."

A shout sounded from outside, and the rebel camp was stirred into a rush of activity. The two pistols turned away from Tater, much to his relief, and covered the door. The Confederate officer came stamping past with several of his men, and the fugitives had no trouble hearing his words as he bellowed to the sergeant.

"There's a Yankee patrol out of Alexandria camped just a few miles up the road. Leave the details covering the roads and bring the rest of the men. We'll see if we can't do something to spoil those Yankees' sleep a little."

The troopers rushed to mount, and soon only empty tents remained in the yard. Tater Williams dusted his shoulder and looked proud as he crowed, "Ah also told one o' 'em road guards thar was a whole passel o' Yankees a-comin' down 'long the river road." He met their quizzical stares and shrugged innocently. "Thar is! Thar's always a passel o' Yankees somewheres 'long the road."

A smile of hope brightened Alaina's face as her eyes met Cole's. "Maybe we can sneak past and get you to the Yankee patrol."

"Hain't much chance o' that," Tater scoffed. "Them Yankees don't git too far afore they draws a swarm o' grayback hornets. They jes' feel around a bit, then head back when the goin' gits hard."

Alaina's shoulders slumped in disappointment, and the strain of the long night and day showed in her face. Her features were drawn and tight, her eyes downcast as she tried to think of a way they could avoid the roadblocks and get out of Cheneyville safely.

Tater hunkered down on his heels until he caught her gaze. "Miz 'Laina?"

Alaina's jaw sagged, and a startled look came at the

use of her name. At that moment Cole began to seriously wonder if he was the only one she had fooled with her disguise.

"Shucks, Miz 'Laina," Tater smiled gently. "Ah knowed right off ya weren't no boy, an' ah didn't know any other friend o' Saul's what fit yer size. Ah also knows what Emmett done ter ya when the Yankees was up here last year. Ah always liked yer folks. They was good ter me, an' my pa sez y'all was fine, upstandin' folk, an' it were a shame 'at y'all weren't 'round here no mo'. Miz 'Laina?" He reached out and tugged at the cuff of her sleeve to bring her tear-filled eyes back to him. "They built this here steam engine track right outside the door. It were s'posed to go clean down ta New Orleans, but this is as far as they got afore the war. My pa was sayin' as how he worked on it back then, an' as how they got the levee built for it almost down ter Holmesville afore they quit. They ain't no iron or wood on top of it, but my pa said it'd be a good way ter go if'n a body wanted ter git south a ways and not be seen. Them Johnnies got the road blocked, but they's mostly from other parts an' don't know nothin' 'bout this. Y'all can catch a road east or one south along the bayou, which ever way you have a mind ter go."

Alaina doffed her hat and, sniffing loudly, wiped her face on a sleeve and leaned forward to give the boy a brief hug of gratitude. Tater rose quickly to his feet and was suddenly fumble-footed in confusion. After a moment of indecision, he mumbled a few words about luck and home, then slipped out the door and was gone.

Darkness descended over the small town with the setting of the sun, and a scattered layer of fluffy clouds played tag with a bright half-moon. Saul slipped out and steathily crept about the minimumly guarded camp, coming back with several appropriated blankets. In the warm weather of the southern land, it was a matter of speculation as to what he needed them for until he began to wrap the iron rims of the hearse's wheels and gathered squares of the same to muffle the horses' hooves. Cole checked his pistol and settled into the open coffin as Saul and Alaina eased open the doors of the shed.

The hearse rolled out like a silent ghost as Saul led the horses forward. The doors were closed behind them, and the wheel ruts were erased, then Alaina followed, dusting away all signs of their passage, while Saul guided hearse and horses onto the tracks until the wheels straddled one of the rusty rails. As soon as Alaina climbed into the seat, he shook the reins, urging the team into motion.

Noiselessly they passed lamp-lit houses at the edge of town and were behind a masking copse of trees before the barking of dogs roused anyone to see. A few yards further on, the rails ended, and soon the regular jolting of wheels over ties also ceased. The smooth rise of the railroad embankment extended straight ahead into the swamp, leaving behind the roads and the Confederates who guarded them. The first of several trestles was still boarded over, a necessary convenience for the passage of horses and wagons during construction, and the team trustingly followed Saul as he led them over it.

Before dawn they were on the road east of Holmesville heading toward the rising sun and the Mississippi. With the coming of daylight, Cole retreated like a vampire into his crypt, and as the morning wore on, began to realize the full stricture of his confinement. The swelling of the upper leg had extended to the knee, and his ankle grew tight in the boot. Though the small blocks of wood at the head of the coffin lid held it open enough for an occasional wisp of air to enter, Cole could barely move in the narrow confines. Each lurch or bounce sent a stabbing pain through his leg, and his head thrumped on the bare wood planking of the coffin. He gritted his teeth and forced his mind away from his present plight. He tried to form a mental picture of Roberta. Her sultry beauty and the round, ripe curves of her body could have been a delight had they also been imbued with a like measure of life and spirit. Recalling her dark, foreboding frowns and the bite of her vitriolic tongue, he failed miserably in his effort.

Slowly, unbidden, and in relaxing distraction, a vision of thickly fringed, clear gray eyes crept into his mind and played a gamut for him as they squinted in jest, widened in wonder, laughed, teased, feared, threatened, raged, cried. A slim, straight but pert nose joined the mesmerizing pools of gray and rivaled them in its expressions. Soft, full lips gently smiled and beckoned, parting beneath his. Young, tender breasts heaved with every gasping breath as she answered his hard, thrusting body, and her arms—

Enough of that! Cole savagely attacked his rebellious thoughts until they cowered in meek submission back into a corner of his mind. But his heart was pounding, and sweat was pouring from his brow. There was no way he could fully ascribe his state to the growing warmth of the coffin.

Cole turned his reluctant musings onto a fresh track, considering the possibilities of the near future. The plan of progress was loose, to the point of being undefined and flexible enough to accommodate a multitude of unknown eventualities. In the hope that some of these might be bypassed with viable tender, he had given Alaina a small packet of gold coins and several silver dollars which he had hidden in the bottom of his bullet pouch and which had remained a secret even when Emmett had worn the pistol belt. Now all he had to do was keep his patience and bide his time until that moment he would be free of his narrow prison.

Around midmorning, the hearse approached a crossroads just as a troop of gray-clad cavalry arrived at the juncture. Alaina reached back and gave a quick double rap on the body of the hearse, warning Cole to be quiet, as Saul drew rein well back from the detail and called out the usual warnings about yellow fever, pointing to the flags that decorated the corners of the hearse. The officer waved them on, but, after they passed, the patrol fell in behind, keeping a safe distance away. They provided the fugitives with an unwanted escort for the rest of the morning, but at noon the patrol drew off the road into a spot of shade, halting for a rest and a quick meal. Saul restrained his urge to race the team away, but once safely out of earshot, he guided them into the next side road, one that bordered a lazy bayou. Though the new path wound tortuously to and fro, they saw no more of the soldiers.

Beneath the noon sun, the coffin began to take on all the aspects of an oven, causing Cole much distress to which his repeated, and highly colorful protestations left little doubt. Saul finally stopped, and they opened the coffin to give the complaining Yankee a breath of cooling air. By now his temper was well frayed. He was drenched with sweat, his face beet red from the heat. Even Alaina dared no retort as he glared at her, but mutely handed him a bucket of water as he stripped off the woolen blouse and the shirt beneath it.

The sun was several hours past its zenith when the hearse came to a juncture of two waterways and the end of the road, a short distance from where a small cabin squatted amid cypress trees. It would be a long delay to backtrack to the main road without considering the risk involved, but it was openly apparent that they had little choice but to do so.

A thin, bearded man left his rocking chair on the rickety porch of the cabin and, cradling an earthern jug fondly in the crook of his arm, meandered in their general direction. Alaina pulled down the rim of her hat, squinted her eyes to hide the gray of them, and leaned back against the high seat of the hearse.

"Y'all be wantin' ter cross?" the man called in a thin, reedy voice while he was still some distance away.

"Yassuh," Saul's voice boomed. "We is takin' de po' massah back to his kinfolk, but ah doan rightly see as to how we is gonna git dere."

The man snickered in his beard and took a long pull at the jug without lifting his eyes from them. "W-a-a-l-l," he cleared his throat hoarsely as he wiped his mouth on a sleeve. "Mos' folks hereabouts use the ferry. 'Course, ah don't take jest anybody. Only those what got the fare. You got any money?"

Alaina fished a hand in her pocket and, drawing out a silver dollar, handed it to Saul. The black passed it on to the thin man who tested it with his teeth, and frowned thoughtfully as he remembered the clink of coins he had heard.

"W-a-a-a-l-l," he drawled even longer than before. "Hit be Yankee money, and it's good all right. 'Course, it ain't near enough."

The man eyed the pair as Alaina tugged at Saul's sleeve. When he leaned down to her, she whispered in his ear and held out her hand as if to show him something. The huge black turned to him and, with wide eyes and a doubtful tone, worried aloud.

"We'uns only got two more o' dem. De ol' massah didn't have too much, an' de undertaker man, he give us all de big white ones and keep only de little yeller ones fo' hisself."

"Hain't near enough fer me ter risk my good health with a fever victim," the man whined. "Yo' sure the man didn't leave you a couple o' dem lil' yeller ones?"

"No, suh!" Saul shook his head vigorously. "But de massah, he doan pass away ob no fever. De massah, he done got hisself kilt in dat fight wide de Yankees way up river. De undertaker man, he say de lil' yeller kerchiefs on de dead wagon keep de Yankees from pokin' 'round."

"W-a-a-l-l, in that case, an' cause ah is a loyal Confederate man, ah's gonna take y'all across fer only three dollars."

Saul grinned from ear to ear, despite the fact they both knew the usual fare for such a service was closer to a quarter. After testing the additional coins, the man sauntered along a narrow path that ran beside the bayou, and he was gone for so long they began to fear that they had been further cheated. Then an ancient wooden barge came floating into view. The flat-bottom hull had been planked over to form a deck and a rickety railing of poles surrounded the whole of it which looked barely big enough to accommodate the long hearse and the horses too. Saul ran to catch the rope the thin man tossed ashore and hauled the barge snugly against the bank. The boatman reached up and pulled down a stout hemp cable that stretched across the bayou, slipping it beneath iron guides at the front and rear of the craft, then lowered the rear rail and slid wide planks out to form a bridge to land.

The barge dipped precariously as the weight of the horses came upon it, then lurched heavily in the opposite way as the heavy hearse was drawn aboard. Saul coughed loudly to cover the explosive curse that came from the coffin, then hastened to kick chunks of wood beneath the wheels to block them in place as the boatman eyed him closely.

"You oughta do somep'n 'bout that there cough, boy," he commented. "Sounds like you might have a touch of the ague." He patted the jug which he had wedged securely against the post. "Got a sure cure for it right here. If'n y'all had 'nother dollar, I'd sell you some for a dosage."

Saul stared at him blankly, blinking his eyes, and made no comment, much to the man's disappointment.

"Here, boy! Ah'm gonna need some help if'n y'all 'spect ter get across with this load. Y'all jes' grab that rope up front and walk toward the back. Like this!"

When the barge entered the main current, the eddies in the flood-swollen waterway took the ferry against the guiding cable and tipped it from one side to the other as Saul labored to haul them across and the thin man struggled to keep the top-heavy craft at least generally upright with the large sweep oar. The ferry dipped and plunged precariously, and Alaina clung to the high seat of the hearse, fearing for their safety, while the blindfolded horses stood stock-still and trembled when the motion was unusually severe.

Boxed in the dark interior of the coffin, Cole could only wonder at what his end might be. The incessant heaving and rolling rapidly affected his equilibrium. His stomach knotted as his black, cramped, hot, and airless world seemed to turn itself end for end. It was too much! If he was going to drown, it would not be trapped inside a coffin. He pried the lid up with his elbow until he could get a hand out through the crack and grasp the edge. Gaining some leverage, he braced a shoulder and lifted the heavy lid enough to pull away the black crepe that covered the casket.

As Cole shoved the lid free of the box, a strange warbling half-scream, half-moan caterwauled through the air. The boatman, staggering back with horrified countenance, could only gape as Cole sat upright in the coffin. Then the man whirled and before anyone could stop him plunged into the water. A frothing, splashing geyser of water marked his rapid approach to shore, leaving Alaina and Saul howling and slapping their legs in glee as they watched his flight. Once the boatman gained solid ground, he set his feet to widening his margin of safety from whatever creature it was he left behind him. Without so much as a single backward glance, he streaked into the thick growth of brush and trees and disappeared from sight.

Saul came to help Cole from the hearse, but the two had no time to exchange banter for the current swung the unsteered barge against the restraining cable and began to drag the upstream rail slowly downward. Alaina shouted and pointed above them, and as their eyes followed her direction, the two men saw an entire uprooted live oak being swept down upon them by the rampaging water. If it struck the barge, they would be taken under and hard pressed to escape swirling murky destruction. There was no alternative but to slip the cable and drift with the current.

The cords of Saul's neck stood out like heavy ropes as he brought the cable down and out of the iron guide. The sluggish craft swung, lurched, and bucked. The frightened horses stamped and snorted nervously at the motion. Saul slipped the front guide, and thus freed, the barge righted and ceased its plunging battle as it rode easily with the current.

The ferry landing fell back behind a curve in the bayou as Saul manned the sweep and kept them in the mainstream, away from the stumps and dead trunks that filled the shallows near the banks. It was a tiresome task as they wound endlessly through the black-water swamps.

An hour's passing of the sun brought them out of the bayou into the muddy ocher flow of a broad river. They were on the Red River, somewhere above Simsport. The stronger currents made the unwieldy barge sway, dip, and turn until Saul was dripping wet with sweat from the effort of keeping it straight.

The bow of the barge began to ride low in the water, lifting the stern until steerage was even more difficult. Alaina opened a small trap door in the deck by its iron ring and found the forward hull over half full of water. The hull was divided into several compartments by bulkheads, but it was a simply constructed craft and was not meant to bear the stress of a weighty load in a forceful current. Cole found a length of rope and tied it to a handle of a bucket, while Alaina lowered herself into the hole. She began to bale with vigor, and bracing himself against the flimsy rail, Cole hoisted the full pail up and dumped it over the side. They soon brought the barge back to an even keel, but at intervals had to repeat the process in order to keep it so.

The sun lowered in the sky as the laboring craft was swept along by the river. They were going in the right direction, but staying afloat was their main worry. No relief appeared in sight as the fiery, heavenly sphere sank below the treetops.

Suddenly the scream of a steam whistle tore the evening's hush asunder, and the tall form of a paddlewheeler came snorting around the bend behind them. At sight of the strange craft that lay in its path, the steamer repeated its whistle. The white-winged curl of wake beneath the prow faded as the huge wheels slowed, and the small, bale-protected cannon atop the promenade deck was quickly manned. The ship closed cautiously, the barest of ripples showing in her wake.

Cole snatched off his blue jacket and waved it above his head. Any ship this far south on the river had to be Union. A man left the pilothouse and, raising a long telescope toward them, scanned the tiny craft carefully. Cole slipped the blouse back on as he bade Alaina and Saul to quickly pull the yellow flags from the hearse. The packet gave up its caution and was soon nudging against the barge.

The exertion of battling the sinking craft and signaling the steamer had cost Cole much of his strength. He leaned weakly against the railing until he was helped aboard the larger vessel. The horses were hoisted over, but the sinking ferry with its black hearse was cut free and left to meet its end in whatever manner fate decreed.

The packet was bearing wounded to the New Orleans hospital, and after a brief examination of his injury, Cole was established in a vacant cabin. None of the officers aboard could see any reason not to grant his request and allow his companions to join him since the steamer would be docking in the morning. After all, the officers were told, the pair had saved his life.

Throughout the night, Cole dozed only fitfully as the pain gave him no ease. Saul snored, sprawled out on the floor, while Alaina curled in a chair beside the bed to nap. Dawn was lightening the sky when Cole roused from a half slumber to see Alaina standing at the window, gazing pensively out at the new day. He called her name softly, and she came to the side of his bed. As she faced him with a gentle, tired smile, he could not remember what it was that he had meant to say. A thousand inanities filled his head as he sought to find some way to express his gratitude. He selected one with all the adroit idiocy of a besotted wooer.

"Alaina—you may keep the money," he whispered unwisely. "I will see that Saul is also rewarded."

The smile faded and was replaced by an expression of pained sadness. "You may know the body, Doctor Latimer, but you have much to learn about the person." Her voice was tiny and oddly strained. "The money is in your bullet pouch where it was before. I don't think you could buy Saul or me for a hundred times as much."

Solemnly she turned and went out of the cabin, leaving him to stare at the closed portal. In the silence that followed, the steamboat whistle shrieked twice, signaling the sighting of New Orleans.

Chapter 22

BY the time the influx of wounded arrived at the hospital, the place was a frenzy of activity. Sergeant Grissom had stationed himself by the door and directed the litter bearers as they carried the wounded in. Alaina was in no mood to cool her heels outside and, towing a reluctant Saul behind her, pushed her way in immediately after Cole. The sergeant's eyes passed briefly over her without a hint of recognition, went to rest on the towering black, then returned with an abruptness that left his jaw aslack.

"What the hell—?" He peered closer. "Al? Is that you?"

"Yassuh." Alaina slipped into the swaggering role of youth with a practiced ease. "I had to put some darkening on so's the two of us"—she jerked a grimy thumb over her shoulder at Saul—"could get the cap'n back here. Some of dem rebs ain't too 'ticular about how young a soldier is."

"You men bring the captain along." Sergeant Grissom gestured to the bearers, then leaned out the door to call outside. "Just leave the rest of the men on the litters in the hallway." He paced alongside Cole's stretcher. "Doctor Brooks is busy with the wounded, but I'll see if Major Magruder can't have a look at your leg."

Cole made no comment as the man left him outside the operating room, but a look of apprehension came onto his face at the mention of the major's name.

"You gonna let ol' meat-ax Magruder cut on your leg?" Alaina questioned none too gently.

Before Cole could reply, there was a heavy tread of boots in the hall, and a red-faced Magruder glared angrily at the slim snipe.

"Meat-ax, is it? You little twirp, I'll have you court-martialed for desertion."

"I ain't one of yer bluebelly sojers," Alaina snapped

defiantly. "And I didn't desert neither. I jest went home for a spell."

"Leave the boy alone, Major." With some effort Cole propped himself up on an elbow. "If Al hadn't gone home, I'd probably be in some stinking rebel prison right now."

Magruder's countenance showed some surprise. "Well! Captain Latimer! Speak of the devil! We just got word you were missing in action. It seems you've managed to become something of a hero. Let's see now, how did it go? The old sergeant was most glowing in his report—you stayed behind to cover the retreat of the wounded, he said. Single-handed against a regiment of cavalry and a battery of artillery."

"Actually it was just a small patrol and a gun they had captured," Cole responded laconically.

"Hm, it must give you a sense of accomplishment to know that out of the nearly four hundred wounded left behind at Pleasant Hill, those from your hospital camp were the only ones who made it back."

"I was not even aware of it, major."

"Whatever." Magruder shrugged and wiped his bloody hands on a towel. "I'm sure a board of inquiry will be interested in learning just how you turned up here while the rest of the army is still in Alexandria."

"I'm not sure I can explain all of that myself," Cole muttered. "I spent a good deal of the time wrapped up in a coffin. But thanks to Al and his friends, I am here to tell whatever I can about it. And I did bring a bit of souvenir with me."

"Ah, yes—your wound, of course. We'll have to take a look at that." Magruder knelt beside the litter and, taking a pair of scissors from his pocket, snipped away the bandage, then peeling it free, he probed the wound with the point of the scissors and pulled the ragged edges apart. He callously ignored the grinding of Cole's teeth and the sudden beads of perspiration that broke out on the patient's brow. Alaina cringed, biting her lip and, with a strange sound, turned her face to the wall, shaken by the fresh flow of blood.

Saul's gaze fixed on the major, and he made several accurate conclusions on the man's character in those brief moments. This was one Yankee to avoid if a body was hurting.

Magruder rose from his examination. "A rebel shell, you say. That means it will be brass with a good deal of lead in it. Matter of weeks your blood will be poisoned. No doubt about it. That leg will have to come off."

Cole managed a hoarse question though his lips were white and stiff with pain. "Can't you get the fragment out? I've had the leg with me for some time, and I've grown quite attached to it, and I would be most loath to lose it."

The major shrugged. "I've seen it before. The metal is wedged tightly against the bone. Probably have to break the leg to get it out. Too many arteries—vessels close by. Nick one of those, and it will be gangrene. Again, just a matter of time."

"I don't think so," Cole managed. "The gun was a Wilkinson—breechloader with saboted steel shot, not brass. If you can't get the piece out, just close the leg up and leave it."

"I disagree, Captain." Magruder was arrogant. "But whatever I do, it will be up to me. You will hardly be in a position to argue, now will you?"

Cole stared at the smirking man and laid back on the litter. "Perhaps not, Major, but I can arrange a pair who will." He reached back to the roll he used as a pillow and withdrew the Remington .44. "Al?"

The one called turned.

"You still have your pistol?"

"Right chere, Cap'n." She patted the heavy pouch slung over her shoulder.

"Loaded?"

"Yessuh," she replied with a firm nod of the head.

"Saul, you know how to use one of these?"

"Well, Cap'n," the big man said, grinning. "Ah ain't so fast on the loadin', but ah sho' knows how to unload it right enuff."

"Here!" Cole handed over the pistol. "You both come into that room with me, and if anybody touches anything that looks like a saw, you just start blazing away."

Magruder spluttered as the bearers lifted Cole. "Do you really expect me to operate with a stripling boy and an ignorant nigger holding guns on me?"

"You'll figure out something, doctor," Cole replied dryly. "Just be gentle, and be careful that you don't pick up a saw."

The orderlies placed Cole on the operating table, and he relaxed a bit as Alaina and Saul took up stations in a corner of the room. Sergeant Grissom lowered a gauze pad over Cole's mouth and nose, then, lifting a small, brown bottle, let drops fall on the cloth.

The room grew quiet. Magruder labored, pulling, testing, tugging at the piece of metal firmly buried in the heavy bone. He even forgot the pair of pistols that followed his every movement until he reached out a hand and fumbled at the tool tray beside him. A loud double click echoed in the room, and the doctor froze, slowly raising his eyes to find Al's heavy Colt centered squarely on his chest. He looked to his outstretched hand and began to sweat as he saw that it hovered over a narrow bone saw. Carefully and deliberately he moved the erring hand and lifted a pair of forceps he had been searching for.

The piece of metal was solidly stuck, and in the deep, lacerated wound, there was no place to gain a hold for leverage. A shadow moved over Magruder's hands, and he glanced up to find that Doctor Brooks had joined him.

"You'll never get that out," the elder doctor observed. "There's not really enough to grasp."

"Hm, yes," Magruder agreed, then enlarged upon his statement. "It is steel, though, and not rebel lead, or brass. I could just close it up and hope."

"The only thing to do." Doctor Brooks rubbed his chin. "It's either that, or lop the leg off."

Magruder stared at the old man for a long moment, then shook his head as he pointed at Al and Saul with his forceps. "I wouldn't even think of it, Doctor Brooks."

Saul was extremely uneasy with all the blue uniforms about, and he took himself off to the Craighughs', while Alaina chose to stay behind, just until Cole came around, and then she would perhaps see if Mrs. Hawthorne would put her up for a night or two. She repeated her story of Cole's rescue to appease the curiosity of the hospital staff, and was finally admitted to the small, narrow room where Cole had been taken, on the excuse that she had to see that the captain got his gun back. Her eyes lingered on his lean profile. She had never seen him so still before, and it brought all her fears into focus. What if he took a turn for the worse—like Bobby Johnson?

She shook her head vehemently, rejecting that morbid

bend of mind. He would be all right. He just had to be.

The door opened, and Doctor Brooks came in. Several hours had passed since the operation, and it was nearing the end of the workday. Alaina allowed him a tired smile as he gave her shoulder a reassuring pat, but she drew herself up as Magruder and General Mitchell came in to check on Cole. She listened to their voices droning on without hearing the words as she waited for that time when Cole would regain consciousness, and she would be assured that all was well.

There was a dull thudding in Cole's head as he slowly roused and an ache that pulsed in unison with it. Though the draperies were drawn, the light was far too bright for his eyes and their thin, dry, scratchy parchment lids. He recognized Al's small shape against the far wall, but he could banish neither the stiffness from his lips nor the dullness from his brain to give her a reasonable greeting. He blinked his eyes several times and saw there were others in the room also. Doctor Brooks stood near Alaina and Magruder was, as usual, at the surgeon general's elbow, rattling words that grated against Cole's jangled nerves.

"It's amazing the captain survived this ordeal," the major observed officiously. "He was certainly lucky that Al found him and brought him back."

"Captain, huh!" Mitchell snorted. "It will be major soon enough if I have anything to do with it. After all, it's not every day that one of our doctors must defend his charges as well as mend them."

Magruder's smile drooped into hanging jowls of displeasure, but the general gave him no notice as he turned to Al.

"You saved us a most valuable man, young sir. We'll have to see what we can do about that. I think it not improbable that I can get you some kind of commendation—perhaps a monetary reward would not be out of order."

Magruder, now red-faced and silently raging, was unable to make any excuses for his hasty departure. He stalked to the door, and when he snatched it open, the startled dark eyes of Roberta met him. Again words failed him. Brushing brusquely past her, he strode down the hall toward the dayroom where he could be away from the mewling concern everyone seemed determined to bestow upon the captain.

Alaina, sharply aware of her own haggard and filthy state, shrank back into the corner behind Doctor Brooks as her cousin swept into the room. The woman was the epitome of high fashion. Though promptly informed of Cole's return and his condition, her preparations had obviously been lengthy and detailed. Every tress was artfully curled into ringlets that bounced coyly as she moved. The striped taffeta gown flared over wide hoops that seemed to fill the narrow space of the room.

Giving forth a dramatic sob, Roberta flew to Cole's bedside and, flinging herself upon his chest, began to weep sorrowfully. "My poor darling! My poor wounded darling!"

General Mitchell stepped solicitously forward, momentarily interrupting her tearful display. "Your husband's leg has been seriously damaged, Mrs. Latimer, and still bears a fragment of the shell in it. I fear he'll be spending a good deal of time abed to affect a proper healing."

Collapsing upon Cole again, Roberta renewed her solicitous sobs. "Oh, darling—darling! If only you had stayed here with me—"

Cole submitted to her embrace in stoical silence until the two doctors, much embarrassed by the emotional spectacle, made their excuses and departed. Then, not surprisingly, as the door closed behind them, Roberta straightened her stance and cooled her manner sharply.

"Well, you certainly did yourself in fine." Her tone had an undisguised sneer in it. "All for the little tramp you bedded." Tugging off her gloves, she tossed them carelessly on the bedside table, then halted as she caught sight of the slim figure in the corner. Her face hardened to a stern glower, and there was pure venom in her voice as she mocked, "And look here! You've got her tucked beneath your wing again."

She advanced upon Alaina with eyes narrowed, demanding, "What's this I hear about you dragging my husband halfway across the state, and in a hearse, at that? If you two think you can put anything over on me—"

"I can assure you, dear Robbie," Alaina cut in abruptly, "that we were well chaperoned. Mostly by Saul, but for a time we were escorted by enough Confederate soldiers to please even your exceptional standards. Then on the steamboat, there were plenty of bluebellies to fill the requirement." Her own eyes took on a flinty hue. "May I be so blunt as to say that you should be thankful he's back alive?"

"If he had listened to me in the first place, he would never have gone," Roberta observed caustically. "We could have been in Washington by now."

Cole rolled his head on the pillow as his dulled and confused senses tried to follow their argument. The aftereffects of the chloroform relentlessly sought to drag him back into oblivion.

Alaina gave her cousin a bland smile. "I shouldn't wish to upset your ambitions, Robbie, but I don't think you'll be going to Washington anytime soon. Apparently you didn't listen when General Mitchell tried to tell you. Your husband will have a long recuperation ahead of him, and as I've heard it, Magruder has volunteered to go in the captain's place."

"What do you mean?" Roberta became incensed. "Of course we'll go to Washington! A doctor wounded in the line of duty—" She laughed. "Why, we'll be the hit of the social season, and under my guidance, Cole will probably be a general before the war is over."

"He's already made major—without your help," Alaina couldn't resist goading. "And without going to Washington."

Roberta's eyes narrowed with hatred. She was sure her cousin was smirking in glee. The little bitch would do anything to have Cole near her, even if he were a cripple.

With a sense of outrage, Roberta flung out an arm toward the door. "Get out of here! Your services, whatever they be, are no longer needed. I can take care of my own husband from now on. I don't need you meddling in our affairs."

Alaina shrugged, undismayed, and, wrapping the belt around Cole's holster, stepped to the bed to place it beside his pillow. "Anytime you want me to hold off another bluebelly, Captain, just give me your word."

Cole laboriously focused on the gamin's visage, searching the features for the woman he knew was there. She was vaguely visible behind the lingering traces of stain and shaggy hair.

"Where are you going?" he asked thickly.

Alaina lifted her slim shoulders beneath the baggy coat. "Who knows?"

He gave her a faint frown and opened his mouth to question her further, but she stepped away. Briefly meeting Roberta's glare, Alaina settled the top hat on her head, then strode to the door, throwing back a parting comment. "Hope you won't be regretting that I brought you back this time, Captain."

As soon as she was out the door, Alaina released a long, dismal sigh. There was something about leaving an injured man with a caustic-tempered witch that made her protective instincts come alive. But having been ordered from the room, she could hardly stay and provide Cole protection from his own wife.

In front of the hospital, she found Doctor Brooks waiting in his buggy. "I thought you might need a ride." He patted the seat beside him. "Come on. I want to talk with you."

She hesitated, wondering if he might again be the bearer of bad news. "It's not anything—serious this time, is it?" she asked haltingly. "I mean, the captain is going to be all right, isn't he?"

The old doctor chuckled. "This, I think, will be more to your liking."

Relief flooded her, and she was happy to settle her tired, aching body into the empty space beside him.

"Mrs. Hawthorne and I have come to a decision," he announced matter-of-factly.

Alaina looked at him wonderingly. "I didn't know you were a friend of hers."

"We've known each other for a number of years, but this is the first time we've collaborated on our ideas."

"From what I know of Mrs. Hawthorne," Alaina said cautiously, "I won't be a bit surprised if it's something outrageous."

A jovial chuckle came from the man as he stared at the road ahead. "You know her that well, eh?"

"Well enough!" In spite of her casual attitude, Alaina's curiosity was aroused. "How do you propose to twist the Yankees' tail this time?"

"My child, how would you like to discard those filthy garments and dress yourself as a young lady should?"

For a moment she sat stunned. Almost hesitantly she asked. "You mean wear real dresses and things?"

"And all that other paraphernalia you young ladies garb yourselves in." He glanced aside and saw that he had ignited a spark of enthusiasm in her gray eyes. "I take it the idea meets with your approval?"

"Oh, yes! Yes!" she laughed and, sweeping off her hat, hugged it close to her bosom. "It would be so good—but are you sure?—What made you decide?"

"Mrs. Hawthorne was quite firm in her belief that you would come back." He shrugged. "Some woman's intuition, I suppose. She sought me out, asked if I could get a job at the hospital for her niece—"

"You mean—this hospital—the Yankees'?"

Doctor Brooks nodded. "I have already inquired, and you'll be starting Monday morning—providing you can scrub yourself pink again."

That night, in Mrs. Hawthorne's house, Alaina scrubbed and soaked in a large tub of hot water until the very last traces of stain were scoured from her skin. Afterward her flesh bore a rosy blush that hinted of her determination to rid herself of the darker color. Her wardrobe became the remodeled garments of Mrs. Hawthorne's own daughter, and though plain, they boosted her spirits tremendously. She assumed the identity of one Camilla Hawthorne, Mrs. Hawthorne's newly acquired niece. The elderly doctor had been more successful in securing her an adequate wage than the captain had been, and she was to be employed by the hospital at a very substantial salary.

Bright and early Monday morning, her heels tapped rhythmically through the hospital entrance. Her short hair had been pulled away from her face and secured beneath a rolled chignon, a switch of hair that she had purchased with the monetary reward Mitchell had spoken of. Her gown was a simple gray and, once about her labors, a starched white apron and long, elbow-length cuffs were to be added.

It encouraged her greatly to find no hint of recognition in Sergeant Grissom's countenance as he directed her about the wards. She listened attentively, seeming to hang on to his every instruction, though she perhaps knew better than he what was to be done and where everything was kept.

It was midday when she finally managed to appease her curiosity as to Cole's convalescence. Balancing a food tray on one hand, she rapped lightly on the door and entered at his muttered command. He half sat, half reclined against a pillow that was propped against the headboard, and was intent upon trying to shave himself. Without glancing around, he indicated the table beside the bed, knowing by the rattle of dishes what it was.

"Leave it there," he ordered gruffly.

She complied, then paused to watch his progress as he stroked the straightedge razor along his cheek, leaving in the blade's wake a path free of soap and whiskers—all without the aid of a mirror.

"May I be of assistance?" she murmured in an easy, but unaffected Southern drawl. The silky smoothness of her voice almost sent shivers down Cole's spine as he remembered that same voice in a dark room on a singular night not too long ago. His head jerked around, and he found the gray eyes smiling at him with warmth.

"Alaina!" He raised himself up, ignoring the pain that pierced through him. "What are you doing here? I mean, with the tray and apron and all?" His gaze took in her feminine attire with eager appreciation. "Are you working here? Is it safe?"

"Alaina? Why, Captain, you must be delirious. My name is Camilla Hawthorne, and if you must be so forward, please remember it."

"Are you sure it's—I mean—I don't think I've—" He cleared his throat in a half-angry manner. "Are you new here?"

"I've been to the city before. But this time I'm just down from Atlanta for a spell to visit my aunt. And rather than sit around twiddling my thumbs all day, Doctor Brooks suggested I might work here. It seems you have lost some of your staff lately, and since the Yankees have managed to give me a tolerable salary"—she stressed the word to gently goad him—"I'm doing fairly well."

Understanding dawned with her meaningful gaze. "You seem to be enjoying yourself here, Miss Hawthorne."

"Camilla, please, Captain."

He looked at her with a doubtful eye. "I think I shall use Miss Hawthorne for a while. The formality of it tends to trip my tongue less than that familiarity."

Her slender shoulder lifted in a brief shrug. "Suit yourself, Captain. And why shouldn't I enjoy myself?" She took the razor from his hand and, turning his cheek, plied the blade carefully along the lean contour of his jaw. "You won't believe it, but I have seen scrawny lads with filthy hair and dirt on their faces thick enough to scrape. I'm so glad I don't have to live like that."

"Hm, yes." Cole considered her askance. "I seem to remember one like that. Filthy little beggar, he was. Always looked like he needed a good bath. Had a mouth almost as dirty as the rest of him."

Alaina carefully applied the razor to that area just beneath his nose. "Did you ever see the rest of him, Captain?"

"Uh-huh," he replied with certainty, somewhat wary of moving his lip beneath the sharp edge of the blade.

"And was he really as dirty as you say?"

This time his answer took longer, and though his eyes smiled, his lips remained motionless. "Huh-uh."

She laid down the razor and gingerly dipped a towel in the basin of steaming hot water. "I would say, Captain," she mused thoughtfully, "that there must have been other things you were just as mistaken about."

Before he could answer, the steaming towel was dropped onto his face.

"Lie still," she commanded, pushing his head back down on the pillow. "You're liable to hurt yourself."

A half angry, half pained groan emitted from the cloth, but her hands held it firmly in place until his came to snatch it away.

"You've done it again, wench! I swear you'd see me roasted alive!"

"Why, Captain." She smiled sweetly into his reddened face. "It was just a lil' bit warm. What's all the fuss about?" With a quick flick of her skirts, she moved toward the door, calling back over her shoulder. "I'll pick up the tray later."

In the days that followed, Cole came to recognize the energetic click of heels as Camilla Hawthorne passed in the hall or brought his lunch with regular punctuality. It became a pleasant, but torturous moment when every second day she remained a while to shave the stubble from his face. It was a favor she bestowed upon many in the wards, and it never failed to disproportionately brighten some lucky soldier's day. When not busy serving the meals to those who could not go for themselves, she gathered sheets, changed linens, dusted, and did light duties.

The heavier labors, for which "Al" had once been hired, were done by a new chore boy, and though the lad's appearance was neater than Al's had been, his accomplishments did not prove of the same merit as his predecessor. When there was time, Camilla collected letters, dispersed the mail, pausing here and there to talk with the men, sometimes reading books to them. She reveled in acting out the choicer parts of the stories, spicing them up to a delightful degree with her imagination, charm, and wit, and an unsuspected talent for mimicry.

Major Magruder was the only one who seemed puzzled by her. No one else had ever taken more than casual notice of the sprite, Al, but when the major asked her outright if he had ever seen her someplace before, she laughed warmly and countered with a question of her own. "Have you ever been in Atlanta, Major?"

It was during this time that Cole gained the official promotion to major, and this so irritated the older officer that Magruder's thoughts turned away from the young woman and became, instead, entrapped in the resentment he felt for Cole.

He had no special license to that emotion, however, for Cole Latimer himself suffered from like emotions, though they were directed elsewhere. It was a matter of aggravation that a young lieutenant, who had been assigned to the surgeon's staff, appeared heavily smitten by the attributes of Camilla Hawthorne and showed no hesitation in applying his own best qualities to a form of mild courtship. While the new major was forced to lie on his back in bed, the young officer was free to range the halls and wards at his whim. Though the object of his attention firmly rebuffed the lieutenant's sometimes jocular advances, the man's mobility seemed an unfair advantage. It only added to Cole's frustration that he could make no open objection, being otherwise committed.

That commitment showed itself in its fullest feminine form when one day, a full week hence, Roberta visited at the unusually early hour of eleven in the morning and was primly seated at his bedside when Alaina brought the tray bearing his noon meal. Following her, much to Cole's irritation, was the lieutenant carrying a basin of hot water for the ritual shaving. Alaina paused briefly at the door, surprised to see Roberta present. It was first time the woman had visited since the day of her husband's admittance.

"Good-day, major." Alaina proceeded as cheerily as was her custom and placed the tray on the bedside commode, giving a nod of greeting to her cousin. "Mrs. Latimer."

Cole struggled to rise to a half sitting position in the bed, somewhat chagrined at his unshaven appearance when the other officer was crisply neat. Alaina took the basin from the lieutenant and, placing it beside the tray, made the introduction.

"Mrs. Latimer, I don't believe you've met Lieutenant Appleby. He's the new surgeon on the staff."

Roberta graciously extended her hand, and dutifully the lieutenant bent over it in the best of the high court tradition, but quickly returned a hopeful smile to Alaina. "Would you like some help here, Miss Hawthorne?"

"I can manage well enough, Lieutenant. Thank you," she smiled. "Perhaps you'd better return to your duties now. I've taken up enough of your time as it is."

Roberta chafed beneath the stricture of wedlock. The lieutenant was quite handsome, and it provoked her that Alaina always managed to affect an easy manner around men, as if she had no fear at all of their baser nature. Roberta yearned to test her own charm on the fellow, just to see how quickly he would forget about the younger cousin.

Finding no excuse to remain, Lieutenant Appleby departed the room as Alaina busied herself setting out the shaving implements. Roberta rose, crossed the room to carefully close the door, and returned to stand at the end of Cole's bed. Her eyes bored into her cousin as she hissed, "Just what do you think you're doing here?"

The girl looked up with a casual shrug. "I have to earn a living, and Doctor Brooks got me a job. I work here."

"Sneaking in and out of bedrooms, I suppose." The woman's tone was something less than polite, and she ignored the warning frown from Cole.

Alaina fixed her cousin with a cool stare. "I don't have

to sneak, Roberta. I leave that for others." Turning back, she began to wet the towel.

Roberta grasped the brass rail at the foot of the bed with such intensity that her knuckles whitened. "And what do you think you're going to do with that?"

"I'm going to give Major Latimer a shave," Alaina answered. "It's part of my duties."

"I'll tend to that!" Roberta snapped. "You just get out of here, and stay out!"

"Whatever you say, Mrs Latimer." Alaina dropped the towel into the basin and, at the door, glanced around as she pushed the portal wide. "We leave this open here on the second floor, Mrs. Latimer, so the men can call if they need help—or anything."

She was gone before an answer could be made, leaving Roberta fairly seething.

"I always said that little tramp would be the ruin of us someday. She's got all of us living in fear that someone will recognize us as her kin. It's just terrible!" Roberta mewled as she sought her chair again. "You can't even say her name without having people look at you in suspicion. And now she's here, working amongst all these men, just like a busy little courtesan."

Cole leaned back and watched his wife from beneath gathered brows. "I think you're being harsh with her, Roberta. You know as well as I do that she is innocent of what she has been accused."

"And I think you're being far too easy on the little hussy," Roberta objected. "How can you be so blind, Cole? You saw the way she acted with that lieutenant. Why, she's leading him around by the nose. She acts as if every man were her consort—as if she were a queen—or some special gift to men."

Cole held his silence, though his mind agreed, She is!

"I remember when we were children. It was always Alaina who played with the boys. If you wanted to find her, you found the boys, and more often than not, she was with them and usually dressed just like them, while I played with my dolls and minded my virtue."

Cole propped on an elbow and raised a brow, unable to resist the question, "How is it then, my dear, that she managed to keep hers longer than you did?"

For a moment the dark eyes narrowed and glared, then she sneered, "Humph! As scrawny as she was, what boy would have taken her seriously? If you want to know the truth of it, Cole Latimer"—Roberta gathered herself in erect self-righteousness—"had she been mature enough, she'd have given up her virginity long ago."

In some exasperation Cole reached for the shaving mug and, wetting the brush, began to lather it.

"And what are you going to do with that?" Roberta questioned quickly.

"I'm going to lather my face and then I'm going to shave," Cole stated the obvious bluntly.

"I'll do that! Just lie back a little."

Cole was suddenly apprehensive. "You don't need to, Roberta. I think I can manage."

"I said I'd do it!" She rose and took the brush and mug from his hand.

It was late in the afternoon, and well after Roberta had left, when Alaina returned to Cole's room for the dirty dishes. He was lying flat in the bed with a wet towel pressed to the lower half of his face. As soon as he saw her, he glared, and though his voice was muffled behind the cloth, his indignation was bold and rampant.

"Good lord, woman! Your cruelty is beyond reason! Helpless as I am, you left me with that butcher!"

He snatched away the towel, and Alaina gasped. His face was nicked and cut in a full score of places and still oozed red from at least a dozen.

"Fetch that new surgeon friend of yours before my weakened life is spent this day," he snapped. "Or better yet, fetch me a lump of alum that I might stem the flow from my wounds. I swear a week in the swamps with an open leg bled me less than this afternoon at Roberta's hands."

Alaina's footsteps and laughter echoed in the hallway as she ran to fetch the alum. When she returned, he glowered at her again above the towel. She wet the lump in the basin and, still trembling with an occasional giggle, applied it to his battered face.

"I've not yet decided, girl," Cole informed her sternly as she tended him, "whether you may have done me more injury from your desertion this day or on my wedding morn."

"Be that as it may, sir." Her voice was low as she bent

far too close to him. "But this time, you can hardly claim mistaken identity."

Now that Roberta knew Alaina was working at the hospital, she strove heartily to visit Cole every day at an early hour and did not deem it within her duty to leave until all visitors were dismissed for the night. Though she appeared adamant in her purpose to minister to him, he was just as determined that she would not shave him again. Rather, he grumbled, he would grow a length of beard before allowing her to do a like service again.

The week was filled with malicious tidbits and insinuations of Alaina's conduct, past and present. Now that the truth of her identity was out, the older cousin actively sought to sway Cole's regard for the younger. It was a barrage of half truths and bold lies, attacks that struck while he was frustratingly confined to bed and forced to witness the attentions of Lieutenant Appleby. Some dark, growing anger churned at the young surgeon's tenacious pursuit of Alaina, though he knew he had no right to protest or feel resentment. Still, it was like a wound festering in his vitals, and he could find no cure.

By Monday morning, Cole had come to the definite conclusion that he had had enough of his mattress-bound incarceration. Just after dawn, he bade an orderly to fetch some crutches, then stiffening his jaw against the stabbing pain that bloomed from the area where the piece of metal was lodged against his bone, he left the bed, though weak and unfamiliar with the walking aids. His muscles had become flaccid from inactivity, yet with dogged persistence, he forced himself to exercise. From the bed to the wall and back again, slowly, painstakingly, over and over, he hobbled until cramps began to knot in his shoulders and legs. Still, he drove himself, refusing to give in to the throbbing, searing pain that continually reminded him of his impairment.

Just after the morning help began to arrive, he paused to listen as familiar footsteps came down the hall toward his room. Then, those of a bolder, more manly stride joined the quick, light steps.

"You're looking quite delectable this morning, Miss Hawthorne." Appleby warmly applied the compliment, and Cole could imagine the man avidly leering at those soft, feminine curves.

"Oh, Lieutenant," Alaina responded in a more serious tone. "Major Magruder was just asking where you were. You're wanted in surgery immediately."

"Duty calls," the young surgeon sighed forlornly. "But my heart remains with you."

Derisively, Cole raised his eyes to the ceiling. If the man only paid as much attention to his work as he did to Alaina, there would be no telling what manner of miracles he could perform.

Lieutenant Appleby hurried away, and the click of high heels continued on their way. Cole glanced around as the sound stopped in his doorway. He saw the surprise in Alaina's face as she stared at him, then she entered the room, setting aside the stack of linens that she carried over her arm.

"Are you supposed to be up?" she questioned suspiciously.

With riant ill humor he retorted, "Better up than to bear another day in bed."

"You look as if you can stand a rest. Sit down while I change the bedcovers, then I'll walk with you for a spell until Roberta comes. She'll be glad to see you up."

"Don't coddle me, woman!" He waved her away as she stepped forward to escort him to a chair. "I don't need a nursemaid watching over me while I walk."

"Well, somebody should be here to see you break your silly neck," she retorted spiritedly.

"You can let your young friend practice on me if I do. I'm sure he needs the experience. He seems much more adept at courting women than he does at handling a scalpel."

"You can't possibly know anything about his skills," she protested. "You've never been with him in surgery."

"No, but I've seen him running up and down the halls like a panting pup after you often enough. When does he have time for his duties?"

Alaina raked the dirty sheets from the bed. "Lieutenant Appleby is just being nice, and you have no reason to be so caustic."

"Have you ever considered cooling his ardor?" Cole questioned curtly.

"I do not encourage it, I assure you, Major," she snapped. She stalked to the door and threw the dirty sheets into the hall, then came back with the fresh ones, glaring at him. "I have done nothing improper."

"You haven't discouraged him either. I've seen the way he looks at you, like some rutting young whelp over-anxious to catch you in the nearest corner. You act as if your mother never warned you about such men."

"Oh, she warned me about them all right," she laughed jeeringly. "But it was your kind she failed to mention. Shall I depend upon you, Major, for advice about that which you have already taken? Indeed, beside you, I would consider Lieutenant Appleby a saint."

She turned away to spread the sheet across the bed, but Cole was unwilling to let her have the last word. Forgetting the crutches, he reached out to grasp her arm, then suddenly found himself twisting slowly on the unwieldy sticks. He caught at the foot of the bed to keep himself from sprawling full face, and the crutch under his right arm skittered away, rattling across the floor. Pain shot through his leg as his weight came full upon it, and the weakened member began to fold. Words that Alaina meant to issue with rancor turned to a gasp of dismay as she saw him crumpling. She flew to his side and, thrusting her shoulder beneath his arm, checked his fall and held him upright.

"Are you all right?" she inquired anxiously.

Slowly he straightened and gazed down into her worried gray eyes, impressed with the clearness of them and the fringelike thickness of her silken lashes. She possessed quite a lovely and expressive mouth, one that needed to be kissed—!

Alaina felt his arm tighten across her back, and before she could gather her wits, she was lifted to meet his lowering, parted lips. Open-mouthed, the kiss vividly betrayed his hard-driven desires, going through her like a searing bolt of lightning, stripping naked her own needs and passions. Fighting desperately against the madness that threatened to envelop her, she twisted away and staggered back a step, shaken and shocked by the stirring rush of excitement that had catapulted through her. She struck out, as much in shame as with a sense of outrage that he should dare accost her in such a public place. The room echoed with the resounding crack of her open palm meeting his cheek. In the next instant, she whirled and flew toward the door, yearning to find someplace where she could be alone and unleash the agonized sobs that were near to bursting forth.

Heavy-booted heels struck against the marble floor in the hallway outside Cole's room, and with an effort, she collected her dignity. It was a hard won triumph when she stepped into the corridor with a restrained and cool manner, but her poise was nearly shattered again as an oddly familiar voice called:

"Why, Mrs. Latimer!"

She whirled to see Lieutenant Baxter hurrying toward her, and could only stand in mute confusion as he neared. She could think of no graceful or easy escape from the predicament she found herself in.

"You remember me, don't you, Mrs. Latimer? I mean—we actually never met that night at your husband's apartment—but I'd recognize you anywhere. And I never forget a face." He laughed as he added. "Especially one so lovely."

Alaina was too stunned to make an answer, but the man rushed on with his inquiries, unaware of her distress.

"How is the major anyway? I've heard of his heroics and promotion. He has a right to feel proud of himself."

"Major Latimer—is doing—well," she answered haltingly. "Did you—want to see him now?"

"Actually," the officer laughed to cover his embarrassment. He could hardly boast that he had boils on his backside. "I have a bit of a problem that I must attend to first. Is one of the doctors available?"

"Why don't you check with Sergeant Grissom," she suggested disconcertedly. "If he's not at his front desk downstairs, just wait there. He'll be able to find a doctor for you, and it will save you some wandering around."

"Thank you, Mrs. Latimer."

She opened her mouth to correct him, but he swung around and hurried off, leaving Alaina staring for one shocked moment into the wide, blazing eyes of her cousin. Roberta had been coming down the hall behind Lieutenant Baxter when he called out and had been halted by the exchange.

"You dare portray yourself as Mrs. Latimer?" Roberta gritted between gnashing teeth as she came forward. Threateningly she shook a fist beneath the girl's nose and swore, "You'll have him and that title over my dead body!"

Brushing on past, Roberta entered Cole's room and slammed the door behind her. The major immediately fell victim to a vivid and most insulting description of his character, and Alaina fled, not wishing to hear the vulgar accusations that her cousin made against them. It was a much later hour when she sent around an orderly to finish making the bed.

The major's homecoming to the Craighugh household was celebrated with a stoical greeting from at least one member. Angus Craighugh had been hoping for the worst, and disappointment reigned along with the usual resentment he felt for his son-in-law. That same afternoon Cole was ushered to the guest bedroom, and Roberta made a lengthy explanation as to how he would be more comfortable there, now that he had the lame leg to consider. Not that Cole wished differently, but he noted that Roberta was exceptionally pleased with herself for having thought of the arrangement.

After playing the dutiful wife for so long, Roberta was restless beneath its restricting role. Now that Cole had been removed from Alaina's daily presence, she wasted no moment resuming her social life, attending teas with military wives and accepting luncheon engagements with high-ranking officers whom she hoped might aid in furthering her husband's career.

It was July when Doctor Brooks, escorting Alaina home to Mrs. Hawthorne's after a day at the hospital, stopped at the Craighugh house to deliver a message for Cole. It was an official letter informing the major of his pending medical retirement from duty. Leala sent it directly upstairs with Dulcie, while she invited the guests in for some cooling refreshments, but the black woman was intercepted at the major's door.

"I'll take that," Roberta held out a hand expectantly as she came down the hall. "Go on back to your work."

The woman glanced worriedly toward the major's door. "Miz Leala say gib dis here letter directly to de major."

Roberta glared menacingly. "Give it here, I said!"

The portal was snatched open as the black woman debated her alternatives. Gratefully, Dulcie handed over the letter to him, then retreated rapidly as she caught Roberta's angry glower. Returning to the parlor, Dulcie was in the process of serving the refreshments when a horrendous screech rang through the house, fairly trembling the glass in the windowpanes. For a moment, all the faces in the room were awe struck, and in the stunned silence, an upstairs door was heard opening and then Cole's casual tone, "Good-day, madam."

The door was gently closed, but only briefly before it was snatched open again. Roberta's enraged tones scattered through the house, loud enough for anyone's hearing.

"Don't you walk away when I'm talking to you!" she railed. "We could have gone somewhere, been somebody, if you hadn't insisted on the foolhardy campaign!"

"More lemonade?" Leala nervously offered in an attempt to divert the guest's attention from her daughter's caustic sneer. Her effort was ineffectual as Roberta raised her voice to a screech.

"I want this settled here and now!"

"There's nothing to settle." Cole's tone was almost pleasant as the sound of his footsteps and the thump of his cane were heard from the stairs. "I am being retired for medical reasons. It's as simple as that."

"You spineless, gutless, filthy Yankee! You made me believe we were going to Washington, while all the time you were planning on getting out so you could stay here with the dirty little tramp you bedded beneath our noses! I should have let Daddy marry you off to Lainie that night instead of saving you from her! That little traitor! She'd have dragged you down with her! And all you can mewl about is how I tricked you into marrying me! You can't see what I've done for you! Why, you should be grateful for everything I've done!"

Alaina bowed her head over her glass in abject embarrassment as the other occupants of the parlor turned to gape at her. Her humiliation was painful, yet Roberta was unwilling to relent in her tirade as she followed Cole down the steps, showering him with a deluge of verbal blows.

"Sometimes I think you dreamed up this whole charade just to keep me from having any fun!"

Cole continued his painful progress with only a muttered comment. "Washington was your idea, madam, not mine." He reached the bottom and, oblivious of the slack-jawed stares he won as he came into view of those in the parlor, turned back to face Roberta. "There'll be no Washington now, Roberta. It's all done with. I'll be mustered out as soon as we reach Minnesota."

"Minnesota! A-r-r-g-h!"

Roberta's hand appeared and snatched the cane from his grasp, flinging it against the wall. "You and your damned bloody leg! I wish they had chopped it off!" Her foot lashed out from beneath her skirts, striking Cole full on the right thigh. He half turned and stumbled back with a harsh grunt of pain, catching himself against the frame of the parlor door.

The enraged Roberta stepped forward, following until Cole reached down to seize the cane by its lower end, lifting it like he would a club. Growing wary, Roberta backed around into the parlor as he stumbled after her, his face white and bearing a grimace of pain.

"Woman," he snarled, "if you ever do that again, I shall—"

He halted abruptly as his eyes went over her shoulder and took in the astonished faces turned toward them. Only Alaina sat with her head bowed, her slender hands clenched tightly in her lap. Cole fought for self control and slowly straightened himself, finally extending a brief nod of greeting to Doctor Brooks.

Roberta whirled at his gesture, and her face burned bright crimson as she realized her vengeful act had been well witnessed. No less flushed was Leala's own as she sat rigidly erect and stared into the distance.

"Roberta? Cole?" Her voice was small even in the dead silence of the room. "We have guests."

"I'm going out for a ride," Cole reported curtly and limped away from them. "I don't know when I'll be back."

Roberta, finding no way to excuse her actions, beat a hasty retreat upstairs to her room. Doctor Brooks could do nothing to ease either Leala's or Alaina's mortification. Bidding the older woman a rather stilted good-bye, he escorted the girl to the door and they made their exit. Dulcie wandered off to the kitchen, shaking her head sadly, while Leala sat much in a daze, wondering how a sweet, dark-eyed daughter had come to this pass.

Chapter 23

THE heat of the summer bore down on the southern fields that continued to lie fallow as the war progressed. It was largely a summer of defeat for the Confederacy. Grant assumed command of the Eastern Department of the Union Army, and Robert E. Lee proceeded to fight a series of retreats in a war of attrition that he could not afford, as he fell back upon Richmond. Sherman attacked Johnson in the Central Department, and that stalwart fought a flawless retreat to Atlanta. Hood, the gallant one-armed Texan, replaced Johnson, and began to fight the battle for Atlanta, while the city itself fell into a panic of evacuation. In the Western Department, known on the Confederate side as Trans-Mississippi, Kirby Smith failed to catch Steele in Arkansas, then returned south in time to let Banks escape across the Atchafalaya. August waxed with its exhausting heat, and the blue-clad soldiers in southern Louisiana became almost rare as Sherman and Grant's armies demanded replacements for their losses.

On a late Saturday afternoon in early September, Alaina and Mrs. Hawthorne were at work in the flower garden when a rhythmic rattle of hooves came down the road toward the house. Alaina straightened as a horse and buggy came into sight, the latter bearing the impeccably uniformed Major Latimer. He drew rein beside the hitching post and decorously tipped his hat to them.

"Good afternoon, ladies."

"Why, Major Latimer, how nice of you to come calling!" Mrs. Hawthorne greeted with warmth. "Would you like to come in for some tea, or a bit of sherry perhaps?"

"No, thank you, m'am. Actually I came out to talk over some matters with Alaina. I'll be leaving in a few days—going home—and there are a few affairs that need to be settled before I leave."

"Of course, Major." The woman smiled warmly. "I understand. I shall be in the house for a while—if you two should need me." Just before entering, she paused at the door and looked back over her shoulder. "If we don't get to talk again, Major, I do wish you a safe journey home. Godspeed!"

"Thank you, m'am." Cole touched the brim of his hat politely and waited until she had disappeared into the house before his gaze came around to rest upon Alaina who carefully tended the shrubs.

"Can you stop that for now?" he asked quietly. "I'd like to have a talk with you."

Though her mind was not on her labor, Alaina continued to trim the withered blossoms from the greenery. "What we have to talk about, Major, can be discussed while I'm working."

Cole rubbed the cool leather of the reins beneath his thumb. "I came to talk with you privately, Alaina, and I would be grateful if you would go for a ride with me and listen to what I have to say."

She turned and stared at him for a long, indecisive moment, then approached the buggy.

"Get in," he bade gently and reached out a hand to offer her assistance.

Alaina stared up at him. He was darkly bronzed from the sun, and in contrast his pale blue eyes seemed to shine like bright gems. Just when she had thought that she would not be affected by his presence, he appeared, and all her carefully tended illusions were cruelly sundered. Why hadn't he just gone away and let her be reconciled to his leaving? Why did he have to prolong her misery?

"I beg your indulgence, Alaina. I'll be gone in a few days, and I desire a few moments of your time, if you can spare them."

Reluctantly she removed her apron and gloves, hanging them on the hitching post, and climbed in beside him. Cole lifted the reins, and headed down along the river road, halting only when he found a dapple-shaded spot, well secluded from the main road by a grove of trees.

"I do hope your intentions are honorable, Major." She tried to sound flippant. "I seem to be at your mercy, and you appear quite determined to compromise my reputation."

Cole wrapped the reins about the whip staff, and leaned back in the seat. Unbuttoning his blouse, he reached within it and drew out a small derringer which he handed over to her. Bemused, Alaina raised her gaze to stare at him wonderingly.

He gave her a slow smile. "To soothe your fears, madam."

She examined the small, double-barreled pistol, then observed wryly, "It's unloaded."

"Of course," he grinned, setting aside his hat. "I'm not a complete fool." He took the weapon from her. "Do you know how to use one of these things?"

"It's rather ineffective without proper loading, that much I know."

Ignoring her quip, he began to slip the brass cartridges into the chamber. "Pay close attention," he admonished. "This little lever on the side is a safety and will prevent an accident."

"And your reasons for this gift?"

Cole slapped the chamber shut and briefly aimed the gun at a distant wildflower before meeting her inquiring stare. "After I leave, you may have need of some convincing protection, and since you've attracted the likes of Jacques DuBonné, who knows what could happen. This is the only thing I can offer toward your safety. It's part of a farewell gift, I guess you might say."

"You mean there's something more?"

He shrugged casually. "Are you of a mind to go into a business of your own?"

"That would be nice, but I'm afraid my funds are rather limited."

"I can provide those funds," he said slowly. "I can have it arranged before I leave, and if there's any problem in the future, I've hired an attorney in the city to deal with some of my affairs here. You need only contact him."

"Thank you, Major, but I do not wish to be kept by you, or by any other man. I am fairly self-sufficient, and I prefer it that way."

"Dammit, Alaina, I'm not asking you to become my mistress. I just feel obligated—"

"You needn't," she interrupted coolly. "You owe me nothing, and I will take nothing from you."

"I have money with me—at least two thousand in gold, and the key to my apartment. I've made arrangements to keep it as long as you're here in the city. I want you to take them both—"

"No!" She was just as adamant as he. She had her pride and her reasons, which she would not discuss with him. "And you can't force me to take them!"

Cole sighed heavily. "You are a stubborn woman, Alaina MacGaren." After a moment, he reached behind the seat and handed over a large, ornately carved wooden box. "The last of my gifts," he announced wryly. "And this, I think, will not greatly compromise your reputation."

Suspiciously she glanced at him, then lifted the lid. A gasp of astonishment came from her as she saw what lay in the bottom of the velvet-lined box. It was a miniature of her parents that had once hung on the wall of her bedroom. "But how? How did you get this?"

"My hand touched it as we were leaving your bedroom that night. I had noticed it on the wall earlier, and I thought you might like it as a keepsake."

"Oh, yes!" The shine of tears were in her eyes as she gazed into his. "It's the most beautiful gift of all! Thank you!"

On impulse she leaned toward him, pressing her lips against his brown cheek. Cole's head was suddenly filled with the fragrance of her hair, and something wild escaped within him, something too strong to fight against. As if he had no will to stop them, his arms came around her, gently molding her to him. He had a man's desire, and it had been many months since it had been soothed with the softness of a woman.

"Alaina—Alaina—I want you." His voice was a hoarse, ragged whisper in her ear, and it burrowed down in her soul, unlocking all the forbidden passions that she had held in check. His mouth found hers, and for a moment there was an eager meeting of lip and tongue, of passions winging out of control. Her breath caught in her throat in a small, sobbing gasp as he held her hard against him. Every fiber in her being yearned for him, but her mind rebelled. He belonged to another woman, and in a few days would be gone from her. If she allowed some tenderness between them now, his leaving would be that much harder to bear.

"Cole—no," she choked out, turning her face away, and struggling against his broad chest. "We can't do this."

Cole's need had been physically stirred by her all too

fleeting response, and his mind was enflamed with the desperation of starving passions. "Come to my apartment, Alaina," he pleaded as he pressed warm, ardent kisses upon her cheek and the slim column of her throat. "Stay with me there. Let me love you as I yearn to do. We only have a few days left."

Shaking her head, Alaina pushed herself from him and pressed a trembling hand to his chest to hold him away. "I'm not one of your common doxies," she whispered weakly. "I won't be left to bear a child in shame, while you boast of one more bastard. Whatever happened between us was a mistake—"

He caught her hand and held it fast within his grasp. There was an ache in the lower pit of his belly that could not be appeased with denials and rationalizations. "There are some mistakes, Alaina, that cannot easily be put aside." He stared intently into the wavering depths of her eyes as he stated slowly, desperately, "I need you, Alaina."

"No," she moaned and tried to turn away.

Cole caught her by the shoulders and forced her to face him, giving her a small shake to bring her gaze up to his. What he saw in her eyes was in complete variance with what her lips conveyed, and there was a shivering tremor in her slender body that belied her words of denial. His lust overcame his common sense. *Silence her protest,* he thought, then her heart would follow his leading. He grasped her tightly to him again and covered her gasping mouth with his. But he misjudged her. There was a sharp pang as her small teeth clamped down on his lip. He snatched away, tasting blood, and threw up an arm in defense as her hand came around to deliver a blow to his cheek.

"You may force me, Major, if that is your desire." She made her vow in an ice-hard voice that hissed as if it struck hot steel. "But I will be no more yours after, than I am now."

"I should have chained you to me that night," he swore. "It's been my hell to pay since."

She snatched up the miniature, spilling the box to the floor of the buggy, and before he could stop her, she stumbled down the step and, glaring back through tears, stalked away. "I won't be your hell anymore, major!

You are free to go and live with Roberta in Minnesota. I don't ever want to see you again!"

"Alaina! Come back!" he shouted as she ran stumbling down the lane. "Dammit, Alaina! Get back in here!"

"Go on! Go live with your precious wife!" she railed. "And you can take your money, your apartment, and your key and give them to your mistress!"

Cole mumbled several curses as he swung the buggy about. "Alaina, get into the buggy," he commanded, slowing the buckboard beside her. "I'll take you home."

"And what price the ride?" she sneered over her shoulder. "Another night's toss in bed?" She laughed harshly as she continued to stamp her way indignantly along the path. "Begone with you, Yankee! Out of my sight!"

"You're being unreasonable, Alaina!"

"Unreasonable? Because I won't bed down with you and get with child? You, my dear major, are the one who's being unreasonable! In a few days you'll be gone, and you'd be free of any obligations you'd leave with me!"

"Do you think I'm like that?" he demanded. "Do you think I wouldn't come be with you—"

She stopped and faced him squarely, setting her arms akimbo. "And what would you do with Roberta? Set her aside so you could put a name to a child of yours? Forget it, Major. You can't give me what I want."

She whirled and strode angrily along her way, while he paced the horse beside her.

"What do you want, Alaina?" He watched her as she paused to shake a pebble from her worn slipper.

"I want what every woman wants," she stated, raising her eyes briefly to his. "And that's not to become the mistress of a Yankee womanizer."

"Believe what you will," he began, "but I am no—!"

"You're right! I'll believe what I will!" She was final in her dismissal of him as she walked on, ignoring his pleas to get into the buggy, though he followed her all the way back to Mrs. Hawthorne's drive.

Cole halted the buggy and watched her as she ran across the porch. The door slammed behind her, and he heard her running footsteps in the house. He did not enter the lane, but urged the horse around, returning to the city, all the while wondering how he had ever managed to make such a stupid, blundering mistake.

Long into the night, Mrs. Hawthorne lay awake,

listening to the racking, bitter sobs that drifted from Alaina's room. Her own heart ached for the girl—and for the major. It seemed the two were caught in something that could not easily be cooled—and she doubted that distance would have any effect on the burning fires of their emotions.

A shudder ran through the riverboat as the last hawser was cast off, and the threshing paddlewheels took her from quayside and into the main current of the river. Leala wiped her eyes and frantically waved the kerchief as her daughter departed, while Angus stood stiff and unyielding beside his wife, knowing full well that with his own part in Roberta's marriage, he could now voice no objection.

As for Roberta, she was enraged that she was being dragged off into a wilderness from where tales of wild Indian savagery drifted and which was known to be populated with cloddish lumberjacks and half-breed trappers. The reality of it all came home to her as she stood on the upper deck of the river steamer. Her dreams of Washington and *haute société* faded to leave a bitter taste in her mouth. Somehow she translated her loss into the fact that Cole had used and then betrayed her. The tall, handsome man, leaning on a slim cane beside her, became anathema to her.

Roberta raised her gaze and saw a small, slender figure garbed in a pale muslin gown standing alone and silent near the levee's crest.

"Alaina!" The name came like a curse in Roberta's mind. *She knows what she's done to me! Oh, she knows all right, and how that little bitch must be chortling at my fate!*

"Did you speak?" Cole turned from his own musings to face her with the question.

Roberta stared up at him, and all her frustrations and hatred made itself known in the sudden snarl of pure rage that twisted her face into a hideous mask. She could bear no more of this!

Abruptly she whirled and ran to their cabin, hiding her face behind a gloved hand. Cole followed more slowly, but when he tried the doorknob, he found the passage locked against him. He paused for a moment in deep reflection then, leaning heavily on his cane, he limped to the purser's office to arrange for separate accommodations.

Later in the afternoon Alaina was puttering in Mrs. Hawthorne's back yard when the woman called her to come around to the front porch. When she did, she found Saul standing in the yard with hat in hand. Since their return from Briar Hill, he had been working at the Craighugh store, and she had seen little of him. He looked at her rather sheepishly, stirring her curiosity, then her gaze went past him, and she saw Cole Latimer's buggy and horse in the drive.

"De major say to bring it here, Miz Alaina, and not to take no for an answer. He say it's yours now, ter do with whatever yo' wants." Saul turned the hat around in his hands, sliding his fingers nervously over the brim. "De major also say, if'n yo' doan want ter raise Mistah Angus's brows more'n a mite, yo' won't be trying to give it back to them."

"How am I going to take care of that animal?" Alaina protested.

"Well, de major say for you not to worry 'bout that. He done take care o' that. Dere'll be some feed and stuff delivered here ever so often, an' all yo' gotta do is sign for it."

Alaina gritted her teeth and peered at the black suspiciously. "That's not all, is it, Saul?"

"W-a-a-l—" He lowered his gaze and shrugged lamely.

"Spit it out," Alaina commanded.

Reluctantly he withdrew a key from his cotton coat and handed it to her, then reached to take a pouch from his belt. "De major say dere's two thousand in gold right here, and that there's a key to his 'partment. Ah was ter see dat dey got here to you without Mistah Angus knowin' 'bout 'em."

"Saul Caleb!" Alaina cried in outrage. "You mean you took money from that Yankee for me!"

"Now, Miz Alaina." He glanced in appeal toward Mrs. Hawthorne who was staring off into the distance. He found no escape from his predicament in that corner. "Ah tole de major yo' was gonna be hot and mad 'bout this, and he say he was gonna be hot and mad if'n ah didn't do what he say."

"A fine kettle of fish you've gotten us into," Alaina fussed.

"Yas'm, ah know. But de major say ah was not to go back to Mistah Angus's widout givin' de money and hoss to yo', an' he made me promise, Miz Alaina."

She sighed heavily. "Leave the horse and buggy. You can take the money—"

Saul shook his head passionately. "No'm! Ah promished ah wouldn't! 'Sides, de major done gone and left me money, too."

"Supper anyone?" Mrs. Hawthorne inquired sweetly as she rose to her feet. "I believe I smell it burning."

"Oooooohh!" Alaina flew to the door, yanked it open, and disappeared into the house, leaving Saul to stare glumly at the pouch.

"If you would like, I'll take it for her, Saul," Mrs. Hawthorne smiled gently. "Just in case an emergency arises and she needs the money."

Saul was glad to be relieved of his burden, and he hurried to unharness the animal and put the buggy away, not wishing to stay around long enough to enter into another debate with the tenaciously stubborn girl.

Mrs. Hawthorne made her way leisurely into the house and put the pouch away in an armoire. There would come a day when the girl might have second thoughts about the major's possessions. Until then, the money could be discreetly kept or used for her.

Chapter 24

IF it was a summer of defeat, then it was a winter of disaster. Lee was besieged in Richmond, Atlanta fell, and Sherman marched to the sea, cutting the eastern Confederacy in half and leaving a path of destruction sixty miles wide. As the South awakened in spring, the last hopes of the Confederacy dimmed. Lee fled Richmond, and the city lay naked beneath Grant's heel, and finally, on April ninth, driven back upon the Appomattox, Lee could find no more cause to support and surrendered his starving, ragtag army. Five days later a greater disaster struck; Lincoln was assassinated! The South crumbled as Johnson, Taylor, and Smith surrendered in turn. The fleeing Jeff Davis was captured on the tenth of May, and with a full blood of vengeance up, the Northern congress slashed the South with savage blows. The destitute Confederacy was punished piecemeal for its arrogant disobedience, and a locust horde of rapacious carpetbaggers descended like vultures to pick the bone-thin carcass clean.

Louisiana was ruled by an implanted governor, basically honest but extravagant, to whit: a ten-thousand-dollar chandelier for the statehouse, and gold spittoons for every office. As a port, New Orleans thrived with the return of foreign shipping. As a city, it tore itself apart. The cheap black labor clashed with the Irish, Scottish, and German immigrants, and the Federal troops were called back in to quell the riots.

The hospital became more and more a civil establishment. Although nominally still under the control of the army, a single ward now served the soldiers, and Doctor Brooks gained position and respect as the administrator. Alaina still served as she had, with an outwardly gay and cheerful spirit, but even Mrs. Hawthorne's companionship could not lessen her attacks of abject loneliness. She turned away Lieutenant Appleby's proposal of marriage and discouraged other suitors as she had no interest in being courted.

It was a quiet afternoon when she was called to Doctor Brooks's office. On arriving there, she found the aging man staring at the top of his desk with his white head braced in the palms of his hands. His eyes rose slowly as she slipped into a chair across from him, and he solemnly folded his arms on the desk.

"I have just returned from the Craighugh house," he informed her. "And once again the news I have to bear is sad."

Alaina stiffened, and her thoughts flew. *Uncle Angus? Aunt Leala? Dulcie? Or Saul? Who?*

"Leala has just received a letter from Minnesota—"

Alaina gritted her teeth, and her insides went cold with dread, yet she could not voice her fear even in her own mind.

The old man continued haltingly. "Roberta has passed away. It seems she had a miscarriage. A fever consumed her, and she weakened and died."

Although Alaina felt no exaltation, overwhelming relief flooded through her, leaving her weak and thankful. She waited for the pang of sadness, but none was forthcoming. Quietly she excused herself and took the rest of the day off, making her way dutifully to the Craighughs' with the thought of offering her services in whatever way they might be needed. Dulcie answered her knock on the door, and after a tearful greeting, the black woman's face took on a deep frown of concern.

"De doctah gib Miz Leala some powders, and she's sleepin' upstairs. Massah Angus, he gone back to da store. Miz Alaina"—the woman twisted her hands in her apron —"ah jes' doan—know what to do. Massah Angus is ravin' as how yo' brought da Yankee here, and dat caused Miz Roberta to die. Dey is both downright blue, Miz Alaina, and ah jes' think it's best, chile, if yo' waits a while befo' coming to visit."

Alaina nodded mutely and returned to her buggy. Sadly, thoughtfully, she made her way toward Mrs. Hawthorne's house. Perhaps, after all, it would have been better for everyone concerned had she stayed at Briar Hill and never ventured away at all.

After his daughter's death, Angus Craighugh lengthened his hours at the store, working feverishly into the late hours. Even then, he was inclined to stop and sample the wares of nearly every tavern he passed, and, more often than not, arrived home in no condition to negotiate the stairs without assistance. Thus, it was no surprise when a letter came from Leala pleading with Alaina to return and live with them. Several weeks passed while the girl pondered the decision. She was more than reluctant to go, for the Craighugh mansion had the capacity to arouse too many memories, most of them bad. Although she understood and sympathized with the loneliness of her aunt, it was not until the older woman visited her at the hospital and made a tearful plea that Alaina yielded the point, agreeing to move in with them.

Almost immediately it became apparent that Leala expected Alaina to be her daughter, in fact as well as in fancy. She constantly pressed the girl to go out shopping for clothes and other accoutrements so that she might be dressed as befitted one of Craighugh stature. Leala even went so far as to suggest that Alaina might be more comfortable in Roberta's old room, and seemed stricken by the young woman's refusal. It was an innocent slip of a wishful tongue when Leala called her niece Roberta, jelling the mild resistance that had been born in Alaina's mind. Alaina knew that she must set this dream at rest before it became a nightmare, and she faced Leala in firmness well tempered with tribulation.

"Aunt Leala, I live here because it seems to please you, but I am not Roberta. I cannot replace her, and I will not be Roberta."

Leala twisted her hands in sudden nervous confusion, and tears came to her eyes as she avoided Alaina's gaze. "I am sorry, child. I did not mean to make you my own. It's just that it's so easy to forget—"

"I know," Alaina sighed. "I love you, and I understand. But remember that I am someone different. A guest, for a while. Nothing more."

Leala seemed to brighten a bit each day after that, coming out of her doldrums. Having once faced the loss, she found it bearable.

Uncle Angus, on the other hand, did not fare well in his time of testing. He stayed away from the house as much as he could, as if the very sight of the niece in his home rankled him. With shipping at its peak, his business was flourishing, and he drove himself mercilessly in a never ending effort to get another dollar ahead.

With Alaina's reappearance in the Craighugh house, another threat loomed over the girl, one she became aware of on a morning in July as she turned the buggy off the avenue where her uncle's house was located. Seeing a large landau blocking most of the road, she slowed the buggy to pass around it, then gasped in surprise as Jacques DuBonné, stepped down from the carriage. Wearing a cocky grin, he strode toward her and set a booted foot on the buggy's step, very self-assured and prosperous looking in clothes that hinted more of good taste than his garments of earlier days. In fact, he was garbed more like a wealthy gentleman than a backwater's roué.

"Good-morning, madam." He tipped his hat decorously. "I am pleased we meet again. I had almost given up hope of finding you, even though my men have been haunting these streets, looking for the widow. May I be reassured that you are no longer in mourning?"

"Monsieur DuBonné, I don't think you should be reassured at all where I am concerned. I do not like you, and I do not care to change that situation in any way. Now, if you don't mind, I'll be on my way." She lifted the reins to urge the horse forward, but Jacques placed a delaying hand across hers. Alaina stared at the short, blunt fingers with a mild showing of distaste, then slowly raised her gaze to meet the shining black eyes which rested upon her. "Was there further business you wished to discuss with me, sir?"

His fingers traced along the fragile wrist, while his gaze held hers imprisoned. "It had come to my attention that your benefactor has left the city."

She slowly arched a brow. "And who might that be, sir?"

Jacques smiled leisurely. "Monsieur Doctor Latimer is the one of whom I speak." His caressing fingers traveled further up her arm. "And now you have no one to see to your care, so I think perhaps I should offer to you my protection."

"How kind of you, sir." Her smile was bland. "But I see no need for your guardianship." The last word was stressed with open mockery.

Tossing his dark head back, Jacques laughed in amusement. "Oh, but, mademoiselle, you do not understand. Unless you will allow me to bestow upon you my protection, you will find no peace either day or night."

"Are you threatening me, sir?"

He shrugged his shoulders and spread his hands. "I would not like to frighten you, mademoiselle. I am more willing to soothe your fears—"

"At what cost?" she asked bluntly.

His hand slipped down to rest possessively upon her knee. "I should like to be intimate friends with you, mademoiselle."

Alaina rose to the challenge with fire in her eye. "Get your hands off me."

The sound of his mirth rang again as he stroked upward along her thigh, but in the next moment, Jacques found himself staring into the bore of the small derringer that she had snatched from her handbag. He needed no command, but cautiously lifted his hand from her leg, then stepped back in urgent haste. At that, the wheels of the buggy nearly marked the toes of his boots as Alaina slapped the reins against the horse's back and sped away, leaving Jacques standing in the middle of the street, staring after the fleeing coveyance.

The huge black stepped from behind the landau and, climbing into the driver's seat, urged the horses forward, bringing the carriage to his employer.

"Zat hospital boy-girl, massah?"

The Frenchman's gaze came around to stare at the negro. "What do you mean?"

The broad shoulders shrugged. "She looked like hospital boy-girl."

"You mean the one who throw the bucket of water on me?"

"Yassuh—zat hospital boy-girl." He patted his chest. "Under coat, she girl—woman. I pick her up, and she soft—woman."

Jacques caught the black's meaning. "The same boy-girl who also held gun on us at Madame Hawthorne's?"

The black nodded vigorously.

"I see!" Deep in thought, Jacques climbed into the landau and signaled the black to drive on. Why would a young woman pose as a boy he wondered. Unless of course there was something she wished to hide. But what was that? And how could he find out?

Dully, Angus Craighugh rose from his store desk as the door opened and a wealthily garbed man strolled in, followed by an oversized black who resembled Saul in bulk and height.

"May I be of service, sir?" Angus solicitously asked as he moved forward to meet the men.

Jacques DuBonné smiled graciously and lightly caressed a bolt of silk on the table beside him. "Very good taste, monsieur."

"Are you interested in some materials, sir? I just received a shipment of rare, fine silks from the Orient."

"Ahh, but it must be a coincidence."

"A coincidence? In what way, sir?"

"It has come to my attention that a ship from the Orient was seized in the Gulf, divested of her cargo, then was sunk with all aboard."

"What has that to do with this silk, sir?"

"The cargo just happened to be silks and ivories, the rarest carpets—such as you might have there, sir." Jacques waved his hand toward a rug displayed on the wall.

"I assure you, sir"—Angus reddened at the subtle insinuation—"I have paid good money for these articles, and if they were pirated, it was not of my doing."

Jacques laughed casually. "In this day and age of carpetbaggers and high prices, isn't it strange to come upon good bargains? A man, unless he is completely scrupulous, would not question his good fortune in finding such a bargain. He is grateful for the opportunity to make a profit, and would not think of questioning his suppliers."

"What are you suggesting, sir?" Angus questioned indignantly.

"I am saying that you must have been aware of some chicanery, but chose to overlook it with the hope that you could add some wealth to your pockets."

"That is preposterous!" Angus objected strenuously to the suggestion that he might be less than an honest man—a little frugal perhaps, but certainly not a thief. He blustered, "What interest do you have in this matter? Was it your ship that was pirated?"

"Let us say, monsieur, that Jacques DuBonné has a way of knowing certain things, and is interested in all happenings here in the city." He waved his fingers in a mysterious gesture, and glanced about him. "One never knows when a disaster can strike. A fire, perhaps. Vandals maybe." He shrugged. "I have many friends, some to whom I can offer protection since I've become a very important man in this city. A word here or there will keep the authorities from involving themselves in affairs that are no concern of theirs. Sometimes a bit of information might suffice to soothe my yearning to see justice done."

"Are you blackmailing me, sir?" Angus questioned suspiciously.

Jacques chuckled. "No indeed, monsieur. I would never dream of offending a man of your integrity. I was merely curious about a certain young lady you have living in your home. Is she kin to you, monsieur?"

Angus's brows lowered darkly, and his face flushed with color. "No kin of mine," he replied savagely. "She is just a guest in my home—for a time."

"I'm aware that she left your house for a time and lived someplace else. Where did she go?"

"As you know all things, sir, I would suggest that you rely upon your friends to gain the information for you. I am much too busy to answer your questions"

"If that is your wish, monsieur. *Bonjour!*"

The next day Angus stormed home in a rage because two Yankee officers had come into his shop and demanded to see certain bolts of cloth. In the days following he found no peace from their presence in his store. It became the usual thing that an officer would meander in to look about or buy a plug of tobacco or some other trivial thing at odd hours of the day.

It also became apparent to the Craighughs that the house was being watched. A man was usually in sight while Alaina was home, and could be openly seen lounging against a tree, sitting on a horse, or relaxing in a carriage. Saul became Alaina's guardian once more, driving her wherever she needed to go while he continued to help Angus at the store.

Jacques waxed bold in his courting and visited Alaina at the hospital, finding her in a rare quiet moment alone in the officer's dayroom.

"You cannot escape me, Mademoiselle Hawthorne," he laughed confidently as she felt a presence at the door and turned to find him standing there. "I know now where you work and where you live. I know many things about you."

"Indeed?" She displayed little interest in him as she continued with her dusting.

"I also know you worked here as a boy—the one who doused me with water."

Alaina carefully kept her gaze on the surface of the table. "A prank—nothing more."

"I would like to point out to you, mademoiselle, that I have become a man of some power and circumstance," Jacques stated, as if he sought to convince her of his importance. "I have acquired many things, and can pass as a gentleman wherever I go."

Alaina let his statement pass without verbal comment, for she had already noted that his speech now wavered somewhere between the lazy drawl of a Southern gentleman and a blooded Frenchman. He even dressed the part of an aristocrat.

"I have acquired a valet from one of the best families in town, and he has taught me much about a gentleman's way. I can escort you about this city in a manner worthy of royalty."

Alaina smiled serenely as she gazed at him. "Not probable sir since I have yet to give my consent to be escorted anyplace by you and I doubt if ever I will. You don't seem to understand that I am quite satisfied with leading my life without you. Now good-day, sir."

"Not just yet, mademoiselle." He laughed and strolled arrogantly forward.

She watched him warily as he halted close before her. Reaching out a hand, he cupped her chin, turning it up until her eyes met his and tightening his fingers when she tried to turn her face away.

"I can take you here and now, mademoiselle, if it met my mood. You would not be able to stop me. But I offer you something better. To be my companion—a hostess when I entertain, or sometimes, when there would just be the two of us. I would dress you in rich gowns, and you would be the envy of every woman in this town—"

"As your mistress?" She laughed in amazement. "Sir, you are dreaming."

He caught her roughly by the arms and snatched her close to him. "Don't laugh at me again, mademoiselle." His words took on the rushed Cajun accent. "You would only regret doing so. A face such as your does not bear well under a fist. It is too fine and fragile."

"I will be no man's mistress, sir," she hissed, glaring into those dark eyes.

"I have ways to convince you," he smiled lazily.

Alaina shivered at the callow crudeness of his threat, and again she tried to turn away, dragging her eyes away from those burning black ones that bore into her. Then, over Jacques's shoulder, she saw a familiar form paused in the doorway. Doctor Brooks stepped forward, loudly clearing his throat, and Jacques jerked around at the intrusion.

"Miss Hawthorne, are you all right?" the doctor questioned.

"You should have made your presence known, old man," Jacques sneered angrily.

Doctor Brooks fixed the younger man with a stern glower. "And you, sir, should not go about my hospital accosting and threatening defenseless girls. Begone from here before I set the sheriff on your tail, and don't ever let me see you in here again."

"You think to threaten Jacques DuBonné?" the roué scoffed. "I will cut you up in little pieces for the alligators, monsieur. No one tell Jacques what to do."

"And I, sir, will rouse the gentlefolk of this city to a rat hunt if I ever catch you laying your hands on this young lady again."

Jacques's nostrils flared with indignation, but he saw the truth in the old gentleman's angry glare. "I will go, but not because you say." He turned and sneered at Alaina. "I assure you, mademoiselle, we are not finished with this."

Alaina stared after the Frenchman as he made his departure, and finally, after a long moment, met the old doctor's gaze. "I fear Mister DuBonné is becoming a bit overzealous in his determination to have me." She tried to sound flippant, but she failed miserably as her voice quavered unsteadily. With more truth, she admitted, "I think he poses a bigger threat to me than I can handle just now. Saul drives me to work, then comes to pick me up. I never leave the house unless I'm with someone—either Jedediah or Saul. Who knows what that man will do, and if it's a matter of his pride, he will not ease his attentions until he has satisfied it."

It seemed only a series of harassment tactics that found Angus vehemently denying that he had any part in the Yankee payroll robbery which the renegade Alaina MacGaren had been involved in. Several bank notes that he had deposited in the bank were identified by their serial number as those taken in the theft, and immediately a swarm of Yankee officers descended upon his store to question him at length. He could only explain that he had haplessly accepted the money as legal barter for some merchandise he had sold. The Yankees could not prove otherwise, and thus were helpless to pursue the matter. Long after they left, Angus sat at his desk and stared unblinkingly at the packet of letters he had received from Roberta before she died. The back door swung open, and Saul leaned in to announce that he would be going now to pick up Alaina.

"Was dere anything else yo' was wantin' me ter do befo' ah goes, Mistah Angus?"

Angus heaved a laborious sigh. "No, Saul. You can be on your way."

The door closed gently behind the huge black, and it was a long while before Angus stirred himself enough to reach for the packet of letters. He opened the second envelope from the top and folded out the letter to examine the bank notes it contained, a part of the same that he had innocently deposited. They were crisp and unused, and in this one letter there was at least two thousand dollars in paper money tucked within it. The other letters contained like amounts, and the total wealth they contained approached almost twenty thousand dollars in crisp Yankee currency. Where his daughter had gotten them, he did not know—only that she had instructed him to keep them for her until she returned home again.

Angus hastily put away the money as a knock came at the back door, and at his call of admittance, Doctor Brooks escorted Tally Hawthorne in. Angus rose to meet them, and pulled out a chair for the old woman.

"We've come to talk with you about Alaina," Tally stated bluntly.

Angus frowned heavily. "I don't know why you came here. The girl is no concern of mine."

"She's your niece," the woman reminded him pertly.

"Of late, I've been trying to forget that fact."

"Angus! How could you! She's such a dear, sweet child!" Tally scolded angrily.

"Not as dear as my Roberta," Angus commented caustically. "She's meant trouble for me ever since I took her into my house, and I am forever hounded by her presence. I pray that I may be besieged no longer. I am an old man, and I am weary."

"Do you know anything about Jacques DuBonné and his threats against her?" Doctor Brooks inquired impatiently.

"His threats against her! My lord, it is his threats against me that have laid me low. Any day I fear he will set a torch to my store, or my home, or that some other disaster might befall my family. Why should I worry about her when I have my own problems with Mister DuBonné?"

"I have taken the initiative and written Cole about this matter," Tally informed him imperiously.

"Cole? That bas—?"

"Angus!" Tally snapped sharply. "Control your tongue!"

"That Yankee killed my daughter!" Angus barked.

"You're being ridiculous! It was not Cole's fault," Tally declared.

"He got her with child!" Angus shouted.

"Angus, I would suggest that you listen to what Tally is trying to tell you," Doctor Brooks coaxed. "Cole has sent a reply to her letter, and it might be an answer to your difficulties."

"Anything that Yankee offers I am not interested in," Angus vowed vehemently.

"He has asked for Alaina's hand in marriage," Tally serenely conveyed.

"What?!" Angus's eyes nearly bulged from his head as he glared at the old woman.

She nodded, undismayed. "Cole agrees that Alaina should be gotten out of New Orleans, and has offered the solution with his proposal."

"Never! Never!" Angus bellowed, shaking his fist at them. "I'll see him rot in hell first!"

"I'm sure you will be there to greet him should he fall victim to that wayward path," Tally replied calmly.

Angus's jaw thrust out as he questioned sneeringly, "You come here and judge me, Tally Hawthorne, when you've managed to do well for yourself playing both sides of the fence, Yankee against rebel?"

She smiled almost gently. "Angus, nobody seemed to bother what my opinions were, neither your high-and-mighty Confederate friends nor the Yankees, so I simply kept them, uncertain as they were, to myself. And with the exception of Mister DuBonné, no one has bothered me. I come here not to judge, but to plead with you to consent to this marriage as Alaina's only kin. She will only come to harm in this city when Dubonné has every intention of making her his mistress. You must not let that happen—if you are at all a man of mercy."

"Leave me!" Angus thundered. "I'll hear no more of this! Begone with you both!"

"Very well, Angus." Tally sighed and rose to her feet. "But let me warn you that if you do not soon relent, you may regret it for all your remaining life."

"Does Alaina know anything about this proposal?" Angus demanded.

"We wanted to talk with you first," Doctor Brooks explained.

"You will say nothing to her!" Angus insisted.

"I'll give you a while to think about it," Tally threatened. "Then, who knows?"

They left without another word, closing the door behind them and leaving Angus standing alone in the darkening shadows of his store. He paced restlessly about, loathing the thought of satisfying any part of Cole's desires, yet he knew that Jacques DuBonné was just waiting to spring a trap from which there would be no escape. And if the man learned that his niece was the one and only Alaina MacGaren, then it would be hell to pay for sure. Angus was greatly troubled. What was he to do when he wanted to exact some type of revenge on the man who had taken his daughter and when, at the same time, he would be placing himself in jeopardy if he did not consent to the marriage?

He mulled over the suspicions that Leala had roused in his mind, but he dismissed them as untruths. Roberta could not have played such a trick on anyone. Yet if Cole and Alaina were attracted to one another and if he consented to the marriage, then the Yankee would be well contented with her as his wife—unless they were somehow kept apart.

Angus paused in his pacing to stare down glumly at his shoes, and pondered the options open to him. What should he do? What should he do?

The heat of August descended upon the city with a merciless vengeance, and only in the cooler temperatures of the evening could a small measure of comfort be found. As she sat alone on the Craighugh porch, Alaina stared into the star-filled darkness of the heavens, wrapped in the aura of a melancholy mood. Supper had long since passed, and Angus, for a change, had arrived home at a reasonable hour and in a more sober state of mind than was his custom of late. For at least a week now, Jacques had kept his distance from the store, but his absence had all the feeling of a lull before the storm. It was hard for any of them to relax.

The front door creaked open, and Alaina glanced around as her uncle stepped out onto the porch. He approached the swing where she rested and cleared his throat sharply as he settled himself in a nearby chair. It was apparent that he had something on his mind, but a long moment of silence passed between them before he came to the point.

"I have written to Cole pleading with him to help you out of this predicament you've gotten into with Jacques." Angus cleared his throat as if a bitter gall welled up within it. "He has offered to let you come north and stay in his house for a while until this trouble has passed. I, of course, reminded him that your reputation might be greatly compromised with such an arrangement. I further suggested marriage as a solution to the problem. He has tentatively accepted, providing—ahem—"

Alaina waited rigidly, not feeling particularly complimented by her uncle's account of his exchange with Cole. She was even less flattered when he continued.

"Cole will accept on the grounds the marriage is considered to be only a temporary affair and that it be a titular arrangement, a marriage in name only—an affair of convenience to be annulled as soon as your problems are resolved."

"I see!" Alaina replied caustically, feeling more hurt and degraded than she cared to admit.

Angus rushed on to reason with her before she could express her indignation. "I see no other option open to you, Alaina, or to me. Jacques DuBonné is becoming too much of a threat for us to live here safely together. If he should learn that you are Alaina MacGaren, there'll be no hope for you. But as the wife of a retired Yankee officer, and one who was a hero besides, you'd be relatively safe. With Cole lending you his protection, you can leave the city without suspicion, and Jacques would not dare interfere."

"Thank you for your concern, Uncle Angus, but I'd rather not inconvenience Major Latimer. I can leave the city without his protection."

"You can't even leave this house without one of Jacques's men tagging behind. The man will not let you escape him. He knows your disguises, and no doubt has cautioned his men to be wary. As long as you're living here with us, he's probably hoping to persuade us in a more peaceable fashion to give you over to him—"

"Peaceable!" Alaina scoffed. "Is that what you call it?"

"Jacques has boasted of greater brutality. If he had some serious threat to hold over our heads, he'd be in here in a moment with his men to seize you. But now, he's just feeling around, looking for some handle he can grasp in order to frighten us into submission. As long as he doesn't have it, he's probably as afraid of the authorities as we are. I do not believe that he is a very honest man."

"I'll not become a burden to any man, and I won't accept Major Latimer's charity," she gritted.

"If you will not think of yourself, then consider what your aunt will have to suffer if you are taken," Angus argued.

"I'll go away if you wish! I don't have to stay here!"

"And where will you go? Mrs. Hawthorne's perhaps? Doctor Brooks's? Will you put them in danger, too?"

In roweling frustration, Alaina shot to her feet, but Angus held up a hand to stem the flow of tempestuous words.

"Think about it. You owe us that much."

Alaina whirled and ran into the house, knowing all the hurt and humiliation of being rejected by the one man who haunted her dreams. In the quiet that followed her departure, Angus gazed out into the dark-filled night. Now that he was set on a course of action, he could not easily be swayed from his purpose. As much as he loathed to, he'd enlist the aid of Tally and Doctor Brooks to help convince Alaina that marriage with Cole was the only resource of freedom open to her. By the time his niece arrived in Minnesota, she would be, he vowed, so embittered with Cole Latimer that there would be no help for the two of them.

It was late in the afternoon of the following day when Alaina received word that she was wanted in Doctor Brooks's office. Whenever such a summons had come before, she had been met with bad news, and she wondered what cataclysmic event confronted her this time. When she entered his small office, he rose from his desk and moved past her to close the door. It was then that her eyes fell on Mrs. Hawthorne who sat haughtily erect in the narrow corner behind the door. The old woman looked like a majestic queen with her wide hat and her veil tucked beneath her chin. She rested both hands on the handle of her parasol, the tip of which she had braced on the floor before her. She smiled sweetly and nodded her white head in greeting, and Alaina turned wonderingly back to Doctor Brooks as he reclaimed his chair. He leaned back, playing with a scalpel that lay on the desk top, and watched Alaina over the rim of his glasses. She glanced back and forth between the two elders, growing more and more confused by the vague signs of disapproval that she noted in their faces.

"Have I done something wrong?" she questioned hesitantly, unable to bear the stilted silence any longer.

Mrs. Hawthorne lowered her eyes briefly and toyed with the handle of her umbrella. "Not really wrong, Alaina, just utterly stupid."

Alaina sat down abruptly in a chair, more than a little stunned. Her gaze went to Doctor Brooks, and she caught him gazing thoughtfully into the distance, but nodding his head ever so slightly as if in agreement. Alaina was crushed that the criticism of these two friends and benefactors should descend upon her, and she had no clue as to the reason. She looked down at her suddenly clumsy hands and clasped them tightly in her lap to cease their fumbling. She heaved a long sigh against the urge to tears and shrugged.

"I—don't know what you disapprove of," she murmured softly.

Mrs. Hawthorne glanced at Doctor Brooks and received his nod of approval for her to proceed. "The doctor and I," she began in a rather brittle tone, "went to considerable effort to arrange a way for you to leave Louisiana. At least, until things cool down a bit. We had to twist Angus's arm nearly off to get his endorsement and cooperation. Now, we find that you have rejected the whole thing out of hand."

Alaina stared at her in amazement. "You mean you and Doctor Brooks—But Uncle Angus said that he—" She was more confused than ever.

"Bah!" Mrs. Hawthorne barked. "For a man of otherwise intelligence, Angus Craighugh is a fool when it comes to matters of delicacy."

Doctor Brooks chuckled at Mrs. Hawthorne's blunt appraisal. "Now, Tally," he reproved gently. "Be fair." He took on a slightly lecturing tone as he faced Alaina. "Angus did inform us of the fact that he had written Cole several letters—and what Cole's suggestions were. It seems to me, Alaina, that you made your denial in an emotional gesture which, though understandable, we are here to implore you to reconsider."

"I did not!" Alaina decried, a trifle insulted at the doctor's judgment. "I was not angry. I listened to all of Uncle Angus's reasons, and simply disagree that I should flee halfway across the country to let things simmer down."

Doctor Brooks leaned forward and began to tap the blade of the scalpel on a blotter. "I wonder, Alaina, if you have really considered the full depth of your predicament. Jacques has gained enough stature in the city's affairs to be dangerous, and we know him to be most persistent. He will not leave you be. He bides his time until the moment is ripe, and then, my dear, you will find yourself in dire straits. Angus made his arguments, yet I doubt that he went this far. Angus can handle the accusations that Jacques makes against him because he is an honest man in his business, and can no doubt prove it. But if you are found out, both Angus and Leala will be judged harshly. For harboring a person who is believed to be, by both North and South, a most despicable criminal, they can be stripped of everything they have and thrown into prison.

"Indeed, if the full story is brought out, even Tally and myself could join them. If Alaina MacGaren disappears for a while, what proof will there be that she was actually residing here among us? If you go away, there would be time to search out and correct the false accusations that have been leveled against you. It is most urgent that you leave, but where do you go? Back home? To hide in the swamp and hope that the Gilletts or someone as mean can't ferret you out? If we can send you to some far-off city, how would you travel and how would you live? Certainly you cannot be known as Alaina MacGaren. Every riverboat captain, every sheriff would be suspicious of a young woman traveling alone. Then again, if you travel as the bride of a well-respected doctor, a wounded hero, who would be the wiser? I doubt that they would consider Mrs. Latimer as a suspect, and you would reside in a remote frontier community, free of Jacques, free of suspicious lawmen, free to relax and enjoy a bit of peace and gracious living."

Doctor Brooks paused, and Alaina raked her brain for some logical denial. Mrs. Hawthorne took up the standard.

"You are dear to us all, Alaina," the old woman began her argument. "And we would not see you tortured or abused on a whim. But you simply must understand that you are a burden to us all, one we would gladly bear, yet one we are most fearful of losing through a chance mistake. If you are safe and far away, we would be free to defend ourselves, should the need arise, and far better able to defend you as one who has been deeply wronged. Major Latimer has assured us by letter that he understands the entire situation, but he also assures"—Mrs. Hawthorne's lips twitched beneath the spurs of a threatening smile—"that he heartily doubts that you would have the wisdom to accept. I believe he said—" The woman fumbled in her handbag and drew out a letter to scan it quickly. "Ah, yes—here it is." She raised the thin parchment and read. " 'She has a penchant for foolishness and trouble that outweighs all the considerations of common sense. I extend the suggestion most willingly and wish you luck in your attempts to convince her, though I doubt much will come of it. Will be anxiously awaiting your reply.' "

Mrs. Hawthorne folded the letter primly and tucked it away. Alaina's face was flushed as she stared down at her white-knuckled hands. Doctor Brooks and Mrs.

Hawthorne exchanged the briefest of glances and nods, then watched the young girl as they waited for her response.

Alaina's mind flogged itself in a confused melee. *Outweighs all common sense! That blithering bluebelly idiot!* She could just see his gaping grin above his broad brass-buttoned chest. That miming jackanapes! He pities me and plays his savior's role most heartily, but he does not want me as a wife.

Her mind hardened, and her neck stiffened. *Well, I don't want him as a husband!*

And all the arguments rolled endlessly back on her like a flooding tide, and slowly her defenses crumbled. Burden! Threat! Danger! Stupid! Foolish! And one that had been unspoken—Unwanted!

She straightened and, in a small voice, conceded. "All right. I'll go away. I'll marry him—I'll stay until I'm a danger to no one—but only until then."

The two elders relaxed and smiled. They had gained the first step of their plan. But soon the girl would be out of their hands, and they would have to depend upon a greater guidance for its full consummation.

Chapter 25

AT times Jacques DuBonné was a lender of money at high interest rates. He expended very little risk since, for his investment, he was careful to command property of much higher value as security. It was in this capacity as usurer that one bright September morn he entered a merchant's shop across the street from Angus Craighugh's store and sought out the owner.

"You are far behind in your payments, monsieur. Jacques DuBonné does not have great patience in the matter of moneys. Either you pay your debt, or you will lose your shop. Do you understand?"

"It's obvious that you've intended this very thing from the beginning," the merchant accused. "I have seen you come and go over there, and I would say that you've supplied Angus Craighugh with money and merchandise so he could lower his prices and gain all my customers. You'd do that for the uncle of that thieving and murdering Alaina MacGaren, and where I am an honest man in a bit of difficulty, you take advantage of my plight."

"Pardon, monsieur. What was it you say?"

"I said that you've planned this from the first!"

"*Non! Non!* I mean about this Alaina MacGaren."

The merchant glared in heated ire. "Anybody who knows him can tell you that Angus Craighugh is the uncle of that traitorous bitch!"

Jacques leisurely straightened his tall hat on his head and tapped the handle of his ornate walking stick against the man's chest. "You have until tomorrow evening to satisfy your debt, monsieur. I would not waste another moment if you hope to keep your shop."

The Frenchman strolled from the shop, cast a long and thoughtful glance toward the Craighugh store, then climbed into his landau. Sometimes a man profited from biding his time.

A light mist was settling upon the city, turning the trees and houses along the way into indistinct shadows as Saul and Alaina wended their way home in the gathering shrouds of dusk. At the Craighugh house, Alaina ran to the back door, while the black man drove the buckboard into the carriage house. As she entered the kitchen, Dulcie glanced around from her work and announced: "Miz Leala's in de parlor, chile. And dere's a gen'man with her. Ah doan know what he's here for, but he done come all de way from Minnesotee, and he been sent by Mistah Cole."

Alaina smoothed her damp hair. "I guess everyone neglected to tell you, Dulcie. I'm about to follow in Roberta's footsteps."

"Huh?" The woman looked at her suspiciously, raising her brows.

"I'm going to marry Doctor Latimer."

Dulcie gaped in awe, then slowly whispered, "Lawsy! Ain't dat a wonder!"

"A wonder," Alaina mumbled disconcertedly. Despite herself, she had been counting the days past, wondering if each would be the one that heralded her Yankee rescuer. September was already full upon them, and no word of his intended arrival had been received. She took a long, steadying breath. "I'd better see why the man is here."

Alaina passed through the house, her footsteps echoing in the hall. At the sound, the voices in the parlor halted expectantly, and as she entered the room, a rather small, thin, nattily dressed man came to his feet. A large leather case sat beside his chair.

"Alaina, child, this is Mister James," Aunt Leala said in introduction. "He's an attorney Cole has sent."

"It's a pleasure, Miss Haw—uh—Miss MacGaren," he corrected himself and smiled kindly. "Doctor Latimer went to some length to explain your situation here, but I'm afraid he failed to inform me of your youth and beauty."

"Doctor Latimer has been rather hampered in the past by the presence of soot and grime," Alaina replied. "He's never been able to see past it. But tell me sir, how has such a gracious man come to know Doctor Latimer?"

Mister James was confused by her veiled jibe and

politely explained. "I have been associated with the Latimer family for some time. I knew his father."

"And you are here to arrange the details of the marriage. I suppose you have copies of the letters, agreements, and such?" Alaina regarded him curiously, half expecting him to give some reason why the marriage should be put off.

"It is my prime purpose, and I have the necessary entitlements." He nodded, then hastened to place the leather case in front of her. "Doctor Latimer has also sent a gift of clothing for your wedding and the trip up north."

"That wasn't necessary," she responded cooly. "I have managed to acquire a sizable trousseau, and I do not intend to accept more of Doctor Latimer's charity than I can afford."

Mister James coughed delicately. He had been warned, of course, of the young woman's stubborn independence and tried to soothe her ire as much as possible. "Perhaps you might look over his gifts just the same. There might be something in the case you'd like to have."

"When is Doctor Latimer arriving?" she asked bluntly.

"Oh, I don't think you quite realize why I'm here. I bear Doctor Latimer's proxy and am prepared to accomplish the service in his absence."

"Do you mean that bluebelly Yankee couldn't even come to his own wedding?" Her voice grew louder with each word.

"Doctor Latimer has been a trifle inconvenienced of late—"

"Inconvenienced!" she railed. Her color mounted high in her cheeks and warmed her ears. Mister James was taken aback by her outburst and spluttered to explain, but with a strangled cry of outrage, Alaina whirled, throwing back a comment that left both of the elders gaping as she fled the room. She hit the front door running, struck by a mad, impelling urge to get away from the house. Leala hurried after her, pleading with her to come back, but Alaina was incensed. She quickened her pace as she heard her aunt calling for Saul. Her eyes burning with tears, she ran across the wide lawn and into the street, fleeing through the fog-filled night as if the hounds of hell dogged her heels.

After a time, some sanity returned, and she realized she had come some distance from the house. Her side ached, and she gasped for breath as she leaned against a tree by the roadside. At first glance, shadows seemed to flit along the street, three on either side of the avenue. But even as she paused, they retreated and faded from view. Then, in the night, a new sound came, the measured clip-clop of horses' hooves on the stone street and the slow creaking of carriage wheels.

Clasping her side against the pain, Alaina began to walk away from the sound. The shapes came back, vague movements on either side, gone before the eye could focus, and somewhere behind in the night, the relentless plodding pursuit of the carriage. She came to an intersection where a streetlamp glowed dimly in the fog, and gladly entered its narrow nimbus of light as if it provided a haven from the surrounding darkness. She tried to peer through the thick haze, then slowly, almost magically, a darker shadow took shape and drew near. It was a magnificently matched pair of black horses drawing a low-slung landau of the same hue. The carriage halted, and Alaina gasped as the driver stepped down. It was the huge black who served Jacques Dubonné as coachman and bodyguard. A few steps away from her, the man paused and cocked his head as if listening.

"Miz Alaina? Miz Alaina?" Saul's voice, muffled by the fog, came faintly through the black gloom.

"Saul!" she shrieked with all her strength. "Here! Help me!"

She turned to run again, but the black driver was on her before she could take a step, his arms encircling her and preventing flight. Even as she drew a breath to scream again, he spun her around, and his massive fist came forward almost gently to tap the point of her chin. Strangely the light disappeared, and she floated into a limbo, a void as black and bottomless as the deepest, darkest hole.

Jacques's huge servant, Gunn, picked up the limp form and turned in time to see the other large black charging him. But before Saul could reach his quarry, he was swarmed upon by a half dozen waterfront toughs. He struggled to cast his assailants off, gritting and gnashing his teeth with his effort as he saw Gunn carry Alaina to the carriage, hold her face up into the light as if for inspection by someone inside, then open the door and place her within it. A moment later the man's sharp whistle set the magnificent black team in motion, and the carriage disappeared into the night.

Saul turned to the several matters at hand. He grasped the arm of one of the men who wielded a heavy wood truncheon and seemed intent upon splitting a black skull. A twist of the man's wrist brought a scream of pain, and Saul lifted the club from the slack fingers, laying it about him in a hasteful, wasteful manner. A surprisingly brief time passed before Saul crouched, gasping for breath, over the still forms of the six men. Turning them over, he recognized two as the minions of one despicable Jacques DuBonné.

Tucking the truncheon into his belt, he raced back to the house. His feet took him flying across low shrubs and fences, but scarcely outdistanced his mind. There was no use in telling the household since the only news he had was of the worse kind. Angus would probably explode, and Leala would be a nervous wreck before the night was over. Thus Saul went directly into the stable. He slipped a bridle over one of Cole's finest horses and led it carefully through the gate to the front of the house before he threw a leg over its bare back, thumping his heel into its ribs to send it flying like a hunting bird through the dark of night.

When they entered the shantytown of the emancipated Negroes, he tied the horse in a tumbledown shed of a friend and went the rest of the way by foot, seeking out those who had a knowledge of the underworld current in this gray, dingy, half-civilized city. A word here, a word there, a reluctant forced piece of information, and soon he knew where the worst corruption on the waterfront was headquartered.

Alaina stirred, then moaned. A dim light threw eerie specters on the back sides of her eyelids. A quaking ache throbbed at the base of her skull, and her head swam as the ache splintered and became a dull, pounding pain somewhere behind her eyes. She eased her eyes open and saw a dim, blurred figure of a man seated beside what seemed to be a table with a lamp on it. She blinked away the fog and repented the act as she recognized the leering grin of Jacques DuBonné. He leaned back in the chair, the tails of his coat hitched over his thighs, and his bandy legs spraddled wide.

"Ah, my dear Mademoiselle Hawthorne." He fairly chortled with glee. "Welcome back. I had almost begun to fear that Gunn might have been over harsh with you."

Ignoring the man for the moment, Alaina took in her surroundings. She lay on a bale of cotton over which a bolt of rich silk brocade had been carelessly tossed. The room was small but as quiet as a cave. No outside sounds came in, and the walls, though piled high with crates and barrels, seemed hewn of stone block. She could think of no part of the city where such a place could exist.

"Are you feeling well enough to discuss a few things, *ma chérie?*" Jacques's mewling voice drew her attention once more.

Alaina tried to answer, but a thick croak was all that issued from her parched throat. She managed to sit up, but braced herself as her head swam with the motion.

"Well, be that as it may, I'm sure your voice will return in a few moments. I've never known a woman who could be silent for very long."

Alaina slid her feet to the floor, then had to lean back and grasp the bale as a sickening dizziness swept over her.

"Remember the feeling, Miss Hawthorne." Jacques's voice was flat and deadly. "And remember Gunn's gentleness with you. It could save you much pain in times to come."

Alaina stared at him in frustrated anger. She croaked again, then gestured questioningly to where a bucket and dipper hung near the door.

"Please, *ma chérie,* help yourself," Jacques acceded lightly. "Whatever you wish—within reason, of course."

Alaina had regained much of her senses, but made it a point to stagger and stumble a bit as she went to the water. The stuff was tepid and stale, yet its wetness was most welcome. She drank deeply before she replaced the dipper, then leaned against the wall, rubbing a hand over her brow as her other hand crept toward the door latch. With a sudden rush, she lifted the bar and threw the portal wide, but halted in her tracks with such abruptness that her skirts swirled about her ankles. Gunn was already waiting in a half crouch, his arms spread wide to block her passage whichever way she turned, and with a grin that split his face from ear to ear. As she stared at him in stunned dismay, he began to laugh, a low, rolling thunder that began deep in his chest and grew until it echoed in the stone-walled corridor. She slammed the door in his face, then leaned against it as the high cackle of Jacques's laughter drove punishing shards of despair through her.

"Well, Miss Hawthorne, I hesitate to say that your sudden departure is not within reason. After all, we have come to no understanding as yet."

Alaina found her voice and hurled back. "Do you think you can abuse me and find safety anywhere in the South? Why, every gentleman, Southern or Yankee, will hunt you down like a mad dog."

"For Camilla Hawthorne? True, as you say." He favored her with a sneering grin and shrugged. "But for the murderess, thief, traitor Alaina MacGaren? Hardly." He considered the back of his hand. "Why, they even might award me an honorarium—or a medal."

Alaina set her jaw and glared her hatred through the sudden fear that threatened to engulf her. She knew the full folly of her stormy flight from the Craighugh manse now, and retribution had come swiftly for her foolishness.

Jacques rose to his feet, and straightening his coat, began to pace the room, strutting like a banty rooster ruffling his feathers for a desirable hen. "I have met many haughty wenches before, *ma chérie.* There was a Creole bitch who considered herself a prize for the most handsome roué of the Delta. In a matter of days she came crawling, begging me to take her to my bed. Then, there was a Southern belle who came down from Memphis after the siege. Oh, she was most arrogant. But slightly more than a week of my hospitality brought her to see the light, and she came to me willingly."

"Do you think to frighten me," Alaina railed, "with a simpering account of your conquests?"

"Frighten you?" Jacques stopped, and his dark eyes raked her boldly. "Why, of course not, *chérie.* If I wished to frighten you, I would call Gunn, or a dozen of my men. They would most enjoy frightening you. Indeed, they would vie heartily for your screams. I do not wish to frighten you, Alaina, only to point out the advantages of my continued protection."

Alaina swallowed an urge to vomit and could only glare at him in silent defiance.

He began to pace again and instructed her further in a most casual and offhanded tone. "I know of some hostelries—several down along the coast—some well back in the swamps. They cater to that brand of men who found the dangers of war not at all to their liking and fled—from both sides, mind you—to find some place of peace far from the conflict."

"Deserters!" Alaina snarled.

"Hm, whatever. Then, there were those who were not always discriminating about the ownership of articles they wished to sell."

She named them as well. "Pirates. Blackguards, one and all."

"Perhaps." He took off his hat and smoothed the bright panache. "Then, there would be a whole host of others, most who cannot stand the rigors of civilized society. The only flaw is that there are few women in these places. They mostly abhor the roughness of life there. Thus, the men are most eager when a pretty young thing is put at their disposal. Sometimes they wax most rough—one might even say crude or brutal. Ahhh—but there, Mademoiselle MacGaren!" He jammed the plumed hat on his head again. "There you have it! Why, if a pretty young thing went there for a few months, think of the things she could learn. How to please a man in—oh, so many ways." He paused and stared at her, his nostrils flaring. "And when she returned, she would be more aware of the benefits of the gentler life here in the city—one considerably less repetitious and tiresome."

Alaina looked at him for a long moment, and her decision formed with a finality of a door closing in her mind. There could be no yielding. Beyond this point, there was only freedom or death. Somehow she would find a way to kill either him or herself.

"Do you think to convince me, sir, of your gentle manner?" she laughed.

Jacques's black eyes narrowed dangerously. He stepped toward her, drawing himself up to his full, stunted height.

"I have warned you, mademoiselle, do not laugh at me." The guttural backwater French crept into his voice.

"Ahh, Jacques DuBonné! The gentleman always," Alaina sneered and flung a further taunt full into his face. "You are unfit company for the gentlefolk, Mister DuBonné. And more's the pity that you will never know why."

"I am Jacques DuBonné! The gen'l'man of New Orleans!" His face flushed crimson as his rage showed white around his eyes. He caught Alaina's arm roughly and threw her away from the door. "I am Jacques Dubonné!" He jabbed a thumb at his richly garbed chest. "I come with nothing from up the river!"

"From a backwater houseboat, most likely," Alaina interjected, rubbing her arm and backing warily away from him.

"And now I am rich! And own much of the city!"

"Stole much of the city," Alaina corrected sharply.

"From the lazy and stupid who could not hold it!" Jacques raged on. "And from the blind Yankees who polished the buttons and prance the horse along the street. I play the game, and I beat them all! Me! Jacques DuBonné!"

"You have never played your game with men, you arrogant fop. You played your game with old women, widows, and children." Alaina carefully placed the table between them.

Jacques's eyes glittered hard in the dim light of the lamp, and his yellowed teeth showed in a ragged snarl as he slowly stalked her.

"I have seen you belly-crawl too many times when you face a man," Alaina goaded. "You are a miserable little man."

"Little man!" A hoarse screech twisted his face. He lunged forward, feinting to his left, then darting to his right to catch her arm as she fled. Jacques aimed a vicious slap at his tormentor's head, but she ducked beneath it, and her heel came down on his instep. He gasped in pain, and she snatched free, leaving a shred of cloth in his grasp.

"I will teach you, little bitch!" he wheezed as he limped after her. "You will crawl and call me Massah DuBonné like a good black sow."

"You betray yourself! You are a pig, with all the wallowing grace of one." She whirled away, avoiding his rush. "You stumble over your fine leather boots," she chided as he lurched around. "Are you more at ease barefoot in the mud?"

They were like two wild animals half crouched, circling each other.

"Do you think," Alaina ground out deliberately, "that I will give myself to the likes of you—ever? Do you think you can get me alive to one of your filthy pigsty wallows? I served you mop and bucket well, sir, and if you come to me, I will serve you much, much more, you cackling little crow."

Jacques could stand no more. With a bellow of rage, he launched himself in a soaring leap and came down upon her, his arms flailing wildly. Alaina's fist thrust up with every ounce of her strength and, though unaimed, the blow caught Jacques squarely in the groin. He sagged against her, his arms now clutching for support, his eyes wide and glazed as he gagged for breath. Alaina tried to push him off, and her hand slipped under his jacket beneath his left armpit. In reflex she grasped the smooth butt of the small derringer and, putting her shoulder against the man's chest, pulled it free.

Jacques felt her movement and, seeing the pistol, seized her wrist with his left hand. His attention was divided between the struggle and the sickening pain in the pit of his belly. Alaina twisted her wrist and sank her teeth into the base of his thumb until he screeched and jerked away, dragging her hand with his, unwilling to loose it for fear of his life. Both hands and the gun thudded solidly into the side of his head along his cheek, and the small derringer barked. A neat round hole appeared briefly in Jacques's left ear before the blood gushed forth. He staggered back whimpering, until he realized he was still alive and only slightly harmed. Alaina struggled with the unfamiliar weapon, trying to flip the second barrel into place. It turned just as Jacques lifted the glass lamp from the table and held it high over his head as if to throw it. She snapped the barrel into place and, aiming at the light, closed her eyes and squeezed. The echoing report blended with the shattering of glass and a scream from Jacques.

Alaina's eyes flew open to see Jacques standing, his raised arm ablaze like a torch, with oil and glass flying everywhere. In the next instant Jacques's entire side was aflame and he gave another shrill scream as he fell to the floor rolling, spreading flames in his wake. He came up against the cotton bale and, scrambling to his feet, wrapped his arm in the silk brocade to smother the fire that engulfed it.

A look of deadly purpose came into his pain-twisted face. He ignored the flames that now covered half the room and, raising his left arm to the back of his neck, slowly drew out the long, thin stiletto.

"You have won your dying place!" his strained hiss sighed over the roar of the fire. He moved toward her and Alaina raised the pistol again.

"Have I not served you enough?"

"It is empty!" His pain-tightened voice sneered. "Two shots—no more."

There was a shout from without, then a deafening crash as the thick, but age-weakened door splintered inward. Alaina and Jacques gaped in stunned surprise as a towering black shape rose from the floor. It was Saul!

Alaina cried his name and saw, as he came to his feet, the unstirring form of Gunn sprawled motionless on the door. Jacques retreated quickly back through the flames as Saul stepped forward and, with a casual flip of his thick arm, reached out and hurled the table at the other. The stiletto flew from Jacques's hand, and with an enraged scream, the man leaped atop the bale and hauled himself upward toward a small trapdoor between the massive rafters overhead.

The smoke swirled chokingly into the chamber as the fire grew, testing the taste of other goods stacked against the walls. Saul caught Alaina's hand and led her toward the door. Gunn moaned and stirred as they stepped over his body to dash down the narrow passageway. The corridor was lined with inert shapes of several more guards, but Saul paid them no mind. Pulling her along behind him, he charged up a flight of stairs and entered a large warehouse stacked to the rafters with row upon row of cotton bales, some labeled with the cryptic block letters "C.S.A.," then crossed out and with new letters "U.S.N." beneath. The wild tale had floated downriver when Porter's fleet journeyed north as to how the Union navy came to be called the Cotton Stealing Association of the United States Navy. These were some of the bales that had caused the caustic comments.

Saul mumbled a quick apology, then slipping an arm

beneath Alaina's trembling legs, laid her over his shoulder and ran. A flickering light began to grow behind them before they found the door and dashed through it. There were angry shouts, then a high-pitched voice screamed, "Find her! Find her! A thousand dollars for the one who brings her back!"

"Huh!" Alaina grunted out between the long, jolting strides of Saul's gait. "The—Yankees—offered—much more."

They raced along the top of a levee, the river on one side, a long row of warehouses on the other. After they passed several of these, Saul ducked into a narrow alley between two of them. Alaina gasped as he half sprinted, half leaped down the steeply sloping incline of the levee, and then they were in the runs and warrens of the black waterfront section of the city. Saul lowered her to the ground and they proceeded on more deliberately. They passed a board fence where someone had left a dark blanket to air. Saul snatched it down and spread it over Alaina's shoulders, covering the light color of her dress and forming it into a cowl to hide the pale shape of her face.

The hue and cry followed them, and they crouched beneath a low tin shelter as Jacques's men raced by. The pursuit grew distant, but now a new furor mounted. Flames licked high into the air from the roof of Jacques's warehouse and dined with hungry vigor at the bales within. The clamor grew around the burning warehouse.

Even Jacques's toughs were loath to spend much time in the colored section, and groups of them muttered solemnly as they withdrew past the fugitives. After a while Saul led Alaina through the narrow alleys and streets to the house of his friend where he had left the horse.

Alaina could not return to the Craighugh house, nor was Mrs. Hawthorne's any longer a safe haven. Doctor Brooks was known about as her friend, and she would not do well hiding in the store. There was only one place where she could hide.

The Craighugh household was in a dither when Saul returned. He explained that Alaina was safe and began to lay out the plan they had made. It was near midnight when Saul left the house, a satchel and a large bundle beneath his arm. He placed them in the rear of the buggy and mounted to the seat, clucking the horse into motion and going leisurely down the street, not seeming to notice the pair of men who followed at a discreet distance.

When Saul was out of sight, Jedediah and Angus dragged a large steamer trunk out to the stable and placed it aboard the decrepit old wagon. A few moments later Jedediah drove the wagon around the front and headed off in a direction opposite the one Saul had taken. A man followed him also.

Dulcie and Angus meandered casually over the grounds until they were sure no other lurking men remained, then steathily Angus eased open a narrow little-used gate behind the stable, and Dulcie's eldest daughter, Cora Mae led Ol' Tar through it and across the neighbor's yard where she climbed to the nag's back and, keeping to back roads and alleys, wound her way toward the hospital. The hour of midnight was striking on Doctor Brooks's tall, grandfather clock when the housekeeper was roused by a persistent tapping on the rear door. Muttering dire threats about the lateness of the hour, the black woman slipped into her robe and opened the kitchen door to find a young negro girl patiently waiting.

"Ah's got a message for Doctah Brooks."

"Git yo'self 'way from here, chile," the housekeeper fretted. "Ah ain' gonna wake the doctah dis time o' night. Yo' come back in the mornin'."

The woman closed the door, and the tapping resumed as before.

"Ah is got a impo'tant message for the doctah," the girl repeated as the door was snatched open again. "De massah done said ah is to gib it to him, and don't let nobody put me off. Yo' tell de doctah it's about Miz Lainie."

The older woman glared down at the child and sputtered angrily. Cora Mae smiled and started over from the first.

"Ah is got a impo'tant message for the doctah—"

Even the half-asleep housekeeper could recognize determined persistence. "Ah know! You said that! You said that!" She shook her finger at Cora Mae. "Ah is gonna go tell the doctah, and if he doan say it's impo'tant, ah is gonna come back here and whip yo' blind."

Cora Mae waited patiently outside the open door, her hands folded in front of her as the housekeeper went grumbling off. A few moments passed, and a man's voice sounded somewhere in the house, then a quick *slip-slap* of slippers coming down the stairs, followed by the disgruntled tones of the black woman.

"Hmph! Chil'uns dese days ain' got no respec'. Hauling de older folks outa dere beds at all hours."

The fussing stopped as the kitchen door swung open, and Doctor Brooks pushed through, trying to tie the belt of his robe with one hand while he settled his glasses in place with the other.

"Come in, child. Come in," he bade the girl, and when she had complied, he then asked, "What is it, Cora Mae?"

The girl cast a leery eye toward the woman who had taken up a stance beside the hearth. "Ah ain' s'pose ta tell no one but you."

"It's all right, Cora Mae." Doctor Brooks looked over the top of his glasses at the housekeeper. "Tessie would only listen through the door. She knows everything that happens in this house anyway."

The black woman gave an injured sniff, but made no move to depart as Cora Mae drew a small envelope from her pocket and handed it to the doctor. He opened it, withdrew the key it held and stared at it blankly.

"Dat is de key to—ah"—the girl rolled her eyes upward for a long moment—"Miz Roberta's captain doctah—his—his place—down at the 'Talba house."

Doctor Brooks raised his brows. "You mean Major Latimer's apartment at the Pontalba place?"

Cora Mae nodded vigorously. "Yassuh, dat's what it's for."

"And what does this have to do with Miss Alaina?"

"W-a-a-l-l." Cora Mae raised her hand, spread her fingers, and began to count off the points she had been told. "Miz Lainie, she say she ain't mad 'bout the weddin' no more—and she will do it wid"—the girl paused and looked up questioningly—"wid the lawman? But some man—" She moved on to the next finger. "Jack DeBone, I guess it were. He done caught Miz Lainie and got her in trouble." Cora Mae moved back to the first finger, shook her head, then moved on to the third.

"Miz Lainie say—or Saul say, Miz Lainie say—for you to come pick her up wid the key, and the two of you go to that Pon—Pon—where dat key fits—and wait dere inside." Cora Mae moved to the fourth finger and stood in deep thought for a moment. "Dat's right! Den Mistah Angus, he gonna bring de lawman—and de preacher man—and yo' is gonna get de weddin' done with."

The girl dropped her hands and held them behind her back, grinning broadly at the success of her mission, while Doctor Brooks tried to sort out the facts as he had just heard them and the housekeeper stared fixedly at the wall, muttering beneath her breath.

Doctor Brooks looked at the key and began to repeat carefully, "Now let me get this straight—Miss Alaina wants to go through with the marriage—" Cora Mae pulled out her hands and began to tick off her fingers as the doctor continued. "Because Jacques DuBonné caught her and caused a lot of trouble. And I am supposed to take this key, pick up Miss Alaina, and go to Major Latimer's apartment where we will meet Angus, the lawyer, and the minister."

The girl nodded her head, then suddenly her grin faded, and she stared down blankly at her still-raised thumb. "Yassah! Yassah!" She worried. "But dere's somep'n mo'. I used all o' dem when dey said it. Dey is somep-n mo'—" Her voice trailed off as she became lost in thought. Her audience waited with bated breath.

"Oh!" The grin came back wider than before, and she proudly pushed the thumb down. "Miz Lainie is waitin' up where dem—where dem hurt rebel soldiers used to be."

"In the hospital?" Doctor Brooks asked urgently. "In the old Confederate ward? Of course, I would have guessed it. You've done very well, Cora Mae, and I hope Miss Alaina—" he glanced again at his housekeeper who shook her head in confusion—"will answer any further questions I might have. But tell me, child, why did you come sneaking through all the shrubs to the back door?"

"Saul say dat DeBone man gots a buncha white trash out on de streets, an' dey is lookin' fo' Miz Lainie, and we is gots to be careful dey don't find her."

"Very well, Cora Mae. Do you have a way home?"

"Ah gots Ol' Tar. He down the street a ways."

"Then go back home, and be just as careful as you were on the way here."

When the girl was gone, he turned to the housekeeper. "I'm going to get dressed. I'll take a horse and buggy from the hospital stable. If anyone asks, tell them I was called out to the hospital."

PART TWO

Chapter 26

A light mist had settled on the river, mottling the surface of the water into a dull brownish gray and muting the autumn colors of the thick forests. Alaina leaned against the forward railing of the upper deck, letting her eyes skim over the panorama of this northern land as the packet slid through a jumbled, island-filled stretch of water. Low limestone bluffs began to grow on either side. Then, a darker current on the eastern bank slowly expanded until, beneath a high cliff, it became another river that spewed its clearer waters into the Mississippi. The tributary was the Saint Croix, she was informed, and another hour or so would see them to their destination.

Once again, a riverboat carried her away from the smell of ashes and into a new phase of her life. Alaina could hardly deny a feeling of expectation, yet a sense of strangeness roamed restlessly within her. The awareness that she was now Cole Latimer's wife burrowed down in her mind, leaving her nothing more than a thin facade of composure to mask her disquietude. The closer she came to her destination, the faster her thoughts churned in fretful turmoil, and a full night of restful sleep had slipped beyond her grasp. This morning she had risen before dawn after much tossing and turning, packed her few belongings, and thrust her wicker valise, along with the leatherbound case, into the larger steamer trunk wherein she had started her voyage. In deference to the light drizzle that threatened to continue, she had been reluctant to wear one of her better gowns for fear of having it ruined by the rain and mud. Instead, she had donned the reliable black dress with its newly added adornment of ecru lace. Her haste to be ready gained her nothing, for she had to wait out the remainder of the morning with only the changing countryside and her own thoughts to occupy her. She chafed, not with eagerness, but with something more akin to anxiety and dread. She had hoped to meet Cole with at least some semblance of dignity, but her appearance was far from being at its best. Rather, she feared that she might be mistaken for someone's poor relation. Yet her Scottish blood would not allow her to subject any other item of her carefully replenished wardrobe to the elements for the sake of mere pride. The black bonnet and the homemade woolen cloak of Confederate gray served to protect her from the cold, damp wind even if it lent nothing to a stately grace.

The unrelenting, dark rust hue of the autumn oaks gradually gave way to occasional houses that stood close upon the riverbanks. The sternwheeler rounded a bend to the left, and ahead of them, beyond a last small island, a cliff separated the rivers like a huge ship's prow. High on its summit sprawled a stone-walled fort that flew the stripes and blue of a Federal flag. A precipitous road led down the left face of the hill to a narrow bank below where a cluster of wooden buildings squatted along a low stone landing. As they neared shore, the captain came out of the pilothouse and directed the helmsman until the steamer carefully nudged against the quay.

"Secure her!" he bellowed to the deckhands below, then to the helmsman, "Shut her down!" The man reached up and pulled a lanyard down. The ship's whistle emitted a single, piercing shriek, and the stern paddle wheel halted its restless churning.

Several wagons awaited the packet's arrival, and a short distance from these a large, enclosed brougham was visible. A pair of figures stood beside it, and with a woman's sureness, Alaina knew the tall, lean one was her husband. All about her, passengers were drifting from the railing, but her own limbs felt leaden. She stood as one mesmerized, not able to lift her gaze from the man leaning on a slim, black cane.

Farther aft, Mister James hurried from his cabin with a parcel of papers clutched in one hand and his valise in the other. When he saw Alaina, the small, dapper lawyer came to stand beside her. Resting his satchel between his knees and the railing, he held a tactful silence.

A sudden gust of cold wind swept across the deck and struck Alaina full force with a spattering of raindrops. She huddled deeper into the warm folds of her cloak, pondering on the events that had made such an unmatched pair as she and Cole, man and wife. He waited on the dock like some dark Teutonic lord, seeming much in accord with the dreary, rain-swept landscape. Even without an exchange of words between them, she was taken with the chilling thought that this whole affair had been a terrible mistake. In more ways than one she would soon step from the temporary haven of the steamboat into a new world, and she felt much the foreigner in it.

Mister James waved until he gained his client's attention. Raising his head, Cole returned the gesture in acknowledgment. Almost immediately his gaze shifted to the trim figure of the woman who stood beside the rail. Alaina's knees had a moment of weakness as she waited for some evidence of recognition. Among the families of the South a mild show of warmth and greeting would have been in order, but he gave no sign of welcome, not even to move from his stance beside the carriage.

Mister James respectfully tipped his hat to her. "If you are ready, madam, we'll go ashore now."

Alaina nodded her agreement, lifted her resolve, took a firm hold on her courage, and followed the lawyer down the stairs. On the lower deck they were joined by Saul who had slung across his back the threadbare blanket that held his belongings. Hoisting Alaina's large trunk onto a broad shoulder, he followed behind them.

With a word to his driver, Cole left him and, leaning on his cane, moved carefully toward the packet. The chill damp air bit through the greatcoat he had shrugged about his shoulders, settling like a numb lump in his thigh. Since the ride out, his leg had stiffened from the cold and inactivity, giving him cause to regret the fact that the steamer had docked here at the Fort Snelling landing and not at the more comfortable one at Saint Anthony, but it carried supplies and mail for the fort and, after a stop here, was bound up the Minnesota River.

As Cole neared the steamer to receive his bride and party, his gaze found the huge black who trailed her, and he knew a moment of relief, for he had often wondered if Saul had survived the war and the upheaval after it. But Cole's attention was drawn back to Alaina, and his brows drew together beneath the wide brim of a black, low-crowned hat. He was anxious to fathom her mood. But where he had known her earlier as a quick-tempered, many-sided vixen, he now perceived an air of seriousness about her. She displayed none of the frivolity that was common in other young ladies her age. She moved with a fluid grace, but with an intent directness that was at once both pleasing and a trifle disconcerting. It was as if she had carefully considered all the alternatives and, having made up her mind, was not to be swayed from her purpose. Perhaps the hardships and tribulations of the war had stripped all humor from her. She bore no hint of the saucy "Al" as she came across the landing ramp, but was as cool and aloof as if she were a nomadic queen holding herself from a distasteful event. He could guess at the depth of her reluctance to be here among the hated Yankees, and no less would be her distaste with being married to one. Cole braced himself but could not shrug off a dismal bend of mind. He had come full circle, from the vivid rages of Roberta, to the cool disdain of her cousin, and the outlook seemed far from bright.

Alaina studied her new husband surreptitiously as he stepped to the end of the gangplank. Beneath the greatcoat casually draped over his shoulders, he seemed somewhat thinner. His long, muscular frame was well turned out in black, the color's starkness being broken only by a double-breasted vest of silver brocade and a crisp, white shirt of silk. He had the look of a riverboat gambler and appeared most worldly. It was the first time she had seen him garbed in anything other than a military uniform, and it was like coming face to face with a stranger. It frightened her, especially when those thoroughly blue eyes locked on her and slowly raked her. She had forgotten how brilliant and clear they were. In some magical way they seemed capable of stripping the lies from whatever passed before them. It was all she could do to face his unspoken challenge and not retreat to the safety of her cabin.

The change, she sensed, had more substance than the clothing. Measure by measure, the realization dawned that this was a man none of them had known. He had been an intrusion into their lives, and a desperate Roberta had seized upon the hope that he could lift her above the depravations of the South. Now his manner bore an odd touch of threatening boldness. He appeared able to hold himself apart from the world, and yet, with his mere presence, dominate the scene around him as he did now. He tipped his hat to her, and Alaina almost expected him to click his heels in a mocking bow. But then, the scrap of metal in his leg had left him somewhat less than agile.

"I trust you had a comfortable journey, madam." His voice had the same rich timbre, and Alaina began to wonder if he had any flaw she could touch upon and draw some strength from. His brow raised as he took in the detail of her long cloak and recognized the black gown she wore beneath. "Mourning garb, Alaina?" He smiled ruefully as he chided. "Usually a marriage is more a time for gaiety and laughter."

She opened her mouth to reply, but a frigid gust of wind slanted stinging droplets down upon them and swept the breath and words from her. Gasping, she turned her face away from the pelting raindrops, and Cole moved close until his bulk sheltered her. He carefully refrained from touching her, remembering all too well Al's reluctance to be fondled.

Saul set the trunk to the ground beside them, drew the collar of his thin woolen jacket close about his neck, and stamped his feet in an effort to banish the prickling iciness from them. His well-worn shoes afforded little protection against the cold and wet.

"Good heavens, man!" Cole thrust out a hand in welcome, and the other took it in his huge one. "Didn't anyone warn you about the weather up here?"

"No, suh!" Saul's face split into a wide, white-toothed grin. "But ah is learnin' mighty fast."

Alaina felt a need to explain the man's presence. "I had to bring him along—for the same reason I had to come," she ventured, at first apologetically, then realized that in this matter she had no cause to be contrite. "I assure you, Major Latimer, we're not asking for more charity. I paid for his passage myself, and Saul can find work. If not with you, then with someone else."

"With someone else?" Cole's tone was scoffingly incredulous. "Madam, I will hear of no such thing. The man saved my life." He faced Saul with the statement. "I'm in need of a new foreman for the field hands. Have you had any experience along those lines?" At the man's eager nod of affirmation, he settled the matter. "The position is yours if you wish it."

Saul grinned, lifted the steamer trunk again, and made his way to the back of the brougham where he deposited it in the boot.

Brushing aside Alaina's attempt to thank him, Cole gestured to his driver who came at a run. "Olie, see Mrs. Latimer to the carriage. I'll be along shortly."

"Yah, sure t'ing, Doctor Latimer." The brawny, pale-haired man, of an age more than two score, lifted his odd little, narrow-billed cloth cap and gave Alaina a jerky nod. "Olie vill get yu out of dis cold, yah?"

Alaina thrust down the feeling of pique at being brushed off into another's care, reasoning it was probably just as well she avoided the close attention of Cole Latimer. Stiffly smiling her assent, she allowed the driver to escort her to the brougham.

Left alone with Mister James, Cole turned to the lawyer with a question in his eyes, yet as the man began his tale, Cole could not resist the view of swinging skirts and trim back he was afforded over the lawyer's shoulder. Even as he watched her go, Cole counted it strange that the memory of one night shared with her long ago should return to warm his loins this strongly.

Alaina paused before accepting Olie's assistance into the carriage and glanced back over her shoulder toward the two men. She was startled to find the blue eyes locked on her with a frowning intensity. It was like being caught naked in a public place, the way he looked at her. Returning his stare with haughty gray eyes, she gave her hand to Olie and mounted to the carriage. She knew full well what the lawyer was relating to her husband.

The rear seat was spread with a large fur robe, and though it looked warm and inviting, Alaina settled herself on the forward seat. As she relaxed to await her husband's pleasure, her eyes watched the slow, meandering river, but in her mind, she saw only those startling blue eyes. A rueful smile slightly touched her lips. Ignore her that Yankee might do, but sooner or later he would have to deal with her.

Mister James handed over the marriage documents to Cole, assuring him, "Once away from New Orleans, the rest of the trip was uneventful."

Cole's brow was harshly furrowed. "You say she was

reluctant to accept the proxy contract until Jacques kidnapped her?"

"Indeed, Doctor Latimer. When she found out you hadn't come, she flew off in a tizzy." The man cleared his throat apologeticaly. "I believe her words were something to the effect that you could rot in a hot place before she would marry you."

Cole unconsciously rubbed the aching leg and swore beneath his breath. The little twit! She had always been too stubborn and proud for her own good, and if that weren't enough, she seemed to have a special knack for getting into trouble.

"Jacques's men were determined to find her, sir," Mister James informed him. "We had to hide your wife in a trunk to carry her safely aboard the packet. Indeed, she caused a great deal of stir in New Orleans, considering a good bit of the waterfront burned along with Jacques's warehouse. I can imagine that Mister DuBonné is hiding out after the sheriff took an accounting of the cotton bales the man had tucked away in his storehouse."

Abruptly Cole gestured to one of the wagons. "Murphy came with us to pick up some supplies. If you wish, you can catch a ride home with him. Mrs. Latimer and I will be stopping at a hotel, and I am not sure when we will continue home. Otherwise, I would invite you to join us."

"No need of either, sir. I boarded my buckboard and horse at a livery near here. If Murphy can take me that far, I'd be obliged."

Cole withdrew a flat purse from inside his coat and passed several bills to the lawyer. "Here! Give this to Murphy and ask him to outfit Saul in some warm clothes before the man freezes to death."

"Of course, Doctor Latimer." Mister James accepted the money and hurried to the wagon, leaving Cole frowning thoughtfully as he gazed toward the brougham and the slim, cool features of his young wife.

Returning to the carriage, he threw his greatcoat and hat into the seat opposite Alaina, then climbed in to take a place beside her. He swept the fur throw from beneath his coat and spread it over her lap, leaning across to tuck the robe securely into the corner behind her. Though Alaina avoided meeting his eyes, she was vividly aware of the clean, fresh scent of his cologne. But where he was concerned, she wished to remain distinctly detached and erected an icebound wall of silence to achieve that end. It had been an affront to her pride to be informed that, while he could receive her as his wife, he did not desire her as a woman. Had it been some other man, she might have wondered at his virility, but in Cole's case, she knew better. He was certainly not impotent, whatever the disabilities caused by the injury to his leg. Indeed, if their last meeting had been any indication, his appetites ran toward the satyr and he had the tendencies of a hot-blooded roué. The fact that he had looked to her as easy prey for his lusts was a thorn in her side now that he had stated his preferences for their marriage. Her pride ached for some assuaging vengeance.

The driver shouted, and as the brougham began to move, Cole clasped the hand strap by his window. Alaina noticed that his only concession to the cold was to drape a corner of the fur throw over his right leg, as if the wound made it more tender to the weather. Otherwise, he seemed scarcely affected by the chilly dampness.

She paid no heed to the motion of the brougham until a hard-sinewed arm suddenly reached across her, drawing her complete and immediate attention as he braced a hand on the window molding beside her and rested the back of his arm with bold familiarity against her bosom, pressing her firmly back into the seat.

Alaina's temper flared at this open affront. That he should dare! She opened her mouth to vent a caustic reprimand. In the next instant, the coach lurched upward, and had it not been for the restraint, she would have been spilled ignominiously to the floor. The rebuke dwindled to a gasp, and she clutched the now-welcome arm tightly, securing her dignity.

Olie whistled to the team and cracked his whip over their heads. The animals lunged against the traces, dragging the sturdy carriage upward along the steep road. Finally, with a last scrambling charge, they topped the brink, and the teamster pulled the steeds back into a more leisurely pace. With as much grace as she could muster, Alaina loosened her firm grasp, allowing her husband to withdraw the restraint. With the ride more stable now, Cole moved to the opposite seat where he could take full advantage of the view. Indeed, he made no effort to limit his perusal to anything superficial, and Alaina felt his eyes move with exacting slowness over every part of her.

Let him stare! she thought indignantly and turned her face to the window. *He's at least bought the right to look.*

They passed the main gate of the fort and crossed the wide, cleared area that encircled the walls. The carriage darkened abruptly as they entered into a towering elm forest, and a mile or two further on, the road dipped downward into a shallow valley. Soon, the brougham was rattling across the rock-strewn bed of a small stream. The low murmur of tumbling water came to Alaina's ears, but she could see no sign of a falls. As the carriage plunged and bucked on its way, she kept her gaze fastened out the window, little aware of the scenery they passed. Her mind churned with festering resentment as she continued to be subjected to a most familiar scrutiny that gave no hint of ending soon. She cursed the day she met Jacques DuBonné. But for him, she would not be here now, married to a cocksure Yankee who had the audacity to openly ogle her as if she were some tender morsel expressly prepared for his enjoyment. She was almost glad she had worn the widow's black, for in anything else she might have felt herself ravished by those piercing blue eyes.

Suddenly realizing Cole had spoken to her, Alaina glanced around. He held a cigar in one hand, a match in the other, and was apparently waiting for her consent. "Do you mind?" He lifted the cigar questioningly.

"No, of course not." So he would smoke and look, she mused testily as she again directed her attention out the window. They were splashing through the muddy outer streets of a rapidly growing city, but she had no time to dwell on their surroundings before she was brought once more to the awareness that Cole was speaking to her. Her eyes quickly met his. "I'm sorry, I didn't hear—"

"Would you mind taking off that silly bonnet?" he repeated and punched the match into the tip of the cigar, opening a small hole in the leaf. "I would like to have a better look at you."

Alaina's temper rolled over restlessly at his request, but she obediently removed the bonnet and self-consciously tucked a stray darkly burnished curl into the simple coil at her nape. Having had only a small hand mirror on board the riverboat, she could imagine that her appearance not only resembled a pauper, but was greatly disheveled at best. The scowl that came to Cole's brow made her all the more uncomfortable. He still held the unlit cigar and was fairly flaying the end with the butt of the match.

"Do you frighten children with that frown, Major?"

Irritably, Cole jammed the cheroot into his mouth and, striking the match on the sole of his boot, puffed the thing aglow. His blue eyes considered her through the wraith of smoke that curled into the air.

Alaina swept a slim hand toward the window, feeling a need to turn aside that audacious stare. "I've heard many stories of wild Indians, of snow deeper than one's head, and of great wolves ranging through the streets. I see nothing of that. Instead, a city growing in the midst of a wooded land."

"Your tales were not unfounded, madam." Those clear, bright orbs of blue regarded her with an intensity that made her warm with embarrassment. He gestured with his cigar. "That robe is made from the pelts of several winter wolves."

She smoothed the long, silky fur in wonder. "I would have thought them hoary beasts, short of coat and stiffly furred."

Cole winced suddenly as the brougham bounced over a pothole. They were coming into the center of the metropolis where a scattering of stone and brick buildings were settled in a crowded nest of smaller ones. Some were wood with high false fronts, others monolithic structures of stone, two, three, sometimes four stories high. Raised boardwalks provided passage from one edifice to the next, a necessity since the streets were unpaved and well churned to a muddy depth.

Tight-lipped, Cole drew a small flask from a carriage pocket and, after a long draught, relaxed a moment before he dismissed the unspoken question he saw in her eyes. "That piece of metal does me ill. It has a harsh way of reminding me of its presence."

"Major Magruder thought he had a better idea," she murmured. "Have you changed your mind?"

Cole snorted and drew again from the silver flagon before tucking it away. "Better that I have the ache to remind me the leg is still there than the itch of an empty stump."

Reaching out to her gray cloak, he plucked at its cloth. "Why didn't you wear the clothes I sent to you?"

Alaina's gaze grew distant as she remembered her first glimpse of Mister James and the leather case. It had taken an abduction to convince her she should carry through with the wedding and not send the lawyer back to his client with the sting of heated words. She longed to say them now, but knew from experience that to confront Cole squarely would lead to argument and strife. It was best, for the moment at least, to avoid any confrontation that might end as their last meeting. As gently as she could, she spoke about a subject that sorely pricked her pride. "You have done me great service, Doctor Latimer, in exchanging proxy vows and thus making it possible for me to come here and escape an intolerable situation. For this, I owe you much. Much more than I can repay in any foreseeable time. It seems I must continually remind you that I am not wealthy—"

"You are my wife." His voice was soft, though his smile was knowingly chiding.

Stubbornly Alaina shook her head, rejecting his statement. She blushed with frustration at having to explain her situation. "I repeat, I am not wealthy, but I have a desire to pay what debts I knowingly incur. A few months should give even the Federals time to catch up with Jacques, now that he is found out. Perhaps by spring I will be able to return and see to the clearing of my name. You must know I am sorely put to task with having to beg your indulgence until then. Thus, if I accept the clothes, fine and rich as they are, it would only extend an obligation which I am already at heavy odds to repay. I am quite capable, otherwise, of seeing to myself."

Cole leaned forward until the wide, sparkling gray eyes came to meet the mocking smile in his. "Were you wise enough to see to yourself, Alaina Latimer, you would not be here."

Her face burned at the truth of his statement. She had little left to be proud of. Even her independence had been stripped from her, and it goaded her that she must now rely upon this, of all men, for her support. As dearly as she wished to hurl an angry denial in his face, she could not. Though the truth of it stung, there was none to hurl. Still, she was determined not to be a burden to him, socially or financially. At least that way she could manage to retain some shred of self-esteem.

Cole leaned back and drew on the cigar thoughtfully. "The clothes were a wedding gift, Alaina, and I take it much amiss that you go about looking like a homeless waif."

"Wedding?" She laughed with disdain. "Is that what you call it?"

His face was inscrutable through the drifting smoke. "Ah, yes. Mister James told me of your reluctance to be married."

"Forgive me, Major, if I do not feel wed. Had I been given any other choice, I would not be. But Mister DuBonné left me with no other alternative."

"So kind of you, madam"—he smiled with sarcasm—"to consider me the lesser of two evils."

"The lesser of two evils is still evil, Major Latimer." Alaina dipped her head and continued calmly. "I thought it was the best I could do at the time. I may yet reconsider."

"And you sacrificed yourself, agreed to marry me, though I am still the enemy?" His voice betrayed an overtone of satire.

"There was no sacrifice." Her voice was hard and crisp. "The marriage can be annulled and declared void if you chafe under it. For the last, I do not regard you as an enemy. The war is over."

Cole carefully knocked the ash from his cigar and watched her doubtfully. "It would appear, madam, that this one is only beginning."

Chapter 27

THE carriage tracked a new path through the muddy streets until Olie pulled it to a halt before a tall brick building. A sign on the corner of the cream-colored edifice labeled it as the Nicollet House. In deference to his employer's lameness, Olie had maneuvered close to the boardwalk, allowing them to descend to a level footing on the wooden planks. The rain was falling more heavily now and quickly dappled Cole's hat and greatcoat when he stepped out.

"Got baggage?" a muscular youth called from the protection of the door.

Alaina glanced up in surprise as Cole gestured toward the boot. She had not considered that she would be ensconced in a hotel with him for any length of time. As she moved to the door of the carriage, Cole slid his hands about her narrow waist and swung her easily across the boardwalk into the shelter of a second-floor balcony that jutted out over the main door, forming a canopy of sorts. Whisked briskly into the lobby on her husband's arm, she was made acutely conscious of the contrast between her dreary garb and the rich trappings of the interior. It was not long before she also became aware of having collected the attention of most of the men who stood about the room. She could not fully concede that she warranted such admiring regards, and wondered laconically how long it might have been since they last had seen a woman.

Gesturing upstairs, Cole dropped a key into the lad's waiting hand. The youth hurried off with her trunk, and the major turned, resting his hand possessively on the small of his wife's back. As he guided her across the foyer a few men, meeting his eye, nodded a brief greeting, but recognizing the challenge in his gaze, turned away and proceeded about their business.

In the sparsely filled dining room, the couple enjoyed a relatively restful repast, though Alaina found Cole's stoical frown rather forbidding. She was devouring a rich dessert with an eagerness that hinted of her long separation from sweets when the boy returned with the key and went off again happily counting the coins he had received.

They left the dining room, and after a full flight of stairs, Alaina was prompted to protest the hand that grasped her elbow somewhat less than gently. He seemed unaware of his almost bruising hold. "Major, please! Are you afraid you'll lose me?"

Halting before a door, Cole unlocked it and pushed it wide, commenting as he drew her within the suite. "My past experiences with you, madam, have made me understandably cautious. You have a way of vanishing at the damnedest times, leaving a man in dire straits."

The barb pricked, but Alaina was quick with a retort. "Had I stayed, sir, you would have no doubt found yourself forced into marriage with me rather than Roberta. Would you have seen that as an improvement?"

"A lesser of two evils, surely," he mocked.

Those bright eyes taunted her, and Alaina felt the heat rise to her cheeks.

"As you said, madam, better me than Jacques." With his cane he pushed the door closed behind her. "And better you than Roberta."

"The way you fought with her, I can hardly feel complimented," she stated crisply.

"We had little regard for each other, it's true," Cole admitted. He laid aside his hat and coat, smiling wryly. "All things considered, you and I got along much better."

Alaina felt as vulnerable as she had that first night in his apartment. She crossed the room, nervously placing herself well out of his reach. "Must I remind you, sir of our countless arguments?"

"I remember a few times when you lost your temper—such as in the hospital after I was wounded. You undoubtedly thought it was a crime because I desired you."

"You were a married man!" Alaina gasped. "And I didn't take kindly to being seized and pawed when anybody could have walked in."

"My apologies, madam." He smiled sardonically and

gave a curt bow. "I should have waited for a more opportune time and place."

"You know that's not what I meant," she managed in some dignity.

"You made your way through the wards raising a lot more than the soldier's spirits," Cole declared bluntly. "Indeed, Lieutenant Appleby seemed anxious to play the rutting stag, while I had to lie there and watch him panting after you like some overeager schoolboy. And you allowed it!"

"And why not? It was rather pleasant being courted by a gentleman for a change, and despite what you might have imagined, he was always a gentleman. He was also unattached, if you'll remember, while you were not. *You* only wanted another mistress to add to your stable, while he was after a wife."

"Did he propose to you?" Cole demanded harshly and, at her nod, further questioned, "Then why didn't you marry him?"

"I was quite wary of Yankee soldiers, especially officers." Arching a brow, she gazed at him meaningfully. "Besides, I wasn't in love with him."

Cole snorted derisively. "You're not in love with me either. You've made that abundantly clear."

Alaina turned away with a frown and shrugged lamely. "You've been as blunt."

Restlessly she moved away from his scowl. She was becoming less and less sure of her reasons for marrying him. The way it looked, the two of them were not likely to lead a docile life. She was tired of struggling for survival. All she sought was a brief time of peace and contentment. Yet, with Cole as her husband, that seemed well beyond her grasp.

She wandered into the bedroom, then hastily returned, and Cole caught the covert glance she cast his way. He knew her well enough to read the quizzical quirk that touched her soft lips. But then, he was fully aware that the suite had only one bedroom. He moved past her as she stood in the doorway and, entering the room, doffed his coat and cravat, and leisurely opened his vest and shirt.

"I thought we would be going on to your home before nightfall," she ventured rather shyly.

He glanced up briefly and began folding up his shirt

sleeves. "We'll get there soon enough, Alaina. Have no fear."

"If you have business in town, Major, perhaps Olie can find Saul or Mister James before they leave town, and I can go with them. I will only be a hindrance to you here."

Cole's jaw tensed. So, she would play the reluctant virgin to the hilt, when both of them knew she had no cause. "I'll not have you bumping along the roads on the back of a wagon like the meanest serving wench. I assure you, madam, that I will see you to my home with more dignity than you seem concerned about."

"You Yankees have a way of prattling on about pride and dignity," she replied loftily. "Those have been luxuries I can ill afford of late."

Cole stepped close, and Alaina almost retreated from those suddenly fierce eyes. But she steeled herself and held her ground before his glare.

"You may enjoy what luxury *I*—" he tapped his chest to stress the word—"can afford." He straightened, squaring his wide shoulders, but his eyes still held hers in bondage. "I suggest you put aside this damned silly notion you have about the clothes I bought you. If you cannot accept marriage with me privately, then you had better consider what you must do for the sake of appearances." He raked her with a brazen stare. "It shouldn't be too difficult for you, my dear, since you've played so many parts already."

Alaina held her tongue, not with acquiescence, but when she was just as determined not to let her emotions get entangled with being his wife, it was best to remain silent. As he seemed to expect some response from her, she shrugged flippantly. "I just didn't expect to be nestled in so cozily with you, that's all."

"Does the idea of sharing a bed with me strike you as distasteful?" he asked sharply.

"It's not just the sharing of a bed that worries me. It's what might happen in it." Her pert nose elevated to an imperial angle, she left him and returned to the sitting room.

Cole swore beneath his breath. He had erred in deeming her down-trodden. She was the epitome of the stubborn, prideful South itself, one of the most loyal of that breed of humanity. Bested by circumstances for the moment, she was little daunted. Yet for all of her fire and spirit, she displayed none of the underlying viciousness of Roberta, and although she adroitly evaded him, he found himself neither repulsed nor greatly discouraged by her manner. Indeed, he found the whole affair rather challenging.

He followed her and solicitously moved to lend his assistance as Alaina struggled to untangle the knot she had unwittingly set in the ties of her cloak.

"I can manage alone, thank you," she said, shrugging off his helping hand.

Cole leaned casually against the doorway she had just vacated. "Suit yourself, madam. It will be interesting to see just how long you can remain detached from this marriage."

"If it were any kind of proper marriage, I don't see how I could keep myself apart from it." She finally freed the knot and doffed the woolen garment. "But it's not a bond of marriage we have here, sir. It's an arrangement, and most temporary."

She turned, smoothing her hair, then halted as she found Cole once more scrutinizing her with a thoroughness that made her feel undressed. His gaze moved unabashedly over her high, full breasts and trim waist, then meandered leisurely along the full length of her.

"I hope I do not disappoint you, Major."

"On the contrary, madam," he replied easily. "You have blossomed beyond my wildest expectations." He scratched his palm thoughtfully. "I was just considering the frenzy you'll create among the gossips when I present you as my wife."

"Because I am from the South?" Alaina queried, mistaking his meaning. "Or because you've remarried so soon after Roberta's death?"

Cole was amused. "This is still a frontier, madam. A man is not expected to remain a widower when he might have to spend the winter alone."

"Unless you have spoken of my circumstances with someone, sir," she argued, "I cannot imagine why I should be of interest—"

"I'm not in the habit of bending the local ears with matters personal to me," Cole assured her shortly. He half turned to a nearby bureau, on the top of which was a tray bearing several decanters and glasses. At his questioning gaze, Alaina declined with a shake of her head, and he poured brandy in a snifter for himself. "How I managed to obtain such a beautiful bride without leaving the territory will be the question on everyone's lips. 'Roberta's cousin?' they'll surely whisper, and then ask each other, 'Do you think perhaps she and he were once lovers?' " He laughed aloud at the glare Alaina tossed him. Sipping the liquor, he limped around her to take a seat on the settee. As she faced him again, his gaze ranged slowly over her. "In truth, Alaina, it would seem that you have outdone your cousin in every respect."

Not knowing whether to feel flattered or insulted, she bestowed upon him a smile that was brief and tight. "I don't want to appear dim-witted, sir, but what exactly do you mean by, 'in every respect'?"

Cole countered with a question of his own. "Do you know how beautiful you are?"

Alaina was taken aback by his inquiry. Beautiful in widow's weeds? Sensing some affront, she asked cautiously, "Is this some attempt to play me for a fool?"

He looked at her doubtingly. "Still virginal, Alaina?"

A hot flush of color burned her cheeks. "You, sir, of all people, should know better! But then"—her voice carried a sharp tone of reproof—"I must remember that you mistook me for Roberta."

Staring at her, Cole tasted a small draught of the amber liquid. "Not entirely."

"Oh?" Her disbelief betrayed itself in a voice dripping with scorn. "You mean you weren't duped as you once claimed?" She laughed scoffingly. "My ears did deceive me then. I could have sworn you groaned in agony over your marriage with Roberta."

Cole's eyes passed over her lightly. "Unfortunately it was only after the vows were spoken that I was able to realize that passion was not one of Roberta's strong points, certainly different from the girl I originally bedded in the Craighugh house."

Alaina whirled away, unable to bear his sardonic grin. "If you don't mind, Major," she flung over her shoulder, "I would like to freshen up."

"By all means, madam." As she hurried to the bedroom door, he scanned her trim and shapely back before he halted her with a comment. "The widow's weeds are not unbecoming, Alaina, but they tend to overshadow everything with gloom." Icy gray eyes cut back to him. "It is my desire that you wear a gown more appropriate to the occasion."

"Occasion?" she repeated coolly. "I wasn't aware that we were celebrating anything, sir."

"I've made an honest woman of you," he drawled leisurely. "Isn't that enough cause?"

Her ire was ill suppressed as she ground out between clenched teeth, "You muleheaded Yankee! It took you long enough to find the right woman!"

Laughter gave evidence of his amusement as Alaina stalked into the bedroom. Her color was high, her eyes ablaze. Pure rage roiled through her veins. How dare he harass her about her lost virtue when it was he who had stripped it from her! He had touched a most vulnerable spot in her facade, and the desire was in her to retaliate in some way, subtly perhaps, so he might not readily discern it as revenge. Or even boldly, that he might feel the point of the thrust. But what would penetrate that thick hide of his, she could not imagine.

Alaina locked the door and doffed the black dress, thinking many ill thoughts of the man in the next room. He seemed to know just what it took to prick her temper.

She washed her face and shoulders, drawing in her breath at the bracing cold water. Yet it served in some degree to cool her temper as it thoroughly chilled her.

She brushed her hair to a silky sheen, parted it down the middle and, turning under the softly curling ends, gathered the sleek mass into a pale gray silken net. Between her breasts and behind her earlobes she applied the perfume that she had taken from the case he had sent to her. She had been unable to resist the delicate and elusive, hauntingly seductive scent, but she would never tell him of her weakness. Let him guess, if he could.

Her eyes ran warmly over a day dress of silver gray silk she had taken from her faithful wicker case. Cole would be surprised to realize that she was not a complete pauper, and she relished that thought. Carefully she raised the full-skirted gown above her head and guided it down into place. It was a garment she had managed to purchase with hard-earned coins but, like most of her wardrobe, it had been previously owned by another, a young friend of Mrs. Hawthorne who had arranged the whole transaction. The bodice simulated a jacket of Zouave design and was edged with pleated charcoal gray ribbon. Embroidered lawn duplicated a square-necked blouse of mauve, and *engageantes* of the same cloth filled the open sleeves of the jacket. At least, wearing this, she could hardly be accused of looking like a homeless waif.

Cole had leaned back into the soft comfort of the settee to await the end of his wife's toilette, and when she finally emerged from the bedroom, his gaze lifted from a sober contemplation of a tabletop. Nothing was more obvious to Alaina at that moment than those eyes that immediately took in every detail of her appearance. The greatest compliment he bestowed on her was rising quickly to his feet. Yet his visage betrayed his confusion.

"I don't remember that gown among the ones I sent you."

"I had some money," Alaina murmured and lowered her gaze from his openly admiring regard, strangely thrilled by it, and a trifle pleased with herself because she had been successful in taking him aback a small degree.

"It's most becoming," he admitted.

Alaina acknowledged the compliment with a soft, tactful smile. It came to her that she might have approached this whole marriage business unwisely. Roberta would have been more cunning, using her wiles to win the advantage. At times, the older cousin's methods had proven most effective. A little showing of the bosom, a little batting of the eyelids, and a little sweet talking went a long way to handling a man. Yet Alaina found it difficult to imagine Cole being maneuvered so easily.

Her eyes never wavered from his as he stepped near, and she had to still an urge to withdraw as he reached a hand to the top of her gown. His fingers were a brand of fire against her skin, slipping down within the crevice between her breasts to pluck the medallion from its warm nest. Drawing it into view, he examined it wonderingly.

"I thought you would have given up wearing this by now."

Alaina met his questioning stare, fearing she had lost

more ground than she had gained. Where his fingers had touched still burned, and she could not draw an even breath. "I wear it to remind me of foolishness past, sir."

"Foolishness, madam?" He raised a brow. "Yours or mine?"

"Take it as you will." She shrugged. "Can that moment be called anything but?"

Contemplating her flushed cheeks, he guided the golden disk back into its soft crevice and, with lavish care, straightened the chain around her neck. Alaina remained pliant beneath the roving hand, meeting his expectant gaze with a cool smile of mild amusement. Uncle Angus had taken great pains to warn her before she left that the law did not recognize the chaste marriage. Indeed, he had chastened further, the state of abstinence was to be diligently pursued as her only means of escape from wedlock when conditions warranted. His words came back to her with vivid clarity, "The man is a Yankee, and he has already abused my poor Roberta unto her death. I should be remiss in my guardianship if I sent you unprepared into a vile situation. And I shall further caution you that neither Doctor Brooks nor Mrs. Hawthorne bears any responsibility in this matter. That falls on my shoulders alone."

Yet, here she stood confronting this "lecherous Yankee carpetbagger" in his plush lair, and her concern was more with her own response than with his lingering touch. Her breath nearly halted as his hand wandered downward over her breast and came to rest possessively on her hip. She raised an innocent brow to him, and like a stretching cat, tested the honeyed claws of her well-boned will.

"Doctor Latimer," she murmured sweetly. "I believe we both agreed this would be a marriage in name only. Have you perchance forgotten?"

"I wonder," he mused aloud, "if the agreement will outlast the testing of the flesh."

Alaina laughed with velvety softness, recalling to Cole's mind a burning vision of a young woman naked in his arms. "Nothing like vows of virtue to heighten one's desire, eh, Major?" She tapped his lean wrist gently. "And where is my virtue but rent asunder on a Yankee's couch?"

"So therein lies the rub." Cole withdrew his hand and,

struggling to subdue the hunger rising in his loins, faced the window. "Taken on a Yankee's couch, you now seek vengeance."

"Vengeance, milord?" Her chuckle was deep and low, gently chiding. "Pray tell, sir, what revenge can a Southern lady rest upon her Yankee husband?"

Cole swung around to face her and glared with some dark anger knitting his brows. "I believe, madam, I need not tell you that, for it seems to be very much within your knowledge."

Alaina was aware that she had found a chink in his armor-plated hide, yet she was not quite sure what had opened it.

A moment sauntered past, widening the chasm between them. Cole's scowl grew ominous, leaving her little of the reckless bravado that had carried her thus far. She was much relieved when a light rap came upon the door. Her gaze followed Cole's limping progress to the door, and before he reached for the knob, she found the voice to speak. "Major, if that is someone you're expecting, or have business with, and you wish to be alone, I can retire to the bedroom."

Cole found it aggravating that she chose to use so formal an address with him. "Stay, madam," he bade firmly. "I'll inform you when I desire privacy. Until then, you have my permission to remain."

Alaina folded her hands, feeling like a child rebuked, and wondered if he realized yet that she was a grown woman.

The door was opened, and at Cole's urging, a portly man waddled in. After removing a heavy layer of wrappings from his short body, the rotund fellow picked up the small valise that he had rested between his feet and glanced about expectantly.

"Ah, I presume this is your wife," he chortled and, hearing no denial, crossed to Alaina. "You won't believe what your husband has ordered for you, madam. The very best! Absolutely!"

"Really?" Quizzical wonder betrayed itself in her lovely visage as Alaina glanced toward a suddenly stoical Cole.

"Oh, yes indeed, madam!" the obese one bubbled. Half facing the tall, lean man, he gestured to the case. "With your permission, doctor."

Cole gave a curt nod, and eagerly the fellow unstrapped the valise. With an air of suspense gleaming in his eyes, he slowly lifted the lid of the case to display the contents before Alaina.

Stunned amazement swept over her, for there, arranged on dark velvet, was a small collection of precious jewelry that, she guessed, might be worthy of a queen. Surrounding a wide, gold ring, elaborately encrusted with diamonds and rubies, were several long strands of pearls, an emerald necklace, earrings to match, and a cluster of large diamonds mounted in an intricately worked gold pendant, with brillant teardrop earrings placed beside it.

Leaning on his cane, Cole came to stand beside his wife and reached down to inspect the pieces.

"Everything's perfect, sir," the jolly jeweler beamed. "I checked it all myself. Here, look at these diamonds. Have you ever seen any so brilliant? Will the madam try it on?"

Cole lifted the necklace and turned to Alaina. Short of angering him in front of the jeweler, she had no choice but to let him placc it about her neck. He stood before her and leaned over her shoulder to secure the catch, and for a moment Alaina was overwhelmingly aware of his loosely encircling arms and the hard, furred chest partly revealed by his open shirt.

"Beautiful!" Cole murmured in appreciation, hardly glancing at the pendant.

"Yes! Yes, indeed!" the portly man chortled.

"Alaina, my coat please." Cole nodded toward the bedroom. "Can you fetch it for me, sweet?"

"Certainly," she whispered, strangely warmed by the endearment and yet knowing it was only, as he had said, for appearances, just like the clothes and jewelry. His intention was to put on a grand front, and he expected her to do the same.

In the bedroom Alaina folded Cole's jacket over her arm and thoughtfully smoothed the rich cloth. It was almost as if some magical presence were embodied within it, for she was caught for a moment by a yearning so strong and physical she found it hard to draw a breath. How easy it would be to let appearances slip into reality —if only there were not this arrangement between them.

Cole was handsome and still young. Even if none of the gentler emotions such as love were present, they could still have a marriage. Who could predict what miracles the future might bring? Yet, it was his word that had set the boundary between them and her pride refused to let her cross it.

Cole accepted the coat from her when she returned to the sitting room and, drawing out his flat leather purse, counted out several large bills, and gave them over to the man.

"It's been a pleasure doing business with you, Doctor Latimer. You will let me know when I can be of further service, won't you?"

Cole led the man to the door, politely assuring him. The jeweler nodded a farewell to them both and left.

Now the charade was over, Alaina mused wryly. At least, until that time when they would again be in the company of others. Cole could forget about tender endearments. And she had to remind him of her position.

"Major, I'm afraid it is impossible for me to accept the jewelry. I would never be able to repay you."

"Don't be absurd, Alaina," he replied and reached down to lift her ring from its nest. "Of course you will wear these, and I will expect it." Lifting her left hand, he slipped the brightly glittering band onto her third finger. "And this piece, madam, will never leave your hand."

"A wedding ring?" Alaina whispered, staring at it in disbelief.

"Is it so strange an item for a husband to give his wife? Or is it that you entertained doubts of receiving one? I must apologize for the delay. It took some time to get the ring here." He shrugged carelessly. "Some confusion about the inscription inside, I suppose. Perhaps the name baffled them."

That was understandable since there were other variations of spelling her name. But that was not what concerned Alaina. Taking into account the arrangement, the cost of the ring seemed far out of proportion to their marriage. "Major, we're not really—I mean—" Explanation seemed momentarily beyond her capability. "We are married, certainly. But then, we're not really—" Cole watched her curiously until she blushed and turned away in confusion. "I just didn't expect it, that's all. I didn't expect any of this." She swept her hand to indicate the case. "I can't possibly accept this."

"That's utter nonsense, Alaina," he answered impatiently. "The value of the gems is not lost if you wear them, and you will. You will be presented as my wife, and you will dress yourself in a manner befitting your station."

Appearances again! Her life was becoming a whole series of charades and false fronts. Somewhere she had to claim that right of just being herself.

"If, as you say, the pieces lose nothing of their value from use, then I consent to wear them." She was not incapable of logic. "But the clothes, sir, are a different matter. I will wear them only when I can afford them."

"How do you expect to afford them when you won't even take money from me?" he demanded.

Alaina shrugged. "I cleaned the hospital for a wage. I can clean your house for the same."

Cole flung up a hand derisively. "I have all the servants I need."

"Then, in your practice perhaps. I've assisted Doctor Brooks—"

"That's fine and good, madam." His tone was caustic. "But unfortunately, I don't have much of a practice anymore."

Alaina's brows knitted in bewilderment. "You mean you gave it up?"

"Something like that," he said crisply and waved away further questions.

She had no wish to test his temper further. Nevertheless she stated her ultimatum firmly. "If you cannot find employment for me, Major, I must refuse the gowns."

Cole's frown was fierce. He knew the twit too well to treasure any hope that she would change her mind in a few days. But he was just as determined that she would not go about in rags. He laughed suddenly, drawing her somewhat leery regard, and posed the question, "Have you considered working at being my wife?"

Alaina stiffened, wary of what direction he would lead this conversation. "As the contract has been drawn, sir, no one will suspect I am anything less. Just what did you have in mind that I should do to earn wages?"

As if pondering her inquiry, Cole placed a thin knuckle thoughtfully against his lips. "I have a housekeeper, two cleaning maids, a cook, a boy to fetch, and a man to answer the door. If we exclude those duties, what else is there?"

The most obvious duty of a wife was boldly left unmentioned, but she would not fall prey to his buffoonery. "Sir, since we do have the arrangement between us, I must assume that you are talking about the duty a wife must perform as a hostess."

"A hostess? Mistress of my house?" His gaze leisurely swept her. "Unskilled?"

"I learn quickly," she informed him bluntly.

"Perhaps I have something else in mind," he pointed out.

Calmly Alaina met his gaze. How she yearned to erase that smirking grin from his lips. Coolly she queried, "And what is your suggestion, sir?"

Cole opened his mouth to answer her, but some turmoil twisted just behind his face. From perplexity he changed swiftly to anger. "As you suggest, of course—a hostess," he replied ungently. "You will provide me with a haven from a worrisome society of mothers who seem to detest the fact that an eligible man should remain single and from fathers with overlarge pistols. You will be my representative, my delegate-at-large, so to speak. That will be your duty!" He snatched his coat from the back of the settee and began buttoning his shirt. "And in return, madam, you will dress the part as befits my wife!"

She had no chance to argue, for he limped to the door, jerked it open, and sharply suggested over his shoulder. "Make yourself comfortable, my love. It might be a while before I'm able to remember that I'm still a gentleman."

With that, he slammed the door behind him. Alaina heard the key turning in the lock before his uneven footfalls went down the hall. She released a trembling breath, realizing she had held it almost from the first moment of his tirade.

She passed shaking fingers across her brow. A prisoner she might be. After all he had locked the door. But at the moment, at least, she was free of his overwhelming presence.

Numb to the luxury around her, Alaina returned to the bedroom and put aside the silk gown and necklace. A great weariness descended upon her, and she felt in dire need of a nap. Matching wits with Cole had drawn heavily on her ready store of energy, and the few brief snatches of sleep she had been able to acquire during the night would be insufficient to uphold her resistance for long in the face of his assault. It loomed prominently in her mind that a night on the settee was well within the realm of possibility, for she could only consider that any bed and Cole Latimer was a combination for despair, and it was best to avoid that mixture like the pits of hell.

Thoughtfully, she pulled the encompassing net from her hair and shook out the luxurious russet mane. She reached behind her and tugged at the ties of her corset, but to her dismay the ancient lacings parted, and the stricture of the garment loosened itself, giving her a more rapid freedom than she had planned. In exasperation she threw the stays onto the low chest and, gazing down at them ruefully, began to free the waistband of her petticoat. She would have to borrow the lacings from the corset Cole had purchased for her, or go without. Sometimes this refusal to wear his gifts weighed more heavily on her than on him.

Much to her amazement, she heard a key rattle in the lock once more. Unable to fathom why Cole should return so quickly, she was somewhat fearful, knowing that the costly jewelry had been left in her care.

Snatching her woolen cloak about her shoulders for modesty, she stepped to the bedroom door and waited there to see the identity of the intruder. Instant relief swept her as Cole came through the portal. Scowling darkly, he tossed aside the coat he had flung over his arm, and when he turned to close the door behind him, Alaina saw that his trouser seam had separated down the whole length of his leg, leaving in view the white legging of his undergarment.

"Whatever happened?" she asked worriedly.

"I caught it on a damned nail," he growled.

Alaina restrained the urge to giggle and, as she turned back into the bedroom, suggested over her shoulder with riant undertones. "If you will take your pants off and hand them in here, I'll mend them for you."

She took out her sewing kit and opened it on the bed in preparation, but Cole's angry bark came from the other room. "Dammit, woman! Do you think I'm going to stand out here in my skivvies? I'll just change, and the hotel can have these repaired."

Alaina cautiously eased the door shut to deny his entry into the bedroom, but found to her dismay that the key was gone. A dull glimmer near the wall rewarded her hopeful glance about the floor, and she was just bending over to retrieve the wayward latchkey when the door swung open, rudely striking her broadside. She straightened abruptly, as if she were the stiffest of springs, and, feeling completely ridiculous, faced Cole's harsh perusal.

"I find your penchant for privacy wears thin, madam. I have no intention of hopping about the parlor like a naked crow while I change my pants. I will do it here, in my bedroom, where it is fitting and proper."

She gave him an impatient toss of her head. "Then, sir, I will wait without."

As she stepped toward the door, Cole's eyes swept her, and with sudden decision, he reached out a long arm and slammed the portal closed in front of her. She halted in startled surprise and looked up at him, meeting his suspicious glare.

"With the key in your hand ready to lock me in? And your cloak on ready to fly?" he demanded. He snatched the key from her grasp. "I think not, madam. You will wait with me until I am at least garbed to pursue."

He took the thing and sealed the portal quickly, then withdrawing it, tossed the key over his shoulder with careless finality. His blind accuracy was amazing, for after rebounding off the wall, an almost musical chord rang in the room as the key rattled into the large, brass spittoon.

Alaina's eyes had followed its arching flight, then after a brief pause, she raised a noncommittal brow to her self-sure husband. "I think you may have difficulty retrieving your key, sir."

Cole glanced at the spittoon and shrugged indolently. "It belongs to the hotel. Let them retrieve it."

Alaina matched his shrug with one of her own. She turned away from him, the cloak spreading wide and displaying to his gaze her well-mended petticoat.

"What on earth!" He reached out and pulled the cloak from her shoulders, casting it behind him into a chair. She faced him again with a mild question in her gaze as he stared in reproof at her hooped undergarment.

"Great Caesar's ghost, madam! I have seen better on a ragpicker's wife."

"Your attention to the detail of woman's garments is truly amazing, sir. Indeed, you seem quite knowledgeable about feminine underthings and such," she replied spritely, then half apologized as she smoothed the offending garment. "But this has served me well, and I keep it in a good state of repair."

"A labor of lengthy diligence, madam, to be sure," Cole snorted, and, with a quick movement, reached behind her narrow waist and tugged the bow free.

"Sir!" Alaina gasped as the petticoats fell to the floor.

His eyes took in the simple cotton pantaloons which, though of an inexpensive cut, snugly fit her slim though well-rounded hips. He could admire what they contained far more without their blighting presence.

"I have a wife who garbs herself like a farmer's wench," he growled half to himself, "though I've provided her with far better things."

In exasperation he stepped to the bootjack and applied its ministration to his footwear. Glancing back over his shoulder, he found her regarding him with a tolerantly amused smile as one would a child in a tantrum. It outraged his sense of righteousness. In the face of her blatant patronage, he ignored good sense and deemed it timely to exercise his authority. He restated his earlier words, but this time with a firm directive. "Henceforth, madam, you will garb yourself as befits the position of Mrs. Latimer."

She calmly replied. "When you are gone, sir."

"Now!"

She met his gaze squarely. "I will not!"

Almost incredulously he asked, "What did you say, madam?"

Something prickled at Alaina's consciousness, but she did not take heed of his oftentimes coolly controlled temper. "I said, I will *not!*"

The little ragged wench! She all but dared him! Cole sailed his shirt and vest into a chair, stepped to her open trunk, and removed the leather case he had sent to her. Unhooking the fasteners, he flung open the top and rummaged through the contents, carelessly spilling them over the bed.

"Here!" He flung a delicately made, gossamer thin chemise to her feet. "You will wear this! And these!" He tossed lace-bedecked pantaloons, sheer silk stockings, frilly petticoats, and a satin and lace corset in rapid succession. The last garment he withdrew was a deep green velvet traveling dress, richly trimmed with leather piping and tiny buttons of a dark tan hue. This last he laid on the bed with more care and jabbed a commanding finger at it. "And this! I want to see you in this!"

Alaina had regained her composure and struck a motherlode of stubbornness at least as rich as his. She left the garments at her feet, and though no word passed her lips, the look in her eyes as she silently met his gaze was pure mutiny. Deliberately presenting her back to him, she folded her arms and stood with one slippered toe beating a rapid tattoo on the floor.

An almost lecherous smile tempted Cole's lips as his eyes swept the bed. He would not have her see it and replaced it with his best ominous frown. He limped forward, moving close behind her, as his hand dipped low to lift the scissors from the sewing kit. His quick fingers pulled out the waistband of her pantaloons, and after a deft snip, they sagged loosely downward. With a startled gasp, Alaina snatched for them and retrieved her modesty, but, with a surgeon's sure hand, Cole reached out to her shoulders and cut through the straps. Unhampered, the shift plunged and was barely caught at the brink. She whirled, an expression of indignation frozen on her face.

"Ahhh," Cole smiled condescendingly. "I have your attention now." He made a leg and bowed his half naked torso in a courtly gesture. "At your leisure, madam. The day is still young."

Alaina clutched the freed garment higher over her heaving bosom, aware of the presumptuously possessive gaze that swept her. Leisurely he turned and, selecting a pair of trousers from his case, laid them on the bed. Unbuttoning his fly, he peeled his trousers down and seated himself on the edge of the bed to remove them. But his curiosity plagued him, and he could not resist a glance over his shoulder. His wife had moved, leaving the fine garments where they had fallen, and now stood facing the corner of the room, resolutely refusing to watch him. His eyes coursed down the fine curves of her stiff back, from the slim erect column of her neck, to the beckoning fullness of her hips. The all too apparent womanliness of her evoked a strong stirring of desire, and he felt a familiar hardening beneath the snug fit of his undergarment.

He rose and moved to stand behind her, not touching, but near enough that she was trapped and could not move without coming into contact with him. He braced his forearm against the wall and gazed down upon the tantalizing curve of her breasts that swelled almost free of the damaged chemise and the hand that held the garment in place. He ached to caress the womanly softness of her, to hold her close, and ease the lusting ache that gnawed at the pit of his belly.

"You are woman, Alaina," he murmured huskily.

"Indeed?" she sniffed and clutched her precarious modesty all the closer, pressing the fullness of her bosom upward until it fair besotted his senses. He lusted. He craved. He burned with desire. And all for her.

"Enough to drive a man insane," he breathed. Strange lights danced in her shining hair, and her slender shoulders gleamed with a soft, creamy luster.

"I had no idea," she apologized brightly though his presence nearly overawed her spirit. "But perhaps you wish to prove your words."

"Prove?"

"Your insanity! Your madness!" She struggled to sound flippant and casual. "But you need not burden me. A few flecks of foam upon your lips would serve as well to prove the claim."

The heady scent of her perfume mingled with the essence of pure woman, filling his head and warming his blood. The heat of his hunger spread with eager bounds through his loins. " 'Tis well you are married, Alaina, for if not so bonded, you would have ended as the paramour of some European prince. You were made for love."

His nearness threatened to destroy her composure. But alas, only threatened. "Married? An arrangement of temporary nature? Your proxy sent to a far-off place to exchange words with a woman who has no other choice? Marriage? Is that what you call it?"

"Yes." His hand reached out to caress the silky smoothness of her bare shoulder. "Legal and binding in any court of law."

She pulled away from his touch, unable to breathe. "It was more an agreement, I'd say."

"Of course," he chuckled. "An agreement to ease the qualms of your uncle so he would sign the papers. By any definition, you are my wife."

"Of chastity and restraint," she continued, struggling to steadfastly keep her thoughts on what she was trying to express, and in the course of such, missing the meaning of his words. Beneath her bosom her heart thumped far too wildly for her to claim a mere tolerance of him.

"We are man and wife," he said huskily. "What chastity and restraint does that forebode?"

"We are Doctor Cole Latimer"—her voice came as a flat, toneless drone—"wounded hero of the Union, and Alaina MacGaren, wanted for murder, treason, thievery, spying, and other assorted crimes."

"You are here because I married you."

She laughed briefly. "I am here because I had no other choice."

"Choice? Yes, indeed." He turned her angry words aside. "Choice you are, my love." He ran his fingers down the shining darkness of her hair, smoothing it as if in awe. "The very cream of the lot."

His soft answer and soothing caress awoke tingling answers in places she tried to ignore. This betrayal by her own body aroused an impatient vexation. She had foolishly thought that all the quickening fires she had once felt in his presence would be cooled by now, and if not thoroughly squelched by the insult of his proposal, then surely slow to rekindle. But she was becoming increasingly aware of the folly of that conclusion. He touched; she burned. It was a hard fact for her pride to accept, especially when it was he who had demanded a chaste marriage. What did he expect her to be? Some limp-willed twit who catered to his mercurial moods?

"You treat the word love lightly, sir, when that same emotion should be a prior test of devotion and commitment before the vows."

Cole lowered his face to stir her hair and breathe deeply of its fragrance. For Alaina, it was as if some discordant screech had sent a shudder through her. She pressed forward against the wall, trying to break the contact that so bestirred her.

"Cool your heels, sir," she warned crisply. "This is not of our agreement."

"To hell with agreements and prior things," Cole muttered thickly. "Your need is that which only a man can fulfill, and I would have no other do it but myself."

Pulling her away from the wall, he bent and lifted her in his arms as she struggled to keep herself covered.

"Major!" she panted breathlessly. "This game has gone far enough. Put me down!"

"Games are for children, my love. But this is something more between a man and his woman." His eyes burned into hers as he strode purposefully to the bed with her. "There'll be no more pretenses between us in our marital bed."

Kneeling on the mattress, he lowered her to its softness and, before she could move, his arms came down like sinewed pillars on either side, trapping her between them. He lowered his weight until he half lay upon her, pinning her arm (and her hand that had held the pantaloons) beneath him. She dared not attempt to free it lest she touch some portion of his loins and needlessly confound what meager defense she could muster.

It was all too vivid in her memory that she had fought him on that first night long ago and that physical resistance had been useless against his unswerving seduction. His mood now seemed of the same bent; he had no apparent intentions of releasing her until their vows were tied securely in a most physical knot of passion.

His fingers slowly slid up her arm to the hand that grasped the top of her shift, his thumb brushing over the soft peak of her breast, quickening her breath and her heartbeat, before he gently caught her hand. Pressing a warm kiss upon her knuckles, he drew her arm around his neck, then his mouth dipped downward to hers. It was a teasing kiss, brief and light, his tongue leisurely tracing the contours of her trembling lips, while she tried to chide her wayward will into obedience. His warm breath touched her ear, and his teeth nibbled at the base of her neck, sending delicious shivers through her. She closed her eyes, relaxing in his arms, growing warm and pliant. Then suddenly her eyes came open with a start, a gasp born on her lips. The loose shift had been easily brushed downward, and now his mouth was a hot, searing flame against her breast. She writhed beneath the slow, flicking tongue of fire, feeling consumed by its heat. She knew a growing tightness in the pale, roseate peak and an almost driving urge to rise against him, to open her shaking limbs and let the boldness of his manhood fill the aching void.

Still, some last shred of reason deep within her screamed in terminal agony and beat with frenzied fists against the soft underbelly of her sagging resolve. *No! Stop him!* the voice roared in stentorian conscience. *Set him back! 'Twas his fancy to have the bargain! Hold him to it!* Her mind resumed its function, casting him as a spoiled child who had never been taught the meaning of *no!* What woman he wanted, that woman he took. How long would it be before he saw another wench to his liking? Her ire thus awakened, she directed it well, letting her body go limp and lifeless beneath his caresses.

Cole's hand had slipped down to the severed pantaloons, pulling them free as he slowly stroked the smooth velvet curve of her hip. His fingers wandered beneath the fabric, downward across her belly as his lips returned to take hers. With a small turning of her head, she managed to avoid his kiss.

"Is this the way it's to be?" she whispered. "The same as it was before?"

He raised slightly, frowning down at her in puzzlement.

Her lovely mouth curved in a soft, haunting sweet smile as she continued, staring up into those fiery blue brands that rested upon her. "You've already given me the jewels. What's to be my worth this time? Should I hold out for the clothes?" Her arm slid from around his neck, and her fingers toyed with the medallion, bringing it to his attention. Its bright golden chain gleamed tauntingly against her soft creamy nakedness. "Do you have another one of these? Oh, Major," she laughed softly. "You do wax extravagant in your lusts."

The softness of the tone did not disguise the bitter satire of her words. Cole felt his desires flagging beneath the sting, but in an attempt to ignore it, he bent closer, lowering his lips toward hers.

"Is this the way you plied Roberta—with sweet devotion?" she asked innocently.

Cole ground his teeth and jerked away in frustration. He rolled off the bed and, with nostrils flaring, glared down at her. She sat up, glancing at him apprehensively as she clutched her arms over her naked bosom.

"Am I not worthy of the price?" she asked in well-feigned hurt.

A savage curse came from his lips and, snatching up his clothes and boots, he limped from the room and out of sight. A moment later Alaina appeared in the doorway, the long cloak providing her with cover as she watched him fasten his trousers with quick, taut jerks. He sat down to tug on his boots, but winced slightly as he donned the right one. He straightened his leg, rubbing his thigh as if some pain had struck him, then his gaze raised and caught her look of worried concern.

"Hold your pity, madam," he growled. "I am not some crippled beggar to be satisfied with the crumbs of your compassion. It's plain to see you share the blood of the Craighugh brood."

She raised her chin, slightly miffed at his conclusion. "Is holding you to your promise a wound so deep you cannot bear it?"

"Madam, the sharpness of your two-edged tongue does flay a man more deeply than Roberta ever contrived to do. Like her, you have a way of tempting a man until he fairly simpers at your feet, but when the truth of the matter is hot in hand, you set it aside like some trophy torn from the loins of a living beast."

"How can you claim that my simple refusal rends your manhood?"

He stared at her, his face rigid, then rising to his feet, snatched his cane and coat. "I yield to you, madam," he barked. "I'll have the carriage brought around, and I shall take you home."

As he limped to the door, Alaina calmly reminded him. "You forgot your hat."

Cole faced her with amazed disbelief. No one had baited him with such boldness since he was a child. Even Roberta had known when to cease. Not daring to vent his rage, he strode from the room, slammed the door behind him, and glowered at a startled bellhop who stepped quickly aside as he hurried past.

Alone once more, Alaina did not yield to a feeling of smugness, but, rather, a worried fear that she might have gone too far.

Chapter 28

THE northwestering road meandered across low, rolling hills and wandered through tall forests of elm and oak that mingled their rain-darkened autumn colors with the impassioned greens of interspersed pines. The gale that had driven sheets of rain slashing down upon the brougham as they left the city receded once again. The rain dwindled into swirling shreds of drifting, grayish mists, as if Cole's decision to continue the journey home had left the elements with no other choice but to retreat from their violent display. The countryside lay in breathless repose. Indecisive raindrops trembled on the tips of long, green needles, while on the ground, the thick carpet of wet leaves cushioned the thud of horses' hooves.

Alaina sat tense and silent in her corner, all too aware of Cole's scowling brow silhouetted in bold profile against the far window. He had taken the place beside her and stretched out his right leg, propping his boot upon the opposite seat in an effort to ease his discomfort on the long ride. Though the steady, rapid pace of the well-matched team pushed the miles behind them and dusk was rapidly darkening the leaden sky, few words had been exchanged between them. It was a brooding silence, and in no manner peaceful.

The road traced a path along a river, and the brougham slowed as they approached a sharp bend. Suddenly, from a distance, a shout rent the serenity of the forest, and Olie hauled on the reins to bring the animals to a halt. Cole dropped his foot from the seat and leaned out the window to search the road, while Alaina watched him anxiously. She was not fearful by nature, but she had heard enough gruesome stories about the Sioux uprising to make her somewhat leery of this wilderness and its inhabitants. Her qualms eased greatly when Cole relaxed back into the seat and leisurely withdrew a cigar from his silver case.

Through a small, rear window of the brougham, Alaina soon sighted a man on horseback riding hard to catch them. When he drew near, she saw that he wore the clothes of a gentleman and, in a rough way, was rather handsome. He was a large man, broad shouldered and thick chested. Beneath the brim of a beaver hat, short wisps of reddish brown hair curled upward. He halted his mount beside the carriage, hooked a knee around the saddle horn, and leaned an elbow upon it to peer into the dark interior.

"Damme, Cole," he swore. "Have you forgotten you have neighbors?"

Cole glanced up at the man and, without giving answer, casually struck a sulfur match and lit the cigar. Seemingly unburdened by the major's indifference, the stranger stepped down from his stallion and walked to the back of the brougham where he tied the reins. He came back to open the door, and as if he were one with either much authority or much audacity, he sailed his hat onto the empty seat and climbed in.

"The least you could have done was to stop and let us have a look at your new bride," he chided his host. He rapped his knuckles against the roof and called up to Olie, "Be on your way, man. I'll ride with you up to the house." He settled his outsized frame in the seat opposite them and grinned as he looked Alaina over carefully. "How long do I have to wait, Cole, or do you expect me to be introducing meself?"

Reluctantly Cole yielded to the formalities. "Alaina, may I present one of our neighbors. The first and the nearest, Doctor Braggar Darvey."

She extended a cautious hand, not certain if it were a game or not. The guest responded by taking her fingers and gallantly brushing a kiss upon them.

"The pleasure is all mine, I assure you, Mrs. Latimer." Sitting back, he braced his thick-thighed legs wide against the roll of the coach as it started into motion. His bulk nearly filled the width of the seat as he propped his arms akimbo with a sigh. " 'Tis only that I am ever bound to curse the day that my father, God rest his soul, gazed upon his firstborn and, remembering his great grandfather's name, decided to lay it upon his son." His voice seemed to thicken with an Irish brogue as he continued, and the twinkle in his eyes could not disguise a threatening smile. "To be sure, 'tis a brave name, and that good sire of old would tremble in his grave until the moors quaked were I any less than proud of it. But it takes a skillful, sober tongue to get the twist of it just right." He inclined his head to Cole, who held himself aloof from these inanities by staring out the window, and spoke low to Alaina as if imparting a deep secret. "I have learned that a drunkard's slip is not the price of my ire and give such credit as might be due. Since yer mister will not be telling ye, I shall." He drew himself erect and assumed a tutoring tone. "Me name is Braegar—spelt: B-r-a-e-g-a-r. Try it."

"Bri-gar," Alaina breathed slowly. "Braegar Darvey!"

"Oh, sure and begorra!" the big man roared. "Ye must be a sweet colleen o' the green sod."

Alaina affected her own burr with a gentle laugh. "Me own fahter was a Hi'land Scot, sir, and I can lay ye the tartan and arms to prove it."

"Well! We're nearly kin, we are. The Irish and the Scots have done well for the country, do ye not agree?"

"Of course!" she smiled.

Cole snorted in mild derision, drawing a quick glance from them both.

"Since the good man, Doctor Latimer, is so reticent, I shall be conducting the amenities in me own way," Braegar announced, crossing his legs and resting his riding crop on the upper knee. "In the old days"—he leaned back and sighed as if relishing the memory—"we were about the only people in these parts, the Latimers and the Darveys together. Cole and I were raised almost as close as brothers, what with his mother passed on, and me own mother a widow. But somehow the war separated us, and your husband has not been able to overcome his jealousy." He grinned a bit wickedly. "Really, Mrs. Latimer, it is I who should be jealous—all that travel and adventure and whatnot."

Alaina sensed that Cole was not entirely pleased with the presence of Braegar Darvey, for her husband's frown had deepened ominously from the moment the man bent over her hand. "I'm relieved to know you are a friend, Doctor Darvey, and that you're not after my scalp."

Braegar laughed aloud, a great big booming sound

that displayed his zest for living. "I suppose strangers are a little frightened by what they be hearing of us. 'Tis sorry I am if I caused you any dismay."

"Hardly dismay, sir." Alaina rewarded him with a gracious smile. "More like absolute terror at the thought of being assaulted by red savages. Your outcry was what I would have expected of them." She grew serious as she carefully queried, "But as my husband's—ah—almost brother, were you also in the army?"

A trace of humor played across his lips. "I have a defect that prevented my serving in the military."

Alaina was taken aback, for he seemed so hale and hearty. She could detect no flaw, yet she could hardly press the matter lest it prove some private thing.

Braegar saw her consternation. "A mental defect of sorts—"

"He's insane!" Cole commented bluntly.

The Irishman hurried on to explain. " 'Tis only that I knew from the start that the rigors of the military would not agree with my gentle nature."

"What he really means," Cole grunted, "is that he's a completely undisciplined bastard!"

Alaina stared at her husband, aghast at his insult. Braegar grew serious also as he frowned at Cole, but it was almost as if he tried to fathom that one's mood. "Your husband is jealous of my unspoiled condition," he admonished in light banter. "That scrap of metal in his leg has made him a bloody ornery cuss." He flashed a wide grin toward Alaina. "Should you ever grow weary of his ogrelike disposition, be aware there's a haven close at hand, and one as beauteous as you, Mrs. Latimer, would always be welcome. Indeed, I would be greatly tempted to steal you away from this blackhearted rogue."

Her responding smile hinted of a certain good-natured distrust. "Sir, I presume when one makes such a scandalous suggestion in front of a lady's husband, one doesn't really mean a word of it." She raised a lovely brow and chuckled as she warned. "Should you ever seek me out in private, I'll be more wary of your motives."

"Well, now," Braegar drawled with humor. "Cole is a right good shot with a gun. Sneaking behind his back could be damned deflating."

"And he's a lecher of the first water," Cole muttered dryly, keeping his gaze on the passing forest, which had become little more than dark shadows in the thickening fog. "His intentions are to dishonor every woman who is foolish enough to fall for his golden tongue."

Braegar accepted the riposte with a long, heartfelt sigh. "My family also complains and my mother threatens to disown me. You can't imagine how my gentle nature is taken advantage of by women."

Convinced he was making a spoof of it all, Alaina giggled, but quickly straightened her manner when Cole peered at her askance, raising his brow. As she lowered her head and busily smoothed the fur throw over her lap, his gaze lifted disdainfully to the black bonnet. She had donned it again, knowing full well how it aggravated him.

Braegar missed the exchange between the couple. "Mother was hoping you would soon be back, Cole," he continued. "She has the wayward notion that she must give her approval to this match, and she's anxious to meet your bride. If it's convenient, she'd like you to bring Alaina over for dinner tomorrow night."

Cole frowned. "Unfortunately, I've an attorney coming out from the East to talk over some affairs." He shrugged as he glanced into Alaina's troubled countenance. "However, I see no reason why the dinner should be curtailed for business. If you would like to bring Carolyn and your mother over to join us, I'm sure Alaina would enjoy their company."

In jovial curiosity Braegar queried, "Am I also invited?"

"I suppose Annie will be delighted with your presence," Cole replied curtly. "You Irish have a mindless way of sticking together."

"Annie is a rare jewel, Cole," Braegar laughed. "You ought to realize that."

His host carefully knocked the ash off his cigar. "I don't think you can tell me what or whom I should appreciate."

Braegar passed his brown, dancing eyes over Alaina lighty, unheedful of Cole's face hardening as he witnessed the perusal. "I guess you've done all right without my help. But your young bride seems to be your best effort yet." He winked into the gray eyes as they rose to meet his and offered, "Should your business take you away tomorrow night, Cole, I will do my uttermost to entertain your wife."

The bright blue eyes considered the other without a hint of expression, then with slow deliberation, Cole removed the cigar from his mouth and half turned it, staring at the glowing coal at its tip. He raised his eyes, and had it not been for the coldness in them, his reply might have passed as a flippant remark. "Then I shall simply have to take your presence into consideration and adjust my affairs accordingly."

Alaina saw the uncertainty that flickered across Braegar's brow, cutting through his friendly demeanor.

"Now, Cole, you cannot be worrying about my reputation, are you? You must know 'tis naught but gossip and wishful exaggeration."

Whether it was chagrin or irritation Alaina saw in Cole's face, she could not rightfully determine. But the muscles in his cheek flexed tensely as if he bit back a reply. Impatiently he tamped out his cigar and, for some time afterward, stared solemnly out the window.

The brougham plunged ever onward through tall trees, now and then meeting the river before retreating to the thicket again. The dim, hazy glow was fading from the sky, but off to the northwest, lightning flashed, illuminating the heavy clouds. The wind touched the top of the trees, ruffling the uppermost heights and shredding the mists, while closer to the ground barely a whisper of a breeze stirred. When they broke from the protection of the woods, it was like opening a door upon a raging tempest. Violent gusts lashed the countryside and whipped the horses with flying leaves.

Briefly Alaina glimpsed a large, gray stone mansion perched on a bluff overlooking the river, then the brougham rounded a bend, and trees blocked the structure from sight. The carriage was soon halted before the towering edifice, and Olie jumped down to seize the bridles of the skittish team, while Cole pushed open the door and stepped to the ground. Leaning on his cane, he contemplated the turbulent dark grayish-green clouds churning overhead, then faced the occupants of the brougham, addressing Braegar rather curtly. "You won't make it home before we get the worst of this storm. You'd best join us for dinner."

The large man alighted and, hooking his thumbs in his vest pockets, leaned his head back to scan the low, roiling sky. A fierce gust of wind swept through the trees, stirring them into a new frantic rhythm, while lightning danced across the heavens with carefree abandon.

"I'll help Olie get the team stabled," he announced and casually waved a greeting to Peter as the driver's son ran across the porch to help his father unload the baggage. Mischievously, Braegar tugged at his earlobe and grinned, peering at Cole and speaking in such a tone that Alaina could not hear. "I'm not one to impose upon a man and his wife their first night together. Still, were I you, Cole, I would have stayed at the hotel in town for a goodly while before coming out to this house full of servants."

Braegar hit more squarely than he knew. Chuckling at his own humor, he swung onto his mount and charged off down the hill, leaving Cole's brow heavily creased.

Alaina came to the door of the carriage, and Cole stepped close to lift her down. A strange smile touched his lips, as if he were amused by some wry jest, and when he stood aside, he swept his hand mockingly toward the dark hulk.

"Latimer House bids you welcome, madam."

Twisted pines, cedars, and a few stunted deciduous trees, gnarled and broken by the winds and shriveled by the cold winters, huddled close about the house, masking many of the windows of the lower story. Thrusting up from this greenery, the gray hewn stone leaned inward to form a flat, plain wall with a subtle tumble home. Where the second story began, brick took over the structure and the detail became more ornate. The upper windows were tall and narrow, with small panes of leaded crystal that winked sporadically in the sundered lightning flashes. It seemed an afterthought that a porch had been added across the face of the house. The steep, gabled roof plunged upward with a vengeance, and a widow's walk spread its overly ornate iron railing between towers that raised the eaves at either end. The whole made a jagged, haphazard silhouette against the maddened sky, all purples and grays and blacks dimly lit by the last, murky presence of light.

For a moment, Alaina was struck with the thought that on the brow of the cliff crouched some awesome, ancient, many-eyed beast hugging its belly in agony and watching her as if to ferret out what further torment she might be bringing. Silently rebuking herself for such foolish imaginings, she thrust down the dour thoughts. She knew nothing of this place, but given half a chance, ere long, laughter might ring within its walls. Too much of her world of late had been cheaply spent in pain and strife. This was a time to forget the old and seek out the better moments of whatever life had to give.

Alaina blinked her eyes against the splattering of wind-hurled droplets and looked up at Cole as he jerked his head toward the house. He spoke above the rising, keening wind. "We'd better get inside before this storm breaks."

The buffeting wind whipped and snatched at their garments. Hampered by her petticoats that seemed determined to drag her back, Alaina fought against its force, almost straining for each step. A sudden gust tore the black bonnet from her head, and before she could catch it, the ribbons, loosely bowed beneath her chin, snatched free. The hat sailed off in a riotous dance of freedom, eluding her attempts to retrieve it.

"Let it go!" Cole bellowed with unwarranted gusto.

Helplessly Alaina watched the bonnet tumbling away into the deepening darkness. It was well beyond her reach now. Pushing back the flying wisps of her hair, she turned to Cole. He had also paused to witness the bonnet's departure but with something of a pleasured smile on his face.

"You don't have to look so pleased," Alaina snapped and stalked past him, ignoring the wind that whipped her skirts out behind her.

Cole gave a last wry grin over his shoulder and followed. Even as they were climbing the front steps, large drops of rain began to fall. It was only a signal for the more punishing downpour that quickly followed. As Cole hurried her across the porch, a tall, wiry man swung open the massive oaken door to let them in. The butler stood aside as they entered and accepted his employer's outerwear.

"We were doubtful that you would return tonight, sir. Murphy mentioned that you might be staying at the hotel."

"A change in plans, Miles," Cole answered, taking Alaina's wrap. The introductions were briefly made, before Cole announced, "Doctor Darvey will be along shortly. Will you advise Annie that he may be staying for supper?"

The butler nodded, surreptitiously observing the new mistress as he received the cloaks. Her gown was drab and colorless, even worn, but she complimented it with a grace and poise that was a pleasure to behold. She seemed quiet and reserved, yet quick and observant. He wondered if anything escaped those alert gray eyes. When she faced him, there was a gentle honesty within them that was disarming at the very least. Still, she would bear watching, he avowed, determined to be far more cautious this time. The first Mrs. Latimer had been beautiful also, but had soon proven the shallowness of that quality.

The young man, Peter, had paused at the bottom of the main stairs to get a glimpse of the new mistress for himself, and when Miles passed, the older man nudged the youth to remind him of his duties. The sheepish smile Peter bestowed upon Alaina was suddenly swept away by embarrassment, and in clumsy haste, he hurried up the stairs with her trunk.

"You bedazzle the youth," Cole observed brusquely when the men had gone. "I've never seen him so smitten."

Alaina descended the steps from the small entry vestibule and strolled across the hall, rubbing her hands along her arms to ward off the chill that permeated the mansion. "Perhaps, Major, he's just afraid of you."

"I've never noticed that kind of behavior before."

"As I cannot judge that for myself, I will not argue the point, but I scarcely suspect that my mere presence can disrupt your household, however much you may wish to claim that it will"—she half turned with the question—"how did you put it—'raise a lot more than the boys' spirits'?" She eyed him coolly. "I assure you, sir, it is not my intention."

Directing her attention to something less provoking than his mildly amused stare, Alaina glanced about her. The oil lamps did little to erase the shadows and lighten the mood of the hall. The massive, ornately carved rosewood staircase clung to the wall that faced the entrance, and the vine-clad theme of the elaborate woodworking was carried out in the pillars and posts positioned throughout the hall. In all, the decor was rather garish and cluttered, though everything gleamed with a tidiness that was more characteristic of its owner.

Bracing his hands on his cane, Cole spoke ruefully. "You'll get used to it in time."

Wondering if her distaste was so apparent, Alaina ran a hand along a richly carved column. "I was just admiring the woodwork—"

Her husband descended the two steps separating the entrance from the hallway and stared at her dubiously. "I have often respected your frankness, Al, even when it was less than complimentary. Will you compromise your standards to please a Yankee?"

Alaina's spine stiffened at his mockery, and her tone was brittle as she lashed out with a stinging reply. "Whatever standards I might have had, have been so completely tarnished that they bear no resemblance to those bright and shining values of my youth." More gently, she conceded, "I fear it is a part of growing up. To give up one's dreams for reality is the cost we all must pay."

Cole smiled without a trace of rancor. "Well said, madam."

Confused, Alaina met his gaze, sensing his approval but wary of his sincerity. His eyes were warm and laughing, which only added to her bewilderment. Then slowly he lifted his gaze above her head and stared toward the dark beyond the top of the stairs. She turned to follow his gaze, but found only shadows and gloom.

"Mindy?" Cole's voice was soft, questioning.

Alaina faced him, wondering what he had seen in the blackness beyond the balustrade. A quick sound of furtive movement came from above, but when she looked again, there seemed only fewer shadows than before.

Hardly a second had passed before quick footsteps sounded from the opposite direction, and with a rustle of stiff taffeta, a dark-haired woman came into view, and crossed to the top of the stairs. There, in shrouding shadows, she paused as her attention fell upon the lower hall. In the briefest span of time, she seemed an illusion, an unfinished portrait that some artist had abandoned when he realized his subject had aged beyond the beauty of womanhood and that he had unwittingly captured her just as she was. The black hair, lightly touched with gray, was pulled back severely and rolled into a simple bun at the nape. A long, linen apron was attached to the bodice of her black gown which, with its crisp white cuffs and collar, painfully reminded Alaina of her own rather austere apparel.

"Good evening, sir. Madam." Her dark eyes briefly touched Alaina and betrayed a mild degree of surprise as she quickly perused the widow's weeds. "Peter brought up the madam's baggage, sir, and I was wondering what room I should make ready."

Cole drew out his watch to hide his sudden ire. The merest thought of the arrangement raised his hackles. "You may show Mrs. Latimer upstairs, Mrs. Garth," he bade curtly. "The choice will be hers."

A sedate nod of obedience answered him before the woman directed her gaze to the new mistress. "If you will please follow me, madam."

Aware that Cole's stern attention came upon her and remained, Alaina mounted the stairs stiffly. The choice might well be hers, she mused, but it was also understood that the master's suite was not open for selection. He could entertain himself when it met his whim, but that was as much as he wanted of marriage—and of her.

The housekeeper led her past the open balustrade and down the hall. "I'll show you the late mistress's bedroom," she announced. "It has a view of the river and is most elegant. She preferred it above the smaller rooms."

"And the master?" Alaina could not help inquiring. "Where does he sleep?"

The housekeeper displayed no surprise at the question. "Doctor Latimer sleeps where he wills, madam. Except when his leg is bothering him. Then, I think, he doesn't sleep at all."

Pushing open a door, Mrs. Garth entered a dark room and moved about, lighting the lamps. As she did, Alaina's vision of it enlarged by slow degrees. Dark red velvet covered the walls. Even the high ceiling was draped with scarlet silk that came together above the ornate gold and crystal chandelier. It gave one an illusion of being inside an elaborate tent. Reds and lavish gilts were plentiful, while the floor was cushioned with wildly patterned Oriental rugs. Large pillows were tossed haphazardly upon the floor in front of a richly carved marble fireplace, and a luxuriously tufted chaise stood nearby. If any windows existed, they were well hidden behind heavy drapes edged with thick-corded golden tassels. In the midst of all this grandeur, the lavishly draped gold satin bed reigned dominant. In all, the decor was a gaudy, overworked kind of richness that miscarried to the point of being vulgarly distasteful, much like the heavily carved baroque furnishings.

Not noticing her mistress's lack of enthusiasm, Mrs. Garth opened the massive armoire. Crowded within were the gowns Roberta had feverishly collected but had scarcely worn. The sight of them was enough to bring Alaina to her senses. Without word or explanation, she whirled on her heels and retreated through the nearest door. Across the hall, another door stood ajar, and inquisitively she pushed it wider. In comparison to the chamber she had just fled from, it was rather stark and barren. The brick fireplace was dark and clear of ashes, and Alaina felt a chill draft in the room. A four-poster with a simple patchwork quilt covering, a small bedside table, a straight armoire and a large wing chair were the extent of the furnishings. The floor was bare wood with only a pair of small throw rugs in evidence. But the room, situated on the back corner of the house, had a sweeping view of the river and, to the west, the hills. The windows were meagerly adorned with linen curtains, but during the day, there would be an abundant supply of sunlight to warm her.

"Is this room occupied?" Alaina inquired as Mrs. Garth came to stand in the doorway behind her.

"No, madam."

"Then you may tell Peter to bring my baggage here."

"Yes, madam." The housekeeper moved past her and opened a door, revealing a separate bathing nook. A metal tub, a washstand with white porcelain basin and pitcher, and other conveniences, plain but serviceable, were present, all a person would need for simple comfort.

Cole's uneven footsteps were heard in the hallway outside the room, and as he entered, he glanced about him with the same wry grin he had worn when her bonnet went sailing off down the hill. At his nod of dismissal, Mrs. Garth hastily withdrew, closing the hall door behind her. Lifting a brow, he regarded his wife for some time until she chafed at the unsuppressed humor she saw dancing in his bright eyes. At her glare, amused laughter broke from him. "So! You didn't care for the red room."

Alaina watched him narrowly, wondering what he had found so entertaining about her selection. "I would sooner be in a sultan's tent with the threat of ravishment imminent. At least, I've had enough experience to know that I can live through that."

Cole dismissed her jibe and limped into the bathing chamber where he briefly inspected the water pitcher before facing her again with that same infuriating grin. "What is there about the red room that you find disagreeable?" He shrugged casually. "Roberta liked it."

Alaina gritted her teeth in frustration. "You confused us once before, Major."

"So you keep reminding me." He dropped a hand on the knob of the far door in the bathing chamber, but as if reconsidering, returned through her room to the same portal Mrs. Garth had left by. "Annie will be serving dinner shortly," he announced. "I'll wait for you downstairs in the parlor."

Alaina felt his eyes glide over her, and though unspoken, his meaning was clear. She must make herself presentable for dinner.

The storm had descended upon the house with the ferocity of a maddened beast. Rain cascaded down the leaded windows in heavy torrents, while lightning sizzled and cracked with increasing crescendo. As she joined the men in the parlor, Alaina managed to maintain an outward show of calm despite the turbulence that brewed beyond the haven of the house. She presented a most respectful and pleasing appearance now, having laid aside the black gown, with some relief, and donned the gray silk.

Cole had been standing with his back to the fire, but turned to face the door as Braegar halted in mid sentence and came eagerly to his feet.

"You are stunning, madam," the large man proclaimed, stepping forth to escort her to a chair across from the one he had just left. "Yours would slight the beauty of a magnolia blossom in spring bloom."

"Are you that familiar with magnolias, Doctor Darvey?" she questioned. Her soft, floating laughter was as pleasing as the delicate tinkle of silver bells on a still winter's night. It threaded through Cole's head, twining, twisting, weaving a spell. His eyes fed upon the beauty of her as she slipped into the chair, but unlike Braegar, he reserved comment on her appearance.

"Before the war, I went to Louisiana several times," Braegar answered as he resumed his seat. He was anxious to converse with such a gracious and lovely lady, and he grinned wickedly as he teased. "Had I known it to be your home, I would have threshed through the deepest, darkest swamp to court you."

Cole snorted. "Her guardian angel must have been working overtime."

Braegar replied in undaunted spirits, his eyes gleaming devilishly. "I could believe that, yet—she is married to you." Directing his gaze toward Alaina again, he leaned forward, bracing his elbows on his sturdy knees, and cradled his brandy snifter between long, blunt fingers. "Frankly, I'm beginning to think that I erred by not enlisting and lending my services to the cause. Cole seems to have been more than adequately compensated for what he suffered. Indeed, I'm rather envious of his good fortune in meeting you."

Alaina chuckled warmly. "And I am beginning to think that you are an outrageous flirt, Doctor Darvey, and your zeal seems not at all deterred by the fact that I am married."

"Married women are safer," Cole muttered in his glass. "No telling how many husbands have been cuckolded because of him."

Braegar spread his hands wide in plaintive appeal. "I'm harmless!"

"I wonder," Cole grunted.

A sigh of relief slipped softly from Alaina as Miles entered to announce dinner. The dining room, like all the main rooms of the house, was burdensomely ostentatious. The table was overlong, the chairs overlarge. Everything was rich, heavily carved, and obtrusively grandiose. Cole watched her reaction as she glanced about with a carefully blank expression, and she dared no response that would prompt him to question her credibility again.

Bay windows overlooked the land to the east, and when

lightning shattered the ebony darkness of the stormy sky, the crystal panes glittered with myriad spots of raindrops. Beyond the windows and below the cliff, the meandering river was visible through the swaying trees snuggled close about the house.

Shortly after Cole seated her at one end of the table, himself at the other, and Braegar took a place halfway between, the swinging door to the kitchen opened, and a plumpish, gray-haired woman bustled energetically in. She was intent upon carrying a large bowl of steaming hot potatoes to the table and positioned the dish squarely in the middle of it before she stood back with a sigh of accomplishment. Setting chubby hands on round hips, she greeted Braegar and then carefully scrutinized Alaina.

"Aye, a pretty one to be sure," she nodded finally and introduced herself. "Me name's Annie, love. Annie Murphy. 'Tis been me duties to tend the kitchen and cook the meals." She threw a sharp glance toward Cole and gestured with her thumb in his direction. "Though me labors have been mainly unappreciated by milord here. 'Tis a cruel shame I have to be introducing meself when he's dallied so long with his own comforts." At that, she cast her eyes meaningfully toward the snifter at his service.

"You're a nag, Annie Murphy," Cole avowed.

"Huh! I'll thank ye kindly, sir, ter keep yer muckraking comments to yerself. Ye wouldn't want me ter say what I thinks of yerself now would ye?"

"Heaven forbid!"

"You ought to be the gentleman like himself here." She nodded toward Braegar. "A foin manner he has, always a-laughin' and speakin' well of people." She paused, considering the distance between mistress and master, and screwed up her mouth thoughtfully. On leaving the dining room, she commented wryly in an overloud whisper. "And Mister Braegar is a lot friendlier, too!"

The Irishman gave in to choking laughter, while Alaina looked directly toward Cole and smiled charitably, delighting in the angry flush of color that suffused his face.

"As you must have guessed," Cole warned, "Annie says and does much as she pleases. Since she's been here at least a score of years, she has the idea I won't dismiss her, and has become quite unmanageable."

"I think she is just delightful!" Alaina shrugged and

daintily bent her attention to the potage, dismissing any further comment.

Throughout the meal, it was Braegar who entertained her, for Cole stiffly held his silence. Casually she noted that her husband ignored the potatoes and dined mainly on meat and other vegetables, while Braegar ate heartily of everything. The butler, Miles, was formal in his service about the table and most respectful of his employer. Annie's effervescent cheeriness was a sharp contrast, yet they seemed to get along well with each other. Even when the cook jabbed the man in the ribs to draw his attention to the potatoes on Alaina's plate, Miles only smiled and nodded.

"Now there's one who knows what's good for her," the cook declared, then looked askance at Cole. "Not a bit like yerself, sir."

Cole didn't glance up, but, as he cut his meat, was heard to mutter dryly, "A body can learn to tolerate just about anything if he's been close enough to starvation."

"Aw, get on wit' ye!" Annie shook her head as she stomped off into the kitchen, mumbling to herself about certain people who thought themselves above good Irish staples.

As the rain seemed destined to continue through the night, a bedroom was provided for Braegar. Eventually the storm passed but well after midnight, leaving in its wake a silent stillness. Mists cloaked the earth with wisps of white, while higher above, the moon played chase with the shredded vapors. Long after she had curled herself beneath the down-filled bedcovers, Alaina lay awake, listening for the footfalls that were familiar to her now. This was no chaste marriage they had between them, not with the outpouring of passions that had already been displayed. Love, hate, rage, lust—were those emotions so different from one another after all?

Alaina drifted to sleep, never hearing what her ears strained to catch, and slowly, effortlessly, she sank into the vague world of dreams. She glided along the surface of a bright blue sea in a ship with towering masts and wide, white sails billowing out above her. The rhythmic creaking of the masts whispered and sighed in her brain, as if the dream sought substance. Then, abruptly she was awake, and in a rush she knew what had disturbed her sleep. She had felt a presence beside her bed, a tall form dimly silhouetted against the moonlit windows of her bedroom.

"Cole?" she sighed.

The door latch clicked, and Alaina turned her head to stare at the closed portal, knowing that she was alone again. Yet it was a long, long time before she could banish the illusive shadow from her mind.

Chapter 29

ALAINA awakened with the dawn and, for a space, burrowed deep into her warm quilts, dreading that moment when she would have to set foot on the cold floor of her bedroom. Finally, she yielded to the inevitable, tossed aside the covers, and gathered a shawl around her shoulders against the crisp chill. For all its stone and brick and fortresslike exterior, the cliff house was cold and drafty. Her thin wrapper would be no protection come the long, hard winter if this was only a sampling of its frigid breath.

She ran quickly across the oak floor and perched cross-legged on the raised hearth, savoring even the meager warmth that it retained. Splinters of kindling went onto the bedded coals, and with the bellows, she worked until tiny flames leaped upward around the chips. The pile was rapidly enlarged until split logs were feeding the flames, and soon the heat drove her back. Warmed now, she went to stand at the window to have her first view of the countryside. Her eyes eagerly feasted upon the breathtaking splendor of it all, touching the languid river, the light mists that drifted over the surface of the water, the brilliance of the trees, and the steep cliff on the opposite side.

It took an effort, but she stirred herself from the sight and set her attentions toward a bath. However, the lack of water in the small nook posed a problem. Reluctantly she donned her thin wrapper and went downstairs to seek out Annie in the kitchen. A large copper boiler of water was already simmering on the wood stove, and when Alaina made her request known, the cook was garrulously apologetic until breathlessly she assured, "I'll send Peter up with it the minute it's hot, dearie. And now that we be knowing ye're an early riser, they'll be no more delay."

On retracing her steps through the hall, Alaina noticed that the door to Cole's study stood ajar, and out of curiosity, she went to peer in. The stale odor of smoke and liquor that permeated the room made her wrinkle her nose in repugnance, yet here at last was a place where she could feel comfortable. Books lined the rosewood-paneled walls, and a large desk stood before tall bay windows. A leather tufted sofa faced the stone hearth, and before it, two tall leather chairs faced each other across the surface of a low table. There was a manly flavor about the room, and it seemed much more in accord with the personality of Doctor Latimer, than did most of the house.

In the dim early morning light filtering through the drapes, Alaina became aware of the long form of her husband in the chair that faced the window. His feet were propped on a leather ottoman, and a thick woolen blanket covered his legs. The collar of a velvet smoking jacket was pulled close beneath his chin, as if the night chill had found him out. Quietly she moved to stand beside his chair, and her eyes went to the small side table where an open wooden box of long cigars rested. Near it, a heavy glass dish bore the remains of several of the same. All this was shadowed by a large snifter that contained the last dregs of liquor in its bottom. As she weighed the evidence displayed before her a sudden urge made her lift her eyes, and as they touched Cole's face, she saw that he had awakened and was watching her quietly. Self-consciously, Alaina pulled her muslin wrapper tighter about her narrow waist and realized the room was chilly to a fault.

"You spent the night here?" she questioned softly, her curiosity piqued.

Cole scrubbed a hand across his bristly cheek. "At times, the leg bids me sit rather than lie, and even thus sated, demands an exercise every few hours or so. I have all but given up the comfort of a whole night's rest in a bed."

His answer evoked a memory of a tall form beside her bed during the night, and she wondered what had gone through his mind as he watched her sleep. She reached down a finger to rub it around the lip of the snifter and teased, "There's always Magruder's solution."

Cole frowned harshly. "Your sympathy is too much to bear."

Alaina tipped the glass slightly. "You seem to rely heavily on spirits for your comfort."

"I know of nothing else that will give me like comfort without an undue amount of complaint," he rejoined meaningfully.

"I shall assume you refer to your late spouse," she replied brightly, "since I complain not at all."

Cole snorted. "True! But I'm wary of turning my back for fear you'll find a handy weapon and take your revenge."

"And I, sir"—she raised a brow—"will be more cautious of my bedchamber hereafter." He looked up at her, and she questioned innocently. "Or did you have some matter you wished to discuss with me?"

He reached for a cigar and carefully inspected it. "In truth, madam, there is much that we have to settle between us."

Alaina leaned forward until she drew his gaze. "Was I mistaken, sir? I thought we ended that discussion at the hotel."

Cole flicked a thumbnail against the head of a sulfur match and watched it flare into a bright flame. "Do not be mistaken, Alaina. The argument is far from settled yet."

Footsteps came across the hall, and with a brief knock, Mrs. Garth entered, carrying a tray that bore a cup of steaming coffee and, beside it, a crystal decanter of brandy. Placing it on the table before Cole, the housekeeper poured a liberal draught of liquor into the coffee, and after emptying the ash-filled dish and removing the dirty glass, she quietly excused herself and left.

"Is that what you have for breakfast?" Alaina asked in amazement.

"You should try it, my love," he responded mockingly. "I have heard that it warms the coldest of hearts."

"I have seen no evidence that it has warmed yours, Major," she retorted glibly, and with a fine flick of her heel, she left him, not waiting to hear his grumbled reply.

Once in her room, Alaina set about choosing her apparel for the day. Her wardrobe was barely adequate, but limited as it was, no room remained in the tall armoire. It was jammed full of the same sort of gowns, cloaks, and dressing gowns that had filled Roberta's, leaving no space for her own meager possessions. Some other place would have to be found to store her cousin's garments, she firmly decided. She didn't want them in her room.

An armful of costly gowns came out and were tossed upon the bed. Cloaks followed, long and short. Coats, shoes, bonnets. Most of the clothes displayed no sign of ever having been worn, and she became utterly amazed because Roberta's castoffs were far richer than anything a MacGaren had ever known. The selection of the clothes had been well exercised, for each garment was exquisite in detail, structure, and design. There were silks and plush velvets, plaid taffetas and plain, hats with plumes or feathers or with drapings of sheer cloth that would sweep dramatically beneath the chin. She was greatly saddened by the waste, and she had to fight a feeling of depressing envy that threatened to undermine her pride. How very easy it would be to relent to Cole's demands and allow him to dress her in such a grand manner.

A half dozen large buckets of hot water had been placed in the bathing chamber, and with five of them, Alaina indulged herself in a leisurely bath. After having to contend with the grime of Al's masquerade, she had promised herself, once free of it, she would enjoy the luxury of being a woman. With that purpose firmly in mind, she used the perfumed oils Cole had sent, reasoning that her utilization would not greatly compromise her refusal to wear his gift of clothes. She rubbed lotions into her freshly bathed skin and savored the sumptuousness of her toilet. She brushed her hair until its sheen matched the costliest satins and left the softly curling mass hanging free while she dragged on cotton pantaloons. Trying not to dwell on the soft and dainty undergarments Cole would have her wear, she perched on the edge of the chair in her bedroom and donned knee-length black cotton stockings. The laces had been taken from the new satin corset to replace the broken ones in the old, and she had repaired her undergarments. Even after his assault on her clothes, she had only been reduced to accepting the lacings. But no one knew what a great temptation his gifts really were. The silk stockings were a luxury she had never known, while the corset was a dreamy vision for her hungering eye.

A door slammed in the room beyond the bathing chamber, and Alaina froze in sudden horror. Someone was there! Someone with a cane and a limp! A tall, standing mirror had been added to her bedroom furnishings sometime during the prior evening's dinner hour, and she gaped at her reflection, elbows jutting above the head, bosom bare beneath the binding, half-donned camisole, and gray eyes wide over the top. With belated perception, she realized what had so amused her husband the night before and just where his bedroom was. Of all the rooms in this overstuffed house, she had to pick the one that joined on to his.

Alaina gritted her teeth at the thought of her own foolishness and jerked the shift down, though it seemed each rustle of cloth would remind him of her presence. Still wiggling to set the undergarment in place, she stepped to the dressing room door and eased it shut with as little noise as possible. The door had no lock, as she had discovered the night before, and abruptly it came to her that she had seen none in the house except on that huge front door.

Much to her consternation, the far door in the bathing chamber opened. Water splashed in the basin, and an unfamiliar noise puzzled her until she realized he was stropping his razor. Alaina hurriedly resumed her dressing. If he meant to shave, she might have a few moments to adequately garb herself.

She eased into the old corset, fearing to breathe lest she make some small sound that would draw Cole's attention. The new laces, drawn through the smaller eyelets, tangled themselves hopelessly into a knot, frustrating her every effort. Chewing her lip nervously, she fumbled behind her back and finally tugged the garment around to better fight the knot. The best her haste accomplished was a broken fingernail and the loss of her temper, for without warning her dressing room door was pushed open. Wearing nothing more than trousers, Cole leaned casually against the doorframe and wiped the last of the lather from his face as he contemplated her plight.

Venting a groan of despair, Alaina presented her back to him and jerked the corset about until it approximated its proper position, all the while savoring several fates that could befall the inconsiderate oaf who would so rudely intrude upon a lady's privacy.

"Are there no locks in your house, Major?" she asked in rancor.

"I have never found a need for them," he replied confidently. "Everything in this house is mine."

Alaina considered him coolly over her shoulder. "I suppose that includes me."

"Most especially you, my love," he laughed. He threw the towel over his naked shoulder and limped across the room to take the knotted corset strings in hand. As if by magic, the cords came free beneath his fingers. With a deft motion, he settled the stays into place and began tightening the laces.

Alaina tried to look more indignant than she felt as she gazed over her shoulder, but the truth of the matter was that she enjoyed the husbandly service he performed. Besides, he managed the laces so well, it seemed to her advantage to let him.

His labor finished, Cole caressed the well-rounded posterior fondly, then brushing aside her hair, he leaned down to murmur in her ear, "I've heard it often said: all's well that ends well. But you, girl, are the best ended thing I've seen—well, in a long time anyway."

Still not ready to forgive him, Alaina whirled to face him, but immediately realized her mistake. She was far too close to that hard muscular chest, and a brief glimpse of her reflection warned her that she was not as well covered as she had supposed. A trembling set in, and it had naught to do with fear. She saw an excuse to gain some distance from him without retreat seeming obvious and sought out her petticoats. In an attempt to ignore him and thus urge him on his way, she slipped them quickly over her head. She had no wish to appear vulnerable, but Cole Latimer posed a definite threat to her peace of mind and composure.

"Was there some reason you came in here?" she asked through the cloth.

"There was a matter," the reply came.

Alaina snatched the petticoats down into place and found Cole leaning against the bedpost counting out several large bills. Drawing near, he reached to the top of her chemise and stuffed a large roll of notes down between her breasts. "You were a charming hostess last night. Braegar was most impressed."

Cheeks hot with indignation, Alaina snatched the wad of bills from her bosom and, copying his bold manner, hooked a finger into the top of his trousers and tucked the roll inside the front of them. She smiled tightly. "I wouldn't take your money in a month of Sundays, Major Latimer."

He raised a quizzical eyebrow. "Have you changed your mind?"

"Oh, don't worry yourself, Major. I'll be here to protect you from your frivolous affairs, but you can keep your money."

Cole limped back to the bed and lifted a sleeve of a pink taffeta. "If you will not accept the money, then this should be worth about as much."

Alaina was astounded at his suggestion—and hurt to the quick. "You'd have me wear Roberta's clothes?"

The scowl that came on Cole's face made hers seem gentle by comparison. "Do you think I would garb my wife in secondhand rags?" The notion made him irate, and he swept his arm around to indicate the large heap of clothes on the bed. "These were purchased all for you, madam!"

"Oh, Major," she moaned, suddenly chagrined by her error. "I can never repay you for even a small part of—"

"Major!" he roared, and his voice carried thunder. Rage gathered like a storm cloud across his face. "By damned, woman, have you also set your fangs to striking me? Will you greet my guests this evening and make of me a miserly penny pincher? I forbid it!"

The force of his words made Alaina grind her teeth in stubborn defiance. Eyes flashing fire, she flared, "I will be garbed in such a manner that you will have no qualms, Major Latimer!"

"You will garb yourself as befits my wife! And if you can bring to tongue no better form of endearment, you will at least address me in the presence of others by my given name!"

Cole spun on his left heel, and a moment later the slamming of the bathing room door made Alaina's ears ring.

Breakfast passed much as dinner had the night before. Cole was tersely silent, while Braegar supplied all the conversation. After the meal, the glib Irishman said his farewell with the assurance that he would be back that evening with his kin. Left alone with Cole in the dining room, Alaina felt his gaze move dispassionately over her simple printed gown of wine muslin as she moved to stand before the windows. To avoid another confrontation, she directed the subject to a less volatile matter.

"I should like to look about the house if it's permissible."

"Of course. I'll have Mrs. Garth show you about," he muttered into his cup. "I have some accounts to look over in my study."

"I wasn't asking to be escorted," she carefully explained. "I don't wish to put anyone to any trouble."

"Madam," he sighed wearily. "I have never known you to ask for anything, and I find that almost as maddening as Roberta crying for the moon. The servants are here for your convenience, as well as mine. Mrs. Garth will escort you."

On that final word, he rose from the table and limped from the room. Several moments later, when Alaina crossed the hall to the stairs, she noticed that the study door was closed against any casual intrusions. Even Mrs. Garth, as she led the tour about the mansion, avoided that portion where the master chose to remain closeted.

The house was a mystery. The rooms were either overly embellished or, in sharp contrast, stark and barren. Only the servants' quarters on the third floor seemed appropriately furnished. The tour did little to lighten Alaina's mood, and she was almost regretful of having asked to see it. An aura of gloom pervaded the rooms, and she was glad when the tour was ended and she could escape from the house. The study door was open when she passed it, and she could only guess that Cole had finished his business and left for some other part of the house.

From the porch, she let her eyes feast upon the natural beauty of the hills and forests. The bracing breeze had only a hint of chill in it, and she filled her lungs with its heady autumn scent. She meandered the length of the veranda and back, peering off into the distance from each end, familiarizing herself with the landscape of this northern clime that intrigued her more than the house could ever do.

A large bell was mounted on the post beside the front steps, and she watched in wonder when Miles came out and rang it, striking it twice, apparently as a signal, then, after giving her a polite nod, reentered the house.

On the west side Alaina roamed through the weed-filled rose garden, but the sight of the stunted bushes and the spindly yews were hardly pleasing to the eye. She knelt beside a thorny bush where a lone flower struggled for survival and plucked the weeds from around it, but her attention was rather belated, for the evening frosts had already nipped the edges of the leaves.

Alaina paused, suddenly convinced that someone was watching her. Shading her eyes, she looked up and realized Cole's bedroom window overlooked the garden above the parlor. The polished glass was a black void, preventing any glimpse behind them. Yet, as her eyes raised, Alaina thought she caught a fleeting shadow on the widow's walk. Was he up there? Was he still brooding? Was he sorry he had married her?

The questions were not for her to answer. Indeed, she might never understand him, for he seemed intent upon keeping himself apart from her.

A buggy came briskly up the lane to the house, and Alaina recognized Olie in the seat. When it stopped, the man jumped down, tipped his hat, and called a cheerful morning greeting to her. "Yu be out here enjoying the sunshine, missus?"

"Oh, yes," she laughed. "It's a beautiful day. Much better than yesterday."

"Yah! Yah! A goot day for a ride, maybe?"

Reluctant to admit that Cole had not invited her, Alaina nodded toward the bell. "What's it for, Olie? I heard Miles ring it some time back."

"Oh, dat be the signal to let us at the barns know if the doctor be wanting the brough'am, or dis here buggy. It be a fur piece to come 'cause the old master had this here big house built after the outbuildings were raised down yonder a ways."

"And this rose garden, Olie. Is there no one to tend it?"

"Maybe no." He lifted his cap and thoughtfully scratched his head. "We not see the last gardener for some time now. The first one never come back from de war."

"Were you in the war also, Olie?"

"Yah, I tend de horses like I do now."

Cole came out onto the porch, casually dressed in narrow black trousers, silk shirt, and leather vest of the same hue. With a wave, Olie hurried to meet him, and they talked for some moments as Alaina unobtrusively observed her husband. She could not help but admire his tall, lean but muscular physique and the tanned handsomeness of his features.

In the hushed stillness that followed Olie's return to the stable, Cole half turned to stare at her. The low-crowned hat shaded his eyes, but she was aware of the harshness that still marred his brow. Alaina waited for him to speak, lifting her woolen shawl closer about her shoulders. A long moment passed, and he did not. Then, without a word, he climbed into the buggy. Propping his left foot on the dashboard, he lifted the reins, but paused, staring at the horse's rump. Eyeing him furtively, Alaina walked slowly around the end of the porch toward the front steps and was about to climb them when he relented.

"Was there something you wished, madam?"

She turned hesitantly. "I haven't seen Saul around, and I was wondering how he's faring. He has so few clothes—"

"Climb in," Cole urged, sliding over to make room for her. "I'll take you down to see him."

"I'll get my cape," she said with more enthusiasm. Before she could open the door, Miles pulled it wide and stepped out to hand her a long, hooded cloak her husband had purchased for her. "You will be needing this, mum."

Alaina glanced back at Cole, wondering if he had ordered the butler to fetch the garment, but he stared off into the distance, appearing unmindful of the exchange. Whether he had or not, she was caught, and rather than air her arguments before the servant, she accepted the cloak.

Taking the hand Cole offered her, Alaina climbed into the buggy and settled herself in the space provided on the narrow seat. He held her hand longer than seemed necessary, and when she looked up into his face, she saw that his frown was tempered by the barest hint of a smile.

"I warn you, madam, there is a cost to this. For the duration of the tour you will utter only kind words."

She was suddenly contrite and lowered her eyes to the open collar of his shirt. "Cole—" Her voice was tiny. "I'm sorry about the clothes. If you will be patient with me, I'll try not to embarrass you. But I cannot accept more than I can repay."

"Why not?" he asked quietly and met her gaze directly. "I owe you and Saul more than I can repay." He dropped her hand and smothered her reply in a command to the horse, giving her no choice but to clutch the armrest of the seat for security. In the brisk morning air, the steed's high-heeled trot stretched out until they fairly raced down the hill toward the thicket of trees Olie had disappeared into. After skidding around the trunk of a huge, spreading, autumn-painted elm, they entered a narrow lane bordered on either side by towering maples. The buckboard dashed through the sun-dappled shade with a speed that dazzled the eye and, a brief moment later, burst out into a sprawling field where a nest of buildings clustered together in the middle. Among them were several small houses, a long shed, and a huge barn that dominated the rest like a mother hen does her chicks. As they neared the barn, a loud baying heralded their arrival, and Cole slowed the horse to a more sedate pace. A huge black dog, bigger than a colt, broke from the thicket alongside the road and loped along with them. When Cole drew the buggy to a halt, the beast sat on his haunches and waited until the man stepped down, then, with a glad bark, he charged, swung aside at the last moment and made a lap around the buggy and horse before skidding to a stop before Cole again. He seemed confused and disappointed when Cole reached up to lift Alaina down.

"What on earth is he?" she gasped.

"A dog, of course." Then at her exasperated glare, Cole laughed. "A mastiff."

"He's beautiful," she murmured.

"Hardly," Cole grunted. He snapped his fingers and commanded, "Soldier Boy, come here and greet the lady."

The beast trotted forward, and Alaina's eyes widened a trifle as she realized his head came well above her waist. Unconsciously she took a step backward, but with slow deliberation, the dog sat in front of her and lifted a paw, cocked his large, square head, and peered up at her with yellow eyes, as if to fathom the spirit of this new arrival.

"He expects you to shake hands with him," Cole informed her softly.

Bravely she took the proffered paw, and a long, pink tongue lolled out the side of the huge jaws almost in a smile.

"He is safe, isn't he?" Alaina questioned cautiously when the animal went off to inspect the buggy wheels. "I mean—he doesn't eat people, does he?" Warily she sidled closer to her husband as the mastiff came trotting back and was much relieved when Cole bade the dog to sit and to stay.

Cole looked down at her curiously, amazed that she should fear anything. Roberta had hated the animal vehemently and had refused to have it in the house, but had never displayed any such trepidation when the beast was around. Incredibility was strongly rooted in his tone as he questioned, "Is this Al? Frightened of a harmless beast?"

Alaina straightened the cloak, somewhat embarrassed that her bravado had slipped so badly. "Didn't say I was frightened of him. I just like to know where I stand with Yankees and their critters."

For this quick moment, her mannerisms were so blatantly Al's, the memory of the ragged urchin was brought fully to Cole's mind. He contemplated the features he had once accepted as boyish, but could find no reason for the success of her charade. What he saw now was delicately feminine and finely boned. Out here in the open, with darkly lashed gray eyes bright and irrepressibly gay, with the sun highlighting her dark, auburn-highlighted hair, she was close to dazzling. Had she really changed so much since Al? Or must he lay the cause to his own blindness?

"If you would rather not have him at the house, I'll keep him down here at the barn."

Alaina shrugged prettily. "If his manners are better than yours, bring him back. I think I may have need of a guard."

"Ah, madam," Cole sighed with a laugh. "The cost is dear indeed. Only kind words, if you please.

"Sorry." She scratched her nose in embarrassment. "I forgot."

Witnessing the strange mixture of Al and woman so neatly packaged into one being, Cole realized that watching her was fascinating. "You're going to parch your nose if you go about without a bonnet," he smiled.

"If you care to remember, sir, I no longer have a bonnet."

"You have others," he pointed out.

Alaina peered up at him askance. "You have others, Major! I have none."

His brows arched in a half frown, but before he could retort, a shout interrupted the exchange.

"Miz Alaina!"

At the sound of her name, she turned from the shadowed face and saw Saul running toward them. A broad, white-toothed grin fairly split his black face as he reached her, and not forgetting his manners, he snatched the cloth hat from his head.

"Why, Saul," she laughed, surveying the red woolen shirt he wore and the new trousers that were held up by bright suspenders. He also sported tall, laced boots and a hide vest. "I almost didn't recognize you in your finery."

"Yas'm, Miz Alaina. Ah reckon ah ain't never been so rich. Why, ah gots me mo' clothes than I can wear at once. Even one o' dem union suits, begging yer pardon, Major, with one of dem button up cellar doors in de back." He appeared briefly pained as he scratched his ribs. "Though I been fearing dey done sold de chiggers with it."

"Wool can get right prickly on a warm day," Cole chuckled as he considered the other's layered clothing. He glanced briefly over his shoulder toward the bright autumn sun before questioning, "Are you cold, Saul?"

The black beamed. "No, suh. Ah's fine, thankee."

"That's good." Cole smiled. Placing a hand on Alaina's back, he nodded toward the barn. "Olie wanted to show me something. I'll be back in a bit."

The dog ambled after his master, and slowly Alaina turned her gaze from the limping figure of her husband as she realized Saul was rambling on.

"Mistah Cole gave me a house all to myself, Miz Alaina. For a Yankee, ah reckon he ain't so bad."

Alaina smiled. "You've been treated well then? And you like it here?"

"Well—de people—dey's good, and de house is fine, and de clothes is warm. But, Miz Alaina"—his face grew serious—"ah sho' do miss dat nice warm sun we had back home. Don't seem like this one up here does the same kinda job."

"It's the same one we had," she murmured, "though perhaps a little less friendly up here." Staring off toward the barn, she mused aloud, "The major doesn't seem to suffer unduly from the cold. Perhaps it's all a matter of viewpoint."

"Yas'm, maybe it is." He gestured over his shoulder. "Guess ah'd best get back to de job now. Ah gots to work off all dese clothes and all, so's ah don't leaving owing Mistah Cole."

"Leave?"

"Oh, ah don't mean to say ah'm rushing off, Miz Alaina. But comes de day when ah can, ah think ah'll mosey on down home. If yo' finds yo' is of de same mind, let me know. We'll skedaddle jes' like we came."

"Thank you, Saul." Her voice was barely a whisper. "But like you, I've run up a debt with the major, and I have no means of repaying him." She paused as Soldier Boy came trotting out of the barn, and she knew that Cole would not be too far behind. "We'll talk about this some other time. I think the major is coming."

Saul nodded. "Yo' take care of yo'self now, Miz Alaina. And like ah said, we'll skedaddle right quick outta here whenever yo' say. We can always send Mistah Cole what we owe 'em."

As the black hurried off, Cole stepped from the barn, and by the frown he wore, he didn't look at all pleased. From its lofty elevation, the windmill groaned and creaked noisily. The breeze rustled through the trees that shaded the yard, sending brightly colored leaves scurrying frantically before it and whipping them against Cole's legs.

"Is something wrong?" Alaina asked when he drew near.

He lifted her onto the buggy and climbed in beside her before he answered. "Someone threw several saddles and harnesses into the watering trough during the night and dumped salt over them."

Alaina could well imagine the time and effort it would take to make the leather pliable and serviceable again, or the cost of replacing them. "Why would anyone want to do such a thing?"

Cole sighed heavily. "I cannot imagine."

"Has anything like this ever happened before?"

"No, never before," he muttered.

Alaina's brows drew together in sudden worry. "If you're thinking that maybe I—Why, I didn't even know where the barn was until you brought me here."

"I know that, Alaina," he assured her quietly.

"And Saul wouldn't do it either!" she declared emphatically.

"Dammit, Alaina! I'm not accusing either one of you."

"Considering we're the only Johnny Rebs around here, it figures we'd be the ones blamed!" she insisted.

"Well, maybe someone else thought that same thing!

Or maybe they figured I'd given enough aid to the enemy. Who the hell can say! It's just a damn waste, that's all."

Soldier Boy sat on his lean haunches besides the buggy and scuffed up a cloud of dust with his wagging tail, waiting for some word from his master. His yellow eyes danced in anticipation until Cole shook out the reins, urging the horse into motion, and whistled sharply.

"All right, Soldier Boy. Come along."

The dog barked and took off like a shot, matching the speed of the buckboard. The wild ride left Alaina no breath for conversation, and as Cole lent nothing to breaking the silence, they raced along, seeming oblivious to the other. The road passed beneath large trees, and though the land had flattened out, the horse did not slacken its pace one whit. The brush alongside the road opened suddenly into a clearing, revealing a large, vine-covered house deep in the copse. Cole passed without a glance, but Alaina was most intrigued and turned to stare. Though the brownish red mass of leaves hid much of the detail, she caught the soft glint of leaded diamond panes through the tangle of ivy that covered the dark, close-clapboarded siding and, above it, the dull gray weathered cedar shakes of the steep roof and tall, brick chimneys.

"What is that?" Alaina pointed with her chin as she maintained her hold on the seat.

"The old house," Cole answered without turning. "The Cottage. It was the first house my father built when he came here." A frown briefly touched his brow as he added, "He had the big house built for my stepmother."

Though she waited, he said no more. She was curious, but he apparently did not wish to discuss the matter further, and she let it be, for the time being at least.

"You were very generous with Saul. I wish to thank you," she murmured.

"Simply trying to repay my debts."

"And what do you think you owe him?" she questioned.

They had come to a fork in the road, and Cole pulled the horse to a halt, half turning to meet her face to face. "The two of you saved my life," he remonstrated. "That is worth whatever repayment either of you should need."

"Is that why you agreed to this marriage?" Alaina pursued her subject with straightforward diligence.

Agreed? Cole leaned back against the seat, thoughtfully rubbing his right thigh. What game was she playing now? Did she want some pat answer that would assuage whatever violation she thought she had suffered? Well, if that was what she craved, he'd give it to her. "I felt a certain obligation—and you were kin—Roberta's cousin."

A long moment passed as they considered each other in silence. Cole realized his answer was not even close to the one Alaina sought and leaned forward slightly.

"What I fail to understand is why you bothered at all to save me, or risked your neck doing so."

The slim nose turned upward with all the haughtiness of a much nobler one. When no answer came, Cole pressed on with a stubbornness of his own.

"Why?"

Alaina shrugged indifferently and, accentuating her drawl, gave him some of his own medicine. "You were kin, being Roberta's husband and all. Then, I've got this thing about hurt animals. I just can't bear to see them suffer."

A strange expression came over Cole's face as he regarded her. "And that is all?" he asked. "Just because I was kin?"

Alaina faced straight ahead. "That's the way I said it, Yankee."

Scowling, Cole shook out the reins and, no whit wiser, turned onto the road away from the house. This time there was a definite, almost tangible silence between them, though neither could long ignore the close contact of their bodies as they sat atop the narrow seat. Cole's thoughts drifted on to other things, but it was no simple matter to ignore the proximity of the woman who so completely engaged his attention.

"With all the faces of your masquerade," he finally said, "I could not settle on which would greet me at the dock, if you would be the sprite, Al, or better, the slim-hipped, but ever-chiding widow, or even the tantalizing young Camilla Hawthorne. Then, there was another one, and though I held her close, I never saw her clearly."

"I have no wish to recall that night, sir," Alaina stated priggishly. Too many whispered pleas and stirring kisses had been exchanged in the dark of that night for her to feel comfortable airing the memory.

She turned her face away from his laughing eyes, and

for a long time, she watched Soldier Boy loping alongside the buggy. Sometimes, she thought dismally, it seemed that she would never outlive her role as chore boy, or the other parts she had had to play.

The winds of the storm had gone far in stripping the trees of their brilliant leaves. Only the stubborn oaks retained more than a smattering of autumnal color. The mastiff ranged the woods on either side, and when the road neared the river and traveled along the bank, the hound splashed joyfully through the shallows, yelping at frogs and fish that scattered from his path, and leaped into the air as a pair of mallards flushed from a backwater pool. As they neared the outskirts of Saint Cloud, Cole slowed the buggy, whistled Soldier Boy into the back of it, and bade him firmly to "Stay!"

"He's gentle enough," Cole anwered Alaina's unspoken question. "But people often mistake his smile for something else, and then, he doesn't fare well with strange horses."

Alaina opened her mouth to speak and, remembering her promise to be nice, swallowed the comparison she had been about to make. It was a well-known adage that if one could not say good things, one should hold one's peace. Thus, the ride progressed in silence.

Several blocks of merchant stores were passed, and at the end of the wide, muddy, well-rutted street they traversed, a yellow brick warehouse squatted. It was to this Cole guided the horse. As they neared, Alaina saw a goodly number of men lounging or napping on the broad wooden loading dock. One of the wide doors had been painted with a gaudy beer advertisement, while the other was crudely lettered with the legend:

Worker's Hall
Beer 5¢
Food 50¢
Bed: Overnight 25¢ w/ pillow, blanket, 50¢

Cole halted the buggy parallel to the dock and looped the reins around the whip staff, then reached beneath the seat and lifted out, not his usual cane, but a heavier, gnarled walking staff. It was well rubbed with a dark stain, and a knot on its thicker end formed the grip. He smiled wryly at Alaina as he flexed his wounded leg, which had grown stiff on the long ride.

"I have to post notice for hire here," he explained, and hefted the walking stick. "Some of the lads wax enthusiastic in their zeal to prove their worth, and more than a couple employers have been put to the test. However, if all goes well, I shan't be more than a few minutes." He tucked a rolled poster beneath his arm and placed a foot on the dock before he turned a warning eye to her. "I implore you, madam, do not venture from the buggy."

"I think you need have no fear on that account," Alaina assured him soberly as she eyed the men on the dock who were beginning to show some interest in the couple.

Cole hoisted himself onto the platform, then snapped his fingers sharply. Soldier Boy leaped from the boot and stood alert where his master indicated. "Sit!" The dog complied. "Stay! Watch!" The long tongue flicked over the broad jowls, and the yellow eyes began to scan the crowd of men.

After taking a last look around, Cole made his way to the door and entered the hall. Once he was out of sight, the men crowded in for a closer look. It was not every day that they were treated to such a comely sight, and the long months in the remote logging camps were drawing steadily nearer. Alaina appeared not to notice them, yet she casually lifted the buggy whip from the staff and toyed with the butt of it, letting the tip dangle over the side of the buggy where it would be clear for a blow.

One of the men, a huge specimen with long blond hair down to the collar of his plaid wool jacket and a beard that hid the full width and length of his bullish neck, grew bold and strode to the edge of the dock beside the buggy. A low rumble began in Soldier Boy's chest, but the man ignored him and lifted a foot as if to rest it on the buggy.

"I wouldn't, if I were you," Alaina warned him direly.

"Oh, liddle lady, I really worry 'bout dat dog." The man guffawed loudly, and a round of snickers marked appreciation for his humor. "I break him, so!" Massive hands twisted in a quick, explicit demonstration. "You like de dog, liddle lady, you tell him quiet."

The man kicked a foot sideways, and Soldier came to a half crouch, his jowls curling back to display inch-long fangs. The rising hackles formed a wide crest down his spine.

"By chiminey, dog! You got no damn respect!" He searched about, then shouldered several others aside and came back with a yard-long length of board. "I teach you, dog!"

He swung the club in a sideways blow, and Soldier took it square across his wide chest. It was like hitting a solid tree trunk. The hound's jaws dipped down, caught the cudgel, and with a quick jerk of his head, he snatched it from the man's numbed hand and tossed it aside. The yellow eyes glared hatred, the long fangs gleamed white, and the growl became a snarl as the huge, black hound moved forward threateningly.

"Soldier!" Cole's voice rang sharp, and the dog froze. "Down!" Soldier retreated to the spot beside the buggy and obeyed, though his eyes remained watchful and his hackles still stood erect.

The brawny man faced Cole and boasted. "You lucky, man! Gundar break de wolf so!" The hands twisted again in a snapping gesture.

"You were lucky!" Cole snorted and pointed his staff at Soldier. "His kind hunt the wolf down and kill them for sport. Their real work is to drag down wild bulls and the big bears. Soldier would have made short work of you."

Gundar's face showed brief awe then anger that he had been made less than a bull or bear. "Ach! You talk too many!" He sought to regain the admiration of his fellows. "You go! Gundar like the liddle lady. We talk more!"

He turned his back on Cole, took one step toward the buggy, then seemed to dive at Alaina only to fall short, sprawling at the edge of the dock with his head jutting out over it. His ankle had been neatly caught by the hooked head of Cole's heavy cane. The blond man rolled over and sat up, favoring Cole with a furious glare. He thrust a finger into the side of his mouth, then withdrew it, holding the digit before his face to stare at the blood on it. His next few words may have been in English or some other language, and perhaps it was best Alaina could not understand them, but they were as badly chewed as the man's tongue.

"The little lady," Cole mocked, smiling down at the injured one, "is my wi—"

The Dane seemed to explode from the planking of the dock with a slanting trajectory, catching Cole about the thighs in a bruising hug and carrying him upward and backward until they slammed squarely into the middle of the beer advertisement. With a gasp, Alaina half rose from the buggy seat, the whip gripped tightly in her fist as if she had every intention of using it. The dog set up an angry barking seeing his master pinned against the door by the snorting Dane who clawed upward for whatever was vulnerable. Cole thrust the heavy cane under Gundar's chin and over his shoulder, then levered back hard. The Dane was peeled away as his head was forced back, and his opponent dropped to his feet. Alaina sank back to the seat, but every muscle in her body was tense and rigid as she watched the battle.

The grimace on Cole's face was as much from pain as from the struggle, but this was no time to pamper a pet leg. He stepped aside and dusted the Dane's broad rear with the cane, eliciting a bellow of rage for his effort. The man whirled, and Cole jabbed with all his strength, catching the other in the stomach, just beneath the ribs, with the blunt head of the staff, and driving the breath from him. Gasping, Gundar staggered back as Cole reversed the cane and followed. He smote the left side of the huge noggin, then the right. It was like hitting a barrel; there was sound but no effect! Cole brought the heavy knotted end up from the ground. This time Gundar's head snapped back with the impact, and his eyes glazed a trifle.

Cole changed positions of the staff, holding it across his chest like a rifle, and struck out with the thick butt, rolling the Dane up on his heels until he staggered back for balance. At the edge of the dock, Gundar teetered like a tall pine ready to crash down. Cole decided the matter with a light push of his staff against the man's chest. The resulting geyser of mud startled the horse and caused it to prance nervously. Alaina caught the reins and spoke in a soothing tone until the steed calmed.

Cole braced on his cane and surveyed the crowd with a challenging gaze, but none seemed eager to take up the gauntlet for the fallen Gundar. The groggy Dane pulled his mud-covered form up against the edge of the dock as Cole gingerly lowered that part of his person which had first hit the wall into the seat beside Alaina who watched him worriedly. Cole whistled and slapped the back of the seat to bring Soldier to his place, then with a flip of the reins, the roan lifted his feet high and took the buggy away from the hall.

"Are you all right?" Alaina questioned with anxious concern. "Did he hurt your leg?"

"It's a bit bruised perhaps." He glanced aside at her. "But it will be all right."

Alaina looked back over her shoulder to where several of the men had hauled the Dane back onto the dock and were busily dousing him with buckets of water. She shivered at the thought of the icy bath. "They seem to enjoy fighting almost as much as drinking," she observed laconically.

"A rowdy bunch," Cole agreed. "With a stringent pecking order, but good workers all, once they are out of the town."

"You need more men at the farm?" Alaina asked in wonderment.

"Not at the farm," he replied. "I have some good timberland up north, and it's about time it was worked over."

She noticed that they were traveling along the river but not in the direction of home. "Where are we going now?" Her voice held a note of excited curiosity. "Are you taking me to meet your mistress?"

Cole's stare was at first one of amazement, then he saw the threatening smile on her face. "Not hardly, madam," he chuckled at last. "There was a message for me in the hall that an old friend is visiting in town. The man would be an excellent foreman for the crew up north."

Some moments later the buggy neared a large, white house decorated with intricate gingerbread workings. A tall, lean man, of almost Cole's size and build but younger, came out onto the front porch as the buggy rolled to a halt before the hitching post.

Cole whistled shrilly and pointed. "Kill Soldier!"

The mastiff bounded from the buggy with enough force

to rock the seat precariously. Alaina caught her breath, aghast at the command, but the dog barked joyfully and charged up the steps, leaping to place his paws on the man's shoulders and growling in mock ferocity.

"Down, you misbegotten son of a moose!" the assailed one laughed as he tried to avoid the licking tongue. "Cole! Call him off!"

"That should teach you to foist off your castaway mongrels!" Cole laughingly called as the blond man subdued Soldier's capricious play.

"Mongrel! Huh!" Alaina heard the man's reply. "He probably has a better-documented lineage than you do."

Cole threw his legs over the side and slid to the ground. Alaina saw the back of his neck stiffen as his feet touched, and it was a long moment of testing before he rested any weight at all on the right leg. He fumbled under the seat and lifted his slim black cane, using it to take most of the strain off his leg as he limped around the buggy to lift her down. He caught her hand and tucked it within the crook of his arm as he made a cautious way up to the house. "My wife, Alaina," he presented as they climbed the steps. "Franze Prochavski, a simple Polish fellow."

"Not Polish!" Franze laughed in a charming, almost boyish manner. "Prussian! And like any good solid German, Cole can't understand the difference."

"Austrian!" Cole corrected with a grin.

"Of course!" Franze's dark eyes gleamed with merriment as he satisfied his revenge. "My apologies, Herr Latimer."

An attractive young woman, obviously pregnant, swung open the front door and came out to join them. Happy twinkling blue eyes shone with as much warmth and friendliness as her quick smile.

"My wife, Gretchen," Franze announced to Alaina.

"We did not get a chance to meet Cole's first wife." Gretchen's light, German accent was just enough to be completely captivating. "So we make a special time to meet you. I am so happy to see that he has done well." She took Alaina's slender hands in both of hers. "I hope this time Cole will get a chance to make a baby also, yah?"

Under Cole's gaze, Alaina felt her face grow warm and in her sudden confusion, mumbled a few words she hoped would be accepted as a suitable reply.

"This second time for us to make a baby," Gretchen confided, but continued a little sadly. "But that was before Cole came home from the war. The midwife say the baby come wrong, and the cord choked the breath from it. This time, Cole take care of it all, yah?"

"You put too much trust in me, Gretchen," he gently admonished.

"That's because I know you best doctor around here. You not say no, yah? You come up north, all right?"

"I've given up my practice," he said quietly.

"No!" she gasped, eyes wide with disbelief. "But you loved it so! How come you to do that?"

It was Alaina's turn to watch him, and she was even more curious than Gretchen. With a troubled frown, he stared down at the planking beneath his feet, shrugging off an answer. "Circumstances were such that I decided it was best to give it up."

The woman turned to Alaina, honestly concerned that a doctor of his abilities should be forced to make such a decision. "Can you persuade him to change his mind?"

"I don't know," Alaina murmured softly. "He hasn't told me why he gave it up." As Cole raised his gaze, she looked straight into his eyes, adding, "It seems a shame, though, since he was so good at what he did."

Gretchen felt reassured as she observed the couple. If anyone could influence Cole, she sensed that it was this young woman, whether he was ready to admit it or not.

Gretchen would have it no other way but that they share a pot of tea, and this was soon extended to include some of the most delectable sweet breads Alaina had ever sampled. As they sat about the table before the warming hearth, Alaina learned that the house belonged to Gretchen's parents who were gone for the afternoon and that the young couple was visiting from a farm they were struggling to establish near Cole's holdings.

It was well into the afternoon before business matters were settled and Cole escorted Alaina to the buggy. Gretchen stood at the door until the buckboard had disappeared from sight, then she turned with a gentle smile to her husband, assuring him, "Cole will come north when the time nears for the baby to be born."

Franze stared at her, totally perplexed. "How do you know?"

Her smile widened. "I just know."

Chapter 30

JUST before dusk, a warm, southwesterly breeze sprang up to set astir the slumbering countryside. Alaina paused in her toilette to open a window and enjoy the gentle caress of the warming air. The river curled away on either side of the cliff and lazily glistened in the lowering sun. Now and again a breath of wind skimmed across the surface, rippling and stirring the water as it traveled the winding course. Much in the same fashion, thoughts touched her mind, disturbing the smooth peace of lassitude. Memories caused waves or made strange patterns against the rocks hidden just beneath the surface. It was a mammoth boulder that Cole had married her simply because he felt it was the right thing to do, and its roiling disturbance muddled the flow of her logic. Her own casual acceptance of events was the unsettling breeze that whispered through her musings until it became a tumbling troubled tide of confusion. She argued that her sensibilities had been abused, yet she could find no righteous anger to deal sharply with him as he deserved.

Releasing a pensive sigh, she returned to her dressing, donning her own best evening gown of yellow taffeta woven with fine, black stripes. A wide band of black lace was draped diagonally across the front of the gored skirt which flared out with great fullness at the bottom. A pleated berthe adorned the bodice, and puffed sleeves were trimmed with black lace. The tiny buttons that fastened the back caused her several moments of regret that Cole was not handy to assist her. But the lawyer from Pennsylvania had arrived shortly after they returned, and the two men had withdrawn into the study to indulge their business, leaving her to fill out the afternoon with idle meanderings.

Ruefully Alaina removed the chair she had carefully

wedged against the door that led to her husband's bedroom. It had been a wasted gesture, for no slightest sound had come from that direction. A clock daintily chimed the half hour, and Alaina glanced in surprise toward the fireplace mantel, realizing that some time during the day an ornate timepiece had been added to her bedroom decor. In another thirty minutes or so, the Darveys would arrive. She was dressed and ready, while Cole still had not come upstairs to change for dinner.

As the moments flew by, she opened the hall door so she might hear the clapper that would herald the guest's arrival. In a last effort to search out whatever flaws there might be in her appearance that would thwart Cole's approval and blatantly remind him of her refusal to wear the clothes he had purchased, she returned to stand before the mirror. She had taken unusual care to brush her hair until the dark tresses gleamed richly. Parted down the middle, it was drawn away from her face, and an openly woven black silk net held the full, sleek mass of it. It was a rare experience to feel pretty and feminine, but she could not savor the moment with the uncertainty of Cole's reaction yet to be resolved. The teardrop diamonds dangling coyly from her earlobes might pacify him to some extent, but she could hardly base her hopes on the unpredictability of her husband.

Some minute whisper of a sound penetrated Alaina's consciousness as she stood before her reflection, and the hair on the back of her neck began to crawl. Suddenly, a vague movement in the mirror caught her eye, and she whirled, only to find the doorway empty. Taking up a lamp, she hurried to investigate, but the hallway shadows were void and barren, although she walked the length of the corridor and back. She left the lamp on a high bracket in the hall to dispel the darkness. The stealthy visitor would have to brave the light it cast, an unlikely probability since he seemed to prefer the shadows.

Voices trailed upward from the front hallway, and Alaina realized that Miles was already greeting the guests. She drew a deep, steadying breath, and prepared herself to meet Cole's friends, to enter her role as mistress of the house. Still, as she made her way down the hall, her mind was plagued by the fleeting shadow she had glimpsed in the mirror. Who was this Mindy Cole had spoken to the night before. What had she to do with this house—and with Cole?

The rustle of her taffeta gown caught Braegar's attention as she came down the stairs. Glancing up, the man immediately forgot that he was helping his sister off with her wrap, for the apparition descending toward them wiped his mind clear of anything but sheer appreciation. He hastened across the hall to greet their hostess, leaving Miles to assist his kin out of their wraps.

Clicking his heels, Braegar affected a fine, courtly bow, then taking Alaina's hand, bent over it in the best of old world tradition. "Madam, you surely warm these northern climes with the sunshine of your beauty."

"You are most gallant, sir," she replied, smiling graciously.

Allowing Braegar to escort her across the hall, she paused briefly as the butler turned with their wraps over his arm, murmuring to him discreetly, "Miles, will you inform Doctor Latimer of our guests' arrival?"

"Yes, madam." The thin servant gave a disjointed bow and, with a deliberate tread, crossed to the study door where he rapped lightly.

Casually the sister assessed the new Latimer woman. "I had speculated on just why Braegar was so anxious to get here this evening," she commented wryly. "Now I can plainly see his reason."

Alaina was not quite sure how to accept the compliment, but whether future ally or foe, the woman was a guest in her husband's house, and was to be treated to a bit of warm Southern hospitality. There was nothing like a bright smile to confuse an adversary or charm a friend. Alaina's soft, pink lips curved graciously as she extended her hand. "You must be Carolyn."

In belated gallantry Braegar swept an arm toward his relatives. "I would have you meet my most sainted mother, Mrs. Eleanore McGivers Darvey, and, as you have guessed, this is Carolyn, my aging, spinsterish sister."

The fair-haired woman drew a stiff smile. "We've been anxious to meet you, Mrs. Latimer." The title felt clumsy in her mouth. "And since you're already acquainted with Braegar, you may understand why I am as yet unwed." She looked straight at her brother. "Few men wish to marry into a family where congenital idiocy is rampant."

Alaina smothered her laughter, but could not hide the

shine of it in her eyes. Hopefully it was only the woman's dry wit that made her seem at first unfriendly.

Braegar drew himself up in exaggerated shock, but his planned rejoinder was quickly squashed by his mother. "Children! Children!" Eleanore protested. "What can this young lady think of your buffoonery except that I have raised a pair of jackdaws?"

"No, indeed," Alaina reassured the woman pleasantly. "It recalls fond memories of my own family."

A polite enough answer, Eleanore mused distantly, but she was not willing to accept Cole's young bride so readily. In her own mind she had placed the fault of his earlier marriage directly on him and berated his lusting foolishness. Once she had held visions of him marrying Carolyn, but however much she had hoped for that, his eyes had cast elsewhere, overlooking the carefully brought up girl close at hand. Perhaps he and Carolyn had been too close, and he had not been able to think of her as anything more than a sister. Yet after Roberta's death, Eleanore's aspirations had been revived. She had expected him to come to his senses and look closer to home for a bride. Instead, he had taken a complete stranger to wife. God forbid, another Southern wench! And poor Carolyn was still a spinster at the age of twenty-seven.

The door of the study opened, and Cole's voice came from within. "I'll rely upon you to handle it, Horace."

Putting on a brighter smile, Alaina turned as the two men entered the hall. Cole still wore the dark garb of the earlier hour and leaned heavily on his cane as if in need of its support. There was a whiteness about his tensed lips that bespoke somehow of pain, and when he paused in what might have been a casual stance to allow him a glance about the hall, Alaina wondered if it wasn't a ploy to give his leg a rest. His eyes lingered on her a moment, taking full note of her attire, before they moved on. He gave Braegar a curt nod and, as he limped toward them, smiled briefly at the two women. He introduced the gray-haired lawyer to the Darveys, then slipping an arm possessively about Alaina's waist, concluded the formalities. "And you met my wife this afternoon."

Horace Burr took Alaina's hand into his. "I apologize for taking so much of your husband's time, Mrs. Latimer. Will you forgive me?"

"Only if you grace us with your company at dinner

tonight, Mister Burr." As Alaina played the congenial hostess with guileless warmth and radiance, the honest scents of sweaty leather, cigar smoke, and brandy that clung pleasantly to Cole stirred her awareness and roused feelings she could not even explain to herself.

Horace laughed with pleasure. "I shall be delighted to join such gracious and lovely company." He moved to take Mrs. Darvey's hand. "At last I have the honor of meeting you after hearing the Latimers rave about you all these years."

A widow for more than a decade, Mrs. Darvey was not immune to the gallantry of the older gentleman. She was still an attractive woman and enjoyed the attention Horace Burr chose to lavish upon her.

Finding a discreet moment, Alaina turned within Cole's embrace and, placing a hand familiarly against his chest, looked up into those blue eyes which rested upon her as boldly as ever, drawing a warm blush into her cheeks. "Do you wish to change before dinner?"

Although hardly more than a murmur, her voice reached Carolyn, prompting that one to recall the first wife's diatribes when Cole had not been properly attired or on time. "Come now, Cole. We've known each other too long for you to worry about such formality." Her voice dwindled as she lost the courage of her first thrust. Where once she would have jested in light repartee, the stiff coolness in Cole's manner as he glanced toward her destroyed all thought of such banter. Perhaps her tone had carried some implication of her readiness to find fault with his new wife, for he seemed most protective of the girl. "I mean—" She could only finish lamely. "This is just a friendly dinner for neighbors, and certainly no high affair."

Braegar held title to no such reservations. "As long as Cole doesn't smell of the barn, I can tolerate him as he is." He straightened his coat. "And there's no sense standing here discussing it when there's some excellent brandy in the parlor."

As the guests were drawn into the parlor by the brash Irishman, Cole paused a moment with Alaina. His hand lightly traced the buttons running down her slim back, while his eyes searched hers, delving into those smiling gray depths for some clue to her game. Her lips curved softly beneath his stare, and she reached to straighten his collar, smoothing the shirt familiarly.

"Am I not providing a suitable haven from worrisome mothers?"

The muscle in Cole's jaw twitched. He should have known better!

Alaina slipped her arm beneath his, ready to accept his guidance, but when he moved, she was at once both amazed and frightened by the unsureness of his step and the weight he placed on the cane. Anxiously she questioned, "Are you all right?"

He grunted, brushing off her concern. "The hours of sitting have made the leg stiff. It will loosen up in a bit."

In the parlor, Cole stood beside her chair and, after Miles had served the libations to the guests, caught the servant's eye and inclined his head toward the crystal decanter. The butler obediently poured a dram or two into a snifter and held the glass up for his employer's inspection. Cole frowned a bit until Miles, with the slightest of shrugs, complied, bringing both snifter and decanter to set them on the table beside Alaina's chair. Cole tossed down the first drink, then reached to pour himself another, briefly meeting his wife's troubled gaze.

"Is that all for you, Cole?" Braegar queried with humor. "Or will you let Miles pass it around again?"

Cole nodded curtly toward the butler, and from a second decanter, the butler quickly replenished Braegar's supply.

"I prefer Cole's custom of enjoying the brandy before dinner," the Irishman commented jovially. "It is most civilized."

Eleanore sat in her chair like a displeased matron and briefly graced both Cole and Braegar with a cool glance. "It comes to me that an overaffection for spirits could well be a man's undoing."

When Miles came to announce dinner, Alaina rose and, slipping an arm through Cole's, took the initiative as hostess. "Mister Burr, would you be so kind as to escort Mrs. Darvey into the dining room?"

Seeing that Alaina's escort was already chosen, Braegar reluctantly lent his arm to Carolyn and followed after his mother. Thus, as Alaina had intended, Cole's pace was unhurried by the presence of anyone behind him. With a gentle pat on his arm, she left him beside his chair and proceeded to her own at the far end of the table, there accepting Braegar's ready assistance. The chair slid forward beneath her, and the Irishman claimed the place at her immediate left, leaving the two of them separated from the others by the length of the table. Alaina's casual glance caught Cole's sharp glare fixed upon her, and she raised questioning brows, wondering what she had done to deserve his anger.

Horace was helping Eleanore into her seat, and of a sudden, Cole realized Carolyn had been left to her own end. He hastened to limp around his own chair to hers, but before he could reach his objective, the lawyer moved to accomplish the necessary service.

"Rest yourself, Doctor Latimer," the older man bade him. "I know your leg is bothering you."

Cole flushed in prideful embarrassment. It seemed he could not perform the simplest chivalry with grace anymore and was ever reminded of the fact that he was lame. He slid into his own chair and hitched it forward, mumbling caustically, "I'm not a doctor anymore. I've given up my practice."

Astounded by his colleague's reply, Braegar leaned back in his chair to consider its import. He was totally unable to comprehend what had caused Cole to lose interest so completely in the work to which he had once been so devoted. Of the two of them, Cole had been the serious doctor, serious in his studies, serious in his concern for his patients, while Braegar realized that his own practice was carried on quite casually and that he relied as much on his good-natured affability as upon his skill to keep his patients content. Frederick Latimer had led them both as youths into the profession and encouraged them with his own zeal and love for it, but he had instilled something special in Cole, a gift for surgery Braegar had never managed to acquire.

"Perhaps he worries that his skill has been impaired somehow," he mused and, catching the sidelong glance from the clear gray eyes beside him, perceived that he had spoken aloud. He hurried to set aright any possible misunderstanding. "Cole is the best surgeon around here, barring none. I can't imagine why he has given it up."

Cole finished another snifter of brandy without gratifying Braegar's curiosity. It was the Irishman's proximity to Alaina that aggravated him more than that one's conjectures.

Serious conversation halted as the first course was served and the meal was entered. The appetizer was small, sweetened meats cooked in a zesty sherry sauce. Annie proved that whatever her politics, she was no simple Irish potato boiler but an accomplished cuisinière, well schooled in the tastes of a dozen countries.

When the talk was resumed, Eleanore could no longer resist broaching a subject that challenged her curiosity. "Cole, you haven't told us anything about Alaina, how you came to know her, or why you arranged a proxy marriage. To be truthful, I'm not at all sure about this proxy thing. It is legal, isn't it? I mean, you didn't bring that poor child up here on some base pretext, did you? Good heavens!" Mrs. Darvey pressed her hand to her cheek as if aghast at her own thoughts. "You are married, aren't you?"

Even with the distance between them, Alaina saw the tenseness in Cole's face and manner, though from anger or pain she knew not which. "You may rest at ease, Aunt Ellie," he assured the woman. "The exchange of vows was quite legal."

"But hardly Christian, Cole," Eleanore said in a reproving tone. She paused as Miles served her plate from the tea cart and, when the man had moved on, continued chidingly, "I don't think your father would have approved. A good church wedding would have been so much more reassuring. Perhaps you should prevail upon the reverend to perform a church ceremony, just to put aside any gossip."

"To hell with the gossips!" Cole growled. "I will not give them more meat to chew."

"Mama, you know that Cole's wound makes traveling difficult for him," Carolyn interjected. "And I'm sure that Mister Burr, being a lawyer, can attest to the legality of a proxy marriage."

"Indeed, madam. It fulfills every letter of the law," Horace affirmed.

Only Alaina saw the scornful glance Annie threw over her shoulder as she pushed the serving cart through the swinging door into the kitchen. The delicious main course of braised veal was consumed with appreciation between comments, but Eleanore was not yet ready to be convinced of the properness of Cole's marriage.

"How do your parents feel about you exchanging vows in such a manner, Alaina? Surely they must have felt some reticence."

"My parents are dead, madam." Alaina experienced a brief rise of irritation, but forced it down as she realized the question was put in all innocence. How could she expect someone who had remained so distant from the conflict to understand? "My father and brothers were killed in the war. My mother died trying to work our plantation, while the Union soldiers played their mischief on our crops and animals. I fled to New Orleans to escape the unwelcome attentions of a Yankee officer who swore he would see Saul and me hanged for spies. I met Cole on the dock the day I arrived, when he saved me from a mauling several drunken soldiers intended. That was two years ago, madam. Doctor Latimer was my cousin's husband, and when she died, he offered marriage. To avoid being forced into a questionable relationship with a backwater river rat, I accepted his proposal." She folded her hands sedately in her lap and met the troubled look of the older woman with a calm, level, but tightly controlled gaze. "Is there anything else you wish to know, Mrs. Darvey?"

Embarrassed by the result of her unchecked inquisitiveness, Eleanore replied contritely, "No, child. I believe you answered my questions quite adequately."

A moment of strained silence passed. Half smiling, half frowning, Cole considered his young bride over the rim of his brandy snifter. A man could hardly find favor in being reminded that he had been his wife's last resort. There would have to be much more resolved between them than just the matter of clothes, he thought.

"Drunken soldiers mauling young ladies?" Eleanore turned on him without warning. "Good heavens, Cole! What has our army come to? I begin to think I should talk this over with the governor."

A commotion followed, a chattering discord with everyone talking at one time. Cole gave up trying to explain, and gradually the others subsided, all except Braegar who was bent upon directing an apology toward Alaina. "Forgive us for being so damned impertinent with our inquiries—"

Eleanore straightened herself indignantly in her chair. "Watch your tongue with that young lady, Braegar Darvey! And I should like to remind you that even in my dottering age, I am as yet capable of apologizing for my own errors—if the need should arise!"

The man grinned and laid his hand over Alaina's. "Then I humbly apologize for my behavior, though I'll wager you've heard as much from your own dear husband's lips, for I fear he's a proper scalawag like myself."

Alaina smiled in an easing of spirit until she glanced toward Cole's end of the table and found him watching her broodingly, then she sobered. His anger seemed to be at odds with anything Braegar Darvey did or said, and she could not fathom his reasons. She dismissed jealousy as a cause for Cole was far more handsome and manly, to her way of thinking. At times Braegar reminded her of a puckish little rascal, intelligent but decidedly mischievous. She found it equally hard to accept that Cole might feel remorse in the fact that Braegar was whole and hearty while he was something less than an able man. The reason seemed more personal than that and obviously of far greater consequence.

"Somehow, I cannot imagine that Cole married you just for the sake of duty." Braegar shrugged carelessly. "It is typical, of course. He was always the upstanding gentleman in love, as in war. To hell with self, so to speak." He caught his mother's warning glare and tried to refrain, for the moment at least, from using any harsh language. "My saintly mother can vouch for it, and if there's one who will speak the truth, she will." He leaned forward and looked down the table at Cole to receive a dispassionate stare which might have hinted at a growing vexation. "As for myself, I would have more reason to marry a beautiful woman than for honor, and I can't believe Cole and I are that far different." A pause followed while he let the others consider this, then he raised his glass in salute to the newly wedded couple. "Here's to your marriage, Cole, for whatever reason it came into being. But if it was for honor, your taste in women has certainly improved."

"Braegar!" His mother was astonished at her son's crudity. "What kind of toast is that? Mister Burr will go home thinking we're the rudest family he's ever met."

Braegar shrugged. "I was just pointing out that if Cole married the first time for love and the second time for honor, he made the better contract in the latter case. If I am too blunt and honest, then you'll have to bear with me. But if the man is too blind to see what a precious treasure he has gained, I say he's a blasted fool!"

"I don't think Cole is blind or a fool, Braegar Darvey!" Carolyn objected.

Her brother again lifted his heavy shoulders to convey his indifference. "You always claimed to understand Cole better than I could anyway."

Annie Murphy came in with the cart again and accepted the empty plates Miles removed from the table and handed him the smaller ones from the tea cart. The butler was the epitome of proper decorum as he placed the dark plum pudding smothered in rum-sauce before the guests. His eyes never raised as Braegar continued.

"It would still be a damned waste if Cole married Alaina for mere honor's sake and not for his own."

"You only met her yesterday," Carolyn reminded him tartly. "How can you judge anyone in that short a time?"

With an impatient gesture, Cole shoved his dessert plate aside, ignoring Annie's obvious disapproval as he slid back his chair and pushed himself to his feet.

Carolyn glanced up in surprise. "Where are you going, Cole? This pudding is delicious. You should eat yours."

"He didn't like me calling him a fool," Braegar offered with humor.

"Sweet merciful heavens!" Cole swore to the ceiling. He braced himself against the edge of the table and favored each of the Darveys with an ill-humored smile. "I feel much like a wounded mouse beset by a flock of crows. Sooner or later you will pick me apart and leave nothing but bare bones."

"Crows, indeed!" Eleanore raised her aging chin imperiously.

Cole pressed on, ignoring the interruption. "Can the fact not stand that I simply married two women who happened to be cousins? Both well-bred ladies of the South? Both beautiful?" He held up his hand, palm outward, as if swearing an oath. "Perhaps it was not done as much in gallantry as your conjectures would have it. Rather, we were simply brought to the altar by—" he glanced at

Alaina and finished the sentence more kindly than she had expected—"fate. In either instance, marriage seemed the only solution."

Alaina was pricked by his rather cavalier explanation. To her way of thinking, he stood in dire need of a comeuppance, the application of which she could not resist. Smiling prettily, she leaned her elbow on the table and crooned with honeyed sweetness dripping from an exaggerated, deep Southern drawl. "You thick-witted Yankee, if you ever put me in the same class with Roberta again, I'll light into you so hard, you'll think the wh-o-o-ole Confederate Army marched over you, mules, wagons, and all."

The gentle, smooth tone of her voice and the radiance of her smile were such that a long moment passed before the impact of her words sank in. Cole raised an eyebrow and gave her an odd quirk of a grin. Horace Burr cleared his throat loudly and busily polished his glasses. Carolyn squelched a giggle and struggled to keep a straight face, while Eleanore's eyebrows were unmercifully stretched upward. Braegar came to his feet in applause. When the furor died, the dining room was silent except for the sound of unbridled laughter drifting through the still-swinging kitchen door. The tea cart, stacked with dirty dishes, remained near Cole's chair, mute evidence of the haste of Annie's departure.

"I beg your pardon, Al," Cole drawled. "It was the last thing I meant to—"

"Al!" Carolyn choked and gave up all thoughts of humor as she gaped at Cole. "You mean—that—she"—Carolyn gestured lamely toward the other end of the table—"is—" She could go no further. Her mind raced over the details of Cole's relationship with "Al," at least as much as he had related through his letters.

Mrs. Darvey was almost afraid to venture a question and yet could not resist just one. "This is the same Al—who—scalded you?" Their whole family had chuckled long and hard over the tales which now came back to haunt her.

Braegar sank back into his chair with a stunned expression that changed to a thoughtful one as he, too, recalled the many mentions of "Al" in Cole's communications. He also recalled that the merest mention of Al had been enough to send Roberta into a shrewish frenzy.

Carolyn's reeling mind had been snared by the threat Cole had made soon after he had met the urchin, that one day he would peel down the lad's britches and blister his pampered behind. It ran over and over in her thoughts as she stared in mute shock at Cole. In fact, they all gawked at him, awaiting his answer, while Alaina, in pleased satisfaction, leaned back under Cole's pained frown and, with a bland smile, refused to say another word. She was interested in seeing just how he would explain it all to them.

Cole sat down and glared around the table. "One and the same!" He pulled out a cigar and bit off the tip, while the Darveys waited expectantly. "Alaina disguised herself as a boy to pass the Union soldiers unmolested. At that time, I was just another bluebelly to be avoided. I took the lad 'Al' to his uncle's house and was introduced to Roberta that very same day. I was not—ah"—he stared at the cigar in his hand—"let in on the secret until after Roberta and I were married."

"Impossible!" Braegar denied.

"How terrible it must have been!" Carolyn wrinkled her nose. "Dressed like a boy?" She peered down the table at Alaina and found it hard to accept.

"You poor dear!" Eleanore consoled and, rising, went to stand near Alaina. "With all the things you've been put through, child, I would not blame you if you hated us all."

Alaina smiled down the length of the table at her husband and, in the guise of innocence, questioned, "Did Cole tell you about the time in the stable?" Beneath his warning scowl, her grin deepened. "Or our dip in the watering trough? Did he mention the fight in the kitchen when Dulcie stopped him from thrashing me?"

"You poor child!" Eleanore gasped, then glared at Cole. "You beast!"

Irritably Cole jammed the cigar in his mouth, flicked the sulfur match alight with his thumbnail, tendered the flame to the end of the cheroot, drawing deeply. All the while his eyes never left his wife.

Eleanore fanned the air as the smoke curled upward. "Cole! I declare! I don't understand what you like about those foul things!"

Alaina slipped to her feet. She thought it best to escape gracefully while she could. After all, there were no locks on the doors to save her from being turned across Cole's knee—as he had so often threatened to do with Al.

"Perhaps the ladies would rather retire to the parlor and leave the men to their cigars and brandies," she suggested in the manner of a cordial hostess.

When she reached the door, Alaina glanced back over her shoulder and found Cole's gaze still resting on her. Those bright eyes burned with something other than anger, something she could not quite lay a finger to.

Mister Burr rose with the men and made his apologies, explaining that he had to start his travels early the next morning. "You'll hear from me as soon as possible, Cole," he said as his host led him to the door. "Be assured that I will do all I can to set aright the problems we discussed." The older man thrust out a hand, and his eyes twinkled as the other clasped it in friendship. "You've got quite a family here, Cole, and a most charming wife. I shall look forward to returning with my report."

The man took his leave, and Cole closed the door behind him. A quick grimace of pain flashed across his face as he stepped down from the vestibule, then realizing Braegar waited at the study door and contemplated him with close attention, he steeled himself against any further display as he made his way to the study.

In the parlor Alaina barely followed the uneasy chatter of Eleanore Darvey, for in her mind the memory of those blue eyes resting upon her was far too vivid. Lately it seemed a recurring affliction that her thoughts should be solely occupied with Cole.

Mrs. Darvey hardly dared pause in her long-winded discourse, afraid she might waver in her resolution to accept Cole's proxy marriage without further inquiries. Carolyn was too busy trying to sort out the details of his tour in New Orleans and make them match with what she had heard at the table to give her mother much heed. The house was amazingly quiet beyond the drone of Eleanore's voice. Then abruptly the serenity was broken by a shattering of glass and the roar of Cole's voice.

"Dammit, man, I've heard enough!"

"Cole, listen!"

"Get out! Get out of my house before I throw you out!"

The women were jolted by the command. Helplessly, Alaina rose with the guests and followed them into the hall where she quietly bade Miles to fetch their wraps.

Braegar burst from the study and strode angrily down the hall, his face red, his eyes blazing as he muttered to himself, "Damned ornery cuss!"

He cut his words off sharply as he met Alaina's worried gaze. Murmuring an apology, he took her hand, but Cole, bracing a hand high against the doorjamb of the study, glared at them until Braegar, seeing the burning rage in the blue eyes, stepped away. He nodded crisply and, pivoting on a boot heel, stalked out of the house. Bewildered, Eleanore stared at Cole for a long moment before she followed her son. Just as confused, Carolyn took her cloak from Miles before she turned to Alaina. She opened her mouth to speak, reconsidered, and took her leave as gracefully as she could. Miles closed the door behind them, but refrained from meeting Alaina's gaze. Dutifully he went into the parlor to bank the fire before making his way toward the back of the house. Alaina faced Cole, seeking some explanation for his outburst, but meeting the question in her eyes, he only snorted in derision, stepped back into the study, and slammed the door.

Alaina's chin came up. She felt as insulted as if he had slapped her. Stiffly she mounted the stairs and sought out the privacy of her bedroom. If the master of the house could sulk in solitude, then so could the mistress.

The house gradually settled into the quiet routines of late evening. For a while Annie and the servants could be heard cleaning up the dining room, then Peter closed the back door as he departed for his father's house. Soon all was silent, and no sound intruded upon the stillness of the bride's chamber except the low creaks and groans, the ever-present mutterings of the stone-and-brick manse. Even the chimes of the clock seemed somehow subdued as they struck the midnight hour.

The tension and excitement of the evening waned more slowly and left the young bride wakeful and depressed. Sitting solemnly before the fireplace, she stared into the brightly flickering flames, pondering the state of her life. In her desire to show herself reasonably dressed, she had spent what money she had earned on her trousseau and Saul's passage. There had been precious little, and to leave even a few coins in her purse, she had sacrificed on the least important items. The nightgown she wore was threadbare and had been repaired too often to bear any resemblance to a bride's negligee. She fingered it distractedly and lifted her gaze to the mirror. The silvered glass gave back to her the portrait of a woman, no longer thin or bony, but slender and softly rounded. The long hours of toil had not been to her disadvantage, for the sleek, healthy tone of her body brought as many admiring stares as Roberta's ever had. Still, Cole was not satisfied. He would have her wear the clothes he had purchased for her—the rich, elegant gowns she craved to wear, but could not afford. And his purpose? To have her continue with another charade and thus convince the world that they were a most loving couple, while all the time the animosity between them still raged.

Alaina stared into the troubled gray eyes reflected in the mirror. She knew what plagued her, what bore on her mind more than anything. Those moments in the hotel—she could not strike them from her mind. Each touch, each kiss had been branded on her memory with a clarity that set her body aflame and left her aching with her own needs.

Uneven footfalls sounded out in the hall, and Alaina tensed, listening over the wild hammering of her heart. Would he come to her this time in anger or in lust? Did he expect to stand above her bed and watch her sleep again? Or was there some other purpose to his coming?

The steps halted at her door, and abruptly the portal was flung wide, bringing her to her feet. Cole limped across the threshold, his jaw set, his eyes red, his brow furrowed. He still wore the narrow black trousers and silk shirt, but the latter had been opened to the waist and revealed his firm, well-muscled chest. The suspicion that he was drunk penetrated her consciousness, but it was only her instincts that warned her, for he displayed none of the obvious signs. Indeed, he seemed well in control of his faculties.

The long moment stretched longer as his eyes bore into her, and Alaina could find no strength in her limbs. The oil lamp on the table behind her silhouetted the womanly shape of her through the thin, loosely flowing nightgown, and his eyes ravished the bounty of her meagerly clad charms. Her breath trembled from her lips as she waited, frozen by the chair, then he limped nearer, spurring her to seek the doubtful protection of her robe.

"Do you wish to discuss something with me, Major?"

She moved past him to close the door, not wanting to portray herself as some weak-kneed schoolgirl. His eyes followed her, and she returned to the hearth where she sat cautiously on the edge of a chair to ease the trembling in her limbs.

In a halfhearted attempt to set aside the thing that was gnawing at him, Cole tried a gentle approach. "You were beautiful this evening, Alaina."

Her unanswering silence chafed. He limped to her wardrobe and, with the tip of his cane, stirred the hem of the petticoat that she had left hanging over the armoire door. He was clearly displeased by its tattered state and prodded the door open with his cane. Though the wardrobe was stuffed once more with rich garments, the black dress was easily accessible to hand.

"When you came across the gangplank yesterday, I almost expected Al to be lurking somewhere within these skirts."

Alaina looked at him askance. "You always had a problem with that."

"But it's obvious that Al has departed forever." Despite his care, his words sounded coarse and curt, and he berated himself as he saw her chin raise slightly in defiance.

"The lad was never really appreciated by anyone, Major."

"There are some who would argue," he murmured distantly.

She raised her eyebrows and stared at him in mild amusement. "Really, Major?"

The title irritated his sorely strained good humor. "Dammit, Alaina!" The curse was sudden and explosive, startling her. He threw open the other door of the armoire and flung his hand toward the contents angrily. "You have a full closet of finery at your disposal, and I come in here to find you in rags!"

Alaina rubbed her slim nose with the back of a knuckle. "Quite right, sir. Beggarish though they be, they're mine to wear." She sat proud and stiff-necked in the chair. "Did I disappoint you this evening? Did I embarrass you in front of your guests?"

"No, of course not!" His tone was harsh as he waved away her inquiry. "You were a credit to my house."

"Thank you, sir!" The reply was prompt, but the title smarted a bit. He did not meet her gaze, but glanced restlessly about the room. Everything was neatly in its place. Not at all like Al, he mused, but very much like this switch of a lass he was just beginning to find out about.

"I thought perhaps I might have displeased you," she said softly, folding the flap of her robe over her knees. "You frowned so much—"

"It was only that damned pompous ass! That licentious Lothario who wheedled his way to your side. Undoubtedly he has been much attracted to you from the beginning." His eyes raked over her, making Alaina acutely aware of the scantiness of her garb. His voice deepened. "But I do not intend to share you with him."

As soon as the words left his lips, Cole had the distinct impression that he had just foolishly stirred a volcano and was about to see it erupt in his face. On a later day he would decide this had only been a warning whiff of smoke. The sting of his insult brought Alaina immediately to her feet, and she faced him with eyes blazing.

"I don't think you need worry overmuch, *Doctor* Latimer! I am not a pawn to be used at anyone's convenience!" She strode irately about the room, questioning almost sneeringly, "What kind of man are you? What kind of man is it who invites people to dine, then orders them out of his house? Your skill as a host leaves much to be desired! Indeed, you behaved just like an army mule—"

Cole cut her off with a snarl. "I only ordered Braeger out."

"Why do you hate him so?" Alaina demanded, whirling to meet his gaze. "Is it because he's still capable of being a doctor?"

"Doctor, pah! That ham-handed—"

"Enough!" Her voice was sharp as she realized he intended to give only insult to the man.

"He, too, bade me chop off my leg!" Cole raged on, unmindful of her command. "Cut it off and be done with it, the man said!"

"Stop it!" The rising fire of the volcano showed in her eyes. "I care naught for your hard-minded ravings. You've grown hateful and mean!"

"Od's blood!" He laughed caustically. "I vow you and Roberta were closer kin than you claim. Hateful and mean! Her exact words on many occasion. You set upon me with the same fangs your cousin laid to my neck!"

His voice was hoarse and cracked. His eyes blazed fiercely with the battle that raged within him. He could not shake the lustful cravings in his loins or the urge to clasp her to him and smother her struggles in a passionate embrace. "But you have done your cousin one better. She promised what she could not give. You deny me what you can give!"

The volcano rumbled. Alaina's own eyes flashed a dangerous steely blue as she took a step toward him. "I warned you about comparing us before, bluebelly!"

"Ah, yes, the innocent now!" He trod the trembling ground with a fool's boldness. "You left—she came! Trick the Yankee! Trap the bluebelly! Drag him down! Tear him apart! How much did your bitch of a cousin pay you to waste your virgin's blood on me?"

Whaap!

The sound of Alaina's hand striking Cole's cheek echoed in the room. He caught her wrist, and in the next instant she was crushed unmercifully against his naked chest. His open mouth plummeted down, covering her protests in a brutal kiss, his lips forcing hers apart and his tongue thrusting through with overwhelming savagery. The restrained desire broke through him in a rush, and he yielded to the rutting heat of his lust, lifting her feet clear of the floor until her soft thighs were snugly settled against the manly fullness in his loins. Alaina's whole being burned with the brazen boldness of his onslaught. She could not draw a breath. Her mind would not form a sane thought. Her breasts ached against his hard chest. Her loins throbbed with the scalding heat of his arousal. She could find no strength to hold him off, nor the desire. Then abruptly Cole released her, and she staggered back, breathless, drained of all anger.

"Be warned, madam," he rasped hoarsely, shattering her trance. "I have known the follies of marriage much too well, but no more. You are mine, and I will take from you whatever I desire, and whenever—"

"You agreed—" A weak, unconvincing whisper of denial was all she could muster.

"Whenever! Wherever!" Cole reasserted. He retrieved his cane from the floor and limped from the room, closing the door behind him.

Like a sleepwalker, numb, stunned, Alaina moved about the room, lowering the lamps until deep shadows filled the chamber. Robe and all, she crawled beneath the covers and curled herself in a tight ball, hugging her knees. Yet the haunting pressure of his excitement still burned in the depth of her being. It was a wee small hour in the morning before sleep finally came to her dazed mind.

Chapter 31

THE early morning mists still wreathed the valley when Alaina rose and carefully dressed herself, intending to confront Cole about this matter of their vows. They'd either have a marriage or they would not, but she would not straddle the fine wire of his mercurial disposition.

When she descended the stairs, Miles came rushing from the back of the house, hurriedly shrugging into his vest. As she moved toward the closed study door, he positioned himself obtrusively before it.

"Good-morning, madam." He was still knotting his tie.

Alaina gave him an elegant morning smile. "I was just going in to see if my husband is up and about."

Miles moved to block her way more completely. "Begging your pardon, madam, but the doctor gave me strictest orders that he was not to be disturbed by anyone. And"—he swallowed nervously—"begging your pardon again, madam"—he cleared his throat—"most especially, not by you." He lowered his gaze quickly and fumbled with his watch fob.

In the brief silence that followed Alaina could hear the off-rhythm thump of Cole's cane beyond the study door, as if he paced the room. As graciously as possible, she released the poor butler from his embarrassment. "I understand, Miles."

She ate breakfast alone, while the chair at the far end of the table remained conspicuously empty. Cole's service had not even been set, and though tasty, the food on her plate was barely touched. Alaina left the dining room to retire upstairs, and as she entered the hallway, Mrs. Garth was just raising her hand to knock on the study door. The housekeeper paused as Alaina passed and slowly lowered her arm. In her other hand she carried a silver tray that bore an unopened bottle of brandy. It was obvious to Alaina that the woman was deliberately waiting for her to leave. In quiet dignity Alaina crossed to the stairs and mounted them. Just before reaching her room, she heard the light rap of Mrs. Garth's knuckles against the heavy oak of the study door.

Alaina frowned. It seemed as if everybody else in the house knew what was going on and was determined to keep her apart from it. If Cole was attempting to drink his problems into submission, then the servants had their orders; he was not to be disturbed.

Well! A finely shaped jaw thrust out defiantly. That, too, would pass. He has to come out sometime.

In the afternoon, Olie dragged a chair into the hallway and leaned it back beside the study door. There, he reposed in guardianship while Miles attended other duties. Through the thick oak door, Cole's voice drifted, chanting a singsong ditty, the words of which were slurred beyond recognition.

In the evening, Peter took up the station, and the next morning Miles was up earlier, puttering about in the foyer when she came down. Appraising the situation, Alaina made no attempt to approach the door, but answered Miles' greeting with a nod of her head and went in to breakfast. Sometime around the noon hour Peter returned to guard the study door. At the evening meal no sound came from the study, though Olie was taking his tour of duty.

The third morning Alaina came down slightly later than usual. She had been especially careful in her toilet, brushing her hair until it fairly gleamed and pinching her cheeks to a brighter color. Surely, she thought, even Cole had taken enough solace from the bottle. But the door was still closed, the study quiet, and Miles was, as usual, present before it. Annie brought Alaina's breakfast under a silver cover and again the mistress of the house ate alone. Heaving a weighty sigh, Alaina took a cup of coffee with her to the large window that provided a splendid view of the river. All her resolutions of confronting Cole had mellowed to a desire just to see him. But even that seemed too much to hope for.

The first sense of being watched was a crawling of hair on the nape of her neck, yet this time Alaina continued sipping her coffee until the first flush of fear died away. There was no threat here; that much she realized. Without giving an indication of her intent, she whirled. The kitchen door creaked as it swung closed.

There was someone! Alaina dashed forward, setting the cup on the table, and threw open the betraying portal. She took a step through, then stopped, listening carefully. No one was in the room, but she heard a low humming, a wordless song coming closer. The door leading from the fruit cellar opened, and Annie stepped into the kitchen, cradling several crock jars against her plump bosom. When she saw the new mistress in her kitchen, she stopped in surprise, ceasing her melody.

"Did you see anyone come through here?" Alaina queried in confusion.

"No, mum." The portly cook heaved a breathless sigh and set down her burden. "As ye can see, I was down in the cellar fetching some vittles. How would I know if anyone came through here or not?"

"I guess you're right." Alaina chewed thoughtfully on a lip as she returned to the dining room. She grew vexed with herself because it seemed as if she had resorted to chasing shadows through the house. It almost had her doubting her own sanity.

She realized with some irritation that she had been doing too much sitting and thinking of late. If this was the best she could find to occupy her time, she'd soon be in need of some of Cole's brandy to fortify her wits. The interior of the house was well kept, but the exterior made many silent demands. The rose garden was there, waiting—

Quicksilverishly her mood changed as she found something to distract her thoughts away from Cole. She hurried upstairs and, giving no serious mind to his disapproval, she donned her meanest dress, the widow's weeds, leaving off the dainty cuffs and lace-flounced collar. She found a pair of old shoes she had brought with her and a kerchief to gather her hair in, another to tuck in her waistband, and a rather ancient pair of gloves.

Alaina approached the rose garden with caution until she was sure the drapes in Cole's study were tightly closed. Having acquired a shovel and a rake from the toolshed at the back of the house, she set to work with diligence, on her knees, snatching out handfuls of dried weeds and leaves, and carefully replacing the small border stones that had been tumbled away. Her need was as much to let off tensions that had mounted within the last days as to improve the appearances of the small garden.

The warmth of the autumn day and her labors began to find her, and she straightened to loosen the neck of her dark dress and unfasten the buttons that trailed to the elbow, rolling back the sleeves. Using the shovel, she turned the earth until it was fresh and brown beneath the thorny bushes. The work was hard, and after a time, she stepped back, as much to catch her breath as to survey the results. The soil clung to the front of her skirt, resisting her best effort to brush it away. She pulled the kerchief from her belt and wiped the perspiration that trickled down between her breasts, then, patting dry her neck, she raised her head and froze. Cole stood casually watching her through the open window of his bedroom. He was neatly groomed, fresh of shirt, and here she was sweaty, dirty, and wearing the dress he hated.

Leisurely Cole took the cheroot from his mouth and blew a long streamer of smoke toward her. Alaina dropped her gaze and stared at the stone facade of the house, seeing nothing, despairing all. She groaned inwardly in frustration. Three mornings up! Three mornings dressed to the hilt! Two days of waiting for the master to appear! And what good had it done her?

The window above her closed with a snide *snick,* and when she glanced up, Cole had retreated from view.

"Oh, why did he have to catch me like this?" she fretted aloud.

"My apology, madam!" a voice responded from the front of the house, wrenching a startled gasp from her as she jerked about to face the intruder. It was Braegar, sitting on the back of one of his long-legged thoroughbreds.

"Would it suffice," he called as he dismounted, "if I went back and promised not to look this time?" He picked his way through the remains of a picket fence, draping the reins of his horse loosely over the slat of a decrepit arbor.

Alaina wiped apologetically at her soiled skirt, hoping that the blush on her cheeks was not too apparent. "Doctor Darvey! I wasn't expecting visitors!"

"Be that as it may." Braegar loomed over her as she bent to retrieve the kerchief she had dropped. "I shall simply have to make do with whatever beauty is at hand."

With the last word, he reached out to assist her to her feet.

For a brief moment Alaina stared at him in open confusion, then laughed as she realized his compliment and accepted his hand. She enjoyed his game and dropped into a curtsy. "You are most gallant, sir, and you have boosted my spirits as much as this fine day." She swept her hand about to indicate the vibrant blue of the sky and the rich autumn colors of the hillside. "If your winter is at all like this, I think I'll be able to tolerate it."

"Winter!" Braegar snorted. "My dear, innocent Alaina, I shall warn you that this is only a brief warm spell of Indian summer. Better that you brace yourself for the winter that's on its way." He gestured to the rosebushes. "You know they'll be dead come spring if you leave them that way."

"Oh?" She glanced back in sudden dismay to think all her labor might be for naught.

Braeger assumed his best lecture tone and enjoyed the opportunity to discourse. "Perhaps if you will heap the soil over them and top them off with a thick layer of leaves they'll survive."

"Is that all?"

"I think so." But he suddenly appeared doubtful. "It seems to work on ours."

Alaina smiled. "And you came all this way to help me tend the roses? You're truly a gentleman of the first blood!"

He swept his hat from his head. "Madam! I would come a million miles to glimpse your fair face!"

She chuckled disbelievingly. "Sir, I must tell you truly, I've never heard blarney quite as rich as yours."

"Madam!" he pretended injury. "Do you believe me insincere?"

"I am somewhat skeptical, sir, of Irishmen and Yankees," she rejoined pertly.

Braeger peered at her with laughter sparkling in his eyes. "And you've come to tame us all, eh, Alaina?"

She nodded stoutly. "As much as I can, Doctor Darvey."

"And you'll do it too, I'll swear!" Braeger vowed jovially.

Alaina removed her gloves and tucked them within her

apron. "I didn't think I would see you again after the other night."

Braegar grew serious as he admitted, "Cole and I have had our differences before." He sighed heavily. "I came—" The usually glib tongue was at a loss for a moment, and she waited patiently. "I felt—a need—for some kind of an apology."

Alaina slowly shook her head. "I can give you none, sir. It will have to come from Cole."

"No—no." He waved his hand in a half-angry gesture. "I meant from me. I guess it was my fault. I just can't seem to talk to Cole of late. Whatever the topic, I always say the wrong thing. I don't know what it is." He stepped aside, and they strolled together toward the front of the house. "It could be him. It could be me. If I am the cause, I don't know what to do, but Cole has been different since he came back from the war." With obvious agitation Braegar stared into the distance. "He volunteered, full of patriotism and loyalty, boldness and courage. But I could see no reason to risk my life in this foolishness called war, so I paid another to go in my stead."

Braegar gathered his horse's reins, and they walked along in silence, while Alaina thought of her own father and brothers. Finally she halted, and when he too stopped, she caught his gaze and held it with unwavering gray eyes. "In a way you're right," she stated bluntly. "It takes a special kind of man with a special kind of cause to go into battle. I can't agree with you. I won't approve of your actions." She shrugged. "But I won't condemn you either. There were several times when I might have fled had I been given the chance."

Braegar studied her a long moment. "You're a special kind of woman, Alaina Latimer, and you're kinder than most. Is that what Cole holds against me? That I am whole, while he is less so?"

"I think not," she murmured. "Somehow that just doesn't seem to fit."

Braegar was greatly perplexed. He tossed the reins over the horse's neck and settled his hat into place. "Maybe someday I'll find out what's eating at him, and then we'll have it out." He touched the brim of his hat in a quick salute and mounted his steed. "With any luck, I'll see you again. Convey my apologies to your husband. I have a rich patient with the gout waiting."

Alaina was standing on the porch watching him ride away when the door opened behind her. Certain that it was Cole, she waited until he came to stand beside her before she spoke.

"You needn't worry. He's gone." No answer came and after a long pause, she sighed. "He came to apologize." She faced her husband squarely. "For whatever it was that he said."

Still, Cole made no reply, and Alaina's eyes lowered uncertainly, skimming the tall, lean narrowness of him which was complimented by the flawless tailoring of white silk shirt and dark pinstripe vest and trousers. He looked tired and drawn, even pale, and Alaina thought to herself that it was a shame he abused himself so.

"I've been waiting to discuss some matters with you." She broached the subject tenderly but without hesitation.

"I'm sorry, madam." He glanced down at her briefly. "I was indisposed."

"So I noticed," she retorted crisply, then bit her lip. She hadn't meant to sound so caustic.

Cole made no excuse, but stared off across the field to the sunlit hills.

"We had an understanding, Major," she began, but lost some of her purposefulness when his brows gathered in a harsh frown. She finished in a barely breathed whisper. "You accost me whenever the urge strikes, and I wish to know your intentions."

Cole gave her a quick, curt bow of apology. "Why, honorable of course, madam. Was that not part of the vows we exchanged? I believe something was said to that effect—for better or for worse, until death us do part."

Her pride was nipped by the brusque manner in which he dismissed his actions. She could have been Al as much as he seemed to care for her feelings. Perhaps, once again, he had trouble thinking of her as a woman. He had admitted the existence of that problem whenever she wore her widow's garb.

Irritably, she folded down a sleeve of the black gown and began to button it. She could not fathom the reason for the resentment she felt toward him at the moment. "We had an agreement, sir," she pressed, hoping to probe some reply from him that might assuage her pride. "You promised—and you've broken your word—"

"I have taken many oaths, madam," he interrupted.

"One as a doctor, one to my country, two as a husband—and I have come to the realization that in the taking of them, I have made many contradictions."

The conflict of vows had become apparent to him when he had been ordered to leave the wounded and retreat from Pleasant Hill. In outright disobedience of that command, he had chosen to stay. The consequences of his defiance of orders gave him little ease from pain, although he had been honored as a hero. Still, he had felt it his duty to stay and find conveyances for the wounded.

His oath as a doctor had conflicted with his marriage to Roberta. She had repeatedly lied to the patients who had come calling, turning them away. The last had been a tiny, gravely ill girl who had been brought to the house by her parents. Roberta had seen the family coming and had met them on the front porch to inform them that he couldn't be reached, though he had been no farther than the cottage. Braegar was favoring a comely patient at the time and was not available. The child, as he learned later, died that same afternoon, but when confronted with the truth, Roberta had only shrugged indifferently, sneering that the world was better off without the likes of that backwoods trash.

Thus, it seemed that every oath he had ever taken had in some way turned its sharpest edge toward him, and this last one no less than the others.

"You mention honor, sir." Alaina prodded him from his thoughts with the reminder. She was not about to let her question die a beggar's death. "But the vow was threefold. What of love and cherish?"

A brief moment's pause ensued before Cole chose to give her an answer. "I cherish you."

She could find no satisfaction in his reply. "And what of love?"

Cole chafed uneasily. "I have always been suspicious of this flaring thing that occurs on first glance," he muttered. He favored her with a quick glance and spoke with deliberate slowness. "How can I determine what love is? When a man and a woman begin to understand each other, love begins small and grows with the passage of time. It is that which a man holds within himself until it blooms to its fullest."

Angry frustration ran rampant through every fiber of Alaina's being, and her argument burst forth in a torrent.

"With all due respect, Major," she curtsied politely, "but I think you're a blind, bloody fool! A baby is begun in a few brief moments, but it endures a lifetime! An acorn will lie in the crevice of a rock for years, but when the winds tumble it to fertile ground, then it sprouts in the first warmth and wet of spring to become the mighty oak which will last a century or two. As for the holding of love, it's the only thing that must be given away to be held dear in one's heart. It must be shared, or it withers!" Her eyes flashed, and expressions changed her face in a fleeting panorama of emotion. "You, Major, are like a huge, black cloud on a hot summer day. You rumble and crash and fill the air with great sounds. Your lightning flashes with awesome power and sends small, frightened creatures scurrying for cover. But until the rain falls, until that which you hold within you is shared, the land and life will remain as parched and dry as they were before. Until then, you will only tumble and roil and tear yourself apart. In other words, sir, until some good is done, the noise and show are all for naught!"

Before Cole could lift a brow in amused condescension, she turned and stalked across the porch, leaving him to watch the tantalizing twitch of her skirts as she flounced into the house.

His entrance into the hall was much more orderly, and as he descended the foyer steps, he saw the last flick of petticoats passing the upstairs balustrade, then a short moment after, he heard the definite closing of her bedroom door. Miles glanced his way warily, and Cole subdued the smile that threatened.

"Have Peter fetch the madam some water," he requested. "She'll no doubt be wanting a bath."

"Yes, sir. And will you be wanting your breakfast now, sir?" Cole's affirmative nod seemed to relieve a small measure of the man's anxieties. "Annie will be happy to hear that, sir."

Cole seated himself at the dining room table and accepted a cup of brandy-laced coffee from Mrs. Garth. He struggled to shake a feeling that was familiar from his childhood. The one thing his father had been intolerant of was willful foolishness, and Cole had learned at a tender age that if he persisted in an obvious folly, his father would usually seek out a pliable willow switch and firmly instruct the son on the rewards of traveling such paths.

Afterward, the son had suffered deep chagrin at having tested the limits of propriety with such inane boldness. It was this selfsame chagrin Cole struggled with now. The only thing missing was the sting of the switch, and yet he could not truthfully retrace the line over which he had obviously stepped.

He finished his breakfast, choosing to ignore the plate of fried potatoes, and sat back to sip the steaming coffee, even forgetting to add to the second cup the usual draught of spirits. He wished now that he had paid more attention to Alaina's words. It had taken an extreme effort on his part to maintain a stern demeanor and disguise his fascination with her open bodice. Her glistening bosom had heaved with each angry breath as those soft lips berated him. What he could remember of her lecture, he sensed in it a hint of sincere wisdom that belied her years. But he had already recognized that behind that comely face was a brain—and an active, alert one at that!

Alaina's snarl came from the hallway, and Cole set his cup on the saucer in surprise, pushing his chair back just as she rounded the wide doorway from the hall. In the next instant there was a flash of yellow and black as her evening gown was hurled into his lap. He started to rise, but realized she was suddenly near, almost treading on him. She planted her small feet firmly between his and furiously shook a fist before his nose.

"You bluebellied swamp rat!" she hissed like a fighting-mad wildcat. "I'll go naked before I wear a stitch of the clothes you bought!"

At very close range Cole saw the burning, spitting rage that fairly sizzled in her clear gray eyes. "I wouldn't mind that, madam," he drawled calmly. "But what has brought this on?"

Alaina snatched the dress from his lap, and at the violence of her movement, Cole half expected something more disastrous to befall him. "Don't patronize me, you muleheaded Yankee!" She shook out the dress for his inspection until his gaze was properly directed toward the large charred holes burned through the bodice and skirt.

"Do you think I would do that?" He raised his own incensed glare. "Be damned, woman! I did not!"

Alaina fingered the burned edges as she remembered her desire to please him, and she could not restrain the tears that came into her eyes.

"Alaina." Cole's own wrath ebbed as he confronted that misty gaze. He laid a hand on her slim waist as he attempted to console her. "I cannot imagine who in this house would do such a thing. Is it not perhaps possible that a gust of wind blew it into the fire?"

"There was no fire," Alaina murmured softly. Her ire had fled, but was replaced with a growing tightness in her chest. "Someone lit the kindling in the fireplace and threw the gown on top of it." She folded the gown carefully over her arm and smoothed the unsinged sleeve with her hand.

"I ask you to believe"—Cole tried again—"that I would not do such a thing. But who would? Can you name anyone else?"

"It doesn't matter." She spoke so softly Cole had to strain to hear her voice. She clutched the dress closely and, sniffing, turned her face away from him. "It was one of my best. Mrs. Hawthorne helped me to find it." Her voice began to break. "I wanted you to be proud of me, not because of what you could give me, but because of what I could bring to you."

Cole had faced Roberta's tantrums until they had become just another fact of life, but he felt helpless and unsure before the tears of this small wench.

Ah, damn! The wisdom burned in his brain. *Chide her! Get her dander up a bit! Anything is better than this*—he thought.

"What am I seeing?" he pondered aloud in a gentle, half-teasing tone. "Is this the one who took a mop to a man? Is this the one who dragged me from the river and saved my life in the middle of a war? Is this the same one I see crying over a spoiled dress? Is this Al?"

Alaina faced him, and Cole realized his failure in the same moment. The tears flowed freely now, making light paths through the smudge on her cheek. Her voice trembled with suppressed sobs.

"I was a young girl with hair hanging past my waist, raised in a fine family to be a fine young lady." She breathed deeply, trying to fight the heartache and tears. "I watched them all go, one by one. I buried my mother, then I had to cut my hair short and ragged. I had to rub dirt into it and on my face. I had to wear old, stinking clothes from somebody's ragbag. I had to learn to walk like a boy, talk like a boy, fight like a boy. I had to listen to you prattle about giving me a bath"—she was sobbing aloud now—"when I felt so filthy I could have died." She leaned forward, and the gray eyes searched his face in wonder. "Don't you understand? Don't you know?" Her voice broke in a sorrowful wail. "There was no Al! It was always me!" She beat a clenched fist against her bosom. "I have always been Alaina! There—never—was —any—Al!"

The sobs broke, and Alaina fled, still clutching the yellow gown. The sound of her grief dwindled until the bedroom door shut them off, leaving him to bear the oppressive silence alone.

Chapter 32

THE gown was irreparable, but Alaina was of much more sturdy stock. By nightfall, she had come to the determination that she could bear the loss of the garment sufficiently well. In this calmer state, she realized she had, in her dismay, thrown herself on a deep green velvet chaise that had not been in her room when she had left to tend the garden. She found it rather strange the way items of comfort were moved in during her absence; she surely had not expressed a need for any of them. First, there had been the standing mirror, a day later the mantle clock, then the thick Oriental carpet, and finally the rich, overstuffed chaise placed in front of the windows where she might relax and enjoy the scenery. She could no more explain the reason for these additions to her room than she could the damage done to her gown.

The night echoed its misery through the house. The wind changed, and howling gusts whipped the trees into a frenzy, stripped the last leaves from the branches, sending them scurrying, and left the bare limbs to twist as if in agony before its fury. Blinding bolts of brightness lanced across the night sky and faded to deafening crashes of thunder. Rain spattered the windows forcefully and washed down them in tiny rivers. Then, as quickly as it had descended, the storm passed, and all was quiet again. Serenity settled into sleep, and the house grew dark and still as the lamps were blown out, and each sought his own bed. Late in the night, Alaina thought she heard the restless roaming of her husband down below in the study, but even that eventually ceased. The moon broke through the clouds, and she came again to the fringes of sleep. In a floating limbo of darkness, serenity was dispelled by a strange scuffling and dragging that seemed to come from somewhere in the depths of the house. Soldier whined in the hall outside her bedroom, an eerie sound in the dark of night when other ghostly noises pervaded the manse.

Determined to be brave despite the uncertainty of what lay beyond her room, Alaina struck a sulfur match to a candle and, slipping into her wrapper, carefully opened her door. Soldier sat on his haunches before Roberta's door and was only momentarily distracted by Alaina's entry into the hall. He scratched at the portal and whined, as if wanting to be let into the room.

"Come away, Soldier," she coaxed. "Nothing is in there."

He growled as if in disagreement, bringing a trembling to her hand that nearly made her drop the candle. Realizing he would not go away until his curiosity was satisfied, Alaina squashed her fears and pushed open Roberta's door. The hound thrust through and made several circuits about the room, sniffing and then pausing as if to listen. Alaina glanced about. Nothing seemed out of place. The window was open, and the drapery billowed out, making a flapping noise. Sure that she had discovered the source of the disturbance, Alaina breathed a sigh of relief.

"That's all we heard, Soldier." She made the statement aloud as if to convince herself. She went to close the window and was amazed to find the draperies dry and untouched by the rain that had been forcefully driven against the house from nearly every direction. She could only surmise that one of the servants had opened it after the storm to let the rain-sweetened breezes freshen the room. A wintry chill had also been admitted, and its breath went quickly through Alaina's gown and wrapper. Roberta's suite was not a place where she desired to be, and the frosty, tomblike atmosphere did not encourage her to linger. She called to Soldier, but he was preoccupied, sniffing and whining at a wall where small, square plates of silvered glass were fitted snugly together, creating an illusion of a larger mirror. An alcove of sorts framed it, and the whole was draped in scarlet velvet. Standing before his reflection, the mastiff seemed convinced that he had found another animal in the room.

"Out with you, Soldier!" she scolded. "Out, I say!"

The dog tucked his tail between his legs and reluctantly made his exit. Still, with the door of her own room closed safely behind her, it was a long time before Alaina could put to rest her disquietude.

At breakfast her place at the table remained conspicuously empty throughout the meal, and though the master of the house made inquiries among the servants, he received only a vague explanation from the upstairs maid that the mistress was not feeling well this morning. Determined to find out more on the matter, Cole made his way to the door of his wife's bedroom and for once paused to rap lightly on the wood. Hearing a murmured reply from within, he pushed the portal open and found her seated on the edge of the chaise as if about to rise. Seeing who it was, Alaina huddled back on to the cushions, tucking her bare feet beneath the hem of her nightgown and pulling her thin wrapper close about her neck. Half mumbling a greeting, she replaced a cloth over her brow and eyes, dismissing his presence from her sight.

The chill in the room became immediately evident to Cole. The fire had burned low, and the gusty wind that whipped around the corners of the house sucked a hearty draft up the chimney.

"You should have summoned the servants to stoke the fire, Alaina," he gently scolded. "You'll catch your death in this room."

She sniffed noncommittally beneath her mask and sank deeper into the soft cushions, listening to the sound of his irregular footsteps as he crossed to the fireplace. He shut the damper down a bit before throwing several slabs of dry wood onto the glowing coals, then approached the chaise where he stood for a long moment considering the slight figure of his wife.

"Is it my understanding, madam, that you are not well?"

"Nothing out of the ordinary, sir," she murmured.

"I thought you might still be lamenting the loss of your gown."

"I have put it behind me, sir, as you suggested."

"If you would like a replacement for it, it will be an easy matter to accomplish. I'm sure the dressmaker in St. Cloud can find the same cloth and lace—"

"I can manage without it. I have other gowns, perhaps not as nice, but they'll suffice."

Cole searched for some path to break this polite but restrained stalemate. "I'll be going into town to talk over some business with Franze, and I was wondering if you would care to ride in with me."

Alaina raised a corner of the cloth and peered at him, then lowered it again. "I'm sorry, sir, but I am indisposed today."

Cole scowled deeply. She had used almost the same words he had uttered in a brusque apology the day before, and he wondered if this was some attempt of hers to retaliate. Illness was a ruse Roberta had often resorted to. "If your head aches, madam, I shall advise Annie to fetch some ice from the icehouse. It has a soothing effect—"

"My head is fine, Major." She stressed the title.

Cole reached down and slipped a hand over her brow, receiving a glare from her as the cloth toppled to her breast.

"I don't have a fever either, Major," she informed him crisply.

"Then I am bemused, madam—" he began, but Alaina snatched the cloth and flung it angrily to the floor.

"Bemused? Doctor Latimer!" she gritted and blushed profusely at the necessity of having to explain. "Is it beyond your capability to realize that I am a woman? Do you know so little about women that you cannot imagine why I am genuinely indisposed?"

The dawning came, and Cole did his best to hide a smile of amusement. "I'm truly sorry, madam. I was not aware that your state was of such a delicate nature. As a husband I should realize your womanly inconveniences, of course, but being less than intimate with you, I am somewhat at a disadvantage."

"Go away," Alaina groaned in abject misery. Hoping sincerely that he would leave her in peace, she closed her eyes and leaned her head back against the chaise. She could not help but wonder how it always happened that she was reduced to the very shambles of her dignity whenever he was about. Why couldn't he, just once, see her as a proud lady, dignified and serene? It seemed that Roberta had always been able to accomplish that feat with ease. Why couldn't she?

"I will leave you, my dear, after I have seen to your comfort."

She raised herself somewhat apprehensively as he went into his bedroom. He reappeared with a decanter of brandy and a snifter. After splashing a small draught into the bottom of the glass, he offered it to her. Alaina wrinkled her nose in repugnance and listlessly turned her face away.

"I think I would prefer to remain sober and suffer in solitude."

"Come now, Alaina," he chided with humor. "The brandy will sooth and warm you and perhaps alleviate some of your discomfort. As a doctor, it is the best I can prescribe for your plight."

She sniffed as she reluctantly accepted the snifter. "I thought you had given up your practice."

"How can I resist when I have a captive patient?" he grinned.

She glared at him, but he seemed unaffected as he spread a lap robe over her legs and tucked it around her cold, bare feet.

"Is there something your pride will allow me to purchase for you while I'm in town?"

The pert nose lifted sufficiently to convey that she was slightly miffed by his question.

"Bonbons, perhaps?" he inquired, regarding her closely.

His suggestion made her forget her irritation. She hadn't tasted bonbons in years! Her eyes were eager as they found his, and he laughed when he saw his answer.

"I'll buy you so many, my pet, you'll get fat if you eat them all. Then you'll leave me no other choice but to annul our marriage."

She saw the teasing sparkle in his eyes, and her own smile warmed. "Just a few will content me, sir."

"I may not get back until late, however," he warned. "I'll be hiring lumberjacks to go up north with Franze, and I'm not sure how long it will take."

Alaina leaned her head back against the cushion and hid her expression of disappointment beneath the cloth, carefully spreading it over her eyes in silent dismissal.

Cole stepped to the door. "I shall most probably dine in town. You need not hold dinner for me."

She lifted the cloth from her eyes. "And I, sir, will most probably dine in my room. If your concern bends to that matter, I shall be most cautious in my selection of guests."

It was Cole's turn to scowl, but after a moment, a laconic smile twisted the corner of his mouth. "At least, madam, I need have no fear of Braegar Darvey and his attentions for a space."

The gray eyes took on the cold glint of ice. "Major Latimer, you seem to have a most curious morality. You took me readily enough in New Orleans when you thought me a woman of the streets, and no doubt have had many women. I suppose your excuse is that it's simply the relief of a physical need. On the other hand, you choose to interpret the most proper graciousness as if it were some sordid betrayal and vent your spleen accordingly."

"There are many things you don't understand, Alaina."

"In that, sir, you are entirely correct!" She gave him a perplexed half smile, half frown while she waited patiently in hopes he would explain them.

Cole opened his mouth to retort, then steeled himself against a weakening urge. He opened the door, nodded a curt farewell, and left her staring after him, as much bemused as she ever was. She listened to his footsteps going down the hall. How could she ever understand him when he seemed intent to surround himself in a sea of silence?

It was nearly midnight when she heard Cole come into his room and move about in the bathing chamber. His footsteps paused beside her door. Somewhere she heard the thump of Soldier's tail on the floor, then the footsteps went away. Long into the black hours of the night, she listened to his restless pacing in the study below.

The next morning Alaina halted in surprise just within the wide doors of the dining room. Placed on the table before her service was an ornately painted tin box and a nosegay of small, yellow daisies tied with a ribbon. At such a time of year, it was a most refreshing sight.

A soft smile touched her lips as she sank into her chair, noting the card that was braced against the tin and lettered simply, "Alaina." She lifted the bouquet and gingerly tested the pungent fragrance, warmed by Cole's thoughtfulness. She knew the tin contained the candies he had promised, and it occurred to her that such candies were usually made in the large cities in the East and required a great deal of careful handling to transport them this far afield. Why had she never doubted Cole when he had so very casually said that he would bring some to her?

Almost as swiftly, the answer came. Roberta had loved bonbons. Indeed, she had demanded them even in the hardest times. Now the woman was dead. But would she ever go away? Would she ever stop haunting their lives?

The kitchen door creaked as Cole pushed it open, then he paused, seeing his young wife framed in a swirl of warm, shimmering gray silk. The early morning light bathed her in a soft halo that made her seem like a dreamlike apparition, and he had to fight a feeling of awe as he stared. Slowly her gaze raised to meet his, and the mysterious smile that touched those soft, fertile lips nearly drew his breath away.

"Thank you, Cole."

"Do the bonbons meet with your approval?" he asked softly.

She laughed gaily as if she were about to plunge into some strange, thrilling adventure. He watched the entrancing play of her features as she lifted the lid and parchment paper beneath it. Her eyes widened in amazement at the wealth of confections he had purchased for her. Lifting a tidbit, she tasted it delicately, then sighed and closed her eyes as if transported into some pleasure beyond this world.

"Absolutely wicked!" she giggled, licking her fingers. "Will you have some?"

Cole retreated to the safety of his place at the table and rejoined ruefully, "Olie swears such sweets will destroy one's manhood."

Alaina regarded him with a smile twitching at the corners of her lips. "Do you lend a great deal of credence to old men's tales, Doctor Latimer?"

"Madam, of late, if one declared a like effect from water, I would have no way to prove the contrary," he commented dryly.

She leaned her elbows on the table and lifted a chocolate to consider in museful deliberation. "Perhaps you should try several. They might ease the lustful side of your nature."

"Thank you for your suggestion, madam." He met her gaze directly. "Though I daresay my lustful side has had little opportunity to assert itself, I shall try to restrain it better in the future." He considered the silver hound that formed the handle of his cane and pondered aloud as if to himself, "I had no idea that marriage bore such a resemblance to the monkish style of life."

A dozen or more chiding comments were ready on her tongue, but she had no mind to further erode the pleasantry of the morning, and thus held her silence for the sake of peace. There would no doubt come a time in their somewhat unsteady relationship when she could remind him that he was getting just what he had asked for.

The next morning Alaina came down at her usual time and found Annie dancing about in a fair fit of distress in front of the dining room fireplace. An odor of burned chocolate filled the room, and when the cook moved aside, Alaina saw the reason. The banked coals of the fireplace were covered with a sticky black scum. The tin box lay bent and twisted on the fire grate, the bright paint now scorched and brown.

With a cry of dismay, Alaina flew to the hearth and reached to pull the container out. Just as quickly, she withdrew her fingers and shook them to ease the pain, for the tin had proven quite hot. More wisely she lifted the box free with the poker.

" 'Tis a heathenish thing, mistress," Annie sobbed. "I cannot say who would do such a thing, but 'tis a devil, whatever name he be called."

The tin had obviously lain on the fire for most of the night to have been seared so badly by the low, ash-covered coals. Whoever had conceived the notion, had deliberately emptied the candy on the fire, then had mutilated the box. Not an act of momentary anger to be sure, but one of cold, calculated hatred. Someone in the house apparently bore a deep enmity for her.

"What's happened here?" Cole demanded sharply from the doorway.

Both women whirled, Alaina blinking back tears and Annie with her mouth aslack. As he glanced from the mangled box to thc two women, the cook rushed to explain.

"The tin was there, sir, when I come in to set the table. Some villainous creature is at work hereabouts, and I have naught a ken as to what his name might be."

"Perhaps the other servants might shed some light on this matter," Cole replied. "I will speak to them immediately."

" 'Twas no accident, sir," Annie stated emphatically. "This was pure meanness at its blackest."

"So it would seem," he responded brusquely. "But one

way or another, such happenings will cease, even if I must dismiss the entire staff."

The cook wrung her hands fretfully. She would be sorely distressed to have to leave. After working for the Latimers for so long, she felt as if she were part of the family and the master himself more like her own son. Yet she could understand that his commitment to his young wife came first.

Alaina's own spirit was much humbled by Cole's threat. Struggling to control an urge to tremble, she murmured an excuse and left the room. Concerned, Cole followed her to stand in the hall, and watched as she slowly mounted the stairs. He could think of no comforting words that might soothe her. She moved on past the balustrade out of his sight, leaving him to stare in troubled silence at the shadows she had just left. He was about to turn away when she appeared again, this time ramrod stiff and pale of face.

"Doctor Latimer?" Her voice trembled with emotion. "Will you come up here a moment please?"

He hurried up the stairs at the best gait he could manage with the aid of his cane, wondering what damage had been done now. Mentally he began sorting out the dire proceedings he had threatened should his fears prove correct. But when he stepped into his wife's bedroom and saw what had aroused her, he laughed aloud in relief.

"I see nothing amusing in this!" Alaina snapped, white lipped. "Something is always being moved in here while I'm gone! And now this! What kind of fool jest is this, anyway?"

She lifted the small, painted tin box that had been left in the middle of her bed and handed it resentfully to Cole. It was less than half the size her own box had been, but bore the same rich bonbons inside.

"It's Mindy's," Cole answered. "I think you have gained a friend."

"Mindy!" Her voice cracked with ire brought forth by his jovial grin. "Who is this Mindy? Is she some paramour you have kept in this house beneath my very nose?"

"Paramour?" He chuckled in amazement. "I would guess she has need of love, at that, but not the sort you mean. Perhaps it's time you meet Mindy. Come along, my pet."

Giving her no choice in the matter, he caught her hand and led her down the hall to a bedroom on the far side of Roberta's suite. He pushed the door wide and drew her in with him. The room had a strange, untouched look about it. Indeed, no sign of habitation existed. Cole grunted, then pulled Alaina back through the hall to the stairs and descended them.

"Cole!" she hissed, trying to pry his long, thin fingers loose from her wrist. "Let me go! What will the servants think?"

"This is my house, madam, and I don't give a damn what anybody thinks!"

She was still in tow when they passed Miles and Mrs. Garth in the dining room. The servants paused to stare in surprise, and Alaina attempted to appear quite composed and dignified as Cole pulled her unceremoniously through the swinging door that led into the kitchen, leaving the two servants gaping in astonishment. Having had to match the limping pace of her husband's long legs, Alaina was slightly breathless when Annie turned from the wood stove with a ladle in her hand.

"Now this be a rare day, to be sure! Both the mistress and his lordship coming to visit me at the same time." She looked at them suspiciously. "Gives me to wonder what's brewing in the mill."

Cole shushed her with a wave of his hand, further rousing the cook's curiosity. She maintained an obedient silence, but contemplated him narrowly as he glanced about the kitchen. He checked beside the wood box and in the pantry, then stepped out the back door onto the small, enclosed porch.

"There you are," he said to someone whom Alaina could not see. He held out the tin. "Did you give this to the lady after her box was burned?" Though no sound came that Alaina could hear, he apparently received an affirmative reply, for he smiled. "She would like to thank you, and I think it's time you stop hiding and come out and meet the lady. Come on. You needn't be afraid of this one," he coaxed, reaching behind the door. "Her name is Alaina, and she's a very nice lady."

Alaina gasped as he brought into view a child, a girl no more than six or seven years of age, clutching a tattered cloth doll close against her. She was wearing a long ankle-length, faded calico dress beneath a woolen coat that was at least a size or so too small, and though the kitchen was warm, she was shivering like a frightened rabbit. Large, dark eyes cast a quick, furtive glance around at Alaina, but after that, she refused to lift her gaze again and held it fastened on the worn toes of her black, high-topped shoes. The thin, tiny face was smudged and blackened with soot and grime, while the long, badly snarled braids indicated much neglect.

"She doesn't say much," Cole informed his young wife. "But this is Mindy."

"Good heavens, Cole! What on earth have you been doing with that child?" Alaina demanded, horrified at the girl's bedraggled state. "She's filthy!"

"I bought her clothes"—he shrugged—"but she won't wear them. There is a bedroom for her upstairs, but she refuses to sleep in it. She seems to prefer it here in the kitchen. In a quiet way, she is very independent, much like another one I came to know quite well in New Orleans."

Glancing away from his pointed stare, Alaina realized that Annie was closely following their exchange and watching them attentively over the tiny wire-rimmed spectacles that perched on the end of her nose. Cole turned, following his wife's gaze, and Annie hastily busied herself with scraping a carrot for the soup. Yet it was not in her character to withhold comment.

"Mindy don't take ter people as a rule, and I guess I can't blame the poor tyke. The old mistress used to rant and rave 'bout havin' ter share her house wit' every raga-muffin brat the mister be finding. Even took a razor strap to Mindy, one time she did, but the mister showed up afore any real harm was done."

"Annie, your tongue rattles far too much too often," Cole observed gruffly.

The woman appeared undismayed. "I'll be speaking me mind with no adornments, to be sure. But the child seems to have taken right well with the new mistress. Mindy's been watching her for days now." Annie sniffed loudly as she continued. "In fact, she was so worried 'bout the mistress, she give up her own tin what the mister gifted her with. Ye cannot be disputing the gentle heart she has, poor wee orphan."

"Doesn't she have any kin?" Alaina asked.

"She had an uncle," Cole stated. "He worked as our gardener for a while after I came home from New Orleans, but no one seems to know what happened to him. Mindy's been here ever since he disappeared."

"But where are her parents?"

"The massacre three years back," he whispered softly and shook his head to warn her away from the topic.

Alaina took the tin from beneath Cole's arm and held it out to the girl. "I'll need help eating all these. Would you mind keeping the tin for me and helping me along with them?"

Mindy blinked her large eyes and looked inquiringly at Cole as if seeking his guidance. He nodded his approval, and hesitantly her gaze came back to the lady. Accepting the box, she immediately clutched it to her breast, then sidled nearer the door, anxious to escape.

Alaina had known firsthand the fear, the hunger, the displaced feeling of not having a home, and could well understand the young child's anxieties and fears. Her ragged appearance alone could wrench the heart of anyone capable of having compassion for another being, and Alaina was most susceptible. Tenderly she bade the girl to come near, assuring her, "I won't hurt you."

Mindy crouched in sudden trepidation, not willing to trust her, and started through the door, but Cole caught her arm, forbidding her escape. "Here now! Where are you going? Didn't you hear the lady?"

Dark eyes grew enormous with panic as he drew her back. In nervous apprehension Mindy clasped her possessions to her and balked at being dragged past his leg, which she clung to desperately

Alaina's mother had raised her children with a firm but gentle hand. She had never been harsh, but she had not been overly lenient with them either. It was this kind of upbringing that Alaina fell back on now.

"I would like a closer look at you, Mindy. Come here." Her voice, though soft, brooked no disobedience. Reluctantly Mindy moved nearer, and Alaina made a slow tour around her, lifting a braid to peer at a well-crusted ear, scanning a dirt-caked neck, and turning small, thin hands to stare with disapproval at the soiled palms and begrimed knuckles. Finally Alaina raised her gaze to Cole who watched her in wry amusement. "You've let this child live in your house like this? You? Of all people?"

Cole chafed beneath her tone of reproof almost as much as Mindy had under her inspection. "Madam, you may ascribe to me a great deal of experience where woman are concerned, but I assure you, this one falls outside of that realm. If you can enlighten me as to the best way to deal with her, I would be most grateful."

"What every child needs, sir, is a good guiding hand and to be told when to bathe and how to keep clean. And that, Doctor Latimer, will be the next step here. Now come along, Mindy," she said, taking the child's arm. "We'll deal with a few of your most obvious problems first."

A bit of rebellion showing in her dark eyes, Mindy pulled herself away. She had been perfectly satisfied to lead her life the way it was and could do without the likes of a bath! Her uncle hadn't cared one whit about seeing her tidy, and though Doctor Latimer had insisted, she had hidden from the servants until they were too busy with other chores to take time for her. Thus, she had maintained her present state of comfort, and was not anxious to see it end.

Calmly Alaina faced the show of obstinance and nodded, folding her arms sedately. "Well, I suppose I could call Peter, Miles, and Mrs. Garth to help hold you while I give you a bath. It makes no difference to me whether it's by force or consent, but either way, you're going to have a bath."

The girl glanced quickly to Cole in hopes he might save her from this woman who was making such threats against her. After all, he had rescued her often enough from the first mistress. But now he seemed most disinterested in her plight as he drew out his pocket watch and casually noted the time. With that last appeal spent, Mindy had no other option open but to yield. Glumly she hung her head in submission.

"Come along then," Alaina urged and took the girl's narrow fine-boned hand. "Doctor Latimer?" The gray eyes came back to him. "I may need your able assistance should I meet resistance along the way. Will you join us?"

"I'll have Peter fetch some hot water for you, mistress," Annie offered enthusiastically. She was much impressed with the common sense displayed by this young woman and agreed with a goodly measure of gentle force. It was the unnecessary violence of the first mistress that she had abhorred.

Cole was also impressed. "Madam, if you can perform such miracles as leading her calmly to a bath, then perhaps you can get her to sleep upstairs in a bed."

Mindy passionately shook her head.

"But why not?" Alaina asked, pausing at the swinging door.

Annie coughed loudly to gain their attention and interjected, "Pardon me interruption, mistress, but as I said afore, the first Mrs. Latimer was real spiteful to the girl whenever the master weren't about, and little Mindy was given the bedroom right next to the red room. I would be thinking the dearie is afraid that Miss Roberta will come back. It's a fact that she fears being up there by her lonesome."

"We'll see what can be done about that," Alaina replied.

Upstairs in his wife's bedroom, Cole laid more wood on the fire as she brushed the tangles from the child's hair. Mindy obediently put aside the tin box, but refused to give up her doll even while her coat and gown were being removed. Alaina wrinkled her nose at the grubbiness of the garments, and was struck with the memory of the garb she had worn as "Al." At least she had been clean beneath the clothes, while Mindy was not.

Cole contemplated the small, trim woman who had taken charge of the child. It seemed with each day's passing that his knowledge and understanding of her increased tenfold, yet he doubted that with all the facets of her personality he would ever know her completely or cease to be amazed and intrigued by some newly discovered characteristic. He saw the warm look of determination in her eyes as she rolled up her sleeves and pinned an apron to her bosom. She was quite a spirited woman, and he wished to tame nothing more than her heart.

At her bidding, he lent his assistance by pouring fresh water from a pitcher, while she painstakingly rinsed the soap from Mindy's hair over a basin in the bathing chamber. When faced with the prospect of putting aside the doll while she bathed, the girl clutched it all the more fiercely to her. Alaina was not disturbed.

"That's fine. She looks like she needs a bath, too. Only, you'll have to be careful with her. She's far more delicate than you are, and it would be a shame if she came apart in the water."

Cole smiled as Mindy, on second thought, carefully perched the doll on the bench beside the tub. No fuss, no furor, just a little calm-voiced logic that the child could comprehend. He returned to the bedroom, lifted a glowing stick from the fireplace, and touched it to the end of his cigar before leaning back in a chair to smoke and muse upon his young wife. He could guess that along about now Mindy was regretting that she had offered her box of bonbons as a replacement for the burned chocolates, for Alaina had set to scrubbing her with nearly as much vigor as she had the floors of the hospital.

It was a much cleaner, pinker, sweeter-smelling Mindy who, after a time, emerged from the bathing chamber bundled in two large towels. Alaina led the child to him and was strangely warmed when he threw away the cigar and lifted Mindy onto his lap.

The smaller armoire in the girl's room was full of new clothes as Cole had indicated, but Alaina discovered something very strange in her search for apparel for Mindy. Every garment, even the lace-edged bloomers and petticoats, had been deliberately slashed, cut, or torn in some way, then carefully returned to the chest so the mischief would not be readily noticeable. She went through the clothes carefully, selecting the necessary articles that could be repaired the most easily, and returned to her own chamber. She fetched comb, scissors, thread, and needle from her bureau and, in passing the chaise, swept up the goose down comforter. Kneeling before Cole, she beckoned Mindy to stand, discarded the towels, wrapped the child in the quilt, and began to gently comb the snarls from the wet strands.

"I cannot say why or when," she murmured in a calm, unhurried tone, "but all the clothes you bought for Mindy have been deliberately damaged." Cole's amazement changed to silent anger, and she returned the girl to his knee, adding, "I didn't think you knew, but I believe that's the reason why Mindy refused to wear them."

The small girl hid her face against Cole's shoulder as Alaina lifted the red velvet gown with its broad collar and cuffs, displaying the parted seams. She held up the undergarments for his inspection and pointed out the lace that had been torn free. Cole's face darkened.

"There were even burrs in the stockings and butter in the shoes." She shook her head in dismay. "I've wiped off the shoes as best as I could." She sucked her finger where a burr had maliciously pricked her. "But the stockings proved a little more difficult."

"Roberta!" Cole growled.

"Do you think so?" Alaina glanced up from threading the needle.

"The gardener disappeared a couple months before Roberta died, and when I took the child in, she threw the usual tantrums. It seems very likely that she avenged herself on the clothes when I wouldn't let her abuse the child."

Alaina sewed in silence for a long space, wondering how her cousin could have been so vindictive. Roberta had wanted for nothing, but for some reason had not been able to find the contentment to enjoy anything. How miserable she must have been.

Mindy had dismissed their presence, having found a haven in Cole's cradling arms where she now slumbered most contentedly. Alaina lifted her gaze from the child, moving her eyes caressingly over the man's features until he glanced up, then she hurriedly bent her attention to her needle-work, hoping he would not notice the flush of color in her cheeks. She slipped the needle through the fabric, jerked the thread until the knot caught, and innocently presented an inquiry.

"Did you know Mindy's uncle very well?"

Cole snorted. "Well enough to know that he was a bastard. He and Roberta would have made a likely pair."

"What do you mean?"

"Mindy was as afraid of him as she was of Roberta. The man seemed to delight in punishing the child. I once threatened him with dismissal if I ever caught him beating her again. Shortly after that he disappeared, leaving the girl behind."

"I think Mindy can do without the likes of him," Alaina stated. She glanced askance at her husband. "But you, Major, seem to have a way about you. Indeed, Mindy seems quite taken with you. Perhaps you should adopt her."

Cole arched a brow and gave her a crooked smile. " 'Twas my understanding that fatherhood came more gradually. First the bedding, then the diapering. Isn't that the way it usually goes?"

"You should know, sir."

He laughed in amazement. "Madam, I have never fathered any children—believe me!"

She considered him dubiously. For all of his criticism of Roberta, they must have found some common ground between them. "What about your first wife? Was she not in a child-bearing state when she died?"

Looking down at the small form in his arms, Cole tucked the quilt carefully around the thin shoulders as he replied. "Roberta and I did not share a bed—or anything more intimate after my return from the Red River campaign. She became pregnant by some other man."

Dropping her gaze, Alaina stared unseeing at the velvet gown in her lap. "I'm sorry, Cole. I didn't know."

"No need for apology, my pet. It was by mutual consent. She didn't miss it, and I—"

Alaina glanced up as he halted and wondered what he had been about to say.

"—Didn't either," he finished stiffly. "At least, not from her."

"She must have loved you, Cole."

"No." He shook his head. "I don't think she was capable of loving anyone. She enjoyed playing the wealthy mistress. Perhaps she was even proud to claim me as her husband before I was wounded. She enjoyed dressing herself in expensive clothes and liked to show off her beauty, but it wasn't for me. That was about as deep as her love flowed. She was like a shallow stream, all bright and pretty on the surface, but murky and dark with slime underneath."

Alaina held up the repaired dress, seeking to divert the conversation to a less disturbing topic. "You have excellent taste, Doctor Latimer, and this color should suit Mindy's fair skin and dark hair quite well. She'll be a little beauty."

Cole rubbed his leg as a cramp began to grow in it; it was what Alaina had been watching for, that slight indication that he was in discomfort. She rose to her feet and sought to take the child from his lap, but he laid a hand on her arm, delaying her.

"You have quite a mothering instinct, madam. You ought to have several of your own."

Their faces were only a short distance apart as her translucent gray eyes, glowing with warm lights, shone into his. Her voice was low and husky as she questioned, "Are you suggesting something, sir?"

Cole leaned his head against the tall, tufted back of the chair and arched a brow wonderingly. "And what if I am?"

She lifted the child from his lap and smiled poignantly. "Then I would remind you, sir, of our marriage arrangement."

A lesson in the proper morning grooming of a young lady preceded breakfast with Doctor Latimer the next morning. Having frequently watched Alaina from hiding, Mindy readily copied her manner. The example was already set, and the child was as swift of mind as she was at mimicking. But then, there was something about the lady that had sparked a memory of her own mother.

In the ensuing days Mindy responded readily to the firm but loving warmth of Alaina's attention. After the discovery of small, dried thistles hidden beneath the child's lower sheet, Mindy's aversion to the bed became understandable. Still, a goodly measure of reluctance to be left alone in the room remained in the girl. Thus Alaina sought out Cole and asked his advice. His solution was to move the child into another bedroom where she would be away from that cauldron of hatred that had been well steeped into the old mistress's rooms. The idea seemed to delight the child and her eagerness was readily apparent as she helped move her clothes and possessions to the new location.

Alaina gave a last pat to the freshly made bed in the newly occupied room and sat down on it, facing Mindy. She smoothed the quilted bedspread beside her as she asked, "Will you sleep here now?"

Mindy's nod came without hesitation, but again there were no words, only the fleeting smile, then a wide-eyed attention as if she waited, almost fearfully, for some bad dream to return.

"Oh, Mindy." Alaina's heart twisted in pity. "Poor child." She held out a hand and, when the small girl took her offer, gathered Mindy into her arms. She lifted the thin body onto her lap and caressed the soft hair. "We're a pair, the two of us," Alaina whispered sadly.

"But at least my trials were a matter of choice, and I know full well why the choices were made. But yours were none of your own making."

Mindy bathed that evening in Alaina's tub and, when she had dressed herself in a long nightgown and warm robe, sought out her doll and the empty candy tin, gathered them into her arms and allowed Alaina to tuck her into the new bed without a whimper. She listened to a brief prayer as Alaina knelt at her bedside, then closed her eyes and when the lady pressed a kiss to her forehead, a tiny smile came—and stayed.

Chapter 33

ALAINA had already realized that when Cole Latimer set his mind on having something, he was not easily dissuaded from that end. Indeed, he could be steadfastly persistent, never wavering far from his purpose. Most often he won the prize of his attention through relentless pursuit. Thus, when Alaina found herself to be the thing he purposed to have, she knew that she faced a struggle of temperaments ahead, hers pitted against his. As yet he had not issued forth with any verbal commitment that would reassure her she was not going to be used for a whim, and she was most reluctant to trust his amorous attentions.

He became outright bold in the way he courted her, not making any attempt to conceal the fact that he wanted to bed her, or that he considered her to be his property that he could casually touch and freely handle. He restrained himself only to the point that he didn't force her to serve his pleasure, but Alaina was not quite sure just how long he would hold himself in check.

He introduced her about as his wife, and because he had business in St. Anthony, took her with him, acquiring a hotel suite with two bedrooms only because she had gently insisted that they should take Mindy along.

She had shared one of the rooms with the child, leaving Cole to take the other, but he had even gotten around that marital separation, at least for a night, by accepting an invitation to stay with friends after the theatre. Alaina had no choice but to share his room in order to keep up appearances, an arrangement that left her more than leery. While Mindy was safely ensconced in a room of her own down the hall, Alaina had to face the prospect of not only sharing quarters with her husband, but a bed besides.

"You'll, of course, be sleeping in a chair," she remarked hopefully when he started undressing for bed.

Cole looked at her in surprise. "It was not my intention at all, madam. The bed is large enough for the two of us."

"I thought you had trouble stretching out in bed with your leg."

His smile brazenly hinted of his amusement. "Does bedding down with a Yankee frighten you so much?"

Alaina glared at him coolly. "You don't frighten me at all, sir."

"Pray tell me then, madam, why you have turned out all the lamps to undress?" His chiding laughter struck a cord of irritation in her. "If not for the fire in the hearth, I swear I'd have to fumble around in the dark to find my own clothes."

"It would help considerably if you did find some," she retorted with rampant sarcasm.

"My apologies." His long, naked torso bent slightly in a mocking bow. He seemed casually unconcerned that the shifting firelight boldly portrayed him as a man. "I was not aware that your nature was so tender to the honest sight of a little bare skin. However, I must warn you. I do not intend to keep myself forever bound in a cocoon for your peace of mind."

Modestly Alaina clutched the folds of her nightgown to her bosom as he neared the darkened corner where she had sought seclusion to undress. She had only been successful in removing her gown and petticoats, having found the corset strings as difficult as usual. He saw the hesitancy in her eyes as she raised her gaze to his, and smiled gently.

"Do you wish some help?"

Uncertainly Alaina presented her back, allowing him access to the corset strings. It was a long quiet moment that passed between them as he concentrated on the task at hand, but once free of the garment, she waited, scarcely breathing, as he caressed her loosened hair and the silkiness of her bare arms. Stepping nervously away, she pulled the nightgown over her head and released her undergarments beneath its protective shield.

Limping to the head of the bed, Cole folded aside the top covers and sat on the edge, taking up a cheroot to light as he casually observed her progress in modesty. After donning her robe, she came around to the other side of the bed and, quickly slipping beneath the covers, stayed as close to the far edge as allowable without falling to the floor and clutched the silken quilt high beneath her chin. She was no more willing to spend the night in a cold, hard chair than he was, and had quickly given up the idea when she saw what choices were open to her.

Raising the bedcovers, Cole slipped in beside her, keeping his leg bent to ease the drawing tightness in his thigh. As he smoked his cigar, he noticed that she lay with her eyes open, watching the trail of smoke curling upward toward the ceiling. He could not help but wonder at her thoughts. She had been most charming throughout the evening, acting the loving wife for the benefit of his friends and, with her simplest touch, arousing his desires more than she could know. After Roberta, his friends had been much taken with her graciousness and cheerful wit. He couldn't blame them any. She was quite a delectable bit of fluff.

He rolled his head on the pillow to whisper a question. "Warm enough?"

Alaina nodded shyly. "And your leg? Does it hurt?"

"Nothing to worry yourself about, madam." He shifted the cigar to his other hand and reached across to pull the downy quilt over her shoulder.

"Thank you for letting Mindy come with us, Cole."

"Hmm." It was his only reply as he continued smoking. Before he finished the cigar, his wife was asleep, but it was a long time before he could find that same nectar of peaceful repose.

Alaina's slumber deepened as the moon continued its flight across the heavens. She nestled against the warm body beside her, liberated in the blanketing arms of Morpheus. Then, there was a tickling in her ear, a whisper so soft she could not distinguish it from her dreams.

"Alaina, are you asleep?"

"Cole?" she sighed in a soft, drowsy breath, unable to break the lingering essence of silken sleep. She pressed closer, lulled in the security of his presence. He rose above her slightly, laying an arm along her back and nuzzling his nose into the fragrant, curling tresses above her ear, while his lips moved against it.

"Unless you wish to fall victim to circumstances which could rapidly advance beyond my control, Alaina, I suggest you remove yourself—at least, to a more modest distance."

Her eyes flew wide as she realized full well of what he

spoke. She lay on her side facing him with her left leg raised and resting intimately across his bare loins. The branding heat he displayed was graphic proof of his words. His manhood was firm and hot against her, searing her flesh.

"Excuse me," she mumbled in roweling embarrassment and moved quickly to the far side of the bed where she lay staring at the ceiling. Now they were both wakeful, their nerves stretched taut like the strings of an archer's bow. It was a long time before dawn came to release them from this mutual torture chamber.

Once at home again, Alaina felt on safer ground, though she still had to bear his untimely intrusions into her bedroom. Sometimes at night she would awake to find a long shadow beside her bed, and there was be no mistaking his broad, naked shoulders against the moonlit windows. Once again his restless prowling had brought him to her side.

She had all but given up barring the doors with chairs, for she could not bear his sarcasm that ridiculed her fear of him. She was just ornery enough to show him that she was not afraid of him, but then, after discontinuing the use of such safeguards, she could not dismiss the idea that she was playing right into his hands, for he now went in and out of her rooms as he pleased. He seemed especially wont to intrude upon her baths.

"I would enjoy the privilege of showing you off about town this evening," he announced after such an interruption. "And this time," he drawled leisurely as his eyes dipped meaningfully to the pale breasts she sought to cover, "wear something that will compliment you as a woman. You must forgive me, but I'm a bit tired of the gray."

Compliment me as a woman! Alaina's mind railed as he withdrew from the bathing chamber and wisely closed the door. She restrained the urge to throw something at the portal, but only because he'd just laugh at her display of temper. By heavens, she vowed, she would show him just how much of a woman she really was!

She labored most of the afternoon to make adjustments to a velvet gown which, other than the gray, was the last of her personal wardrobe worthy of compliments. As she studied the neckline, pondering whether it should be demure or bold, something savage rose up within her, and she applied the scissors until the décolletage was well below what propriety dictated. Cole seemed to have a penchant for bosoms, and she was well fired to whet his appetite to the full measure!

When it was time to dress, she propped a chair against her bedroom door to prevent Cole from wandering in unannounced. She wanted the shock to be sudden and ruthless, and she was determined that after tonight, he would never again question her womanhood.

At her light rap on his bedroom door, she heard him call out, bidding her admittance, and primed herself as much as Roberta had ever thought of doing. As she entered, Cole turned, working the studs through the tiny openings in his shirt. He halted as his gaze came upon her and boldly stared his appreciation until Alaina had the distinct feeling that his imagination plunged far below the limits of her gown. In that same moment she realized that she had struck her goal as well as could be expected, for Cole absently tried to work a stud through his shirt where no hole existed.

"You're not dressed," she murmured.

Cole limped near and, at closer range, leisurely inspected her, letting his gaze follow the course of the golden chain that disappeared into the deep, inviting valley between her breasts. An enticing bit of lace had been added where the neckline plunged sharply down the crevice, and its transparency stirred his curiosity no small amount, for he could only wonder at the brevity of the shift she wore, if she wore one at all.

Though Alaina was bound and determined that he would never again treat her casually, she realized, as her own pulse throbbed an unsteady beat, the possible danger for herself. Cole was no dawdling schoolboy, and she would have to be cautious, lest the limits of his self-control be exceeded.

She smoothed the deep, rich burgundy velvet. "Is this womanly enough for you?"

Cole laid a hand on the slim column of her throat, feeling the rapid pulse beating there and, with a thumb, lifted her chin until her eyes raised fully to his. "Were it any more womanly, madam, you would not escape my bedroom tonight. It is as much as I can bear and still retain my modesty." His hand slid downward over her breast and around her waist, then slowly up her back, gently pressing her closer to him. "Are you sure," he whispered hoarsely, "that you would not rather spend the evening right here?"

Alaina braced her elbows on his chest to prevent her bosom from coming in contact with him and laughed softly as she inserted the studs into his shirtfront with quick dexterity. "Mind your manners, sir," she cajoled. "Olie will be upon us to find out the delay. I heard him bring the carriage around sometime ago."

Cole released her and picked up his cravat, muttering angrily, "Olie! Mindy! Annie! Miles! Someone is always threatening in this house." He snugged the cravat about his neck. "I shall dispense with the lot of them"—he moved to the mirror as she flipped the striped silk into place—"and rape you at my leisure."

Light laughter echoed through the bathing chamber as Alaina retreated to the shelter of her own room. "So the cock crows," her voice came chidingly. "Search out your vest and coat, milord. We are late."

Cole gave a lecherous grin to the image in the mirror before hastening to comply. Taking up a tall hat and throwing an evening cloak over his arm, he stepped from his room and met his wife as she entered the hall. He was taken aback a notch or two to find that she had donned the hooded, fox-trimmed cloak he had bought for her and had covered her charmingly upswept coiffure with an exquisite black lace shawl.

Master Latimer was at his very best behavior as he handed his wife into the waiting brougham. He slid into the seat beside her and thumped the head of his cane against the roof, signaling Olie to get under way, then leaned back to place an arm about his wife's shoulders and bestow upon her his full attention. The carriage lanterns leaked their shifting light in upon her, casting a soft glow on the enticing cleavage as he plucked away the sheltering folds of her cloak.

"It pleases me that you've worn the cloak, my love," he murmured huskily. "It suits you."

The endearment came from his lips like a tender caress, strumming the strings of her heart. Yet for all of her longing to be soft and responsive to him, she was most wary. She could hardly feel confident in her ability to handle him, having failed at least once before. In many respects he was like some sharp-fanged, wary-eyed wolf, ready to devour, but at the moment, temporarily pacified. She had cause to be cautious.

"I've never worn anything so luxurious before, Cole." She smoothed the fur trim shyly. "It's beautiful."

"Only because you're wearing it, my love," he breathed as he bent his head near to brush his lips against her hair. "You smell as pretty as you look. All woman, soft and sweet."

Alaina privately conceded that his taste in perfumes suited her mood of the evening, but she was becoming increasingly aware that her ploy as temptress was quickly diminishing to the role of cornered hare. He had latched on to the game with fervor, and was chasing her down, wearing down her resistance with honeyed words and gentle caresses. What woman wouldn't find her defenses much askew when boldly courted by the likes of such a handsome and zealous suitor? She was not to be blamed because she wanted it to continue, even though somewhere further on she must find the will to hold him off.

Sometime later Olie pulled the carriage to a halt before a large, three-story, yellow building, the high gables of which were elaborately decorated with openwork. A porch, bearing the same plethora of gingerbread, stretched across the face of the structure.

"What kind of place is this?" Alaina questioned eagerly as Cole handed her down from the brougham.

"The best the town has to offer," he stated with a grin. "But then, madam, you must remember that this is not New Orleans. Hardly comparable to the St. Charles as a hotel I'm afraid."

"Hotel?" She stared at him in wide curiosity.

"Stearns House, madam. We'll have a bite to eat here," he obliged her further. "I've heard there's a traveling troupe in town. Perhaps we can catch a performance after we dine."

"Will we be staying the night here?" Her voice was soft but the question blunt.

"That remains to be seen, madam." He smiled debonairly. "It's not outside the realms of possibility, if you should feel inclined to stay."

"We have no baggage." She made the statement as if to dismiss the feasibility of such a happening.

"Then I would say that dispenses with the problem of you wearing a robe to bed," he grinned.

She blushed profusely, remembering that other night with embarrassing clarity. "You are a conniving rogue, sir."

"Madam, let me assure you," he responded lightheartedly, "that I will not press you overmuch to do anything against your will." The light of humor sparkled in his eyes as he offered his arm, and he covered her hand warmly with his when she slipped it through the crook. "You must forgive me, my sweet. You play the loving wife so well, I catch myself getting lost in the role of husband."

"And sometimes, sir," she replied in a gentle but more serious vein, "I find myself completely baffled by you and this marriage of ours."

In the rich foyer a uniformed maid took their outer garments, and demurely Alaina drew the lace shawl about her shoulders, gathering it over her bosom. Whatever her casualness might be with Cole, she lacked the boldness to lend herself to the stares of other men.

The hostess turned to lead the way, and Cole slid his hand along his wife's back, settling it possessively upon her narrow, corseted waist. They passed through a parlor adorned with long, gilt-framed mirrors, velvet drapes, and twinkling chandeliers. In the dining room, they were led to a secluded table in the corner. As the hostess bustled off to fetch them wine, Cole assisted Alaina into a chair which faced away from the other occupants of the room, shielding her from their overly curious stares. He nodded to several casual acquaintances before seating himself beside her, stretching out his leg beneath the table.

Cole gathered his wife's slender fingers into a gentle grasp, admiring her beauty and the vision she made. He was stirred by the nearness of her and most enchanted with the detail of her features, the way her eyes tilted upward beneath their thick fringe of black lashes, the gently curving bow of her soft lips which he craved to caress with his own.

"You hand is cold," he whispered.

"And yours is warm," she murmured, snuggling her other hand into his and unconsciously bringing her shoulders forward until the gown gapped open, revealing the pale, lustrous swell of her breasts to his rapidly warming perusal. The bodice teased him, ever threatening to yield a view of the tantalizing peaks he longed to touch. There was a sweet, nagging ache growing in the pit of his belly, a hungering he yearned to appease.

"We've become something of a curiosity among the gossipmongers hereabouts, my sweet," he commented with a wayward smile. "Perhaps we should allow them the opportunity to see that you're not a jackal with two heads."

"And what do you suggest, sir?"

He gazed down into the warm, gray eyes. It was easy to become mesmerized in their clear depths. "A small celebration, I think, to honor the new Latimer woman. Nothing extravagant, a few neighbors and acquaintances over for some wining and dining and a bit of dancing."

A burst of laughter came from the entrance, and the sound of mixed voices chattering gaily approached the dining room. The Latimers turned as Braegar and Carolyn Darvey, accompanied by another man and a woman, swept through the doors. A muffled groan came from Cole as he silently cursed the fate that had brought them to the hotel at this particular time, and when Alaina looked at him, he was pressing a hand against his face as if the whole side of it ached while he gazed steadfastly out the darkened window.

"Cole, be nice," she pleaded. "Remember, he did make his apologies."

"Madam," her husband sighed heavily. "You can't understand my present urge to throttle him."

Catching sight of the couple, Braegar flashed them a broad grin and waved a greeting.

Cole smiled stiffly, nodded, and muttered beneath his breath, "Have you ever seen so many teeth in one man's mouth?"

"Oh, Cole, please!" Alaina begged softly, her eyes appealing to him in humble supplication.

"Cover yourself, my pet," he bade gently. "I have a strong aversion to that man ogling you."

She gathered the shawl to cover her bosom, her cheeks pinkening as she realized what the degree of her exposure had been. Carolyn was already leading the procession toward them, weaving her way past other tables and people. Cole struggled to his feet, realizing there was no escape, no back door he could pull Alaina through.

"Alaina!" Carolyn bent to affectionately press her cheek against the younger woman's, then straightened to do the same with Cole. "What a pleasure it is to run into you like this."

"Good-evening, Miss Darvey." Cole's voice was flat and dry, barely meeting the definition of polite greeting.

"Miss Darvey, indeed!" she laughed, resting a hand on his arm. "Good heavens, Cole! You're as stiff as a mossy old board. You know you really should learn to relax more. No wonder your leg bothers you so much."

Braegar came to stand beside them, offering an explanation. "Our carriage wheel broke just down the street, and it cannot be fixed until the morning. We were worried that we'd have to stay the night, but since you're here, Cole, perhaps we can beg a ride home—" He left the sentence hanging expectantly.

It was even worse than Cole had first imagined. He saw the whole evening wasted and his intentions put to naught. They couldn't possibly know how outraged he felt at their intrusion or understand his frustration. Hoping to dissuade them, he displayed his reluctance to leave. "We just got here."

"Oh, well, that's just fine!" Braegar rejoined. "We'll join you and have a bite to eat."

"Braegar, you haven't made the introductions," his sister reminded him.

"Of course!" He laid his arm around the small, red-haired woman's waist. "Cole, I believe you know Rebel Cummings and Mart Holvag, our senior knight of the law and order forces."

Cole translated the introduction as he presented his wife. "Martin is our deputy sheriff, and this is Rebecca Cummings." He saw the perplexed look that flickered across Alaina's brow and explained further. "Most of her friends call her Rebel. She spent several months with her father down in Vicksburg after the siege." He smiled ruefully. "When she returned, she had been infected with a drawl." He nodded briefly toward Braegar. "It appears that she's living up to the title."

Braegar gave no sign that he had heard Cole's gentle barb as he swept his hand ceremoniously about to indicate Alaina, but his own rejoinder struck its mark. "And this fair lady is the latest mistress of yon Bluebeard's castle, my friends."

"Braegar! How could you?" his sister gasped angrily. "That wasn't funny."

His thrust had been sharp enough to make Cole stiffen. Alaina, seeing the stone-chiseled set of her husband's features, slipped gracefully to her feet and slid her hand through his arm, meeting his eyes with her silent plea until she felt him relax. She could not shake the mild feeling of disappointment at the intrusion these people forced upon them. The growing realization that she was beginning to enjoy Cole's courtship more and more brought an odd but undeniable radiance to her existence and being. Except for Jacques's crude abuse and the lieutenant's halfhearted wooing, she had never known the warm attentions of a handsome man, but this, she realized, was something beyond the simple gratification of a woman's desire to be wooed. Something entirely different.

"Are y'all really from the South?" Rebecca asked sweetly in wide-eyed wonder. "Cole seems to have such a preference for Southern belles, I was just wondering what it is about y'all that he finds so intriguing."

"My Southern accent perhaps?" Alaina queried, miming the other's innocence, but couching her reply in a crisp English twang. "It really is amazing how being in a new place can affect one's tongue. Why, after being around Cole for so long"—she smiled up at her husband solicitously and felt warmed by his approving stare—"I've learned words I never knew existed."

"Truer words might never have been spoken," Braegar avowed. "I've heard him range the length and breadth of the language and then some."

"Oh, faith and begorra!" Carolyn threw up her hands in despair. "Here's an untutored Irishman laying claim to the English tongue!"

"I have been well tutored by him." Braegar shrugged.

"Like the kettle tutors the pot in blackness!" His sister retorted.

"He has the advantage of his youth and wide travels with the army," Braegar excused lamely.

"But you have the natural talent!" Carolyn accused, shaking her head in exasperation.

Braegar favored her with a doting smile of appreciative thanks and deftly changed the subject. "You don't mind if we join you two, do you, Cole? Here! We can take this table over here and put it up against yours."

Cole himself could hardly dissent, but he drained a glass of wine in a single gulp and pointedly abstained from assisting with the required table maneuver. When the seating arrangements had been adequately modified, Carolyn was on Cole's right, and on her right, Martin. Braegar slid a chair beneath his companion on Alaina's left, retaining the choice space between them for himself. In doing so, he unknowingly increased Cole's consumption of strong liquor and completely withered that one's high spirits of a few minutes before.

The meal progressed with liberal conversation, and gaiety abounded in all but one. Cole sat glumly morose, nodding stoically when directly addressed. For the most part he watched his wife, admiring her easy wit as she engaged in lighthearted repartee, countering Rebel's seemingly guileless barbs with subtle humor. The moment to depart for the town hall came and passed unnoticed. It was not until the last dishes were being removed that Cole drew out his watch and uttered a sharp expletive as he noted the time. His exclamation halted the conversation as all turned to stare at him, and he tucked away the offending timepiece as he offered an explanation for his outburst.

"There was a traveling troupe performing at the town hall tonight, and I had planned to take Alaina. But I'm afraid we've already missed a good half of it."

"Oh, Cole, it's too late in the season for really good troupes to venture this far north," Carolyn offered. "Besides, I have it on the best of authority that this one is completely boring. You are better off for having missed it."

"I guess there's nothing for you to do, Cole," Braegar smiled wisely, "but take Alaina home and go to bed."

Cole held his breath, knowing the jest, yet despairing that he could disentangle Alaina and himself from the group and have such good fortune actually descend on him.

"We should be getting back," Carolyn commented, trying not to yawn. "Cole, you don't mind that Martin and Rebel will be coming, too, do you? Rebel will be staying overnight with us, and Martin has his horse to fetch."

"I wonder if there'll be enough room," he muttered.

"We'll make room!" Braegar declared.

When Olie brought the brougham around, it was the others who paused to discuss how best to arrange the seating. Cole pushed through the group and, grasping Alaina by the waist, lifted her bodily into the carriage. He climbed in behind her, squeezed past, seated himself with his good leg against the far side, then pulled his wife down upon his left knee, holding her firmly in place with an arm about her waist. Alaina gasped and struggled to control her hooped petticoats which threatened to rise above her head in the confined space and cause her acute embarrassment. Cole caught the edge of her cloak, and flipped it over the velvet skirt in order to protect it, then, lifting his right boot, laid the heel on the lowest hoop and crushed the willful thing into submission. He gazed with amusement over her shoulder at the four stunned faces still outside.

"My wife and I are going to leave for home shortly. We invite you to join us, but we do not mean to tarry overlong while you goggle."

There was a shout and a rush for the carriage, and the ensuing lurch of the vehicle nearly launched Olie from his high driver's seat. Carolyn and Rebel, taking advantage of the fact that they were deemed to be ladies, laughingly tumbled into the unoccupied front seat and Deputy Holvag brushed Braegar aside to follow closely. Martin's face broke into a wide grin, the first Alaina had seen from him, as he wedged himself into place between the "ladies" and consolingly put an arm around each.

Braegar was left to stare at a wealth of petticoats and pantaloons while he pondered how to make room for himself. Finally he stepped in, avoiding skirts and white lace, and was about to suggest that Rebel accommodate herself on his knee as Alaina had on Cole's when he was jolted into the vacant place beside his host. With a shout, Olie had set the team into motion. Braegar leaned out, caught the swinging door to latch it, and settled back with crossed arms and sulked.

"If this is to be the way of things, Doctor Latimer," he snorted. "I'm going to go out and get me a coach worthy of the name!"

It seemed an endless ride to the Darveys', but finally Olie, sawing on the reins and with a heavy foot against the brake lever, hauled the brougham to a trembling stop before their stoop. The driver jumped down from his perch and hastened to open the door for his passengers. All that greeted him was a wild tangle of petticoats, boots, and trimly slim ankles. He could not determine a spot where he could politely reach a hand in to lend assistance.

"Dumb nonsense," he mumbled and left them to their own ends. He returned to his seat and tried to ignore the sounds coming from within.

Braegar had slid to the floor with the sudden halt and couldn't lift himself without the risk of compromising the modesty of the ladies. Crawling out head first from the floor of the carriage, he stepped to the ground where he rearranged himself, then, with a small bit of dignity regained, reached back a hand to assist a giggling Rebel to a safe landing. As a matter of convenience, Martin descended next and ably handed Carolyn out.

As the carriage was emptied, Alaina moved to the seat beside her husband, her manner much becalmed. Entrapped as she had been between Cole's thighs, she had felt the solid thud of his heart against her arm the entire distance from town, and when she had innocently sought to shift her weight a trifle lest his leg grow weary with her weight, the beat had grown heavy and swift. In wonder she had turned her gaze to him, then realizing the reason, blushed as the blue eyes met hers boldly and without wavering. Thankful for the darkness, she had dared no movement thereafter, not wishing to arouse him unduly.

Olie pulled the brougham out of the Darveys' drive, and Alaina huddled beneath her cloak, chilled by the crisp night air and deprived of Cole's warm, encompassing arms. She accepted the fur robe her husband tucked around her, snuggling gratefully beneath its comfort.

"Slide over here, my pet, and rest against me," Cole urged. "We might as well be warm together, and it will help my leg."

Hesitantly Alaina complied and, in a moment, was nestled against his warmth. She could not deny that her comfort rapidly increased. The place seemed made for her, and the pleasant heat that seeped through her garments lent her an odd sense of security. His arm curled about her, pressing her closer, and she found no cause to resist. Her head found a place of its own against his shoulder, and she banished all thoughts of hungry wolf and captured hare. Yet, with all of her comfort, there was a strange sense of dissatisfaction at the knowledge that he had put such limitations on their marriage and she was not free to enjoy a more intimate relationship with him.

"I had planned the evening quite differently," he confessed against her hair. "At least, something more private." His hand stroked along her arm. "I think I shall take you with me to St. Paul. There'd be less chance of an interruption that far from home."

"And what would be your intent, sir?" she asked quietly.

Cole reached a hand to play with the silken fasteners of her cloak, guilefully plucking them free as he replied, "Perhaps to keep you captive in a hotel room for a week or more, to make love to you as I yearn to do."

Lifting her head from his shoulder, Alaina frowned into his shadowed face. "You confuse me mightily, Major. I just don't know what to expect from this marriage."

"It might be better, my love"—he tried to keep the strain out of his voice—"if you accepted our marriage to be as any other and expected from it what any bride might. You must be aware of my eagerness for that end. I ache with the need to make you mine once again, Alaina. It is constantly in my thoughts."

Alaina's breath caught as his hand found the opening of her décolletage and slipped within to find the naked fullness of her breast. Wildfire spread through her, scalding every nerve, leaving her panting as his lips sank hungrily to her throat. He was leaning back in the seat, tightening his arm about her and drawing her down upon him. In another moment he would have her beneath him, and she would be hard pressed to stop her careening world. Breathlessly she braced a hand against his chest and pushed herself away from him, sacrificing the comfort of the robe. With shaking fingers, she tried to repair the disarray of her bodice. There was a throbbing tightness in the pit of her belly, making her painfully aware of her own passion and desires. She avoided him as he reached for her again and voiced her protests feebly.

"But it's not just any marriage, Cole. It's mine, and it's a disaster."

"It wouldn't be if you would let it take its natural course."

"It's not my fault," she cried plaintively. "You seem willing to shift the blame from where it truly belongs, and you have been most zealous in your accusations. You accused me of betraying you—of helping trap you in a marriage you abhorred, while you, Doctor Latimer, appeared quite willing to seduce Roberta on your own." She flung up a hand to halt his angry interruption. "You cannot deny it! I was on the porch when you came to the Craighughs' for supper. I didn't mean to spy, but I was trapped on the stairs when you walked out onto the porch. You kissed Roberta with certainly more enthusiasm than seemed proper."

"And why not?" he demanded. "She was a young woman who appeared starved for passion, and I was a lonely soldier in a land where most were wont to affix various derogatives to my name. If I take you in my arms and kiss you, does that make me a lecher or pervert? Or is it only that you detest the fact that I choose to treat you like a woman?"

"Oh, I enjoy being treated like a woman," Alaina assured him fervently. "And especially by you."

"Then forget these senseless quarrels, Alaina." He grasped her arms and turned her to face him. "I am a man, and you are my wife. You have no right to deny me."

"You agreed that this would be a marriage of convenience only."

"Bah!" He gave a derisive snort and leaned back angrily against the seat.

"Tell me what I must expect," Alaina pleaded in an unsteady voice. "You vow that this will be a chaste agreement, but you accost me in broad daylight only moments after my arrival, intending to take your pleasure of me, by force if necessary. Then you come into my room and threaten dire violence at your whim. Now, you would seduce me in your carriage. I cannot help but wonder where this marriage will end, for you seem most fickle!"

"Madam, I am not fickle!" He pressed on, though she would have interrupted. "I have had enough of crows picking at my bones." He leaned forward, and his voice cracked with the intensity of his emotions. "I have had enough of harpies screaming 'bout my head. You walk before me and greet my guests and play the part of wife so well. Then I see you cringing before me when I am stirred to take you in my arms. I see you kneeling in the rose garden, and the urge to take you then and there sets red-hot coals adancing in my belly. You sit beside me, prim, aloof, guarded, while the lust within me is like spurs tearing at my groin."

As the words tumbled from his lips. Alaina's eyes widened in amazement. He continued in a hoarse whisper as his hard fingers bit into the soft flesh of her arms.

"I see you beautiful and cool, bending, touching, turning, playing your bittersweet song upon the gutstrings of my need, and always you are just beyond my grasp." He caught her hands in his and held them when she would have drawn them back. "I cannot promise I will never take you by force. I do not know that I can long endure this way. I want you willing in my arms, but I warn you, madam, you fill my mind both night and day. I dream of your lips on mine, your bosom warm and eager pressed to mine. I have a thousand visions of you, and the first of those burns my memory with soft, white flames which devour me more surely than any volcano's fire. Think well upon it, madam, and have a care for how you tease me with a little showing of your bosom, lest we both discover the limit was not where we thought it to be."

Alaina would never be sure whether she escaped or he let her go. She folded her hands in her lap and stared down at them. "This bond or vow between us—we have built a fragile thing, you and I." Her words were strangely muted. She shook her head and blinked back tears. "Am I to be your plaything then? Shall I ever sit and wonder if today I might have overstepped the bounds? Whether you will come to me in rage tonight? Or with pleasant cajolings? Or perhaps not come at all? What do you intend of this marriage, Doctor Latimer? Will we just say good-bye one day and never see more of each other? I warn you, sir, I want more than that."

"The vows we exchanged were permanent enough for me." He sounded tired now. He sat back in the corner, his face hidden in dark shadows.

"I exchanged some words with Mister James, not with you. And there was a prior agreement."

"I have questioned Mister James to some length on that account, and I understand that the vows were made until death us do part. Yes, I believe those were his very words. Since he bore my letter of proxy, duly witnessed and sealed, do you not think those vows, made before God's witness, supersede any other agreements?"

"But did you not agree that I could leave when I wanted to?"

"And do you? Is that why you've denied me? Do you have some other man you wish above me?"

She couldn't bear the ragged, raking tone of his voice. "There's no one else, Cole. I do not wish to leave here—without you."

A long silence followed until they both noticed that the carriage was standing still. In fact, it had been stopped for some time, and furthermore, it was halted in front of the hill house. Olie was not in attendance, and Cole helped Alaina down in museful silence. They found the driver leaning against the wall in the vestibule, conversing with a yawning Miles. Cole stared at Olie until the man reddened and shuffled his feet in embarrassment.

"Yu were—uh—busy," he explained. "An' it vas cold up dere."

Cole gave him a curt nod of dismissal while Alaina brushed past the men, fleeing up the stairs in painful humiliation.

Chapter 34

COLE was gone the next morning when Alaina ventured downstairs. Miles dutifully informed, upon her question, that the master of the house had traveled to St. Paul where he intended purchasing supplies to last the logging crews through the winter.

Alaina was surprised that Cole had not even seen fit to tell her he was going. "Murphy was sent for supplies just the other day," she said carefully. "Did he forget something?"

"I think not, madam." Miles saw her bewilderment and sought to ease whatever disappointment she might be feeling at the doctor's absence. "Doctor Latimer decided to have his properties worked for timber this year, and with the crews about to leave, there've been extra supplies to buy. Murphy was not that familiar with the purchase order, madam, so the doctor went along."

Alaina's confusion grew despite Miles's best efforts. "Doctor Latimer went to St. Cloud to post a notice for hire the day after I arrived. I thought it was something he had decided upon some time back."

"No, madam," Miles replied. "The doctor had no intentions of sending a crew up before he went down to fetch you."

"But how do you know?" she asked in amazement.

The butler was most patient with his explanation. "Mister James has often approached the doctor on the financial advantage of working his lands for the timber, but until you came, Doctor Latimer displayed no interest in it." Miles flushed as he realized he was being much too verbose with a lady he had cautioned himself not to trust.

"When do you expect the doctor to return?" she queried softly, unable to find a reason for Cole's sudden preoccupation with business except that he had somehow felt driven to it by her presence in his house.

"They took several wagons with them, madam. I would guess it will be a few days before they're able to get all the supplies they need and return. If you desire to venture out during the doctor's absence, madam, he left the brougham and Olie to see you about."

"That wasn't necessary," she murmured. "I have no place to venture to."

The following days Alaina occupied her time in companionship with Mindy, though she was far from content. The house seemed alien to her, and the foreboding gloom heightened in Cole's absence. Now that he was gone, the mansion appeared to come alive every evening in the wee hours past midnight. Strange sounds emitted from Roberta's room, and Alaina could find no explanation for them. Once, she even thought she heard a woman humming off key behind the closed portal of the red suite, and a memory was brought hauntingly to mind that Roberta had never been able to sing, even passably. It was just like her yellow gown and the charred bonbons. There seemed no reasonable explanation for the happenings, but she could only guess that someone in the house did not like her.

Another time, on leaving her own room to investigate a noise that sounded much like the shattering of glass, she saw a thin thread of light shining from beneath the door. Since Cole's departure, Soldier had taken up the custom of sleeping beside her bed, and it was only the dog's presence that lent her enough courage to try the doorknob. This time, to her amazement, she found the passage blocked from within. Some barrier had been placed against it.

"Stay, Soldier! Watch!" Alaina was determined to get to the bottom of this nonsense one way or another. She didn't believe in ghosts, and she doubted that even Roberta had the power to come back and haunt her. Therefore, it had to be a living, breathing creature behind that door!

Running back to her room, Alaina put on her old robe, then caught sight of her reflection in the mirror. A thinly clad image stared back, with taut nipples straining against the fabric of the light wrap. She could not expect to accost the servants in such dishabille. Reluctantly she sought out the heavy, satin-lined, velvet robe that had remained unused in the armoire and slipped into it. The immediate increase of comfort was most thrilling, and temporarily discarding her proud forbearance, she also donned a pair of slippers before leaving her bedroom.

She rapped insistently upon Miles's door until a mumbled reply bade her to wait a moment, but on retracing her steps to Roberta's room with the groggy butler, whose woolen robe had been hastily donned, she saw only darkness beneath the door.

"Whoever is in there can't have gotten out, not with Soldier guarding the way," she reasoned aloud, though her voice shook with the excitement of the moment. "They must still be in there."

Solicitously Miles turned the knob and pushed against the door. It creaked open easily, much to Alaina's bewilderment. Regaining her senses, she followed Miles into the room and shivered as a cold draft swept through the chamber.

Miles touched a match to the wick of a lamp and carried it about the room as he made a careful inspection of every corner, nook, and cabinet until all possible hiding places were searched. But to no avail. There was simply no one in the room.

Soldier seemed quite docile as he returned briefly to the mirrors to inspect his reflection, but in bored disinterest, came back to plop himself at her feet.

"There was someone in here, I tell you!" Alaina cried in frustration. "I heard something break, and I saw a light under the door!"

No sign of broken glass was visible, but Miles was not one to dispute the mistress's words. Yet he found it hard to accept the possibility of someone disappearing into thin air.

"I'm sorry I disturbed you, Miles." Alaina didn't want the servants to think she was losing her mind, but neither would she plead for the butler's discretion. It was rather difficult not to question her own sanity when such things happened. "It appears that it was nothing more than my own foolishness and imagination."

" 'Twas no trouble, madam," he assured kindly. "And please don't fret yourself. I can't explain what went on here, but if you say it happened, I believe you." He was suddenly convinced of his own sincerity in making such a statement, though he failed to understand his reasons. Indeed, he barely knew this young woman.

Alaina smiled gratefully. "Thank you, Miles."

"You'll be safe enough with Soldier watching over you, madam. Try to get some rest."

The house grew still once again, and with Soldier sleeping beside her bed, Alaina managed to ease her trepidations enough to find the slumber she sought. But as she slid into its restful arms, she had one last conscious thought of how sweet a relief it would be to hear the tap of Cole's cane coming down the hall.

Two nights hence, Alaina was awakened by the creak of the floor outside her bedroom door. Soldier's head raised from his massive paws, and the ridge of hair along the broad back stiffened. Whoever it was, it was certainly not Cole. The doorknob turned ever so slowly, and the hound was at the portal in a leap, fangs gleaming white in the moonlit room. The silence was rent by his rumbling growl, and quick footsteps fled across the hall. When Alaina opened her door a moment later, the corridor was empty. The mastiff searched about, leading her once more to Roberta's room, but just as before, nothing was even remotely out of the ordinary. This time Alaina refrained from disturbing Miles, not wishing to cause herself greater embarrassment, and returned to her bedroom where she braced a chair against the door.

During the next days Alaina grew quite attached to the idea of having the huge dog sleep in her room. They struck up a friendship of sorts, and, with Mindy, ranged the wooded hills together, outings which Alaina actively sought in order to be free from the gloomy atmosphere of the mansion.

It was toward the end of the week when Alaina was again awakened by small noises intruding into her sleep, but this time the sound came from Cole's bedroom. Grabbing up her wrapper, she hurried through the bathing chamber where Soldier sat on his haunches, whining and pawing at his master's door. A dim light filtered from the crack beneath the door, and when Alaina turned the knob, she found no barrier. The hound was through the open door in a rush, wagging his tail joyfully as he bounded toward Cole who stood before the open doors of his armoire unbuttoning his shirt. The man affectionately patted the beast's head before the blue eyes raised to meet Alaina's surprised gaze, and the slow smile that came upon his handsome lips was one of warmth and welcome.

"Cole!" She laughed in glad relief. "I didn't know you were home!"

"I arrived back only a short time ago. I'm sorry if I frightened you."

She shrugged happily. "I'm just thankful it's you! Someone I can see, for heaven's sake! I was ready to believe you have a ghost in this house."

"I did frighten you," he said in wonder.

"Oh, it wasn't you!" she assured him. Her world seemed safe again now that he was home. "This house is so big, and every little sound echoes through it. It's almost as if something here doesn't like me. I feel out of place." She lowered her eyes from his questioning gaze and stared at the floor in self-conscious confusion. Finally, in a rush of half apology, half sheer elation, she added, "Anyway, I'm glad you're back, Cole."

She couldn't bear the long silence that followed her statement and, without looking up, fled back to her room, closing her bedroom door behind her.

The next morning she was half dressed when a sharp, angry curse came from the bathing chamber where she had heard Cole moving about. The explosive expletive did not trouble her half as much as the silence that followed. Tying a knot into the waistband of her petticoat, she approached the door and rapped lightly on the wood.

"Cole? Are you all right?" she questioned through the barrier. Receiving no answer, she leaned close to listen. "Cole?" Her tone became insistent. "Are you all right?"

A muffled grunt gave answer but hardly relieved her concern. Indeed, it sounded more like a groan than anything else.

"Cole?" She knocked on the door again. "If you don't answer me properly, I'm coming in."

Abruptly the door was opened, and Cole, wearing only a large, linen towel about his middle and clutching a small cloth against the side of his mouth, stood aside and swept an arm about to gallantly invite her in.

Angrily Alaina set her arms akimbo, ignoring the audaciously bold stare that, in a twinkling, divested her of chemise, petticoats, and corset. "I thought you were hurt!"

"I am," he stated and removed the small towel to disclose a long, clean cut that ran across the corner of his mouth. "It hurts when I talk."

The sight of so much blood brought a gasp of alarm from Alaina. "What happened?" she demanded. She took up a clean cloth, dipped it into the pitcher of water, and began dabbing at the gash, cleaning away the blood.

"I cut myself shaving," Cole mumbled beneath her ministering.

Alaina arched a dubious brow. "For a surgeon, you're rather unhandy with anything sharp. Hold still!" she admonished as she applied a lump of alum to the cut. "It's plain to see you're out of practice."

He frowned at her chastening humor. "Would you also accept that I need more practice at being a husband?"

"Poor darling," she crooned, as if in sympathy. Her eyes were wide and innocent as she needled, "Does milord chafe beneath the bridle of restraint?"

Cole peered down at her. "You've become quite saucy in my absence."

She smiled serenely. "I've learned that, in this house there's something worse than a lecher, my love."

"Indeed?" It was his turn to arch a brow. "And what is that, my sweet?"

Alaina chuckled and, with regal dismissal, dropped the cloth onto the washstand. Flippantly she shrugged. "His absence."

With a flick of her petticoats, she spun about on a heel and returned to her bedroom. A moment later, when she looked over her shoulder, she found Cole leaning against the doorjamb, watching her with a hopeful, if somewhat lopsided, smile on his face. "Is it in your mind to be reasonable about our marriage then?"

Her jaw sagged at the question. "Me? Reasonable? Of all the nerve!"

"Never mind!" He cut her off sharply. He half turned, but paused and looked at her again. "Before I left, I informed the servants that we would be entertaining come the week's end." His face was stiff as he examined a snagged fingernail. "It's about time I let our neighbors meet you."

Alaina raised her chin proudly. She resented being set

aside, shut off from his presence, then brought out like some fragile porcelain doll that could not withstand the strain of being overheld, overloved, or overused, and be commanded to perform for his guests. "Am I, then, to be displayed like some possession of yours, Major? To satisfy the wagging tongues hereabouts?"

His face tense and unsmiling, he stepped to her dressing table and began trimming the nail with a pair of small scissors he found there. "Did you not inform me that one of the duties of a wife is to perform as hostess for her husband?"

Her words smarted on the rebound, and she wished vehemently that she had never said them.

"There shouldn't be too much left to do," he stated, dismissing the argument. "The servants are usually quite dependable, but I will ask Carolyn to help you if you need assistance in some way."

He stood indolently studying the nail with a total disregard for his state of undress, and she wanted to disrupt that arrogant complacency, if just for a moment. "Why not her brother?"

The blue eyes raised slowly until they met hers in the mirror, then he went back to clipping the snag. "I shall endeavor to protect your reputation as much as I can by not asking for his assistance."

"It's a bit late to be concerned about my virtue, don't you think, Major?" she replied with a bitter laugh. She shrugged, pushing a fallen tress from her brow, as he scowled at his hand. "I mean, you might have exercised as much caution the day I dragged you from the river."

He tossed the scissors down with an impatient gesture. "At that time, madam, I believed you were what you claimed to be. Thus, you must accept part of the fault. You were most convincing."

His remark stung like salt in an open wound. "You must have been very gullible that night, sir," she replied with rancor. "You believed the lie Roberta told, too."

"But yours was the one that settled the matter," he remarked tersely, and for a moment Alaina was frozen by those eyes that swept her, peeling away the meager covering of her shift until she felt ravished by his stare. Then he returned to the bathing chamber and closed the door behind him without further comment.

Cole leaned back against the portal to slowly release his mind and body from the iron restraints of his self-control. His insides were churned to a painful depth, for it had taken all his will power to refrain from a physical display. Somehow he must conquer this ingratiating weakness of his.

Chapter 35

THE upstairs maid, Gilda, had been originally hired as personal maid for Roberta and timidly offered her services to the new mistress in styling an upswept coiffure for the evening's festivities that would be held at Latimer House. Alaina had never before had her hair dressed by anyone other than her own mother or herself, and it was a luxury she found most enjoyable. The dark, burnished tresses were artfully woven into a swirled grandeur that even complimented the widow's garb she had temporarily donned to see to some last minute chores.

One of those labors was the supervision of Mindy's bath. The girl had not yet conceded that washing was particularly good for a body, or, for that matter, even necessary, and unless encouraged, she avoided the toilette entirely. She was to be allowed to attend the festivities for a short time, at least long enough to sample Annie's delectable confectioneries and to meet some of the guests when they arrived. Breathless with anticipation, she fidgeted nervously as Alaina helped her dress and repeatedly inspected her lace-edged smock of white and the new royal blue velvet gown. Then, in a most genteel and ladylike fashion, she descended the stairs and perched her tiny frame in the hall where the parlor settee had been moved to provide room for the dancing. There, she was prepared to meet the first arrivals.

Alaina hurried down the hall to her own chambers, and as she neared them, was struck once again with a feeling of being watched. This time she knew the source was not Mindy. She slowed to a hesitant walk and, reaching her door, half turned and peered down the lighted hall. There was no place for even a small form to hide. Then, as her eyes scanned the corridor again, she noticed that the door to Roberta's suite stood slightly ajar. Curious, she returned to the portal and pushed it wider. The room was dark, and no movement hinted of another's presence.

"Cole? Cole, are you in there?"

No answer came to reassure her. Taking a lamp from the hall bracket, she cautiously entered. Her eyes moved about the room, roaming the deep shadows beyond the glow of the lamp. As the light fell upon the bed, a gasp was torn from her throat. On the gold satin coverlet lay a ball gown of blood red hue, the sort that Roberta might have worn. In such a dress she would have demanded the attention of every young swain in attendance.

A chill went up Alaina's spine. She almost expected her cousin to flit gaily from some darkened corner and swoop up the dress to don it, while laughing at the ruse that had been played on the unsuspecting "Lainie." Here she was all this time, she would warble, right beneath a MacGaren's nose, still married to Cole, and he part of the scheme to dupe the younger cousin. Only a prank, she would shrug. Only a prank to fool "Al."

Alaina took a firm grip on herself, thrusting down those errant fears that threatened to cartwheel out of control. Someobdy in the house was playing tricks all right, but hopefully not the sort that she imagined.

The lamp shed a dim aura of light as Alaina lifted it higher. A reflection from Roberta's writing desk caught her eye, and she remembered that the desk had been closed several days before when she had entered the room. Now it was open, and a journal was spread wide beneath a quill pen that slowly leaked a dark blot onto the page, forming an outsized and misshapen period to the writing. The blot was still wet beneath her testing finger, and as Alaina looked closer, she recognized the elaborate script as Roberta's own.

Her hands trembled as she set the lamp on the desk and lifted the book to read the last page of the dead woman's memoirs.

> "I see it in Cole's eyes. He stands at the end of the bed, knowing what I've done, knowing I'll soon be gone from this world. He makes a pretense at helping me, but I know he's anxious to be with her again—that little tramp cousin of mine, and he'll go to her again when this is done—this dying. Oh, why —why did I let myself be used like this?"

Alaina's heart took up a frantic beating as she flipped back through the pages to where her husband's name again caught her eye.

> "I almost wish Cole could have seen me today, spreading myself for that stinking oaf's delight and pretending to swoon with passion when he took me. How I loathe them both, Cole for all of his lusting after Lainie, his tricking me, and this fool I killed with kindness—"

Alaina turned forward several pages, and her puzzled gaze scanned the writing she found.

> "I need no fool to tell me what must be done. Cole would be amused if he knew. He's not tried my door since he learned that Lainie was the whore in his bed that night. But I will not give him the pleasure of knowing my condition. I've been told there's a woman in town who will help me rid myself of this thing. I must not delay."

Pages flitted through Alaina's fingers, and her eyes searched each with an eagerness that was spurred ever on by the writings.

> "The filthy fool thought to have me at his beck and call because he caught me hiding my treasure, but my secret is safe again, well hidden from prying eyes and such scum as he. It's mine now, and I'll leave here rich!"

Alaina was not sure how long she read bits and parts of the diary, but she suddenly became aware of Cole calling her. Voices were drifting up from the downstairs hall—a good many voices mingled with laughter. It suddenly penetrated her awareness that the party was well on its way without her, and that Cole was searching for her.

Tucking the book beneath her arm, she lifted the lamp and hurried from the room. She found Cole pacing her bedroom in a very agitated state. When he saw her, he appeared much relieved.

"Madam, where have you been?"

"Cole, just look at this—" she began, holding out the book toward him.

"There's no time, Alaina." He took the diary from her and tossed it casually upon the bed. "Half the guests are here, and they're threatening to tear the house apart if you do not soon appear."

"But the book is important," she insisted. "It's Roberta's diary!"

"Forgive me, madam, but I am not the least bit interested in reviewing what she might have written. I am more interested in getting you downstairs. At least half the guests have vowed that they will take the house apart stone by stone if I don't return with you posthaste."

"Really, Cole," she chided. "You exaggerate."

"Madam, you do not know my guests! They've already depleted the wines that were brought up from the cellar and have begun to raid the pantry for more." He pulled her across the room as quickly as his awkward gait would allow and halted before the armoire. Impatiently he flipped through her personal wardrobe, then growled, "There must be something better than this." He turned to her, slipping into his military tone of command. "I care not for the color or pattern, but tonight you will garb yourself as befits a Latimer woman."

His haste drove all caution from his mind, and he forgot the fate of those who dealt roughly with this small wench. Her suddenly angry glare should have warned him away from further foolishness.

"Sir," she snapped. "I will garb myself as befits a MacGaren."

"A MacGaren!" he barked unreasonably loud. "Kin to one of those damned Irish clans, I'd wager!"

"Eh, nay, sir!" She rolled the *r* in a manner that would have made her father proud. "Nane o' yer flatland Irish litters, but one o' the foinest highland Scots!"

"A bunch of paupers, by the looks of you and that damned black rag!" He flicked the open collar with a derisive snort. The sight of it was too much for his pride to bear.

"Black rag!" Her voice rose in incredulous question. "It's a fine piece, and it's served me well! And if I see fit, it will serve to greet the best o' yer Yankee backwoodsmen!"

Cole peered at her closely, irate suspicion boiling near

the surface. "And you'd do it, too, just to humble me in front of my friends." Her look of defiance boded ill. "Well, madam, we shall see about that."

Before Alaina could move or retreat, he reached out and, catching his hands in her open bodice, split the gown and, because she wore no corset, all beneath it to her waist. Alaina stumbled back and gaped down at her overextended décolletage. She raised her gaze just enough to see his vest, and her eyes flashed with wicked intent for the barest moment, then she became all woman, soft and appealing as she moved toward him apologetically.

"Cole?" she murmured softly and smiled up at him as she rubbed a hand against his chest.

Now, when Alaina MacGaren Latimer became sweet and gentle, Cole had learned to be wary. He tried to brace himself against whatever it was she intended, but he knew not from which direction it would descend upon him. Her hand slipped down and began to slowly undo the buttons of his vest.

"I—was—wondering"—she worried coyly at the last button—"How"—smiling sweetly, she tugged his shirt free of his trousers—"you would like"—a sound much like a purr came from her throat as she laid her hands on the front of his shirt—"your clothes"—then she snarled in rapid fire—*"torn off you!"*

With a quick movement she sent a full front of shirt studs sailing about the room and, in the process, laid bare his chest. Satisfied, Alaina smiled and flicked a finger against his loosely dangling cravat before she stepped away, leaving him to stare down in absolute stunned amazement at his ruined clothes. Having a choice of further violence or retreat, the master of the house wisely chose retreat and started for the bathing chamber door and the shelter of his own rooms, only to find that his wife had proceeded him.

"Use the other door, please," she bade him pertly. "I'm going to finish my toilette." Before he could protest, she stepped within and closed the portal behind her.

Muttering to himself, Cole opened the hallway door, but as he limped to his door, he immediately wished that he hadn't, for Carolyn was at the head of the stairs conversing with Miles. Her jaw sagged in astonishment when she glanced down the corridor and caught sight of him. Miles turned slowly to follow her stare, and a wide range of expressions crossed the servant's face in the half second before he regained control. Cole gave a curt nod of greeting to them, then, opening the door, entered as casually as possible.

A few moments later, with a fresh shirt donned, he was amid his guests and renewing acquaintances that had sagged in disrepair for many months. As he waited for his wife, he noticed that every time he turned, Carolyn was watching him, but whenever he caught her eye, she quickly hid her face behind a gloved hand or faced in another direction. Though he was the prime target of her curiosity the whole evening, the sight of him obviously upset her.

He had only consulted his pocket watch thrice when suddenly the room grew quiet and the guests moved aside, opening a corridor before him to the parlor entry. Alaina stood in the open doors, her wide-hooped skirt brushing either side. The silence in the room was as much stunned awe as anything. There had been rumors drifting through the area about Latimer's new wife, but most had dealt with a small, plain-looking woman. Nothing had prepared them for this.

Cole felt the weight of her beauty, and if any tiniest bit of irritation remained at her tardiness, it immediately vanished at the sight of her. To his supreme gratification, she was wearing a gown he had purchased for her, a most charming creation of pink taffeta that bared her shoulders sublimely. She saw him, and it was as if the whole room brightened in the dazzling radiance of her smile. He moved toward her and decorously presented his arm, while his eyes glowed warmly into hers. Turning to the guests, he introduced her, immensely proud that he could say the words.

"Ladies and gentlemen." His voice rang out loud and clear. "My wife, Alaina."

Immediately a buzz of voices filled the silence, and guests came eagerly forward, bestowing good wishes on the newly wedded couple and clasping Alaina's hand in ready friendship. Names became a blur of confusion for her as Cole introduced their guests. His arm remained about her, claiming her as his possession, as he lightheartedly conversed and bantered with acquaintances.

Through the maze of faces Alaina caught sight of Braegar and nearly broke into laughter at the outrageously lecherous leer he cast toward her. At his elbow Rebel obviously found his humor wanting, for she gave his sleeve an angry jerk and tossed a glare toward Alaina.

When some of the throng moved away, Alaina found Mindy's hand snuggling timidly into hers and the dark eyes proudly perusing her as if to convey a certain satisfaction that no other lady was quite as pretty. An affectionate hug from the young woman made those eyes even more radiant.

"Madam, I believe this is our dance," Cole announced as he signaled the musicians to begin. He smiled into her amazed countenance. "I believe I can manage the slow steps, never fear."

She blushed lightly at his gentle chiding. "It's just that I never considered that you'd be dancing."

Bringing her into his embrace, he swept her into the waltz. "I may not be the most graceful of your suitors, my sweet, but I must be the most determined. And I'll not give you up without a struggle to the hordes of fawning youth who are waiting to claim a dance with you."

"I would say that you dance much better than most," she stated with truthfulness. Indeed, he waltzed with a sureness of step that gave no hint of his affliction. Meeting that engulfing blue gaze with warmth, she relaxed against his arm and questioned, "Do I meet the standards of a Latimer woman, milord?"

"Madam, I fear not." Cole swung her in a dizzying whirl, then brought back her smile as he continued. "They are dashed beyond repair. You have set such standards I seriously doubt that they'll be matched for at least the next thousand years."

"And do I meet your standards, sir?"

The heat of his stare lent the weight of truth to his words as he gave an answer. "Were we alone, my love, I would swiftly prove the ardor you have stirred."

"What about the arrangement?" she reminded him gently.

"Blast the arrangement!" He lowered his voice as eyes turned to stare at him curiously. He brought her nearer. "I have a far better arrangement in mind, much more in keeping with the whole idea of marriage."

Something caught at Alaina's heart, a warming hope that all would be well between them and that they could enjoy each other without restrictions. Still, she was hesitant and murmured, "We should discuss this further."

"You are right, of course. But in a more private place."

"My bedroom?"

"Perhaps. Or mine."

"Later?"

"As much as I would like otherwise, it must be."

Alaina's left hand rested on his shoulder, and few of the other dancers noticed that it crept upward until it reached the top of his starched white collar where it dallied, gently caressing the nape of his neck.

"Aren't you the tiniest bit interested in the book I found this evening?"

"Roberta's diary?" He arched a brow questioningly. "Should I be?"

"It was a very personal account of her thoughts."

"Then I think I am better off not knowing them," he said, derisively.

Alaina searched his face. "Roberta once declared that she would never have a baby, and from what I was able to gather from her writings, she tried to do something about her condition—and that you knew what she had done."

"I was aware of what she had done after she went to the butcher," he admitted. "I tried to do what I could to save her, but the fever took her."

"Uncle Angus blames you for her death."

"I guessed as much."

"He blames me for bringing you to the house."

Cole grinned suddenly. "I think I should have taken you in to live with me the first time I saw you. The one thing I would have done was clean you up a bit, then your secret would have been out for sure."

"I probably would have shot your leg off, or something worse," she chuckled. "I had a real aversion to Yankees then."

"What about now?"

"I can stand a few," she smiled, and her eyes glowed as he squeezed her hand in warm communication.

As far as Mindy was concerned, heaven began the moment the master of the house asked her to dance. They walked through the steps, and under Cole's guidance, she caught the rhythm, following his deliberate small steps with a natural grace. The young girl beamed, and for a few moments at least, Cole took his attention away from Alaina as she was swept about the room in another man's arms.

"Mistress Mindy, have you considered that you're the belle of the ball?" Cole asked debonairly, smiling down into the child's radiant face.

A quick, negative shake of the dark head and a nod in the direction of Alaina answered him. Cole had to agree with the girl. Alaina was like a shimmering butterfly, rid of its dour cocoon, now bright, beguiling, mesmerizing, a fascination to watch.

Sometime later, after Mindy had been tucked into bed, Alaina caught sight of Cole making his way toward her through the maze of dancers. He came steadily nearer, his gaze fastened intently upon her and eating of her every movement. As Braegar waltzed her about, she found her vision barred by the man's massive shoulders and craned her neck to see past his arm, drawing that one's inquisitiveness. When he glanced around to see what she was staring at, he groaned aloud as he saw Cole only a short step away from them.

"I should have known! The first dance with her, and you take her from me. 'Tis cruel you be, Master Latimer. Have you no sense o' sharin'?"

"None at all," Cole replied easily, taking Alaina's hand and drawing her into his arms.

Except for the Virginia Reel and the faster steps that were beyond his agility, Cole proved to be most truthful to his statement. He refused to give in to the growing ache in his thigh and Braegar's attempts to waltz with Alaina, but claimed her hand whenever the music permitted.

Cole could not be found when Alaina sought an escape from the zealous males who had given her no moment of respite. Pushing open the study door, Alaina slipped within, glancing hopefully about for Cole. The room was empty, and only the firelight from the hearth illuminated the shadows. With an exhausted sigh, she sank gratefully into the large wing chair and lifted her daintily slippered feet to the low stool that sat before it. There was much to be said about being a hostess; one just had to be endlessly gracious and stouthearted enough to endure the trampled toes and the heavily whiskeyed breaths in performing such duties. She didn't care what Roberta's preferences had been; being the grande dame of the ball was certainly more choresome than being on intimate terms with one's husband—especially when that husband happened to be Cole.

The door hinges squeaked slightly as the portal was pushed ajar, and Alaina waited to hear the welcome sound of his halting step. But the heavy footfalls that entered were not Cole's, and her disappointment stirred.

Braegar Darvey came to stand before the hearth, unaware of her presence and, in a rare quiet mood, stared pensively into the flickering flames while he sipped his brandy.

"You seem deep in thought, sir," she murmured.

Braeger looked around in surprise, then chuckled as his eyes found her in the overlarge chair. "I must have been if I failed to see such a pretty thing as yourself sitting there."

"Is something troubling you?"

"Aye, girl," he admitted. "But as you're Cole's wife and were Roberta's cousin, I think I best not air my problems. I do not feel right speaking ill of the deceased."

"Cousins or not, I'm afraid that Roberta and I were not the best of friends."

"She hated you, I know." He nodded. "Whenever Al's name was spoken, she'd fly into a fit. Especially if it was Cole who mentioned it."

Alaina turned her gaze to stare into the fire. "I suppose she had cause."

"Aye?" His tone betrayed a doubtful acceptance of her statement. "As I've known you both, I'd say the cause was of Roberta's own making." He stared at her with a frowning intenseness until her eyes came to meet his. "Do you know what a bitch that woman was?"

"If you think to surprise me about her, I doubt that you can."

Braegar took a healthy draught of his brandy and, waving his glass, began to pace back and forth in front of the hearth. "The very first day they met, she gave Carolyn to understand that she was not to be seen within earshot of Cole, in public, in private, or otherwise."

Alaina smiled at his subtle quip. "A common threat of Roberta's, to be sure, Braegar Darvey."

He strode toward her again. "She even went so far as to tell my mother that there was nothing about Cole that needed her attention, and that she—Roberta, I mean—

would take care of whatever did need attention. She could not abide my friendship with Cole. Why, she had the gall to try to get me in bed at first. Oh, not because she wanted it, mind you. She just wanted to hurt Cole, and throw it into his face that his best friend had gone behind his back to do him dirt. That's all it was, I could swear on it. Why, she'd fawn all over me, and rub herself against me, and on several occasions that I know of, told Cole that I tried to—uh—"

It was amusing to see the big Irishman stumble over words. Had his topic been less serious, Alaina might have smiled.

"I mean, that I tried to—maul her! She even came to my office in St. Cloud and, once alone with me, began to —take off her clothes—insisting that I giver her a close examination. I'm afraid I became rather angry and bundled her up and sent her off with a firm lecture on the proprieties of being a good wife. I didn't see either of them for some time. Then, just before she died, I passed Cole in town, and he refused to even speak to me. After that, he began to act the way he does when I'm around. I don't know! I just don't know!"

Resting an elbow on the mantel and rubbing a fist against his forehead, he heaved a laborious sigh and continued. "It has to be something that she told him—and I've got to find some way to set the record straight."

"Braegar," Alaina murmured softly. "There are three things the Irish do well. They are drinking, talking, and worrying. Thus far, you have not disappointed me in any of them."

He stared at her for a moment, his mouth open as if he were caught in the middle of a word, then he laughed and mimicked in his thick brogue. "Ah, me darlin' Alaina, ye have such a tender way o' touchin' a man's heart. Oi've been kicked by horses and felt the pain less."

Alaina rose to her feet and faced him squarely, giving him a troubled smile. "Roberta was a strange one. She demanded love from everyone, and her definition of the word meant blind, unquestioning obedience. She would have been more at ease in some far, secluded kingdom devoid of women, rich of appointment, and with a full table of the young, chaste, brightly armored knights to do battle for her and court her, but never to win her. She found the well-preened public role of woman to her liking, but all the private scenes were burdensome and boring to her and she only accommodated them when they built her pedestal to a better height. It was perhaps her torment that she should ever pursue the role of wife, but never enjoy it."

Braegar set down his drink and lightly applauded. "Ah, madam fair, you have dispelled the meanest rumor of the ages and made me own heart glad to see it."

He waited, a strange light twinkling in his eyes, until she took the bait like a fine, wee trout. "And what was that, sir?"

"Why, madam," his brown eye winked impishly. " 'Twas the one that a Scottish lass could be na but a mindless, working drudge." He rushed on as she gasped in indignation. "Of course, it could be nane but some jealous English wench that set the word on high, for as anybody can see, ye have a good head on yer shoulders, and a great heart full o' compassion and understanding. And, oh lordy, a foin, foin flask to put it all in." He took her hand and bent over it briefly, then straightened with a broad grin lighting his face. "Were ye not so heavily committed, I would me own self sample yer brew to the last of its dregs."

Alaina took the backhanded compliment in stride and gave as good as she got. "Bragger Darvey, 'twas a master stroke of the fates that yer father should have laid the name upon ye to warn the rest o' mankind, and, saints forbid, all o' womankind."

"Ye turn the screws with the best of 'em, lass. But 'tis a blessed man the good Master Latimer be to have found such a one as you for his life's mate."

"I'm glad you admire my taste in women so much!"

They turned as Cole's voice came from the doorway, and from his viewpoint, their movement seemed furtive, almost guilty. Many glasses of brandy had failed to ease the painful throbbing in his leg, but had sadly blunted the edge of his judgment. Or perhaps he judged himself, for he would have given no pause with the tables reversed and Alaina the woman concerned.

Cole slammed the door behind him as he entered and, bracing both hands on the handle of his cane, favored them with a glower meant to bestir the hearts of weaker spirits. "I'll share my brandy, and I'll share my horses, but, sir, I will not share my wife."

"Cole Latimer!" The one of sweet, fair form positioned herself before him with arms akimbo and cheeks flushed with outrage. "How can you be so crude! You have no reason to accuse either of us!"

Braegar stepped beside her, and Cole faced him with obvious ill humor. "I have taken much from you in friendship, Cole, and my temper grows weak with the effort. If you have a complaint, then air it now or—"

"Friendship!" Cole snorted. "Friendship!" he barked. "I have been cuckolded in my own house, and you say you have borne much in the name of friendship!"

"Cuckolded?" Braegar stared at him in amazement, no less stunned than Alaina herself. "Man, I believe the pain has finally addled your mind. Cockolded? Do you think that this—Me? Ye're insane or drunk, but either way, ye're a blithering fool. Ten years ago I'd have called you out for the likes of this!"

Braegar turned away in frustration, but Cole grabbed his sleeve. "Ten years ago? And what stops ye now, me foin Irish boy?" he mocked. "Do ye have no stomach to fight a cripple?"

"Cole!" Alaina gasped in horrified apprehension.

A red flush crept upward from Braegar's collar, and his brow darkened. The blunt edge of judgment turned upon Cole as he flailed onward.

"Aye, and the pox on the likes of you who prattle blithely in your simpering delights, but, when faced by a sterner caste, turn tail and run."

Braegar's head snapped around with such force that his hair fell tousled on his brow. "Who prattles, lord?" he sneered. "We simple folk of the Irish clans? Or you whelps of the narrow, pale-born German ilk who sell their swords to the highest bidder and serve a foreign king, then call it honor?"

"I served in the Union when it called," Cole snarled. "I paid no man to bleed for me."

"I see." Braegar stared at Cole. "And you have a cause to slander folk while you wear your limp and cane like some great bejeweled badge."

Alaina glanced between them fearfully. They stood nose to nose with savage snarls twisting their faces, their eyes red and fierce.

"I'd trade the shell and scar for a good night's rest and a day free of pain," Cole grounded out. "But as for the cane—" He tossed it up and caught it in his fist. "Ten years or no, 'twas made to thrash a thickset skull with an Irish lisp."

"Irish lisp! Fey, man. Ye've gone too far!" Braegar snatched the stick from Cole's grasp and sent it sailing across the room. In the next moment, Cole was lifted by the shirtfront and slammed back into the bookshelves.

"Braegar Darvey!" Alaina shrieked and pushed between them, her back toward Cole, her hands thrusting at the Irishman's great barreled chest. "Let him go! Let him go!"

Master Darvey regained his temper and backed away, releasing his host. Alaina waited until there was a good space between the men before she turned and faced Cole. Her heart sank. Red-faced, he glared at her with a hateful leer.

"I do not need your skirts to protect me, madam," he sneered. He raised his glower to Braegar. "There is not room for both of us here—"

"Cole!"

His eyes lowered to find a look of utter contempt on his wife's face. He remembered her rage the last time he had ordered Braegar from the house and could not bring himself to do it again. Instead, he bowed mockingly. "Therefore, I shall leave until a sweeter clime is met."

Brushing past her, he retrieved his cane, took a full bottle from the cabinet, and left the room.

The Darveys made an early departure, and as the party wound down in the not-so-wee hours of the morning, Alaina stood alone in the foyer bidding the guests good-night. No sound came from Cole's room when she went upstairs. She did not care that Roberta's diary was not where it had been thrown, but as the room had been neatened, brushed it off as having been put away by one of the servants.

She rose with the sun to breakfast alone. The study door was still ajar, and the room was empty. It stayed so throughout the day. There was no sign of Cole.

Night came, and she worried, but could find no way to ease her concern. She took herself to bed at an early hour, leaving a dimmed lamp burning in the hall and another in Cole's room. It was much later when she was roused from a restless sleep by a low rumble from Soldier and, lighting a lamp, found the mantel clock indicating the time to be nearly midnight. After a moment, Soldier quieted and returned to his nap. She turned the lamp down, but left it burning for her own peace of mind. She had barely climbed into bed when Soldier raised his head again, his ears stiff and alert. He padded to the door, sat for a moment, then returned and thumped down on his usual rug. It was too much!

Alaina rose and, slipping a warm robe on, found the derringer and tucked it in her pocket. She pulled on her slippers and, holding the lamp high, called Soldier and ventured with him into the hall.

It was empty and shadowed, and as she roamed the upper rooms found them quiet and still. Cole's bedroom was just as it had been, and Roberta's door firmly shut. Mindy blissfully slumbered in her own room.

Soldier trotted along behind Alaina, showing no interest at all. It was the dog's relaxed disdain for the whole affair that calmed her fears as she crept down the stairs. He plunked himself down in the hall while she checked the parlor and the study, giving her no mind as she passed through the dining room and pushed open the swinging door to the kitchen. A turned-down lamp had been left burning, as was Annie's habit. The warmth from the huge cookstove gave the place a cheery, homey feeling. Of all the rooms in the house, this seemed to be the most welcoming as it retained something of Annie's cheerful nature in it.

Alaina set her lamp on the table as she returned to the dining room and straightened Cole's chair, which had been turned askew. Suddenly, without cause, the hair on the back of her neck began to crawl. She glanced back at the kitchen door. It was still and closed. The windows were blank and featureless and too high from the ground for anyone to peer in. She turned to leave, then gave a gasp. Her hand flew to her throat while the other clawed in the pocket of her robe for the derringer. A tall, darkly clad form stood in the hall doorway, the top half hidden in shadows.

"Cole!" The word escaped as she recognized him, and she leaned back against the table, weak-kneed with relief. Releasing the derringer, she pressed her hand over her pounding heart. He stepped forward and leaned against the doorjamb, a brandy snifter with a sip left in it dangled loosely from his fingers.

"You were looking for someone, madam?"

She tried to find the sureness of her voice, but realized she had failed when she answered him in a whisper. "Soldier heard something—and was restless. I didn't know you were down here."

He swept his hand that bore the snifter about the room. "I see you have no guests."

"I never had any." Alaina lifted her chin. "They were all yours." She tried to see his face in the shadows. "I presume since you're back that you find a sweeter clime about the place."

Cole glanced back over his shoulder and snorted. "Madam, I fear your presence is the sweetest clime this dismal place has ever known." He stepped forward until the light cast its glow upon his face and searched her eyes for a long moment, his features troubled and harsh, then he lowered his gaze to his drink and turned the glass slowly in his fingers. "Madam, I think I should make it clear that I was berating that damned fool Irishman, not you. I did not mean to suggest that you have been anything less than a proper lady."

"I fear your aim was bad," she murmured, pulling the robe tighter. "I've heard it said that either strong drink or anger can make a fool of a man."

"And surely to combine them would make of him a raving idiot," he continued for her. He sipped thoughtfully from his glass, then, meeting her silent gaze, dipped his head in submission. "I stand guilty, madam."

She gestured toward the kitchen. "Would you like something to eat? Annie baked fresh bread, and there's some ham—"

Cole shook his head. "I dined with Olie."

She looked at him narrowly for a moment. "And where did you spend the night?"

He glanced away as if reluctant to answer but as a long, waiting silence ensued, he sighed, "With the horses—in the barn."

Alaina fought against a smile. "And did you find a sweeter air there, milord?"

Cole lifted a brow. "I could say that I found the conversation of a gentler sort than I've heard here of late. But then, I cannot swear that there is not an Irish ass or a Scottish mare among the brood."

Ungrateful at his comparison, Alaina snugged her robe tighter across her bosom. "Excuse me, milord. Might I have your permission to return to my room? The air grows chill."

She did not wait for an answer, but made her exit with a last, meaningful glare.

Chapter 36

THE carriage negotiated a twisting alleyway as it approached the rear of the millinery shop, then it left the dirt path and halted behind a sheltering clump of spruce and pine trees. It seemed that Olie was opening the door before Cole had a chance to bestir himself, though in reality the driver had waited some moments for the doctor to disembark by his own volition.

Cole stared at the trellis-covered path that led to the owner's private quarters for several long moments before he stepped to the ground. Olie gently closed the carriage door and inquired in a subdued voice, "Vil it be the usual time, sir?"

"What?" Cole stared at him, as if awakening from a trance.

"Du yu vant me to pick yu up here like usual?" Olie patiently inquired. "Or vill yu be staying the night?"

"No!" Cole's reply was so sudden and sharp Olie was startled and much bemused. But then, Olie hadn't reckoned that the doctor would be seeking out his mistress so soon after his marriage.

"The usual, I suppose," Cole sighed heavily.

With a nod Olie climbed to the driver's seat, and a moment later the carriage rumbled off down the narrow lane. Cole approached the back door. It was not because he was lame that he dragged his feet. He was hard pressed to keep his hands off Alaina, and it had come upon him suddenly this morning as he watched his wife sitting so innocently at the opposite end of the table that he needed an immediate outlet for what was brewing within him. Outside of force, only one choice appeared open to him—Xanthia Morgan.

He raised the handle of his cane to rap on the door, then froze as an illusion of Alaina flooded through his brain, cauterizing his very thoughts. He closed his eyes to savor the vision more fully, but it was as quickly gone, vanished from his grasping mind. He was suddenly unsure that this course would solve his problem, and he lowered the cane as he tried to sort out his thoughts. His options vanished as the door opened and he faced the long-legged, auburn-haired, and exceptionally well-formed Xanthia Morgan.

"Cole!" she exclaimed in relief. "I saw your shadow and thought it might be some miscreant intending harm." She lifted her hand to betray a small double-barreled derringer and, with some embarrassment, tucked it back within the folds of her skirts. "Come in! Good heavens, it's been so long! I was afraid you wouldn't ever come again." Smiling with warmth, she caught his hand, and he was helplessly drawn into the house. Eagerly she took his hat and gloves, left them on the hall table, and led him into the parlor, there pouring a libation for him. As she pressed it into his hand, she coaxed, "Sit down, darling, and I'll help you off with your boots."

"No—I mean—" He saw the worried curiosity come into her eyes and finished lamely. "In a moment, 'Thia."

"Your leg is stiff again," she stated matter-of-factly. "I shouldn't wonder, the way you roam around. You should either settle down and take care of it, or see what can be done." His noncommittal shrug warned her away from the subject. "Will you join me for dinner? Can you stay the night?"

"I'll have to be getting back soon." He read the disappointment in her eyes and, then gazed down into the amber pool of brandy in his glass. "Olie is waiting for me."

"Olie is always waiting, darling," she reminded him calmly. "Sometimes I think he enjoys that stint in the tavern."

"No doubt." For lack of something better to say, he took a shallow sip of the brandy.

In an attempt to break his preoccupation, Xanthia ran a hand caressingly over his lapel, asking quietly, "Did you get that business arrangement settled?"

Cole glanced at her briefly, unable to defeat the scowl that creased his brow. "It was carried out by proxy before she came up here."

"I heard it rumored, of course," Xanthia admitted, turning aside to hide her displeasure. "The gossips never forgave you for marrying Roberta, and they've been clucking like hens all over town about your new wife. You must be keeping her well hidden because the few who have seen her are lording it over the ones who haven't, and I can tell you, Cole, their curiosity is eating them alive."

She waited, but he made no effort to appease her own burning inquisitiveness. She tried again, knowing that she erred, but was helpless to resist. "Miss Beatrice showed me some of the gowns you had her make for your wife." He looked at her sharply, and she rushed on to explain. "Oh, darling, you needn't worry. Miss Beatrice doesn't know about us. I was just in her shop for a fitting when she started raving about some of the clothes you had ordered." Xanthia paused until she could continue in a casual manner. "You sly rogue, it must have warmed her heart considerably to have received such a rich gift."

"Alaina—is different," he muttered.

"In what way?"

His silence was an eloquent declaration. Xanthia sensed she would do well not to inquire further about this new wife of his, this Alaina. She rose on tiptoes to press her lips to his and was somewhat surprised by his coolness. "Cole?" His eyes turned to gaze down into hers, and she ran a well-manicured finger about his ear as she questioned softly, "Do I have too much competition?"

He sighed and stared into the crackling fire. "I explained her terms and the reason I was marrying her before. Nothing has changed."

"I probably know you better than anyone, Cole," she murmured low. "But sometimes I wonder if I know you at all. You say she saved your life, and I guess I wouldn't fear so much if I really believed you were doing all this out of gratitude."

"I don't wish to talk about it, 'Thia."

She stroked his lean knuckles, urging, "Finish your drink, darling. I won't be long."

Before he could stop her, she was gone. Cole realized now that he had made a mistake in coming here. This had been a haven from Roberta, but somehow its quality had flown. It was no longer a place for escape but, in some strange way, had become a place for cheating. Suddenly it was the wrong place, the wrong time, and the wrong woman. He was uncomfortable, and he wanted to be away, anywhere but here.

Setting the snifter down, he left the parlor and made his way down the hall to the familiar bedroom. The door was open, the bedcovers folded down invitingly. Xanthia sat on a stool before a wide mirror, brushing out her long hair. When she caught his reflection in the glass, she smiled and began to loosen her bodice.

" 'Thia—" She paused and looked up, her eyes finding his in the silvered glass. "I'm going now."

She turned on the stool to face him. "But you just got here."

"I know," he admitted. "And it was a mistake."

Her hopes were crushed, and she asked in a husky voice, "Is it something you want to talk about?"

"No."

"Will you be back?'"

He met her gaze directly. "I don't know."

Xanthia stared at him a long moment, fighting to control the mistiness that suddenly affected her vision. "It was nice of you to come and tell me, Cole," she said slowly. "I appreciate that. Should you change your mind, you know you'll always be welcome."

He nodded. "You were a friend when I needed one, 'Thia. If there's anything you ever need, don't hesitate to call on me."

She straightened her spine and did her best to smile. "I'm afraid what I need most, someone else already has."

"I'm sorry, 'Thia," he apologized. "I just haven't worked this out for myself yet."

He withdrew a flat purse from his coat and dropped a wad of bills into a vase beside the door. "Good-bye, 'Thia."

She listened to his footsteps and the tap of his cane as he went down the hall, and after a time she heard the gentle closing of the back door. For all his prattle about his second marriage being nothing more than a business arrangement, he must have found something in it which intrigued him. She would have to meet this Alaina Latimer and see for herself just what it was that spurred this sudden attack of fidelity in him.

The evening mists had risen, and the cold dampness began to work its painful presence into Cole's leg. He walked for a space, then paused to ease the throbbing in his thigh, and after a rest, he marked a careful path down the road again, leaning heavily on his cane. The tinkle of a piano wheedled its way through the still night air, and he knew that for an able man, the saloon was only a short jaunt up the street from Xanthia's millinery and gift shop. Usually the tavern closed its doors before he was ready to leave his mistress's arms, and Olie would bring the carriage to wait at the spot behind the trees. Now Cole cursed his own folly for coming. It had been a damned fool idea!

Olie had settled his large bulk at a table in the corner. It was his wont to stand at the bar and engage in gay camaraderie with the transients of the tavern, but this evening he had felt more in need of some deep pondering in hopes that he might make some sense of events of late. The barkeep's wife had brought him a tankard well afoam with a dark amber brew and left it on the table without a comment. Though he had left payment for his share, she was probably still piqued over the minor damage to several bar chairs and a table that had occurred on his last visit.

A goodly portion of the tankard had provided ease for a huge thirst before Olie lowered the mug to the table and stared bemusedly at it. He had known the good Doctor Latimer for quite a number of years, and he was disturbed because the man seemed bound along a path to some sort of debauchery. Of course rumors were roaming wildly about Latimer House, and his own son, Peter, had hinted that there were, in fact, separate beds for master and mistress, just like it had been with the first wife. Not one to lend too much credence to whispering servants, Olie had watched the couple for himself. At church, for instance, with the child between them, and every head coming together behind the Latimer pew like eggs rolling from opposite hills and meeting in wild confusion in the middle of a vale. Afterward, the very air outside the church had buzzed with the gossip, because Doctor Latimer hadn't attended services since he had been home from the war, and now all of a sudden he showed up with a new wife and a child besides, and hardly no time married! The fact that Mrs. Latimer was from the South didn't seem to concern them as much as their speculations as to how young she might be, why Doctor Latimer had married her, and just what kin the child was to her? Well, Olie thought, anyone could see that she was too young to have a child that old, and that Doctor Latimer might have married her simply because she was a right comely young lady. Despite all the rumors of separate beds, the doctor appeared quite taken with his young bride and, one might say, most anxious to protect her from the stares of every swain they met. Then, there had been the outing along the river on a rare warm day. Mindy had smiled with a radiance she had never shown before when they unpacked the basket Annie had prepared for the picnic. Olie had shared the food and the pleasure of the day with them. He had seen for himself the politeness that was congenial yet not quite as intimate as would be normal between a man and his wife. And he had witnessed the almost hungering eye of the doctor fastened on the lady as she skipped and played with Mindy. Laughing, she had thrown her arms wide in carefree abandon until her bodice had stretched taut against her soft bosom, and Doctor Latimer had flushed a deeper shade when he realized Olie had caught him ogling his own wife.

A second tankard's contents were being carefully sampled for quality when, in some astonishment, Olie paused with the mug almost to his mouth. He stared over its rim until, without a word of explanation, his employer lowered himself in the chair opposite him. Even with the noisy din of the piano player's melody, the rowdy laughter of some loggers, and incessant giggling of the saloon girls, Cole had no trouble hearing Olie's statement.

"I been tinkin' yu're a fool, and now I know. Yu can't get along with either of them."

"When I want some of your Norwegian logic," Cole retorted tersely, "I'll ask for it."

"Yah!" The blond head nodded as if he sorely lamented the plight of the other. "Yu've tied yourself a few good knots this time." Olie slammed a brawny fist down on the table before Cole could reply and bellowed to the bartender. "Sweyn! Bring the bottle and two short glasses."

In a moment a quart of whiskey of questionable age was placed before them and two glasses were slid across the table. Olie waited until the barkeep had left before he shared a bit more of his wisdom. "When I feel good,

I drink beer. When I got voman trouble, I need a little somet'ing stronger to take the edge away."

Cole lifted his brows in amazement. "It's not you who has the trouble!"

The driver shrugged his thick shoulders and spread his hands. "Yu got trouble—I got trouble." He tossed down a shot of whiskey and followed it closely with the beer. Cole copied his example and was astounded that his throat should feel completely seared all the way down to his stomach. A trifle wide-eyed, he reached for the stein of beer in hopes it would put out the fire.

"That's enough!" he wheezed and pushed his glass away.

"Nah! Nah! Two women are too much trouble for one drink." Olie poured the glasses full to the rim, and the bottle was half empty when Cole spread a hand over his own glass and put a halt to the infusion of the dark whiskey.

"Women can be damned sobering," he muttered crossly. "Especially that bit of fluff I've married, and it's a dreadful shame to waste good whiskey." He eased himself to his feet and paused a moment to let the world settle down around him, while Olie tucked the bottle affectionately beneath a heavy arm and plowed his way toward the door. There, he had a moment of lucid recollection and bellowed to the barkeep that the whole was to go on Doctor Latimer's account. Cole cringed at the overloud shout. He was beginning to consider that he had underestimated the strength of Olie's whiskey. Yet he managed to follow his driver with a quieter dignity.

It was a long ride home, perhaps even longer tonight because Olie chose to weave his way through the city at a snail's pace. It gave the cold, snapping air some time to affect a sobering on Cole, but the slight, discomforting ache that came and went somewhere behind his eyes made the memory of the strong brew a trifle less than enjoyable. To make matters worse, Miles met him at the door with a displeasing announcement.

"Doctor Darvey is here, sir. We didn't know when you were to return, and finally the madam started dinner without you, sir."

Cole was further irritated by the fact that Braegar had seated himself neatly at Alaina's right, while he had to cross to the far end of the table and take his own place.

"Tell Annie to get those damn potatoes off the table!" Cole snarled, venting his wrath on the first inanimate thing that pricked his ire.

"The likes o' you insulting good Irish food!" Annie squealed indignantly. She had heard the command in the kitchen and came bristling through the swinging door with her face redder than a scarlet banner and her dander up and flying high. "Seein's as ye be naught but a poor German immigrant yerself, sir, I guess I must be making allowances."

"Austrian!" Cole corrected darkly.

Annie stood her ground before his glare and slid the potatoes closer in a challenging manner. "If ye knew what was good for ye, sir, ye'd put some meat beneath yer hide with a plateful of 'em."

Cole stared incredulously, certain the woman had taken leave of her senses. Alaina knew him well enough to realize this quarrel boded ill. Slipping hurriedly from her chair, she reached the bowl of potatoes and moved it out of harm's way herself. Placing the dish in the cook's hands, she gently guided the woman back into the kitchen.

"It's best to humor him tonight, Annie. No doubt his leg is bothering him again." She didn't know if it was or not, but at least the cook's anger dwindled to nothing more than an occasional sniffle of indignation.

The task of calming the woman performed, Alaina returned to the dining room, only to find Mrs. Garth setting out large snifters and a decanter of brandy. Alaina had already noted the woman's penchant for liberal draughts and quickly moved to halt her. Master Cole Latimer appeared to have imbibed far too much as it was, without adding more kindling to the fire. "I'll do that, Mrs. Garth. See if you can help Annie in the kitchen."

The housekeeper nodded stoically and complied, leaving her mistress to measure out the portions. In comparison to the woman's generosity, Alaina was definitely stingy. Solicitously she placed a snifter beside her husband's service, feeling his harsh stare.

"Annie is warming your soup," she murmured. "Can I get you some coffee?"

He replied in the affirmative only to keep her there at his end of the table a bit longer. She smelled sweet and fresh, with a hint of an essence that never failed to stir his blood. Her hair was gathered off her neck in an informal cascade of loose curls, and even the high-necked gown of wine muslin seemed fetching by candlelight.

"Where is Mindy?" he asked softly.

"You were so late, I let her eat and go to bed."

Much to his chagrin, she resumed her seat, and the soft feelings dwindled as he watched her beside Braegar. As the meal continued, Alaina noticed the deepening darkness of his mood and watched him apprehensively, praying the storm would pass without being unleashed. Braegar also considered his host in a museful bend of mind, wondering if he should broach the subject that had caused the heated quarrel the other night and find out at last what was eating at Cole, but in the mood he was in, Braegar did not press the matter.

"Weren't you two ever told it's not polite to stare at a cripple?" Cole quipped sharply, and reached for his snifter of brandy to sip it with glum disinterest.

He finished the dinner in piqued silence, sampling the coffee perhaps more than the liquor. As soon as they left the table, Braegar made his excuses, and Alaina paused just long enough in the hall to bestow a withering glare on her husband before she stiffly mounted the stairs to her bedroom. Cole followed to his own and slammed the door behind him, growling something about having a houseful of cantankerous women to contend with. Almost immediately the portal between his room and the bathing chamber was opened. He turned, peevishly sailing his frock coat into a chair, and faced his young wife who stood in the doorway glowering at him while she angrily jerked open the buttons on her long sleeves.

"You, sir, have proven yourself an absolute boor. There were times when I had my doubts about you, but tonight you have proven it. You are undoubtedly the orneriest man I've ever had the displeasure to meet!" She spun on her heel and flounced back into her bedroom, but Cole was not in the mood to let this affront go unchallenged. He limped after her, the look on his face thunderously black.

"You call me a boor when, as soon as I leave, you beckon that sniveling lout here to my house and entertain him!" He wrenched off his cravat and began working at the buttons of his vest while he raged on. "You set him down at *my* table and served him *my* food! Madam,

I must say you are a poor judge of character! That coxcomb seizes upon any excuse to sniff around this place while I'm gone! And you invite him, knowing how I feel about him!" He snorted in derision and left her staring agape at the empty portal as he stormed back into his room.

"Poor judge of character!" she railed, wrestling the gown over her head. She flung it over the armoire door and retraced what was quickly becoming a well-worn path through the bathing chamber, while she plucked at the ties of her petticoats.

"Invite him! What do you mean, invite him?" she demanded.

Cole paced restlessly about his room, snatching open his collar and unfastening his shirtfront. "He obviously knew I was gone."

"He dropped by to see *you,* sir!" she explained irately. "And stayed until you came home! When it became apparent that you were not in the mood to discuss anything with him, he left. Do you find that questionable, sir, or imagine it as some illicit affair? Will you say you've been cuckolded again?"

She wiggled out of her petticoats and, tossing them over her arm, stalked back to the armoire where she dragged forth her overly mended gown and wrapper. Cole returned to her door, pulling the tail of his shirt from his trousers. Letting the shirt fall open, he braced a hand high on the doorsill while she, in tight-lipped silence, pointedly ignored him.

Cole knew he was being unreasonable, but he plunged recklessly through this madcap folly with the gift of a fool. "You have many admirers, madam, but in this case, have not the sense to know what that bastard is after."

Alaina threw her night garments on the bed, incensed by his insult. She faced him with arms akimbo, well fired to lead a crusade against ridiculous nonsense despite the fact that she wore nothing more than camisole, pantaloons, and corset. Indeed, the garments might have served her as more gallant armor in a different joust had she given even the merest thought to her state of dress.

"I was well chaperoned, sir! A full half dozen of your servants can vouch for my conduct. Ask Annie, Miles, Peter, or Mrs. Garth! You may question them all if you doubt that I was anything less than proper."

"Proper! Ha! Sitting at the table, letting him drool over you! As for the servants, I'm beginning to think the lot of them would lie themselves blue in the face to protect you!" He jerked off the shirt and rumpled it into a ball as he returned to his own chamber.

Alaina was only a step behind as he entered. "Lie to protect me! You boneheaded mule! They are *your* trusted servants! Why, they've been giving me excuses all afternoon and so sheepishly that, were I the suspicious sort, I could believe you had run off to seek your pleasure with some loose-minded hussy!"

Cole flung the shirt across the room, thrust his right foot into the bootjack and began to carefully work the boot off. "And what if I did?" he ground out. "Have I been awarded such favors in this place that my honest urge would be dampened?"

She glared as he seated himself on the foot of his bed to tug off the other boot. "Well, Doctor Latimer, you sent your man quickly enough when the terms were drawn! So now you can stew in your own kettle!"

She retreated into her bedroom and kicked her slippers into the corner, nearly sizzling with indignation. That he should dare accuse her of withholding her favors when it was he—

"Did you fear that it would be 'Al' who would greet you at the dock, Major?" she called through the open bathing chamber. She perched on the stool in front of the dressing table and rolled down the knee-length stockings, dropping them carelessly to the floor. "You bawl so loudly about your restrictions now, you undoubtedly expected me to be less than worthy of your attentions."

"Oh, I knew you to be worthy all right." His voice came angrily through the open doors of the bathing chamber. "It was your game that set the trap for me. If not for you, I would never have married Roberta."

Alaina shot to her feet and strode barefoot through the middle room, seeking some outlet for the indignation she felt. "And you never once doubted that it might have been somebody else!"

Cole threw up his hands in exasperation. "How the hell should I have known? I thought there were only two women in that house." Standing tall, lean, and muscular in the narrow fitting underwear that boldly displayed the bulge of his manhood, he casually arched a brow at her and mocked, "Should I have given the credit to your aunt, my dear?"

"Ooooohh, you're a cad!" she cried and padded irately over the familiar trail to her haven.

"Perhaps I should have blamed that dirty-faced Al," he followed her to scoff. He destroyed the idea with a quick slashing of his hand. "Absurd! I would have thought, not knowing of course that he was a she lurking beneath a rascal's garb. Nor would I have expected a proper young lady to disguise herself as a woman of the streets and apply herself to the part with such vigorous enthusiasm."

Alaina gasped in outrage and dashed after him as he strode arrogantly back to his room. If he thought to leave on that last word, she had something more to say in her behalf. Undaunted by his broad shoulders and bare back, she caught his elbow and tugged him around until she could glare up into his face.

"For your information, sir, I did not apply myself like that at all!"

"You came to my room willingly enough."

"You were drunk, and I was afraid you'd wake the house and get shot for an intruder."

"So! Should I be grateful for what you did?" His tone was caustic. He left her standing with hands clenched in rage, throwing back over his shoulder, "Do you mind if I was not too overjoyed with being left in Roberta's care?"

Alaina scuffed a small, bare foot against the floor as she meandered back to her room. "You were so eager to give her all the honors. How could I have stopped the marriage? Had I spoken up, I might have rotted away in one of your filthy Yankees prisons."

"So you saved yourself," he jeered through the doors.

Pricked by his scorn, she flicked the hem of several skirts hanging in her armoire. "And you, sir, think to compromise me with fine dresses and costly gems!" She moved toward the door, wanting to see his face when she hurled the full accusation in it.

Cole jammed his trousers in the wardrobe and slammed its door. That little, virgin-minded temptress! He would see that she understood the full weight of what she had started.

They met at the foot of the tub, angry face to angry face.

"Perhaps you have women you can buy so cheaply, Major, but I'm not for sale!"

He laughed in derision. "If it's a matter of cost, madam, what do you think that medallion you wear around your neck is worth?"

His taunt was too much! She would give the blasted thing back to him! She jerked the necklace off, unintentionally striking him across the face with the light chain as she whipped it over her head. Her arms were raised, and it seemed to Cole that she meant to vent her rage in a more physical manner. He caught her slim, corseted waist and snatched her to him to prevent her from striking again.

Alaina's breath left her in a sudden gasp. She was immediately aware of his naked chest and the manly feel of his lean, muscular body pressed to hers, while he was made totally conscious of her meagerly clad form. They stared at each other for a second of suspended time, which could as well have been a century or two. Then slowly, almost haltingly, Cole lowered his mouth to hers.

The shock was abrupt, and the first gentle touch of his lips turned to a heated, crushing demand. Rage had become raw hunger; agreements and contracts were cindered beneath the white heat of their mutual desires. It all came upon them in a rush, the awakened fires, the hungering lusts, the bittersweet ache of passion so long restrained. Cole knew the lithe form in his arms from a half dreamed night long ago, and the warmth and softness of her set his mind and body aflame.

Alaina clung to him, aware of his desires, knowing what he wanted her to yield. She waited again for the screaming denial to come from some dark, unfeeling recesses of her brain, this time determined to squelch its intrusion. But strangely she found only empty silence as if her conscience watched in amused approval.

Cole straightened slightly, and his blue eyes burned into hers with an unspoken question: Would she deny him again, as she had in the past? Would he be turned away once more with this craving hunger still gnawing at the pit of his belly?

The pendant slipped unheeded to the floor as Alaina raised on slim toes, reaching parted lips to meet his and sliding silken arms tightly about his neck. She came to him with an eagerness that astounded him, having no thought of holding back or refusing him. This was Cole—man. And she was Alaina—woman. No hint of Al remained between them, and each found the other as a long-tended seed came to fruition. Their lips blended with an impatient urgency, and, locked in each other's embrace, they were caught up in the fierce tide of passion.

Muttered, unintelligible words tumbled from Cole's lips as he pressed fevered kisses along the ivory column of her throat and the beginning swell of her breasts, arching her backward over his arm, while his other hand stroked the roundness of her buttock and a shapely thigh. There was a haste in him to know and touch every part of her, to claim her as his own, to let his lips wander at will over her soft flesh. His lean fingers worked between her breasts until the chemise fell open above the corset, exposing the tantalizing fullness of her naked bosom to his sight and hand. Glowing waves of pleasure spread like quickfire through Alaina's body as he caressed the silken curves. He bent and swept her up into his arms, and his eyes met hers with an intensity that took her breath away. Then, as she stared, his gaze lowered, and she was devoured as he boldly drank his fill of the vision of her creamy flesh. His head came down, and a breathless moan slipped from her as his mouth caressed a pink, pliant crest. His tongue branded her with its fiery torch, and her lithe form shook with the fervor that built within her. Her lips brushed his cheek, and she traced the tip of her tongue around his ear. His face turned, and his mouth was suddenly there, tasting hers with a hunger they both shared.

Vaguely Alaina was aware of the tremor in his arms, of his movement toward the massive four-poster in his room. They were in a world alone, apart from the whale oil lamps that were left burning, the scratch of the barren limbs against the windows, the crackling fire in the hearth. Even the realization of his wound was dimmed, for he moved with an easy strength that belied his lameness.

Beneath the edge of the heavy tapestry that bordered the high tester, Cole withdrew his arm, letting her legs slide down against him. Before her feet touched the floor, the corset fell upon it. The blue flame in his eyes flared brighter as the underbodice parted to the waist. His mouth lowered to savor the sweet, heady wine-nectar of her lips, and his tongue chased hers in a provocative play that traversed the warm cavities of their mouths. The straps of her chemise were brushed from her shoulders, and Alaina shivered in ectasy as his hands leisurely stroked downward over the heaving roundness of her breasts. They swept her hips, loosening the pantaloons, and aided their descent to the floor. His hand slipped between them and released his undergarment, and for Alaina the shock of his bold, manly flesh was renewed and remembered, just as startling and awesome as that night long ago.

Like two feathers caught on an airy breeze, they drifted down to the soft comfort of his bed, their mouths clinging, their sighs mingling into one breath. His hand stroked her body in a long caress, then wandered along more intimate ground, stopping her breath with his boldness. Her thighs quivered and loosened beneath his questing search, and her eyelids fluttered as a rapturous bliss washed through her. Her breathing was shallow and rapid, while her heart thudded a wild, frantic rhythm.

"Oh, Cole," she sighed in a soft, trembling breath. "What are you doing? Is this some torture you've brewed for me?"

"Eh, no torture this," his ragged whisper came against her lips. "But love, as we make it together."

"Then love me more," she pleaded. "And let me love you." Hesitantly she brushed her fingers along his scarred thigh. "Is it—permissible to touch you?"

Cole held his breath as he guided her hand to the hard, heated shaft where throbbed the pulsing hot blood of his desires. His whole being turned to liquid as her cool, gentle fingers explored his man's body, igniting too many fires for his crumbling restraint. Shaking, he raised above her and lowered his hips between her thighs, pressing his entry home as his hard belly caressed the softness of hers.

It was a merging. A blending. A coming together. Man with woman. Husband with wife. Softness yielding to hardness. Wonder turning to rapture. Bodies straining and cleaving together. Two beings wrapped in the pure bliss of their union, proceeding in eager, uncaring haste, giving all to the other and in return finding everything and more.

And it came, just as it had before, whatever it was that made their coupling unique. As waves of pure physical pleasure washed over her, Alaina could only sense that theirs was a special nectar of love. Cole knew it. It was what had held his mind in tow all these many months, and now he poured himself into her, groaning, shuddering, reaching into her very soul with his possession of her and binding their heaving bodies in total consummation.

A fine film of sweat glistened on their bodies as they lay entwined in the afterglow of love, their passions spent, their muscles drained of strength. Cole turned his face into the rumpled, fragrant hair that spilled across his shoulder and inhaled the delicious scent of her, remembering the many nights of torture when he had not been able to banish her from his mind. For some time he had known that she was the catalyst that stirred his blood until his passions seethed. He had been a man burning with desire —but always for her. Now sated, he could only marvel at the peace of contentment.

Freezing temperatures after a heavy fog had frosted the barren limbs of the trees, dressing the landscape in a bedazzling array of crystals that shimmered and danced beneath dawn's rising sun, that same which tentatively thrust its rays into the room to awaken the sleeping woman. Alaina stretched languidly beneath the cozy luxury of the down-filled comforter before she realized she was alone in the oversized bed. Clutching the covers to her naked bosom, she sat upright and glanced about the empty room. A crackling fire danced in the hearth, chasing the chill from the room, but it was a poor substitute for the warmth she felt in Cole's presence. Then, from the open door of the bathing chamber, drifted reassuring sounds of his proximity. Wrapping the sheet about her, Alaina ran across the cold oak floor into the adjoining room where Cole sat relaxing in a steaming bath. Her mood was gay, almost flippant as she rushed forward to bestow a lingering good morning kiss upon his lips, sending his mind reeling back to the memory of her shy but captivating boldness of the night before. He found himself much enamored with this lighthearted sprite who had come into his life with her unquenchable élan. There was more woman here than he had ever realized, and it was not the calculated femininity of Roberta, but an easy, natural thing that never failed to stir his ardor. He savored the warmth of her mouth eagerly conforming to his and sighed as her lips left his. Her eyes sparkled above a puckish smile as she gave him a long, deliciously lecherous perusal that took his breath away.

"Need any help, Yankee?"

"As a matter of fact," he breathed, crooking an arm behind her neck and pulling her back for another kiss, "I am in dire need of a little feminine companionship."

The sheet dropped as he tugged it free, and he pulled her down on top of him, spreading wanton kisses upon her mouth and bosom.

"Finally," he murmured huskily against her throat, "my threat has been carried out. But little did I think when I issued it that bathing you would be so pleasurable."

Chapter 37

XANTHIA Morgan descended from her modest carriage with the help of her driver and paused on the front steps of Latimer House to cast her eyes toward the dark, lead gray sky that hovered close above the rooftop. Her breath was an icy frost in the chill air, while the crisp sting of the north wind hit her full in the face. She would have to conclude her business here quickly if she intended to make it back to St. Cloud before the gathering storm descended.

Shown into the parlor by the butler, she seated herself on the settee to await the entrance of Alaina. Earlier in the morning she had seen Cole pass the shop in his buggy, and she had seized upon the opportunity to meet his young bride. At least she had the advantage of surprise. The girl would be totally unprepared.

Slipping off her gloves, Xanthia glanced about the room with a critical eye. Roberta's tastes had always leaned toward the garish, and this crowded, overdecorated room suited the woman's overbearing personality. Of course, there really hadn't been time for the new mistress to change things, but Xanthia was most curious to see if Alaina was of the same type. Rumor had it that she was hardly more than a child, and from Rebel Cummings's careless chatter, a cloying little mouse of a girl. Though men could be unpredictable in their tastes, Rebel's opinions could not be relied upon either.

Roberta's haughty arrogance had displayed itself on her many visits to the millinery shop. In search of some trinket to appease a momentary whim, she had often ripped off a veil, flower, feather, or whatever ornament she had found displeasing on a hat, then, upon trying it on, she had many times decided she preferred something else entirely.

Quick footsteps sounded in the hall, almost running,

and a breathless voice addressing the butler, "Oh, Miles, will you ask Annie to prepare some tea?"

The chimes of the clock brought a gasp from the unseen woman, and her distress was obvious in the barely subdued whisper that reached Xanthia's ears. "Two! Half the day is gone! Why didn't someone wake me sooner?"

Xanthia did not lay the cause of the girl's tardy rising to a night and morning spent in amorous lovemaking. She could only think that the new mistress was as lazy as the old.

"Doctor Latimer left explicit instructions that you were not to be disturbed this morning, madam," Miles quietly informed his mistress. "And he said to tell you that he had business to attend to in St. Cloud and would return as soon as possible."

Xanthia's eyes were fastened on the door when Alaina finally stepped into view, her cheeks slightly flushed from hurrying which made the gray eyes seem all the brighter and clearer. The sight of her momentarily scattered the older woman's defenses, for Alaina was exactly what Xanthia feared most. This was no graceless gosling of Rebel's descriptions, but one with a young exuberance, a joie de vivre about her that was unmistakably intriguing. Though Xanthia had expected her to be wearing much richer garb, the plum muslin with its high neckband, long fitted sleeves, and narrow bodice was pert and pleasing. With this first glimpse of Alaina Latimer, Xanthia wholly understood Cole's infatuation, and it frightened her more than she had imagined anything could.

"I'm sorry to keep you waiting, Miss—ah—" Alaina smiled expectantly.

"Mrs., really." It was best to set the matter straight right from the beginning. "Mrs. Xanthia Morgan." She moved her handbag and the package she bore to the settee beside her for the present moment. "There have been so many rumors flying about town, Alaina, I had to come and meet you face to face."

Not unaware of the woman's exacting perusal, Alaina asked quietly, "And do I meet with your approval, Mrs. Morgan?"

Xanthia nodded concedingly. "You're really quite beautiful."

"Might I return the compliment, Mrs. Morgan?"

Xanthia was a bit at odds as to how best to proceed. "I suppose you are curious about me."

Alaina nodded. "Are you a friend of my husband's?"

Xanthia's mind groped like some creature caught on a bed of quicksand. The question blunted the force of her intended attack, and her reply seemed somehow trite. "I own a shop in St. Cloud. Cole purchased it for me."

Xanthia paused as the butler brought in the tea service, and if she had hoped to see a flicker of emotion pass across the girl's face, she was disappointed.

"My husband is a man of many occupations, many of which I have yet to learn about, Mrs. Morgan," Alaina answered softly. "You must forgive me for being unaware of your particular establishment. He speaks so rarely of his business affairs."

Xanthia pointedly waited until Miles had taken his reluctant leave. Declining both sugar and cream, Xanthia accepted the cup of tea Alaina handed her. "I've been acquainted with Cole for some time now. Seven years at least."

Alaina lowered her gaze from the woman's curious stare and sipped her own tea. Of a sudden she wished she had worn one of the gowns Cole had purchased for her and paid more attention to her hair instead of quickly sweeping it from her face and leaving the mass to curl in carefree abandon around her shoulders. The auburn hair of the other was exquisitely coiffed, and she was gowned in costly good taste, a rich brown silk gown with hat and muff of plush sable. Desperately, Alaina tried to crush the apprehension that had stirred restlessly at her first sight of the woman.

"Mrs. Morgan—" she began in a questioning tone.

"Xanthia, please. I haven't been called Mrs. Morgan since I left the graveside of my late husband. And I assure you, I have few worthwhile memories left of him."

Alaina's raised eyebrow betrayed some amazement, but out of good manners she didn't dare question one of such brief acquaintance.

"Oh, it's no secret," Xanthia assured her, shrugging. Her voice bore a soft, husky quality within it as she continued. "Everyone in town knows about my marriage to Patrick Morgan. He was a drunk, a gambler, a no-good man about town." She idly traced the rim of her cup handle with a long fingernail. "I was from a good family, you understand, and I had never met anyone else quite like Patrick Morgan. I fell hopelessly in love with him, married against my parents' wishes, and followed him out here. Oh, I would have followed him anywhere the first month of our marriage." She released a long sigh as she mentally recounted the times in their brief marriage that Patrick had beaten her and left her sobbing and heartbroken. "I conceived within the first few months of our marriage, but my husband didn't want any responsibilities like that." She waited until she could control the slight quaver in her voice. "When I began to show my condition, he started running around with other women. After a particularly wild night in town, he became violent, and as a result I lost the baby. I would have died had it not been for a friend taking me to a fine, young doctor." A long pause ensued before she murmured. "That was when I met Cole. Some hours later they dragged my husband from the river. Witnesses said he swam out with his horse to catch the ferry which had already started for the other side, but he had been drinking far too much and couldn't save himself in the swift current."

Alaina folded her hands sedately in her lap. "Why are you telling me this, Mrs. Morgan?"

Xanthia set her cup down on the saucer and let her words fall like a dead weight upon the girl. "I have known Cole about as well as any woman can."

"Oh?" Placing her own cup and saucer on the table before her, Alaina asked in feigned surprise. "Were you married to him?"

Reluctantly Xanthia replied in the negative.

Alaina's inquiry came shyly, hesitantly. "You knew him before Roberta?"

Xanthia braced herself. "Yes."

Without meeting the woman's eyes, Alaina examined the back of her hand and fidgeted with the large stoned ring on her finger. "He's married two women since he's known you?"

Xanthia could find no answer for the question. At least, not one she wished to entertain. "I'm in love with Cole."

Alaina fought the conflict raging with her, and with a soft, wistful smile, she picked up her cup of tea again. After a moment her eyes raised until she met the other's apprehensive gaze. "Then I think we are not so different, Mrs. Morgan, for I love him, too."

"How can you? You barely know him!" Xanthia demanded in a desperate rush.

The younger woman shrugged indolently. "I have known him as well as you have, Mrs. Morgan. Perhaps not as long, but surely just as well."

Xanthia felt her heart sink to the very depths of despair. She chided herself for not being more calm and deliberate in this matter, but she was fighting for something as vital to her happiness as anything she could imagine. Purposefully she opened her handbag and drew out a roll of bills. "If it's a matter of money, I will meet your needs. Whatever your—arrangement is with Cole, I'll make it worth your while if you will leave here and go someplace else."

"Put away your money, Mrs. Morgan," Alaina murmured softly. "I do not plan to give up my husband because of another woman's infatuation. I've been through that before, and I shall fight with every ounce of my being to keep it from happening again."

Xanthia thrust the roll back into her handbag with a vigor that seemed unwarranted. This was going to be more difficult than she had imagined. "Cole told me you saved his life. Obviously he feels indebted to you."

"For saving his life?" Alaina sipped her tea, hardly tasting it. "I should hope it's for something far more personal and intimate."

Xanthia betrayed her exasperation. "You'd hold a man by playing upon his indebtedness to you?"

Alaina met the trembling rage of the other with well-feigned assurance. "He's my husband to have and to hold, is he not?"

Xanthia felt her cheeks grow hot with the sting of defeat. She drew a breath, let it out slowly, and advanced to her next ploy. "You're an intelligent girl, Alaina, and I sense that you have a great deal of pride. People around here resent Cole marrying a Southern girl. They won't accept him, and they won't accept you."

"Then I guess I've met a lot of nobodies who like Cole despite his marriages," Alaina answered softly. "And they seemed so gracious, too."

Xanthia rose, her back rigid, and picked up the package. "Will you give this to Cole? I discovered it after he left yesterday." She tore back the paper to display one of his white silk shirts. "I washed and ironed it just the way he likes."

"My husband has always been so careless about his clothes." Alaina managed with a gay laugh. "Why, he even lost a whole uniform once—and while he was wearing it, too! There he was in his skivvies, and I had to sneak him into my uncle's house without being caught. But I will warn him to be more careful. A thing like that can compromise your reputation. It nearly did mine."

White-lipped, Xanthia put on her gloves and walked stiffly toward the door.

"Will we be seeing you again, Mrs. Morgan?" Alaina questioned politely.

"I doubt it," Xanthia replied in a muted voice. "Good-bye, Alaina."

The clock struck three some moments after Xanthia Morgan left. Shortly after it struck four, Mindy looked into the parlor, but decided not to disturb Alaina, for she seemed deeply occupied in thought. Alaina had not stirred when the small chimes of the clock tinkled through the half-hour mark, nor even a few moments later when the buggy drew up in front of the house. Or when Cole's voice called out to Peter as the latter took the buggy back to the barn. Or when Cole slammed the door and asked Miles of his wife's whereabouts. It was only when he came limping into the parlor that she came out of her chair. In the same moment her hand swept the package from the table. She took a step toward him and, as he came near, flung the half-wrapped shirt into his face, smothering his smile and the greeting he had formed on his lips.

"Your mistress left this for you," she snarled through the red glory of her rage. Another step forward, and her small, doubled fist slammed into his hard belly just above the lowest button of his vest. Caught by surprise, Cole had his breath driven from him. "But that's from me, Yankee!"

She was by him in a flash, snatching up a shawl and running past an astounded Miles. She flung open the door and ran onto the porch.

"Alaina!" Cole regained his voice with the realization she was leaving the house. "Alaina, come back!"

Blindly she stumbled down the stairs and hurried across

the drive. As soon as she left the bulk of the structure, a cold north wind, mingled with icy sleet, struck her full force. She caught her breath against its numbing blow. Something at the bottom of her mind warned her that she was making a mistake, that she was not dressed for this weather. But rage overshadowed reason, and she would not go back. Anywhere, but not back!

She saw Peter's head disappear beneath the brow of the hill. It was as good a direction as any to take. She raced after him as fast as her feet could fly across the frigid turf.

A dull pain grew in her side, and she slowed her headlong pace to a more sedate walk. Far ahead Peter turned into the lane to the barn and disappeared from sight. The slope of the hill had steepened, and Alaina hastened her step. From behind her came the urgent ringing of the bell. Once! Twice! Her feet flew faster. The double peal rang again, quicker and with a note of impatience about it. From ahead, she heard Peter's whistle as he urged the horse into a gallop. A sense of fear seized her. She must not be seen! Cole would be after her in a flash. She stepped from the lane and slipped into a clump of bushes, crouching low to hide her slightest shadow. The buggy careened back into sight and rushed past her with Peter leaning far forward and swinging the ends of the reins against the rump of the racing mare.

As soon as he was past, Alaina was on the road again. Then her gaze caught on a dark shadow in the trees. The cottage! It offered a haven from the cold, if not from eventual discovery. She was chilled through and shivering uncontrollably, and though she found a small bit of protection from the wind behind the shrubs, she longed now to find some meager warmth well away from the frigid air.

Trying the door and finding it unlocked, she slipped within and closed the heavy portal behind her. The hall was dark and eerily shadowed with doorways leading to other rooms. At the end of the corridor that ran the full depth of the house, a large window outlined the stark, barren balustrade of a stairway. The silence was tomblike, and only the mournful wail of the rising wind and her own harsh breathing intruded upon the stillness. She tried several doors, but in each room was presented with a forbidding sight of pale, ghostly shapes of furniture spread with dustcovers. They promised no hint of the warmth she sought. She returned to a wider passage of double folding panels just to the left of the entryway and, flipping open the latch with trembling cold fingers, pushed the doors wide. A brighter scene greeted her, one still wanly lit by the failing winter light, but her first impression was that the room had been struck by some inhuman destructive force. Chairs were tumbled over, papers were scattered helter-skelter, leather-bound volumes raked from their shelves. Through the maze of debris, a huge, stone fireplace beckoned to her sense of comfort. It was firm in her mind that she must find warmth soon or beat an ignominious retreat to the house on the hill. Her pride preferred the first choice.

Firewood and kindling filled the woodbox, and with cold, numbed hands, Alaina fumbled along the mantel, searching for matches or anything she might start a fire with. Her fingertips brushed an icy object, and she brought a small metal box into sight. Fighting a shuddering clumsiness, she pushed open the sliding lid and sighed in relief. It was a tinderbox.

Soon brightly flickering yellow and orange flames licked with hungry abandon at the dry wood she heaped over the blazing kindling. Alaina stretched out her hands before its warmth and grimaced as the fleeing cold left her fingers prickling with a pain like a thousand tiny needles. The winter night was settling rapidly over the land, and only the glow of the fire threatened the deep shadows in the house. Alaina ventured to light a lamp to chase the darkness to the far corners of the room, fairly confident that the dense brush and evergreens growing close about the house would mask the windows from casual view.

Alaina's shivering slowly abated, and her curiosity grew apace. Several tall, glass-fronted cases, the likes of which she had seen in the hospital, stood beside a long, waist-high table. One cabinet held dully gleaming instruments, while another was filled with vials and bottles, boxes and canisters, all neatly labeled in a careful hand. Still another bore stacks of bandages and other assorted wrappings. The room had all the appearances of a doctor's study, no doubt where Cole and his father had rooted their practice.

A portrait of a woman hung above the mantel, and the resemblance she bore to Cole was unmistakable. This was undoubtedly his mother. But what of his stepmother? Alaina glanced about with curiosity. No indication here of another woman. And there were no portraits in the hill house.

Thoughtfully Alaina lifted a heavy chair before the fireplace and set a small table upright beside it. She set aright a tall, wide-backed, well-used leather chair, and almost without thinking, slid it before the massive desk that sat before the windows. As she did, a small, twisted gilt-framed miniature lying on the desk caught her eye. It was partially hidden beneath wildly tossed papers and an overturned brass scales. She picked it up, shaking the shattered glass away from the picture, and took it closer to the light.

The photograph had been chopped off in such a manner that the main figure was now a woman in a dark dress and wide, starched apron. A sudden suspicion began to tickle her mind. Carefully she plucked the last particles of glass from the picture and held it beneath the lamp, then gasped in surprise as she realized it was a likeness of herself. She stared at it, her mind racing. A photographer had come into the hospital during the latter days of Cole's convalescence and had taken a picture of a small group of wounded men and had bade her to stand alongside them. Apparently Cole had witnessed it all, and somehow had managed to obtain a copy.

A heavy crease marred the middle of the photograph as if someone had repeatedly twisted the frame trying to tear the whole of it in half. Alaina sensed the utter rage that had been vented on it and on this study, and as her eyes moved about the room again, she could only wonder if this holocaust of loathing had been directed entirely at her.

"Little fool!" The words rang sharply in the room, and Alaina whirled with a small cry of alarm, then nearly crumpled to her knees in relief as she recognized the tall form of her husband in the shadowed doorway. Struggling to control the trembling that threatened to reduce her to tears, she leaned against the desk and pressed a hand over her pounding heart.

"Good heavens, Cole!" she railed weakly in freshening temper. "Must you always make it your habit to scare the wits from me? Couldn't you have made your presence known in a gentler fashion?"

"What, and have you run out on me again?" he questioned angrily. "You didn't care that you left me fearing for your safety."

"I told you before. I can take care of myself."

Cole flung his fur cap into a chair. "This is not the soft winter of the South, my love, and you'd best learn to respect it." He crossed the room, and Alaina noticed both his pronounced limp and the absence of his cane. He stood close in front of her and yanked off his gloves as he enlarged upon his earlier declaration. "A lesson of missing fingers or toes is harsh, Alaina, but a life can fade quickly in the freezing winds of this clime. One who ventures out in the face of an impending storm or blizzard without the slightest thought of protection can only be termed a fool."

Alaina's wits had been well flayed throughout the afternoon, and no tough hide was left to absorb this verbal chastisement. "How did you find me?"

"I saw the sparks fly from the chimney when I passed in the buggy. If you haven't looked outside lately, a freezing rain is coming down, coating everything with ice. I was about to go back and call out the servants in an effort to find you when I happened to glance this way."

"I stand rebuked, milord." Her manner bore the submissive tones one might expect of a slave. "Shall I return to the house, or await your—pleasure—here?"

Cole ignored her overstated humility, and she did not raise her gaze to see the smile that played for the briefest moment about his lips. He grew serious as he noticed the mangled photograph she held and reached out to take it from her.

"A keepsake I cherished from my tour in New Orleans," he murmured distantly. "Roberta said she threw it into the river, but I guess she lied about that, too."

He placed the frame on the desk, then went to stand in front of the fire, placing more logs on it before spreading his hands before its warmth.

"This was my father's study." He folded his hands behind his back and stared thoughtfully into the flames. His deep voice seemed to fill the corners of the room as he continued. "I used to come here to find some peace, to think, to get away from"—he shrugged—"whatever bothered me." He turned and unbuttoned his greatcoat, sweeping the room with his gaze. "Roberta came here looking for me about a week before she died, but I had gone into town. She found your photograph and flew into a rage." Slowly his hand ranged about to indicate the mangled interior. "And you knew Roberta well enough to believe that when I returned the next day, she was still fit to be tied." He chuckled briefly. "Miles had taken the day off, Annie was hiding in the fruit cellar, the upstairs maid and the downstairs maid were cringing in their rooms. Mrs. Garth was the only one who dared move about. Roberta accused me—and you, for that matter, of plotting the whole thing against her." His lips twisted in a bitter smile. "She demanded to know where I was keeping you hidden."

Alaina was confused. "But why did you keep the photograph?"

His eyes raised slowly to meet hers. "Don't you know, Alaina?"

What she wanted to believe could not be reasoned out, not when the memory of Xanthia Morgan was harsh in her mind. She stiffened her neck and turned away from him, gathering the scattered papers into a neat stack.

"Did Roberta know about Mrs. Morgan?" she asked caustically over her shoulder.

"No," Cole replied flatly. "And neither do you."

She whirled, ready to beard this stumbling brute. "I know you were there yesterday—*before* you so tenderly came to me."

"That's true." Cole stretched his shoulders back as if something in his chest pained him. "I went to her with the meanest of intentions, but nothing came of it. I realized before I passed through her door that it was a mistake. I could not reach out—or touch her—or find any desire to hold her. And nothing more happened, Alaina. Olie may attest to that. I joined him only moments after he left me at her door. He and I shared a cup—or two—or maybe it was three, I forget. If you wish, you may condemn me for the thought, but you must pardon me for the act."

A warmness grew within Alaina that was not of the fire burning in the hearth. Her voice was tiny and hesitant as she questioned, "Why did you keep the photograph?"

Cole heaved a long sigh and, taking her hand, settled himself in the large overstuffed chair that faced the fire and pulled her down onto his left thigh.

"Is it so hard to understand, Alaina?" he queried, half

frowning, half smiling into her searching eyes. Slipping off her damp shoes, he tucked her cold, stockinged feet onto the seat of the chair, snuggling them intimately between his thighs and bracing a hand on her buttock to hold her. "I have been in love with you for some time now. Even before I left New Orleans. I tried to discount it and lay it to infatuation, but I had to finally face the truth."

"Impossible!" Alaina flung out a hand in a wild, flamboyant gesture as she protested his claim. "Our marriage proves it! If you had loved me, then you would not have demanded the arrangement."

"Madam, you jest!" He laughed in amazement. "I never demanded anything of the sort."

"But Uncle Angus said you did!"

"Then he lied and played us against each other, for I have a letter from your uncle stating it was your desire to have a titular marriage—and that you would not come up here unless I agreed to such an arrangement." His hand stroked upward along her arm. "I suppose Angus decided to brew the mischief after I wrote to Doctor Brooks and Mrs. Hawthorne asking them to approach him with my proposal."

"You wrote first?" Alaina probed the translucent depths of those clear blue eyes.

"Mrs. Hawthorne wrote to inform me of the trouble you were having with Jacques. She said that if I cared for you at all, I'd forget about trying to appear indifferent and do something to help. I took her advice and offered marriage. If she hadn't written, I might have wasted some time floundering around for an excuse to ask you to marry me."

"Was it so difficult to propose?" she inquired softly.

"You put down my overtures so firmly in New Orleans, I had some doubts as to whether you would accept. I was after better odds."

"You honestly wanted to marry me?" she questioned in amazement.

"Madam, I wanted you any way I could get you, and that's no lie."

Tears filled her eyes, and a softening warmth replaced the anger and mellowed her emotions. After all their battles and arguments, could she believe that he cared for her? Was this what she had coveted all those months when he had been with Roberta? His tender regard and his arms about her? Could she relax her distrusting vigil and be the warm, gentle woman she longed to be in his presence?

Almost shyly she slipped her arms about his neck, and as his open mouth found her lips, she returned his ardor hesitantly. Slowly the trembling lips parted and yielded to his passionate kiss.

Alaina pulled away slightly and tried to put her reeling thoughts in order as she leaned her brow against his cheek. She had to take this more slowly, get her mind organized. It was all happening too quickly, and she cautioned herself against stripping her vulnerable emotions bare too soon. She had hidden them so well for so long, it was hard to turn loose.

She steadied her quaking heart and postponed making important decisions by turning the subject away from her. "This place—tell me about it. Tell me about your family."

Cole leaned his head back against the chair to stare up at the painting above the mantel. "There's little to tell, really. My father built this house for my mother shortly after they moved here from Pennsylvania. She died after my first year, and he married again—I suppose he thought he was providing me with a mother. My stepmother demanded a better house be built for her. She designed and furnished the one we now live in, and my father was too busy with his patients to give much heed to what she was creating until it was finished. She might not have been altogether pleased with the house either, for it wasn't six months after it was completed that she ran off with a gambler. It was the last my father saw of her. He was rather bitter you might say. When she left, she took what money and valuables she could lay her hands on. My father swore then that she'd never get another cent from him. He disinherited her and any offspring she might claim as his." Cole rested his cheek against the softly flowing russet tresses as Alaina nuzzled her face against his throat. "It would seem that the Latimer men have not been altogether successful with their women—at least, not until now."

There had been so much strife between them, Alaina longed now only to relish the tender, the softer emotions. It was much later when they returned to the house. Wrapped in a buffalo robe for the short ride home, she was scarcely aware of the fierce wind that swept icy rain down upon them. She needed only the presence of the man beside her to be content with her surroundings.

Cole halted the buggy in front of the house and, lifting her still bundled in the robe, carried her indoors where they were met by the anxious looks of the servants who gathered in the hall. Worry turned to relieved laughter as Cole unwrapped the pelt, presenting her safe and sound to the household. Mindy came timidly forward to clutch Alaina's skirts and refused to relinquish her grasp until the young woman tucked her gently into bed and quietly assured her that she would not run away again.

Some time later, when Alaina entered her own bedroom, she came to an abrupt halt and glanced about. Her first thought was that someone was playing tricks with her. The armoire was gone. The rug had disappeared along with the chaise. Even the clock had been removed from the mantel. The room was no different from the first time she had seen it, the only exception being that several comfortable-looking chairs had been placed before the fireplace.

She swept a full circle in dismay and was ready to fly downstairs in anger. Then she heard Cole moving about in his bedroom, and a new thought dawned. She followed the mental urging and passed through the bathing chamber. His door stood wide, and she halted within its frame. Everything was there, the chaise before the window, the mirror in the corner, her armoire beside Cole's, and the clock on the mantel as if it had always been there. Even the bare floor that had chilled her feet only that morning was now covered by the soft carpet that had been in her bedroom for these many weeks.

Cole sat before the cheery fireplace, his knee propped high to ease the tightness in his thigh. His eyes raised as she came to stand beside him, and her own shone softly.

"You've been playing games with me, milord, and adding my men to your side of the board."

He smiled with disarming gentleness. "What better way to lure you into my bedroom?"

"We do have a marriage then?"

He arched a brow wonderingly. "Of course, my love. Have you ever doubted it?"

"On occasion, sir. But what once seemed a dismal bargain seems to have turned into something almost too good to be true."

"And will you henceforth share the bed and the room with me, Mrs. Latimer?" he queried.

"Wait for me?" she questioned in a shy, soft whisper.

"Don't be long."

Pausing briefly to select a nightgown from her armoire, she retired to the bathing chamber to garb herself as befitting a bride. She was just slipping into the grayish blue gown when she heard Cole's footsteps come to the door and pause on the other side, as if he were impatient with her toilette. After a long moment, the footsteps went away, leaving her to hastily brush out her hair to a soft, silky sheen.

No great amount of time had passed before she heard Cole return to the door and stand once again on the other side of the unopen portal. Smoothing her hair, Alaina slowly pulled the door open. He was there, tall and slender in a long velvet robe. The heat of his gaze ranged the full length of her in a long, slow, appreciative stare, pausing on the soft, pale nipples showing provocatively through the lace and admiring the womanliness of her that was readily visible to his hungering eye. It was unmistakably a gown he had purchased for her.

"You're beautiful," he breathed almost in awe.

Smiling timidly, Alaina reached out a hand, and with a single tug, the belt of his robe fell limp. She spread the garment wide and stepped close to him until the heat of his naked body blended with the warmth of hers. Then her arms were around his neck, and her lips met his with a fevered eagerness that never failed to amaze him. His arms swept her up. The bed beckoned, and they sought its downy comfort together as one, man and wife. For Alaina, it was like being home after an eternity away. He was home to her, and she was safe in his arms.

Chapter 38

IT was a swiftly fleeting hand of time that swept the days of the month past, speeding on the hours that were too sweet to lose so quickly. Yet now there was always the promise of more rapturous moments just ahead.

As Alaina contemplated leaving the cozy comfort of their bed this morning, she grew warm with the memory of the past month when in the hours of night she had lain in Cole's arms before the crackling fire and answered his kisses and caresses, or talked quietly with him of intimate things and shared remembrances. She smiled as she thoughtfully fingered the medallion that was once again about her neck. The addition of precious gems had enhanced its beauty, but the script still boldly read, PROPERTY OF C.R. LATIMER. Now that they had a real marriage between them, Alaina found herself even more deeply in love with Cole. Though she would have denied it, and her pride and prejudices had struggled against it, love had rooted itself firmly within her heart long ago, moving out hate and intolerance.

Retrieving her gown from the floor, Alaina slipped it hastily over her head and donned her robe. She remembered that Cole had been restless during the night and had seemed in a great deal of pain after he had slipped on a loosened strip of carpet on the stairs. He might have plunged headlong to the bottom had he not fallen against the balustrade and managed to grasp the railing. She had noted the long bruise on his scarred thigh as he undressed for bed, but forgot about it when he came to her and began to remove the gown she had only just donned. The memory of what had followed brought a light blush of pleasure to her cheeks. Not too long ago, there had been a time when she would have torn the heart from anyone who would have dared to suggest that a bluebelly Yankee officer would be the doting joy of her life. Now he seemed the center of her very being.

Alaina's slippered feet skipped lightly down the stairs. But halfway in her descent of them, she halted in surprise. Miles was stationed in front of the closed study door and appeared once more on guard against any possible intrusion. The servant hesitantly met her troubled gaze and conveyed his apology in his eyes. It was as before; she would be forbidden entry into her husband's private domain.

"Doctor Latimer offers his apologies, madam," he murmured in pained embarrassment. "And he begs you to forgive him. He will be unable to join you for breakfast."

Alaina struggled through the day as best she could, unable to understand Cole locking himself in the study and setting guards at the door to keep her out. Later in the day, Olie relieved the butler, and Alaina's vexation showed in her frowning visage as she faced her husband's driver with arms akimbo. The man squirmed uncomfortably on his chair and, whistling an airless tune, fixed his attention on his feet.

The servants tirelessly guarded the study door for four straight days and were well into the fifth when Alaina lost patience with the lot of them. She could hear the faint, singsong voice of her husband behind the barrier they provided and the closed, forbidding door. As far as she was concerned, Cole had already steeped himself in too much privacy and brandy, and she grew incensed at the loneliness of her bedroom.

It was Peter's misfortune to have drawn the afternoon watch at the door when Alaina's pique reached its limit and she entered the hallway, determined to put an end to Cole's monkish whimsy. The young man had been most wary of the first mistress, but this one he had come to idolize and consider her much in the same light as a small, delicate, fragile, china doll. Younger than she by only a hand's count of months, he had led a sheltered life in this secluded place and had never known the shattering effect of a full broadside of feminine wiles.

His heart pounded as she came toward him with a smile designed to melt honey from any comb. He came to his feet in an awkward scramble, ignoring the book that spilled to the floor.

"Keep your seat, Peter," she bade the youth sweetly. "I was just going to have a word with the doctor."

Peter began to obey, then his bedazzled mind recalled the reason he had been posted at the door. "Uh, mum?" He hastily took a position in front of the portal to deny her entry. "Doctor Latimer's orders were to—uh—keep you out."

"Oh, really, Peter!" Alaina placed a hand gently on the lapel of the boy's coat and observed that he seemed to be having some trouble with his breathing. "You know it's touted that a man can't have any secrets from his wife. Now, I realize the doctor likes a fine brandy now and then, and of that I have no complaint. But this sort of drinking is ridiculous. I simply must discuss this with him!"

"Oh no, mum! It ain't the drinkin'—I mean—that's part of it I guess, but really it's more his—!"

"Peter!" The name cracked in the silence of the hall as Miles came from the back of the house. "You know what Doctor Latimer said, Peter."

Although Miles's voice was harsh in reproof, Peter seemed relieved to have his supporting presence. Miles took up station beside the lad, drawing himself into a stiff caricature of the proper butler.

"Do you really think to keep me from my husband?" Alaina questioned almost incredulously as she considered the pair.

"Yes, madam," Miles answered sternly. "On his orders, madam, we are to insure his privacy." Miles's eyes stared down from either side of his thin, hooked nose as if he were sighting a weapon at her.

Calmly Alaina took Peter's chair and slid it a good distance down the hall, positioning it in a corner facing outward. She returned to stand before the two men, while they obviously fretted beneath her deliberate stare. She lifted a hand and pointed to the chair.

"Peter, sit there." Though still gentle, there was something in her voice that did not encourage argument. Peter obeyed with alacrity, and Miles faced her alone, fixing his gaze on the far wall as tiny beads of sweat appeared on his forehead.

"Miles?" He flinched at the sound of her smooth, silky voice.

"Yes, madam?" A nervous tic began at the back of his right arm.

"Do you consider yourself a gentleman?" Alaina began to pace back and forth in front of him.

"Yes, madam, of course." Miles sniffed. "One of the best schools in England and one of the best families. In fact, I have instructed at several schools on the continent."

"Indeed, a professor!" Alaina nodded. "Of the manly arts, I presume?"

"Yes, madam. You might say that."

"And you are a gentleman of the old school."

"Yes, madam."

Alaina halted her pacing and stood directly in front of the butler, her arms akimbo. He stared at the wall over her head, and the sweat began to trickle down his face.

"Have you ever struck a lady?" Her voice took on a crisp note of inquisition.

"No, madam! Of course not!" He was aghast.

"Have you ever used force against a lady?"

"No, madam!"

"Do you consider me to be a lady?"

"Oh, yes, madam. Decidedly so, yes." His voice dwindled as he began to feel the bite of the trap. A long pause followed with only the sound of Alaina's toe tapping on the hall floor.

"Then please step aside, Miles." Her tone was one of brisk command. "Or I shall destroy your reputation on the spot."

His eyes flickered downward briefly to hers, and he saw no mercy in the steel gray. Nervously he sidled away from the door.

"Pa!" Peter's plaintive wail trembled in the hall, and as Alaina laid her hand on the doorknob, Olie thundered in from the kitchen, a napkin still tucked in the neck of his shirt and his cheeks bulging with a healthy portion of his meal.

Her hand still on the latch, Alaina turned to face him, a quizzical brow raised to silently ask his intent. Olie could no more lay a hand to her than could the others, and the three men stood helplessly by while Alaina pushed open the study door and entered.

The drapes were tightly drawn, and the sickening reek of whiskey and stale cigar smoke was enough to make

Alaina choke and cough. Cole had been pacing in a small circle along the edge of a round rug before the fireplace, but at the intrusion of her cough, he jerked about, finding her through the gloom of the room.

"Dammit, Alaina," he barked. "Get out of here!"

Closing the door firmly behind her, she leaned against it and let her gaze roam over him derisively. What she saw was hardly the neat, well-groomed man she had always known him to be. His face bore the stubble of a half week's growth, and a long dressing robe hung in loose folds to his ankles. His eyes were red rimmed, puffed and bloodshot, his mouth distorted in a grimace as he braced himself on the black cane.

"Isn't it time you come to your senses, Doctor Latimer?" she inquired.

"Leave me be, woman!" he commanded hoarsely. He swept his cane across the surface of the table which stood between them, sending the articles it held crashing to the floor. "Get out, or I'll have the servants throw you out!"

"That will do you no good, sir," she answered serenely. "They are now more afraid of me than they are of you."

"As I see! The lot of them cannot keep one wee wench from this room!" Rashly he boasted, "So if I cannot trust my servants, then I will tend to you myself!" But as he advanced toward her, Alaina became amazed by the awkwardness of his gait. He all but dragged his right leg behind him, and he made his way slowly, his teeth gritted against the pain.

"Cole?" She began to fear for him and stepped forward to meet him. "Let me help you."

"No!" he cried, moving away from her reaching hand. Embarrassed by his unsightly appearance, he ducked away, but his cane slipped on the bare wood floor, and he stumbled against her. Her weight too meager to stop him, Alaina fell with him. As he hit the floor, Cole rolled away from her, writhing in agony, grinding his teeth to keep from groaning aloud. Alaina rose to her knees beside him, then sat back on her heels, staring in astonishment at his right thigh which the parted robe revealed. He was naked beneath the garment, for a pair of trousers would not have slipped over his swollen thigh which was half again as large as his left. The bruised, discolored look of the limb roused a new anxiety in her, and her fingers trembled as she reached out to touch the purple, distended flesh.

"Good lord, Alaina," Cole choked hoarsely as he struggled to cover himself. "You unman me."

"Is this why you stayed in here?" she demanded incredulously. "Because of your leg?"

"I can do nothing but walk to keep the blood flowing in the leg and pray that I don't lose it."

Her emotions were mixed between relief and anger that he had so foolishly secluded himself from her. "And you believed that I would think less of you because of this?" She flung out a hand to indicate his leg, her tone one of disbelief.

"You would not have been the first."

"Like I told you before, Yankee, I ain't Roberta!" With that, she came to her feet and, stepping to the door, snatched it open. "Olie! Miles! Peter! Come in here. Now!"

"Alaina!" Cole barked, struggling to rise. "Close that door!"

Alaina saw Mrs. Garth coming across the hall with a fresh supply of brandy and jerked her head toward the stairs. "Take it upstairs to the bedroom."

"Blast you, woman!" Cole bellowed. "I need that to kill the pain!"

His wife ignored him and stepped aside as the three men entered the study. "Take the doctor upstairs and put him in his bed immediately."

"Like hell you will!" Cole thundered. "I'll dismiss the lot of you if you come near me!"

Olie's gaze shifted uneasily toward Alaina who retorted boldly, "Then I'll hire you all back again." She waved a hand to her husband. "Now stop this shilly-shallying and take him upstairs. And for the sake of heaven, be brave about it! You're three against one!"

Cole brandished his cane like a weapon, and his raving curses burned Peter's ears, prompting Miles and Olie to glance uncertainly from the master of the house to the mistress, each hoping that the wrath about to descend upon them would not be of a permanent nature. Either way, they were bound to catch hell.

Olie stepped forward, nervously rubbing the tip of his nose with a forefinger, and peered down at his employer. "She say we take yu up. I t'ink we take yu up!"

A long string of oaths christened them as Olie and Peter lifted him and Miles carefully supported his leg. As soon as Cole was deposited safely in his bed, he found himself faced with a new threat, that of being at his wife's mercy. She began giving orders as if she were born to command.

"Mrs. Garth, you may air out the study and see that it's given a proper cleaning. Peter, fetch hot water for a bath and put a kettle of the same here on the hearth. I'll need some linens, too. Miles, you and Olie may bring the doctor's chair from the study up here. He'll be needing it close by for a while. And I want a bucketful of snow and ice, preferably before any of it melts."

Cole had no time to question her instructions before the servants hurried off to see them carried out. Warily he asked, "Now that you have me up here, what are your intentions?"

Alaina folded back the bedcovers and stacked several pillows beneath his knee. "I would not presume to tell you what to do, my love, but it seems to me that a doctor should take better care of himself than you appear to be doing."

"You have not answered my question," Cole pressed.

"Would you like to take your robe off before I start the compresses? I'll fetch you a fresh nightshirt if you wish."

"Compresses?" Cole raised himself apprehensively.

"Hot and cold compresses to make the swelling go down. That much I know about home remedies." She gestured casually. "The robe, please. I plan to see to the entire man. After we've tended your leg, I'll shave and bathe you."

"I'm not an invalid, madam," he assured her. "I can bathe myself."

"You'll have difficulty getting into the tub. It will be simpler if you're bathed here."

His brows crinkled thoughtfully. "All over?"

Alaina's eyes raised slowly to his. "I think you can manage a few places."

"You've crushed my hopes."

"Serves you right," she chided with a smile twinkling at the corner of her mouth. "Anyone who would walk on a leg like that deserves nothing more than a good ear washing."

Cole had second thoughts as to her charity when she slapped the frigid bulk of snow onto his leg, almost bringing him straight out of the bed. And if that was not enough, she nearly scalded him again, this time with a steaming towel still dripping wet from the kettle.

"Be careful with that thing!" he yelped. "You could end our hopes for a family altogether."

"I'll try to be more careful," Alaina apologized, sweetly contrite. "But I don't think you have anything to worry about, my love."

Olie and Miles wrestled in Cole's large leather chair as Alaina withdrew the lukewarm linen from his leg, replacing it with more snow. Covering his nakedness, Cole watched the men. The removal of his chair from the study foretold a change in his habits. He could no longer closet himself in seclusion, but then, a more appealing condition appeared in the offering. To be ensconced in a bedroom with a fetching wench was not altogether displeasing.

Though not tutored in the ways of cures or medicines, Alaina found her meager knowledge successful. By evening the swelling had gone down, and with his leg carefully propped, Cole was able to rest peaceably. To keep Alaina pacified, he stayed in bed through the next day, but no amount of cajoling would keep him bedridden the following morning.

Chapter 39

DECEMBER had come upon them with a flourish, and the north wind blew its snow-laden breath across the land, cloaking the countryside with a mantle of white. Mindy, who had never known the import of the season, listened with enraptured awe as Alaina spun tales of fact and fancy about the event. In anticipation, the child hung a stocking from the parlor mantel and eagerly awaited the day, while Alaina diligently fashioned the remains of the charred black and yellow evening dress into a tiny gown for the new china doll that Cole had purchased for the girl. He constructed a wooden crib for the old rag doll and placed the gifts away in the attic in readiness for the holiday.

Horace Burr journeyed back for a visit one day, and thereafter Cole held tight rein on his own impatience to present a very special gift to his young wife on Christmas morn. Alaina planned her own surprise beyond the smoking jacket she made for her husband, and in preparation for the more important gift sent a servant to bid Braegar Darvey to stop by the house for a few moments while Cole was in St. Cloud attending to business.

It was not in her scheme that her husband should finish his business early and return home. The presence of Braegar's horse was cause enough to tweak Cole's temper, and to find the parlor door closed against intrusion, set all the old jealousies astir. If the man's friendship had not held him from pressing Roberta into an affair, then surely with Alaina, being the more desirable of the two, the Irishman would be wont to press his attentions upon her all the more readily. Cole was determined that such a thing would not happen again.

He brushed past the waiting butler and pushed the sliding doors of the parlor wide. Braegar had been leaning forward in his chair, his head close to Alaina's and a drink dangling from his fingers, but as Cole opened the doors, he straightened and leaned back, sipping from the glass with casual demeanor.

Cole handed his hat to Miles and shrugged out of his greatcoat. Favoring the two with a sneering leer, he leaned his cane against his leg and began to work his gloves off. Hesitantly Alaina rose and, smoothing her gown self-consciously, moved toward her husband, her eyes downcast and a warm blush pinkening her cheeks.

"By God," Cole rasped, unable to find innocent cause for her obvious dismay except that of guilt. He glared at Braegar accusingly. "Every time I leave this house, I return to find you in it sniffing after my wife. From your zealous attentions, I would say you haven't had a woman for some time."

Alaina's eyes widened and snapped steel gray with rage. "Cole! How can you say such a thing?"

"Because I know the bastard!"

"I invited him here," she grittingly stated.

Cole stared at her, an array of fleeting emotions crossing his face. The spurs of jealousy were sharp and pricked him to a painful depth. Huskily he answered her. "Then perhaps I'd better hear more of this, madam, because I know you can't be wanting for attention."

The insinuation stung Alaina at a moment when she was most vulnerable.

"You utterly boorish oaf!" she choked and, bursting into sobs, fled the room and raced across the hall. She flung her cloak about her shoulder and slammed the door behind her as she left the house.

Cole would have gone after her, but with quick, running steps, Braegar caught him at the front door and, having the advantage of at least a hundred pounds, slammed him face forward against it.

"Your wife sought out my services, Doctor Latimer," the Irishman snarled, "because she wanted to be sure of the signs before broaching the subject with you. Like it or not, man, you will become a father in the summer."

Cole's eyes grew wide and, with a burst of strength, he pushed the heavier man aside. Reaching again for the door, he flung it open. As he ran out onto the porch, the cutter was just moving away from the house. Alaina cracked the whip to urge the mare into a faster pace, ignoring his cry.

"Alaina! Wait!"

The only mount present was Braeger's, and that one's ownership gave Cole no pause whatsoever. For a man of hampered ability, he was down the steps in a thrice and, snatching the reins from the hitching post, swung onto the horse's back. The stallion skidded on the hard-packed snow and ice as it pranced in a wide circle, skittish beneath the unfamiliar weight. Cole's bootheels dug into his sides, and the steed caught the full import of the message. He leaped forward and charged after the fleeing cutter. The stallion drew abreast of the racing conveyance, but when Cole shouted for Alaina to stop, she ignored him and cracked the whip harder. It was a breakneck race down the slippery lane, and Cole urged his mount on ever faster until he could crowd the mare into the deeper snow and brush that grew alongside the road. The mare was forced to slow and finally the cutter, plunging through the low, snow-covered growth, dragged her to a halt. Braegar's stallion pranced several steps farther in a splendid neck-arched display despite Cole's best efforts. Impatiently he jerked the headstrong stud into a reluctant halt and dismounted.

Alaina had been caught in an upheaved plume of snow and came to her feet, brushing its fine powder from her face and cloak as she gasped against its icy sting. Breathlessly she sobbed, "You blithering, bluebellied—cutthroat excuse for Yankee sawbones!"

She seized the reins, trying to urge the mare out of the snowdrift, but Cole ran toward them.

"Alaina, calm down before you hurt yourself," he cried. Nearing the frightened animal's head, he reached up to grab the bridle. But as he did so, his feet slipped, and he slammed into the mare's shoulder. The horse reared, jerking the bridle from his grasp. Cole fell flat on his back beneath the steed's pawing hooves, and with a strangled cry, Alaina came to her feet. The animal came down, and her hoof landed squarely on Cole's right thigh. There was an audible snap as the bone gave, then the brittle air was set atremble as a hoarse scream of pain broke from Cole's lips.

Frantic, Alaina scrambled out of the cutter and, heedless of any danger to herself, ran around in front of the horse, throwing up her arms with a shout until the mare sidled away from this new threat. When the animal regained the hard-packed snow of the lane, she stood snorting and trembling, though gradually she calmed. Cole rolled in agony in the snow, his teeth gnashing in pain until Alaina fell to her knees beside him and caught his twisting shoulders in her arms.

"Oh, Cole darling, be still," she whispered urgently. "You'll only do more damage."

He caught the collar of her cloak and pulled her close above him, pressing his face against her bosom as he hammered his will into iron self-control.

"The beast!" he snarled through gritted teeth. "That damned evil beast! She's cost me my leg for sure."

"Hush, my darling," Alaina pleaded. Slipping the skirt of her heavy cloak beneath his thinly clad back, she wrapped him in its warm confines and rolled the hood into a pillow, shivering violently as the cold wind penetrated her velvet gown. "Don't try to move. I'm going back for help."

"Wait!" Cole gasped, fighting the pulsing flood of agony that threatened to engulf him.

Alaina leaned toward him as he caught her hand. "I'm just going for help," she assured him gently. "I'll be back in a moment."

"Alaina"—he grimaced as the tide of pain washed over him, and he struggled to resist its assault. "I'm sorry—for what I said. It's just that—I lost you once—I don't want to lose you again. And I cannot trust—Braegar. He seduced Roberta—and got her with child—and then sent her off to some back room hovel to get rid of it."

Understanding dawned in Alaina's mind and swept away all the hurt she had felt at his words. Though she couldn't believe that Braegar was of such low character that he would cuckold his best friend and inadvertently kill that one's wife, she knew that Cole believed Braegar to be guilty of all he accused.

Blinking at the moisture that blurred her vision, she snuggled the cloak more warmly about his neck. "I told you before, Yankee, I am not Roberta, and whatever she did has nothing to do with me."

"I'll never—make the comparison again," he rasped, trying to smile.

"Then hold on to this thought while you're waiting for me," she whispered, caressing his cheek and gazing down into the clear blue of his eyes. "We're going to have a child, and so you'll never doubt my loyalty or love, he'll have the biggest, brightest blue eyes on the face of this earth."

"She!" Cole corrected. He paused a moment, gritting his teeth against the white shards of pain that were shooting up his leg, then managed a further statement. "I have a fancy for a wee daughter who has her mother's nose and mouth."

Alaina smiled tenderly and, brushing a soft kiss upon his chilled lips, rose to her feet. Her shoes slipped on the hard snow as she struggled toward the stallion. Catching the dangling reins, she tossed them over the mane, then grasped the high saddlehorn and placed her foot in the stirrup to haul herself astraddle, no mean feat with a full skirt. The heels of her light slippers thudded hard against the mount's ribs until he scrambled and clawed his way up the ice-crusted lane. As soon as she came in sight of the house, she waved an arm frantically to Braegar who stood on the porch waiting the return of his mount.

"Ring the bell three times!" she shouted. "Cole's been hurt!"

With the signal of distress pealing through the wintry air, Alaina whirled the horse about and went thundering back the way she had come. By the time Braegar came panting down the hill, she had Cole's head cradled in her lap. The Irishman quickly doffed his greatcoat and placed it around Alaina's shoulders, then laid his attention to the broken leg.

It was only a few moments later when a wagonload of men came careening around the road from the barn. At Braegar's bidding, they lifted Cole into the bed of the wagon, taking care not to unduly jostle his leg. Even so, the effort cost Cole his grip on consciousness, and he fell into the black void of oblivion.

"It's just as well," Braegar stated. "Let's get him to the house before this frigid clime takes a further toll on his health."

Braegar and Alaina rode with Cole, while Olie and Saul simultaneously took to the wagon seat and the other hands returned on foot to the barn. When the wagon reached the house, the three men carried Cole to the upstairs bedroom. Miles fetched Braegar's black bag with its full complement of ominous instruments, and while Annie set kettles of water boiling on the cookstove, Mrs.

Garth collected several bottles of brandy and, as bade, left them beside the bed.

Firmly, Braegar set Alaina from the room, bidding Saul to stay, for as the black had more of a knowledge of healing and medicinal cures than the others, the Irishman chose to enlist his aid.

Alaina waited in her old bedroom, restlessly pacing the floor and anxiously twisting her hands as the moments dragged into an hour and an hour into an enternity. Dusk had begun to settle over the land before the bathing chamber door creaked open and Braegar came in with a piece of cloth folded in his hands.

"It was a clean break and not difficult to set," he stated.

"But what took so long?" she questioned anxiously.

Braegar turned the cloth in his hand and gave her a considered grin. "It just might be the best break that muleheaded ape has had since he married you." He carefully unfolded the cloth and showed her a jagged, slightly curved strip of metal of a spotty blackish hue. "I took the initiative and found this after a bit of digging around. It was loosened by the break, and though I fear Cole will miss it, he's probably better off without it."

"But will he be all right?" she pressed.

Braegar pursed his lips and slowly nodded. "If he doesn't take on an infection, the leg should be better than before." He lifted a small brown vial from his bag and laid it in her hand. "This is laudanum. Just a small spoonful should do when the pain gets bad, or when he needs to sleep. I know he hates the stuff, but it will help him rest, and his leg needs that."

Alaina followed him down the stairs. "Will you come back tomorrow?"

Braegar nodded again as he donned his hat and coat. "Of course. I wouldn't miss it for the world. At last I have that skinny oaf just where I want him."

He noticed her puckered brow and laughed heartily. "He can't kick me out, and he can't get away. This time I'm going to have it out with him once and for all and find out just what is bothering him."

Alaina opened her mouth to warn him of the seriousness of Cole's beliefs, but as Miles waited beside the door to let the doctor out, she refrained, not wishing to air personal matters before the servants, though she had great doubts whether too much escaped them.

Alaina had no more than dozed off when a light stirring in the master bedroom brought her to full alertness. She slipped out of the bed in her old room and donned a pair of slippers against the chill of the cold floor before she made her way through the bathing chamber. Cole lay still in the bed, though the light of the flickering fire betrayed the fact that his eyes were open. She passed the bed and laid a fresh log on the fire, completely unaware in a fresh naive way of the figure she made as the firelight cast shadows through the light fabric of her gown. Even the pain in Cole's leg could not quench the sudden rush of blood to his loins or the trip-hammer pounding in his chest.

Fascinated with the way the gown puckered tauntingly over the cold tightened peaks of her bosom, he watched her in silence as she moved about the room. She paused beside the bed for a moment, soft sympathy shining in her eyes, then a shiver shook her body as the inescapable chill of the house crept through the gown. Cole reached out his arm and turned down the covers beside him, and Alaina gladly accepted the invitation. When she was snuggled closely against his side, she lay her head back against his arm to better observe his face. Her hand rested on his furry chest, and she was boldly aware of the deliberate thudding of his heart beneath it.

"I love you," she whispered and sighed. "Though I would have been the last to admit it, I think I loved you even before that night you took my virginity."

Cole raised his brows in amazement, silently questioning.

"When you left New Orleans, I went dead inside," she timidly admitted. "I thought I would never see you again."

"We shared the same loneliness then," he murmured huskily.

"You needn't be afraid of Braegar, you know. I've never been interested in anyone but you."

His hand slid down the warm, smooth curve of her back. "I suppose you want me to thank him for mending my leg."

"It wouldn't hurt." She reached behind her to the table and, holding the piece of metal up in the firelight, displayed it for his benefit. "He thought you could do without this. He said the break loosened it, and he took it upon himself to remove it from your leg."

"He's always had a mind of his own," Cole commented laconically.

"Strange, but he said much the same about you." Alaina ran her fingers through the crisp mat of hair covering his chest. "Aren't you glad that he removed it?"

"I'll be glad if nothing worse comes of it."

"And you will tell him you're grateful?" she gently urged.

"Perhaps."

"And you will tell him why you're angry with him?"

"I cannot do them both in the same day, madam. The one tweaks my pride and the other my ire."

"Try." She kissed his lips lingeringly, flattening her breasts tightly against him until Cole's thoughts could not move beyond the awareness of her taut, little nipples boring holes in his skin even through the cloth of her gown. He could only groan at this torture and kiss her fiercely, forgetting everything else, even the burning pain in his thigh.

The sight of his wife moving about the bedroom in the lamp-lit predawn darkness as she renewed the fire, dressed, and combed her hair, which by now was long enough to reach well down her back, forming a rich, dark flowing mantle over her shoulders, was for Cole such a pleasurable experience that it left him both lusting and content. Before she went downstairs to set the house astir, Alaina bent to brush a kiss upon his lips, and Cole had only just begun to miss her cheery presence when she returned, bearing a tray laden with his breakfast. Once the tray was in place across his lap, she perched cross-legged on the bed beside him and helped herself to samples of his meal. Her dancing eyes and quick smile made his morning sublime.

After she removed the tray, Alaina was gone for some time, while Cole pored over a long ignored stack of medical publications. He was engrossed in acquainting himself with new techniques when, from the corner of his eye, he caught a movement at the door and raised his gaze to find Alaina framed in the portal, her hands folded and an odd look of barely contained expectation on her face. She spoke no word, but stood aside to let another enter.

"Good morning, Doctor Latimer!" Braegar Darvey's booming voice suddenly filled the room.

"It was good for a little while anyway," Cole muttered only half under his breath and caught Alaina's quick, sidelong glance. He hauled himself upright as much as the cumbersome splint would permit and accepted his wife's assistance as she tucked several pillows behind his back.

Braegar seemed unusually lighthearted as he strolled across the room. Leaving his black bag in a chair, he stepped before the fireplace to warm his front side, then turned to give the other side a fair share of the heat. Hunching his shoulders, he peered at Cole. Lifting his coattails, he asked cheerfully, "And how is my distinguished patient this bright morn?"

"I fear that my temper has taken a decided turn for the worse," Cole mumbled, avoiding his wife's gaze.

"Aye, lad, and there lies the root of it." Braegar made a show of swinging a chair to face his patient, well out of reach of course, and placing a footstool in front of it before settling himself within it. "It sets heavily on my mind that I have been the one to bring the brumes upon ye much of late. It seems only right to me, since the good Lord has seen fit to remove the aggravatin' steel from your leg, that I should do my best to remove the aggravation that stands between us."

"And that's to be the way of it then?" Cole ground out.

Braegar nodded and, pulling out a pipe, began to tamp tobacco into the generous bowl. He was apparently waiting for his host to begin.

Cole caught Alaina's hand. "My love, will you have Annie send us up some coffee and perhaps a bit of brandy to add to it." If he lost his temper with the man again, he didn't want her witness to it.

"I've already told Mrs. Garth to bring up coffee and cakes, and there's brandy here beside the bed," she answered sweetly.

"Then perhaps you have something which would better occupy your time," he urged. "This will probably be nothing more than a long, dry discussion."

"I have nothing at all pressing," she assured him in a

most charming guise of innocence. "And I'd much rather stay here with you."

Braegar chuckled past his pipe. "Well, doctor, you may as well set your mind on having it out since you cannot leave and neither of us is likely to."

Cole folded his arms and leaned back with a stubborn frown growing on his face. "Then I choose to maintain my silence."

"I came here to have this out once and for all," Braegar insisted. "We may discuss whatever you wish, but unless I am satisfied, I will be here tomorrow, and the day after, and however long it takes for you to get to the point."

"Dammit, man!" Cole's ire rose again. "Do you expect me to discuss the details of your reputation in mixed company?"

"My reputation, as you well know, Cole, is much a matter of gossip and wishful dreaming." Braegar relit his pipe, and wreaths of fragrant smoke billowed about his head as he pulled on it.

"It's not as much a matter of reputation as it is of pure ethics. I can forgive you for betraying my friendship and having an affair with Roberta, but sending her to a sleazy midwife when she came with child, it was a cheap thing for you to do."

Braegar strangled and coughed into his pipe, then had to hastily wipe at the shower of sparks that descended on his trousers. When the danger was past, his attention returned to Cole, and his surprise was blatant in his expression. "Roberta?" he managed to choke out. "And me?"

"She said as much," Cole stated. "On her deathbed she swore you were the father."

"A bloody lie!" Braegar protested adamantly. "Roberta did make advances toward me, probably because she wanted to hurt you, but I swear, Cole, that I had no time for the woman, and I made no secret of the fact. I put her out of my office on two occasions and earned her everlasting hatred for it." He set the pipe aside and leaned his elbows on his knees. "She could hardly have come to me for the care you suggest, for she knew I would have no part of it, even if the child had been mine."

"Cole," Alaina's voice was soft and pleading. "I believe him. You know yourself that Roberta was capable of lying—even on her deathbed. If she found my photograph in the cottage, she might have used this form of revenge."

"Vengeance is a cruel, driving master," Braegar commented wryly.

Cole's anger was gone. "You're right about Roberta. She never gave herself unless she had a purpose. As much as I have been blind to the fact until now, she never seemed greatly tolerant of Braegar—or of me, for that matter."

"But if neither of you were the father," Alaina mused aloud, "then who might it have been?"

"There you have a complete freedom of choice, my love," Cole responded. "I have not a ken as to the man's name and will probably never know now."

"It doesn't really matter anyway now that you know Braegar wasn't the one." Alaina caressed her husband's arm and gazed down at him expectantly. "Wasn't there something else you wanted to discuss with Braegar, my love?"

Cole crinkled his brows at her, realizing how effortlessly she was maneuvering him. The fact that he didn't mind and was more interested in the memory of her breasts pressed warmly against his chest was a sure sign he was mellowing. He frowned in mock anger, not willing to let her see just how deftly she could handle him.

"Alaina informs me that I should be indebted to you for taking the piece of metal from my leg."

Braegar shrugged. "I was curious. Saul told me that the metal had been embedded in the bone of your thigh and couldn't be gotten out. But whenever I touched it, there was enough movement that I was sure it had been loosened. I took the chance of losing your friendship completely and made the small incision to see if I could remove it."

"You have a skillful hand, Doctor Darvey," Cole remarked with sincerity. "I am barely conscious of any pain from the surgery. My own father could not have done better."

The Irishman blushed deeply with pleasure. It was no light compliment for Cole to make such a comparison, for he had held his father in great esteem.

"The community could use another doctor if you're of a mind to take up your practice again, Cole."

Eager to convince him of the need, Braegar entered into a vivid account of recent ailments and abnormalities, wounds and infections, asking Cole's advice and soliciting his help. Both men were soon caught up in the discussion, and Alaina noticed the intent interest that came into her husband's face. Braegar was much too descriptive for her tender ears and queazy constitution. The men hardly noticed as she slipped from the room, yet in the cool air of the hallway, she smiled to herself, confident that Cole would soon return to the occupation he loved the most.

Gift giving began very early Christmas morn at the Latimer residence. Dawn had not fully lightened the heavens when Cole, fondly watching his wife sleep, leaned over her to wake her with a soft, tender kiss.

"Merry Christmas, my love," he breathed.

Languidly she stretched and purred in contentment, snuggling close as he laid an arm around her. "And Merry Christmas to you, my darling," she sighed sleepily.

"I have a surprise for you. Would you like to guess what it might be?"

"What more could I want when I have you and your baby growing inside me?" She nuzzled her nose against his throat. "What else could a woman possibly need?"

Cole reached beneath his pillows and withdrew a packet of papers, which he handed her. Puzzled, Alaina searched his face with wide, questioning eyes.

"How about a deed to Briar Hill?"

Alaina gasped and scrambled to her knees in a fit of excitement, fumbling with the string that held the papers secure like a child tearing through the gay wrappings of a gift. At last she unfolded the parchments and eagerly read the words that claimed Alaina Latimer sole owner of the property.

"Oh, Cole!" she sobbed with happy tears flowing unchecked down her cheeks. She flung her arms about his neck and embraced him fiercely, weeping with joy. "I thought it was lost to me forever. Thank you, my darling."

The never ending white of the northern land became drab as the bitter cold of late January continued. The dry brittle air parched the throat and drew the skin taut, and after a few minutes outside, fingers and toes ached and lips grew stiff. Thus, when on the evening of the fourth day of the second month, Cole announced that he would be leaving the next morning for the Prochavski's farm up north, Alaina's fears were not easily put to rest.

"It is within a week of Gretchen's time," Cole explained, "and she'll be less anxious about the birth if a doctor is with her. With any luck I should be back in less than a fortnight."

Alaina's unanswering silence dragged on while her imagination formed a dozen or more visions of Cole caught in a blizzard with a frosty mantling about his head. All the warnings he had issued in the cottage about the folly of journeying out in this wintry clime came back to haunt her.

"I have left instructions as to your care, and either Olie or Saul will sleep in the house so you won't be frightened again."

Cole halted as he took note of a vague look of rebellion that appeared in those brilliant gray eyes.

"And who will look after you, milord Yankee? If you've cared to notice, it's a bit crisp outside. I think I shall not let you go without me."

A smile twitched Cole's lips despite his effort to control it. "My love, I swear you will be more comfortable here, and safer, too. And you must have a care for your condition."

Her pert nose lifted in a manner of prim confidence. "I have every faith in your ability to take care of me."

"But there would just be the two of us alone together in the wilderness for nearly two days going and two days coming back."

"Then you will need the companionship, and Gretchen will no doubt appreciate my womanly understanding with all those lumber-whatever-you-call-'em around."

Cole recognized the stubborn thrust of her lovely jaw and the glint of determination in her eye. "I see you have no intention of relenting."

"Quite right, sir. It's much like you said. I lost you once. I do not want to lose you again. Besides, we've always proven able to take better care of each other than ourselves. That should be enough to convince you that we're not meant to be separated."

He raised a brow in amusement. "You have artfully set aside all my arguments, madam. I can do nothing more than give in to your demands."

A soft expression of warmth and gentleness shining on

her face, Alaina rose from her chair and went to where he half sat on the rolled arm of the settee, slipping her arms about his neck as he brought her within the circle of his embrace.

"I shall try not to be too much of a burden, Cole," she murmured sweetly. "It's just that if I stayed here, I would do naught but worry about you."

"I must admit the thought of getting you alone and all to myself in the middle of nowhere is truly a captivating notion," he smiled.

Alaina chuckled as she leaned back against his encircling arms and watched his gaze sketch the limits of her décolletage with an ogling leer. "Are you sure, sir, that you didn't have this all planned from the beginning?"

He lowered his head and tantalizingly caressed her lips with his tongue, while he pressed her hips closer to his, letting her feel the firm pressure of his manhood. "The idea did flit through my head whenever I thought of leaving you. Two weeks is a long time."

"An eternity," she sighed and ardently answered his stirring kisses.

The next morning the heavier sleigh was loaded and waiting when Alaina and Cole came down the front steps of the cliff house. The hour before dawn was moonless and crisp, and though no hint of a wind stirred the barren limbs of the trees, the air was piercing, numbing the fingers with its cold and tingling the face with its icy touch. Cole settled his boyishly dressed wife into the heap of furs that lined the seat and, tucking his case-bound shotgun in the rear, whistled for Soldier and thumped the place left for the beast on the canvas-and-rope-lashed supplies that had been loaded behind the seat. Lowering himself into the place beside Alaina, Cole nodded assurances to the servants' admonitions to be careful and lifted the reins.

The sleigh bells echoed in the still air as Cole turned the horses onto the lane. For Alaina, warm and cozy beneath a hooded fur coat that closely resembled Cole's, the ride was much like passing through the blanketing wreaths of a dream. Everything about them was hushed and motionless, frozen in a frigid stance, waiting for the magic of spring to release them from the enchantment of winter. Alaina cuddled closer to Cole. At the moment she could think of no words that could express her contentment or her love for him.

The first light of dawn tinged the eastern sky a soft magenta hue as they passed through St. Cloud. They climbed the low bank from the river and headed out Government Road, which followed the Mississippi northward. Late in the afternoon a long, low log structure came into sight. A sloping roof along the back would provide shelter for the horses, and a few yards away a tiny cabin squatted in solitude. It was here they would spend the night, and by noon of the next day, they would reach their destination.

Wrapped in a warm cocoon of furs, they made love by firelight and, with the dawn, rose to resume their journey. Soldier loped alongside the sleigh for a spell, but found the game so sparse that he soon took shelter in the rear with the baggage where he dozed.

Franze Prochavski was chopping firewood beside his cabin when the baying hound and the sleigh came in sight of the small farm. Smiling and calling a greeting, the young man stopped his labors and ran to greet them as Cole halted the team before the house. In a moment Gretchen's animated face appeared at the door. Laughing and waving, she bade Franze to quickly bring them in out of the cold.

"She knew you would come," Franze informed Cole as he helped Alaina from the cutter and with genuine sincerity, the young man added, "And I'm greatly relieved to see you."

Franze gustily pushed them through the open door of the cabin into the warm interior, while Gretchen rushed about putting a kettle of water on the fire for tea and laying out sweet breads and cold meats on the table. Cole knelt to help Alaina off with her boots, and when the fur coat was doffed, Gretchen's quick, assessing gaze found the slight roundness of the girl's belly. The woman nodded in satisfaction, and her face glowed as she came forward to affectionately embrace Alaina.

"It's good that you and Cole make a baby together. It will bind you close to each other."

For Alaina it was a time of renewing the acquaintance she had begun several months before, and Gretchen's cheerful, bubbling personality had an uplifting effect that made the secluded cabin seem as busy as a society gathering.

Cole toured his lands and was much satisfied with the lumber operation. It was what he had started with the hopeful thought that someday Alaina would bear him heirs for his holdings. While married to Roberta, he had felt no driving ambitions to enlarge his wealth. Now, all that was changed, and behind every business transaction was the idea that it was for Alaina and their offspring.

In deference to Gretchen's encumbered agility, the Prochavski's bed occupied the far corner of the cabin's lower room. In the attic beneath the sharply sloping roof, another bed had been prepared near the ever-warm chimney. It was a simple affair of boards with ropes stretched taut between, but the many thick down-filled ticks made it a heavenly trysting place for enraptured lovers, and there the visitors were wont to spend many a blissful hour.

It was late in the evening on the fifth day after their arrival, while the four of them were seated about the table, that Franze attempted to teach the others a new card game, a tangled travesty of misbegotten rules called whist, which he swore had been brought by the latest arrivals from Germany. In the middle of his sixth try at explaining the details of the game, Gretchen suddenly gasped and laid down her cards. After the pain passed, she gave them all a reassuring smile and verified their concern with a simple statement.

"I think it has begun."

The pains were irregular and uneven throughout the night, but it was not a time when rest came easily to anyone. An hour or so before dawn, the contractions stabilized, and as the sun began another day's chapter, a new voice filled the cabin. It was a normal birth, a boy, strong and healthy with lungs that boded that he would never speak in a low voice and a greedy lust for his mother's breast where he smacked loudly in contentment.

Cole's mere presence had given Gretchen the confidence she needed, and though Franze protested, she was up and about by the third day. When time came for the Latimers to leave, Alaina reluctantly laid the sleeping babe in his mother's arms and gathered her belongings into the venerable wicker case.

The next morning was brittle and gray and after partaking of a sumptuous breakfast farewells were said. Cole whistled Soldier into the back of the sleigh and headed the horses southward. They had barely made the river when a fine, white powder began to fall, and the world narrowed down upon them until the dark shapes of the pines along the banks became nearly indistinguishable. Cole and Alaina nestled deeper into the furs, but even there the cold wind reached in to nip at them.

By midmorning the snow swirled fetlock deep, and the sleigh wallowed in the powdery drifts. In the treetops high above them, the wind howled and moaned like a tribe of banshees on a frenzied warpath. Twisting sheets of snow slashed down upon them, and the horses stumbled and slid on the uncertain ice.

Shortly after noon Cole guided the team off the river and into a twisting gulley that cut through the north bank. "There used to be a trapper's cabin here," he shouted above the fury of the storm. "We'll have to take shelter until this blows over."

It was still there, a low, log-walled, sod-roofed cabin that huddled against and seemed part of the embankment behind it. A protected corner, formed by the cabin and bank, had been roofed over and still bore poles that shaped a crude corral. Soldier left to survey the surroundings, while Cole and Alaina investigated the cabin. The rock fireplace was in some disrepair, but proved still usable, and as soon as a fire was flickering on the hearth, Cole ventured out to put away the horses. When he returned, he bore the large basket of food and the encased shotgun. The huge black dog was close at his heels and made a circuit of the interior, sniffing out every corner before he plunked down before the fire.

Their situation, though not without hazard, proved to be not uncomfortable. A small heap of well-weathered hay would augment the bag of grain in the back of the sleigh. A fair stack of firewood was near at hand, and a rusty ax thoughtfully laid in the rafters would provide more if that dwindled. Their supply of food would last several days, and a trip out with the shotgun or pistol would extend it several more. The only thing left was to make themselves comfortable and try to find some way of filling the passing time.

Armfuls of furs from the sleigh secured the first requirement, and the warm, laughing light in Alaina's eyes promised that the second was hardly a cause for worry.

The blizzard shrieked over them, and the small, sturdy cabin became a world unto itself. Soldier was let out for an evening romp, and what ensued in his absence was a most thorough christening of the cabin in a completely marital sense.

In the warm afterglow of the moment, they lay on their sides facing each other, their thighs entwined, their breaths mingling into one as they exchanged slow, languid kisses. Against his hard, flat belly, Cole could feel the fluttering movements of his child stirring within Alaina's womb, and he marveled at the wonder of it. Though a doctor who had just recently experienced the miracle of birth, he counted this moment special. It was something created out of their love, and he prayed that all would go well so that in years to come, they would have much to show for their devotion.

"You have bewitched me, Alaina Latimer," he sighed against her lips.

Alaina rubbed her slim nose against his and whispered as if there were ears to overhear. "How so, my love?"

"From the first night we knew each other as man and woman, I was caught in your spell and thereafter did I yearn for you. Call it love if you will, for I cannot deny that I was enamored with a woman I could put neither name nor face to."

"But did you not say that love has to grow with the passage of time?" she inquired warmly. "And that you were suspicious of any emotion which flared overnight between two beings?"

"Aye, I said all that," he admitted. "But that was a time when I was very cautious of my love and most reluctant to admit its existence."

Alaina chuckled softly as she kissed his lips. "There was a time, my love, when you were an ogre."

He grinned at her, his eyes shining in the firelight. "I still am, but I manage to hide it better." He brushed her hair back from her cheek as he whispered, "But I've given up many of my old ways in favor of something new and bright and shining. And with each day's passing, my love for you has grown untold measures."

"You really loved me from the moment we first made love?" she asked timidly.

"Aye, my sweet. You haunted my dreams. Though I could put no face to you, you were a white ghost in the back of my mind. It was that hope which led me to accept Roberta. The dream faded and came back as a nightmare when I found out who you were. There was cold steel in my leg which tortured me, but there was white hot steel in my mind every bit as painful."

"And what do you dream of now?"

Cole laughed and held her close in his arms, pressing full length against her warm, naked body. "I have changed my ways, madam. I have given up the steel. It flays me no longer, in my mind, or in my leg. My dream comes to me when my eyes are wide open and when I close them, it is in search of rest, not of the vague wraith."

Her body trembled against him, and his lips found hers, and passion stirred anew.

The snow stopped the next day, but the sun was an indistinct glow in the sky as the winds continued to shriek, sweeping the whiteness into unearthly sculptures across the landscape. They stayed in the cabin another day, and that night a bitter cold set in as the driving storm abated to a mere gale.

Cole gathered Alaina into the curve of his body, and they combined their warmth against the persistent chill of the cabin that not even the blazing fire could banish. Soldier had found a soft place on an aged pelt by the fire and, after turning around several times, settled down once again. The small cabin grew still as the wind howled in the pines that sheltered it.

Sometime later Cole's eyes came open, and he was suddenly tense and alert. Soldier was prowling the room, pausing now and then to sniff at the door. The hackles made a ridge down the hound's spine, while the horses snorted and stamped their feet nervously in the corral. Then the sound came again, an eerie moaning that rose above the wind. Soldier crouched with a snarl on his lips, and outside, one of the horses whinnied in fear.

Alaina roused as Cole left her side, Without stirring, she watched quietly as he pulled on a pair of hide britches and donned a woolen shirt, leaving it open down the front. He lifted the .44 from the holster and checked the caps with a quick spin of the cylinder before raising his gaze to find her eyes open and resting on him.

"Wolves," he answered her silently questioning look

and struck a sulfur match to a lantern's wick. "They're worrying the horses."

As Alaina hurriedly wrapped a fur about her, Cole stepped to the door. He threw it wide and squinted beyond the glow of the lantern. At first sign of the light, a half dozen or so gray shapes retreated from the area of the stable, but the bright reflections from their eyes revealed that they had gone no farther than the edge of the pines and were crouched there, still threatening. He took a step outside and, raising the pistol, fired shots into the night until he emptied the piece. The glowing eyes disappeared, but in a brief moment were back, fewer in number than there had been, yet ominously persistent.

Soldier shot past as Cole jammed new charges into the gun. Recognizing a foe they could challenge, the wolves came to meet the dog, snarling viciously as they pressed the attack. Soldier took the first wolf with his shoulder and dipped his head, his huge jaws savagely crunching the available throat, then the still-thrashing wolf was hurled high in the air over the mastiff's back. Soldier had his second adversary by the throat as Cole saw Alaina's shadow pass behind him. A second later a heavy blast deafened him as she let fly with both barrels of the shotgun. One of the charges flipped one of the wolves in an oddly graceful head over heels tumble and plowed him into a drift where he lay still. Cole raised the pistol and shot as a gray form dodged behind Soldier in an attempt to hamstring him. Instead, the wolf was hurled back onto his haunches and, dripping blood from slack jaws, sank into the snow. Cole fired two quick shots at the last intruder he could see, just as Soldier shook the life from the one who dangled limply from his jaws. The dog gave the carcass a last twisting jerk before dropping it disdainfully. He checked each still form for life, then returned to the cabin with deliberate slowness.

Cole glanced down at the gun in his hand. He had heard no report from his last shots. He had felt the pistol jump in his hand and had seen the flash and the beasts that had fallen. But even now, there was only a thick buzzing in his ears. He called to the mastiff and was again amazed that he did not hear his own voice, though the dog responded with a lolling tongue and trotted past his master to flop in satisfied self-confidence in front of the fire.

Cole raised his gaze to Alaina as she rubbed her right shoulder. The still-smoking shotgun lay on the floor where it had fallen from her numbed grasp. Putting an arm about her shoulders, he held her trembling body close to his. Ruefully she shook her head as tears of relief tumbled down her cheeks, then gradually calming, she sniffed and urged him to see about Soldier.

The dog bore a long gash on his chest and several nicks on his head and legs, but was otherwise unharmed and unperturbed. The fire was restoked, the guns reloaded, and the lantern's light doused.

Alaina sat upright in the midst of the furs, waiting for Cole with a glowing softness in the translucent gray of her eyes as she watched his every movement. Cole slipped the pistol into its sheath and knelt beside her. She winced as he examined her shoulder. The bruise was already darkening. She sat pliant beneath his ministering touch as he applied a soothing salve to the silken skin. Her head turned slowly, and her eyes met his with open invitation in them. She was suddenly in his arms, and he forgot the bells in his head as their lips met and mingled, tasting, testing—

A time later Alaina lay sleeping in the crook of his arm as Cole observed the shifting shadows on the rough-beamed ceiling, knowing the special kind of peace that only a loving woman could give her husband—and he could once more hear the gentle sigh of the wind in the pines.

Chapter 40

IN March the winds brought a slow warming trend, and by its end, open stretches of water began to appear on the river. The lake ice grew gray, and the last week in the month brought a refreshing sprinkle of rain. But alas, when darkness fell, it turned into more of the white powdery stuff and blanketed the landscape anew.

April brought warm days and fluffy clouds and the river rose above the ice, widening with the open spots until they connected, and, then, only a thin fringe of ice along the shore remained.

Patches of earth began to show, and the hills took on a dirty, grayish look. The April moon waxed and waned. Geese and swans came honking in the night, and ducks fluttered along the river, seeking the sloughs, potholes, and other nesting places.

A flash of lightning and a peal of thunder in the dead of night brought Alaina upright in the bed. She rose and went to the windows to watch as a thunderstorm marched ponderously toward the cliff, then, with a crashing crescendo, sent driving sheets of rain against the leaded panes. Alaina flinched and stepped back from the bright flash of light.

Cole's arms came around her, and he bent to kiss her soft, white shoulder as his hand caressed the growing roundness of her belly. She turned in his arms and rose to find his lips with hers. He lifted her in his arms and bore her to the bed, and the spring thundershower rolled on across the cliff house, leaving in its wake a soft and tender peace, a warm gentle night wherein two lovers twined at rest in each other's arms.

May brought the promise of spring flowers, and as no gardener could be found, Peter was drafted to conduct a deep spading of the rose garden. Cole had just finished seeing a patient, one of many who had in the last months been admitted into the doctor's study, and Alaina was in the parlor with Mindy when she saw Peter rush past the open doorway in search of Cole. She stepped out into the hall just in time to be nearly knocked askew by her husband and Peter who charged past her on the way out. Curious, she followed out onto the porch but was even more bewildered when she saw both men digging at a hole in the garden. She was about to descend the steps when she felt her skirts suddenly seized from behind. Surprised, Alaina turned to find Mindy desperately clutching two handfuls of her gown as if afraid to let her go.

"Whatever is the matter, Mindy?" she questioned in wonder, but the girl frantically shook her head, her dark eyes wide with fear and the hunted look of a cornered animal. Realizing that something of a serious nature was disturbing the child, Alaina refrained from going after the men and stayed to comfort her. The girl was trembling uncontrollably and with small fists tightly gripping the cloth, she hid her face in Alaina's skirts.

Cole threw down the spade and was about to kneel beside the hole with Peter when he caught sight of his wife and Mindy standing together on the porch. Waving his arm, he gestured her back.

"Take the child and go inside, Alaina," he commanded.

Obediently she did so, though much confused by it all. A short time later Cole came into the parlor where she was, while Peter could be seen racing off down the hill toward the barn. As soon as Cole stepped into the room, Mindy was off the settee, running toward him. Throwing her arms about his legs, she began to sob forlornly. Cole's face softened with compassion. He lifted the tiny girl into his arms and held her close as she buried her face against his shoulder.

"Do you know what we found, Mindy?" he asked quietly, and the girl's nod answered him. She did.

"What is it, Cole?" Alaina inquired, growing more bewildered. "What did you find?"

"We found Mindy's uncle buried beneath the rosebushes. Apparently he'd been there for some time, probably since he disappeared."

Alaina sat down quickly, for the disclosure sapped the stability from her limbs. She shuddered as she remembered having turned the earth in that same area only last fall.

"Peter's gone for the sheriff," Cole reported. "While we wait for them, I'll take Mindy upstairs and have Gilda sit with her for a time. Maybe she'll be able to rest. No doubt the sheriff will want to question her about what she knows."

The small arms tightened around his neck, and Cole patted the girl's back reassuringly as he spoke gently to her.

"It's all right. Nobody will hurt you. We'll take care of you from now on."

As the sound of his footsteps faded across the marble floor in the hall, Alaina sat in the hushed stillness of the parlor. Her strength was drained by the shock, but her mind raced chaotically on several different paths. What fate had brought the gardener to the end he had suffered? Who had buried him? And how, what, and how much did Mindy know about her uncle's demise?

"He was murdered," Cole stated bluntly when he returned. "The back of his skull was crushed, as if someone had hit him from behind. It looked as if he had just tumbled into the hole after he was hit."

"Do you suppose he could have been digging it himself?"

"Very possible, but why? Rosebushes don't require that deep a hole when they're planted, and I can't imagine the man knowingly preparing his own grave."

"Then perhaps he was burying something else."

Cole shrugged. "Unless Mindy can tell us more on the matter, we can only guess at what it might have been. There was nothing else in the grave, certainly no treasure to boast of."

Treasure? The word drifted hauntingly through Alaina's head, prickling the outer core of her memory. Hadn't Roberta mentioned something about a treasure in her memoirs? Or leaving Latimer House rich? It had all been in the diary, but where was the book now? And who had taken it? The gardener's murderer?

The bedroom adjoining their bathing chamber had been recently stripped and refurnished as a nursery for the anticipated arrival of their firstborn. Even with everything taken out of the room, the diary had not been found.

Alaina chewed her lip thoughtfully. Should she give credence to her cousin's meanderings? Perhaps it had just been Roberta's twisted reasoning at work once again, and it would only be foolishness to take her writing seriously.

It was Deputy Sheriff Martin Holvag who answered their summons, being acquainted with the family. He brought two men with him, and while they removed the body from the narrow grave and laid it on a canvas shroud, Martin stood on the porch with Cole and listened attentively as the doctor recounted just how the discovery had been made. Alaina had been interested in the roses, Cole explained, and he had set Peter to the chore of mixing manure with the soil. The gardener's hat had been found first, and that had prompted Peter to probe deeper, therein discovering the body.

The sheriff's men gingerly picked through the gardener's pockets and extracted a plug of tobacco, a knife, a few coins, and from the purse tucked away in the pocket of the man's jacket, three relatively crisp ten-dollar bank notes. Finding nothing of import, Martin presented the possessions to Cole to keep for Mindy as she was the last of kin.

"Since he was the child's uncle and my hired man," Cole proposed as the men lifted the body into the back of the wagon, "the least I can do is buy him a decent grave."

But Cole could only spread his hands and shrug as Martin pressed for more answers. "I'm sorry I cannot add more to the clearing up of this matter. The man disappeared a few weeks before Roberta died. We thought he had run off and left Mindy behind because he didn't want to be saddled with her anymore."

"What about your servants? How well do you know them, Cole?"

"Mrs. Garth, the upstairs maid, and the downstairs maid were all hired by Mister James shortly before I returned home with Roberta. Except for the gardener, whom I employed after receiving word that the old one had been killed in the war, the rest of the help have been here for a good number of years, and were hired by my father."

"Your present wife came after the gardener disappeared, but what about your first wife?" Martin pressed. "Could she have known anything about this?"

"Roberta disliked the man intensely and thought of him only as no-account trash. But then, she had no time for the rest of the servants either."

"Can I talk with Mindy now? Perhaps she can shed some light on this."

Cole nodded toward the house. "She's in the parlor with Alaina. She's quite upset by the matter, and since I've known her, I've never heard her speak, so I don't know how much she will reveal."

"You mean she can't talk?"

"No, I don't believe it's because she's not able to. It's just that she won't."

Martin scraped his boots before he entered the house and clumsily doffed his hat as he nodded a greeting to Alaina. She had been waiting tensely on the settee with Mindy, and as he approached them, the girl shrank backward against the seat, pressing as close to Alaina as she could get. Martin squatted down before them to look Mindy in the eye, but she refused to look up.

"Doctor Latimer tells me that you knew your uncle was buried in the rose garden. Do you know who put him there?"

Mindy turned pale, and her mouth worked convulsively, though no sound escaped. It seemed as if she were caught in a terror all her own.

Alaina glanced pleadingly to Cole, taking the child against her and cradling the small, dark head against her bosom.

"Perhaps this could wait for another time, Martin," Cole interjected in the girl's behalf. "As you can see, the child is frightened nearly out of her wits."

"If you don't mind, I'll take her to her room," Alaina murmured, and was greatly relieved when the deputy nodded in acquiescence.

As Alaina left the room with the girl, Martin broached another subject of concern to him. "I was wondering, Cole, if you might have seen a small riverboat pass on the river—white with red trim, she was. Not too big, a sternwheeler named the *Thatcher*."

Cole had just poured some brandy and handed a glass to Martin. He shook his head. "Not anything recent. About a week or two ago there was one."

Martin's brow furrowed. "This would have been in the last two or three days. No passengers. Just a cargo of plows, wire and cordage. The only thing of real value was a few cases of Winchester rifles. She left the falls last Thursday and was seen passing upriver about ten miles south of here. Beyond that, it's as if she just disappeared into thin air."

Cole sipped on his brandy. "She could have struck a snag. All that iron on board, she'd go down like a rock."

"Well, I'm only asking around," Martin pondered, draining his glass in a single gulp. He glanced out a front window. "I see they've got him loaded and are waiting for me. I'd better get him down to the undertakers."

Cole accompanied him to the door. "I believe the man had a room somewhere in town, and there's an old nag that he and the child went back and forth on. Let me know if you turn anything up."

After the deputy's wagon had rattled off down the road, Cole absently picked up a pile of effects the gardener had left. He lifted the bills and rubbed them between his fingers thoughtfully. They were slick and unwrinkled, yet of a '63 issue. By their crispness, he could almost assume that they had been tucked away somewhere before being buried with the gardener. He peered closer and realized that the serial numbers of all three bills were consecutive, the last digit being the only one that changed. How could a man who worked as a gardener for six dollars a week have had any dealings with a money house or bank?

There seemed to be more than a shallow mystery about this whole affair, but be damned if he could say just what it was. With a sigh, Cole swept the effects and the bills into a kerchief and, wrapping the bundle securely, stowed the whole away in one of his desk drawers.

The gossipmongers reveled in all sorts of conjecture about the finding of the Latimers' gardener beneath the rosebushes. Some would have it that the doctor had attacked the man in a jealous rage, but they could not definitely conclude as to whether it was because of the first wife, or the second. The fact that the gardener had been middle-aged, filthy, far from good-looking and certainly no competition for the handsome doctor seemed of no consequence. A plumpish matron, with a loosely wagging tongue, was sure that she had seen the present Mrs. Latimer cavorting about the countryside with the gardener just shortly after her arrival. She said as much to Xanthia Morgan while in her millinery shop trying on hats, and though Xanthia felt no loyalty to Alaina, she decried the fact that Doctor Latimer would resort to such measures, even out of jealousy. Besides, Xanthia shrugged, she had heard it from a very reputable source that the Latimers' marriage was merely a business arrangement and that the doctor had simply taken the young woman into his home out of compassion for her, much as he did Mindy.

The triple-chinned matron stretched her nearly bald brows upward and looked at the red-headed proprietress with amused condescension. "My dear, it is obvious that you have not seen the present Mrs. Latimer lately."

And smugly superior in her knowledge, she refused to explain further, letting Xanthia's curiosity simmer and stew. After all, Xanthia had put down her speculations as groundless. It would serve the woman right to be the last person in town to know about the expectant state of Alaina Latimer. Business arrangement, humph!

Xanthia paused at the door of her shop that same afternoon as a largc, black carriage swept into town. She would have known it anywhere, just as she would have recognized the tall, broad-shouldered form of the man who owned it. Cole Latimer was in town. The thought raced through her brain. Maybe, just maybe he would come to her one more time.

The carriage halted before Mister James's law office, and Xanthia's pulse quickened a beat or two. It didn't matter that it wasn't at her back door. Her eyes fastened eagerly on the darkly clad figure which descended. He looked good, she decided with a smile. Real good. Yet there was something about him that was different, too. Then it dawned on her that he did not have his cane and was walking without a limp.

He turned back toward the carriage, and her hopes shriveled as a woman appeared in the doorway of the brougham. Cole reached up and carefully handed his wife down and Xanthia realized, as she now saw the young woman clearly, what the portly matron had been so smug about. Despite the lace shawl carefully folded across her protruding middle, Alaina Latimer was obviously well along with child.

A flare of jealousy reared its miserable head as Xanthia observed the other woman. A child was the one thing she had tried to give Cole, but had been unable to regardless of how hard she had yearned to bind him to her with such a link.

Carolyn Darvey descended with the assistance from

Cole, and the three stood a moment as it seemed questions were presented and answered. Cole drew out his pocket watch and noted the time, nodded to Carolyn's inquiry, and shrugged as he replied. The Darvey woman moved away, but paused as Alaina stepped back to her husband and lifted her face. Dismally Xanthia watched as Cole accommodated his young wife, kissing her full on the mouth and much more warmly than seemed proper for a public thoroughfare. Raising his head, he spoke to her in an intimate fashion and squeezed her hand as she moved away. Cole smiled and watched her as she joined the taller woman, and it was a long moment before he stirred himself to movement and entered the lawyer's office.

Nearly an hour's passing had occurred when Xanthia came from the back of her shop to find Carolyn Darvey leading her companion through the front door of her establishment. There was a moment of shock as Xanthia and Alaina's gazes met, but Carolyn was exuberantly examining the merchandise and failed to notice the two women's discomfiture and the vivid blush that came into Alaina's cheeks.

Xanthia stiffly smiled a greeting and refrained from looking lower than the crisply ruffled collar of Alaina's pale blue dress. Though charmingly feminine, the expensive detail of her gown was apparent at first glance, and her ribbon-festooned bonnet would have rivaled the best in the shop. Xanthia crushed the green monster within her beneath the heel of her will and, with a deep breath, entered the role of proper proprietress.

"May I be of some assistance to you ladies?" she asked solicitously.

"I wanted to show Mrs. Latimer those perfectly delightful little baby bonnets you were selling in here at one time," Carolyn bubbled gaily, completely innocent of her blunder in bringing Alaina into the shop. "Do you still have them?"

"Of course." Xanthia stepped past them to open the doors of an armoire and brought out a basket of tiny, puffed bonnets edged with lace or ruffled brims.

"Now here's one for a boy, Alaina." Carolyn held it up for the other's benefit. "Look at this. Have you ever seen anything so precious?"

"Cole is hoping for a girl," Alaina murmured mutedly, wanting desperately to be out of the shop and on her way.

Carolyn was a bit disappointed with Alaina's rapidly declining interest in shopping for the baby and, sensing something was troubling the girl, did not press Xanthia to show them more. She couldn't resist questioning as they left the shop, "Aren't you feeling well, Alaina?"

"Yes, of course, Carolyn." Alaina smiled weakly. "It's just a bit warm today, that's all."

She stepped out onto the boardwalk, then halted abruptly as she nearly collided with a short, wealthily garbed man who was just passing the shop. She was about to murmur an apology when her gaze raised and recognition set goading spurs of terror beneath her tender hide, blinding all reason. Though he wore his hair longer on the left side to cover his ear, there was no mistaking Jacques DuBonné.

His gloved right hand held a silver-handled swagger stick and a second glove. Recovering from his own surprise, he raised his left hand to doff his hat, while his dark eyes took in her burdened state. His face hardened imperceptibly as he did so, and with an almost sneering smile, he opened his mouth to speak.

Pale and shaken, Alaina whirled and stumbled back into Xanthia's shop, not hearing Carolyn's worried questions that came in a rush of confusion. As Alaina pressed against a low table filled with hats, her world dimmed and slowly her knees buckled beneath her. Tiny spots of darkness enlarged until all was empty and black, and she never knew that Xanthia Morgan rushed forward to catch and slowly lower her sagging body to the floor.

"Alaina!" Carolyn gasped in alarm as she went to the red-haired woman's assistance.

Kneeling on the floor with Alaina's head in her lap, Xanthia looked up and stated almost in amazement, "She's fainted."

"I'd better get Cole." Carolyn said. She was at the door before she paused to glance back and ask. "Will you watch her?"

"Yes, of course." Xanthia lowered her eyes to the delicately shaped features of the victor in her game of hearts as the Darvey woman hurried out of the shop. Almost mechanically she loosened the ribbons of the bonnet and, gently lifting the dark head, eased the hat off and laid it aside.

Jacques DuBonné paused in the doorway of the general store and watched the willowy blond as she ran along the boardwalk. She entered a small office down the street and soon reappeared with a man he recognized as the good Doctor Latimer. Jacques sneered derisively. So, it *was* the major who had plucked the fruit and left his seed to sprout.

Xanthia glanced up as the front door of her shop burst open and Cole Latimer came charging through, his concern for his young wife rampant in his face. Much to Xanthia's disappointment, he hardly glanced at her, but quickly knelt to lift Alaina into his arms.

Xanthia rose to her feet as Carolyn joined them and gestured hesitantly to the back of her shop. "There's a bedroom in the back if you'd care to use it."

Cole nodded in silent gratitude and went down the familiar hallway with Carolyn following closely behind. When Xanthia entered the room, he had partially opened his wife's bodice and was bathing her face and throat with a cool, wet cloth as he sat beside her on the bed. Alaina was just rousing from her stupor.

The thickly lashed eyelids fluttered open slowly, and for a moment Alaina stared about her in confusion, then, as Cole leaned over her, her gaze turned to find him, and she was suddenly against him, her arms tightly clasped around his neck. Xanthia glanced away with a heavy heart as Cole kissed the dark head and lovingly brushed the rumpled curls from his wife's cheek.

"Feeling better now?" he murmured with a tender smile.

"Cole, it was Jacques!" she whispered brokenly against his shirtfront. "He's here—in St. Cloud. I saw him!"

Cole pulled away to stare down at her in surprise, his gaze probing hers and finding fear and distress within the translucent depths. Her lips quivered, and she nodded, tears springing forth to overflow the wide, worried pools of gray. She was clearly frightened.

Cole turned suddenly to Xanthia with a question. "Can my wife rest here for a while? I have a matter to take up with the sheriff. I shouldn't be very long."

"Cole, no!" Alaina gasped, clutching his sleeve. "Think of what he can do to us."

"It's all right, Alaina," he soothed. "Trust me."

Her eyes searched his, and though she still trembled, she did not try to hold him. He dropped a light kiss on her forehead and rose, peering inquiringly at Xanthia.

The red-haired woman nodded and resolved herself to

the fact that there was no hope for anything where Cole was concerned.

After he left the millinery shop, Cole went directly to the sheriff's office and, finding Martin Holvag on duty, explained bluntly that there was a man in town wanted by the law and requested that the deputy accompany him. With Martin at his side, Cole first checked at the hotels in town and was amazed to find a message addressed to him waiting at the desk in the Stearns House. It was from Jacques, bidding him to come up to his room. Cole wasted no moment in doing just that. His jaw was set, his brow furrowed as he raised his brown knuckles to rap sharply on the door. It was quickly opened by Jacques himself.

"Ah, good-evening, Doctor Latimer." The Frenchman's speech was precise; only a slight hint of a Cajun accent remained. "I see by your presence that your wife told you of our meeting. My apologies that it should have come as a surprise. I assure you it was my intention to contact you and present my credentials so that your fears would be set aside. If you hadn't come, I would have sent for you."

"Indeed?" Cole's tone was mockingly incredulous.

Jacques's gaze flickered past him to Martin's badge. "Of course, a minion of the law. It is as I expected, and it's just as well that you are here. Come in, gentlemen. What I have to show you will take only a moment."

He closed the door behind them and, lifting his coat from a chair, drew forth a leather bound purse from a pocket, clumsily using his left hand to do so. Cole watched him carefully, noting the gloved hand and, when the long hair brushed aside, the hole in the left ear. Self-consciously Jacques touched the wayward strand into place and flipped open the purse, displaying several officious-looking letters. After waving them briefly beneath Cole's nose, he handed them to the deputy, then directing the doctor's attention with a flourish of his hand, he explained them.

"Just to assure you that I am no longer wanted by the law, gentlemen, these are full pardons from the governor of Louisiana and the Federal officials in that state. And here"—he produced another letter—"is my authority from a Paris-based firm to act as their agent in reviewing possible markets for our wares in this area." He paused to let them digest the documents and his announcement before arrogantly examining the nails of his left hand. "I assure you both that I am in the best of standing with all parties involved, and everything I do here is of an honorable—and legal—intent. Do you have any questions?"

Cole was by no means satisfied and studied the man with open suspicion.

Jacques met his eyes briefly. "In a day or two, Monsieur Doctor Latimer, I will be gone. I have no intentions of returning to this city in the foreseeable future."

Cole put it out plainly for the man. "I don't care if you have a pardon written in stone by God's own finger. If I catch you on my property or in the immediate vicinity of my wife, I will arrange for your next judgment to be on a much higher level."

"You make a threat, monsieur?"

"No, just a simple statement of what our future relationship will be."

Jacques glanced up into the stern face and nodded, pursing his lips. "I think I understand. And considering what has passed, monsieur, how can I blame you. But I only wish to go about my business in peace, and it's been toward this end that I've entertained you."

Cole smiled, though there was little humor in it. "Good, and may I wish you a speedy conclusion of whatever business you have in this state."

"I shall keep your words in mind, Monsieur Doctor Latimer, and a good-day to you also, Sheriff." Jacques opened the door in an overt invitation for them to leave.

"I'm just a deputy, sir," Martin corrected as he led the way through the portal. "But perhaps you're only a bit premature."

Jacques extended his left hand in a parting gesture to the deputy, but Cole pointedly refrained from exchanging any form of gentlemanly cordiality with the man. Settling his hat on his head, he nodded crisply and followed Martin out.

It was a silent, tense ride to the Darveys' where they dropped Carolyn off. The woman had sat across from them all the way from St. Cloud with her lips pursed tightly as she waited for someone to explain the events of the afternoon. Finally in front of the Darvey stoop, Cole relented and, with humor wrinkling the corners of his eyes, confided, "The small man you saw in front of the millinery shop was a blackguard and a scoundrel during the war. His name is Jacques DuBonné, and it was mostly because of him that Alaina had to leave New Orleans." His arm moved from the back of the seat to his wife's shoulders. "For that favor, I could almost thank him."

Alaina gave him a weak, nervous smile. She had held all her emotions bottled up while Carolyn sat across from them, but the moment the carriage was on the road again, her dismay could no longer be contained.

"Why did Jacques have to show up now? What if he tells someone that I am a thief, a murderess, even a traitor?" Her questions moaned agonizingly from her. "He'll see me thrown into prison. Oh, why couldn't he have just stayed away?" Her voice broke, and she pulled a small handkerchief from her bodice to muffle her sobs.

All during her tirade Cole had been struggling to free a thick packet of papers from his coat. He unfolded them and smoothed them out on her lap.

"These should dispel your fears, my love."

Baffled, Alaina lifted the papers, blinking back the blinding tears.

"I just picked them up from Mister James," Cole informed her as she turned a bewildered, tear-streaked visage to him. He smiled. "It seems that Horace Burr did his job well. He contacted the attorneys that I had retained in Louisiana, and his influence with the Federal courts lent them much assistance."

He flipped through the top pages too rapidly for her to see anything but the numerous signatures. "These are sworn depositions from me, from Saul, Doctor Brooks, Mrs. Hawthorne, and various other individuals. But these last are the important ones." Cole reached the final several pages, which were richly embellished, sealed, and stamped. "Documents from the Governor of Louisiana," he read, as his fingers traced the words, "Releasing one Alaina MacGaren from any and all charges so leveled while the State of Louisiana was a member of the Confederacy, et cetera." He turned the page, and his finger pointed out words again as he read in a rapid singsong voice. "From the Union commander of the South Central District. As such charges have been proven false and inappropriate, and since no other evidence of wrongdoing exists, said charges are herein withdrawn and declared null and void. This document to be endorsed by the proper bureau in Washington. And here are the endorsements—" His finger jabbed the stamps and initials at the bottom. "And for your own benefit, madam." He flipped to the last page. "A letter from one General Taylor while still an acting general of the Confederacy, stating that you were no spy but only on one occasion did you deliver the personal effects of a deceased soldier to him."

Cole leaned back in the corner of the seat and pulled out a cigar, savoring its aroma for a moment as he rolled it beneath his nose. "I believe, madam, that you are not the villain you portray."

Alaina stared at the letters and slowly sifted through them, seeing signatures through a teary blur.

GENERAL RICHARD TAYLOR, CSA
MAJOR C. R. LATIMER, USA SURGEON, RET.
DOCTOR THADDEUS BROOKS
GENERAL CLAY MITCHELL, USA SURGEON
REVEREND P. LYMAN

And from some unknown judge, the words:

> "Henceforth let it be known that after careful investigation into the matter and with signed affidavits from witnesses of unquestionable integrity, that it has been found that Alaina MacGaren is innocent of the crimes charged against her and that all rewards posted for her capture have been nullified. Attached are letters from witnesses who have sworn before God and under oath that she was wrongly charged of spying and, further, that it was impossible for her to have taken part in the theft of a Federal payroll on the date specified, being at the time in the company of a Federal officer."

Alaina frowned. "But these letters from General Taylor —from Saul—they're dated long ago!"

"Humhum." Cole was smug in his pleasure. "Some of them were signed before I left New Orleans. I retained the best Southern lawyers Louisiana could offer in your behalf, and Horace Burr is the most influential attorney in the East. I told Horace exactly what happened, gave him permission to divulge your disguises to possible witnesses, and named those places you frequented."

"You told him everthing?" Alaina queried hesitantly.

"I had to, madam, but I made Horace understand that it was my fault and that you were only trying to save me from a dire fate. Doctor Brooks avowed that he heard about the same story from Roberta's own lips. But you needn't worry about Horace Burr spreading rumors. He has been very discreet.

"So, madam! You may cease your worry that our child may be born in some dismal prison. You are—except for the matter of our marriage—virtually a free woman."

Alaina leaned back and laughed, though tears continued to course down her cheeks.

"As to that bondage, my love," she choked through laughing sobs, "I would that I be chained to you forever."

She fell against his chest as racking sobs of relief completely dissolved her composure. Tenderly Cole held his wife in his arms and utterly enjoyed his role of husband all the way home.

Chapter 41

THE month of June was the eighth in Alaina MacGaren Latimer's scheme of accounting time, and the measure of her accuracy was the ever-growing size of her belly. Long ago she had put away her beautiful gowns and adopted a high-waisted fashion better suited to her advancing condition.

As the days grew warmer, the countryside took on a lush green hue, and the scent of lilacs and apple blossoms filled the air with a fresh sweetness. The shaded spots of the forest were a lavender carpet of violets broken only by an occasional yellow patch or the fragile white bells of the trillium.

It was nearing a year since her migration to the north, and letters from the Craighughs were slow in coming. Thus, when a brief note arrived from Leala asking if the Latimers would receive some guests from New Orleans, Alaina was both surprised and elated. Immediately she sent off a dispatch informing her aunt that both she and Cole would be delighted to have company from the South.

They were awaiting further word from Leala, and on this particular day, the third Monday in the month, Alaina was engaged in sewing a small gown in the parlor when the warning bark of Soldier brought her to her feet and across the room to the front window. She stared in some bemusement as a strange procession came up the drive and halted in front of the house. Martin Holvag's wagon was in the lead, and behind it came a monstrous black carriage with maroon and gold trim that would have done grace to some head of state. The vehicle was complete with two guards at the rear and a footman beside the driver who guided a four-in-hand team of well-matched, high-stepping horses.

Alaina made her way carefully to the front door and stood behind Miles as the footman knocked on the portal, while the deputy leaned back in the seat of his wagon and watched the proceedings with a strange quirk in his smile.

Miles peered down his nose as he opened the door for the footman.

"Is this the residence of Doctor and Mrs. Latimer?" the man inquired stiffly.

"Indeed it is," Miles answered just as rigidly.

The other turned without comment and went to fold down the step of his carriage and open the door. He stood aside as a rather small, portly woman pulled aside her skirts and daintily stepped down.

"Aunt Leala!" Alaina's shriek of recognition rang in the foyer, and Miles stood aside just in time to avoid being pushed as Alaina rushed out onto the front porch. Her progress was not as swift as she might have thought, and she met Leala at the top of the steps.

Alaina's arms went around the older woman, and before she knew it, she was sniffing back tears of happiness. Then another hand was on her arm, and she looked up.

"Mrs. Hawthorne!" Alaina fairly gasped. "Great merciful heavens! I never dreamed you would be coming, too!"

"We just had to come." Tally stepped back from the enthusiastic embrace and surveyed the young woman. "The suspense was too great, but"—she gazed pointedly at Alaina's rotund belly—"well worth both the wait and the journey. I was beginning to wonder if I might have been wrong about the whole thing. But I'm glad to see that you and Cole have reconciled your differences. And from what I can see, you two didn't waste any time."

Leala seemed somewhat confused by it all. "I don't suppose there'll be an annulment now."

Alaina laughed and hugged her aunt affectionately. "I don't think so, Aunt Leala. We gave up that idea long ago."

Leala smoothed the softly curling tresses of her niece. "I hope you're not angry, Alaina. Your letters said everything was fine, but I just had to know for sure. Roberta complained so much about living up here, I was worried."

Alaina gave the other another hug for good measure. "I've never been more content, Aunt Leala, and I'm just so happy that you've come that I could sit down right here and just giggle with the sheer pleasure of it."

Suddenly realizing that Cole probably had not been informed of their guests' arrival, Alaina turned to tell Miles to fetch him, but found her husband already close behind her.

"Cole!" Her eyes danced with excitement. "They're here!"

"I had guessed as much," Cole replied with humor. Alaina's bubbling happiness was infectious. "What with all the screaming that's been going on out here, how could I not?" He took the proffered hands of both ladies and gave them a warm squeeze of welcome. "Is Angus with you?"

"No!" Leala's answer was quick and sharp, then she lowered her gaze as if embarrassed. "No, he—was busy with the store." She drew a deep breath and, with obvious effort, struggled to be gay. "It's all going quite well, really. We're doing even better than before the war."

"Ladies?" A tall, handsome, elderly gentleman had descended to the top step of the carriage, and managed at last to gain their attention. "I shall be on my way now. It's been delightful meeting you, and if we should ever meet again, I shall deem it my good fortune."

Alaina turned in wonder to the two women as the grand conveyance went off down the road. "Traveling with strange men, ladies? Tsk! Tsk!"

"It was Tally's idea," Leala insisted, blushing.

"Of course it was!" Tally proudly declared. "He offered to share his carriage with us since he was coming this way, and I saw no reason to decline. Besides, I have passed the age of impropriety. Anything I do now is legal, moral, and decidedly dull."

"Wherever did you meet him?" Alaina laughingly queried.

"In a hotel in St. Anthony, after we arrived on the steamboat," Leala rushed to answer.

"He's a count, or lord, or some such thing." Mrs. Hawthorne seemed unimpressed as she shrugged. "Whatever, a gentleman."

Cole smiled as he watched Alaina escort the ladies inside the house, then descended the steps to stand beside Martin's wagon. After clasping his hand in greeting, the deputy leaned an elbow on the back of the seat and chuckled.

"The ladies arrived in town this afternoon and came directly to the office to ask where you lived. I had to come out anyway, and the sheriff suggested I escort them. They seem like a pair of fine, genteel Southern ladies."

"They are," Cole agreed, then peered up at the man with a grin. "The feisty one—uh—rather arranged, or at least abetted our marriage."

The deputy grew serious as he got down to the real reason for his visit. "We lost another boat on the river, Cole. The *Carey Downs* this time, and just about the same place."

"Strange," Cole mused. "I can't understand how they can go to so much trouble hauling those boats up the falls, then run into something on the river."

"We lost a couple last year, too," Martin informed him. "If it wasn't for the oxcarts and the fur trade, the shipping company would give up going above St. Anthony. We just haven't found any sign of the boats. Not hide, nor hair, flotsam or anything."

Cole delved into conjecture. "If they're on the bottom, they'll break up one of these days, and then you'll find all the evidence you need. I only hope you do as well with Mindy's uncle."

"We found out where he lived. Didn't discover anything though, only a few letters that seemed to indicate that he came up from somewhere in Missouri before he picked up Mindy, then he wandered this way looking for work in the lumber camps. No kin, except for the girl, and no friends anywhere around. But I intend to get to the bottom of it."

"I'll stop in the next time I'm in town. Until then, I wish you the best of luck, Martin."

The deputy tipped his hat, shook out the reins, and guided his team down the lane. Cole stood for a moment watching him go. Martin was intelligent and down-to-earth, much like Carolyn. He had paid little or no heed to the rumors floating about town, and now the gossip was like dead ash on a hearth, no longer of interest to anyone. Yet Martin would be relentless in his pursuit in finding the answers; he was that way. Solid, sturdy, never wavering or fickle. He would make Carolyn Darvey a fine husband.

After supper the two travelers retired to their rooms relatively early, leaving Cole and Alaina to wend a leisured way, arm in arm, to their own bedroom. The house was quiet, except for the usual squeaks, thumps, and groans, sounds that Alaina had come to grudgingly accept. After moving into Cole's room and farther down the hall from Roberta's, she had not been disturbed by the noises in the night, and for the summer, Soldier was often left out at night to range where he would. Thus, if there were any sounds emitting from the red room, she was not made aware of it.

As Cole was more fascinated in observing his wife's disrobing and toilette, Alaina was in bed and waiting while he was still tugging his shirttail loose from his pants. Unbuttoning his shirt, he considered the soft, radiant beauty of his wife as she sat propped against the pillows combing her long hair into a shining mane. The soft light of the oil lamp gave her a glowing halo, and Cole smiled as he admitted to himself that she was indeed quite angelic after all.

He dropped the shirt into a chair and began to free his pants when a soft knocking on the door made him cease and reach for his robe. When he opened the door, he found Leala standing in the dark hallway, twisting her hands in nervous embarrassment.

"Leala! Is something wrong? Can I help you?"

"I didn't mean to disturb you and Alaina, Cole, but I wonder if I could come in and talk with you for just a few moments." Her voice was unsure and hesitant.

"Of course!" He stood aside as Alaina donned her slippers and shrugged into her robe that she had left on the foot of the bed. She swung around her own favorite rocking chair for Leala and, once her aunt was comfortable, went to pour a small sherry from the crystal decanter that sat on a table in the room.

"I seem to remember your preference for a glass of wine, Aunt Leala." She smiled softly as she offered the glass.

"Oh, Alaina child, you will never know how much of a start you gave me that evening you came to New Orleans. Those filthy clothes! Your beautiful hair all chopped off! And with a bold Yankee officer in my own parlor!" Leala smiled and laid a hand on Cole's arm in gentle apology. "It was purely scandalous. But you seem to have tamed the Yankee, your hair is more beautiful than ever, and you have learned to garb yourself in a better manner. I would say you won your portion of the war."

"You're kind, Aunt Leala," Alaina leaned against her husband's chest. "But I'm afraid Cole has done most of it. Why, he got them to drop all the charges against

Alaina MacGaren, and we even own Briar Hill now. We'll be going down late this autumn to look over everything, and Cole has even suggested that we build a house where we can spend some of our winter months. He's brought my life together again, Aunt Leala."

Cole slipped an arm about his wife's no-longer-slim waist. "I say it was your own spirit that refused to admit defeat, my love, and—"

"Enough!" Leala laughed and held up her hands in mock dismay. "I had trouble believing Tally when she said you were both madly in love with each other, but I can see she spoke aright. Heaven forbid that I should cause you to argue over your respective virtues. It is enough for me, Alaina child." She reached out to take the young woman's hand warmly. "If it is all right with both of you, Tally and I would like to stay until after the baby is born. Perhaps you would even forgive a doting old woman if she looks upon your baby as her own grandchild."

Tears came to Leala's eyes as Alaina assured her that her suggestion would not be taken amiss and that they were welcome to stay until the spirit moved them. She heaved a tremulous sigh.

"I fear that Angus might have had something to do with that awful arrangement. Am I correct?"

"Neither Alaina nor I wanted it," Cole conceded slowly, wanting to spare Leala the distress she was apparently suffering.

"I'm sorry for what my family did to you, Cole," she apologized disconcertedly. "And I beg you to forgive Angus and perhaps Roberta—if you can."

"Alaina and I are together now, and that's all that matters to me. Everything else is past and forgotten," he replied kindly.

"Thank you, Cole." She smiled uncertainly. "Had my daughter been less concerned about her own wants and desires, she might have been able to realize how fine a man she married."

Leala became nervous again. "But this is not why I came to you tonight. I have a chore which has chafed me much." Her hands trembled, and after trying to continue, she lifted the glass of sherry and drained it, coughing as if the mild wine seared her throat. *"Sacré bleu!"* she wheezed. "Oh, my!"

When she regained her breath, Leala clasped her hands tightly in her lap, sat up stiffly, drew a deep breath, and began resolutely.

"Several weeks ago I grew lonely in the house and decided to help at the store. Lord knows the place needed a good cleaning, and I was sorting out some old tin boxes that Angus had collected beneath his desk when I came across one that had something in it. I opened it and found this."

She fumbled beneath the folds of her robe and produced a fat brown packet which she handed to Cole. He opened it and looked within, then went to shake the contents out on the bed. Fresh, new bank notes fluttered out, making a small heap of green on the sheet.

Cole's voice was filled with amazement as he stated, "There must be better than ten, or maybe fifteen thousand dollars here."

"Nearly twenty," Leala corrected. "I found the bills in a bundle of letters Roberta had sent to Angus at the store. She bade her father hold the money for her and to secure it in some private place, not in a bank, against her return. She said that she had earned every cent of it, and that it was hers for when she came back to New Orleans. I—confronted Angus, and we had a terrible argument. He kept raving and accusing you of being some kind of thief and saying that Roberta had every right to whatever she had taken from you. He swore he was going to use the money to avenge her death somehow. I never did understand just what he was talking about." Leala stared down at her clasped hands in embarrassment. "Later I packed my bags, took some money from the store and this bundle, and went to Tally's. I had to return this to you, Cole. I just couldn't bear the thought of Roberta being a thief and stealing from her own husband. I know she wasn't what you had hoped for, Cole, but she was my baby, and I can't help blaming myself for all the trouble she caused for both of you."

As Leala dissolved into sobs, Alaina knelt beside her, placing an arm across the woman's shoulders as tears swam in her own eyes.

"Aunt Leala," Alaina murmured softly, "you mustn't blame yourself too much. The war did many cruel things to many people. Roberta was caught in the flower of her youth when she was expecting better things. She just wasn't able to deal with it."

Leala raised her tearful gaze to Alaina's face, then lifted a hand to fondly caress the other's cheek. "Thank you, Alaina. I won't call you child anymore. You're so much more than that now."

Leala drew out a kerchief, plied it, and drew a deep breath. "This has been such a burden." She smiled at Alaina and straightened her shoulders. "But I feel so much better now. I think I shall have a very good night's sleep."

Alaina went to the door with her aunt who paused halfway through the portal.

"Good-night, my dear." She kissed Alaina's cheek. "I shall make a special prayer of many blessings for you and yours." Then she was gone.

Alaina returned to the bed to find Cole staring at the money with a heavy frown. He rubbed his chin with the back of his hand.

"I can't imagine Roberta taking this much and my not knowing it!" He shuffled some into a stack and riffled it. "This money is crisp, new. I haven't seen money this fresh since—" He paused, a look of sudden dawning coming over his face. He tossed the money with the rest and strode from the bedroom, leaving a puzzled Alaina to slip into bed alone. She heard his feet on the stairs, then the squeak of the study door. In a moment he was back to display for her three ten-dollar notes.

"These are from the gardener," he stated and placed the bills near his pillow. Drawing up a footstool, he sat on it and proceeded to arrange the money neatly in rows on the bed and rearranging them as if to match some mysterious order. He formed them into stacks and each bundle was stiff and new, all but the last one which sagged sharply as if it had been folded in half. He showed it to her.

"This money was folded and perhaps stuffed in a pocket or purse. You see the bent edges?" Cole glanced up to receive her nod, though bemusement was still rampant in her eyes. "Now look." He lifted the three tens and placed them with that same stack. They bent alike. "Also, the serial numbers of these three match the rest. They are all in sequence."

"But what does it mean, Cole?"

"It means that probably both Roberta and the gardener had their hands on this money."

"But where did they get it if it was not from you?"

"That, madam, is a question I can only wonder about, or, at best, make wild conjectures as to where it came from."

He gathered all the money as he rose and laid it on the hearth. He doffed his garments, then flopped down on the bed, clasping his hands behind his head and staring thoughtfully into the shadows of the ceiling.

"Martin said the man came from Missouri," he mused aloud. "If he were a member of one of those gangs down there that are robbing trains and such, he might have brought some of the loot with him."

"But how did Roberta manage to get it away from him? Do you suppose he was her lover?"

"I cannot imagine Roberta stooping to entertain the family gardener. Besides, he was filthy, old and haggard, certainly not the sort she would have even flirted with. She hated the man!"

A warm form snuggled against his side, and a small, finely boned hand rubbed his chest and belly.

"Milord Yankee?" Her breath tickled his shoulder. "Are you going to think about Roberta and that money all night? Or are you going to set my jealousy to rest and hold and kiss me and assure me that even with a fat stomach, I'm the light and love of your life?"

Cole chuckled and brought the lamp close to blow it out, then rolled back into her embrace. He kissed her pert nose. "You're my everything, Alaina MacGaren Latimer, and just to prove that I think you're beautiful when you're carrying my child, I will keep your belly filled with many more for years to come."

Alaina leaned her head back and peered up at him with bright, twinkling eyes. "Every year, milord Yankee?"

Cole pondered the question a moment, then smiled down into the visage he loved so well. "Well, almost every."

Early the next morning Cole took the money to the sheriff and offered his theory to Martin. The bank notes only became another piece in the puzzle and lent no more to a solution than any other of the all-too-meager clues.

The memory of it dimmed, and the end of June flowed past like a dream for Alaina. Mrs. Hawthorne and Leala were with her constantly, and no action could she take without coming under their stern scrutiny and guidance as to what was best for the babe.

Her burden lowered, and her pace became labored and clumsy. She awaited her time with a growing expectation and daily inspected the nursery that all might be in readiness. Cole had set the men cleaning out the overgrown yard of the cottage and began to see patients in his father's old office. Braegar visited to complain that some of his patients were seeing Cole now and, after a cursory conference, agreed that Alaina was progressing as she should. He totally captivated the elder ladies with his brash rhetoric and his unpolished political opinions.

It was a pleasurable time for Alaina, and she lived every day fully with her unquenchable zest and enthusiasm. The Prochavski family came to stay on a brief sojourn from the north woods. When all the figures were in, the logging operation proved a profitable venture, and plans were made to continue it the next winter.

The Darveys were invited for an evening meal and graciously accepted the chance for a repast with the Southern visitors. After weeks of a closer seating order, Cole had escorted Alaina to her end of the table and reluctantly had taken his own chair at the far end. At least from there he had admitted that he had the best view of her, and for once, Braegar had chosen a place to Cole's right.

Carolyn left that evening, much amazed by the realization that Cole had changed. He was the man of old again, easy mannered, relaxed, gracious, and yet something more. His concern and care for Alaina was readily apparent even to a casual eye, and still, that was not the key. It was more that he was a man, whole, unhampered, self-assured, confident, made complete by the beautiful woman who now shared his life. He was no longer irascible and curt because, all of a sudden, life pleased him and wonderfully so. He did not doubt Alaina because Alaina left him no room for doubt. He was once again a most handsome man in every way, and at his side, Alaina, even with her hour near, was a woman in the finest and fullest interpretation of the title.

It was during the next evening's meal that a low growl

echoed in the room, and all eyes turned to Soldier who had been dozing just inside the dining room doorway. Now he raised his head, and his ears stood alertly erect.

"Someone's coming," Cole observed.

A moment later the rapid approach of horse's hooves confirmed his statement and brought the Latimers and their two guests to a waiting silence. Heavy footsteps trod across the porch, and a loud pounding sounded upon the door. When Miles answered the demanding knock, Angus Craighugh pushed his way through with a gruff announcement. "I was directed here and informed that this is where Major Latimer resides. Is that true?"

"Doctor and Mrs. Latimer live here, sir." Miles looked the rumpled, red-faced man over with some distaste. One who intruded into his employer's house with such callousness was certainly no gentleman. "Is it your desire to see Doctor Latimer?"

Leala had come to her feet in surprise when her husband entered the house, and now she sank back into her chair and sat with her hands folded as she stared down at them. Sensing her aunt's dismay, Alaina quickly rose from her seat and hurried to the wide doors of the dining room.

"Uncle Angus?" she questioned softly, amazed by his disheveled appearance. He was thinner than she had ever known him to be, and he looked haggard and tired. He had obviously been traveling long and hard. His hair was mussed and unkempt, as if it had not been combed for some time, and there was no sign of a hat on his person. For a usually neatly dressed man, he was a terrible sight. His cravat hung loose about the open collar of his shirt, and his shoes were scuffed and dirty.

At the sound of her voice, he turned, and then stared much agog, his gaze lowering to her rounded belly. His face reddened, and his eyes seemed to protrude forth as he glared. Taking several halting steps toward her, he made an effort to speak through the grinding sneer that twisted his lips. He was almost on her when the words broke through with pure rage.

"You filthy little trollop! It didn't take you long to fall into his bed, did it?"

Incensed, he was oblivious to the horrified gasps he drew from the table, but as he pulled back his arm to avenge his sense of outraged justice upon the girl, quick footsteps sounded behind him, and he was seized by two very capable hands and hauled backward away from Alaina. He was spun about to face blazing blue eyes that bore into him mercilessly.

"Be careful that you never raise your hand to my wife again." Cole ground out the warning. "And if you were anything besides the besotted fool you are, I'd have it out with you here and now. You have abused the privileges of a guest, which you may deem a fair turnabout, but I decry the fact, for the one abused in your house was not the one who claimed it. In my befogged stupor, I allowed you to commit an act of which all of us have been acutely rueful. I warn you now, sir, for the good of all those present, that henceforth when you enter this house or tread upon any of my lands, you strive most heartily to be gentle of tongue and mild of manner—and most respectful to my wife."

"I will not be respectful of a harlot and a thief!" Angus railed.

Cole's eyes narrowed dangerously. "Be careful, man. You slander what I hold most precious to me. She was a virgin when I took her, and she's never taken a cent that was not hers!"

"You are the thief!" Angus glowered.

"Oh, Angus, give it up!" Leala wrung her hands and wailed. "It was Roberta who was the thief. She stole the money from Cole!"

"It was stolen money long before that! It was part of the Yankee payroll money that was taken from the riverboat in New Orleans. Did you not hear me?"

"I think we had better discuss this at some length, Angus," Cole said and reached out to take the man's arm.

"Stay away from me!" Angus bawled as he clawed for the small revolver tucked into his waistband. Just as quickly Cole caught the hand that grasped the weapon and forced the older man's arm upward until the weapon was pointed toward the ceiling. He seized the man's lapel in his other hand.

"Angus! Listen to me!" he barked. "There was another time when you waved a gun at me, and I have suffered much chagrin because I did not take it from you and seek the truth then. You must understand that the money Roberta sent to you was not mine. We found a dead man buried in the rose garden this spring, and he had some of the same bills on him. I suspect that Roberta got the money from him, but I didn't know where he had gotten it."

Angus's bitterness remained unchecked as his sneer betrayed. "Now a blemish is put on my daughter's name."

"You have had your time of blustering, Angus, and I will tolerate no more." Cole dragged the pistol from the man's hand and placed it on the mantel as Leala came out of her chair.

"And I will tolerate no more!" She was furious as she stepped around the table to face her husband. Angus sagged into an empty seat near the door, his face crumpling, his ire dwindling into defeat. "You followed me the depth of the country, outraged because I had taken money you had planned to use against Cole. You came here athundering on your horse in the night with your all-vengeful manhood astir and dare attack Alaina because she had not held herself from a man she loves. Roberta was my baby, too, Angus, and she was so pretty and so fine. But, Angus, you have to realize that she was not a nice person. All our high-minded thoughts about our daughter were not valid. She tricked Cole. She tricked and used Alaina. She tricked and used us. Now you come here with a violent intent and claim to be my husband. Have I had a husband this last year? A man who winds his way home trekking from one tavern to another and on the way sampling from any handy bottle? Was it my husband who stumbled into our bedroom most every night with the reek of whiskey heavy on his breath? I think not." She shook her head slowly. "It was some stranger whom I saw but knew not."

Tears suddenly blurred her vision, and she drew a ragged breath. "Perhaps if I hadn't been so lenient when Roberta—gave herself—to one of her young boyfriends—"

Angus looked up in surprise.

"Oh, yes, I knew she was not—the virgin in Cole's bed. She told me about her friend, and when she promised never again, I didn't even tell you. I know many other things about her that give me nothing but pain. But Angus"—she paused until he met her eyes again—"I'm going to remember her as a sweet, beautiful child and try my best to forget the rest."

Mrs. Hawthorne moved to Leala's side and took the

now-sobbing woman against her bosom. Angus raised his head briefly as he felt her stare.

"You too, eh, Tally?" he muttered.

"I think you've let your grief befuddle your mind, Angus." Mrs. Hawthorne stated bluntly. "I am of a mind that the sooner you get yourself up out of the mud of your wallowing self-pity, the sooner you will begin to enjoy life again. Leala is right. Forget the hurts. You can't change the past. Get out of your hole and live the rest of your life like it means something."

"Why should I, when it doesn't?" he replied sourly.

Tally cocked her head to one side and stared down at him. "That's your choice, Angus. Just don't blame the rest of us if we don't agree."

"Cole?" Alaina's plaintive appeal was barely noticeable to anyone but her husband who turned quickly at the soft summons. His eyes widened as he found his wife half crouched against the door holding an arm over her stomach. "Cole, I think it has started."

A startled hush fell over the room as Cole bent and lifted his wife into his arms. Briefly he turned and caught Mrs. Hawthorne's eye.

"Tally, will you rouse the household for me and inform the servants that Mrs. Latimer's time has come? They'll know what to do."

Cole mounted the stairs with his tender burden, taking them two at a time, and shouldered open the bedroom door. Running footsteps came behind him, and he half turned to see Leala enter the room and wipe her tears dry.

"Pull down the covers," he bade and waited until Leala had hastily complied before placing Alaina gently upon the cool sheets. He yanked off his coat and vest, throwing them aside, then jerked off his cravat and opened his shirt.

"You'll be needing fresh linens, Cole," Leala stated, taking a firm hand in the management of the proceedings. "Where will I find them?"

"In there." Cole nodded to the bathing chamber and bent to remove his wife's shoes and stockings.

Alaina bit her bottom lip as her belly hardened and contracted, then a moment later a small sigh of relief slipped from her as the pain ebbed. She smiled tenderly at her husband's concern and reached out to caress his lean cheek.

"I love you," she whispered.

Cole caught her fingers and pressed them against his lips. "I find myself suddenly atremble, Alaina. A score and more of babies have I guided into this world, but none frightens me like this one."

"You'll do fine, milord Yankee," she assured with soft lights of love shining in her eyes. "And what with being a witness to the birth of Gretchen's babe, if you err," she teased him with a delicious little grin, "I shall set you aright. We have a child coming into the world, Doctor Latimer, and we'll bring it in together." Her gaze became soft and probing as she whispered. "I trust you—beyond anyone else."

Thusly fortified, Cole proceeded with the best of his knowledge and his experience, though he could not detach his heart and emotions from the slim girl who labored and strained, silently gritted her teeth at the pain and came through each one to smile reassuringly up at him. While Mrs. Hawthorne and Leala busied themselves about the room in preparation for the birth, he gripped the slender hands, unaware of the sky lightening to a dusty blue or the mantel clock striking an early morning hour.

As the grinding agony cut through her once again, Alaina caught the twisted spindles of the headboard and bore down as her husband gently directed. Her face contorted in a grimace of victory as she at last felt the baby's head slide from her, and she panted, relaxing, waiting for another spasm to come so she could push the child completely from her. There was a weak, snuffled cry from a voice she had never heard before, and she thrilled with the knowledge that it came from her firstborn.

Cole's hand pressed on her belly, while the other supported the child's head. "We're doing fine, Alaina. Bear down hard now. It's coming."

As the pain washed from her with the birth of the child, she heard Aunt Leala's exhilarated cry.

"It's a girl!"

"She's beautiful!" Mrs. Hawthorne exclaimed in awe.

Cole cradled his daughter into his two hands and grinned broadly as he placed her on her mother's belly.

He peered questioningly at his wife. "Glynis Lynn Latimer?"

Alaina raised her hand and hesitantly touched her loudly squalling child, blinking away tears. "After my mother?"

Cole nodded. "I thought it would be appropriate."

"Glynis Lynn Latimer," Alaina repeated softly. "It has a nice ring to it."

Chapter 42

ANGUS Craighugh had been forgotten by the members of the family, and had been shown to a guest room by the butler who stoically laid out borrowed sleepwear and set Peter to preparing a bath for him. In the quiet, dark solitude of his room, Angus had much to think and ponder on. He had never struck a woman in his life, but just a few hours before, had almost slapped his niece, and she with child. Though at his anxious questions, he had been assured by the butler that Alaina's time had not come early, he still worried and fretted because, in his own mind, he had caused the onset of her labor. He agonized over that fact as he awaited some word or announcement from the Latimers' bedchamber. Considering what he deserved, he thought that Cole had been relatively gentle with him and certainly lenient to let him stay in his house.

In the morning Angus waited in the parlor for the others to wake from their belated slumber and caught the excited whispers of the servants.

"A girl!" "Small!" "Healthy!" "Mrs. Latimer's doing well." "Sleeping!"

Thank God, Angus thought, clasping his hands tightly together on his knees. He would never have forgiven himself if something had not been right.

Sensing a presence in the open doorway of the parlor, Angus slowly raised his gaze. A small, slender girl, barely seven or so, in a pert muslin gown, with long, shining dark hair and luminous dark eyes stood against the doorframe timidly watching him.

Angus blinked and slowly leaned back in his chair. She looked so much like Roberta had when she was a child, it almost startled him. The child sidled around the corner and seated herself in a chair facing him, politely folding her hands and looking at him with those large, beautiful eyes.

Angus cleared his throat and self-consciously rubbed his short, thick-fingered hands along his trousers. "I don't remember seeing you here before."

Mindy cocked her head wonderingly and slowly grinned. It was a matter of fact that she could say the same about him.

"I'm—Mrs. Latimer's uncle," he clarified his identity.

Mindy glanced in the direction of the staircase in the hall and scratched her slim nose. Angus sat forward in his chair almost eagerly.

"Whose little girl are you?"

A small, oval-framed photograph sat on the round table beside the child's chair, and she gestured to it, smiling timidly. Angus rose and went to peer more closely at the picture, then raised his brows in wonder. It was a photograph of Alaina and Cole together. He returned to his seat and stared blankly at the girl until a brief moment later, a discreet clearing of the throat brought his attention to the door where Miles had come to stand.

"Annie was wondering, sir, if you would be wanting to eat now. The others are still sleeping, and it will just be you and the girl."

Angus glanced at the child. "Would you care to join me for breakfast—ah—" He waited expectantly, but Mindy hid a silent giggle behind her hand.

"Mindy, sir," Miles supplied the information. "And you'll not likely get anything from her. She hasn't talked since the gardener brought her here."

"The gardener?"

"Her uncle, sir, but I'm afraid he's passed on now. Doctor and Mrs. Latimer have taken the child in. She's an orphan, sir."

Angus rose and extended his hand to the child in an invitation for her to join him. "I had a daughter once." There was a warmer light in his eyes as he spoke, a spark of life that had been long dead. "She was a beauty, just like you."

Mindy walked beside him to the dining room, her small hand tucked comfortably into his. She smiled uncertainly up at the man as he glanced down at her. It was a good beginning for Angus.

Glynis Lynn spent her first afternoon beneath her father's fascinated perusal. He had never seen such a beautiful baby girl in all of his years as a doctor. Of course, the fact that she belonged to him could have made him somewhat prejudiced, but he'd still argue the point with anyone.

He glanced up as Alaina stirred in the bed beside the cradle, and the gray eyes opened slowly to find him smiling at her.

"She has your nose and mouth," he stated fondly.

Alaina's smile was tender and soft. "How can you tell?"

Cole came around the cradle and sat on the edge of the bed beside her. "Because it's my fondest wish that she should have them."

"Do you get everything you wish for?"

"I got you," he pointed out, as if that ended the argument. "And having you was my most cherished desire."

A timid rap sounded at the door, and Cole went to the portal to find Angus sheepishly waiting in the hall.

"Captain Latimer—uh—Major—Doctor Latimer—"

"Try Cole," his host urged.

"Cole." Angus nodded and gained a small measure of confidence. "I've been thinking for most of the night and day, unable to make heads or tails of it all. Of the money, I mean, and of Roberta and everything else that's happened since we first met. I began to pray—" He chuckled. "I haven't done that in a long time, you know. But it seemed to clear my head. I know what a fool I've been now, and I just had to apologize for my stupidity and for hurting Alaina. I beg your forgiveness."

Cole smiled wryly and extended his hand. He never thought he would be hearing those words from Angus, and clasping hands in new-found friendship somehow made everything right between them for the first time. "Being a fool at times is the whim of man. I fear I've suffered much from it myself. How else would we learn to be wise?"

Angus rubbed his stubbled cheek with the palm of his hand and seemed uncertain once more. "I think—" He paused, then tried again. "I think I'll go talk to Leala for a bit."

Cole nodded in agreement. "Now *that* is being wise!"

The Craighughs and Mrs. Hawthorne departed the first

week after the delivery of the baby. Angus had left store and all to come after his wife, and Leala smiled as she admitted to herself that it was something rare in the history of their marriage for Angus to put aside the making of money to a later time. Angus was much taken with Mindy, and as he left, he anxiously urged the Latimers to visit soon and bring the child with them.

After their visit and the birth of Glynis Lynn, the house seemed less gloomy for Alaina, yet when the sweltering days of August came upon them, the sun and hot, dry winds made a virtual oven of the cliff manse. Even the usually unruffled Miles broke into a sweat, but Alaina knew how to deal with the heat. She loosened her bodice, rolled up her sleeves, and went on about her affairs of motherhood and wife.

In contrast to the hill house, the cottage was cool beneath its towering elms, and more and more Alaina was wont to take Mindy and Glynis and spend her hours of the day near Cole in the shaded rooms. She ordered a thorough cleaning of the place and joined the help in bringing the furnishings to a rich luster or a beauty comparable to its former state. The cottage had a solid feel about it. The floors were thick oak or, as in the kitchen, slabbed stones. Where the hill manor rattled its windows at the slightest breeze and groaned and seemed to creak at the lightest settling of a moth, the cottage was firm and secure, and one could forget the weather outside, be it gale or drenching storm, steaming heat or chilling frost. It had been built with care to last several lifetimes, and Alaina grew attached to its sprawling quietness. She felt more at home in its tasteful decor and subtle elegance than she could ever do in the overly embellished manor on the hill.

It was during an evening meal that Cole brought up the possibility of moving down to the cottage, now that she had become so well ensconced in it. He had noticed the increasing supply of baby garments and towels and linens, not to mention the several changes of clothes for Alaina in the armoire of the master bedroom upstairs.

His announcement left Alaina wondering if he had access to her inner thoughts, and she tried to subdue some of her bubbling excitement over the idea as she replied in agreement. "I think that's a fine idea, milord Yankee."

Cole gestured to Mrs. Garth to bring her attention to

the fact that he was waiting for her to pour his usual after-dinner brandy. She seemed to have been more startled by his decision than Alaina.

"Excuse me, sir," she hastened to apologize and splashed a meager amount of the liquor into the snifter. It had been the doctor himself who had chided her on her penchant for filling his glass close to the brim and now often totally declined, even preferring to sip coffee without additives.

"Have you given any thought as to what you'll be doing with this place?" Alaina asked from her chair at the table, which was now close to his.

"I've a thought that it might be made into an acceptable hospital, certainly more worthy than some of the pest-houses I've seen."

The decanter rattled against the snifter, splashing brandy over the table. Quickly dabbing at it with a cloth, Mrs. Garth blotted the table linen and mumbled an apology before she took herself from the room. Cole peered after her curiously, a wondering brow raised. But he forgot the woman as Alaina, now in the privacy of the dining room, slipped into his lap, winning his complete and immediate attention.

"Oh, Cole, I think that's an excellent idea!" she exclaimed eagerly, wrapping her arms about his neck. "And Braegar can help you. Why, the servants and I can start carrying clothes and things down to the cottage tomorrow, and by the end of the week, or a little more, we can be living down there. Then you can have carpenters in here tearing down walls and opening up some of the rooms for wards. In no time you'll be taking in your first hospital patient."

Cole had suddenly lost interest in the subject. The scant layers of petticoat and muslin gown, which she had adopted for wearing in the heat, allowed him to feel the soft woman beneath. Since the birth of their daughter, he had bided his time until the day they could become once again intimate lovers. It was nearing September, a good month and a half since that event, and he was hard pressed to restrain himself. The pressure of her derriere against his loins set the hot blood stirring, warming his desires.

"Do you realize, madam, how long it's been since we've made love?" He crinkled his brows at her as she turned to gape at him in surprise, taken completely off guard by his sudden change in topics. He toyed with the buttons of her bodice. "I have another excellent idea if you'd be of a mind to hear me out."

Alaina leaned against his lightly shirted chest, and her hand strayed within the garment to caress the firm muscles and furry expanse, feeling the heavy thud of his heartbeat. Her breath brushed against his ear. "Could we discuss this more in the privacy of our bedroom, milord Yankee?"

In the next days they gained a patient for the hospital even before Cole chose to announce his decision to the servants. Rebel Cummings visited with Braegar and, during dinner, listened with apparently meager interest as they discussed the possibility of the men combining their skills in such a manner. Then as they were preparing to leave, she suddenly and without warning swooned, conveniently into Cole's arms. No amount of medical know-how roused her; smelling salts only made her choke and cough and faint dead away again.

Alaina observed the whole thing rather brittlely as the woman all but wallowed against Cole. She was tempted to give Rebel a good pinch to bring her around, but refrained, being a respected doctor's wife. Instead, she stood back and watched, unaffected by the furor. Braegar anxiously insisted that Rebel shouldn't be moved, and a guest room was provided for her. It was not that Alaina was hardhearted or unsympathic to the weaknesses or maladies of others, but she had seen better acting at a Sunday supper with a handful of stiff-necked biddies doing the honors. She didn't know the woman's game, but if it was a play for Cole, Alaina was determined to put aside such advances in the best and quickest way possible. A quiet, heart-to-heart talk with Rebel would do for starters if the need came.

Rebel stayed a course of three days and left after a night of confrontation with Cole Latimer. It seemed she had a tendency to walk about during the wee, tender hours of morning and, in so doing, mistakingly happened into her hosts' bedchamber shortly after Cole roused Alaina from sleep with warm, ardent kisses. If Rebel had gotten herself lost while making her way through the house, then she was brought sharply to awareness of her whereabouts by the sight of the moonlit figures clasped together on the bed. The naked curve of the man's back and the silvery limbs entwining him made it all too obvious to her that she had intruded at a most intimate time.

Cole's savage bark made her jump and skitter from the room, and no amount of her fumbling, embarrassed excuses about how sick she was or getting lost in the house appeared to cool his ire. Olie was ordered to bring around the carriage the first thing in the morning. Declining breakfast and avoiding meeting Cole's frown, Rebel mounted into the conveyance and left.

The sun rose in a clear sky on the second Tuesday in September, but long, high streamers of clouds stretched across the sky before the day had fully crept from its cradle. Alaina had not yet joined Cole at the cottage as was her habit, for the baby was still sleeping and had not yet roused for her morning feeding.

Alaina bathed and dressed in preparation for the short journey down the hill. They would be taking up residence in the cottage on a more permanent basis before the end of the week, and by the beginning of the next, carpenters would be admitted into the hill house to begin their work.

Sensing a presence at the bathing room door, Alaina turned, brushing her hair, then halted in surprise as she saw Mrs. Garth standing in the doorway, holding Glynis in her arms. It was the first time the housekeeper had deigned to touch the baby, but for some strange reason, Alaina found the sight less than soothing.

"I have something to show you, madam," the woman stated in flat, dry tones. "Would you come with me?"

Abruptly Mrs. Garth turned, went again through the bathing chamber, and crossed to the hall door of the nursery. A sense of wariness leadened Alaina's feet, and she was slow to react.

"Well, come along," Mrs. Garth commanded as she paused in the portal and glanced back. Her voice was almost curt. "We don't have all day."

"Let me take Glynis," Alaina urged. "I'll follow you in a moment after I've seen to her diapering."

"It can't wait. Come along."

Alaina realized she had no choice as the housekeeper carried the baby into the hall. Much to Alaina's amazement, they entered Roberta's room, and Mrs. Garth went without hesitation to the mirror set in the alcove. The woman raised a hand to press the upper corner of the silvered panels, and Alaina's jaw slackened in surprise as the mirror shifted beneath the pressure of her hand. It opened to reveal a dark passageway into which Mrs. Garth entered. She turned in an invitation for Alaina to follow, and hesitantly the younger woman did so. Alaina paused at the opening. The mirrored panel had opened onto a dark, square shaft where a flight of stairs hugged the wall and wound endlessly downward. There seemed only a black, bottomless pit beneath the stairs, ending in shadows through which her gaze could not penetrate. Glancing upward, Alaina saw that the stairs extended to the attic level, and above that, a ladder reached to a small door which could only have led to the widow's walk. A tiny window high in the peak gave a weary light to the shaft.

Mrs. Garth had descended a flight and stood with her free hand on a butt of timber that jutted from the wall.

"Are you coming, Mrs. Latimer?" The woman's impatient question sounded hollow in the tower.

"Shouldn't we call Cole or some of the men?" Alaina asked in sudden, worried distress. She bit a trembling lip as she glanced at her sleeping daughter, desperately wanting her back safe in her arms.

"There is much for you to see below, and we don't have time to waste. Come along!"

This last was a command if Alaina had ever heard one. Meekly she followed, for the narrow stair was no place to engage in a struggle for her child. As soon as she cleared the portal, Mrs. Garth turned the timber butt, and with a rattle of chains and pulleys, the panel swung shut behind them. Alaina blinked at the sudden darkness. There was a scratch of a match, then a lantern's wick flared into a brighter light. Holding the lantern high with one hand and cradling the child in the other arm, Mrs. Garth hurried down the winding stairs, leaving Alaina no choice but to follow. A steady draft blew upward past them and seemed to carry minute sounds, muted and distant. They went ever downward until the wooden walls of the shaft turned to stone. Shortly, they became rough and uneven, as if the tunnel were a natural flue in the cliff. The draft carried a damp smell, and the sounds became louder. Alaina glanced up and saw that the small window was only a dot of light far above them. She could only guess that they were well beneath the basement of the house and probably close to the water level.

The walls were wet further down, and from the dark shadows, occasional high-pitched, clicking squeals sounded. Then Alaina realized with a sense of forboding that there were bats clinging in the sheltered crevices of the rock wall.

When they came to the floor of the shaft, a thick wooden door blocked further passage. Mrs. Garth leaned on an upright lever, moving it to one side until, with a clank of chains, the door began to move. When it was open enough for her to squeeze past, she slipped through and waited for Alaina to do likewise. Once on the other side, Mrs. Garth pushed another lever, but frowned sharply as the door left a crack the width of a man's hand.

"Blasted thing! Never did work right!" the housekeeper fussed. Leaving it, she took up the lantern again and hurried on her way. The floor sloped sharply downward, and a new source of light shone from ahead.

Alaina's feet lagged as she glanced about her. Along the walls of the cave dimly lit with lanterns all sorts of merchandise and boxes of goods and wooden barrels were stacked several layers deep. Behind grated doors of a small side chamber sat small kegs of gunpowder and several tiers deep of long boxes with the stenciled shape of a rifle stamped on the side.

"Rifles? Machinery?" Alaina murmured in awe and suddenly remembered Cole telling her about a sternwheeler being lost on the river. It had carried such cargo. Could it be that they had river pirates right in their own basement?

"This way, if you please, Mrs. Latimer." The housekeeper's voice had become almost insulting in its arrogance. "Just a little ways farther."

Mrs. Garth led the way into a small cave that appeared to have been scraped from the soft sandstone to form a rough room. Going directly in, the woman laid the baby on a narrow cot that sat close against the wall. Alaina gave no pause but ran to her daughter, lifting the small form against her shoulder. Then a loud clang behind her made her spin about, and she saw Mrs. Garth fastening a large lock on an ornate gate that transformed the narrow room into a prison cell.

"What do you think you're doing?" Alaina cried indignantly. "Let me out of here!"

Mrs. Garth leered at her prisoner as she slowly unbuttoned the neck of her prim black gown until she revealed the upward swell of full breasts crushed into flatness. She reached up and loosened the pins from the sober bun of hair, shaking it free and letting it fall around her shoulders. The visage was no longer the dull emotionless face of Mrs. Garth, but had taken on new life. Only the life it displayed was bitter, hot red, barely repressed contempt.

"I've done enough bowing and scraping," she sneered. "I'm taking back what was mine from the beginning, Madam Latimer."

Mindy's small hand pressed anxiously at the mirrored glass. She could see herself but not those who had passed beyond its barrier, and that's what fretted her. She had been dressing herself in her bedroom when she heard Mrs. Garth's brusque commands and Alaina's worried reply. Her curiosity had been piqued, and she had followed the sound of their voices that had led her from her room into the dreaded red chamber that had been Roberta's, but only in time to see Mrs. Garth disappear with the baby through the strange opening in the wall. Her sudden anxiety had become dismayed terror as the adored Alaina entered into the dark, frightening maw, and before Mindy could reach the passage, the mirrored jaws had closed behind Alaina. In frenzied fear, Mindy pushed and clawed at the reflecting glass, but it would not open to her. Helplessly she dragged a chair close to the doorway leading into the hall and sat down to wait and watch, ever ready to skitter into hiding if the mirrored door opened again. Agonizingly she counted the slow chiming of the tall clock that echoed through the house from the downstairs vestibule, and each hour it struck she became more anxious. The long striking of twelve was the time she and the Latimers usually returned from the cottage for the noon meal, and she knew that Cole would be coming shortly. He would know what to do. He would see that Alaina and Glynis were safe.

It had been a long wait for a small girl, but on dashing to the window after the hour struck, she saw the nice-faced Cole riding toward the house. Her tiny, slippered feet carried her swiftly down the stairs, and she was on the porch, breathless and chafing with impatience, when the doctor passed Peter who was still waiting on the front stoop to take the mistress to the cottage. Only, Alaina had never come down.

Peter shrugged to the doctor's inquiry. He had been told to come around nine to fetch the mistress, but as anybody could see, he was still there.

Occupied with his thoughts, Cole hurried into the house, never noticing Mindy tugging at his vest. It was unlike Alaina to keep Peter waiting the whole morning, and he was suddenly concerned that she might be ill. He took the stairs two at a time, but found the nursery and their bedchamber empty.

"Alaina?" He walked the hall, pausing at the doors to check the other rooms. "Alaina, where are you?"

His polished boots were a blur on the stairs as he rapidly descended them, brushing past Mindy as she came up. He pushed open the swinging doors of the kitchen and questioned Annie, but the cook only shrugged.

"Not since breakfast, sir."

Mindy halted in her descent as Cole came charging past her up the stairs again, and she stood in trembling frustration, her small hands clenched. She turned angrily and followed the not-so-nice Cole upstairs again. She met him as he came out of the nursery, having once more made a complete circuit of the master bedroom and bath.

"Mindy!" He knelt to her level. "Have you seen Alaina?"

The girl smiled and vigorously nodded. She caught his hand and led him directly into Roberta's room, straight across it to the mirror. She pushed at the middle of the glass and glanced back to see if he understood.

Cole nodded in distraction. "Yes, Mindy. It's a nice mirror, but I've got to find Alaina and Glynis now."

Mindy pointed frantically at her reflection, but dumbfaced Cole had already turned away and was leaving her. Quick tears of distress and disappointment filled her eyes, and she clenched her thin hands into fists again. She remembered adored Alaina explaining about heroes and wise men. Adored Alaina had said that anybody could do things that were easy, but heroes and wise men did things that were so difficult, nobody else would try them.

Well! Mindy wasn't a wise man, but she might have to

be a hero if nice-faced Cole didn't listen to her! Listen to her! Listen! Listen, Cole! Please!

The tears spilled down her cheeks, and her single sob was only a voiceless gasp. She wiped at her cheek angrily and went again to find him. He was questioning Peter.

"No, sir!" Peter shook his head. "Like I told you, she said she wanted the wagon brought up this morning about nine. I've been here since then, and here I still am."

"She didn't come out or anything?" Cole's scowl took on the deeper creases of his growing worry. What if she had gone out the back, walked along the steep cliff? Fallen? Or maybe she was in the woods with a sprained ankle, or a broken leg, and unable to carry the child. Maybe even unconscious! The vision of her and the baby lying helpless somewhere set his mind on fire. He brushed away Mindy's plucking hand and went to seek out Miles.

"No, sir. The last I saw of her was when she went upstairs after breakfast. She did not come down."

Cole knew Miles's alert ear for the comings and goings about the house and could question the man no further. He brushed away Mindy's hands, but they came back to seize the back of his vest firmly.

"Not now, Mindy!" He pried her fingers loose and didn't notice the frenzied working of her lips as she silently begged him to come. "I've got to find Alaina! Don't you understand? Alaina and the baby have disappeared!"

He pushed the clutching girl away and strode into the dining room, his mind ranging over all sorts of horrors.

"Peter!" he bellowed suddenly.

The lad appeared at the door before the echoes died.

"Take the wagon and go fetch Olie and Saul, and keep a good eye out for any sign of Mrs. Latimer along the way. Bring the men back as soon as you can, but check the cottage on the way down to see if she's there."

Peter ran out the door, and the wagon rumbled away as the boy urged the horses into their fastest gait.

Cole paced the floor, his mind recklessly crossing bridges before they were built. He stood at the window overlooking the river and searched for any glimpse of movement along the brow of the cliff.

Annie stood in the hall with Miles, her meal forgotten, a spoon still in her hand, while the butler nervously fumbled with his cravat until it was hopelessly awry.

"There's trouble brewin' in this house!" Annie brandished her spoon like a weapon. "The hackles on me neck is fair crawlin' with it."

Miles could only fidget in anxious vexation. The thought of the house or cottage without the vivacious presence of the mistress and the beautiful Latimers' baby numbed his mind.

A repeated thumping sound drew Cole's attention from the window. He turned to see Mindy beating her small fists on the table. When she saw that she had caught his eye, she stopped and suddenly made a rocking motion with her arms, then jabbed a finger behind her toward the stairs. She pointed upward and made a pushing motion with her hands.

Cole shook his head and tried to be patient. He spoke as softly as he could manage. "Mindy, I don't want to play with you now. I don't want to see the mirror again. Alaina and the baby are gone, and I don't know where. Please understand."

The girl nodded quickly, then pointed to herself, and repeated all the motions she had made before. Cole turned back to the windows to hide his irritation.

"Leave me be, Mindy."

The thumping began again and didn't cease until he whirled, his eyes clouded with anger. Then he saw the tears streaming unchecked down the small girl's face, and his ire dwindled. He could not speak the harsh retort that was on his lips.

Mindy stood, this time with her hands braced wide on the table as her thoughts went back. She remembered being tucked into a clump of brush and warned not to speak or cry out no matter what. She remembered the slow crumpling of her father and the rolling thunder of the smooth-bore trade muskets. She remembered the screams of her mother as the painted faces dragged her from the burning house. She remembered the dull thud of the shovel and the collapse of her uncle as he fell into the hole. Her mind stopped. Now, it was adored Alaina and the baby Glynis whose eyes said such nice things when Mindy leaned over the cradle. The time for silence was long past.

Mindy's mouth opened, and her lips twisted and her chest jerked with her effort, but all that came out were wheezing gasps. The gasps became sobs, and Mindy's hand slowly beat on the table with her frustration. The sobs grew louder until they racked the thin frame, and Cole, watching, knew not how to bring her peace. He came around the table and took the child into his arms. The strangled words first sounded as a whisper in his ear.

"Papa! Papa! Mama! Mama!" Suddenly Mindy pulled back. She grasped handfuls of hair on either side of his head as she looked into his eyes. Her lips worked, and the sounds struggled agonizingly forth.

"Na! Na! Ainya! Ainya!"

"Alaina?"

The small head nodded vigorously. "Nis! Nis! Inis!"

"Glynis?"

"Co! Cole!" She clenched her eyes tightly as she fought to clear her words. "Col! Come!" Tears streamed down her cheeks as she looked at him pleadingly. "Col! Come! Quick! Quick!"

She released his hair and grabbed his hand, jerking at it anxiously. "Col! Come quick!"

The dawning had come slowly, but it finally penetrated. She knew where Alaina was and was trying to tell him. Cole rose to his feet and let her lead him straight up the stairs and back to Roberta's room. Mindy returned to the mirror and spread her hands wide apart on it. She turned to look at Cole over her shoulder.

"Dor! Dor!"

"Dor?" Cole repeated slowly. "Door!"

Mindy leaned a shoulder against the mirror. "Door! Door! Open!"

"The mirror is a door, and Alaina has gone through it?"

Mindy nodded her head eagerly. "Inis! Inis!" She jabbed at the mirror.

Cole glanced around the edges of the mirror.

"Ar—Ar—Arth! Miz Arth!" Mindy slowly mouthed the strange sounds.

"Mrs. Garth?"Cole suddenly remembered that he had not seen the woman in his frantic tour around the house. He stepped close to the mirror and examined it from top to bottom. It had a lightly marbled silvering that marred the reflection, but there was no sign of hinges or knobs. He brushed aside the drapes that framed the mirror, then he noticed a small smudge of a handprint near the upper right corner. Placing his hand over the spot, he pushed, and the mirror moved an inch, no more. He pushed harder, and the silvered glass swung wide.

"Mindy!" Cole faced her. "Olie and Saul will be coming! Bring them up here and show them the doorway."

Mindy ran toward the door, then halted and faced him again. "Co?"

He was dragging a chair to block open the mirror, but paused.

"Minny lo' Ainya an' Inis." The words came slow and carefully.

Cole smiled gently. "I love them, too, Mindy. And Mindy? I love you, too. Thank you."

The girl's eyes glistened. She turned and was gone quickly from sight.

Taking a lamp from a bedside table, Cole passed through the opening and began his descent. If would-be skulkers were waiting for him, they'd be warned by the light. Without it, there was a threat of plunging headlong with an unwary step. Slowly, stealthily, he went down, it seemed, into the very pits of hell. A dim ray of light shone from the crack in the heavy door, and finding level footing, he turned down the wick. It was once again all blackness around him, except for the meager, dull glow that marked the passage. Carefully he crept down and found his way through the portal. His feet sought cautious footing on the slope. Lanterns glowed dimly here, but cast a pitiful amount of light. He paused to survey the cargo and quickly drew his own conclusions and then the small cell in the corner found his attention. The dejected figure within it was the one he knew and sought.

"Alaina?" he whispered and, stepping from the tunnel, found himself face to face with the grinning black who was called only by the name of Gunn. The man's fist shot forward, and the lights flashed in a bright flare of pain, then just as quickly faded into blackness.

Chapter 43

ALAINA'S scream died away in slow degrees as it echoed hauntingly through the cavern. Only a moment before she had been slumped listlessly on the cot beside the sleeping babe, confused and distraught by their present circumstances. Then Cole's whisper had come from the shadows surrounding the huge door, and hope and relief had flooded into her breast, only to be crushed cruelly by Gunn as he laid his massive fist forcefully against her husband's jaw. Now she pressed close to the bars of her prison, watching fearfully as the black lifted Cole into his arms. She had no doubt that Gunn could seriously injure or even kill a man with only a stroke or two from that brawny, hard-knuckled hand.

Mrs. Garth gestured to several men, who came running with her from the opposite end of the cave, hurriedly directing them through the portal that Cole had emerged from. Alaina heard their rapid footsteps in the room beyond and, a moment later, the sound of their heavy boots on the wooden stairs.

Mrs. Garth approached the iron gate, waving Alaina back away from the bars as she withdrew the key from her pocket. Seeing Alaina's gaze fastened anxiously on the limp form in Gunn's arms and noting her obvious consternation, the housekeeper laughed mockingly. "He's all right, Mrs. Latimer. A bit shaken perhaps, but nothing serious. Gunn can be quite gentle—when he wants to be."

She pulled wide the door, and Gunn stepped through with his burden. He dumped Cole carelessly on the cell floor, and Alaina was immediately beside her husband, taking his head in her lap and bending close over him to carefully scrutinize the bruise already darkening on his lean jaw. She had nothing in the way of a balm to apply to it, for her captors had not even allowed her food or water since locking her in this damp, stone prison. She could only be grateful that Glynis had not had to suffer. The baby had contentedly nursed from her breast, played for a time on her lap, then had drifted off again for another session of sleeping.

Mrs. Garth smirked as she considered the attentions the younger woman bestowed on her husband. The slim fingers repeatedly smoothed the tan hair or caressed his cheek, much like a lovebird preening and comforting her injured mate.

"That's the way, dearie," she sneered. "Tend him real good. You might as well have your fun while you can. It will end all too swiftly."

Alaina gripped her floundering emotions with a tight rein of determination. The appearance of Gunn had roused fears she could not afford to entertain. His presence had left little doubt that Jacques DuBonné was a central part of this pack of miscreants. The woman's insinuations added to her growing qualms, threatening to totally destroy her courage and composure.

Feeling helpless in her plight, Alaina could only watch in despair as Mrs. Garth swung the door closed behind Gunn, but as the woman started to lock it, the black tapped her shoulder with a blunt finger.

"Wait!" The single word was not a request but a command, and Mrs. Garth paused, raising a haughty brow to the man. When he walked away without explanation, she glared at his back.

"That filthy black never did learn his place," she muttered angrily when he was out of earshot. "One of these days he'll turn bad and be the death of us all."

Gunn came back with a wooden bucket of water and a handful of rich, embroidered towels which were initialed with an elaborate L, an apparent appropriation done well before now. He swung the gate open with his elbow and placed his offerings on the floor beside Alaina, then straightened, towering above her until she glanced up questioningly. The black's gaze was one of curiosity rather than threat. Reaching down, he felt Alaina's upper arm as if testing the flesh on it, his long fingers easily encompassing the slimness of it. A low chuckle rumbled deep in his chest.

"Little boy-girl good woman! Strong! Give girl first! Good! Get many goats when man comes to marry. Next one boy. Big! Strong! Like Gunn!"

Abruptly he turned and, without further comment, left the cell and departed quickly from sight. Mrs. Garth clanged the door shut and locked it, commenting caustically, "You must have impressed the big ox."

Alaina dipped a towel into the water, wrung it between her hands, and placed it on her husband's chin before she deemed to glance up in question to the woman's statement. "Why do you say that?"

The woman shrugged. "I've never heard him say more than three words to anybody else but Jack."

Alaina sat back on her heels and made an attempt to reason with the woman while Jacques was still in absence. "Really, Mrs. Garth. You should realize that if my husband found his way down here, there will be others coming to help us."

Mrs. Garth scoffed. "It seems to me if there had been others, dearie, then they would have come with him. But no matter. They will be taken care of, should they appear."

"Do you honestly think you can keep us down here forever?" Alaina asked incredulously. "Be sensible, Mrs. Garth—"

"Mrs. Garth! Mrs. Garth!" the woman mimicked in a mock falsetto. "How I loathe that name!" A snide smile twisted her lips, and her superior demeanor drew Alaina's attention as she stated, "I think that it's about time you call *me* Mrs. Latimer."

Surprise touched Alaina's face briefly, but giving the woman a widely doubtful stare, she responded with a bit of her own sarcasm. "Oh? And is your name also Roberta?"

The woman's dark eyes narrowed and glared. "You mistake me, Alaina," she replied, using the more casual address contemptuously. "I was never Cole Latimer's wife, but his stepmother, Tamara Latimer, Frederick Latimer's second wife."

Suspicion became realization for Alaina. Of course! Her mind raced in ever broadening circles. Who could have known more about the secrets of the house than the woman who had had it built? Neither of the Latimer men had apparently known of the secret passage through Roberta's room. Once, those rooms had belonged to Tamara.

Now with the knowledge of the woman's identity,

Alaina's thoughts came together with a myriad of conjectures, and she did not tarry in expressing them. "You were the one flitting in and out of Roberta's room, trying to scare the wits out of me, weren't you?" She laughed disdainfully. "But I didn't frighten quite as easily as you had hoped. Did you really think to send me fleeing from here with your simple efforts? Or break Cole and I apart by making me think he had burned my gown, or cast suspicion on me when you had the harnesses thrown into a salty brine? Weak and simpleminded gestures, Mrs. Garth," she chided, blatantly disregarding the woman's name. "You frightened no one, not even Mindy. You are a bumbling buffoon, just like your friend, Jacques."

"You are the one who's a fool," Tamara accused jeeringly. "You should have gone while you had the chance, or better yet, not come at all. Cole was falling into my hands readily enough with his drinking and depression, and I abetted it in every way that I could. Soon, he would have met with an accident, and as much as he drank, no one would have questioned the affair. Then I would have become mistress of this house once more, as I have every right to be. But you came and turned Cole's mind, urged him back into his practice, and schemed with him to turn my mansion into a pesthouse for disgusting invalids and the diseased." Her eyes flared with her hatred. "Do you think I would have allowed that? Allowed carpenters to touch a wall of my mansion?" The pitch of her voice rose with her ire. "The idea is absurd!"

"What you were really worried about," Alaina replied in a mild, almost pleasant tone, "was that your den of thieves would be discovered and that you would have had to flee or be caught. I would assume you've been carrying on your little games of pirating ships from this vantage point ever since you started working here." She nodded meaningfully toward the stacks of barrels and boxes of rifles. "This cave makes a convenient warehouse for stolen goods. But tell me, how do you manage it all? You would have to bring the ships here to the mouth of the cave and unload them at night when no one could see. But what happens to the riverboats afterwards? Do you burn them? Sink them? How do you make them disappear?"

Tamara smiled smugly. "A little of both, my dear

Alaina." She raised her brow as she added with special import, "And with no survivors."

No survivors! The words tore savagely through Alaina's mind with a vision of bodies crumpling at the merciless crack of exploding guns or the stealthy flick of a knife. She remembered another incident involving a riverboat in New Orleans and wounded Confederate prisoners. Then, there had been no survivors of the latter, and Alaina MacGaren had been blamed for the massacre. At one time or another, during her stay here, Roberta had had her hands on the money plundered from that riverboat, the very same loot that had been found at Briar Hill and that was later taken by Lt. Cox's murderer. Somehow it had found its way up here, no doubt brought by the murderer or one of the thieves.

Alaina's spine began to tingle as she studied the woman with a careful eye for detail. Tamara was small, even petite. In the dark of night she could have passed very well for a younger woman and, with a wig, one with reddish hair. Was she the renowned thief and murderess who had passed herself off as Alaina MacGaren, casting all the blame on the innocent head of the real one? Was she the one who had stabbed Cox?

"You have aroused my curiosity, Tamara." A little friendly cajoling might wheedle the answers quite freely from the woman, and Alaina was willing to use such a ploy to satisfy her suspicions. "I sense that you and I have played many different characters when it's become necessary for our survival or our gain. We are alike, in a way. We have been through much, yet we have weathered it all fairly well. We can go out and seek what we have not. But Roberta was different, wasn't she? She took from us. Connived. Schemed. I had Cole in the palm of my hand, but she whisked him away and claimed him for herself. Lately, it has been discovered that Roberta took some money. Only, it wasn't Cole's, and I've begun to believe that it might have been your money. Are my suppositions correct?"

"The bitch!" Tamara snarled. "She found her way through the mirrored panel and came poking her nose down here when none of us were aware of it! I brought that money all the way from New Orleans, and that busy beaver picked the lock of this cell to get at the chest. It was safe here until she came with her prying little fingers and stuck her nose where it didn't belong. She took it all! Money I had worked hard for! She even killed the gardener after he caught her trying to hide it."

Tamara ignored the horrified gasp she had won from Alaina and continued on venomously. "He was nosey too, and it cost him his life. Roberta played cozy with him when he pressed her to share the wealth, even bedded him to allay his suspicions. Took that filthy slime right into my bed, she did!"

The woman seemed outraged over this fact and thumped her own chest with a forefinger to emphasize her statement. "Into the very bed I had purchased for myself and which she so fondly called her own. I stood at the mirrors and saw it all that night. Heard it all! Realized they were talking about my money. Later, Roberta lured the gardener into digging a hole in the rose garden by letting him believe they would be burying the treasure there together."

Tamara laughed caustically. "He didn't know he was digging a grave for himself. I watched from the widow's walk, and I could see just what she was doing. They had the money beside them, and he had stuffed a few of the bills into his pockets to keep himself happy while he labored. Then, Roberta crept up behind him with a shovel and bashed his skull in. He fell into the hole, saving that lazy bitch the trouble of pushing him, though she scrambled down quickly enough on her hands and knees to remove the money he had taken. She threw the dirt in over him and stuck the rose bushes right on top. After that, I followed her down to the cottage. She had to make several trips to get all of *my* money down there. You've seen that big old hearth in the kitchen? Well, that's where she put it, tucked it on a ledge inside the chimney. It was probably the most work she had done in her whole life. When she left the cottage, I reclaimed it, but she had already whisked away almost twenty thousand. A few weeks later she found herself with child, and she asked me, the reliable housekeeper, if I knew of someone she could go to who would help her and be discreet about it. I recommended one who had never really learned the art of her trade. As I suspected, the woman was careless, and that was the end of Roberta. Good riddance, I must say."

Alaina slowly dipped the cloth into the water again

and reapplied the wet compress to Cole's chin as she carefully asked, "And what is to become of us?"

"You, my dear Alaina," Tamara replied, smiling blandly, "will become nothing more than a wet nurse and servant for your child, while I set myself up as her rightful, if somewhat distantly related, grandmother. I'll run this house the way it should be managed, and there'll be no carpenters tearing down what I created."

"Perhaps Cole will have something to say about that. It's *his* house!"

"It's *my* house! I designed it! I furnished it! It's *mine!* Every last stick and brick of it. Besides," Tamara chuckled softly, "Cole Latimer will cease to exist. He'll be disposed of in an accident. Oh, I'll make sure he'll be identified by the necessary individuals so the Latimer fortune will go to *his* next of kin. I'll need that to establish myself as the child's guardian when you cannot be found."

A shiver of dread crawled up Alaina's spine, but she lowered her eyes to hide the trepidation that she felt and waited until she could control the quaver in her voice before asking, "And this cave? Was it part of your design, too?"

"Of course!" Tamara was smug in her conceit. "Frederick was too busy with his patients to have any care for what I was doing, or to realize this cave was even here before the house was built. Living out here in this godforsaken wilderness, I wasn't about to be slaughtered by blood-thirsty savages. So I made a way to escape through my bedchamber. Frederick conveniently supplied all the money I needed to build the house the way I wanted it. But he disinherited me after I left, and I could not claim it as mine—until now. Of course, it will be in the child's name, as she will be legal heir to the Latimer fortune, but a babe is only a pawn. She can be used and maneuvered. It will be the same as if it were mine again. But you mustn't make the mistake of thinking yourself indispensible, my dear. I just want you around to take care of the child, and if need be, someone else can be hired for that."

"You have it all planned, I see." Alaina's manner was well controlled, though the trembling palpitation of her heart forced droplets of cold sweat from her pores. What they planned for Cole frightened her beyond anything else. "But tell me, Tamara, why didn't you stay here in the first place? It could have been yours without question, and there would be no need for killing."

Tamara yanked at the white cuffs of her gown, tearing them off and crushing them beneath her feet, as if she detested the reminder of her servile position. "Frederick Latimer only wanted me as a mother for his child. But I wanted something more! Fame and fortune! Wealth! He had that, of course, but he cared little for the parties and the grandeur of being rich!" She lifted her chin imperiously. "A man came, handsome, charming. A gambler! I fell in love with him. Oh, you should have seen us, my dear Alaina. We made that old river come alive, from Pig's Eye to the Delta and back again. But there was a child. Oh, not his! Master Latimer's! I had the babe in my belly when I left! Only, I made Harry believe it was his, and I never told the child otherwise. Harry and I worked the steamers, you know. I would signal him when anyone held a winning hand or one that was just a hair less than his. Not that he needed my help, of course. He could make any card you name jump out of the deck. But he liked to play it safe."

She leaned against the gate and stared reflectively down at the toe of her slim, black shoe for a moment. "Then, some of his customers wanted a woman—and I became another kind of shill. I—pacified the heavy losers and—" she tossed her head defiantly "—most of them went away happy and satisfied. But Harry had a temper. He didn't like being called a cheat. He was a good shot, but one night he challenged the wrong man, a Creole buck in New Orleans. They pulled Harry out of the river with a bullet hole square in his forehead." She placed a finger on her own to indicate the spot. "He left me with a year-old baby, but I could handle a pack of cards, too, and if the customers didn't mind playing at the gaming tables with a woman, I usually won a worthy trick or two. When that action was slow, I found another way to stay alive. Then I made a big score and settled down with my boy in a well-secluded little Cajun town. That little scrapper remembered the high life, and I taught him at an early age all I knew. After he got old enough, we took to sharing our ideas, and let me tell you, we had some to brag about."

Tamara shrugged. "Well, I got word that Frederick had

passed on, and I came up here to see what I could do for myself. I was planning and hoping that Cole wouldn't make it back from the war. It would have saved me so much trouble. You see, Frederick never did divorce me. Legally I could have claimed myself as his bereaved widow and, no doubt, turned some judge's heart. I'm still quite a looker, and no one can guess my age. But now, with the girl, all I have to do is convince some official that I am partial to babies and have Glynis's best interests at heart. It will be so much easier claiming her inheritance than trying to reestablish my claim to the Latimer fortune. But—I have talked long enough, and my son will be coming soon. I must leave you for the time being, Alaina. Just don't stray too far, will you?"

Laughing at her own humor, Tamara left her unwilling guest and went off in the same direction that Gunn had taken, leaving Alaina greatly disturbed by the workings of the woman's mind.

Alaina bent her regard to her husband and could not hold back the tears which came at the thought that soon she might be holding his lifeless form in her arms. She choked back a sob and blindly caressed his lean features, forcing back that mental vision. Tenderly she placed wet compresses on his brow until eventually he stirred from his oblivion. He groaned, and his eyelids fluttered open to see her softly smiling face close above his.

"Welcome back, my darling," she murmured.

"Alaina!" He tried to sit up and had to brace himself on an arm until his world stopped reeling. Gingerly he tested his jaw, then peered intently into the gloom where the stolen cargo was stacked. "It would appear we've been sitting on top of a thieves' nest the whole time."

"I believe I came to that same conclusion not too long ago," Alaina observed ruefully. "And there's much more to it than what meets the eye. They're murderers Cole, the lot of them."

"We've got to get out of here." He staggered to his feet and tested the solid gate, then turned to her with a lopsided grin of apology. "But I can't see quite how at the moment."

On the cot, Glynis began to squirm and whimper, and Alaina rose quickly and went to sit beside her, lifting the babe in her arms and cuddling her close while she could. She held out a hand in an appeal for Cole to join her and gratefully leaned into his embrace when he complied.

"Cole, they intend to murder you!" she whispered urgently through Glynis's mewling cry. "They plan to take over Latimer House—"

He laid his fingers gently against her lips to shush her. "We should have some help arriving in the form of Saul and Olie," he breathed, nuzzling his nose into her sweet smelling hair. "So don't fret yourself, my love. We'll come out of this alive and hearty."

Alaina still fretted. "But, Cole, I'm sure they sent some men up to watch the stairs."

"Then we'll wait and see what happens. Saul can usually take care of himself, and with Olie to help, perhaps the thieves have a surprise coming." He hugged her shoulders reassuringly. "I don't plan to be dispensed with quite as easily as they would like."

He lifted his arm from around her and took his dissatisfied daughter on his lap, then complained, "She's wet."

"Is that all you have to worry about?" Alaina laughed in tearful question. She brushed away the wetness at her eyes and swallowed, choking back any further display of her fear. Somehow Cole's calming presence and his assurances made it all seem so less dire. She lifted her skirt and tore another square from her petticoat as she had done before and folded it upon her lap to receive her infant daughter. When the diapering service was completed, Alaina handed the babe back to her father, though Glynis was only mildly appeased and continued to fuss. As Cole tried to pacify her with a gentle jostling, Alaina rested her chin upon his shoulder and imparted another bit of information in a low tone. "I think we're going to meet another friend before the day is out. That was Gunn who dragged you in here."

"Gunn!" Cole rubbed his jaw and rolled his head to ease the ache in the back of his neck. "Of course! How could I forget Jacques's bully?"

"I met him exactly the same way when they kidnapped me in New Orleans," Alaina commented musingly.

Cole tilted his head and fondly considered the delicate line of her jaw before he came to any conclusions. "Gunn must have a touch befitting a surgeon. I've never noticed any evidence of abuse and see none now."

"I think Jacques said something like that," Alaina replied with a smile.

"I'm sorry." Cole touched her lips with a kiss. "I seem to be quoting everyone today."

"That last didn't feel like a quote to me," Alaina murmured softly, staring up at him with eyes brimming with love. "It felt quite like an original."

Glynis's cries soon turned into a full-fledged squalling and only subsided in hopeful expectation when Alaina accepted her return. The babe eagerly rooted at her breast, then whined in disappointment until Alaina, with a timid glance about the dimly lit cavern, opened her dress. When presented, the familiar nipple was latched onto with a lusty eagerness, and Glynis immediately quieted and, in relaxing contentment, kneaded the soft, white breast.

Cole watched with his usual fascination for bare bosoms, little daunted by their plight of the moment. He placed an arm about his wife again, cushioning the stone at her back as they leaned against it together.

"It's odd that I never discovered this cave was here before now," he mused aloud. "But then, I've always hated the red room and only rarely entered it, even when Roberta occupied it."

"Cole, it was Roberta who murdered the gardener, and it was his child she carried. Mrs. Garth witnessed it all."

Cole accepted her statement with mild surprise. "She must have been sorely pressed indeed."

"He caught her with the stolen money and wanted to share it."

"Then I can believe the fact. She was very possessive when it came to wealth."

"We mustn't tell Aunt Leala—or Uncle Angus," Alaina pleaded softly.

"No, I fear the shock would be too much for them."

"There's something else you should know—about Mrs. Garth."

"A very interesting woman," Cole observed ruefully as the one mentioned flitted quickly from one shadowed end of the cave to the other, slipping past the large wooden door after the usual clanking of chains. "And a very busy one."

Placing a hand on the muscular leanness of his thigh,

Alaina drew his attention back to her. "It's something that has to do with you, Cole."

Suddenly mocking laughter echoed from the dense gloom from which Tamara had rushed, bringing their startled attentions to the small, neatly dressed man who stood there with short legs braced wide apart. It was Jacques!

Alaina quickly covered Glynis's head and her bare breast with a corner of the baby's blanket as the Frenchman strode forward to their cell. He was arrogant in his demeanor, confident with Cole behind bars. Her husband stiffened beside her, and with a glance, she saw the muscles in his cheek had tensed and now flexed with his ire.

"And what do we have here?" Jacques jeeringly questioned, halting before the gate. "Doctor and Mrs. Latimer, is it not? How nice to have you both visiting here in my humble abode. And of course, I must not forget sweet Glynis who suckles at your breast, my lovely Alaina. Oh, to be there, *ma chérie*. I would enjoy that greatly."

Cole's eyes were like cold, blue steel as they met the man's amused smile. "Apparently you didn't take my warning seriously when I gave it in the hotel."

"What was it you said now?" Jacques feigned a look of deep concentration. "Something about making sure that I would be judged by the highest authority?" He chuckled at Cole's casual nod. "We shall see who judges whom, *monsieur docteur*."

He leaned a shoulder against the bars of the gate as he made a show of tugging off the glove from his right hand. He withdrew a scarred and withered extremity and held it up for their benefit.

"A gift from your wife, monsieur. As was this." He swept his hat off and brushed his hair aside to display the largely pierced left ear.

"You remember the last time we met in New Orleans, don't you, Alaina? I believe you said you would kill yourself before letting me touch you. Well, this time I have something better with which to make you mind your manners. If you choose not to behave, your husband could die a very slow and agonizing death."

Alaina trembled at his threat and sagged against Cole's arm, pressing close to his side.

"Is that the best you can do with a woman?" Cole sneered. "Frighten her into giving herself? Is that how you make all your conquests?"

His jibe shattered Jacques's composure for a moment, then the man continued on as if he had not heard. "Of course, we plan to do away with the good doctor anyway. But if you cooperate, Alaina, it could go much better for him."

"So much for pardons," Cole scoffed. "You're still a bastard through and through."

"Would you like to see my credentials again, *monsieur docteur?* Here!" He pulled the packet from his jacket and tossed it through the bars. "Peruse them at your leisure. "Oh! And here's another set." He hauled out another packet. "Slightly different, but equally acceptable to the average lawman. And here's a pardon from Mexico, and one from France! You see? Countries vie to give me pardons." His laughter filled the cave, and when his humor ceased, he smirked in self-satisfaction. "Actually, I found a man who had a talent for a pen and a hatred for the world." He shrugged carelessly. "Alas, I gave him a chance to hate the next world, too." He spread his hands in a gesture of helplessness. "You see how confident I am? I will build an empire here, so powerful that no one will dare touch me. All be it, on the bones of the Latimers and their fortune, but I must take into account that both of you have taken much from me. Alaina, my hand and ear. And *monsieur docteur,* the woman I desired for myself. For that, Monsieur Latimer, I am tempted to see you gelded."

As he met Cole's tolerant stare, Jacques ceased his prattle, finding no evidence that he worried the other man. He paced to and fro for a moment, rubbing his chin in deep thought.

"You also seem confident, Monsieur Latimer." He considered Cole with a furrowed brow. "I wonder—could you be hoping for rescue? Could you be basing your hope on the arrival of—" he stepped back and swept his hand to one side, "—this one?"

His uproarious laughter drowned out Alaina's dismayed gasp, trembling the air throughout the cavern, as four men carried a bound and gagged Saul to the opening of the cell where they dumped him. A full half dozen ruffians with various bruises and cuts moved to stand around him, clubs ready in their hands. Saul himself was not without damage. Blood trickled from a swollen gash on the side of his head, and an eye was nearly closed. As one man held the gate open, two others rolled the trussed man into the cell. Cole had risen and was waiting to examine the black's injuries. When the gate clanged shut again, Jacques indolently observed the doctor's ministerings.

"A waste, monsieur. He will be dead in the morning. My men will see to that."

"You could be dead in the morning too, Monsieur DuBonné," Cole responded, freeing Saul of his bonds. He swabbed the laceration on the black's head as Saul tugged the gag loose.

"Still confident, monsieur?" Jacques smirked.

Cole stopped dabbing at the cut and braced an arm on his knee as he squatted on his haunches beside the black. He glanced up with a wry smile. "When a mere girl can set upon you and do as much damage as you have displayed, despite your army of toughs, should I fear overly much?"

The barb struck its mark with accuracy, and the small man stiffened. Irately he gestured his men away, and as their footsteps were retreating, those of another approached. A rustle of taffeta announced Tamara's returning presence.

"We have them all now, eh?" Jacques boasted with a triumphant laugh as he turned to her.

Tamara strolled past the cell. "Things have worked out for us very well indeed. I thought we had lost our chance when the good doctor found his way out of the river and came back to haunt us. But we've got him again, just where we want him. And this time, there'll be no one saving him."

Cole rose to his feet and canted his head as he contemplated the woman carefully. "You were the ones who had me thrown into the river in New Orleans?"

Tamara's brows lifted briefly as she gave a tiny shrug. "Killing two birds with one stone, more or less. When it was found out that you were in New Orleans, after I received word of your father's death, it seemed an opportunity that I could not pass up. And your uniform provided a way into the hospital so we could release the prisoners, a ploy we had used to ruin Alaina MacGaren's name. We did so want that property of hers, and we might have had it, had the Yankees taken Shreveport when they should have."

Everything was going too fast for Cole to digest reasonably. He was openly confused as he asked, "You were informed of my father's death? Why would you have been interested in him?"

"Cole—" Alaina's voice came from behind him, but Tamara cut her short.

"Nevermind, Mrs. Latimer. I'll tell him myself."

"Tell me what?" Cole demanded, half turning to glance inquiringly at his wife.

"You don't remember me, Cole." Tamara drew his attention back with the statement. "You were so young, and that was such a long time ago, though as you can see I've aged very little."

Cole grew even more perplexed. "Should I know you?"

"Well, as I said it's been such a long time you may not remember your stepmother."

"Tamara?" He blurted the name out in surprise.

She inclined her head slightly. "Of course."

"And you're in with this pack of blackguards?" Cole asked incredulously. His hand shot out angrily toward Jacques. "With this good-for-nothing bastard?"

Tamara raised her head aloofly. "He is my son."

Alaina gaped at Jacques, while Cole gave a derisive snort. "Not any kin to me, I hope."

"No kin at all!" Jacques answered sharply.

"Now, Jack—" Tamara sought to soothe him for the coming revelation. "You just—"

Jacques's dark eyes flashed fire. "The name is Jacques, *m'mère*. I would be pleased if you would use it."

Tamara waved a hand aloft in a gesture of impatience. "Oh, Jack, you're getting worse than Harry about that!"

"Henré!" Jacques was even more incensed. "Henré DuBonné! *Ma père!* Henré DuBonné!"

Tamara's eyes sparked with an ire of her own. "Harry never sired a brat in his life."

Jacques drew himself up in outraged disbelief. "You don't mean that I—and he—" He turned a horrified look of disgust on Cole who returned the compliment.

"Half brothers." Tamara cleared the matter of relationship bluntly. "Same father, different mothers."

"Aaaahh!" Jacques threw up his hands in roweling dissatisfaction. He glared at Tamara. "Why did you let me believe all these years that Henré was my father?"

She lifted her shoulders in a shrug, unruffled by his irritation. "There was no sense in telling you while Frederick was alive. He would never have claimed you. He wouldn't have believed me, or you. Why, you don't even remotely resemble Frederick. It was my side of the family you took after. So, I knew it would only lead to your frustration, having the knowledge you were his son and not being able to convince him. It was simpler this way, and you'll have the Latimer fortune through the child."

Jacques mumbled, not totally appeased. "I should have suspected something was amiss when you ordered the *monsieur docteur* thrown into the river."

"It's better this way. Believe me, Jacques," Tamara assured him. "We'll have the Latimer wealth and all that belongs to them through the child. And you can do as you like with her mother. She's in your hands."

"Like hell she is!" Cole barked. "At least, not while I'm alive!"

Somewhat pacified with the idea of having Alaina after all these many months of wanting her, and desiring revenge, Jacques laughed derisively. "That, *monsieur docteur,* will be remedied shortly. She'll be mine, and you'll be dead." His dark eyes found the wide gray ones upon him, and he gave Alaina a brief nod as he promised, "I'll have you before this day is out. Rest assured, *ma chérie.*"

As Alaina fumbled with shaking fingers at her bodice, trying to close it beneath the covering of the blanket, Jacques turned to Tamara with another matter. "You'd better get the men started if they're to catch the riverboat downstream at the bend. It's carrying some valuable cargo that I would hate to lose, and we're getting more orders now than we can fill. The more we seize and the more we sell, the richer we'll be, *m'mère.*"

"We'd better keep a couple of men around just to insure that big fellow doesn't do anything foolish?" Tamara suggested, inclining her head toward Saul."

"Do so," Jacques stated shortly. "Gunn can stay too, but get the rest started. They'll have a ways to go before they reach the bend, and they'll have to get into position before the riverboat comes around it. Our men on board will be expecting their attack."

The woman left to see to his bidding, and Jacques turned upon the occupants of the cell with a look of amused condescension. But his smile faded somewhat when Cole again took a place beside Alaina and pulled her close against his side. It seemed a direct challenge.

Jacques jerked on his glove with a sneer. "You'll have a little time together before I return for her. Duties have a way of pressing in on a man at inopportune times. But rest assured, before I return, I'll have found a place where she and I can have a bit of privacy."

As the man passed from sight, his laughter floated back to them, and Alaina clung desperately to her husband while Cole whispered soft words of comfort in an effort to calm her trembling.

Saul shook his head in worried apology. "Mistah Cole, I sho' is sorry 'bout being taken. Dey was waitin' for me."

"Where's Olie?" Cole whispered.

"He was right behind me, but ah guess he musta heard de commotion when dey took me, and decided not to come through de do'. Or maybe he's gone back fo' more help."

"You see, Alaina?" Cole breathed against her ear. "There's still hope."

"Oh, Cole," she wept against his shirtfront. "I just couldn't go on living if anything happened to you."

"Hush now, my darling," he soothed, caressing her soft hair. "Be brave. I assure you it is my last intention to let these miscreants carry out their plans for us."

Cole glanced around as heavy footsteps intruded upon the silence of the hall. Gunn came into view, carrying a gleaming, brass bound Winchester in his hand. His upper torso was bare, except for a brocade vest which was several sizes too small for him. It was this that sharply tweaked Cole's memory. A bright red patch replaced the piece that had been torn from it, a piece that Cole had often handled in museful contemplation when he tried to decipher everything that he had heard that night at Briar Hill before its burning. The murderer of Lt. Cox had worn the vest then, but he had been a much smaller man than Gunn. However, Jacques was just about the right size.

Gunn halted before the cell and stood, tipping his head

from side to side as he perused Saul. He laid the rifle down well away from them and hunkered down before the black who sat half facing the gate. Saul turned as his shoulder was tapped.

"You big man!" Gunn bobbed his head in self-agreement. "Big like Gunn." He thumped his fist against his chest, then reached through the bars to tap Saul's foot. Holding his hands up, he spread the fingers wide. "This many take you." He dropped one finger until there were nine. "This many, maybe not."

Gunn rose to his feet and looked Saul over ponderingly, as if he debated with himself over some issue. He suddenly grasped the heavy irons of the gate, and the tendons in his bare arms corded and popped as he heaved, trying to tear the bars apart. Satisfied that he could not, he stood back and gestured to the other.

"Gunn not break. Saul try!"

Readily enough, Saul grasped the gate in the same spot and gave it his best attempt. But to no avail. When he gave up and moved back, Gunn laughed heartily and strode out of sight once again, content that the prisoners would remain in their cell.

The sun had set by the time Jacques returned. Alaina had all but yielded hope that Olie would arrive with help in time to save them from the villains, and while Gunn lounged in the shadows, keeping an unconcerned eye upon them, she could not try her hand, as Roberta had done, at picking the lock, even if some implement had been available for her to use.

Behind Jacques, two men and Gunn strode forward, leveling the bores of their Winchesters directly at the occupants. Cole and Alaina tensed in sudden worry, and Saul scrambled quickly to his feet, for he too saw the imminent threat of bloodshed.

Tamara passed through the midst of the large-bodied men and came to unlock the cell, while Jacques stood back and watched with a twisted smirk of a smile. Tamara gestured to Alaina. "Bring the baby here."

Alaina clutched Glynis to her with such fervor that the child awakened and began to mewl softly. The mother's heated glare conveyed her answer.

Tamara stepped back and directed Gunn. "If Mrs. Latimer doesn't do exactly as I say, shoot him." She inclined her head toward Cole. "Just in the legs first. We don't want to lose him too quickly." Tamara paused for a moment, then she added almost as an afterthought, "And if Doctor Latimer makes a wrong move, shoot the girl. Same goes for the black. Shoot the girl."

She saw the sheer hatred in Alaina's gaze and assured her tersely. "As you see, my dear, you're all dispensible. I only want the babe, and if there's one of you whom you needn't be concerned about, it's her. Now bring her here."

Alaina slowly complied and though her lips trembled with suppressed rebellion, she laid Glynis in the waiting arms. After locking the gate, the woman retreated a short distance away, then Jacques strolled leisurely forward.

"She has what she wants." He jerked his head toward his mother. "Now, I will take what I want."

Alaina stumbled back to Cole, reading that meaningful leer in the man's visage.

"Same rules apply, *ma chérie,*" he smiled smugly. "You can have your husband shot by disobeying me."

"You can go to hell," Cole retorted. "I'm not about to give her over into your hands. You'll have to shoot me first."

Jacques shrugged. "Then I suggest, my dear Alaina, that you have your black hold him—if you want your husband to last out the night. I'll see him shot and the black with him, if you do not step out of your own accord."

A bitter, wretched sob attested to the turmoil Alaina found herself in. She knew full well that Jacques would do exactly as he threatened. The rifles were trained almost hungrily on the pair of men who occupied the cell, just waiting for a wrong move. If bending to Jacques's will would allow Cole one more day of life, she thought then it was worth giving herself. After all, if he had a few more hours to live, he might escape entirely.

Tremblingly she pushed herself from Cole, but when he attempted to draw her back, she avoided his grasp, spinning away from him, and threw herself behind the black.

"Hold him, Saul!" she cried through her tears. "If you don't want to see him killed, hold him! For God's sake, hold him!"

Suddenly Cole found his arms seized by the black, and though he struggled violently, he was locked in the embrace of steel.

"Sorry, Mistah Cole." Saul was put through an agony

of his own, and he found little favor in what he had to do. "Miz Alaina say hold, and I gots to."

Jacques motioned Alaina forward as he opened the gate. "Now, come with me, Mrs. Latimer."

"No!" Cole roared, twisting and frenziedly trying to escape Saul's grasp. "I'll kill you if you lay a hand on her, Jacques! By God, I swear it!"

Seeing her husband through a blur of tears, Alaina meekly obeyed Jacques, though Cole's bellow filled the cavern.

"Alaina! Don't!"

The gate was closed behind her, and the key was turned with grating finality. Saul released his prisoner, and Cole threw himself upon the door, grabbing the iron bars and shaking them violently.

"Alaina! Alaina! My God, Alaina!"

Steeling herself against the desperate plea she heard in his voice, Alaina glanced back at Tamara who was jostling the frightened and crying babe in her arms. The woman observed the proceedings with amusement blatantly obvious on her face. As she met Alaina's woeful gaze, she chuckled, then with the sounds of her laughter flowing back to them, she carried the baby to a quieter portion of the cave, out of sight, but surely not out of mind.

The iron gate clanked noisily as Cole shook it, bellowing epithets at Jacques. His half brother leered back at him and motioned the guards away.

"You may go. He can't get loose, and I can order you back quickly enough if there's a need. But there won't be. Will there, Mrs. Latimer?"

He presented the question to Alaina who stood gazing down at the floor. Tears spilled down her cheeks, falling and making wet spots on her gown. She could hear the savage, agonized snarling of her husband as he jerked and rattled the gate. If one, by dint of will, could open the iron portal, then surely it would have been him, for at the moment, he was like a beast gone mad.

Jacques caught her arm roughly, bringing her lithe form tightly against him. Grabbing her hair at the nape of her neck, he forced her head back until their eyes clashed.

"I hate you, Jacques DuBonné," she gritted between clenched teeth. "Whatever you do to me, remember that it's only because you threaten Cole that I yield at all. I have not changed my opinion of you. You're still a little pest of a man."

Eyes flaring, Jacques drew back an arm and slapped her across the face with enough force to send her reeling had he not held her with his other hand.

"Damn you, bastard!" Cole shouted in high fury, and the air fairly crackled with his rage.

Dazed, Alaina slowly straightened, tasting blood in her mouth. Jacques jerked her arm, his fingers biting into her soft flesh, and yanked her along behind him until they reached a small room formed in the interior of the cave. A dim lantern hung from the stone wall, and a pallet had been thrown upon the floor. Jacques swung her upon it and sneered as he began to loosen his cravat.

"Take off your clothes and spread yourself for my pleasure, Mrs. Latimer. My hour of revenge has come."

The maddened strength of the beast increased, and Cole's arm bulged as he strained at the bars. For a moment, Saul watched in awe, amazed by the ferocity of the man. The doctor's face was contorted with rage and sheer, visible determination. Looking on, Saul could only come to the conclusion that if this was what it took to move heaven and earth and bend it beneath one's will, then a little help might hasten the matter along.

Saul threw himself into the task wholeheartedly, adding his strength to Cole's. He had seen the bars give a little when Gunn had tried them. Perhaps there was hope after all.

Saul's bare arms knotted into great strands of muscle which stood out like knots on a tree trunk. The metal groaned and seemed to give away a bit, and they both took heart, each firming their grip and trying harder, straining, heaving, corded veins bulging, and faces twisted in weird grimaces. Beneath their combined effort, the rod bent with a rasping moan, then suddenly snapped, sending both men almost sprawling. Cole was at the door immediately, wiggling his lean frame through the widened hole. If Saul could not follow, then he would return for him—after he found Alaina.

An almost silent hiss came from the wooden door, drawing Cole's wary but immediate attention as the slight, small form of Mindy stepped into the light. She was carrying Cole's Remington.

Cole was beside her in an instant, demanding in a whisper, "Where is Olie?"

"Riber. Gone 'round cliff onto riber. Many man come from cave. Olie, Peter, all men from house, Brag, sheriff—fight them."

Cole tossed the pistol through the bars to Saul and ran into the shadows where he had seen Jacques take Alaina. As much as he could understand from Mindy's muddled speech, Olie, Braegar, the sheriff, and the men from the house had gone by way of the river to gain entrance to the cave, but somewhere along the way had been met by Jacques's men. The outcome of that confrontation was yet unclear, but none in the cave seemed aware of the attack.

He ran like a cat through the night, as swiftly and as dangerously as one from the wilds of Africa, driven on by the torturing vision of Alaina struggling in Jacques's arms.

A weak light shone from up ahead, and he was spurred on as he heard the rending of cloth and Alaina's muffled cries. The sound sent cold, merciless fury charging through every pore in his body, and he hardly cleared the corner of the tiny room, barely saw his wife straining away from Jacques's kisses, before he threw himself at the half naked man who, on seeing him, gave a cry of dismay and stumbled back. But Jacques was unable to avoid the forceful assault of the enraged beast who had appeared out of the blackness.

Shivering and sobbing in relief, Alaina clutched the separated parts of her chemise together as she pressed against the stone wall in an effort to escape the frenzied thrashing of the men who were locked in mortal combat. Jacques's face was a twisted mask of hatred, and his foul, whiskey-laden breath slashed in and out between yellow, gritted teeth. He was small and wiry, but he had the strength of his insane rage combined with the fear that he might be thwarted again. Then, Cole's fist slammed into his jaw, and Jacques sagged limp, frustrating the doctor's desire for further castigation of the man. But as he flung Jacques off with a snarl of disgust, there suddenly came a shot from the part of the cavern where they had been earlier imprisoned, and Cole, realizing that Saul was in trouble, caught Alaina's arm as she was yanking it through the sleeve of her gown and pulled her with him. He ran back through the darkened tunnel. Alaina managed to close her bodice over her meagerly clad bosom as her feet flew beside his. There was no assurance of what awaited them, and she was determined to retain a bit of her modesty.

As they entered the main gate, they skidded to a halt, finding Saul standing off the two white men as well as Gunn and Tamara with the still smoking Remington.

"You fool!" Tamara shrieked. "There's three men here with guns. You'll never escape!"

"Well, ah gots dis heah gun dat maybe can take a couple o' you wid me. Maybe you first, ma'm, if'n yo' don't bring dat chile to its mama."

Tamara faltered in indecision and glared at Alaina.

Saul crooked a large finger at her. "Com'on. Dat's Miz Alaina's chile, and she wants it."

"This is only temporary," Tamara stated when she handed the child over to Alaina. "I'll have her back before the night is done."

"Over my dead body," Alaina replied with finality.

"Saul!"

The bellow echoed in the cave, drawing everyone's notice to the massive bulk of Gunn who strode forward, his arms raised in a challenge. He had left the Winchester leaning against a barrel.

"Saul! Gunn fight Saul! You win, you go free!"

"Kill him, you fool!" Tamara shrieked. "Kill Saul! He can't go free!"

"No!" Gunn's voice rang out again. He turned to his companions and warned, "Saul fight Gunn! Alone! Anyone come, Gunn break!" The twisting motion of his huge hands was aptly graphic.

Saul tossed the pistol to Cole, and as it came around on them, the two men, who had leaped forward to seize the doctor, stumbled back in haste. Cole retreated, keeping Alaina and the babe behind him, then gave a nod to Saul when their backs were to the wall.

The black tore off the remains of his sleeveless work shirt and cast them from him, while Gunn rent the brocade vest in two. Saul spread his hands wide. The gesture was like a signal and both men charged, coming together with a clap as their chests met. They stood toe to toe and strained in a battle of pure strength. Neither could gain the advantage, and they broke apart and began to hammer each other with blows that would have shattered the bones of lesser men, again with no apparent effect.

Like great, black titans, glaring red-eyed with the heat of maddened battle lust, they crashed together again and became a twisting, writhing, struggling mass of muscle. They were locked shoulder to shoulder, head to head, their legs spread wide to provide traction. They took air into their lungs with wheezing gasps as they strained at each other, their backs arched. Then suddenly Saul twisted, and his right arm snaked beneath the left one of Gunn. Locking his hands above the other's back, he levered downward. Gunn began to slip, but he would not yield. The arm bent backward and upward, farther and farther. Gunn gave a grunt of pain, and the snap of breaking bone echoed loud in the stillness.

Gunn sank to the floor of the cave, and Saul braced himself on hand and knees, his head hanging between his arms as his chest heaved in deep gulps of air. Gunn dragged himself across the cavern to lean against the stacks of cargo, then rose to stand erect, his arm hanging at an odd angle and a dull, intent look on his face.

Alaina turned as she heard a sound from behind them and screamed a warning to Cole. He faced the threat, as an enraged Jacques, gun in hand, came tearing from the offshoot of the cave. He dove head first at Cole, and the Remington skittered across the floor as Cole was thrown backward by the sudden assault. Saul caught it up at a run and yanked Alaina out of harm's way as Jacques's pistol waved toward her. Cole's hand struck the gun up just as it fired, and the shot roused a long peal of echoes throughout the cavern. Cole caught Jacques's wrist as the muzzle swung toward Alaina again. The two men rolled on the ground, locked together as Jacques worked the pistol with blind intent. The bullets whined and thudded, while its explosions joined into a continuous thunder. A spout of coal oil sprang from a barrel as a bullet whined through it, and a lantern was shot from its perch above it. The lamp fell crashing to the floor, and in a moment, a gush of flames roared up from the small rivulet of oil. Nearby was the menacing presence of a small keg of gunpowder.

The gun clicked empty, and Cole released the wrist and, now unhampered, rolled onto his back, dragging Jacques with him. His fist again met the other's face, and the river pirate was spun away, whimpering as he clutched a broken mouth.

Suddenly a black arm seized Jacques from behind and dragged him backward, bawling in fear. With his good arm, Gunn wrapped the man in a tight embrace and held firm, though Jacques frantically sought escape.

"Gunn say Saul go free! Gunn never break promise! They go! We stay!"

Jacques shrieked a reply that ended in a quick tightening of Gunn's arm, then Jacques's head rolled limp, and when released, his body sagged slowly to the ground, his neck obviously broken.

Gunn gestured to Saul. "Go!"

"Yassuh!" Saul was eager to comply.

Cole swept the cave with a glance. He could see no sign of his stepmother, but his eye caught a new threat. The flames were working along the path of coal oil to the keg of gunpowder. He sprinted toward Alaina and Saul, shouting for them to run. As he caught up with them, he grabbed Glynis from Alaina's arms and pulled his wife along behind him in the direction of the tunnel. Mindy had hidden herself again by the door, waiting there to make sure they got out, and had the portal open for them.

A part of Cole's urgency seized them, and the bruised, aching Saul could hardly match the pace of Alaina's slim feet. Cole chanced a glance back over his shoulder and saw the fire was feeding around the bottom of the keg. He roared a warning to Saul who flung himself upon Mindy, as Cole dove for Alaina. He sheltered the small form of his daughter beneath him, pulling Alaina under him as well. Then suddenly a deafening roar and a searing blast of heat swept through the cave as the small keg exploded. Barrels, drums, bales, crates ricocheted off the stone walls, bursting and spreading their contents for the hungry flames.

Cole ignored the searing sting of flying ash that settled on his back and, hauling the others to their feet, urged them on into the tunnel that led to Roberta's room. Cole chose not to inform them that as the heat increased below, the draft would build, and the tunnel would become a chimney. Anything in it would be destroyed, and all too soon the house above them would just be dry tinder for the flames.

They took the stairs at a frantic pace, Mindy in Saul's arms, and Alaina being pushed ahead of Cole who held their daughter in a firm grasp. The child was crying and frightened, but there was no time to console her. There was a thunderous crash far below them, and a shower of sparks spiraled up toward them, bringing the uncomfortable heat with it.

"The door's been blown open," Cole roared. "We've got to get out of here, or be roasted alive!"

Alaina was winded, and her side ached. Still, she kept forcing her trembling legs to climb. It was much harder going up the stairs, than it had been going down, and Cole pushed her ever onward, his hand on her buttock as he ascended the steps close behind her. Then smoke began to billow up, choking them and stinging their eyes.

The mirror door was closed. Alaina took the baby from her husband and pointed to the timber on the landing below. Cole leaped down and twisted the latch as she directed, but nothing happened. Then, as they watched, the cables slowly slipped out of the guides and hung free and useless. The ends had been neatly snipped through.

"Tamara!" Cole roared the name like a curse. He should have known that she had left the cave and escaped up the stairs.

"We're trapped!" Alaina gasped.

Saul stood Mindy beside Alaina, then stepped back and thrust a heavy foot at the portal until the recalcitrant door opened for them. They burst into Roberta's room, gasping for air, but in another moment they were sounding an alarm throughout the house.

As they led the way across the front porch, Olie, Braegar, and Peter, and the sheriff were just bringing around a wagonload of trussed-up river pirates and the victorious field hands.

Olie ran forward as soon as he caught sight of Cole and worriedly explained his tardiness. "When I come behind Saul, I knew it weren't no good in tryin' to get through dat way, so I sent Peter to fetch the sheriff and Doctor Darvey, then went by the river to see if I could find the entrance to the cave. By the time I got 'round the cliff, dere was a whole bargeload of men on the river, and I had me a fine tussle with them 'til the sheriff come."

"It's all right, Olie," Cole assured the man. "We're safe now, and the pirates are caught, thanks to you."

As they watched, great gouts of flame began shooting up from the cliff face and far above it, announcing the conflagration to all who could see for miles around. A shrill whistle pierced the roar of the flames and grew lower in pitch as a small flame sprouted from the roof of the western tower and, widening, sent the lesser roof crashing in a shower of sparks down the side of the house. Unhampered, the flames shot high and howled as if in greedy delight. The windows of the house glowed red, then white. The panes shattered outward, sending a leaping spurt of fire up the bricks to lap hungrily at the eaves.

The flames lit the roof, and Braegar caught Cole's arm, pointing upward. High above them on the narrow widow's walk that capped the roof, a strange figure pranced about in a grotesque dance. Her long, black hair swirled about her head as the wind whipped it wildly about. She wore a blood-red dress, and several of the onlookers murmured Roberta's name in stunned awe. The three who had survived the cave ordeal knew the face, and it was not Roberta's. Tamara waved her arms as if supplicating the heavens as she shrieked into the night sky. Then turning, she saw the mass of white upturned faces below her and flung out an arm accusingly. Her high-pitched scream could be heard over the roar of the flames.

"Latimer House is mine forever! You can't take it from me! None of you will have it now!"

"She's out of her mind!" The comment came from beside them, and Cole turned to find Martin Holvag at his side. Then, Cole's gaze passed on to find that Rebel had joined them. Standing beside Braegar, she was twisting her hands and mewling fretfully.

"I know it's in there! I found Roberta's diary, and she said she had hidden a treasure. It has to be in the house, but now it's burning up!"

"You took Roberta's diary?" Alaina questioned sharply in surprise.

"Well, it was just lying there, waiting to be taken," Rebel whined.

"In *my* bedroom!" Alaina snapped.

"How'd I know it was yours? So many rooms in that blasted house, it made me confused!"

"That's the reason you came into our room that night?"

Cole demanded angrily. "Looking for money that wasn't yours?"

Rebel's face crumpled, and she wrung her hands in distress as she looked plaintively up at Braegar who was suddenly looking very disgusted. He turned his back and walked away, leaving her choking on whimpering sobs.

A new flood of fire gushed through the house. Whiter! Hotter! The roof seemed to heave upward, as if it were some living thing caught in roweling agony, then suddenly it crashed downward into the house, accompanied by a strange paean of wild laughter that could only have been formed by their imagination, yet the eerie sound rode the wind into the night.

The night grew still once more as the Latimers retired to the cottage's master bedroom. Only a red glow in the sky beyond the treetops could be seen from the second story room. It concerned them not, for it was here that Cole enjoyed the pleasure of watching his daughter playing, as babies do, with her toes, and it was here that Alaina, almost shyly, set a roll of bank notes onto the bed beside him.

Cole glanced up in surprise as she did so. "What's this?"

Alaina's cheeks pinkened. "You remember the two thousand you wanted me to take from you in New Orleans?"

Slowly he nodded.

"Well, Mrs. Hawthorne gave the rest of it to me while she was here. She said she had kept it for me."

"The rest?"

"There's not two thousand here now," Alaina explained. "I fear she used part of it to help purchase the gowns I wore when I came up here. You see, they were not used gowns, at all, but new, purchased with your money."

Cole laughed incredulously. "You mean, all that time you were refusing to wear the clothes I purchased for you, you were wearing others that my money had bought?"

Alaina nodded gingerly. "I didn't know it, Cole. Will you forgive me for being so blind and so proud?"

"My darling," he chuckled, pulling her down beside him on the bed. "You have added spice to my life that I would have found with no one else. How can I be angry with you for anything? I can only count myself fortunate that you share my life and will continue to do so until we're both old and gray."

"It is my plan, milord Yankee," she whispered against his lips, "and my most heartfelt wish."

Epilogue

IT was late in the evening nearly a month later that Cole found himself alone in the parlor of the cottage. Alaina was upstairs with their daughter, and the house was quiet except for an occasional sound of laughter drifting down the stairs.

Cole paused by a window and stared in some wonder. By the lane in front of the cottage stood the lone figure of a man. He was thin and ragged, and a worn, gray hat sagged upon his head. He perused the house carefully, then consulted a small piece of paper in his hand, but his manner was one of reluctance, as if he resisted approaching the door. In the settling dusk, his face was indistinct but Cole was sure he had never met the man. His curiosity got the better of him, and he went to the door and stepped out to accost the stranger.

As Cole approached him, the man straightened and thrust his hands into the pockets of his shabby coat.

"Do you have business here, sir? Or wish to see a doctor?" Cole asked.

The man was young, perhaps less than thirty, and his gray eyes seemed to challenge Cole before he replied. "Perhaps I have business here, suh." A hint of anger was evident in his voice. "Then again, maybe I don't. I was looking for a Doctor Latimer, and I was given directions to this place."

"You are speaking to him," Cole informed him, studying the man carefully. "You are a Southerner I take it, and though I see no horse or carriage, I must assume you've come a good distance to see me, yet I cannot fathom why. You are obviously not ill."

"I walked here." The statement was terse.

"I can see that you were a Confederate officer." Cole gestured to the man's once gray coat with its faded gold braid and the hat. "And you must realize that I fought for the Union. Could it be that you're looking for some kin of yours perhaps?"

"No, damn you!" The stranger's lips grew white, and his voice was taut with rage. "I have no kin, thanks to you Yankees. I have no home either. When I went back there, I found it burned to the ground. Some Yankee had bought it for a pittance of what it was worth."

"I am sorry you have lost your home and family, and even sorrier that you seem to blame me." Cole shrugged his shoulders and spread his hands in a gesture of innocence, then as the gray eyes flared their hatred, Cole stopped. He tipped his head to one side, and a strange light grew in his own eyes as he carefully studied the man. "Yet I seem to find a hint of your purpose. Could the house you refer to be called Briar Hill?"

"Yes!" The word came almost as an explosion from the man's chest, and he could no longer meet Cole's gaze. He turned away angrily.

"And your name would be MacGaren then?" Cole pressed.

The man only nodded.

"You say you have no family?"

Now he faced Cole with a pained glare. "My father and brother were killed in the war. My mother died of heartbreak. My sister has disappeared. You bluebellies said she was a spy and hunted her. I can only guess her fate in some stinking Yankee prison."

"You seem to have considerable cause to hate," Cole observed. "Could it be that you're Jason MacGaren?"

Again the stiff nod.

"Well, you are right!" Cole went on casually. "I did purchase Briar Hill for the overdue taxes and have kept them well paid since. I assure you it was all very legal."

"Legal!" Jason MacGaren shouted. "Maybe legal, but not right. I have come to get the place back!"

Cole shrugged. "I'm afraid you may have some difficulty there, Captain MacGaren. You see, I bought the plantation for my wife and had the title placed in her name."

"You shame me, suh!" Jason gritted through clenched teeth. He shook himself and fought for a new grip on his emotions. "But then, I have known much shame of late. If beg I must, then beg I will." He crumpled the piece of paper in his hand and hunched his shoulders against the cool breeze. He stared into the distant haze as he continued. "The house is ashes. The outbuildings empty and rotting. The fields are gone to weeds and need tilling. Will you not at least let me sharecrop it and rebuild it?"

Cole considered the man who waited an answer with angry hope unquenched in his eyes. A long moment passed before he reached out a hand and rested it on the other's arm.

"Captain MacGaren, you will have to discuss this with my wife." He stepped aside and motioned for the man to proceed. "Come in. Have a bite to eat with us. She may agree to what you suggest." He glimpsed the man's reluctance and laughed softly. "At least, come in and have a brandy. It's a precious long walk back to town, and I'm sure my wife will be pleased to meet you."

A sour smile twisted Jason's lips, and he gave a shallow shrug before he yielded and walked up the path to the front porch. Cole led him into the parlor and apologized as he poured a liberal brace of brandies.

"My wife is upstairs. It won't take a moment to fetch her. Excuse me."

When he was out of sight, Cole took the stairs three at a time, but he paused before their bedroom door and laid a tight rein on his broad grin. He was calm and offhandedly casual when he entered.

"Alaina, we have an unexpected guest who wishes to discuss a matter or two with you." He lifted Glynis from her lap, and forestalled his wife's questions with a shrug. "Just go down and talk to him. I'll bring Glynis."

"But, Cole—" she protested, smoothing her hair. "Who is he? What does he want with me?"

"He'll tell you that himself. Now hurry, before he decides to leave."

Cole descended the stairs behind his wife, watching her with a grin flitting uncontrollably across his lips. As Alaina entered the parlor, he leaned against the doorway waiting. Jason sat hunched on a small stool, staring at the snifter cupped in his hands. When he heard the swish of petticoats, he came to his feet, yanking off his hat, then he turned—and gaped.

"Jason!" Alaina's cry was a whole chorus of joyful notes. "Oh, Jason!"

Brother and sister were in each other's arms before the universe had spent another second. The man closed his eyes and hid his face against her hair as his arms fairly squeezed the breath from her. When he raised his eyes to meet Cole's smile, tears streamed from them unheeded.

"You're a damned Yankee, Cole Latimer." His voice was hoarse and choked. "I don't know if I can stand you for a brother-in-law."

Alaina leaned back against Jason's arm and smiled through her own tears of joy as she caressed his stubbled jaw softly with her hand. "You have no choice in the matter, Jason MacGaren." Her voice was low and trembling with happiness. "No choice at all."

Lament

Oh, my home!
Your wisdom exceeded far
My meager understanding.
I have *won!*
I am thrice blessed!
You were with me all along, and only slept,
Awaiting this rich soil to spread your roots and grow.
You have taught me this.
And I no more shall fear
The scent of change,
The loss of Yesterday.
Upon its charred remains,
I will build *today!*
And lay the foundation of *tomorrow!*
And nevermore regret,
The smell of ashes in the wind.